The Ultimate Sourcebook of
Knitting and
Crochet Stitches

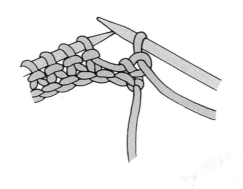

The Ultimate Sourcebook of
Knitting and
Crochet Stitches

Over 900 great stitches detailed for needlecrafters of every level

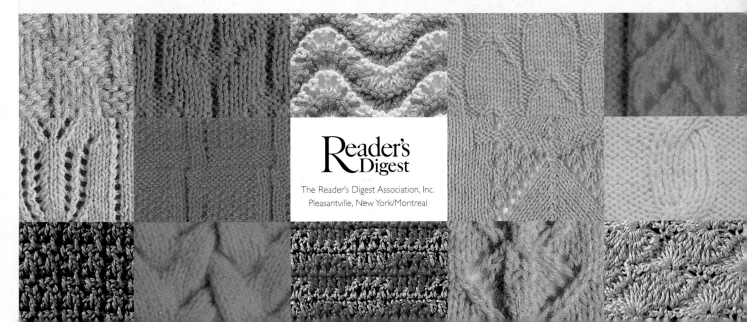

Reader's Digest

The Reader's Digest Association, Inc.
Pleasantville, New York/Montreal

A READER'S DIGEST BOOK

This edition published by The Reader's Digest Association
by arrangement with Collins & Brown

A member of **Chrysalis** Books plc

FOR COLLINS & BROWN
U.K. Project Editor: Emma Baxter
Editor: Eleanor van Zandt
Designer: Ruth Hope

FOR READER'S DIGEST
U.S. Project Editor: Melissa Virrill
Canadian Project Editor: Pamela Johnson
Project Designer: George McKeon
Executive Editor, Trade Publishing: Dolores York
Senior Design Director: Elizabeth Tunnicliffe
Director, Trade Publishing: Christopher T. Reggio
Vice President & Publisher, Trade Publishing: Harold Clarke

LIBRARY OF CONGRESS CATALOGING-IN-PUBLICATION
DATA
The ultimate sourcebook of knitting and crochet stitches:
over 900 great stitches detailed for needlecrafters of every
level.
      p. cm.
      ISBN 0-7621-0405-8
      1. Knitting—Patterns. 2. Crocheting—Patterns.
      I. Reader's Digest Association.

TT820 1.U635 2003
746.43`042—dc21   2002031874

Address any comments about *The Ultimate Sourcebook
of Knitting and Crochet Stitches* to:
      The Reader's Digest Association, Inc.
      Adult Trade Publishing
      Reader's Digest Road
      Pleasantville, NY 10570-7000

For Reader's Digest products and information,
visit our website:
      www.rd.com (in the United States)
      www.readersdigest.ca (in Canada)

Printed in Singapore

10 9 8 7 6 5 4 3 2 1

Contents

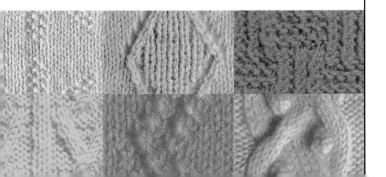

Introduction

How to Use This Book

The craft of knitting has been enriched over the centuries by the creativity of many anonymous knitters who have devised thousands of ingenious and often beautiful stitch patterns. Only a handful of these stitches can be found in the garment patterns available in stores at any given time; but with only a little effort, you can use them to create your own individual designs.

More than 900 patterns have been collected in this book. They are categorized and presented in a way intended to make it easy for you to select the best pattern for a given project. Here is an example of a typical opening page:

Using the Patterns

The simplest way of using one of these stitch patterns is to substitute it for another stitch in a published garment pattern. However, this is possible only where you can obtain the same tension (see pages 15–16) as that specified in the pattern. As always, tension is the key to successful knitting or crochet.

The next test in substituting a stitch is to make sure the multiples will fit across the measurement. For example, if the original garment has 136 stitches across the chest/bust measurement, and your chosen stitch pattern has a multiple of 13 stitches plus 6, the new stitch will fit exactly,

repeated 10 times. If, however, it has a multiple of 14, with no balancing stitches, it will fit 9.7 times, so that 9 repeats produce only 126 stitches and a narrower fabric. In some cases, such variation may not matter greatly; but you must calculate this in advance and decide if the finished size will be satisfactory.

To design a garment from scratch is somewhat more ambitious. The best approach for the beginner is to start with an existing knitted or crocheted garment that fits more or less as you would like the new garment to fit. Choose one with simple shaping, preferably with a squared-off sleeve top. Measure the garment in the

Stitch characteristics typically include the "multiple," or number of stitches in a single repeat of that stitch and, where applicable, extra stitches required to complete the pattern at side edges; the draping quality of fabric knitted in that pattern; and the relative level of skill required to work the pattern.

Pattern instructions may include notes providing special information or explanations of special abbreviations used. (A list of commonly used knitting abbreviations is given on pages 30–31; crochet abbreviations on page 197.)

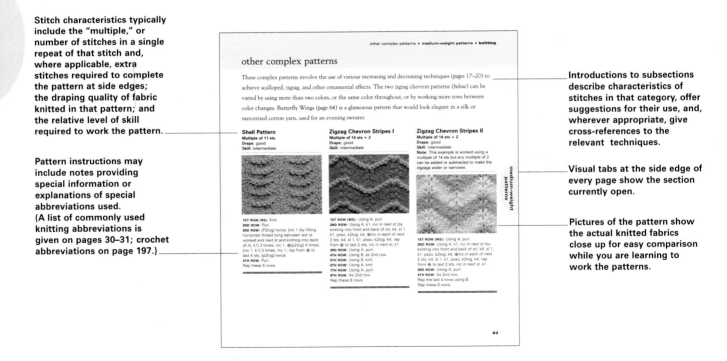

other complex patterns • medium-weight patterns • knitting

other complex patterns

These complex patterns involve the use of various increasing and decreasing techniques (*pages 17–20*) to achieve scalloped, zigzag, and other ornamental effects. The two zigzag chevron patterns (*below*) can be varied by using more than two colors, or the same color throughout, or by working more rows between color changes. Butterfly Wings (*page 64*) is a glamorous pattern that would look elegant in a silk or mercerized cotton yarn, used for an evening sweater.

Shell Pattern
Multiple of 11 sts
Drape: good
Skill: intermediate

1ST ROW (RS): Knit.
2ND ROW: Purl.
3RD ROW: [P2tog] twice, [inc 1 (by lifting horizontal thread lying between last st worked and next st and knitting into back of it), k1] 3 times, inc 1, ✳[p2tog] 4 times, [inc 1, k1] 3 times, inc 1; rep from ✳ to last 4 sts, [p2tog] twice.
4TH ROW: Purl.
Rep these 4 rows.

Zigzag Chevron Stripes I
Multiple of 14 sts + 2
Drape: good
Skill: intermediate

1ST ROW (WS): Using A, purl.
2ND ROW: Using A, k1, inc in next st (by knitting into front and back of st), k4, sl 1, k1, psso, k2tog, k4, ✳inc in each of next 2 sts, k4, sl 1, k1, psso, k2tog, k4; rep from ✳ to last 2 sts, inc in next st, k1.
3RD ROW: Using A, purl.
4TH ROW: Using B, as 2nd row.
5TH ROW: Using B, purl.
6TH ROW: Using A, knit.
7TH ROW: Using A, purl.
8TH ROW: As 2nd row.
Rep these 8 rows.

Zigzag Chevron Stripes II
Multiple of 14 sts + 2
Drape: good
Skill: intermediate
Note: This example is worked using a multiple of 14 sts but any multiple of 2 can be added or subtracted to make the zigzags wider or narrower.

1ST ROW (WS): Using A, purl.
2ND ROW: Using A, k1, inc in next st (by knitting into front and back of st), k4, sl 1, k1, psso, k2tog, k4, ✳inc in each of next 2 sts, k4, sl 1, k1, psso, k2tog, k4; rep from ✳ to last 2 sts, inc in next st, k1.
3RD ROW: Using A, purl.
4TH ROW: As 2nd row.
Rep the last 4 rows using B.
Rep these 8 rows.

medium-weight patterns

63

Introductions to subsections describe characteristics of stitches in that category, offer suggestions for their use, and, wherever appropriate, give cross-references to the relevant techniques.

Visual tabs at the side edge of every page show the section currently open.

Pictures of the pattern show the actual knitted fabrics close up for easy comparison while you are learning to work the patterns.

introduction

following places: around the chest/bust; from the shoulder to the lower edge of the front/back (it is easy to add or subtract length below the armhole shaping); along the sleeve seam; around the lower edge of the sleeve (wrist or arm); from the top (neckline end) of the shoulder seam down to the center of the neckline. Draw a simple diagram of the front, back, and sleeve, and mark these measurements on the three sections. Use the stitch and row tension (see page 16) to calculate the required number of stitches at the width measurements and the number of rows between shaping points. Use graph paper (see pages 16–17) to plan the shaping visually. Then write down your own instructions.

Yarns for Knitting

"Yarn" is the general term used for strands of fiber, or plies, which are twisted (spun) together into a continuous thread. It encompasses both natural (wool, cotton, etc.) and synthetic fibers, as well as smooth and fancy finishes and varying thicknesses and textures.

Knitting yarns are also used for crochet, but crochet also frequently uses fine and tightly twisted cotton threads designed specifically for this craft, which are discussed below.

Yarns used for knitting are sometimes categorized into general weights. These weights give an idea of what thickness the yarn is and are helpful if you need to find a substitute.

Fine Yarns

Very fine yarns are mainly produced for babies' garments and for lacy shawls. Included in this group are yarns called "2-ply" and "3-ply." (Very fine Shetland shawls are knitted from so-called "1-ply" yarn, but this is a misnomer, as at least 2 plies, or threads, are twisted together to form yarn.) The standard gauge over stockinette stitch for "fine" yarns is 29–32 stitches to 4in (10cm).

Lightweight Yarns

Lightweight yarn works well for lacy garments. Yarns called "4-ply" and "5-ply" are included in this group. The standard gauge over stockinette stitch for "lightweight" yarns is 25–28 stitches to 4in (10cm).

Medium-Weight Yarns

This can be used for babies', children's, and adults' garments and is suitable for most stitch patterns, from lace to heavily-textured. "Double knitting" yarns are included in this group. The standard gauge over stockinette stitch for "medium-weight" yarns is 21–24 stitches to 4in (10cm).

Medium-Heavy-Weight Yarns

The most popular yarn of this weight is called "Aran." It covers a range of yarns that have a standard gauge over stockinette stitch of 17–20 stitches to 4in (10cm).

Bulky and Extra-Bulky Yarns

These thick yarns are generally used for loose-fitting outdoor sweaters and jackets.

Crochet Threads

Although crochet can be worked in any of the knitting yarns listed above and all sorts of other materials—from embroidery threads to string and ribbon—certain threads are particularly well suited to the lacy forms of crochet, such as Irish and filet crochet.

Crochet Cotton

Specifically designed for crochet, these are tightly-spun cotton threads that have been mercerized for extra strength. They come in a range of weights, from 100 (extremely fine) to 10 (still quite fine).

Thicker Cotton Threads

Various other cotton threads in slightly heavier weights are available from needlecraft stores. Some embroidery cottons, such as pearl cotton (sizes 8, 5, and 3, the thickest) can be used for some crochet projects.

Choosing Yarns and Threads

When learning either knitting or crochet, it is especially important to choose a yarn that feels comfortable in your hands—one that is slightly elastic and neither slippery nor so highly textured that it will not move smoothly between your fingers. A medium-weight pure wool is ideal for this purpose.

Published knitting and crochet patterns will normally specify the brand to be used for a project. You can often substitute a different yarn for the one specified, provided that you can obtain the same stitch gauge (see page 15), although substituting a different type of yarn—a textured yarn for a smooth one—will obviously produce a different appearance in the finished item.

When doing your own designing, the only rule is: experiment. Try a stitch pattern with different weights and types of yarn and see the range of different effects you can create. With practice, you will learn which yarns are likely to enhance certain stitch patterns, and the occasional happy surprise will add to the fun of creating a new design.

Equipment

Relatively few, inexpensive pieces of equipment are required for either knitting or crochet. Knitting needles and crochet hooks in various sizes can be acquired gradually, as the need for them arises.

For Knitting

Pairs of needles come in a wide range of sizes, from size 00 to size 50 in diameter (see conversion table for commonly-used sizes on page 9), and in various materials, including metal, plastic, wood, and bamboo; choose a type that you can knit with comfortably. Needles also come in several lengths, to accommodate different numbers of stitches.

Circular and double-pointed needles are designed mainly for knitting tubular or circular fabrics (see page 21), but circular needles are often used for flat knitting where many stitches are involved, since they can hold a great many stitches

introduction

comfortably, with the weight of the work balanced between the two hands. Make sure that the length of a circular needle is at least 2in (5cm) less than the circumference of the work, or consult the table on page 9, which gives the minimum number of stitches required at a given gauge for the available lengths of a °circular needle.

For small items, such as gloves and socks, a set of four or more double-pointed needles is used.

Cable needles are short, double-pointed needles, used when moving groups of stitches, as in cabled or crossed-stitch patterns (see page 13). They come in just a few sizes; use one as close as possible to the working needle size, so that it will neither stretch the stitches nor slip out of the work. Those with a kink or a U-shaped bend are easier to work with than the straight kind.

Stitch holders resemble large safety pins. They are used to hold stitches that will be worked on later. Alternatively, a spare length of yarn can be threaded through the stitches and the ends knotted together. Where only a few stitches are to be held, an ordinary safety pin will do.

A row counter is a small cylindrical device with a dial used to record the number of rows, typically between working increases or decreases. Slip it over one needle before starting to knit and turn the dial at the end of each row.

Slip markers are used for marking the beginning of a round in circular knitting and sometimes for marking points in a stitch pattern.

A needle gauge is useful for checking the size of circular or double-pointed needles, which are not normally marked with their size, or for converting needle sizes.

You should have a few **crochet hooks** on hand for picking up dropped stitches (see page 28) as well as for working the occasional crocheted edging for a knitted garment.

For Crochet

Crochet hooks range in size from very tiny steel hooks, 0.60mm or less in diameter, used with fine cotton threads, to chunky plastic size Q hooks, used with thick yarns and string (see conversion table on page 9). Wooden and bamboo hooks can be found in the medium sizes.

Tunisian hooks look like a cross between a crochet hook and a knitting needle and are used for Tunisian crochet (see page 241).

For Knitting and Crochet

A large tapestry, or yarn, needle is used for sewing seams and has a blunt point, which will not split or snag the yarn.

Dressmaker's pins are used for holding pieces of knitting or crochet together for sewing, for marking off stitches on a gauge swatch, and also for pinning out pieces for blocking or pressing. Choose long ones with colored heads. Large plastic, flat-headed pins specially designed for use on knitted or crocheted fabrics can be found in some stores.

A tape measure is used for measuring stitch gauge and also the dimensions of knitted or crocheted fabric.

Small, sharp-pointed scissors are another piece of essential equipment.

Plastic bobbins are used for holding different-colored yarns in some kinds of multicolor work.

A calculator is useful for figuring out the number of pattern multiples in a piece of knitting or the number of chains for crochet and is, of course, essential if you are creating your own design.

Graph paper is another necessary item for planning an original design.

Crochet Hook Conversion Table

Metric Size	10.0	9.0	8.0	7.0	6.5	6.0	5.5	5.0	4.5	4.0	3.75	3.5	3.25	3.0	2.75	2.5	2.25	2
U.S. Size	N 15	M 13	L 11		K 10½	J 10	I 9	H 8	7	G 8	F 5	E 4	D 3		C 2		B 1	
Canadian Size	000	00	0	2	3	4	5	6	7	8		9	10	11		13	13	14

Steel Crochet Hook Conversion Table

Metric Size	2.70	2.55	2.00	1.95	1.85	1.75	1.70	1.60	1.50	1.25	1.15	1.00	0.80	0.75	0.70	0.80
U.S. and Canadian Size	00	0	1	2	3	4	5	6	7	8	9	10	11	12	13	14

Knitting Needle Conversion Table

Metric Size	1¾	2	2¼	2¾	3	3¼	3½	3¾	4	4½	5	5½	6	6½	7	7½	8	9	10
U.S. Size	–	0	1	2		3	4	5	6	7	8	9	10	10½			11	13	15
Canadian Size	15	14	13	12	11	10		9	8	7	6	5	4	3	2	1	0	00	000

Circular Needle Chart (see page 21)

Tension: stitches to		Lengths of circular needles available and minimum number of stitches required						
1 inch	10cm	40cm	50cm	60cm	70cm	80cm	100cm	120cm
3	12	56	69	81	95	109	136	160
3 ½	14	64	79	93	109	125	156	184
4	16	72	89	105	123	141	176	208
4 ½	18	80	99	117	137	157	196	232
5	20	88	109	129	151	173	216	256
5 ½	22	96	119	141	165	189	236	280
6	24	104	129	153	179	205	255	303
6 ½	26	112	138	164	192	220	275	327
7	28	120	148	176	206	236	294	350
7 ½	30	128	158	188	220	252	314	374
8	32	136	168	200	234	268	334	398
8 ½	34	144	178	212	248	284	353	421
9	36	152	188	224	262	300	373	445

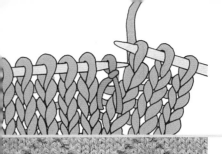

KNITTING CONTENTS

techniques 11

Holding needles and yarn, casting on and binding off, knit stitch, purl stitch, gauge, shaping, increasing and decreasing, circular knitting, cables and bobbles, Aran design, seams, finishing and abbreviations.

medium-weight patterns 32

Suited to summer-weight cardigans and tops, ladies' beach and leisure wear, babywear, wraps, shawls, and scarves.

heavyweight patterns 65

Suitable for garments, summer afghans and cushions, gloves and scarves, children's and baby outerwear, purses, bags, and children's toys.

lace patterns 99

Suited to jackets, coats, winter throws, men's heavy-duty sweaters, fisherman sweaters, and high-use homewear.

panel patterns 132

Suitable for simple stockinette stitch and reverse stockinette stitch garments.

ribs and edgings 165

Suited to collars, cuffs, waistbands and button bands.

knitting techniques

First Steps

Holding the Needles

Before casting on stitches you must get used to the needles and yarn. At first they will seem awkward to hold, but practice will soon make these maneuvers familiar. Use a medium-weight yarn and a pair of size 6 needles to practice with (see conversion table on page 9).

1. For the English method of knitting (see below), hold the right needle in the same position as a pencil. For casting on and working the first few rows, the knitting passes between the thumb and the index finger. As the knitting grows, slide the thumb under the knitted piece, holding the needle from below.

2. The left needle is held lightly over the top. If the English method of knitting is preferred, use the index finger to control the yarn.

3. If the Continental method is used, control the yarn and needles as shown.

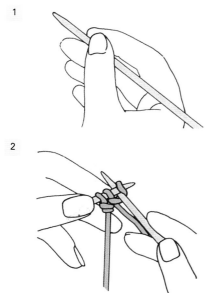

1

2

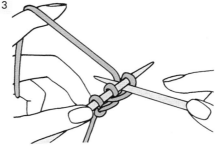

3

Holding the Yarn

The yarn may be held either in the right hand (English method) or the left hand (Continental method). Both are shown here, but the English method is illustrated throughout the rest of this book.

There are various ways of winding the yarn around the fingers to control the yarn tension and produce even knitting.

Method 1: Holding the yarn in the left or right hand, pass it under the little finger of the other hand, then around the same finger, over the third finger, under the center finger and over the index finger. The index finger is used to pass the yarn around the needle tip, and the yarn circled around the little finger creates the necessary tension for knitting evenly.

Method 2: Holding the yarn in the right or left hand, pass it under the little finger of the other hand, over the third finger, under the center finger and over the index finger. The index finger is used to pass the yarn around the needle tip and tension is controlled by gripping the yarn in the crook of the little finger.

Method 1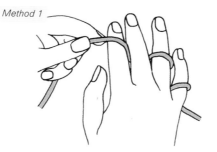

Method 2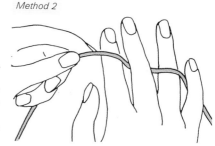

Making a Slip Knot

A slip knot is the starting point for most casting-on techniques.

1. Wind the yarn twice around the first two fingers of the left hand as shown, then bend the fingers so that the two loops are visible across the knuckles.

2. Using a knitting needle in the right hand, pull the back thread through the front one to form a loop. Release the yarn from the fingers and pull the two ends to tighten the loop on the needle, forming the first stitch.

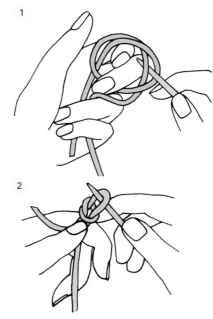

1

2

Casting On

"Casting on" is the term used for making a row of stitches as a foundation for knitting. Each casting-on method serves a different purpose according to the type of edge, or fabric, that you require. It is important for beginners to practice casting on until a smooth, even edge can be achieved.

Thumb Method

This method requires only one needle and is used for a very elastic edge or when the rows immediately after the cast-on stitches are worked in garter stitch (every row knitted).

The length of yarn between the cut end and the slip knot is used for making the stitches. You will learn to assess this length by eye, according to the number of stitches required, but as a general rule the length of yarn from the slip knot to the end of the yarn should be about 3 or 4 times the required finished width.

1. Make a slip knot the required length from the end of the yarn (for a practice piece make this length about 1 yard [1 meter]). Place the slip knot on a needle and hold the needle in the right hand with the ball end of yarn over your first finger. Hold the other end in the palm of your left hand. ✳Wind the loose end of the yarn around the left thumb from front to back.

2. Insert the needle upward through the yarn on the thumb.

3. Take the yarn over the point of the needle with your right index finger.

4. Draw the yarn back through the loop on the thumb to form a stitch.

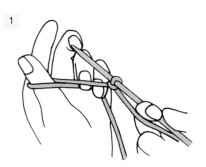

5. Remove the yarn from your left thumb and pull the loose end to tighten the stitch. Repeat from the ✳ until the required number of stitches has been cast on.

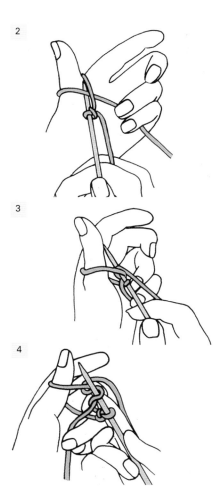

Finger and Thumb Method

This again requires only one needle and gives the same effect as the thumb method of casting on. Once mastered, this technique is extremely quick and efficient and produces a very even cast-on edge. If you find the edge is too tight, hold two needles in the right hand instead of one, as this will give you a looser edge.

1. Make a slip knot about 1 yard (1 meter) or the required length from the end of the yarn and place it on a needle held in the right hand.

2. Wind the cut end of the yarn around the left thumb from front to back. Wind the ball end of the yarn around the index finger of the left hand from front to back as shown. Hold both ends of the yarn in the palm of the left hand. ✳Insert the needle upward through the yarn on the thumb, down through the front of the loop on the index finger, then back down through the front of the loop on the thumb.

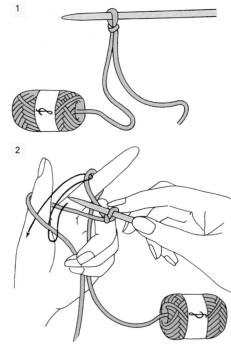

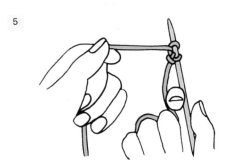

3. Pull the yarn through, thus forming a loop on the needle.
4. Remove the thumb from the loop, then reinsert it as shown, using the thumb to tighten the loop on the needle.
Repeat from the ✳ until the required number of stitches has been cast on.

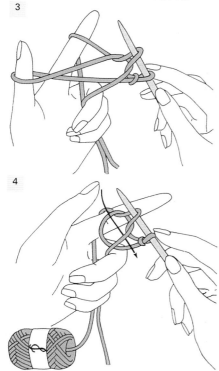

Cable Method
This method gives a very firm, neat finish.
1. Make a slip knot near the cut end of the yarn and place it on the left-hand needle.
2. Holding the yarn at the back of the needles, insert the right-hand needle upward through the slip knot and pass the yarn over the point of the right needle.
3. Draw the right-hand needle back through the slip knot, thus forming a loop on the right-hand needle. Do not slip the original stitch off the left-hand needle.
4. Insert the left-hand needle from right to left through this loop and slip it off the right-hand needle. There are now two stitches on the left-hand needle.

5. Insert the right-hand needle between the two stitches on the left-hand needle. Wind the yarn around the right-hand needle.
6. Draw a loop through and place it on the left-hand needle as before.
Repeat steps 5 and 6 as required.

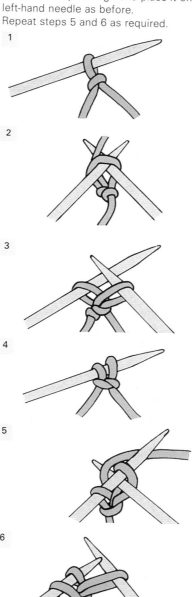

Basic Stitches

There are two basic stitches in knitting: knit and purl. All stitch patterns are based on one or both of these stitches, combined and/or varied in some way. The knit stitch is the easier of the two. Practice this until you can work it smoothly, then move on to the purl stitch. Note that these stitches are abbreviated "k" and "p." Other abbreviations are introduced on the following pages and listed on pages 30–31.

How to Knit
1. Hold the needle with the cast-on stitches in the left hand. With the yarn at the back of the work, insert the right-hand needle as shown through the front of the first stitch on the left-hand needle.
2. Wind the yarn from left to right over the point of the right-hand needle.
3. Draw the yarn back through the stitch, forming a loop on the right-hand needle.
4. Slip the original stitch off the left-hand needle.

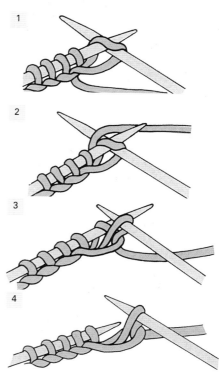

To knit a row, repeat steps 1–4 until all the stitches have been transferred from the left-hand needle to the right-hand needle. Turn the work and transfer the needle with the stitches to the left hand in preparation for working the next row.

How to Purl

1. With the yarn at the front of the work insert the right-hand needle as shown through the front of the first stitch on the left-hand needle.
2. Wind the yarn from right to left over the point of the right-hand needle.
3. Draw a loop through onto the right-hand needle.
4. Slip the original stitch off the left-hand needle.

To purl a row, repeat steps 1–4 until all the stitches are transferred to the right-hand needle, then turn the work, transferring the needles, to work the next row.

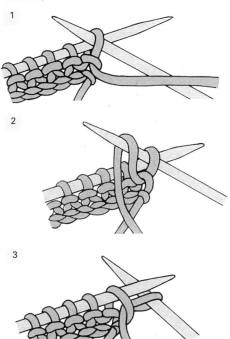

4

Slipped Stitches

It is often necessary to slip a stitch from one needle to the other without actually working it. This can be used in shaping or within a stitch pattern, and is very easy to work.

To slip a stitch knitwise (sl 1 knitwise): Insert the right-hand needle into the front of the next stitch on the left-hand needle as if to knit it, then slip the stitch from the left-hand needle onto the right-hand needle without knitting it.

To slip a stitch purlwise (sl 1 purlwise): Insert the right-hand needle into the front of the next stitch on the left-hand needle from right to left, then slip the stitch from the left-hand needle onto the right-hand needle without purling it.

Unless otherwise stated, when slipping a stitch keep the yarn in the same place as it was for the last stitch worked. If the last stitch worked was a knit stitch, keep the yarn at the back and carry behind the slipped stitch. If the last stitch worked was a purl stitch, keep the yarn at the front and carry it across the front of the slipped stitch. The general principle is that the yarn is normally kept on the wrong side of the work while the stitch is slipped.

When stitches are slipped for a decorative effect, however, as in the patterns on pages 83–93, the yarn may be taken to the right side of the work, and the pattern instructions will tell you to bring the yarn forward or take the yarn back, between—not over—the needles.

If a pattern does not tell you whether to slip a stitch knitwise or purlwise, slip the stitch in

the same way as the rest of the row is worked (knitwise on a knit row or purlwise on a purl row).

Working into the Back of a Stitch

This is a technique that is used to twist a stitch.

To knit into the back of a stitch (k1 tbl): Insert the right-hand needle from right to left into the back of the next stitch on the left-hand needle, wind the yarn around the point of the right-hand needle and draw a loop back through the stitch, dropping the stitch off the left-hand needle.

To purl into the back of a stitch (p1 tbl): From the back insert the right-hand needle from left to right into the back of the next stitch on the left-hand needle, wind the yarn around the right-hand needle and draw through a loop, dropping the stitch off the left-hand needle.

Basic Fabrics

Using the two basic stitches—knit and purl—you can practice making some easy fabrics that occur frequently in knitting. In fact, it will be a lot easier to understand complicated pattern stitches if you realize that a knit stitch and a purl stitch are one and the same thing but formed on opposite sides of the fabric. In both cases you are pulling a new stitch (loop) through an old one. In the case of a knit stitch you drop the old loop off the needle away from you to the back of the work. In the case of a purl stitch you drop the old loop off the needle toward you to the front of the work.

Garter Stitch *(top of page 15)*

This stitch is often referred to as "plain knitting" because every row is knitted. This produces a reversible fabric with raised horizontal ridges on both sides of the work. It is thicker and looser than stockinette stitch. One of the advantages of garter stitch is that it does not curl, so it can be used on its own, or for bands and borders. The same effect is achieved by purling every row, although this is slower to work.

techniques

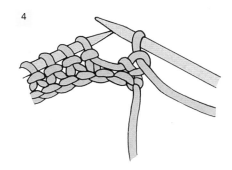

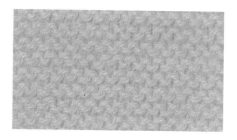

Stockinette Stitch (St st) *(below)*

Stockinette stitch is the most widely-knitted fabric. It comprises alternate knit and purl rows. With the knit side used as right side, it makes a flat, smooth fabric. Stockinette stitch tends to curl at the edges and needs finishing with a band, border, or hem where it is not joined to another piece with a seam. As it is a plain fabric, evenness in knitting is important because any irregularities will be highlighted.

Reverse Stockinette Stitch (rev St st) *(below)*

This is the same as stockinette stitch but with the purl side of the fabric used as the right side. At a distance it may look like garter stitch, but the ridges in reverse stockinette stitch are much closer together and not so distinct. This fabric is often used as a background to cabled fabrics, thus making the cables more pronounced.

Binding Off

The simplest and most common method of securing stitches once you have finished a piece of knitting is binding off. The bound-off edge should have the same "give" (elasticity) as the rest of the fabric. Always bind off in the same stitch as the pattern unless directed otherwise. If your bound-off edge is tight, use a size larger needle.

Binding off Knitwise

Knit the first two stitches. ✳Using the left-hand needle, lift the first stitch over the second and drop it off between the points of the two needles. Knit the next stitch and repeat from the ✳ until all the stitches have been worked from the left-hand needle and one stitch only remains on the right-hand needle. Cut the yarn (leaving enough to sew in the end) and thread the cut end through the stitch on the needle. Pull the yarn end firmly to tighten the last stitch.

Binding off Knitwise

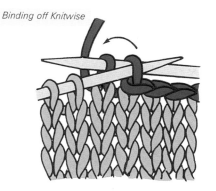

Binding off Purlwise

Purl the first two stitches. ✳Using the left-hand needle, lift the first stitch over the second and drop it off the needle. Purl the next stitch and repeat from the ✳, securing the last stitch as described above.

Binding off in Rib

Always work the stitches as though you were working a row in ribbing, casting stitches off as you go along. For single ribbing, knit the first stitch, purl the second stitch, and lift the first stitch over the second and off the needle. Knit the next

Binding off Purlwise

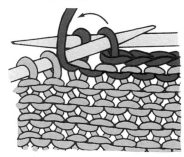

stitch and pass the first stitch over the second and off the needle. Continue in this way until one stitch remains on the right-hand needle, then fasten this stitch off as given before. For double ribbing or any other variation, work in a similar way, knitting the knit stitches and purling the purl stitches. Ribbing should normally be bound off fairly loosely to keep the bound-off edge elastic.

Gauge

"Gauge" refers to the number of stitches and rows obtained in a given stitch pattern worked over a given measurement—usually 4in (10cm). In a published knitting pattern these figures will be stated, along with the recommended needles.

Stitch "gauge" may also refer to the recommended number of stitches and rows worked in stockinette stitch, for a particular yarn: the number that will produce a pleasing fabric—neither too stiff nor too loose and floppy. Often this will be the same as the gauge on a printed pattern using this yarn, at least where stockinette stitch has been used as the standard.

The individual knitter's tension—the degree of tautness with which the yarn is held—will affect the size of the stitches. Some people hold the yarn relatively loosely, which results in fewer stitches per inch; others hold it more tightly, producing more stitches over the same measurement. Neither is "wrong" nor "right"; what is important is to knit with an even tension, which remains the same over the piece of knitting and, when following a pattern, to match the gauge obtained by the pattern's designer.

Before you begin to knit, you must obtain the stated gauge. This involves first knitting up a gauge swatch, comparing the gauge you obtain and, if necessary, changing needles until you achieve the correct result. This step is absolutely vital if the garment is to be the required size. Even one or two more stitches, or one or two fewer, across 4in (10cm) can significantly alter the size of the knitting.

Making a Gauge Swatch
1. The gauge given in a pattern will be over either stockinette stitch or the pattern stitch used for the garment. If it is given over a pattern stitch, it is necessary to cast on the correct multiple of stitches to be able to work the pattern (see Pattern Repeats or Multiples on page 17). Whichever pattern stitch is used, cast on sufficient stitches to be able to work a swatch at least 5in (12cm) in width. Some patterns give the gauge over 2in (5cm), but a larger swatch gives a more accurate measurement. Knit a piece measuring approximately 5in (12cm) square, then break the yarn, thread it through the stitches and slip them off the needle. Do not bind off or measure the swatch while still on the needle, as this could distort the stitches.
2. First take the stitch size. Measure horizontally across the center of the sample where you have relaxed a little after the first few rows. Count the number of stitches stated in the pattern's recommended gauge (e.g. 20) and mark these with pins at either end. Take a ruler or tape measure and check the measurement between the pins; if your gauge is correct it should be 4in (10cm) (or whatever measurement the pattern states).

It is crucial to measure gauge accurately; just half a stitch out over 4in (10cm) becomes quite a large inaccuracy over the full width of a garment.

If the measurement between the pins is more than 4in (10cm), then your knitting is too loose; if it is less, your knitting is too tight. Make another swatch using smaller needles if your work is loose, or larger needles if it is tight. The needles stated in the pattern are the *recommended* size— it does not matter what size you use as long as you end up with the correct gauge.
3. For the row gauge count the number of rows recommended in the pattern vertically down the center of the fabric. Mark with pins at each end and then check the distance between them. (It is easier to count rows on the purl side of a stockinette stitch or reverse stockinette stitch fabric.) Once the stitch gauge is right, the row gauge is most likely to be correct. Any slight inaccuracies could be overlooked, as the lengthwise proportions of a garment are usually given as a measurement.

Measuring Gauge Across a Pattern Stitch
The easiest way to measure gauge over a pattern stitch is to measure the width of one or more pattern repeats. Ascertain the number of stitches to cast on, as explained in Pattern Repeats or Multiples on page 17. After knitting a 5in (12cm) swatch, place a pin in the center of a pattern repeat (e.g. in the center of a diamond), then place another pin in the same place at least 2in (5cm) away from the first pin on the same row of the pattern. Measure the distance between pins. If the instructions state the gauge as the measurement of one pattern repeat, all you need to do is compare this with the measurement you have obtained. However, if the gauge is stated as stitches per 4in (10cm), or another measurement, you must calculate your own gauge in the same terms. Divide the number of stitches between the pins by the number of inches (centimeters) between them. (Using decimal points for fractions of an inch—e.g. 0.25 for ¼—will simplify your calculations.)

Suppose, for example, that the pattern repeat contains 20 stitches, and that one repeat in your swatch measures 2.5in (6cm). Divide 20 by 6 (2.5), which gives 8 stitches (sts) per inch (3.33 sts per cm). Now multiply by 4 (in)/10 (cm), which gives 32 sts to 4in (33.3 sts to 10cm). If the published pattern gauge matches yours, you can proceed with the project; if it differs, you must change needles and try another swatch, see Making a Gauge Swatch.

Problems may arise when the number of stitches in each row does not remain constant; in this case the pattern instructions will tell you which row of the pattern the stitches should be measured over, or the width of one or more pattern repeats will be given. Gauge information for a complicated pattern stitch is sometimes given over stockinette stitch, on the basis that if you get the correct gauge for the plain fabric your gauge should be correct in the pattern stitch.

Designing with Your Own Gauge
When you substitute one stitch pattern for that used in a published pattern, you must again get the same gauge in order for the garment to fit correctly. An alternative is to choose a smaller or larger size to compensate for the difference in gauge. In this case, you must first find the number of stitches per inch (centimeter) in your chosen stitch pattern. Count the number of stitches over 4in (10cm) on your swatch, then divide by 4 (10). Divide the number of stitches across the width of the garment in the larger/smaller size by the number of stitches you get per inch (centimeter) to get the actual measurement across the front/back of the garment. Multiply by 2 to get the total chest/bust measurement you would get if you followed the instructions for that size. Repeat these calculations with another size if necessary.

When you are designing a garment from scratch, you can set your own gauge. Make a swatch in your chosen stitch pattern. If you are pleased with the effect, measure your stitch and row gauge as described under "Making a Gauge Swatch" above. (If the swatch is too stiff or too floppy, try again with different needles.) Then divide by 4 (10) to get the stitches and rows per inch (centimeter). With these two measurements, you can calculate the number of stitches to cast on (or the number across the main fabric if increases are to be worked above the ribbing) and the required number of stitches/rows at other key points of the garment (see page 7). Use graph paper to work out the shaping between these points.

Pattern Repeats or Multiples

Most stitch patterns, unless they are completely random or worked in separate panels, are made up of a set of stitches that are repeated across the row, and a number of rows that are repeated throughout the length of the fabric. If a pattern is symmetrical (for example a diamond pattern), it is important that each row begin and end in the same way to "balance" the row. In other words, if a pattern begins "k3, p1, k5" it should end "k5, p1, k3." (See Abbreviations, pages 30–31).

For a lace pattern, a row that begins with "k2tog, yf" should end with "yf, sl 1, k1, psso," (see Abbreviations, page 30) as the decrease should be in the opposite direction. This ensures that when seams are joined, the pattern is symmetrical on either side of the seam. However, this rule does not apply to non-symmetrical patterns—for example diagonal patterns—which cannot begin and end in the same way.

A pattern repeat within knitting instructions is contained either within brackets or parentheses or follows an asterisk (✳). The extra stitches outside the brackets or before the asterisk are the stitches required to balance the pattern. To work out the number of stitches in a pattern repeat, add together the stitches within the brackets or after the asterisk (i.e. the stitches that are to be repeated). For a lace pattern, either count an eyelet increase (see page 19) as one stitch and a "knit two together" as one stitch or count the "knit two together" as two stitches and do not include the eyelet increase.

To work out the minimum number of stitches required to knit a gauge swatch, ascertain the number of stitches in the pattern repeat and add on the number of extra stitches at the beginning or end of the row. Extra pattern repeats will probably be needed in order to make a swatch of the required size.

Shaping

There are various ways of shaping a knitted fabric. Binding off—or, less often, casting on—stitches will produce an abrupt shaping. Gradual shaping is produced by working two or more stitches together or making two or more stitches out of one. These methods of decreasing and increasing are also used to form stitch patterns.

Decreasing One Stitch

The simplest method of decreasing one stitch is to work two stitches together.

On a knit row insert the right-hand needle from left to right through two stitches instead of one, then knit them together as one stitch. This is called "knit two together (k2tog)," and on the right side of the work the decrease slopes toward the right.

On a knit row

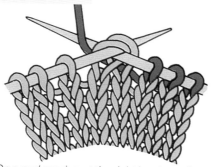

On a purl row insert the right-hand needle from right to left through two stitches instead of one, then purl them together as one stitch. This is called "purl two together (p2tog)." Where this is worked on a wrong

On a purl row

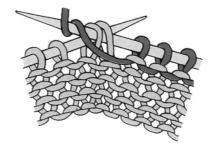

side row, the decrease slopes toward the right on the right side of the work.

To Create a Slope Toward the Left

It is often necessary to create a slope toward the left, either to balance a right slope (for example on opposite sides of a raglan) or in decorative lace stitch patterns.

On a knit row there are three basic ways of creating this effect:

Method 1:
1. Slip the first stitch onto the right-hand needle in a knitwise direction but without knitting it, then knit the next stitch.
2. Using the left-hand needle, lift the slipped stitch over the knitted stitch and off the needle. This is called "slip one, knit one, pass slipped stitch over (sl 1, k1, psso)." Some patterns abbreviate this process as "SKP."

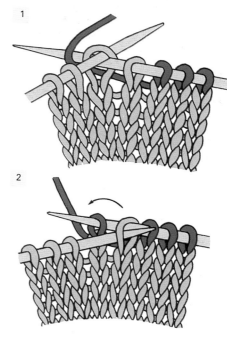

Method 2: This is worked in a similar way to k2tog, but the stitches are knitted through the back of the loops, thus twisting the stitches. Insert the right-hand needle

from right to left through the back of the first two stitches, then knit them together as one stitch. This is called "knit two together through back of loops (k2tog tbl)."

Method 2

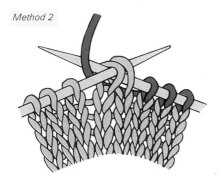

Method 3: Slip the first and second stitches knitwise, one at a time, onto the right-hand needle. Insert the left-hand needle into the fronts of these two stitches from the left, and knit them together from this position. This is called "slip, slip, knit (ssk)."

Method 3

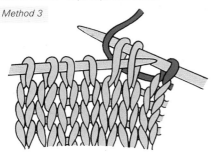

Left slope on a purl row (see top of next column)*:* the stitches are purled together through the back of the loops, which is a little awkward to work. From the back, insert the right-hand needle from left to right through the back of the first two stitches, then purl them together as one stitch. This is called "purl two together through back of loops (p2tog tbl)."

Decreasing Two Stitches

To decrease two stitches at the same point. The following methods are worked on right-side rows, and all create different effects.

Left slope on a purl row

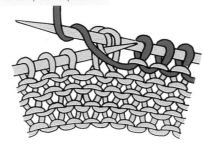

To create a slope toward the left: work as follows:
1. Slip the first stitch onto the right-hand needle without knitting it, then knit the next two stitches together as one stitch.
2. Lift the slipped stitch over the second stitch and off the needle. This is called "slip one, knit two together, pass slipped stitch over (sl 1, k2tog, psso)."

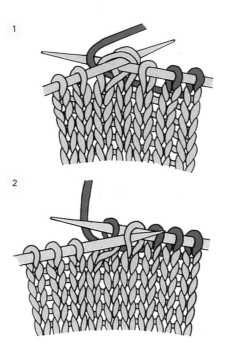

Slope to the right: insert the needle knitwise into the first three stitches and

knit them together as one stitch. This is called "knit three together (k3tog)."

Slope to the right

For a vertical decrease: (one in which the center stitch remains central) work to one stitch before the center stitch and continue as follows:
1. Insert the right-hand needle into the first two stitches as if to k2tog, then slip them onto the right-hand needle without knitting them.
2. Knit the next stitch, then lift the two slipped stitches over the knit stitch and off the needle. This is called "slip two together, knit one, pass two slipped stitches over (sl 2tog, k1, p2sso)."

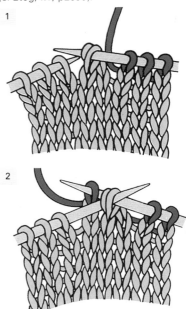

On a purl row the usual method of decreasing two stitches is to work to one stitch before the center stitch, then purl three together (p3tog). Work in the same way as p2tog, but insert the needle through the first three stitches instead of two.

Increasing

The most usual method of increasing is to work twice into a stitch (called "inc").

On a knit row: work into the front and back of a stitch as follows: knit into the stitch, then before slipping it off the needle, twist the right-hand needle behind the left-hand one and knit again into the back of the loop then slip the original stitch off the left-hand needle. There are now two stitches on the right-hand needle made from the original one.

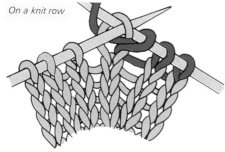

On a knit row

On a purl row: method is similar. Purl into the front of the stitch, then purl into the back of it before slipping it off the needle.

On a purl row

Making a Stitch
Another form of increasing involves working into the strand between two stitches. This is usually called "make one stitch (M1)."

1. Insert the right-hand needle from front to back under the horizontal strand that runs between the stitches on the right- and left-hand needles.

2. Insert the left-hand needle under the strand from front to back, twisting it as shown to prevent a hole from forming, and knit (or purl) through the back of the loop.

3. Slip the new stitch off the left-hand needle.

1

2
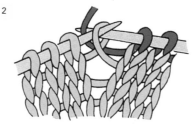

3
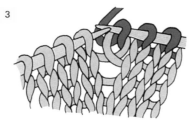

Yarn Overs (eyelets)
Another method is to make an extra loop between two stitches which is knitted or purled on the subsequent row. This forms a hole in the material and is used as a decorative feature. Lace stitches are made in this way and the required position of the hole in the fabric affects the way in which the yarn is wound around the needle. Whether the increase is preceded or followed by a knit or purl stitch, the yarn is always taken around the needle in an anti-clockwise direction—in other words, over the needle from the front to the back.

Between two knit stitches: Bring the yarn forward as if to purl a stitch, but then knit the next stitch, taking the yarn over the top of the needle to do so. This is called "yarn over (yo)."

Between two knit stitches

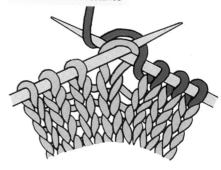

Between two purl stitches: Take the yarn over the top of the needle, then between the needles to the front again before purling the next stitch. This is called "yarn over (yo)."

Between two purl stitches

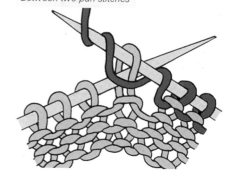

Between a knit and a purl stitch: Bring the yarn forward as if to purl, then over the needle to the back, then between the stitches to the front again before purling the next stitch. This is called "yarn over (yo)." (See Abbreviations, pages 30–31)

Between a knit and a purl stitch

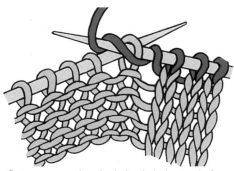

Between a purl and a knit stitch: Instead of taking the yarn back between the needles ready to knit the next stitch, take it over the top of the right-hand needle and knit the next stitch. This is referred to as "yarn over (yo)."

Between a purl and a knit stitch

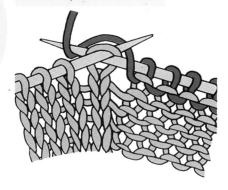

Larger hole within a lace pattern (see top of next column): This is done by making two extra loops instead of one and is normally worked between two knit stitches. Bring the yarn forward to the front, over the needle and around to the front again, then over the needle to knit the next stitch. This is normally referred to as "yo twice."

Increasing Twice into a Stitch

It is sometimes necessary to make 3 stitches where there was only one stitch before. This often happens where an increase is required in ribbing or where a

Larger hole within a lace pattern

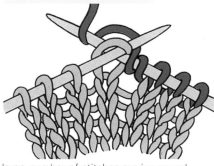

large number of stitches are increased across a row. There are three usual methods of doing this, although a pattern will tell you which method to use.

Method 1: Knit into the front of the stitch, bring the yarn forward and purl into the same stitch, then take the yarn back and knit the same stitch again before slipping the original stitch off the left-hand needle. Work into next stitch (knit 1, purl 1, knit 1 or k1, p1, k1).

Method 2: This method makes a small hole in the work. Knit into the front of the stitch, bring the yarn forward, then knit into the stitch again, taking the yarn over the top of the right-hand needle. Work into next stitch (knit 1, yarn over, knit 1 or k1, yo, k1).

Method 3: This is normally used in stockinette stitch, as the stitch is knitted into three times. Knit into the front, into the back, then into the front of the stitch again, before slipping it off the left-hand needle.

Method 1

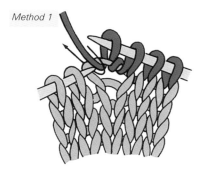

Method 2

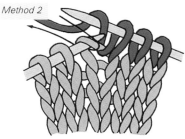

Method 3

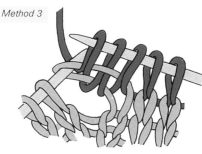

How to Keep Lace Patterns Correct

Complications often arise when a lace-patterned garment is shaped at the side edges—for example, when decreasing for the armhole. Unless row-by-row instructions are given, the knitter will have to use skill and judgment to keep the lace pattern correct. The following rules should help.

Most lace patterns rely on the fact that for every eyelet or hole made there is also a decrease. When shaping, you should regard these as pairs, and not work an eyelet without having enough stitches to work the decrease and vice versa. Check at the end of every row that you have the correct number of stitches, and that the eyelets and decreases are in the correct place above the previous pattern row. If there are insufficient stitches to work both the eyelet and the decrease, work the few stitches at either end in the background stitch (usually stockinette stitch). When only a few stitches are to be decreased—say at an armhole or neck edge—insert a marker at the end of the first pattern repeat in from the edge. At the end of every decrease row check that there is the correct number of stitches in both these marked sections.

For large areas you may find that drawing the pattern and shaping on graph paper helps.

Knitting One Below

The instruction "knit one below," or "K1B," appears in some stitch patterns, such as Fisherman's Rib (page 167). This technique produces an elongated stitch on the right side of the fabric. To knit one below, insert the right-hand needle through the center of the stitch below the next stitch on the left-hand needle. Knit this in the usual way, drawing the loop through, then drop the original stitch off the needle.

Knitting one below

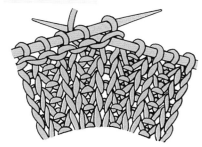

Circular Knitting

Knitting in the round, on a circular needle, or set of four or more short, double-pointed needles, produces a seamless fabric. This technique is used for small items such as socks, gloves, and berets, for polo-neck collars, and for the yoke on an Icelandic-style pullover. It can also be used for knitting the main part of a garment.

There are certain advantages to knitting in the round. If the garment is heavy, the weight of the knitting is evenly distributed between your two hands. And if you are working in stockinette stitch, you simply knit every row, thereby avoiding the problem, common to many knitters, of purling more loosely than they knit and thus producing a slightly ridged effect. Also, there are fewer seams.

Many stitch patterns are easily converted for working in the round. For garter stitch, knit and purl alternate rounds (as you would

for rows of stockinette stitch on a pair of needles). For simple rib patterns you repeat the right-side row throughout. Note that you do not include edge stitches when working in the round, only the multiple, or repeat, stitches (see page 17). Any pattern in which every wrong-side row is purled (or knitted) is adapted simply by reversing this instruction.

Using a Circular Needle

When knitting in the round with a circular needle, you must choose a needle that will accommodate all the cast-on stitches without stretching them. The chart on page 9 shows the minimum number of stitches for a given size of needle.

To start work, cast on onto one of the points the number of stitches required, then spread them evenly along the complete length of the needle. At this stage it is vital to check that the cast-on edge is not twisted before you join the circle of stitches into a ring. If it is twisted you will end up with a permanently twisted piece of material that cannot be rectified without cutting.

The first stitch that you work in the first round is the first cast-on stitch. To keep track of the beginning/end of the rounds, use a slip marker (see below right).

TIP: *The nylon joining the two needle points of a circular needle should be straightened before use. Immerse the needle in a bowl of hot water for a few minutes, then straighten it out by pulling.*

Using a Set of Four Needles

This is the best method to use if you have only a few stitches. Divide the total number of stitches by three and cast on that number onto each of three of the needles (the fourth one is the working needle). Form the three needles into a triangle—taking care that the stitches are not twisted—by drawing up the last stitch firmly to meet the first cast-on stitch.

Use the fourth needle to start knitting. Knit the stitches from the first needle onto the fourth needle. As each needle becomes free it then becomes the working needle for the next group of stitches.

Always draw the yarn up firmly at the changeover point to prevent a ladder from forming between the needles. Alternatively, the changeover points can be altered by working one or two stitches from the next needle on each round. To keep track of the beginning and end of a round, insert a contrasting slip marker.

Although double-pointed needles are usually available only in sets of four or six, any number of needles may be used. Many more may be required for a large number of stitches if a circular needle is not available.

Using four needles

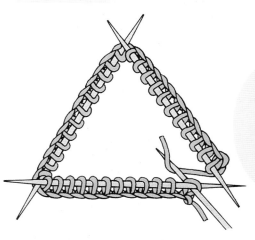

Slip Markers

In circular knitting a slip marker is used to mark the beginning of every round. Slip markers are also used occasionally in flat knitting to mark certain points in a pattern. To insert a marker within a knitted piece,

Slip Marker

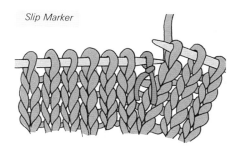

make a slip knot in a short length of contrasting yarn or use a ready-made marker and place on the left-hand needle where indicated/required. Slip the marker onto the right-hand needle on every row as it is reached until the pattern is established or the motif is completed and the marker is no longer required. For circular knitting, leave the marker in place throughout.

Cables and Twists

Cabling techniques are traditionally associated with Aran knitting (see page 25), but they are also used in many different types of stitch pattern. They can be worked in single panels, as all-over patterns or single motifs, or with lace or multicolor knitting, in any yarn thickness or texture.

Cabling or twisting stitches is simply a method of moving stitches across the material, or crossing one set of stitches over another. The following pages give details of how to work the basic cables, twists, and bobbles in knitting. However intricate a cable pattern may appear, the basic techniques still apply.

Remember that all cables pull the fabric in, like ribbing, and the gauge will be much tighter than for a flat fabric. Allowance is made for this in pattern instructions, which normally include a row of increases—either evenly across the row or where cables will be worked—just above the ribbing.

If you wish to add a cable panel to a stockinette stitch sweater, you need to calculate the extra stitches required as follows:
1. Knit a piece of the cable panel with a few stitches extra in the background fabric at either side. The swatch should be a minimum of 2in (5cm) length, or at least one complete pattern repeat if the repeat measures more than this.
2. Mark the edges of the cable panel with pins (inside the extra background stitches) and measure the distance between the pins without stretching.
3. Calculate how many stitches of the background fabric would be required to produce the same width as the cable panel, then subtract this number from the number

of stitches in the cable panel to find the number of stitches to be increased. For example, say the cable panel contains 36 stitches and measures 6in (15cm). The background stitch is stockinette stitch with a tension of 18 stitches to 4in (10cm). To produce 6in (15cm) of stockinette stitch, 27 stitches would be required. The cable panel has 9 stitches more than this (36 - 27 = 9), therefore an extra 9 stitches must be increased to allow for the cable panel and maintain the same width. These stitches should be increased above the ribbing across the stitches to be used for the panel.

Usually cables are worked in stockinette stitch and placed on a background of reverse stockinette stitch to enhance the relief texture. A special cable needle is required to hold the stitches during the twisting process. It is short, double-pointed and should be the same thickness as the main needles (or slightly finer). Look for the cable needles that have a bend in the center so that the stitches do not slide off.

Working a Basic Cable

Cable 4 Back (C4B):
Here the cable panel consists of four stitches in stockinette stitch against a reverse stockinette stitch background.
1. On a right-side row, work to the position of the cable panel and slip the next two stitches onto the cable needle.
2. With the stitches on the cable needle held at the back of the work, knit the next two stitches from the left-hand needle.
3. Now knit the two stitches from the cable needle to produce the crossover.
Leaving the first set of stitches at the back of the work produces a cable that crosses to the right.

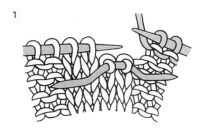

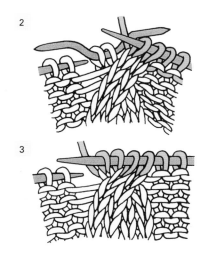

Cable 4 Front (C4F):
1. On a right-side row, work to the position of the cable panel and slip the next two stitches onto the cable needle, leaving it at the front of the work.
2. Working behind the cable needle, knit the next two stitches from the left-hand needle.
3. Now knit the two stitches from the cable needle to produce the crossover.
Leaving the first set of stitches at the front of the work produces a cable that crosses to the left.

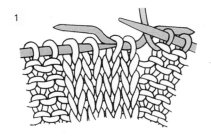

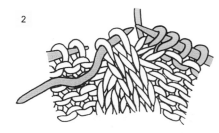

techniques

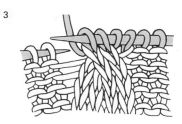

3

The number of stitches crossed can vary to make larger and smaller cables. To practice the basic cabling technique and see the different effects possible, knit some samples, varying the number of stitches in the cable and the number of rows worked between cabling. Attach a tag with the relevant information to each sample and keep for reference. Once you have mastered the basic cabling technique, you can produce any number of variations on it.

Twisting Stitches
Lattice effects and some cable patterns can be worked using twist stitches. These are similar to cables, but the effect is achieved using knit and purl stitches, not just knit stitches. Twist 3 Back (T3B) and Twist 3 Front (T3F) are the most common twists. In the following two examples, two stitches are moved in a diagonal direction across a background of reverse stockinette stitch (St st).

Twist 3 Back (T3B):
1. On a right-side row, work to one stitch before the two knit stitches. Slip the next stitch onto a cable needle and leave it at the back of the work.
2. Knit the next two stitches from the left-hand needle.
3. Now purl the stitch from the cable needle to produce a twist to the right.

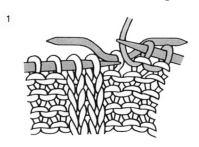

1

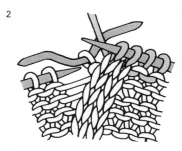

2

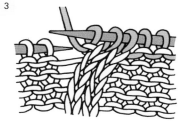

3

Twist 3 Front (T3F):
1. On a right-side row, work to the two knit stitches. Slip these two stitches onto a cable needle and leave them at the front of the work.
2. Purl the next stitch from the left-hand needle.
3. Knit the two stitches from the cable needle to produce a twist to the left.

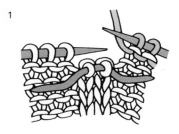

1

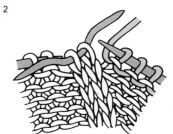

2

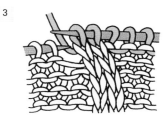

3

The examples given on this page show two stitches twisted to the right (T3B) and left (T3F) over a background of reverse stockinette stitch. As with cables, the number of stitches within a twist can vary. Also, twist stitches can be worked over a variety of background stitches, usually stockinette stitch or reverse stockinette stitch.

Stitches can be cabled and twisted in countless knit and purl combinations. However, the basic principle is always the same. Do not be put off by the complicated-sounding abbreviations for these names as they are required to differentiate all the variations. Just follow the instructions step by step and they will become easy. The more unusual abbreviations are given with each pattern, while the more common ones are on pages 30–31.

Twist 2 Back (T2B):
A small number of stitches can be cabled or twisted without the help of a cable needle, as shown below, or, if you prefer, with one. (See Abbreviations, pages 30–31).
1. Miss the first stitch, then knit the second stitch through the front of the loop.
2. Without slipping the worked stitch off the needle, bring the yarn to the front and purl the missed stitch through the front of the loop; slip both stitches off the needle.

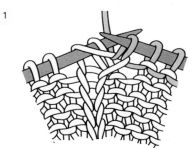

1

techniques

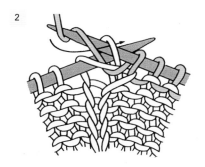

Twist 2 Front (T2F):
1. Miss the first stitch and purl the following stitch through the back of the loop, working behind the first stitch.
2. Without slipping the purled stitch off the needle, bring the needle to the front of the work, take the yarn back and knit the missed stitch, then slip both stitches off the needle at the same time.

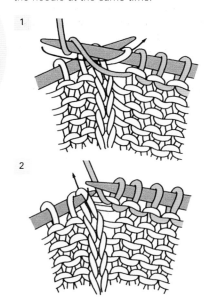

Crossing Stitches

These are very small cables involving only two stitches. Like twisted stitches, they can be done either with or without a cable needle; here they are shown worked without one. (See Abbreviations, page 30, for instructions on using a cable needle.)

Cross 2 Back (C2B):
1. Miss the first stitch on the left-hand needle and knit the second stitch, working through the front of the loop only.
2. Do not slip the worked stitch off the needle, but twist the needle back and knit the missed stitch through the front of the loop, then slip both stitches off the needle together.

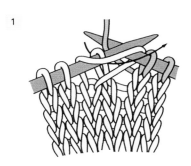

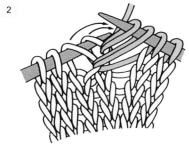

Cross 2 Front (C2F):
Work as given for C2B but knit the second stitch on the left-hand needle through the back of the loop working behind the first stitch.

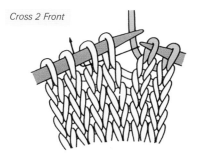
Cross 2 Front

Bobbles

Bobbles are an important feature of textured knitting. They can be used either as part of an all-over fabric or individually, and they can be worked in a contrasting color or in decorative clusters. They range in size from the smallest "tuft" (or "popcorn") to a large bobble that stands prominently away from the background fabric.

Methods vary slightly, but the basic principle is always the same—a bobble is produced either by creating extra stitches out of one original stitch, or between two stitches. These stitches are then either decreased immediately, or on subsequent rows. Alternatively, extra rows can be worked on these stitches but only before decreasing back to the original stitch.

Exact details of how to work a bobble are always given within pattern instructions, but the following example shows a frequently used method.

Large Bobbles

This large bobble is produced by making five stitches out of one and working on these five stitches for another four rows. The stitches are then decreased back to one.

1. On a right-side row, knit to the position of the bobble. Knit into the front, back, front, back, and front again of the next stitch, and slip the stitch off the left-hand needle so that five new stitches are on the right-hand needle instead of one.
2. Turn the work so that the wrong side is facing and purl the five bobble stitches, then turn again and knit them. Repeat the last two rows once more, thus making four rows in stockinette stitch over the bobble stitches.
3. With the right side facing, use the left-hand needle point to lift the second, third, fourth, and fifth bobble stitches, in order, over the first one on the needle. One stitch remains. You can continue to work the remainder of the row as required. Any small gap in the fabric when you continue knitting is concealed beneath the bobble.

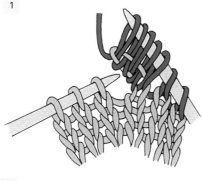

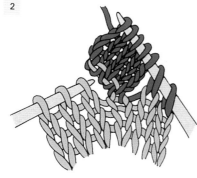

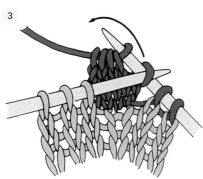

For greater textural contrast against the stockinette stitch fabric, work the same bobble in reverse stockinette stitch, by knitting the bobble stitches on the wrong-side rows and purling them on the right-side rows. Other interesting bobbles can be found among the stitch patterns on pages 235–240. Work a few of these as samples to serve as inspiration for designing.

Designing with Aran Stitches

Once you have gained a little experience in adapting garment patterns and perhaps even designing a simple pullover from scratch, using a favorite stitch pattern, you might like to try designing an Aran-style sweater. This is a very tempting project, for there is an enormous variety of Aran stitch patterns and a virtually infinite number of ways they can be combined. Commercially-available Aran patterns, however, may not include a combination that is exactly to your taste, and if you are going to the trouble of knitting all those cables and bobbles, you might as well include only favorites. By designing your own garment, you can have exactly what you want.

The prospect of combining all those different stitch patterns may seem daunting, but with a little patience and experimentation, as well as some careful initial calculations, you should be able to master it. If designing a whole sweater seems just too much effort, you might simply substitute one cable panel for another. The information below in "Row Repeats" will be especially useful for this.

The main feature of an Aran sweater or cardigan is the panels—cables and other highly textured stitches—that extend down the front of the garment. The garment also includes a background fabric and a ribbed edging, both of which should set off the combination of panels.

Ribbed Edgings

The borders, neckbands and cuffs of Aran garments need to be elastic so that they can stretch and then contract to fit snugly in wear. Ribs are formed by alternately knitting then purling a stitch or stitches to give unbroken vertical lines on both right and wrong sides. Ribbing patterns (see page 165) produce a horizontally elastic fabric. The most common rib patterns used for edgings are 1x1, 2x2 and 3x3 ribbing. These are easy to work and produce a very effective elastic fabric. Fancy ribs are generally less elastic than the more common ribs and are therefore less practical. However, some of the most

attractive Arans have fancy rib patterns as edgings. Ribs are usually worked on a smaller size needle than the main body of the garment to keep them firm. Because many Aran patterns have a relatively high stitch tension, (a high number of stitches per inch [cm]), quite a large increase row usually follows the ribbing. When knitting an Aran with a fancy ribbing, try to work the increases so that elements of the rib pattern continue up into the main body of the garment; this will enhance the finished appearance.

Texture and Background Patterns

These are patterns with small multiples and small row repeats. They form the backgrounds on which cables and more elaborate Aran panels are worked. Texture patterns can also be incorporated within larger diamond and lattice panels. Because cables and lattices are generally worked in stockinette stitch, the most frequently used background stitch is reverse stockinette stitch as this makes the patterns stand out boldly and is also easy to work. Seed stitch, Moss stitch, and Trinity stitch are some texture patterns that are also used frequently within Aran knitting.

Row Repeats

The selection of Cable Panels (pages 132–147) and Aran-style Fabrics (pages 75–77) includes a wide range of row repeats. (Even

Compatible Row Repeats	Largest Row Repeat
2, 4, 8	8
2, 4, 6, 12	12
2, 4, 8, 16	16
2, 6, 18	18
2, 4, 10, 20	20
2, 4, 6, 8, 12, 24	24
2, 4, 14, 28	28
2, 6, 10, 30	30
2, 4, 8, 16, 32	32
2, 4, 6, 12, 18, 36	36
2, 4, 8, 10, 20, 40	40
2, 4, ,22, 44	44
2, 4, 6, 8, 12, 24, 48	48

TRADITIONAL GARMENT DESIGN

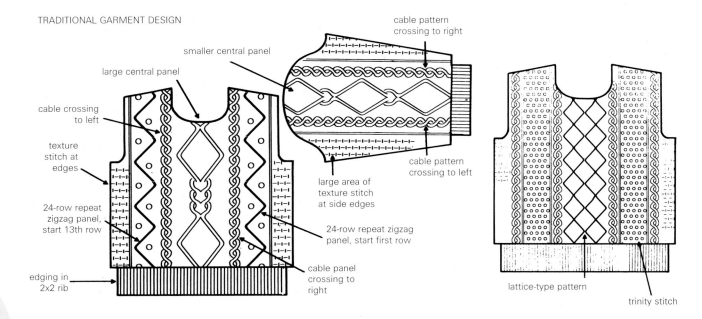

cable pattern crossing to right

smaller central panel

large central panel

cable crossing to left

texture stitch at edges

24-row repeat zigzag panel, start 13th row

edging in 2x2 rib

large area of texture stitch at side edges

24-row repeat zigzag panel, start first row

cable panel crossing to right

cable pattern crossing to left

lattice-type pattern

trinity stitch

longer row repeats can be found in some books specializing in Aran knitting.) It is a good idea, especially for the less-experienced designer, to use a combination of panels that are compatible—that is, one in which each of the shorter row repeats will fit equally into the largest row repeat. This makes it easier to keep track of the pattern rows and is also more likely to produce an aesthetically pleasing design.

If you wish to substitute a panel pattern for one in a published design, choose one with a row repeat that is compatible with the largest row repeat in the existing garment pattern, or alter the length of the repeat as described on page 25.

Altering Row Repeats

If you work a practice swatch of cables, as suggested on page 23, you will see how the appearance of a cable can easily be altered by working more rows of stockinette stitch between cabling rows. You can use this kind of adaptation when combining panel patterns for an original design or when substituting a favorite panel for one in a published design.

Make a swatch to see the effect produced by adding or subtracting rows from the pattern. In some cases the result may not be attractive; in this case, adding stitches to the panel, or subtracting stitches, and thus changing the width to retain the original proportion, may do the trick.

Traditional Combinations

The backs and fronts of traditional Aran sweaters are characterized by a large central panel surrounded by varying numbers of side panels, with a texture or background stitch at either side and between panels. Designs are usually symmetrical to each side of the central panel. For example, a cable panel is often crossed to the right on one side of the central panel and to the left on the other. Also, zigzag panels should be started on different rows at either side of the central panel (see the diagram above) so that they are staggered and form a mirror image.

In order to stand out, panels are usually spaced by a few stitches of reverse stockinette stitch and often accompanied by a single knit stitch or "k1 tbl" to each side.

The side edges are usually worked in a texture stitch, as elaborate Aran patterns would not be seen under the arm and would also be bulky, making the garment uncomfortable for the wearer. The same principle applies for sleeves. Because of size restrictions on the sleeve, a smaller central panel and fewer side panels may be used here.

Working Patterns as Panels

Many patterns work very well over a restricted number of stitches within a traditional Aran combination. Honeycomb and lattice-type patterns are particularly suitable as central panels. Patterns with smaller stitch repeats can be incorporated between side panels.

Positioning Stitch Patterns

There are various ways of approaching the design of an Aran garment, but the following is a good method for a beginner.
1. Using the chosen yarn, knit a gauge swatch (see page 16) in your chosen background stitch. Make a note of your stitch and row gauge.

techniques

2. Knit a sample of each chosen panel, pin it out and measure it, and make a note of the gauge.

3. On a sheet of paper, draw a horizontal line representing the width of the garment front. Mark the positions of the various panels along this line, then write in the number of stitches required for each panel.

4. Using the gauge of the various panels, calculate the width of the combined panels when knitted. Subtract this from the desired width of the garment front, then calculate the number of background stitches required at either side. Mark this number on the plan.

5. Knit a sample of the rib pattern, using needles a size or two smaller. Measure the gauge and calculate the number of stitches to cast on for a snug fit. The difference between this number and the total number of stitches for the main fabric is the number to be increased immediately above the ribbing.

Non-Traditional Designs

Aran techniques lend themselves to be used in many ways. Garments do not have to be designed along traditional lines. Instead of building up a design by combining panels, you can repeat patterns over the entire surface of the garment. The all-over Aran-style fabrics on pages 75–77 can be used in this way to produce garments with an Aran appearance. Also, many of the panels can be repeated, with or without spacing stitches to give an all-over effect.

Basic Color Knitting

The introduction of more than one color to knitting vastly increases the scope for interesting designs.

Horizontal Stripes

This is the easiest way of adding extra color. To work in a stripe pattern, simply work the number of rows required in one color, drop the yarn, pick up the next color, and work the required number of rows. Often stripes are in two alternating colors, or they may be multicolored in a random pattern.

To avoid breaking the yarn unnecessarily, work an even number of rows in each color; this will ensure that the yarn is at the correct edge of the work. However, if an odd number of colors is used, it is possible to work an odd number of rows in each color and still have the yarn in the correct place. Always keep an even number of rows between the last stripe in one color and the next in the same color. As long as there is not too much distance—say a maximum of 2in (5cm) between the end of one stripe and the start of the next one in the same color—the yarn can be carried loosely up the side of the work without cutting it off each time; this will reduce the number of ends to be sewn in. If the stripes are fairly deep, cross the yarn over at the beginning of alternate rows to prevent long loops between the stripes. Sometimes it is impractical to carry the yarn up the side; instead, cut the yarn, leaving a long end when you have finished with the color. When you have completed a section, all the ends must be secured by weaving them into the seam or along the wrong side of the color-change row.

You can achieve a number of interesting effects even with basic stockinette stitch. Changing color produces neat, even lines on the knit side of the work. Turn it over and you will see broken lines of color at the changeover points which make interesting patterns in their own right; this may be used as the right side of the work.

Changing color in garter stitch produces a clean, unbroken line if worked on a right-side row, or a broken line if worked on a wrong-side row. When changing color in ribbing, knit the first (right-side) row of new color (or purl if the first row falls on the wrong side) to produce a clear, unbroken line.

Vertical Stripes

Vertical stripes can be worked by the slip-stitch method (see below) where only one color is used in a row. However, they generally require the use of two or more colors in a row. For fairly narrow stripes using just two colors in a row, you can "strand" the yarns—that is, carry the unused yarn loosely behind the yarn being used, then pick it up again when needed. However, care must be taken not to draw the work together, producing a pleated or gathered effect.

If the stripes are wider than five stitches, it is best to use the "intarsia" method, in which a separate ball of yarn (first wound onto a yarn bobbin to minimize unrolling and tangling) is used for each stripe. Plastic bobbins are available in knitting shops and department stores; or you can make your own from small pieces of cardboard. When changing color, you must cross the old yarn over the new on the wrong side in order to avoid leaving a hole or slit in the work.

Slipstitch Patterns

Slipstitch patterns can be used to give the impression that two colors have been used across a row to create complicated color effects. In reality only one color is used at a time in a simple stripe sequence: the stitches that have been slipped in the previous row are carried up over the contrasting color of the following row.

By varying the combinations of color with knit and purl rows and/or stitches, an infinite number of fabrics can be created. Some designs worked entirely in stockinette stitch with slipped stitches are smooth and colorful; others are much more textured.

Correcting Mistakes

Even the most experienced knitter makes an occasional mistake, but there are very few mistakes that cannot subsequently be corrected.

There are a few ways of avoiding making mistakes, or seeing the error before you have worked too many rows above it. First, try out the stitch pattern in a spare yarn before working the garment. In this way you will become familiar with the pattern and will be less likely to make a mistake. Then, while working the garment, check back after every pattern row to make sure the pattern has been worked correctly. It is far easier and less frustrating to unravel one row than several. When working a lace pattern, check that the number of stitches is correct at the end of the row. If there are too few, you will probably find that an eyelet increase (see page 19) has been missed—check back along the row to see where the mistake has been made. Check that cables have been crossed in the right direction and on the correct row.

Dropped Stitches

This is the most common mistake made by knitters. A stitch dropped a few rows below the work on the needles can be picked up and re-created on each row, so long as the work has not progressed too far. If the stitch has dropped down and formed a ladder, you can easily pick it up and re-work it. However, if you have continued knitting, the stitches above the dropped stitch will be drawn too tightly across the back of the work to leave enough spare yarn to re-create the lost stitch. In this case it is best to unravel the work to the point where the stitch was dropped.

On the row below, picking up a knit stitch:
1–2. Working from front to back, pick up the stitch and the horizontal strand above it with the right-hand needle.
3–4. Insert the left-hand needle through the stitch and lift it over the strand and off the needle.

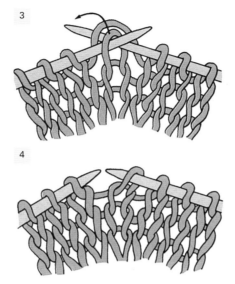

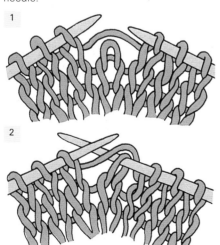

On the row below, picking up a purl stitch:
1–2. Working from back to front, pick up the stitch and the horizontal strand above it with the right-hand needle (the strand should be in front of the stitch).
3–4. Insert the left-hand needle through the stitch, lift it over the strand and off the needle, using the right-hand needle to draw the strand through the stitch, thus forming a stitch on the right-hand needle. Replace the stitch on the left-hand needle to continue.

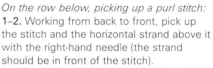

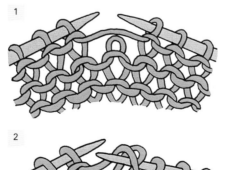

Several rows below: If a dropped stitch is not noticed immediately, it can easily form a ladder running down a number of rows. In this case the stitch must be re-formed all the way up the ladder using a crochet hook. Always work with the knit side of the fabric facing you. Insert the hook into the free stitch from the front. With the hook pointing upward, catch the first strand of the ladder from above and draw it through the stitch. Continue in this way up the ladder until all the strands have been worked, then replace the stitch on the left-hand needle, taking care not to twist it.

Several rows below

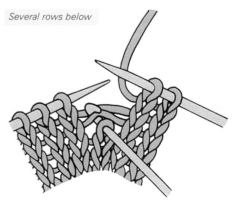

If more than one stitch has dropped, secure the others with a safety pin until you are ready to pick them up.

Unraveling

A single row: This is best done stitch by stitch. Keeping the needles and yarn in the normal working position, insert the left-hand needle from front to back through the center of the first stitch below the stitch on the right-hand needle. Drop the stitch above from the right-hand needle and pull the yarn free. Continue in this way until you reach the stitch to be corrected or picked up.

Several rows: The quick way of doing this is to take the work off the needles and pull the yarn. First, though, mark the row below the mistake and use a spare needle of a smaller size to pick up the stitches along this row, thus preventing more dropped stitches as you try to get them back onto the needle. Unwind the yarn gently—do not tug on difficult stitches or they will become tighter. Waggle the yarn so that the stitches ease themselves apart. You will need extra patience with textured or fluffy yarns. Use small nail scissors to cut away excess fibers forming a knot around the yarn, taking care not to cut the yarn itself.

Yarn that has recently been knitted for the first time can be wound into a ball while it is still attached to the knitting and reused straightaway. If the yarn has been knitted up for some time, it might be too crinkly for re-use—instead, you will have to use a new ball of yarn.

A complete piece of knitting: This drastic form of unraveling is sometimes necessary if you notice a mistake after you have finished a complete section of the garment. It is worthwhile re-knitting if the mistake is noticeable. The work must be pulled out in the opposite direction to the knitting (from the cast-off edge downward).

Correcting Texture Patterns

On a texture pattern you may find that you have worked a knit stitch instead of a purl stitch or vice versa several rows below. To correct, work to the stitch above the stitch to be corrected and drop the stitch off the needle. Unravel the stitch down to the row where the mistake was made, then re-create the stitch using a crochet hook as given for dropped stitches, turning the work as required so that the knit side of the stitch is always facing you. (If the stitch should be purled on the right side, turn the work and work from the wrong side.)

Finishing Knitted Fabrics

Before pieces of knitting can be sewn together, they must be finished in a suitable way.

Blocking

This is the careful pinning out of separate pieces of knitting before pressing to ensure they are the correct shape and measurements. This should always be done before joining seams. Blocking is very useful for smoothing out multicolor knitting, which often looks uneven, and for adjusting slightly the size or shape of a garment without re-knitting it. For blocking and pressing you will need a flat, padded surface covered with a clean cloth, long dressmaker's pins with large colored heads, an iron, and a pressing cloth.
1. Arrange the pieces of knitting wrong-side-up on the padded surface. Place pins at frequent (¾in [2cm]) intervals and angle them through the very edge of the knitting into the padding, avoiding ribbed sections.
2. Check that the measurements are correct and that the lines of stitches are straight in both horizontal and vertical directions. Re-pin as necessary to achieve the correct size and shape, stretching or easing in slightly if required so that the outline forms a smooth edge between the pins.

Pressing

Each pinned-out section of knitting is pressed or damp-finished to give a smooth finish and help it to hold its shape. The characteristics of yarns vary greatly, and information on individual yarns is usually given on the ball band. Some types of knitting or parts of a garment are best left unpressed, even if the yarn is suitable for pressing. These include ribbing and cable and texture patterns. Pressing may flatten the texture and blur the details, and can make the ribbing lose its elasticity. Damp finishing is more suitable in these cases.

If in any doubt about pressing, always try pressing the gauge swatch first to avoid spoiling the actual garment.

Wool, cotton, linen and other natural yarns: Using a damp cloth, steam thoroughly; avoid letting the iron rest on the work.

Synthetics: Do not press yarns that are 100 per cent synthetic. For yarns that are a mixture (containing some natural fibers), use a cool iron over a dry cloth.
1. Cover the pinned-out pieces with a damp or dry cloth, depending on the yarn. Check that the iron is the correct heat, then press evenly and lightly, lifting the iron up and down to avoid dragging the knitted material underneath. Do not press the ribbed edges.
2. After pressing, remove a few pins. If the edge stays flat, take out all the pins and leave the knitting to dry before removing it from the flat surface. If the edge curls when a few pins are removed, re-pin it and leave to dry with the pins in position.
3. After joining the completed pieces of knitting, press the seams lightly on the wrong side, using the same method as before (though without pinning, of course).

Damp Finishing

Damp finishing is suitable for fluffy and synthetic yarns as well as textured patterns—all of which can be damaged by pressing.
1. Lay pieces on a damp (colorfast) towel, then roll them up together and leave for about an hour to allow the knitting to absorb moisture from the towel. Unwrap, lay the damp towel on a flat surface and place the pieces on top of it.
2. Ease the pieces into shape and pin as explained in steps 1 and 2 of "Blocking," above. Lay another damp towel or tea-towel over the top, pat all over firmly to establish contact, and leave until dry.

ABBREVIATIONS

Basic Abbreviations

alt = alternate. This usually occurs during an instruction for shaping; for example: "Increase 1 stitch at end of next and every alt row until there are X sts." This means that, counting the next row as row 1, the increase is worked on rows 1, 3, 5, 7, etc., until the required number of stitches are on the needle.

approx = approximately

beg = begin(ning)(s)

cm = centimeter

dec = decreas(e)(ing). This is a shaping instruction. 1, 2, or even 3 stitches can be decreased in one go during knitting, but if more than this is required it is usually necessary to bind off some stitches. See page 15 for this. For a description of the usual ways to work a decrease see page 17.

garter stitch = every row knit

in = inch(es)

inc = increas(e)(ing). This is a shaping instruction. 1 or 2 stitches can be increased in one stitch (see page 19). However, if more than 1 or 2 are required it is usually necessary to cast on some stitches (see page 12).

k = knit

K1B = knit one below. Insert needle into st below next st on left-hand needle and knit it in the usual way, slipping the st above off needle at same time.

M1 (Make 1 stitch) = pick up strand of yarn lying between last st worked and next st and work into back of it.

M3 (Make 3 stitches) = [k1, p1, k1] all into next st.

psso = pass slipped stitch over. This occurs after a slip abbreviation. Example: k9, s1, k1, psso, k2. This means that you knit 9 stitches, slip the next stitch, knit one more stitch; then you lift the slipped stitch (using the point of the left-hand needle) over the 1 knit stitch and drop it off the needle, then you knit the last 2 stitches. This is a frequently-used method of decreasing.

p = purl

rep = repeat

sl = slip. Example: sl 1, k1. This means that you slip the next stitch onto the right-hand needle without knitting it, then you knit the next stitch.

ssk = slip, slip, knit. Slip the next 2 stitches knitwise, one at a time, insert the left-hand needle through the front of both loops and knit them together.

st(s) = stitch(es)

St st = stockinette stitch. This consists of 1 row knit, 1 row purl, and gives a fabric that is smooth on one side and rough on the other. Keep the stitch at the beginning and end of each row in stockinette stitch. Some knitters slip the first stitch of a knit row, or knit the first stitch of a purl row.

tbl = through back of loop(s)

tog = together. Usually used as a method of decreasing. For example: k2tog.

WS = wrong side

yb = yarn between two needles to back

yf = yarn between two needles to forward

yo = yarn over. (See pages 19–20 for how to make yarn overs.)

Twists and Cables

T2L (Twist 2 Left) = slip next st onto cable needle and hold at front of work, purl next st from left-hand needle, then k1 tbl from cable needle.

T2R (Twist 2 Right) = slip next st onto cable needle and hold at back of work, k1 tbl from left-hand needle, then purl st from cable.

C2PR (Cross 2 Purl Right) = slip next st onto cable needle and hold at back (right side) of work, purl next st from left-hand needle, then purl st from cable needle.

C2PL (Cross 2 Purl Left) = slip next st onto cable needle and hold at front (wrong side) of work, purl next st from left-hand needle, then purl st from cable needle.

T2PR (Twist 2 Purl Right) = slip next st onto cable needle and hold at back (right side) of work, knit next st from left-hand needle, then purl st from cable needle.

T2PL (Twist 2 Purl Left) = slip next st onto cable needle and hold at front (wrong side) of work, then knit st from cable needle.

C2B (Cross 2 Back) = slip next st onto cable needle and hold at back of work, knit next st from left-hand needle, then knit st from cable needle.

C2F (Cross 2 Front) = slip next st onto cable needle and hold at front of work, knit next st from left-hand needle, then knit st from cable needle.

C2BW (Cross 2 Back on Wrong Side) = slip next st onto cable needle and hold at back (right side) of work, purl next st from left-hand needle, then purl st from cable needle.

C2FW (Cross 2 Front on Wrong Side) = slip next st onto cable needle and hold at front (wrong side) of work, purl next st from left-hand needle, then purl st from cable needle.

T2B (Twist 2 Back) = slip next st onto cable needle and hold at back of work, knit next st from left-hand needle, then purl st from cable needle.

T2F (Twist 2 Front) = slip next st onto cable needle and hold at front of work, purl next st from left-hand needle, then knit st from cable needle.

C3B (Cross 3 Back) = slip next st onto cable needle and hold at back of work, knit next sts from left-hand needle, then knit st from cable needle.

C3F (Cross 3 Front) = slip next 2 sts onto cable needle and hold at front of work, knit next st from left-hand needle, then knit sts from cable needle.

C3L (Cable 3 Left) = slip next st onto cable needle and hold at front of work, knit next 2 sts from left-hand needle, then knit st from cable needle.

C3R (Cable 3 Right) = slip next 2 sts onto cable needle and hold at back of work, knit next st from left-hand needle, then knit sts from cable needle.

T3B (Twist 3 Back) = slip next st onto cable needle and hold at back of work, knit next 2 st from left-hand needle, then knit sts from cable needle.

T3L (Twist 3 Left) = slip next st onto cable needle and hold at front of work, work (k1 tbl, p1) from left-hand needle, then k1 tbl from cable needle.

T3R (Twist 3 Right) = slip next 2 sts onto cable needle and hold at back of work, k1 tbl from left-hand needle, then (p1, k1 tbl) from cable needle.

C4B (Cable 4 Back) = slip next 2 sts onto

cable needle and hold at back of work, knit next 2 sts from left-hand needle, then knit sts from cable needle.

C4F (Cable 4 Front) = slip next st onto cable needle and hold at back of work, knit next 2 sts from left-hand needle, then knit sts from cable needle.

C4R (Cable 4 Right) = slip next st onto cable needle and hold at back of work, knit next 3 sts from left-hand needle, then knit st from cable needle.

C4L (Cable 4 left) = slip next 3 sts onto cable needle and hold at front of work, knit next st from left-hand needle, then knit sts from cable needle.

T4B (Twist 4 Back) = slip next 2 sts onto cable needle and hold at back of work, knit next 2 sts from left-hand needle, then purl sts from cable needle.

T4F (Twist 4 Front) = slip next 2 sts onto cable needle and hold at front of work, purl next 2 sts from left-hand needle, then knit sts from cable needle.

T4R (Twist 4 Right) = slip next st onto cable needle and hold at back of work, knit next 3 sts from left-hand needle, then purl st from cable needle.

T4L (Twist 4 Left) = slip next 3 sts onto cable needle and hold at front of work, purl next st from left-hand needle, then knit sts from cable needle.

T4BP (Twist 4 Back Purl) = slip next 2 sts onto cable needle and hold at back of work, knit next 2 sts from left-hand needle, then p1, k1 from cable needle.

T4FP (Twist 4 Front Purl) = slip next 2 stitches onto cable needle and hold at front of work, k1, p1 from left-hand needle, then knit sts from cable needle.

C5R (Cross 5 Right) = slip the next st onto cable needle and hold at back of work, knit next 4 sts on left-hand needle, then purl the st on cable needle.

T5B (Twist 5 Back) = slip next 2 sts onto cable needle and hold at back of work, knit next 3 sts from left-hand needle, then purl sts from cable needle.

T5F (Twist 5 Front) = slip next 3 sts onto cable needle and hold at front of work, purl next 2 sts from left-hand needle, then knit sts from cable needle.

T5R (Twist 5 Right) = slip next 2 sts onto cable needle and hold at back of work, knit next 3 sts from left-hand needle, then purl sts from cable needle.

T5L (Twist 5 Left) = slip next 3 sts onto cable needle and hold at front of work, purl next 2 sts from left-hand needle, then knit sts from cable needle.

T5BP (Twist 5 Back Purl) = slip next 3 sts onto cable needle and hold at back of work, knit next 2 sts from left-hand needle, then p1, k2 from cable needle.

C6 (Cross 6) = slip next 4 sts onto cable needle and hold at front of work, knit next 2 sts from left-hand needle, then slip the 2 purl sts from cable needle back to left-hand needle. Pass the cable needle with 2 remaining knit sts to back of work, purl sts from left-hand needle, then knit the 2 sts from cable needle.

C6B (Cable 6 Back) = slip next 3 sts onto cable needle and hold at back of work, knit next 3 sts from left-hand needle, then knit sts from cable needle.

C6F (Cable 6 Front) = slip next 3 sts onto cable needle and hold at front of work, knit next 3 sts from left-hand needle, then knit sts from cable needle.

C7B (Cable 7 Back) = slip next 4 sts onto cable needle and hold at back of work, knit next 3 sts from left-hand needle, then knit sts from cable needle.

C8B (Cable 8 Back) = slip next 4 sts onto cable needle and hold at back of work, knit next 4 sts from left-hand needle, then knit sts from cable needle.

C8F (Cable 8 Front) = slip next 4 sts onto cable needle and hold at front of work, knit next 4 sts from left-hand needle, then knit sts from cable needle.

C9F (Cable 9 Front) = slip next 5 sts onto cable needle and hold at front of work, knit next 4 sts from left-hand needle, then knit sts from cable needle.

C10B (Cable 10 Back) = slip next 5 sts onto cable needle and hold at back of work, knit next 5 sts from left-hand needle, then knit sts from cable needle.

C10F (Cable 10 Front) = slip next 5 sts onto cable needle and hold at front of work, knit next 5 sts from left-hand needle, then knit sts from cable needle.

C12B (Cable 12 Back) = slip next 6 sts onto cable needle and hold at back of work, knit next 6 sts from left-hand needle, then knit sts from cable needle.

C12F (Cable 12 Front) = slip next 6 sts onto cable needle and hold at front of work, knit next 6 sts from left-hand needle, then knit sts from cable needle.

Bobbles

MB (Make Bobble) = knit into front, back and front of next st, turn and k3, turn and p3, turn and k3, turn and sl 1, k2tog, psso (bobble completed).

MB#2 (Make Bobble number 2) = [K1, p1] twice all into next st, turn and p4, turn and sl 2, k2tog, p2sso (bobble completed).

MB#4 (Make Bobble number 4) = [K1, p1] twice all into next st [turn and p4, turn and k4] twice, turn and p4, turn and sl 2, k2tog, p2sso (bobble completed).

MB#7 (Make Bobble number 7) = [K1, p1] twice all into next st, [turn and k4, turn and p4] twice, turn and k4, turn and sl 2, k2tog, p2sso (bobble completed).

MB#8 (Make Bobble number 8) = [K1, p1] three times all into next st, pass 2nd, then 3rd, 4th, 5th, and 6th sts over first st and off needle (bobble completed).

medium-weight patterns

Endlessly versatile and, on the whole, easy to knit, medium-weight fabrics are the mainstay of the knitter's repertoire. They drape well and make comfortable garments. If you have rarely attempted anything other than the most basic stitches, you'll be delighted to discover how many interesting textures you can achieve with relatively simple techniques.

small knit and purl patterns

Many apparently complex patterns are created simply by alternating ordinary knit and purl stitches (*pages 13–14*). This section includes some of the most versatile stitches, including (below) Seed Stitch, which is often used for borders, and Moss, or Irish Moss, which figures prominently in Aran knitting. Many of these patterns can easily be substituted for Stockinette or reverse Stockinette stitch in a commercial pattern— but check your gauge first!

Seed Stitch (also called Moss Stitch)
Multiple of 2 sts + 1
Drape: good
Skill: easy

1ST ROW: K1, ✳p1, k1; rep from ✳ to end. Rep this row.

Moss Stitch (also called Double Moss)
Multiple of 2 sts + 1
Drape: good
Skill: easy^

1ST ROW: K1, ✳p1, k1; rep from ✳ to end.
2ND ROW: P1, ✳k1, p1; rep from ✳ to end.
3RD ROW: As 2nd row.
4TH ROW: As 1st row.
Rep these 4 rows.

Dot Stitch
Multiple of 4 sts + 1
Drape: good
Skill: easy^

1ST ROW (RS): P1, ✳k3, p1; rep from ✳ to end.
2ND AND EVERY ALT ROW: Purl.
3RD ROW: Knit.
5TH ROW: K2, p1, ✳k3, p1; rep from ✳ to last 2 sts, k2.
7TH ROW: Knit.
8TH ROW: Purl.
Rep these 8 rows.

Seed Rib Stitch I
Multiple of 4 sts + 3
Drape: good
Skill: easy

1ST ROW (RS): P1, k1, ✳p3, k1; rep from ✳ to last st, p1.
2ND ROW: K3, ✳p1, k3; rep from ✳ to end. Rep these 2 rows.

Seed Rib Stitch II
Multiple of 4 sts + 3
Drape: good
Skill: easy

Worked as Seed Rib Stitch I, using reverse side as right side.

Ridged Rib
Multiple of 2 sts + 1
Drape: good
Skill: easy

1ST AND 2ND ROWS: Knit.
3RD ROW (RS): P1, ✳k1, p1; rep from ✳ to end.
4TH ROW: K1, ✳p1, k1; rep from ✳ to end. Rep these 4 rows.

Moss Panels
Multiple of 8 sts + 7
Drape: good
Skill: easy

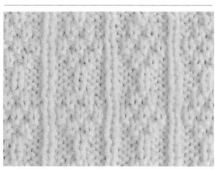

1ST ROW (WS): K3, ✳p1, k3; rep from ✳ to end.
2ND ROW: P3, ✳k1, p3; rep from ✳ to end.
3RD ROW: K2, p1, k1, ✳[p1, k2] twice, p1, k1; rep from ✳ to last 3 sts, p1, k2.
4TH ROW: P2, k1, p1, ✳[k1, p2] twice, k1, p1; rep from ✳ to last 3 sts, k1, p2.
5TH ROW: K1, ✳p1, k1; rep from ✳ to end.
6TH ROW: P1, ✳k1, p1; rep from ✳ to end.
7TH ROW: As 3rd row.
8TH ROW: As 4th row.
9TH ROW: As 1st row.
10TH ROW: As 2nd row. Rep these 10 rows.

Piqué Triangles
Multiple of 5 sts
Drape: good
Skill: easy

1ST ROW (RS): ✳P1, k4; rep from ✳ to end.
2ND ROW: ✳P3, k2; rep from ✳ to end.
3RD ROW: As 2nd row.
4TH ROW: ✳P1, k4; rep from ✳ to end. Rep these 4 rows.

Little Ladders
Multiple of 6 sts + 4
Drape: good
Skill: easy

1ST ROW (RS): Knit.
2ND ROW: P4, ✳k2, p4; rep from ✳ to end.
3RD ROW: Knit.
4TH ROW: P1, k2, ✳p4, k2; rep from ✳ to last st, p1.
Rep these 4 rows.

Little Arrows
Multiple of 8 sts + 1
Drape: good
Skill: easy

1ST ROW (RS): K2, p2, k1, p2, ✷k3, p2, k1, p2; rep from ✷ to last 2 sts, k2.
2ND ROW: P3, k1, p1, k1, ✷p5, k1, p1, k1; rep from ✷ to last 3 sts, p3.
3RD ROW: K1, ✷p1, k5, p1, k1; rep from ✷ to end.
4TH ROW: P1, ✷k2, p3, k2, p1; rep from ✷ to end.
Rep these 4 rows.

Knife Pleats
Multiple of 13 sts
Drape: good
Skill: easy

1ST ROW (RS): ✷K4, [p1, k1] 3 times, p3; rep from ✷ to end.
2ND ROW: ✷K3, [p1, k1] 3 times, p4; rep from ✷ to end. Rep these 2 rows.

Vertical Dash Stitch
Multiple of 6 sts + 1
Drape: good
Skill: easy

1ST ROW (RS): P3, k1, ✷p5, k1; rep from ✷ to last 3 sts, p3.
2ND ROW: K3, p1, ✷k5, p1; rep from ✷ to last 3 sts, k3.
Rep the last 2 rows once more.
5TH ROW: K1, ✷p5, k1; rep from ✷ to end.
6TH ROW: P1, ✷k5, p1; rep from ✷ to end.
Rep the last 2 rows once more.
Rep these 8 rows.

Diamond Panels
Multiple of 8 sts + 1
Drape: good
Skill: easy

1ST ROW (RS): Knit.
2ND ROW: K1, ✷p7, k1; rep from ✷ to end.
3RD ROW: K4, ✷p1, k7; rep from ✷ to last 5 sts, p1, k4.

4TH ROW: K1, ✷p2, k1, p1, k1, p2, k1; rep from ✷ to end.
5TH ROW: K2, ✷[p1, k1] twice, p1, k3; rep from ✷ to last 7 sts, [p1, k1] twice, p1, k2.
6TH ROW: As 4th row.
7TH ROW: As 3rd row.
8TH ROW: As 2nd row.
Rep these 8 rows.

Diamond Brocade
Multiple of 8 sts + 1
Drape: good
Skill: easy

1ST ROW (RS): K4, ✷p1, k7; rep from ✷ to last 5 sts, p1, k4.
2ND ROW: P3, ✷k1, p1, k1, p5; rep from ✷ to last 6 sts, k1, p1, k1, p3.
3RD ROW: K2, ✷p1, k3; rep from ✷ to last 3 sts, p1, k2.
4TH ROW: P1, ✷k1, p5, k1, p1; rep from ✷ to end.
5TH ROW: ✷P1, k7; rep from ✷ to last st, p1.
6TH ROW: As 4th row,
7TH ROW: As 3rd row.
8TH ROW: As 2nd row.
Rep these 8 rows.

King Charles Brocade
Multiple of 12 sts + 1
Drape: good
Skill: intermediate

1ST ROW (RS): K1, ✷p1, k9, p1, k1; rep from ✷ to end.

2ND ROW: K1, p1, k1, ✳p7, [k1, p1] twice, k1; rep from ✳ to last 10 sts, p7, k1, p1, k1.

3RD ROW: [K1, p1] twice, ✳k5, [p1, k1] 3 times, p1; rep from ✳ to last 9 sts, k5, [p1, k1] twice.

4TH ROW: P2, ✳k1, p1, k1, p3; rep from ✳ to last 5 sts, k1, p1, k1, p2.

5TH ROW: K3, ✳[p1, k1] 3 times, p1, k5; rep from ✳ to last 10 sts, [p1, k1] 3 times, p1, k3.

6TH ROW: P4, ✳[k1, p1] twice, k1, p7; rep from ✳ to last 9 sts, [k1, p1] twice, k1, p4.

7TH ROW: K5, ✳p1, k1, p1, k9; rep from ✳ to last 8 sts, p1, k1, p1, k5.

8TH ROW: As 6th row.

9TH ROW: As 5th row.

10TH ROW: As 4th row.

11TH ROW: As 3rd row.

12TH ROW: As 2nd row.

Rep these 12 rows.

Fancy Diamond Pattern

Multiple of 15 sts

Drape: good

Skill: intermediate

1ST ROW (RS): K1, ✳p13, k2; rep from ✳ to last 14 sts, p13, k1.

2ND ROW: P2, ✳k11, p4; rep from ✳ to last 13 sts, k11, p2.

3RD ROW: K3, ✳p9, k6; rep from ✳ to last 12 sts, p9, k3.

4TH ROW: P4, ✳k7, p8; rep from ✳ to last 11 sts, k7, p4.

5TH ROW: K5, ✳p5, k10; rep from ✳ to last 10 sts, p5, k5.

6TH ROW: K1, ✳p5, k3, p5, k2; rep from ✳ to last 14 sts, p5, k3, p5, k1.

7TH ROW: P2, ✳k5, p1, k5, p4; rep from ✳ to last 13 sts, k5, p1, k5, p2.

8TH ROW: As 3rd row.

9TH ROW: As 7th row.

10TH ROW: As 6th row.

11TH ROW: As 5th row.

12TH ROW: As 4th row.

13TH ROW: As 3rd row.

14TH ROW: As 2nd row.

Rep these 14 rows.

Seed Stitch Triangles

Multiple of 8 sts

Drape: good

Skill: intermediate

1ST ROW (RS): ✳P1, k7; rep from ✳ to end.

2ND ROW: P6, ✳k1, p7; rep from ✳ to last 2 sts, k1, p1.

3RD ROW: ✳P1, k1, p1, k5; rep from ✳ to end.

4TH ROW: P4, ✳k1, p1, k1, p5; rep from ✳

to last 4 sts, [k1, p1] twice.

5TH ROW: ✳[P1, k1] twice, p1, k3; rep from ✳ to end.

6TH ROW: P2, ✳[k1, p1] twice, k1, p3; rep from ✳ to last 6 sts, [k1, p1] 3 times.

7TH ROW: ✳P1, k1; rep from ✳ to end.

8TH ROW: As 6th row.

9TH ROW: As 5th row.

10TH ROW: As 4th row.

11TH ROW: As 3rd row.

12TH ROW: As 2nd row.

Rep these 12 rows.

Triangle Ribs

Multiple of 8 sts

Drape: good

Skill: easy

1ST ROW (RS): ✳P2, k6; rep from ✳ to end.

2ND ROW: ✳P6, k2; rep from ✳ to end.

3RD ROW: ✳P3, k5; rep from ✳ to end.

4TH ROW: ✳P4, k4; rep from ✳ to end.

5TH ROW: ✳P5, k3; rep from ✳ to end.

6TH ROW: ✳P2, k6; rep from ✳ to end.

7TH ROW: ✳P7, k1; rep from ✳ to end.

8TH ROW: ✳P2, k6; rep from ✳ to end.

9TH ROW: As 5th row.

10TH ROW: As 4th row.

11TH ROW: As 3rd row.

12TH ROW: As 2nd row.

Rep these 12 rows.

Garter Stitch Triangles
Multiple of 8 sts + 1
Drape: good
Skill: easy

1ST ROW (RS): P1, ✳k7, p1; rep from ✳ to end.
2ND ROW AND EVERY ALT ROW: Purl.
3RD ROW: P2, ✳k5, p3; rep from ✳ to last 7 sts, k5, p2.
5TH ROW: P3, ✳k3, p5; rep from ✳ to last 6 sts, k3, p3.
7TH ROW: P4, ✳k1, p7; rep from ✳ to last 5 sts, k1, p4.
9TH ROW: K4, ✳p1, k7; rep from ✳ to last 5 sts, p1, k4.
11TH ROW: K3, ✳p3, k5; rep from ✳ to last 6 sts, p3, k3.
13TH ROW: K2, ✳p5, k3; rep from ✳ to last 7 sts, p5, k2.
15TH ROW: K1, ✳p7,k1; rep from ✳ to end.
16TH ROW: Purl.
Rep these 16 rows.

Goblet Stitch
Multiple of 6 sts + 2
Drape: good
Skill: easy

1ST ROW (RS): P3, k2, ✳p4, k2; rep from ✳ to last 3 sts, p3.
2ND ROW: K3, ✳p2, k4, p2; rep from ✳ to last 3 sts, k3.
Rep the last 2 rows once more.
5TH ROW: P2, ✳k4, p2; rep from ✳ to end.
6TH ROW: K2, ✳p4, k2; rep from ✳ to end.

Rep the last 2 rows once more.
9TH ROW: Purl.
10TH ROW: Knit.
Rep these 10 rows.

Close Checks
Multiple of 6 sts + 3
Drape: good
Skill: easy

1ST ROW (RS): K3, ✳p3, k3; rep from ✳ to end.
2ND ROW: P3, ✳k3, p3; rep from ✳ to end.
Rep the last 2 rows once more.
5TH ROW: As 2nd row.
6TH ROW: As 1st row.
Rep the last 2 rows once more.
Rep these 8 rows.

Steps
Multiple of 8 sts + 2
Drape: good
Skill: easy

1ST ROW (RS): ✳K4, p4; rep from 8 to last 2 sts, k2.
2ND ROW: P2, ✳k4, p4; rep from ✳ to end.
Rep the last 2 rows once more.
5TH ROW: K2, ✳p4, k4; rep from ✳ to end.
6TH ROW: ✳P4, k4; rep from ✳ to last 2 sts, p2.
7TH ROW: As 5th row.
8TH ROW: As 6th row.
9TH ROW: ✳P4, k4; rep from ✳ to last 2 sts, p2.
10TH ROW: K2, ✳p4, k4; rep from ✳ to end.
Rep the last 2 rows once more.
13TH ROW: As 2nd row.
14TH ROW: ✳K4, p4; rep from ✳ to last 2 sts, k2.
Rep the last 2 rows once more.
Rep these 16 rows.

Diagonal Rib
Multiple of 4 sts
Drape: good
Skill: easy

1ST AND 2ND ROWS: ✳K2, p2; rep from ✳ to end.
3RD ROW (RS): K1, ✳p2, k2; rep from ✳ to last 3 sts, p2, k1.
4TH ROW: P1, ✳k2, p2; rep from ✳ to last 3 sts, k2, p1.
5TH AND 6TH ROWS: ✳P2, k2; rep from ✳ to end.
7TH ROW: As 4th row.

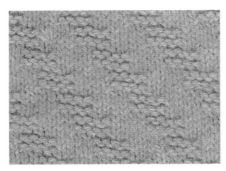

Plain Diamonds

Multiple of 9 sts
Drape: good
Skill: easy

8TH ROW: As 3rd row.
Rep these 8 rows.

Woven Stitch

Multiple of 4 sts + 2
Drape: good
Skill: easy

1ST ROW (RS): Knit.
2ND ROW: Purl.
3RD ROW: K2, ✳p2, k2; rep from ✳ to end.
4TH ROW: P2, ✳k2, p2; rep from ✳ to end.
5TH ROW: Knit.
6TH ROW: Purl.
7TH ROW: As 4th row.
8TH ROW: As 3rd row.
Rep these 8 rows.

Garter Stitch Steps

Multiple of 8 sts
Drape: good
Skill: easy

1ST AND EVERY ALT ROW (RS): Knit.
2ND AND 4TH ROWS: ✳K4, p4; rep from ✳ to end.
6TH AND 8TH ROWS: K2, ✳p4, k4; rep from ✳ to last 6 sts, p4, k2.
10TH AND 12TH ROWS: ✳P4, k4; rep from ✳ to end.
14TH AND 16TH ROWS: P2, ✳k4, p4; rep from ✳ to last 6 sts, k4, p2.
Rep these 16 rows.

Garter Stitch Checks

Multiple of 10 sts + 5
Drape: good
Skill: easy

1ST ROW (RS): K5, ✳p5, k5; rep from ✳ to end.
2ND ROW: Purl.
Rep the last 2 rows once more, then the 1st row again.
6TH ROW: K5, ✳p5, k5; rep from ✳ to end.
7TH ROW: Knit. Rep the last 2 rows once more, then the 6th row again.
Rep these 10 rows.

1ST ROW (RS): K4, ✳p1, k8; rep from ✳ to last 5 sts, p1, k4.
2ND ROW: P3, ✳k3, p6; rep from ✳ to last 6 sts, k3, p3.
3RD ROW: K2, ✳p5, k4; rep from ✳ to last 7 sts, p5, k2.
4TH ROW: P1, ✳k7, p2; rep from ✳ to last 8 sts, k7, p1.
5TH ROW: Purl.
6TH ROW: As 4th row.
7TH ROW: As 3rd row.
8TH ROW: As 2nd row.
Rep these 8 rows.

Squares

Multiple of 10 sts + 2
Drape: good
Skill: easy

1ST ROW (RS): Knit.

2ND ROW: Purl.
3RD ROW: K2, ✳p8, k2; rep from ✳ to end.
4TH ROW: P2, ✳k8, p2; rep from ✳ to end.
5TH ROW: K2, ✳p2, k4, p2, k2; rep from ✳ to end.
6TH ROW: P2, ✳k2, p4, k2, p2; rep from ✳ to end.
Rep the last 2 rows twice more.
11TH ROW: As 3rd row.
12TH ROW: As 4th row.
Rep these 12 rows.

Parallelogram Check
Multiple of 10 sts
Drape: good
Skill: easy

1ST ROW (RS): ✳K5, p5; rep from ✳ to end.
2ND ROW: K4, ✳p5, k5; rep from ✳ to last 6 sts, p5, k1.
3RD ROW: P2, ✳k5, p5; rep from ✳ to last 8 sts, k5, p3.
4TH ROW: K2, ✳p5, k5; rep from ✳ to last 8 sts, p5, k3.
5TH ROW: P4, ✳k5, p5; rep from ✳ to last 6 sts, k5, p1.
6TH ROW: ✳P5, k5; rep from ✳ to end.
Rep these 6 rows.

Fancy Box Stitch
Multiple of 8 sts + 6
Drape: good
Skill: easy

1ST ROW (RS): K2, ✳p2, k2; rep from ✳ to end.
2ND ROW: P2, ✳k2, p2; rep from ✳ to end.
3RD ROW: As 1st row.
4TH ROW: K1, p4, ✳k4, p4; rep from ✳ to last st, k1.
5TH ROW: P1, k4, ✳p4, k4; rep from ✳ to last st, p1.
6TH ROW: As 4th row.
Rep these 6 rows.

Basketweave Stitch
Multiple of 8 sts + 3
Drape: good
Skill: easy

1ST ROW (RS): Knit.
2ND ROW: K4, p3, ✳k5, p3; rep from ✳ to last 4 sts, k4.
3RD ROW: P4, k3, ✳p5, k3; rep from ✳ to last 4 sts, p4.
4TH ROW: As 2nd row.
5TH ROW: Knit.
6TH ROW: P3, ✳k5, p3; rep from ✳ to end.

7TH ROW: K3, ✳p5, k3; rep from ✳ to end.
8TH ROW: As 6th row.
Rep these 8 rows.

Ripple Pattern
Multiple of 8 sts + 6
Drape: good
Skill: easy

1ST ROW (RS): K6, ✳p2, k6; rep from ✳ to end.
2ND ROW: K1, ✳p4, k4; rep from ✳ to last 5 sts, p4, k1.
3RD ROW: P2, ✳k2, p2; rep from ✳ to end.
4TH ROW: P1, ✳k4, p4; rep from ✳ to last 5 sts, k4, p1.
5TH ROW: K2, ✳p2, k6; rep from ✳ to last 4 sts, p2, k2.
6TH ROW: P6, ✳k2, p6; rep from ✳ to end.
7TH ROW: As 4th row.
8TH ROW: K2, ✳p2, k2; rep from ✳ to end.
9TH ROW: As 2nd row.
10TH ROW: P2, ✳k2, p6; rep from ✳ to last 4 sts, k2, p2.
Rep these 10 rows.

Zigzag Moss Stitch
Multiple of 6 sts + 1
Drape: good
Skill: intermediate

1ST ROW (RS): Knit.
2ND ROW: Purl.
3RD ROW: P1, ✳k5, p1; rep from ✳ to end.
4TH ROW: P1, ✳k1, p3, k1, p1; rep from ✳

to end.
5TH ROW: P1, ✳k1, p1; rep from ✳ to end.
6TH ROW: As 5th row.
7TH ROW: K2, p1, k1, p1, ✳k3, p1, k1, p1; rep from ✳ to last 2 sts, k2.
8TH ROW: P3, k1, ✳p5, k1; rep from ✳ to last 3 sts, p3.
9TH ROW: Knit.
10TH ROW: Purl.
11TH ROW: K3, p1, ✳k5, p1; rep from ✳ to last 3 sts, k3.
12TH ROW: P2, k1, p1, k1, ✳p3, k1, p1, k1; rep from ✳ to last 2 sts, p2.
13TH ROW: K1, ✳p1, k1; rep from ✳ to end.
14TH ROW: As 13th row.
15TH ROW: K1, ✳p1, k3, p1, k1; rep from ✳ to end.
16TH ROW: K1, ✳p5, k1; rep from ✳ to end. Rep these 16 rows.

Vertical Zigzag Moss Stitch
Multiple of 7 sts
Drape: good
Skill: intermediate

1ST ROW (RS): ✳P1, k1, p1, k4; rep from ✳ to end.
2ND ROW: ✳P4, k1, p1, k1; rep from ✳ to end.
3RD ROW: ✳[K1, p1] twice, k3; rep from ✳ to end.
4TH ROW: ✳P3, [k1, p1] twice; rep from ✳ to end.
5TH ROW: K2, p1, k1, p1, ✳k4, p1, k1, p1; rep from ✳ to last 2 sts, k2.
6TH ROW: P2, k1, p1, k1, ✳p4, k1, p1, k1; rep from ✳ to last 2 sts, p2.
7TH ROW: K3, p1, k1, p1, ✳k4, p1, k1, p1; rep from ✳ to last st, k1.
8TH ROW: [P1, k1] twice, ✳p4, k1, p1, k1; rep from ✳ to last 3 sts, p3.
9TH ROW: ✳K4, p1, k1, p1; rep from ✳ to end.
10TH ROW: ✳K1, p1, k1, p4; rep from ✳ to end.
11TH AND 12TH ROWS: As 7th and 8th rows.
13TH AND 14TH ROWS: As 5th and 6th rows.
15TH AND 16TH ROWS: As 3rd and 4th rows. Rep these 16 rows.

Diagonals I
Multiple of 8 sts + 6
Drape: good
Skill: easy

1ST ROW (RS): P3, ✳k5, p3; rep from ✳ to last 3 sts, k3.
2ND ROW: P4, ✳k3, p5; rep from ✳ to last 2 sts, k2.
3RD ROW: P1, k5, ✳p3, k5; rep from ✳ to end.

4TH ROW: K1, p5, ✳k3, p5; rep from ✳ to end.
5TH ROW: K4, ✳p3, k5; rep from ✳ to last 2 sts, p2.
6TH ROW: K3, ✳p5, k3; rep from ✳ to last 3 sts, p3.
7TH ROW: K2, p3, ✳k5, p3; rep from ✳ to last st, k1.
8TH ROW: P2, k3, ✳p5, k3; rep from ✳ to last st, p1.
Rep these 8 rows.

Diagonals II
Multiple of 8 sts + 6
Drape: good
Skill: easy

Worked as Diagonals I, using reverse side as right side.

Polperro Laughing Boy
Multiple of 6 sts
Drape: good
Skill: easy

1ST ROW (RS): Knit.
2ND ROW: P2, k2, ✳p4, k2; rep from ✳ to last 2 sts, p2.
Rep these 2 rows once more.
Work 4 rows in St st, starting knit.
Rep these 8 rows.

Lizard Lattice
Multiple of 6 sts + 3
Drape: good
Skill: easy

Work 4 rows in St st, starting knit (1st row is right side).
5TH ROW: P3, ✳k3, p3; rep from ✳ to end.
6TH ROW: Purl.
Rep the last 2 rows once more, then 5th row again.
Work 4 rows in St st, starting purl.
14TH ROW: P3, ✳k3, p3; rep from ✳ to end.
15TH ROW: Knit.
Rep the last 2 rows once more, then 14th row again. Rep these 18 rows.

Alan's Pattern
Multiple of 8 sts + 4
Drape: good
Skill: easy

1ST ROW (RS) Knit.
2ND ROW: K4, ✳p4, k4; rep from ✳ to end.
3RD ROW: P4, ✳k4, p4; rep from ✳ to end.
4TH ROW: Knit.
5TH ROW: As 3rd row.

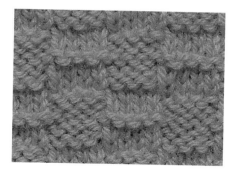

6TH ROW: As 2nd row.
7TH ROW: Knit.
Rep last 3 rows once more.
11TH ROW: As 2nd row.
12TH ROW: As 3rd row.
Rep these 12 rows.

Diamond Web
Multiple of 6 sts + 1
Drape: good
Skill: intermediate

1ST ROW (RS): P3, ✳k1, p5; rep from ✳ to last 4 sts, k1, p3.
2ND ROW: K3, ✳p1, k5; rep from ✳ to last 4 sts, p1, k3.
Rep these 2 rows once more.
5TH ROW: P2, ✳k1, p1, k1, p3; rep from ✳ to last 5 sts, k1, p1, k1, p2.
6TH ROW: K2, ✳p1, k1, p1, k3; rep from ✳ to last 5 sts, p1, k1, p1, k2.
Rep the last 2 rows once more.
9TH ROW: P1, ✳k1, p3, k1, p1; rep from ✳ to end.

10TH ROW: K1, ✳p1, k3, p1, k1; rep from ✳ to end.
Rep the last 2 rows once more.
13TH ROW: K1, ✳p5, k1; rep from ✳ to end.
14TH ROW: P1, ✳k5, p1, rep from ✳ to end.
Rep the last 2 rows once more.
17TH ROW: As 9th row.
18TH ROW: As 10th row.
Rep the last 2 rows once more.
21ST ROW: As 5th row.
22ND ROW: As 6th row.
Rep the last 2 rows once more.
Rep these 24 rows.

Waffle Stitch
Multiple of 3 sts + 1
Drape: good
Skill: easy

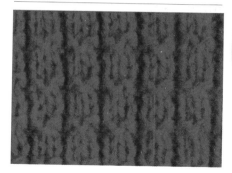

1ST ROW (RS): P1, ✳k2, p1; rep from ✳ to end.
2ND ROW: k1, ✳p2, k1; rep from ✳ to end.
3RD ROW: As 1st row.
4TH ROW: Knit.
Rep these 4 rows.

large knit and purl patterns

The following patterns are also composed simply of knit and purl stitches, although two of them, Stem Pattern and Fancy Basketweave (*page 54*), entail working into the back of the stitch (*page 14*). These patterns give a striking, distinctive look to a garment; however, because of their relatively large multiples and repeats, they entail a bit more design planning. Make your gauge sample (*page 16*) larger than usual—at least 15cm (6in) square—to get a good idea of the finished effect.

medium-weight patterns

Spiral Pattern
Multiple of 7 sts
Drape: good
Skill: easy

1ST ROW (RS): P2, k4, ✳p3, k4; rep from ✳ to last st, p1.
2ND ROW: K1, p3, ✳k4, p3; rep from ✳ to last 3 sts, k3.
3RD ROW: P1, k1, p2, ✳k2, p2, k1, p2; rep from ✳ to last 3 sts, k2, p1.
4TH ROW: K1, p1, k2, p2, ✳k2, p1, k2, p2; rep from ✳ to last st, k1.
5TH ROW: P1, k3, ✳p4, k3; rep from ✳ to last 3 sts, p3.
6TH ROW: K2, p4, ✳k3, p4; rep from ✳ to last st, k1.
7TH ROW: P1, k5, ✳p2, k5; rep from ✳ to last st, p1.
8TH ROW: K1, p5, ✳k2, p5; rep from ✳ to last st, k1.
Rep these 8 rows.

Textured Triangle Stack
Multiple of 10 sts + 1
Drape: good
Skill: easy

1ST ROW (RS): P5, ✳k1, p9; rep from ✳ to last 6 sts, k1, p5.
2ND ROW: K5, ✳p1, k9; rep from ✳ to last 6 sts, p1, k5.
3RD ROW: P4, ✳k3, p7; rep from ✳ to last 7 sts, p3, k4.
4RD ROW: K4, ✳p3, k7; rep from ✳ to last 7 sts, k3, p4.
5TH ROW: P3, ✳k5, p5; rep from ✳ to last 8 sts, k5, p3.
6TH ROW: K3, ✳p5, k5; rep from ✳ to last 8 sts, p5, k3.
7TH ROW: P2, ✳k7, p3; rep from ✳ to last 9 sts, k7, p2.
8TH ROW: K2, ✳p7, k3; rep from ✳ to last 9 sts, p7, k2.
9TH ROW: P1, ✳k9, p1; rep from ✳ to end.
10TH ROW: K1, ✳p9, k1; rep from ✳ to end.
Rep these 10 rows.

Zigzag and Stripe Columns
Multiple of 10 sts
Drape: good
Skill: easy

1ST ROW (RS): P1, k1, p2, k5, ✳p2, k1, p2, k5; rep from ✳ to last st, p1.
2ND ROW: K1, p4, k2, p2, ✳k2, p4, k2, p2; rep from ✳ to last st, k1.
3RD ROW: P1, k3, ✳p2, k3; rep from ✳ to last st, p1.
4TH ROW: K1, p2, k2, p4, ✳k2, p2, k2, p4; rep from ✳ to last st, k1.
5TH ROW: Purl.
6TH ROW: Knit.
7TH ROW: P1, k4, p2, k2, ✳p2, k4, p2, k2; rep from ✳ to last st, p1.
8TH ROW: K1, p3, ✳k2, p3; rep from ✳ to last st, k1.
9TH ROW: P1, k2, p2, k4, ✳p2, k2, p2, k4; rep from ✳ to last st, p1.
10TH ROW: K1, p5, k2, p1, ✳k2, p5, k2, p1; rep from ✳ to last st, k1.
Rep these 10 rows.

Windmill Pattern
Multiple of 20 sts
Drape: good
Skill: intermediate

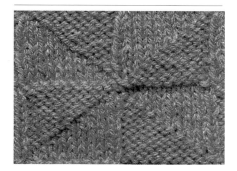

1ST ROW (RS): ✳P1, k9, p9, k1; rep from ✳ to end.
2ND ROW: ✳P2, k8, p8, k2; rep from ✳ to end.
3RD ROW: ✳P3, k7, p7, k3; rep from ✳ to end.
4TH ROW: ✳P4, k6, p6, k4; rep from ✳ to end.
5TH ROW: ✳P5, k5; rep from ✳ to end.
6TH ROW: ✳P6, k4, p4, k6; rep from ✳ to end.
7TH ROW: ✳P7, k3, p3, k7; rep from ✳ to end.
8TH ROW: ✳P8, k2, p2, k8; rep from ✳ to end.
9TH ROW: ✳P9, k1, p1, k9; rep from ✳ to end.
10TH ROW: ✳P10, k10; rep from ✳ to end.
11TH ROW: ✳K10, p10; rep from ✳ to end.
12TH ROW: ✳K9, p1, k1, p9; rep from ✳ to end.
13TH ROW: ✳K8, p2, k2, p8; rep from ✳ to end.
14TH ROW: ✳K7, p3, k3, p7; rep from ✳ to end.
15TH ROW: ✳K6, p4, k4, p6; rep from ✳ to end.
16TH ROW: ✳K5, p5; rep from ✳ to end.
17TH ROW: ✳K4, p6, k6, p4; rep from ✳ to end.
18TH ROW: ✳K3, p7, k7, p3; rep from ✳ to end.
19TH ROW: ✳K2, p8, k8, p2; rep from ✳ to end.
20TH ROW: ✳K1, p9, k9, p1; rep from ✳ to end.
21ST ROW: As 10th row.
22ND ROW: As 11th row.
Rep these 22 rows.

Rib and Arrow Pattern I
Multiple of 14 sts + 2
Drape: good
Skill: intermediate

1ST ROW (RS): K2, ✳p4, k4, p4, k2; rep from ✳ to end.
2ND ROW: P2, ✳k4, p4, k4, p2; rep from ✳ to end.
3RD ROW: K2, ✳p3, k6, p3, k2; rep from ✳ to end.
4TH ROW: P2, ✳k3, p6, k3, p2; rep from ✳ to end.
5TH ROW: K2, p2, k2, [p1, k2] twice, ✳[p2, k2] twice, [p1, k2] twice; rep from ✳ to last 4 sts, p2, k2.
6TH ROW: P2, k2, p2, [k1, p2] twice, ✳[k2, p2] twice, [k1, p2] twice; rep from ✳ to last 4 sts, k2, p2.
7TH ROW: K2, ✳p1, k2, [p2, k2] twice, p1, k2; rep from ✳ to end.
8TH ROW: P2, ✳k1, p2, [k2, p2] twice, k1, p2; rep from ✳ to end.
9TH ROW: K4, p3, k2, p3, ✳k6, p3, k2, p3; rep from ✳ to last 4 sts, k4.
10TH ROW: P4, k3, p2, k3, ✳p6, k3, p2, k3; rep from ✳ to last 4 sts, p4.
11TH ROW: K3, p4, k2, p4, ✳k4, p4, k2, p4; rep from ✳ to last 3 sts, k3.
12TH ROW: P3, k4, p2, k4, ✳p4, k4, p2, k4; rep from ✳ to last 3 sts, p3.
13TH ROW: K2, ✳p5, k2; rep from ✳ to end.
14TH ROW: P2, ✳k5, p2; rep from ✳ to end.
Rep these 14 rows.

Rib and Arrow Pattern II
Multiple of 14 sts + 2
Drape: good
Skill: intermediate

Worked as Rib and Arrow Pattern I, using reverse side as right side.

Flag Pattern I
Multiple of 11 sts
Drape: good
Skill: easy

1ST ROW (RS): ✳P1, k10; rep from ✳ to end.
2ND ROW: ✳P9, k2; rep from ✳ to end.
3RD ROW: ✳P3, k8; rep from ✳ to end.

4TH ROW: ✳P7, k4; rep from ✳ to end.
5TH ROW: ✳P5, k6; rep from ✳ to end.
6TH ROW: As 5th row.
7TH ROW: As 5th row.
8TH ROW: As 4th row.
9TH ROW: As 3rd row.
10TH ROW: As 2nd row.
11TH ROW: As 1st row.
12TH ROW: ✳K1, p10; rep from ✳ to end.
13TH ROW: ✳K9, p2; rep from ✳ to end.
14TH ROW: ✳K3, p8; rep from ✳ to end.
15TH ROW: ✳K7, p4; rep from ✳ to end.
16TH ROW: ✳K5, p6; rep from ✳ to end.
17TH ROW: As 16th row.
18TH ROW: As 16th row.
19TH ROW: As 15th row.
20TH ROW: As 14th row.
21ST ROW: As 13th row.
22ND ROW: As 12th row.
Rep these 22 rows.

Flag Pattern II
Multiple of 11 sts
Drape: good
Skill: easy

Worked as Flag Pattern I, using reverse side as right side.

Chevron
Multiple of 8 sts + 1
Drape: good
Skill: easy

1ST ROW (RS): K1, ✳p7, k1; rep from ✳ to

end.
2ND ROW: P1, ✳k7, p1; rep from ✳ to end.
3RD ROW: K2, ✳p5, k3; rep from ✳ to last 7 sts, p5, k2.
4TH ROW: P2, ✳k5, p3; rep from ✳ to last 7 sts, k5, p2.
5TH ROW: K3, ✳p3, k5; rep from ✳ to last 6 sts, p3, k3.
6TH ROW: P3, ✳k3, p5; rep from ✳ to last 6 sts, k3, p3.
7TH ROW: K4, ✳p1, k7; rep from ✳ to last 5 sts, p1, k4.
8TH ROW: P4, ✳k1, p7; rep from ✳ to last 5 sts, k1, p4.
9TH ROW: As 2nd row.
10TH ROW: As 1st row.
11TH ROW: As 4th row.
12TH ROW: As 3rd row.
13TH ROW: As 6th row.
14TH ROW: As 5th row.
15TH ROW: As 8th row.
16TH ROW: As 7th row.
Rep these 16 rows.

Elongated Chevron
Multiple of 18 sts + 1
Drape: good
Skill: easy

1ST ROW (RS): P1, ✳[k2, p2] twice, k1, [p2, k2] twice, p1; rep from ✳ to end.
2ND ROW: K1, ✳[p2, k2] twice, p1, [k2, p2] twice, k1; rep from ✳ to end.
Rep the last 2 rows once more.
5TH ROW: [P2, k2] twice, ✳p3, k2, p2, k2; rep from ✳ to last 2 sts, p2.

6TH ROW: [K2, p2] twice, ✳k3, p2, k2, p2; rep from ✳ to last 2 sts, k2.
Rep the last 2 rows once more.
9TH ROW: As 2nd row.
10TH ROW: As lst row.
11TH ROW: As 2nd row.
12TH ROW: As 1st row.
13TH ROW: As 6th row.
14TH ROW: As 5th row.
15TH ROW: As 6th row.
16TH ROW: As 5th row.
Rep these 16 rows.

Fancy Chevron
Multiple of 22 sts + 1
Drape: good
Skill: intermediate

1ST ROW (RS): K1, ✳p3, [k1, p1] twice, k1, p5, k1, [p1, k1] twice, p3, k1; rep from ✳ to end.
2ND ROW: P2, ✳k3, [p1, k1] twice, p1, k3, p1, [k1, p1] twice, k3, p3; rep from ✳ to last 21 sts, k3, [p1, k1] twice, p1, k3, p1, [k1, p1] twice, k3, p2.

3RD ROW: K3, ✳p3, [k1, p1] 5 times, k1, p3, k5; rep from ✳ to last 20 sts, p3, [k1, p1] 5 times, k1, p3, k3.

4TH ROW: K1, ✳p3, k3, [p1, k1] 4 times, p1, k3, p3, k1; rep from ✳ to end.

5TH ROW: P2, ✳k3, p3, [k1, p1] 3 times, k1, p3, k3, p3; rep from ✳ to last 21 sts, k3, p3, [k1, p1] 3 times, k1, p3, k3, p2.

6TH ROW: K3, ✳p3, k3, [p1, k1] twice, p1, k3, p3, k5; rep from ✳ to last 20 sts, p3, k3, [p1, k1] twice, p1, k3, p3, k3.

7TH ROW: K1, ✳p3, k3, p3, k1, p1, k1, p3, k3, p3, k1; rep from ✳ to end.

8TH ROW: K1, ✳[p1, k3, p3, k3] twice, p1, k1; rep from ✳ to end.

9TH ROW: K1, ✳p1, k1, p3, k3, p5, k3, p3, k1, p1, k1; rep from ✳ to end.

10TH ROW: K1, ✳p1, k1, p1, [k3, p3] twice, k3, [p1, k1] twice; rep from ✳ to end.

11TH ROW: K1, [p1, k1] twice, p3, k3, p1, k3, p3, ✳[k1, p1] 4 times, k1, p3, k3, p1, k3, p3; rep from ✳ to last 5 sts, [k1, p1] twice, k1.

12TH ROW: K1, [p1, k1] twice, p1, k3, p5, k3, ✳[p1, k1] 5 times, p1, k3, p5, k3; rep from ✳ to last 6 sts, [p1, k1] 3 times.

13TH ROW: P2, ✳[k1, p1] twice, k1, p3, k3, p3, [k1, p1] twice, k1, p3; rep from ✳ to last 21 sts, [k1, p1] twice, k1, p3, k3, p3, [k1, p1] twice, k1, p2.

14TH ROW: K3, ✳[p1, k1] twice, [p1, k3] twice, [p1, k1] twice, p1, k5; rep from ✳ to last 20 sts, [p1, k1] twice, [p1, k3] twice, [p1, k1] twice, p1, k3.
Rep these 14 rows.

Dotted Chevron
Multiple of 18 sts
Drape: good
Skill: intermediate

1ST ROW (RS): K8, ✳p2, k16; rep from ✳ to last 10 sts, p2, k8.

2ND ROW: P7, ✳k4, p14; rep from ✳ to last 11 sts, k4, p7.

3RD ROW: P1, ✳k5, p2, k2, p2, k5, p2; rep from ✳ to last 17 sts, k5, p2, k2, p2, k5, p1.

4TH ROW: K2, ✳p3, k2, p4, k2, p3, k4; rep

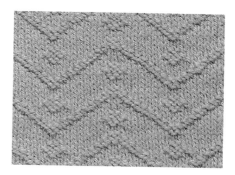

from ✳ to last 16 sts, p3, k2, p4, k2, p3, k2.

5TH ROW: P1, ✳k3, p2, k6, p2, k3, p2; rep from ✳ to last 17 sts, k3, p2, k6, p2, k3, p1.

6TH ROW: P3, ✳k2 [p3, k2] twice, p6; rep from ✳ to last 15 sts, k2, [p3, k2] twice, p3.

7TH ROW: K2, ✳p2, k3, p4, k3, p2, k4; rep from ✳ to last 16 sts, p2, k3, p4, k3, p2, k2.

8TH ROW: P1, ✳k2, [p5, k2] twice, p2; rep from ✳ to last 17 sts, k2, [p5, k2] twice, p1.

9TH ROW: P2, ✳k14, p4; rep from ✳ to last 16 sts, k14, p2.

10TH ROW: K1, ✳p16, k2; rep from ✳ to last 17 sts, p16, k1.
Rep these 10 rows.

Diamond and Lozenge Pattern
Multiple of 12 sts
Drape: good
Skill: intermediate

1ST ROW (RS): ✳K6, p6; rep from ✳ to end.
2ND ROW: ✳K6, p6; rep from ✳ to end.

3RD AND 4TH ROWS: ✳P1, k5, p5, k1; rep from ✳ to end.

5TH AND 6TH ROWS: K1, p1, k4, p4, ✳[k1, p1] twice, k4, p4; rep from ✳ to last 2 sts, k1, p1.

7TH AND 8TH ROWS: P1, k1, p1, k3, p3, ✳[k1, p1] 3 times, k3, p3; rep from ✳ to last 3 sts, k1, p1, k1.

9TH AND 10TH ROWS: [K1, p1] twice, k2, p2, ✳[k1, p1] 4 times, k2, p2; rep from ✳ to last 4 sts, [k1, p1] twice.

11TH AND 12TH ROWS: ✳P1, k1; rep from ✳ to end.

13TH AND 14TH ROWS: ✳K1, p1; rep from ✳ to end.

15TH AND 16TH ROWS: [P1, k1] twice, p2, k2, ✳[p1, k1] 4 times, p2, k2; rep from ✳ to last 4 sts, [p1, k1] twice.

17TH AND 18TH ROWS: K1, p1, k1, p3, k3, ✳[p1, k1] 3 times, p3, k3; rep from ✳ to last 3 sts, p1, k1, p1.

19TH AND 20TH ROWS: P1, k1, p4, k4, ✳ [p1, k1] twice, p4, k4; rep from, ✳ to last 2 sts, p1, k1.

21ST AND 22ND ROWS: ✳K1, p5, k5, p1; rep from ✳ to end.

23RD AND 24TH ROWS: ✳P6, k6; rep from ✳ to end.

25TH AND 26TH ROWS: ✳P5, k1, p1, k5; rep from ✳ to end.

27TH AND 28TH ROWS: ✳P4, [k1, p1] twice, k4; rep from ✳ to end.

29TH AND 30TH ROWS: ✳P3, [k1, p1] 3 times, k3; rep from ✳ to end.

31ST AND 32ND ROWS: ✳P2, [k1, p1] 4 times, k2; rep from ✳ to end.

33RD AND 34TH ROWS: As 11th and 12th rows.

35TH AND 36TH ROWS: As 13th and 14th rows.

37TH AND 38TH ROWS: ✳K2 [p1, k1] 4 times, p2; rep from ✳ to end.

39TH AND 40TH ROWS: ✳K3 [p1, k1] 3 times, p3; rep from ✳ to end.

41ST AND 42ND ROWS: ✳K4 [p1, k1] 3 twice, p4; rep from ✳ to end.

43RD AND 44TH ROWS: ✳K5, p1, k1, p5; rep from ✳ to end.
Rep these 44 rows.

Stripes in Relief
Multiple of 14 sts + 6
Drape: good
Skill: easy

1ST ROW (WS): K6, ✳p3, k2, p3, k6; rep from ✳ to end.
2ND ROW: P6, ✳k3, p2, k3, p6; rep from ✳ to end.
3RD ROW: P9, k2, ✳p12, k2; rep from ✳ to last 9 sts, p9.
4TH ROW: K9, p2, ✳k12, p2; rep from ✳ to last 9 sts, k9.
5TH ROW: P2, k2, ✳p12, k2; rep from ✳ to last 2 sts, p2.
6TH ROW: K2, p2, ✳k12, p2; rep from ✳ to last 2 sts, k2.
7TH ROW: P2, k2, ✳p3, k6, p3, k2; rep from ✳ to last 2 sts, p2.
8TH ROW: K2, p2, ✳k3, p6, k3, p2; rep from ✳ to last 2 sts, k2.
9TH ROW: As 5th row.
10TH ROW: As 6th row.
11TH ROW: As 3rd row.
12TH ROW: As 4th row.
Rep these 12 rows.

Diamond and Block
Multiple of 14 sts + 5
Drape: good
Skill: easy

1ST ROW (RS): P5, ✳k4, p1, k4, p5; rep from ✳ to end.
2ND ROW: K5, ✳p3, k3, p3, k5; rep from ✳ to end.
3RD ROW: K7, p5, ✳k9, p5; rep from ✳ to

last 7 sts, k7.
4TH ROW: P6, k7, ✳p7, k7; rep from ✳ to last 6 sts, p6.
5TH ROW: K5, ✳p9, k5; rep from ✳ to end.
6TH ROW: As 4th row.
7TH ROW: As 3rd row.
8TH ROW: As 2nd row.
Rep these 8 rows.

Slanting Diamonds
Multiple of 10 sts
Drape: good
Skill: intermediate

1ST ROW (RS): ✳K9, p1; rep from ✳ to end.
2ND ROW: ✳K2, p8; rep from ✳ to end.
3RD ROW: ✳K7, p3; rep from ✳ to end.
4TH ROW: ✳K4, p6; rep from ✳ to end.
5TH AND 6TH ROWS: ✳K5, p5; rep from ✳ to end.
7TH ROW: K5, p4, ✳k6, p4; rep from ✳ to last st, k1.
8TH ROW: P2, k3, ✳p7, k3; rep from ✳ to last 5 sts, p5.

9TH ROW: K5, p2, ✳k8, p2; rep from ✳ to last 3 sts, k3.
10TH ROW: P4, k1, ✳p9, k1; rep from ✳ to last 5 sts, p5.
11TH ROW: K4, p1, ✳k9, p1; rep from ✳ to last 5 sts, k5.
12TH ROW: P5, k2, ✳p8, k2; rep from ✳ to last 3 sts, p3.
13TH ROW: K2, p3, ✳k7, p3; rep from ✳ to last 5 sts, k5.
14TH ROW: P5, k4, ✳p6, k4; rep from ✳ to last st, p1.
15TH AND 16TH ROWS: ✳P5, k5; rep from ✳ to end.
17TH ROW: ✳P4, k6; rep from ✳ to end.
18TH ROW: ✳P7, k3; rep from ✳ to end.
19TH ROW: ✳P2, k8; rep from ✳ to end.
20TH ROW: ✳P9, k1; rep from ✳ to end.
Rep these 20 rows.

Polperro Horizontal Diamonds
Multiple of 12 sts + 1
Drape: good
Skill: intermediate

Work 3 rows in garter st (1st row is right side).
Work 3 rows in St st, starting purl.
7TH ROW: K6, p1, ✳k11, p1; rep from ✳ to last 6 sts, k6.
8TH ROW: P5, k1, p1, k1, ✳p9, k1, p1, k1; rep from ✳ to last 5 sts, p5.
9TH ROW: K4, p1, k3, p1, ✳k7, p1, k3, p1; rep from ✳ to last 4 sts, k4.
10TH ROW: P3, k1, ✳p5, k1; rep from ✳ to last 3 sts, p3.
11TH ROW: K2, p1, k7, p1, ✳k3, p1, k7, p1;

rep from ✽ to last 2 sts, k2.
12TH ROW: P1, ✽k1, p9, k1, p1; rep from ✽ to end.
13TH ROW: P1, ✽k11, p1; rep from ✽ to end.
14TH ROW: As 12th row.
15TH ROW: As 11th row.
16TH ROW: As 10th row.
17TH ROW: As 9th row.
18TH ROW: As 8th row.
19TH ROW: As 7th row.
Work 3 rows in St st, starting purl.
Rep these 22 rows.

Polperro Musician
Multiple of 23 sts
Drape: good
Skill: intermediate

1ST ROW (WS): K1, p2, k1, [p7, k1] twice, p2, ✽k2, p2, k1, [p7, k1] twice, p2; rep from ✽ to last st, k1.
2ND ROW: K10, p1, k1, p1, ✽k20, p1, k1, p1; rep from ✽ to last 10 sts, k10.
3RD ROW: P1, k2, p6, k1, p3, k1, p6, k2, ✽p2, k2, p6, k1, p3, k1, p6, k2; rep from ✽ to last st, p1.
4TH ROW: K8, p1, k5, p1, ✽k16, p1, k5, p1; rep from ✽ to last 8 sts, k8.
5TH ROW: K1, p6, k1, p7, k1, p6, ✽k2, p6, k1, p7, k1, p6; rep from ✽ to last st, k1.
6TH ROW: K6, p1, k9, p1, ✽k12, p1, k9, p1; rep from ✽ to last 6 sts, k6.
7TH ROW: P1, k2, p2, k1, p11, k1, p2, k2, ✽p2, k2, p2, k1, p11, k1, p2, k2; rep from ✽ to last st, p1.
8TH ROW: K4, p1, k13, p1, ✽k8, p1, k13,

p1; rep from ✽ to last 4 sts, k4.
Rep these 8 rows.

Polperro Northcott
Multiple of 4 sts + 2
Drape: good
Skill: easy

Work 3 rows in garter st (1st row is right side).
4TH ROW: K2, ✽p2, k2; rep from ✽ to end.
5TH ROW: Knit.
Rep the last 2 rows 10 times more.
Work 2 rows in garter st.
28TH ROW: Purl.
Rep these 28 rows.

Looe Eddystone
Multiple of 11 sts
Drape: good
Skill: easy

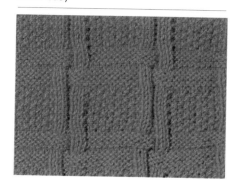

1ST AND EVERY ALT ROW (RS): Knit.
2ND ROW: P2, k7, ✽p4, k7; rep from ✽ to last 2 sts, p2.
4TH ROW: P3, k5, ✽p6, k5; rep from ✽ to last 3 sts, p3.
6TH ROW: P4, k3, ✽p8, k3; rep from ✽ to last 4 sts, p4.
8TH AND 10TH ROWS: P5, k1, ✽p10, k1; rep from ✽ to last 5 sts, p5.
Work 4 rows in St st.
Rep these 14 rows.

Interlocking Pyramids
Multiple of 14 sts + 1
Drape: good
Skill: intermediate

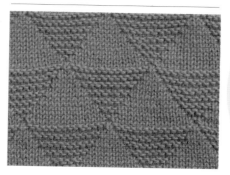

1ST ROW (RS): K7, p1, ✽k13, p1; rep from ✽ to last 7 sts, k7.
2ND AND EVERY ALT ROW: Purl.
3RD ROW: K6, p3, ✽k11, p3; rep from ✽ to last 6 sts, k6.
5TH ROW: K5, p5, ✽k9, p5; rep from ✽ to last 5 sts, k5.
7TH ROW: K4, p7, ✽k7, p7; rep from ✽ to last 4 sts, k4.
9TH ROW: K3, p9, ✽k5, p9; rep from ✽ to last 3 sts, K3.
11TH ROW: K2, p11, ✽k3, p11; rep from ✽ to last 2 sts, k2.
13TH ROW: K1, ✽p13, k1; rep from ✽ to end.
15TH ROW: P1, ✽k13, p1; rep from ✽ to end.
17TH ROW: P2, k11, ✽p3, k11; rep from ✽ to last 2 sts, p2.
19TH ROW: P3, k9, ✽p5, k9; rep from ✽ to last 3 sts, p3.

21ST ROW: P4, k7, ✳p7, k7; rep from ✳ to last 4 sts, p4.

23RD ROW: P5, k5, ✳p9, k5; rep from ✳ to last 5 sts, p5.

25TH ROW: P6, k3, ✳p11, k3; rep from ✳ to last 6 sts, p6.

27TH ROW: P7, k1, ✳p13, k1; rep from ✳ to last 7 sts, p7.

28TH ROW: Purl.

Rep these 28 rows.

Long and Short Stitch

Multiple of 6 sts + 3

Drape: good

Skill: easy

Work 4 rows in St st, starting knit (right side).

5TH ROW: K1, ✳p1, k1; rep from ✳ to end.

6TH ROW: P1, ✳k1, p1; rep from ✳ to end.

Rep the last 2 rows once more.

9TH ROW: K1, p1, k1, ✳p3, k1, p1, k1; rep from ✳ to end.

10TH ROW: P1, k1, p1, ✳k3, p1, k1, p1; rep from ✳ to end.

Rep the last 2 rows once more.

Rep these 12 rows.

Woven Ribbons

Multiple of 10 sts + 6

Drape: good

Skill: intermediate

1ST ROW (RS): P1, ✳k4, p1; rep from ✳ to end.

2ND ROW: K1, ✳p4, k1; rep from ✳ to end. Rep the last 2 rows once more, then 1st row again.

6TH ROW: K6, ✳p4, k6; rep from ✳ to end.

7TH ROW: As 1st row.

Rep the last 2 rows twice more.

12TH ROW: As 2nd row.

13TH ROW: As 1st row.

Rep the last 2 rows once more.

16TH ROW: K1, p4, ✳k6, p4; rep from ✳ to last st, k1.

17TH ROW: As 1st row.

Rep the last 2 rows once more, then 16th row again. Rep these 20 rows.

Basketweave Squares

Multiple of 15 sts + 2

Drape: good

Skill: intermediate

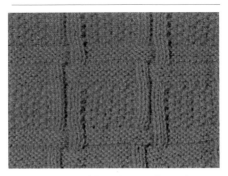

1ST ROW (RS): ✳P13, k2; rep from ✳ to last 2 sts, p2.

2ND ROW: K2, ✳p2, k13; rep from ✳ to end.

3RD ROW: As 1st row.

4TH ROW: Purl.

5TH ROW: P2, ✳k2, p1, [k1, p1] 4 times, k2, p2; rep from ✳ to end.

6TH ROW: K2, ✳p3, k1, [p1, k1] 3 times, p3, k2; rep from ✳ to end.

Rep the last 2 rows 4 times more.

15TH ROW: P2, ✳k2, p13; rep from ✳ to end.

16TH ROW: ✳K13, p2; rep from ✳ to last 2 sts, k2.

17TH ROW: As 15th row.

18TH ROW: Purl.

Rep these 18 rows.

Art Deco Pattern

Multiple of 12 sts

Drape: good

Skill: intermediate

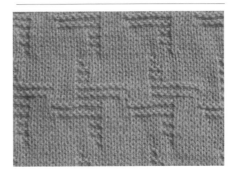

1ST ROW (RS): K4, p1, ✳k11, p1; rep from ✳ to last 7 sts, k7.

2ND AND EVERY ALT ROW: Purl.

3RD AND 5TH ROWS: K4, p2, ✳k10, p2; rep from ✳ to last 6 sts, k6.

7TH ROW: K4, p7, ✳k5, p7; rep from ✳ to last st, k1.

9TH ROW: ✳K4, p8; rep from ✳ to end.

11TH ROW: K1, p7, ✳k5, p7; rep from ✳ to last 4 sts, k4.

13TH ROW: ✳P8, k4; rep from ✳ to end.

15TH AND 17TH ROWS: K6, p2, ✳k10, p2; rep from ✳ to last 4 sts, k4.

19TH ROW: K7, p1, ✳k11, p1; rep from ✳ to last 4 sts, k4.

20TH ROW: Purl.

Rep these 20 rows.

Ridged Ribbons

Multiple of 14 sts + 9
Drape: good
Skill: easy

1ST AND EVERY ALT ROW (RS): P2, ✱k5, p2; rep from ✱ to end.
2ND ROW: K9, ✱p5, k9; rep from ✱ to end.
4TH ROW: K2, ✱p5, k2; rep from ✱ to end.
6TH ROW: K2, p5, ✱k9, p5; rep from ✱ to last 2 sts, k2.
8TH ROW: As 4th row.
Rep these 8 rows.

Diamond Basketweave

Multiple of 14 sts + 2
Drape: good
Skill: intermediate

1ST ROW (RS): K2, ✱p1, k10, p1, k2; rep from ✱ to end.
2ND ROW: P3, k1, p8, k1, ✱p4, k1, p8, k1; rep from ✱ to last 3 sts, p3.
3RD ROW: K4, p1, ✱k6, p1; rep from ✱ to last 4 sts, k4.
4TH ROW: P5, k1, p4, k1, ✱p8, k1, p4, k1;

rep from ✱ to last 5 sts, p5.
5TH ROW: K6, p1, k2, p1, ✱k10, p1, k2, p1; rep from ✱ to last 6 sts, k6.
6TH ROW: P5, k2, p2, k2, ✱p8, k2, p2, k2; rep from ✱ to last 5 sts, p5.
7TH ROW: K4, p3, k2, p3, ✱k6, p3, k2, p3; rep from ✱ to last 4 sts, k4.
8TH ROW: P3, k4, p2, k4, ✱p4, k4, p2, k4; rep from ✱ to last 3 sts, p3.
9TH ROW: K2, ✱p5, k2; rep from ✱ to end.
10TH ROW: P2, ✱k4, p4, k4, p2; rep from ✱ to end.
11TH ROW: K2, ✱p3, k6, p3, k2; rep from ✱ to end.
12TH ROW: P2, ✱k2, p8, k2, p2; rep from ✱ to end.
Rep these 12 rows.

Cross and Lattice Pattern

Multiple of 20 sts + 1
Drape: good
Skill: intermediate

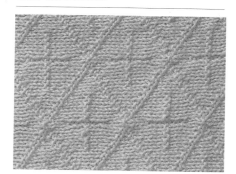

1ST ROW (RS): P1, ✱k7, p2, k1, p2, k7, p1; rep from ✱ to end.
2ND ROW: K1, ✱p6, k2, p3, k2, p6, k1; rep from ✱ to end.
3RD ROW: P1, ✱k5, [p2, k5] twice, p1; rep from ✱ to end.
4TH ROW: K1, ✱p4, k2, p7, k2, p4, k1; rep from ✱ to end.
5TH ROW: K4, p2, k4, p1, k4, p2, ✱k7, p2, k4, p1, k4, p2; rep from ✱ to last 4 sts, k4.
6TH ROW: P3, k2, p5, k1, p5, ✱[k2, p5] twice, k1, p5; rep from ✱ to last 5 sts, k2, p3.
7TH ROW: K2, p2, k6, p1, k6, p2, ✱k3, p2,

k6, p1, k6, p2; rep from ✱ to last 2 sts, k2.
8TH ROW: P1, ✱k2, p7, k1, p7, k2, p1; rep from ✱ to end.
9TH ROW: P2, k4, p9, k4, ✱p3, k4, p9, k4; rep from ✱ to last 2 sts, p2.
10TH ROW: As 8th row.
11TH ROW: As 7th row.
12TH ROW: As 6th row.
13TH ROW: As 5th row.
14TH ROW: As 4th row.
15TH ROW: As 3rd row.
16TH ROW: As 2nd row.
17TH ROW: As 1st row.
18TH ROW: K5, p4, k3, p4, ✱k9, p4, k3, p4; rep from ✱ to last 5 sts, k5.
Rep these 18 rows.

Broken Ridges

Multiple of 26 sts + 1
Drape: good
Skill: intermediate

1ST ROW (RS): Knit.
2ND AND EVERY ALT ROW: Purl.
3RD AND 5TH ROWS: P8, k4, p3, k4, ✱p15, k4, p3, k4; rep from ✱ to last 8 sts, p8.
7TH ROW: Knit.
9TH AND 11TH ROWS: P6, k4, p7, k4, ✱p11, k4, p7, k4; rep from ✱ to last 6 sts, p6.
13TH ROW: Knit.
15TH AND 17TH ROWS: P4, k4, p11, k4, ✱p7, k4, p11, k4; rep from ✱ to last 4 sts, p4.

19TH ROW: Knit.

21ST AND 23RD ROWS: P2, k4, p15, k4, ✱p3, k4, p15, k4; rep from ✱ to last 2 sts, p2.

25TH ROW: Knit.
27TH AND 29TH ROWS: As 15th row.
31ST ROW: Knit.
33RD AND 35TH ROWS: As 9th row.
36TH ROW: Purl.
Rep these 36 rows.

Threaded Ribbons

Multiple of 6 sts + 1
Drape: good
Skill: easy

1ST ROW (RS): K1, ❋p5, k1; rep from ❋ to end.
2ND ROW: P1, ❋k5, p1; rep from ❋ to end. Rep the last 2 rows twice more.
7TH ROW: P1, ❋k5, p1; rep from ❋ to end.
8TH ROW: K1, ❋p5, k1; rep from ❋ to end.
Rep the last 2 rows twice more.
Rep these 12 rows.

Paving Blocks

Multiple of 10 sts + 3
Drape: good
Skill: easy

1ST ROW (RS): P1, k1, p1, ❋k7, p1, k1, p1; rep from ❋ to end.
2ND ROW: K1, p1, k1, ❋p7, k1, p1, k1; rep from ❋ to end.
Rep the last 2 rows once more.
5TH ROW: P1, k1, ❋p9, k1; rep from ❋ to last st, P1.
6TH ROW: As 2nd row.
Rep the last 2 rows once more.

9TH AND 10TH ROWS: As 1st and 2nd rows. Rep the last 2 rows once more.
Rep these 12 rows.

Maze Pattern

Multiple of 24 sts + 2
Drape: good
Skill: intermediate

1ST ROW (RS): P2, ❋k2, p18, k2, p2; rep from ❋ to end.
2ND ROW: K2, ❋p2, k18, p2, k2; rep from ❋ to end.
3RD ROW: P2, ❋k18, p2, k2, P2; rep from ❋ to end.
4TH ROW: K2, ❋p2, k2, p18, k2; rep from ❋ to end.
5TH ROW: P2, ❋k2, p14, [k2, p2] twice; rep from ❋ to end.
6TH ROW: ❋[K2, p2] twice, k14, p2; rep from ❋ to last 2 sts, k2.
7TH ROW: P2, k2, p2, k10, p2, ❋[k2, p2] 3 times, k10, p2; rep from ❋ to last 8 sts, [k2, p2] twice.
8TH ROW: K2, [p2, k2] twice, p10, k2,

❋[p2, k2] 3 times, p10, k2; rep from ❋ to last 4 sts, p2, k2.
9TH ROW: [P2, k2] twice, p6, k2, ❋[p2, k2] 4 times, p6, k2; rep from ❋ to last 10 sts, p2, [k2, p2] twice.
10TH ROW: [K2, p2] 3 times, k6, ❋p2, [k2, p2] 4 times, k6; rep from ❋ to last 8 sts, [p2, k2] twice.
11TH ROW: P2, ❋k2, p2; rep from ❋ to end.
12TH ROW: K2, ❋p2, k2; rep from ❋ to end.
13TH ROW: [P2, k2] 3 times, p6, k2, ❋[p2, k2] 4 times, p6, k2; rep from ❋ to last 6 sts, p2, k2, p2.
14TH ROW: [K2, p2] twice, k6, ❋p2, [k2, p2] 4 times, k6; rep from ❋ to last 12 sts, [p2, k2] 3 times.
15TH ROW: P2, [k2, p2] twice, k10, p2, ❋[k2, p2] 3 times, k10, p2; rep from ❋ to last 4 sts, k2, p2.
16TH ROW: K2, p2, k2, p10, k2, ❋[p2, k2] 3 times, p10, k2; rep from ❋ to last 8 sts, [p2, k2] twice.
17TH ROW: ❋[P2, k2] twice, p14, k2; rep from ❋ to last 2 sts, p2.
18TH ROW: K2, p2, k14, p2, ❋[k2, p2] twice, k14, p2; rep from ❋ to last 6 sts, k2, p2, k2.
19TH ROW: P2, ❋k2, p2, k18, p2; rep from ❋ to end.
20TH ROW: K2, ❋p18, k2, p2, k2; rep from ❋ to end.
Rep these 20 rows.

Little Checks

Multiple of 6 sts + 3
Drape: good
Skill: easy

1ST AND EVERY ALT ROW (RS): Knit.
2ND ROW: Knit.
4TH AND 6TH ROWS: P3, ❋k3, p3; rep from ❋ to end.
8TH AND 10TH ROWS: Knit.
12TH AND 14TH ROWS: K3, ❋p3, k3; rep from ❋ to end.
16TH ROW: Knit.
Rep these 16 rows.

Wavy Ridged Ribbons

Multiple of 8 sts
Drape: good
Skill: intermediate

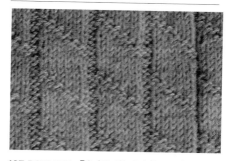

1ST ROW (RS): P1, k6, ✳p2, k6; rep from ✳ to last st, p1.
2ND ROW: K1, p5, ✳k3, p5; rep from ✳ to last 2 sts, k2.
3RD ROW: P3, k4, ✳p4, k4; rep from ✳ to last st, p1.
4TH ROW: K1, p3, k2, p1, ✳k2, p3, k2, p1; rep from ✳ to last st, k1.
5TH ROW: P1, k2, p2, k2; rep from ✳ to last st, P1.
6TH ROW: K1. p1, k2, p3, ✳k2, p1, k2, p3; rep from ✳ to last st, k1.
7TH ROW: P1, k4, ✳p4, k4; rep from ✳ to last 3 sts, p3.
8TH ROW: K2, p5, ✳k3, p5; rep from to last st, k1.
9TH ROW: As 1st row.
10TH ROW: K1, p6, ✳k2, p6; rep from ✳ to last st, k1. Rep these 10 rows.

Curving Ribs

Multiple of 20 sts + 10
Drape: good
Skill: intermediate

1ST ROW (RS): P2, ✳k2, p2; rep from ✳ to end.
2ND ROW: K2, ✳p2, k2; rep from ✳ to end.
3RD ROW: [K2, p2] twice, ✳k4, p2, k2, p2; rep from ✳ to last 2 sts, k2.
4TH ROW: [P2, k2] twice, ✳p4, k2, p2, k2; rep from ✳ to last 2 sts, p2.
Rep the last 4 rows once more, then 1st and 2nd rows again.
11TH ROW: As 2nd row.
12TH ROW: P2, ✳k2, p2; rep from ✳ to end.
13TH ROW: [K2, p2] 3 times, [k4, p2] twice, ✳ [k2, p2] twice, [k4, p2] twice; rep from ✳ to last 6 sts, k2, p2, k2.
14TH ROW: [P2, k2] twice, ✳[p4, k2] twice, [p2, k2] twice; rep from ✳ to last 2 sts, p2.
Rep the last 4 rows once more, then 11th and 12th rows again.
Rep these 20 rows.

Little Tiles

Multiple of 12 sts + 2
Drape: good
Skill: easy

1ST ROW (RS): K4, p6, ✳k6, p6; rep from ✳ to last 4 sts, k4.
2ND ROW: P4, k6, ✳p6, k6; rep from ✳ to last 4 sts, p4.
3RD ROW: K2, ✳p2, k6, p2, k2; rep from ✳ to end.

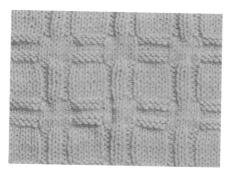

4TH ROW: P2, ✳k2, p6, k2, p2; rep from ✳ to end.
Rep the last 2 rows 3 times more.
11TH AND 12TH ROWS: As 1st and 2nd rows.
13TH ROW: Knit.
14TH ROW: Purl.
Rep these 14 rows.

Rooftops

Multiple of 12 sts + 1
Drape: good
Skill: easy

1ST AND EVERY ALT ROW (RS): Knit.
2ND ROW: P5, k3, ✳p9, k3; rep from ✳ to last 5 sts, p5.
4TH ROW: P4, k5, ✳p7, k5; rep from ✳ to last 4 sts, p4.
6TH ROW: P3, k3, p1, k3, ✳p5, k3, p1, k3; rep from ✳ to last 3 sts, p3.
8TH ROW: P2, k3, ✳p3, k3; rep from ✳ to last 2 sts, p2.
10TH ROW: P1, ✳k3, p5, k3, p1; rep from ✳ to end.

12TH ROW: Purl.
Rep these 12 rows.

Cross Checks
Multiple of 18 sts + 12
Drape: good
Skill: intermediate

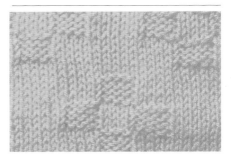

1ST ROW (RS): Knit.
2ND ROW: Purl.
3RD ROW: K4, p4, ✳k14, p4; rep from ✳ to last 4 sts, k4.
4TH ROW: P4, k4, ✳p14, k4; rep from ✳ to last 4 sts, p4.
Rep the last 2 rows once more.
7TH ROW: P4, k4, p4, ✳k6, p4, k4, p4; rep from ✳ to end.
8TH ROW: K4, p4, k4, ✳p6, k4, p4, k4; rep from ✳ to end. Rep last 2 rows once more.
11TH AND 12TH ROWS: As 3rd and 4th rows. Rep the last 2 rows once more.
15TH ROW: Knit.
16TH ROW: Purl.
17TH ROW: K13, p4, ✳k14, p4; rep from ✳ to last 13 sts, k13.
18TH ROW: P13, k4, ✳p14, k4; rep from ✳ to last 13 sts, p13.
Rep the last 2 rows once more.
21ST ROW: P3, k6, ✳p4, k4, p4, k6; rep from ✳ to last 3 sts, p3.
22ND ROW: K3, p6, ✳k4, p4, k4, p6; rep from ✳ to last 3 sts, k3.
Rep the last 2 rows once more.
25TH AND 26TH ROWS: As 17th and 18th rows. Rep the last 2 rows once more.
Rep these 28 rows.

Pockets
Multiple of 20 sts + 1
Drape: good
Skill: intermediate

1ST ROW (RS): K6, p9, ✳k11, p9; rep from ✳ to last 6 sts, k6.
2ND ROW: P5, k11, ✳p9, k11; rep from ✳ to last 5 sts, p5.
3RD ROW: K4, p13, ✳k7, p13; rep from ✳ to last 4 sts, k4.
4TH ROW: P3, k4, p7, k4, ✳p5, k4, p7, k4; rep from ✳ to last 3 sts, p3.
5TH ROW: K3, p3, k9, p3, ✳k5, p3, k9, p3; rep from ✳ to last 3 sts, k3.
6TH ROW: P3, k2, p11, k2, ✳p5, k2, p11, k2; rep from ✳ to last 3 sts, p3.
7TH ROW: K3, p1, k13, p1, ✳k5, p1, k13, p1; rep from ✳ to last 3 sts, k3.
8TH ROW: As 3rd row.
9TH ROW: As 2nd row.
10TH ROW: K6, p9, ✳k11, p9; rep from ✳ to last 6 sts, k6.
11TH ROW: K3, p4, k7, p4, ✳k5, p4, k7, p4; rep from ✳ to last 3 sts, k3.
12TH ROW: P4, k3, ✳p7, k3; rep from ✳ to last 4 sts, p4.
13TH ROW: K5, p2, k7, p2, ✳k9, p2, k7, p2; rep from ✳ to last 5 sts, k5.
14TH ROW: P6, k1, p7, k1, ✳p11, k1, p7, k1; rep from ✳ to last 6 sts, p6.
Rep these 14 rows.

Purl Points
Multiple of 16 sts + 1
Drape: good
Skill: intermediate

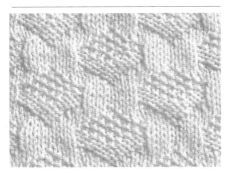

1ST ROW (RS): [K1, p1] twice, [k4, p1] twice, ✳[k1, p1] 3 times, [k4,p1] twice; rep from ✳ to last 3 sts, k1, p1, k1.
2ND ROW: K1, p1, k1, p4, k3, p4, ✳k1, [p1, k1] twice, p4, k3, p4; rep from ✳ to last 3 sts, k1, p1, k1.
3RD ROW: K1, ✳p1, k4, p5, k4, p1, k1; rep from ✳ to end.
4TH ROW: K1, ✳p4, k7, p4, k1; rep from ✳ to end.
5TH ROW: K4, p4, k1, p4, ✳k7, p4, k1, p4; rep from ✳ to last 4 sts, k4.
6TH ROW: P4, k3, p1, k1, p1, k3, ✳p7, k3, p1, k1, p1, k3; rep from ✳ to last 4 sts, p4.
7TH ROW: K4, p2, k1, [p1, k1] twice, p2, ✳k7, p2, k1, [p1, k1] twice, p2; rep from ✳ to last 4 sts, k4.
8TH ROW: P4, k1, [p1, k1] 4 times, ✳p7, k1, [p1, k1] 4 times; rep from ✳ to last 4 sts, p4.
9TH ROW: P1, k4, p1, [K1, p1] 3 times, ✳[k4, p1] twice, [k1, p1] 3 times; rep from ✳ to last 5 sts, k4, p1.
10TH ROW: K2, p4, k1, [p1, k1] twice, p4, ✳ k3, p4, k1, [p1, k1] twice, p4; rep from ✳ to last 2 sts, k2.
11TH ROW: P3, k4, p1, k1, p1, k4, ✳p5, k4, p1, k1, p1, k4; rep from ✳ to last 3 sts, p3.
12TH ROW: K4, p4, k1, p4, ✳k7, p4, k1, p4; rep from ✳ to last 4 sts, k4.
13TH ROW: K1, ✳p4, k7, p4, k1; rep from ✳ to end.
14TH ROW: K1, ✳p1, k3, p7, k3, p1, k1; rep from ✳ to end.

15TH ROW: K1, p1, k1, p2, k7, p2, ❋k1, [p1, k1] twice, p2, k7, p2; rep from ❋ to last 3 sts, k1, p1, k1.
16TH ROW: K1, [p1, k1] twice, p7, k1, ❋[p1, k1] 4 times, p7, k1; rep from ❋ to last 4 sts, [p1, k1] twice.
Rep these 16 rows.

Flat Lattice

Multiple of 15 sts
Drape: good
Skill: intermediate

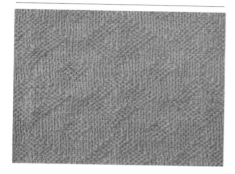

1ST ROW (RS): P1, k4, p5, k4, ❋p2, k4, p5, k4; rep from ❋ to last st, p1.
2ND ROW: K2, p4, k3, p4, ❋k4, p4, k3, p4; rep from ❋ to last 2 sts, k2.
3RD ROW: P3, k4, p1, k4, ❋p6, k4, p1, k4; rep from ❋ to last 3 sts, p3.
4TH ROW: K4, p7, ❋k8, p7; rep from ❋ to last 4 sts, k4.
5TH ROW: P5, k5, ❋p10, k5; rep from ❋ to last 5 sts, p5.
6TH ROW: P1, k5, p3, k5, ❋p2, k5, p3, k5; rep from ❋ to last st, p1.
7TH ROW: K2, p5, k1, p5, ❋k4, p5, k1, p5; rep from ❋ to last 2 sts, k2.
8TH ROW: P3, k9, ❋p6, k9; rep from ❋ to last 3 sts, p3.
9TH ROW: As 7th row.
10TH ROW: As 6th row.
11TH ROW: As 5th row.
12TH ROW: As 4th row.
13TH ROW: As 3rd row.
14TH ROW: As 2nd row.
Rep these 14 rows.

Zigzag Ridges

Multiple of 16 sts + 1
Drape: good
Skill: easy

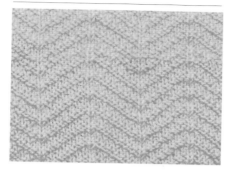

1ST ROW (RS): [K2, p2] twice, k1, p2, k2, p2, ❋k3, p2, k2, p2, k1, p2, k2, p2; rep from ❋ to last 2 sts, k2.
2ND ROW: P1, ❋k2, p2, k2, p3, k2, p2, k2, p1; rep from ❋ to end.
3RD ROW: K1, ❋p1, k2, p2, k5, p2, k2, p1, k1; rep from ❋ to end.
4TH ROW: P3, k2, p2, k1, p1, k1, p2, k2, ❋p5, k2, p2, k1, p1, k1, p2, k2; rep from ❋ to last 3 sts, p3. Rep these 4 rows.

Staggered Ribs

Multiple of 6 sts + 2
Drape: good
Skill: intermediate

1ST ROW (RS): P2, ❋k4, p2; rep from ❋ to end.
2ND ROW: K2, ❋p4, k2; rep from ❋ to end. Rep the last 2 rows 3 times more.
9TH ROW: K1, ❋p2, k4; rep from ❋ to last

st, p1.
10TH ROW: ❋P4, k2; rep from ❋ to last 2 sts, p2.
11TH ROW: K3, p2, ❋k4, p2; rep from ❋ to last 3 sts, k3.
12TH ROW: P2, ❋k2, p4; rep from ❋ to end.
13TH ROW: P1, ❋k4, p2; rep from ❋ to last st, k1.
14TH, 15TH, AND 16TH ROWS: As 8th, 9th and 10th rows.
17TH ROW: As 11th row.
18TH ROW: P3, k2, ❋p4, k2; rep from ❋ to last 3 sts, p3.
Rep the last 2 rows 3 times more.
25TH ROW: ❋K4, p2; rep from ❋ to last 2 sts, k2.
26TH ROW: P1, ❋k2, p4; rep from ❋ to last st, k1.
27TH ROW: As 1st row.
28TH ROW: K1, ❋p4, k2; rep from ❋ to last st, p1.
29TH ROW: K2, ❋p2, k4; rep from ❋ to end.
30TH ROW: P3, k2, ❋p4, k2; rep from ❋ to last 3 sts, p3.
31ST ROW: ❋K4, p2; rep from ❋ to last 2 sts, k2.
32ND ROW: As 26th row.
Rep these 32 rows.

Moss and Furrow Pattern

Multiple of 12 sts + 7
Drape: good
Skill: intermediate

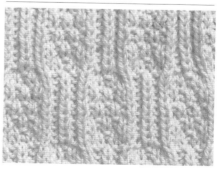

1ST ROW (RS): K3, p1, k3, ❋p2, k1, p2, k3, p1, k3; rep from ❋ to end.

2ND ROW: P3, k1, p3, ❋k2, p1, k2, p3, k1, p3; rep from ❋ to end.
3RD ROW: K2, p1, k1, p1, k2, ❋p2, k1, p2, k2, p1, k1, p1, k2; rep from ❋ to end.
4TH ROW: P2, k1, p1, k1, p2, ❋k2, p1, k2, p2, k1, p1, k1, p2; rep from ❋ to end.
5TH ROW: K1, [p1, k1] 3 times, ❋[p2, k1] twice, [p1, k1] 3 times; rep from ❋ to end.
6TH ROW: P1, [k1, p1] 3 times, ❋[k2, p1] twice, [k1, p1] 3 times; rep from ❋ to end.
7TH AND 8TH ROWS: As 3rd and 4th rows.
9TH AND 10TH ROWS: As 1st and 2nd rows.
11TH ROW: [K1, p2] twice, ❋k3, p1, k3, p2, k1, p2; rep from ❋ to last st, k1.
12TH ROW: [P1, k2] twice, ❋p3, k1, p3, k2, p1, k2; rep from ❋ to last st, p1.
13TH ROW: [K1, p2] twice, ❋k2, p1, k1, p1, k2, p2, k1, p2; rep from ❋ to last st, k1.
14TH ROW: [P1, k2] twice, ❋p2, k1, p1, k1, p2, k2, p1, k2; rep from ❋ to last st, p1 .
15TH ROW: [K1, p2] twice, k1, ❋[p1, k1] 3 times, [p2, k1] twice; rep from ❋ to end.
16TH ROW: [P1, k2] twice, p1, ❋[k1, p1] 3 times, [k2, p1] twice; rep from ❋ to end.
17TH AND 18TH ROWS: As 13th and 14th rows.
19TH AND 20TH ROWS: As 11th and 12th rows.
Rep these 20 rows.

Waving Flags
Multiple of 10 sts
Drape: good
Skill: easy

1ST ROW (RS): P7, k2, ❋p8, k2; rep from ❋ to last st, p1.

2ND ROW: ❋P1, k1, p2, k6; rep from ❋ to end.
3RD ROW: P5, k2, p1, k2; rep from ❋ to end.
4TH ROW: P3, k1, p2, k4; rep from ❋ to end.
5TH ROW: P3, k2, p1, k4; rep from ❋ to end.
6TH ROW: ❋P5, k1, p2, k2; rep from ❋ to end.
7TH ROW: ❋P1, k2, p1, k6; rep from ❋ to end.
8TH ROW: As 6th row.
9TH ROW: As 5th row.
10TH ROW: As 4th row.
11TH ROW: As 3rd row.
12TH ROW: As 2nd row.
13TH ROW: As 1st row.
14TH ROW: ❋P2, k8; rep from ❋ to end.
Rep these 14 rows.

Stem Pattern
Multiple of 10 sts + 7
Drape: good
Skill: easy

1ST ROW (RS): P3, k1 tbl, ❋p4, k1 tbl; rep from ❋ to last 3 sts, p3.
2ND ROW: K3, p1 tbl, ❋k4, p1 tbl; rep from ❋ to last 3 sts, k3.
3RD ROW: P2, [k1 tbl] 3 times, ❋p3, k1 tbl, p3, [k1 tbl] 3 times; rep from ❋ to last 2 sts, p2.
4TH ROW: K2, [p1 tbl] 3 times, ❋k3, p1 tbl, k3, [p1 tbl] 3 times; rep from ❋ to last 2 sts, k2. Rep the last 2 rows once more.
7TH AND 8TH ROWS: As 1st and 2nd rows. Rep the last 2 rows once more.
11TH ROW: P3, k1 tbl, p3, ❋[k1 tbl] 3 times, p3, k1 tbl, p3; rep from ❋ to end.

12TH ROW: K3, p1 tbl, k3, ❋[p1 tbl] 3 times, k3, p1 tbl, k3; rep from ❋ to end. Rep the last 2 rows once more.
15TH AND 16TH ROWS: As 1st and 2nd rows. Rep these 16 rows.

Fancy Basketweave
Multiple of 10 sts + 5
Drape: good
Skill: intermediate

1ST ROW (RS): K5, ❋k1 tbl, [p1, k1 tbl] twice, k5, rep from ❋ to end.
2ND ROW: K5, ❋p1 tbl, [k1, p1 tbl] twice, k5; rep from ❋ to end.
Rep the last 2 rows twice more.
7TH ROW: k1 tbl, [p1, k1 tbl] twice, ❋k5, k1 tbl, [p1, k1 tbl] twice; rep from ❋ to end.
8TH ROW: p1 tbl, [k1, p1 tbl] twice, ❋k5, p1 tbl, [k1, p1 tbl] twice; rep from ❋ to end.
Rep the last 2 rows twice more.
Rep these 12 rows.

twisted stitches and cables

All sorts of intriguing patterns can be created by crossing stitches or moving them across the fabric, and can often be accomplished without the use of a cable needle (*pages 22–24*). The stitch patterns in this section are relatively smooth-textured, compared to most traditional Aran patterns (*pages 75–77*), and thus produce fabrics with good draping qualities. Many, such as Garter Stitch Lattice and Dovetailed Diamonds (*pages 57 and 58*), feature lattice and lozenge effects.

pages 22–24; *pages 75–77*; *pages 57 and 58*

Twisted Arches
Multiple of 8 sts + 2
Drape: good
Skill: intermediate

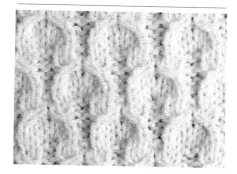

1ST ROW (RS): P2, ✳k6, p2; rep from ✳ to end.
2ND ROW: K2, ✳p6, k2; rep from ✳ to end.
Rep the last 2 rows once more.
5TH ROW: P2, ✳C3L, C3R, p2; rep from ✳ to end.
6TH ROW: As 2nd row.
7TH ROW: K4, p2, ✳k6, p2; rep from ✳ to last 4 sts, k4.
8TH ROW: P4, k2, ✳p6, k2; rep from ✳ to last 4 sts, p4.
Rep the last 2 rows once more.
11TH ROW: K1, ✳C3R, p2, C3L; rep from ✳ to last st, k1.
12TH ROW: As 8th row.
Rep these 12 rows.

Little Cable Stitch
Multiple of 6 sts + 2
Drape: good
Skill: intermediate

1ST ROW (RS): Knit.
2ND ROW: Purl.
3RD ROW: P2, ✳C2F, C2B, p2; rep from ✳ to end.
4TH ROW: K2, ✳p4, k2; rep from ✳ to end.
5TH ROW: Knit.
6TH ROW: Purl.
Rep these 6 rows.

Slanting Lines
Multiple of 12 sts + 7
Drape: good
Skill: intermediate

1ST ROW (WS): [K2, p1] twice, ✳[k1, p1] 3 times, [k2, p1] twice; rep from ✳ to last st, k1.
2ND ROW: [P1, T2F] twice, p1, ✳[k1, p1] 3 times, [T2F, p1] twice; rep from ✳ to end.
3RD ROW: K4, p1, k2, ✳p1, [k1, p1] twice, k4, p1, k2; rep from ✳ to end.
4TH ROW: P2, T2F, p3, ✳k1, [p1, k1] twice, p2, T2F, p3; rep from ✳ to end.
5TH ROW: [K3, p1] twice, [k1, p1] twice, ✳[k3, p1] twice, [k1, p1] twice; rep from ✳ to last 7 sts, k3, p1, k3.
6TH ROW: P3, T2F, p2, ✳k1, [p1, k1] twice, p3, T2F, p2; rep from ✳ to end.
Rep these 6 rows.

Turtle Check

Multiple of 12 sts + 2
Drape: good
Skill: experienced

Special Abbreviations

T4LF (Twist 4 Left) = slip next st onto cable needle and hold at front of work, purl 3 sts from left-hand needle, then knit st from cable needle.

T4RB (Twist 4 Right) = slip next 3 sts onto cable needle and hold at back of work, knit next st from left-hand needle, then purl sts from cable needle.

1ST ROW (RS): K4, p6, ✳k6, p6; rep from ✳ to last 4 sts, k4.
2ND ROW: P4, k6, ✳p6, k6; rep from ✳ to last 4 sts, p4.
3RD ROW: K3, T4LF, T4RB (see Special Abbreviations), ✳k4, T4LF, T4RB; rep from ✳ to last 3 sts, k3.
4TH ROW: P3, k3, p2, k3, ✳p4, k3, p2, k3; rep from ✳ to last 3 sts, p3.
5TH ROW: K2, ✳T4LF, k2, T4RB, k2; rep from ✳ to end.
6TH ROW: P2, ✳k3, p4, k3, p2; rep from ✳ to end.
7TH ROW: K1, ✳T4LF, k4, T4RB; rep from ✳ to last st, k1.
8TH ROW: K4, p6, ✳k6, p6; rep from ✳ to last 4 sts, k4.
9TH ROW: As 2nd row.
Rep the last 2 rows once more, then the 8th row again.
13TH ROW: K1, ✳T4RB, k4, T4LF; rep from ✳ to last st, k1.
14TH ROW: As 6th row.
15TH ROW: K2, ✳T4RB, k2, T4LF, k2; rep from ✳ to end.

16TH ROW: As 4th row.
17TH ROW: K3, T4RB, T4LF, ✳k4, T4RB, T4LF; rep from ✳ to last 3 sts, k3.
18TH ROW: As 2nd row.
19TH ROW: As 1st row.
20TH ROW: As 2nd row. Rep these 20 rows.

Stockinette Stitch Hearts

Multiple of 14 sts + 4
Drape: good
Skill: experienced

1ST ROW (WS): Knit.
2ND ROW: Purl.
3RD ROW: K8, p2, ✳k12, p2; rep from ✳ to last 8 sts, k8.
4TH ROW: P7, C2F, C2B, ✳p10, C2F, C2B; rep from ✳ to last 7 sts, p7.
5TH ROW: K7, p4, ✳k10, p4; rep from ✳ to last 7 sts, k7.
6TH ROW: P6, C2F, k2, C2B, ✳p8, C2F, k2, C2B; rep from ✳ to last 6 sts, p6.
7TH ROW: K6, p6, ✳k8, p6; rep from ✳ to last 6 sts, k6.
8TH ROW: P5, C2F, k4, C2B, ✳p6, C2F, k4, C2B; rep from ✳ to last 5 sts, p5.
9TH ROW: K5, p8, ✳k6, p8; rep from ✳ to last 5 sts, k5.
10TH ROW: P4, ✳C2F, k6, C2B, p4; rep from ✳ to end.
11TH ROW: K4, ✳p10, k4; rep from ✳ to end.
12TH ROW: P4, ✳k3, T2B, T2F, k3, p4; rep from ✳ to end.
13TH ROW: K4, ✳p4, k2, p4, k4; rep from ✳ to end.
14TH ROW: P4, ✳T2F, T2B, p2, T2F, T2B,

p4; rep from ✳ to end.
15TH ROW: K5, p2, k4, p2, ✳k6, p2, k4, p2; rep from ✳ to last 5 sts, k5.
16TH ROW: P5, M1, k2tog tbl, p4, k2tog, M1, ✳p6, M1, k2tog tbl, p4, k2tog, M1; rep from ✳ to last 5 sts, p5.
17TH ROW: Knit.
18TH ROW: Purl. Rep these 18 rows.

Simple Lattice

Multiple of 12 sts + 14
Drape: good
Skill: intermediate

1ST ROW (RS): K4, C3B, C3F, ✳k6, C3B, C3F; rep from ✳ to last 4 sts, k4.
2ND AND EVERY ALT ROW: Purl.
3RD ROW: K3, C3B, k2, C3F, ✳k4, C3B, k2, C3F; rep from ✳ to last 3 sts, k3.
5TH ROW: ✳K2, C3B, k4, C3F; rep from ✳ to last 2 sts, k2.
7TH ROW: K1, ✳C3B, k6, C3F; rep from ✳ to last st, k1.
9TH ROW: K11, ✳C4B, k8; rep from ✳ to last 3 sts, k3.
11TH ROW: K1, ✳C3F, k6, C3B; rep from ✳ to last st, k1.
13TH ROW: ✳K2, C3F, k4, C3B; rep from ✳ to last 2 sts, k2.
15TH ROW: K3, C3F, k2, C3B, ✳k4, C3F, k2, C3B; rep from ✳ to last 3 sts, k3.
17TH ROW: K4, C3F, C3B, ✳k6, C3F, C3B; rep from ✳ to last 4 sts, k4.
19TH ROW: K5, ✳C4B, k8; rep from ✳ to last 5 sts, k5.
20TH ROW: Purl. Rep these 20 rows.

Raised Circles
Multiple of 7 sts + 1
Drape: good
Skill: intermediate

1ST ROW (RS): P3, k2, ✳p5, k2; rep from ✳ to last 3 sts, p3.
2ND ROW: K3, p2, ✳k5, p2; rep from ✳ to last 3 sts, k3.
3RD ROW: P2, C2B, CF, ✳p3, C2B, C2F; rep from ✳ to last 2 sts, p2.
4TH ROW: K2, p4, ✳k3, p4; rep from ✳ to last 2 sts, k2.
5TH ROW: P1, ✳C2B, k2, C2F, p1; rep from ✳ to end.
6TH ROW: K1, ✳p6, k1; rep from ✳ to end.
7TH ROW: P1, ✳k6, p1; rep from ✳ to end.
8TH ROW: As 6th row.
9TH ROW: P1, ✳T2F, k2, T2B, p1; rep from ✳ to end.
10TH ROW: As 4th row.
11TH ROW: P2, T2F, T2B, ✳p3, T2F, T2B; rep from ✳ to last 2 sts, p2.
12TH ROW: As 2nd row.
Rep these 12 rows.

Garter Stitch Lattice
Multiple of 12 sts + 4
Drape: good
Skill: experienced

1ST ROW (WS): K7, p2, ✳k10, p2; rep from ✳ to last 7 sts, k7.
2ND ROW: K7, C2B, ✳k10, C2B; rep from ✳ to last 7 sts, k7.
3RD ROW: As 1st row.
4TH ROW: K6, C2B, C2F, ✳k8, C2B, C2F;

rep from ✳ to last 6 sts, k6.
5TH ROW: K6, p1, k2, p1, ✳k8, p1, k2, p1; rep from ✳ to last 6 sts, k6.
6TH ROW: K5, C2B, k2, C2F ✳k6, C2B, k2, C2F; rep from ✳ to last 5 sts, k5.
7TH ROW: K5, p1, k4, p1, ✳k6, p1, k4, p1; rep from ✳ to last 5 sts, k5.
8TH ROW: K4, ✳C2B, k4, C2F, k4; rep from ✳ to end.
9TH ROW: K4, ✳p1, k6, p1, k4; rep from ✳ to end.
10TH ROW: K3, ✳C2B, k6, C2F, k2; rep from ✳ to last st, k1.
11TH ROW: K3, p1, k8, p1, ✳k2, p1, k8, p1; rep from ✳ to last 3 sts, k3.
12TH ROW: K2, ✳C2B, k8, C2F; rep from ✳ to last 2 sts, k2.
13TH ROW: K1, p2, ✳k10, p2; rep from ✳ to last st, k1.
14TH ROW: K1, C2F, ✳k10, C2F; rep from ✳ to last st, k1.
15TH ROW: As 13th row.
16TH ROW: K2, ✳C2L, k8, C2R; rep from ✳ to last 2 sts, k2.
17TH ROW: As 11th row.
18TH ROW: K3, ✳C2F, k6, C2B, k2; rep from ✳ to last st, k1.
19TH ROW: As 9th row.
20TH ROW: K4, ✳C2F, k4, C2B, k4; rep from ✳ to end.
21ST ROW: As 7th row.
22ND ROW: K5, C2F, k2, C2B, ✳k6, C2F, k2, C2B; rep from ✳ to last 5 sts, k5.
23RD ROW: As 5th row.
24TH ROW: K6, C2F, C2B, ✳k8, C2F, C2B; rep from ✳ to last 6 sts, k6.
Rep these 24 rows.

Ridged Diamonds
Multiple of 16 sts + 1
Drape: good
Skill: experienced

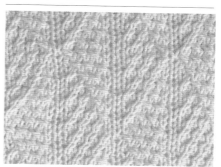

1ST AND EVERY ALT ROW (WS): Purl.
2ND ROW: K1, ✳C2F, [C2B] twice, k3, [C2F] twice, C2B, k1; rep from ✳ to end.
4TH ROW: K2, C2L, [C2R] twice, k1, [C2L] twice. C2B, ✳k3, C2F, [C2B] twice, k1, [C2F] twice, C2B; rep from ✳ to last 2 sts, k2.
6TH ROW: K1, ✳[C2F] twice, C2B, k3, C2F, [C2B] twice, k1; rep from ✳ to end.
8TH ROW: K2, [C2F] twice, C2B, k1, C2F, [C2B] twice, ✳k3, [C2F] twice, C2B, k1, C2F, [C2B] twice, rep from ✳ to last 2 sts, k2.
10TH ROW: K1, ✳[C2F] 3 times, k3, [C2B] 3 times, k1; rep from ✳ to end.
12TH ROW: K2, [C2F] 3 times, K1, [C2B] 3 times, ✳k3, [C2F] 3 times, k1, [C2B] 3 times; rep from ✳ to last 2 sts, k2.
14TH ROW: As 10th row.
16TH ROW: As 8th row.
18TH ROW: As 6th row.
20TH ROW: As 4th row.
22ND ROW: As 2nd row.
24TH ROW: K2, [C2B] 3 times, k1, [C2F] 3 times, ✳k3, [C2B] 3 times, k1, [C2F] 3 times; rep from ✳ to last 2 sts, k2.
26TH ROW: K1, ✳[C2B] 3 times, k3, [C2F] 3 times, k1; rep from ✳ to end.
28TH ROW: As 24th row.
Rep these 28 rows.

Double Moss Stitch Lattice

Multiple of 14 sts + 15
Drape: good
Skill: experienced

1ST ROW (RS): K4, C3B, p1, C3F, ✳k7, C3B, p1, C3F; rep form ✳ to last 4 sts, k4.
2ND ROW: P7, k1, ✳p13, k1; rep from ✳ to last 7 sts, p7.
3RD ROW: K3, C3B, p1, k1, p1, C3F, ✳k5, C3B, p1, k1, p1, C3F; rep from ✳ to last 3 sts, k3.
4TH ROW: P6, k1, p1, k1, ✳p11, k1, p1, k1; rep from ✳ to last 6 sts, p6.
5TH ROW: K2, C3B, p1, [k1, p1] twice, C3F, ✳k3, C3B, p1, [k1, p1] twice, C3F; rep from ✳ to last 2 sts, k2.
6TH ROW: P5, k1, [p1, k1] twice, ✳p9, k1, [p1, k1] twice; rep from ✳ to last 5 sts, p5.
7TH ROW: K1, ✳C3B, p1, [k1, p1] 3 times, C3F, k1; rep from ✳ to end.
8TH ROW: P4, k1, [p1, k1] 3 times, ✳p7, k1, [p1, k1] 3 times; rep from ✳ to last 4 sts, p4.
9TH ROW: K3, p1, [k1, p1] 4 times, ✳C5B, p1, [k1, p1] 4 times; rep from ✳ to last 3 sts, k3.
10TH ROW: P3, k1, [p1, k1] 4 times, ✳p5, k1, [p1, k1] 3 times; rep from ✳ to last 3 sts, p3.
11TH ROW: K1, ✳C3F, p1 [k1, p1] 3 times, C3B, k1; rep from ✳ to end.
12TH ROW: As 8th row.
13TH ROW: K2, C3F, p1, [k1, p1] twice, C3B, ✳k3, C3F, p1, [k1, p1] twice, C3B; rep from ✳ to last 2 sts, k2.
14TH ROW: As 6th row.
15TH ROW: K3, C3F, p1, k1, p1, C3B, ✳k5, C3F, p1, k1, p1, C3B; rep from ✳ to last

3 sts, k3.
16TH ROW: As 4th row.
17TH ROW: K4, C3F, p1, C3B; ✳k7, C3F, p1, C3B; rep from ✳ to last 4 sts, k4.
18TH ROW: As 2nd row.
19TH ROW: K5, C5B, ✳k9, C5B; rep from ✳ to last 5 sts, k5.
20TH ROW: Purl.
Rep these 20 rows.

Dovetailed Diamonds

Multiple of 20 sts + 2
Drape: good
Skill: experienced

1ST ROW (WS): P6, k10, ✳p10, k10; rep from ✳ to last 6 sts, p6.
2ND ROW: K1, ✳C2F, k2, C2F, k8, C2B, k2, C2B; rep from ✳ to last st, k1.
3RD ROW: K2, ✳p5, k8, p5, k2; rep from ✳ to end.
4TH ROW: K2, ✳C2F, k2, C2F, k6, [C2B, k2] twice; rep from ✳ to end.
5TH ROW: K3, p5, k6, p5, ✳k4, p5, k6, p5; rep from ✳ to last 3 sts, k3.
6TH ROW: K3, C2F, k2, C2F, k4, C2B, k2, C2B, ✳k4, C2F, k2, C2F, k4, C2B, k2, C2B; rep from ✳ to last 3 sts, k3.
7TH ROW: [K4, p5] twice, ✳k6, p5, k4, p5; rep from ✳ to last 4 sts, k4.
8TH ROW: K4, [C2F, k2] twice, C2B, k2, C2B, ✳k6, [C2F, k2] twice, C2B, k2, C2B; rep from ✳ to last 4 sts, k4.
9TH ROW: K5, p5, k2, p5, ✳k8, p5, k2, p5; rep from ✳ to last 5 sts, k5.
10TH ROW: K5, C2F, k2, C2F, C2B, k2, C2B, ✳k8, C2F, k2, C2F, C2B, k2, C2B; rep from

✳ to last 5 sts, k5.
11TH ROW: K6, p10, ✳k10, p10; rep from ✳ to last 6 sts, k6.
12TH ROW: K5, C2B, k2, C2B, C2F, k2, C2F, ✳k8, C2B, k2, C2B, C2F, k2, C2F; rep from ✳ to last 5 sts, k5.
13TH ROW: As 9th row.
14TH ROW: K4, [C2B, k2] twice, C2F, k2, C2F, ✳k6, [C2B, k2] twice, C2F, k2, C2F; rep from ✳ to last 4 sts, k4.
15TH ROW: As 7th row.
16TH ROW: K3, C2B, k2, C2B, k4, C2F, k2, C2F, ✳k4, C2B, k2, C2B, k4, C2F, k2, C2F; rep from ✳ to last 3 sts, k3.
17TH ROW: As 5th row.
18TH ROW: K2, ✳C2B, k2, C2B, k6, [C2F, k2] twice; rep from ✳ to end.
19TH ROW: As 3rd row.
20TH ROW: K1, ✳C2B, k2, C2B, k8, C2F, k2, C2F; rep from ✳ to last st, k1.
Rep these 20 rows.

Overlapping Petals

Multiple of 18 sts + 10
Drape: good
Skill: intermediate

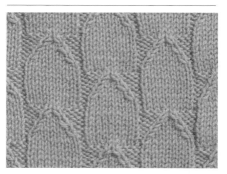

1ST ROW (RS): P1, ✳k8, p1; rep from ✳ to end.
2ND ROW: K1, ✳p8, k1; rep from ✳ to end.
3RD ROW: P1, T2F, k4, T2B, p1, ✳k8, p1, T2F, k4, T2B, p1; rep from ✳ to end.
4TH ROW: K2, p6, k2, ✳p8, k2, p6, k2; rep from ✳ to end.
5TH ROW: P2, T2F, k2, T2B, p2, ✳k8, p2, T2F, k2, T2B, p2; rep from ✳ to end.
6TH ROW: K3, p4, k3, ✳p8, k3, p4, k3; rep

from ✳ to end.
7TH ROW: P3, T2F, T2B, p3, ✳k8, p3, T2F, T2B, p3; rep from ✳ to end.
8TH ROW: As 2nd row.
9TH AND 10TH ROWS: As 1st and 2nd rows.
11TH ROW: P1, k8, p1, ✳T2F, k4, T2B, p1, k8, p1; rep from ✳ to end.
12TH ROW: K1, p8, ✳k2, p6, k2, p8; rep from ✳ to last st, k1.
13TH ROW: P1, k8, ✳p2, T2F, k2, T2B, p2, k8; rep from ✳ to last st, p1.
14TH ROW: K1, p8, ✳k3, p4, k3, p8; rep from ✳ to last st, k1.
15TH ROW: P1, k8, ✳p3, T2F, T2B, p3, k8; rep from ✳ to last st, p1.
16TH ROW: As 2nd row.
Rep these 16 rows.

Conifer Pattern
Multiple of 12 sts + 1
Drape: good
Skill: intermediate

1ST ROW (WS): P1, ✳k4, p3, k4, p1; rep from ✳ to end.
2ND ROW: K1, ✳p3, T2B, k1, T2F, p3, k1; rep from ✳ to end.
3RD ROW: P1, k3, p1, [k1, p1] twice, ✳[k3, p1] twice, [k1, p1] twice; rep from ✳ to last 4 sts, k3, p1.
4TH ROW: K1, ✳p2, T2B, p1, k1, p1, T2F, p2, k1; rep from ✳ to end.
5TH ROW: P1, ✳k2, p1; rep from ✳ to end.
6TH ROW: K1, ✳p1, T2B, p2, k1, p2, T2F, p1, k1; rep from ✳ to end.
7TH ROW: P1, k1, p1, [k3, p1] twice, ✳[k1, p1] twice, [k3, p1] twice; rep from ✳

to last 2 sts, k1, p1.
8TH ROW: K1, ✳T2B, p3, k1, p3, T2F, k1; rep from ✳ to end.
Rep these 8 rows.

Floating Diamonds
Multiple of 18 sts + 2
Drape: good
Skill: experienced

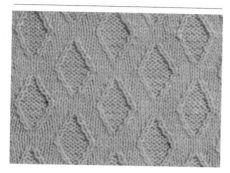

1ST ROW (WS): P6, k8, ✳p10, k8; rep from ✳ to last 6 sts, p6.
2ND ROW: K5, C2F, p6, C2B, ✳k8, C2F, p6, C2B; rep from ✳ to last 5 sts, k5.
3RD ROW: P7, k6, ✳p12, k6; rep from ✳ to last 7 sts, p7.
4TH ROW: K1, ✳T2F, k3, C2F, p4, C2B, k3, t2B; rep from ✳ to last st, k1.
5TH ROW: K2, ✳p6, k4, p6, k2; rep from ✳ to end.
6TH ROW: P2, ✳T2F, k3, C2F, p2, C2B, k3, T2B, p2; rep from ✳ to end.
7TH ROW: K3, p6, k2, p6, ✳k4, p6, k2, p6; rep from ✳ to last 3 sts, k3.
8TH ROW: P3, T2F, k3, C2F, C2B, k3, T2B, ✳ p4, T2F, k3, C2F, C2B, k3, T2B; rep from ✳ to last 3 sts, p3.
9TH ROW: K4, p12, ✳k6, p12; rep from ✳ to last 4 sts, k4.
10TH ROW: P4, T2F, k8, T2B, ✳p6, T2F, k8, T2B; rep from ✳ to last 4 sts, p4.
11TH ROW: K5, p10, ✳k8, p10; rep from ✳ to last 5 sts, k5.
12TH ROW: P4, C2B, k8, C2F, ✳p6, C2B, k8, C2F; rep from ✳ to last 4 sts, p4.
13TH ROW: As 9th row.
14TH ROW: P3, C2B, k3, T2B, t2F, k3, C2F,

✳p4, C2B, k3, T2B, T2F, k3, C2F; rep from ✳ to last 3 sts, p3.
15TH ROW: As 7th row.
16TH ROW: P2, ✳C2B, k3, T2B, p2, T2F, k3, C2F, p2; rep from ✳ to end.
17TH ROW: As 5th row.
18TH ROW: K1, ✳C2B, k3, T2B, p4, T2F, k3, C2F; rep from ✳ to last st, k1.
19TH ROW: As 3rd row.
20TH ROW: K5, T2B, p6, T2F, ✳k8, T2B, p6, T2F; rep from ✳ to last 5 sts, k5.
Rep these 20 rows.

Ribbon Zigzag
Multiple of 16 sts + 1
Drape: good
Skill: experienced

1ST ROW (WS): K1, ✳p7, k1; rep from ✳ to end.
2ND ROW: P1, ✳T2F, k5, p1, k5, T2B, p1; rep from ✳ to end.
3RD ROW: K2, p6, k1, p6, ✳k3, p6, k1, p6; rep from ✳ to last 2 sts, k2.
4TH ROW: P2, T2F, k4, p1, k4, T2B, ✳p3, T2F, k4, p1, k4, T2B; rep from ✳ to last 2 sts, p2.
5TH ROW: K3, p5, k1, p5, ✳k5, p5, k1, p5; rep from ✳ to last 3 sts, k3.
6TH ROW: P3, C2F, k3, p1, k3, C2B, ✳p5, C2F, k3, p1, k3, C2B; rep from ✳ to last 3 sts, p3.
7TH ROW: As 5th row.
8TH ROW: P2, C2B, C2F, k2, p1, k2, C2B, C2F, ✳p3, C2B, C2F, k2, p1, k2, C2B, C2F; rep from ✳ to last 2 sts, p2.
9TH ROW: As 3rd row.
10TH ROW: P1, ✳C2B, k2, C2F, k1, p1, k1,

C2B, k2, C2F, p1; rep from ❊ to end.
11TH ROW: As 1st row.
12TH ROW: P1, ❊k5, C2F, p1, C2B, k5, p1; rep from ❊ to end.
13TH ROW: As 1st row.
14TH ROW: P1, ❊k7, p1; rep from ❊ to end.
15TH ROW: As 1st row.
16TH ROW: P1, ❊k5, T2B, p1, T2F, k5, p1; rep from ❊ to end.
17TH ROW: K1, ❊p6, k3, p6, k1; rep from ❊ to end.
18TH ROW: P1, ❊k4, T2B, p3, T2F, k4, p1; rep from ❊ to end.
19TH ROW: K1, ❊p5, k5, p5, k1; rep from ❊ to end.
20TH ROW: P1, ❊k3, C2B, p5, C2F, k3, p1; rep from ❊ to end.
21ST ROW: As 19th row.
22ND ROW: P1, ❊k2, C2B, C2F, p3, C2B, C2F, k2, p1; rep from ❊ to end.
23RD ROW: As 17th row.
24TH ROW: P1, ❊k1, C2B, k2, C2F, p1, C2B, k2, C2F, k1, p1; rep from ❊ to end.
25TH ROW: As 1st row.
26TH ROW: P1, ❊C2B, k5, p1, k5, C2F, p1; rep from ❊ to end.
Rep these 26 rows.

Linked Lattice
Multiple of 12 sts + 14
Drape: good
Skill: experienced

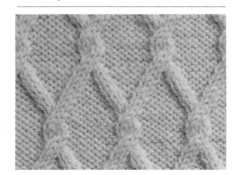

1ST ROW (RS): P5, k4, ❊p8, k4; rep from ❊ to last 5 sts, p5.
2ND ROW: K5, p4, ❊k8, p4; rep from ❊ to

last 5 sts, k5.
3RD ROW: P5, C4B, ❊p8, C4B; rep from ❊ to last 5 sts, p5.
4TH ROW: As 2nd row.
5TH ROW: P4, T3B, T3F, ❊p6, T3B, T3F; rep from ❊ to last 4 sts, p4.
6TH ROW: K4, p2, k2, p2, ❊k6, p2, k2, p2; rep from ❊ to last 4 sts, k4.
7TH ROW: P3, T3B, p2, T3F, ❊p4, T3B, p2, T3F; rep from ❊ to last 3 sts, p3.
8TH ROW: K3, p2, ❊k4, p2; rep from ❊ to last 3 sts, k3.
9TH ROW: ❊P2, T3B, p4, T3F; rep from ❊ to last 2 sts, p2.
10TH ROW: ❊K2, p2, k6, p2; rep from ❊ to last 2 sts, k2.
11TH ROW: P1, ❊T3B, p6, T3F; rep from ❊ to last st, p1.
12TH ROW: K1, p2, k8, ❊p4, k8; rep from ❊ to last 3 sts, p2, k1.
13TH ROW: P1, k2, p8, ❊C4B, p8; rep from ❊ to last 3 sts, k2, p1.
14TH ROW: As 12th row.
15TH ROW: P1, k2, p8, ❊k4, p8; rep from ❊ to last 3 sts, k2, p1.
16TH TO 18TH ROWS: Rep 12th and 13th rows once, then 12th row again.
19TH ROW: P1, ❊T3F, p6, T3B; rep from ❊ to last st, p1.
20TH ROW: As 10th row.
21ST ROW: ❊P2, T3F, p4, T3B; rep from ❊ to last 2 sts, p2.
22ND ROW: As 8th row.
23RD ROW: P3, T3F, p2, T3B, ❊p4, T3F, p2, T3B; rep from ❊ to last 3 sts, p3.
24TH ROW: As 6th row.
25TH ROW: P4, T3F, T3B, ❊p6, T3F, T3B; rep from ❊ to last 4 sts, p4.
26TH TO 28TH ROWS: Rep 2nd and 3rd rows once, then 2nd row again.
Rep these 28 rows.

Elongated Lattice
Multiple of 8 sts + 4
Drape: good
Skill: experienced

1ST ROW (WS): K1, p2, ❊k6, p2; rep from ❊ to last st, k1.

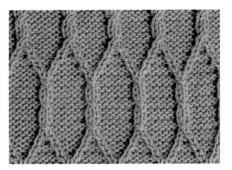

2ND ROW: P1, C2B, ❊p6, C2B; rep from ❊ to last st, p1.
3RD ROW: As 1st row.
4TH ROW: P1, k2, ❊p6, k2; rep from ❊ to last st, p1.
Rep the last 4 rows once more, then first 3 rows again.
12TH ROW: P2, ❊T2F, p4, T2B; rep from ❊ to last 2 sts, p2.
13TH ROW: K3, p1, k4, p1, ❊k2, p1, k4, p1; rep from ❊ to last 3 sts, k3.
14TH ROW: P3, ❊T2F, p2, T2B, p2; rep from ❊ to last st, p1.
15TH ROW: K4, ❊p1, k2, p1, k4; rep from ❊ to end.
16TH ROW: P4, ❊T2F, T2B, p4; rep from ❊ to end.
17TH ROW: K5, p2, ❊k6, p2; rep from ❊ to last 5 sts, k5.
18TH ROW: P5, C2F, ❊p6, C2F; rep from ❊ to last 5 sts, p5.
19TH ROW: As 17th row.
20TH ROW: P5, k2, ❊p6, k2; rep from ❊ to last 5 sts, p5.
Rep the last 4 rows once more, then 17th, 18th and 19th rows again.
28TH ROW: P4, ❊T2B, T2F, p4; rep from ❊ to end.
29TH ROW: As 15th row.
30TH ROW: P3, ❊T2B, p2, T2F, p2; rep from ❊ to last st, p1.
31ST ROW: As 13th row.
32ND ROW: P2, ❊T2B, p4, T2F; rep from ❊ to last 2 sts, p2.
Rep these 32 rows.

Climbing Frame
Multiple of 10 sts
Drape good
Skill intermediate

1ST ROW (RS): Knit.
2ND ROW: K4, p2, ✳k8, p2; rep from ✳ to last 4 sts, k4.
3RD ROW: K3, C2B, C2F, ✳k6, C2B, C2F; rep from ✳ to last 3 sts, k3.
4TH ROW: Purl.
Rep these 4 rows.

Bird's Wings
Multiple of 18 sts + 11
Drape: good
Skill: experienced

1ST ROW: (WS): K4, p3, ✳k3, [p1, k3] 3 times, p3; rep from ✳ to last 4 sts, k4.
2ND ROW: P4, k3, ✳p3, T2F, p2, k1, p2, T2B, p3, k3; rep from ✳ to last 4 sts, p4.
3RD ROW: K4, p3, k4, ✳p1, [k2, p1] twice, k4, p3, k4; rep from ✳ to end.
4TH ROW: P4, k3, p4, ✳T2F, p1, k1, p1,

T2B, p4, k3, p4; rep from ✳ to end.
5TH ROW: K4, p3, ✳k5, p1, [k1, p1] twice, k5, p3; rep from ✳ to last 4 sts, k4.
6TH ROW: P3, T2B, k1, T2F, ✳p4, T2F, k1, T2B, p4, T2B, k1, T2F; rep from ✳ to last 3 sts, p3.
7TH ROW: K3, p1, [k1, p1] twice, ✳k5, p3, K5, p1, [k1, p1] twice; rep from ✳ to last 3 sts, k3.
8TH ROW: P2, T2B, p1, k1, p1, T2F, ✳p4, k3, p4, T2B, p1, k1, p1, T2F; rep from ✳ to last 2 sts, p2.
9TH ROW: [K2, p1] 3 times, ✳k4, p3, k4, p1, [k2, p1] twice; rep from ✳ to last 2 sts, k2.
10TH ROW: P1, T2B, p2, k1, p2, T2F, ✳p3, k3, p3, T2B, p2, k1, p2, T2F; rep from ✳ to last st, p1.
11TH ROW: K1, ✳[p1, k3] 3 times, p3, k3; rep from ✳ to last 10 sts, p1, [k3, p1] twice, k1.
12TH ROW: P1, T2F, p2, k1, p2, T2B, ✳p3, k3, p3, T2F, p2, k1, p2, T2B; rep from ✳ to last st, p1.
13TH ROW: As 9th row.
14TH ROW: P2, T2F, p1, k1, p1, T2B, ✳p4, k3, p4, T2F, p1, k1, p1, T2B; rep from ✳ to last 2 sts, p2.
15TH ROW: As 7th row.
16TH ROW: P3, T2F, k1, T2B, ✳p4, T2B, k1, T2F, p4, T2F, k1, T2B; rep from ✳ to last 3 sts, p3.
17TH ROW: As 5th row.
18TH ROW: P4, k3, p4, ✳T2B, p1, k1, p1, T2R, p4, k3, p4; rep from ✳ to end.
19TH ROW: As 3rd row.
20TH ROW: P4, k3, ✳p3, T2B, p2, k1, p2, T2F, p3, k3; rep from ✳ to last 4 sts, p4.
Rep these 20 rows.

Moorish Pattern
Multiple of 12 sts + 12
Drape: good
Skill: experienced

1ST, 3RD, 5TH AND 7TH ROWS (WS): K2, p2, ✳k4, p2; rep from ✳ to last 2 sts, k2.
2ND ROW: K2, C2B, k4 C2F, ✳k4, C2B, k4,

C2F; rep from ✳ to last 2 sts, k2.
4TH ROW: Knit.
6TH ROW: As 2nd row.
8TH ROW: K3, C2F, k2, C2B, ✳k6, C2F, k2, C2B; rep from ✳ to last 3 sts, k3.
9TH ROW: [K2, p3] twice, ✳k4, p3, k2,p3; rep from ✳ to last 2 sts, k2.
10TH ROW: K4, C2F, C2B, ✳k8, C2F, C2B; rep from ✳ to last 4 sts, k4.
11TH ROW: K2, p8, ✳k4, p8; rep from ✳ to last 2 sts, k2.
12TH ROW: K5, C2B, ✳k10, C2B; rep from ✳ to last 5 sts, k5.
13TH ROW: As 11th row.
14TH ROW: K4, C2B, C2F, ✳k8, C2B, C2F; rep from ✳ to last 4 sts, k4.
15TH ROW: As 9th row.
16TH ROW: K3, C2B, k2, C2F, ✳k6, C2B, k2, C2F; rep from ✳ to last 3 sts, k2.
17TH, 19TH, 21ST AND 23RD ROWS: As 1st row.
18TH ROW: K2, C2F, k4, C2B, ✳k4, C2F, k4, C2B; rep from ✳ to last 2 sts, k2.
20TH ROW: Knit.
22ND ROW: As 18th row.
24TH ROW: K9, ✳C2F, k2, C2B, k6; rep from ✳ to last 3 sts, k3.
25TH ROW: K2, p2, k4, ✳p3, k2, p3, k4; rep from ✳ to last 4 sts, p2, k2.
26TH ROW: K10, ✳C2F, C2B, k8; rep from ✳ to last 2 sts, k2.
27TH ROW: K2, p2, k4, ✳p8, k4; rep from ✳ to last 4 sts, p2, k2.
28TH ROW: K11, ✳C2F, k10; rep from ✳ to last st, k1.
29TH ROW: As 27th row.
30TH ROW: K10, ✳C2B, C2F, k8; rep from

✳ to last 2 sts, k2.
31ST ROW: As 25th row.
32ND ROW: K9, ✳C2B, k2, C2F, k6; rep from ✳ to last 3 sts, k3.
Rep these 32 rows.

Garter Stitch Zigzag

Multiple of 6 sts + 1
Drape: good
Skill: intermediate

1ST ROW (RS): K1, ✳C2F, k4; rep from ✳ to end.
2ND ROW: K4, p1, ✳k5, p1; rep from ✳ to last 2 sts, k2.
3RD ROW: K2, C2F, ✳k4, C2F; rep from ✳ to last 3 sts, k3.
4TH ROW: K3, p1, ✳k5, p1; rep from ✳ to last 3 sts, k3.
5TH ROW: K3, C2F, ✳k4, C2F; rep from ✳ to last 2 sts, k2.
6TH ROW: K2, p1, ✳k5, p1; rep from ✳ to last 4 sts, k4.
7TH ROW: ✳K4, C2F; rep from ✳ to last st, k1.
8TH ROW: K1, ✳p1, k5; rep from ✳ to end.
9TH ROW: ✳K4, C2B; rep from ✳ to last st, k1.
10TH ROW: As 6th row.
11TH ROW: K3, C2B, ✳k4, C2B; rep from ✳ to last 2 sts, k2.
12TH ROW: As 4th row.
13TH ROW: K2, C2B, ✳k4, C2B; rep from ✳ to last 3 sts, k3.
14TH ROW: As 2nd row.
15TH ROW: K1, ✳C2B, k4; rep from ✳ to end.

Squares and Twists

Multiple of 10 sts + 4
Drape: good
Skill: intermediate

1ST ROW (WS): P4, ✳k2, p2, k2, p4; rep from ✳ to end.
2ND ROW: K4, ✳p2, C2B, p2, k4; rep from ✳ to end.
Rep the last 2 rows once more.
5TH ROW: K1, p2, ✳k2, p4, k2, p2; rep from ✳ to last st, k1.
6TH ROW: P1, C2B, ✳p2, k4, p2, C2B; rep from ✳ to last st, p1.
Rep the last 2 rows once more.
Rep these 8 rows.

Wheat Pattern

Multiple of 10 sts + 1
Drape: good
Skill: intermediate

1ST ROW (WS): P1, ✳k2, p5, k2, p1; rep from ✳ to end.
2ND ROW: KB1, ✳p2, C2F, k1, C2B, p2, KB1; rep from ✳ to end.
Rep the last 2 rows 4 times more.
11TH ROW: P3, k2, p1, k2, ✳p5, k2, p1, k2; rep from ✳ to last 3 sts, p3.
12TH ROW: K1, ✳C2B, p2, KB1, p2, C2F, k1; rep from ✳ to end.

16TH ROW: gK5, p1; rep from g to last st, k1.
Rep these 16 rows.

Rep the last 2 rows 4 times more.
Rep these 20 rows.

---

other complex patterns

These complex patterns involve the use of various increasing and decreasing techniques (*pages 17–20*) to achieve scalloped, zigzag, and other ornamental effects. The two zigzag chevron patterns (*below*) can be varied by using more than two colors, or the same color throughout, or by working more rows between color changes. Butterfly Wings (*page 64*) is a glamorous pattern that would look elegant in a silk or mercerized cotton yarn, used for an evening sweater.

Shell Pattern
Multiple of 11 sts
Drape: good
Skill: intermediate

1ST ROW (RS): Knit.
2ND ROW: Purl.
3RD ROW: [P2tog] twice, [inc 1 (by lifting horizontal thread lying between last st worked and next st and knitting into back of it), k1] 3 times, inc 1, ✳[p2tog] 4 times, [inc 1, k1] 3 times, inc 1; rep from ✳ to last 4 sts, [p2tog] twice.
4TH ROW: Purl.
Rep these 4 rows.

Zigzag Chevron Stripes I
Multiple of 14 sts + 2
Drape: good
Skill: intermediate

1ST ROW (WS): Using A, purl.
2ND ROW: Using A, k1, inc in next st (by knitting into front and back of st), k4, sl 1, k1, psso, k2tog, k4, ✳inc in each of next 2 sts, k4, sl 1, k1, psso, k2tog, k4; rep from ✳ to last 2 sts, inc in next st, k1.
3RD ROW: Using A, purl.
4TH ROW: Using B, as 2nd row.
5TH ROW: Using B, knit.
6TH ROW: Using A, knit.
7TH ROW: Using A, purl.
8TH ROW: As 2nd row.
Rep these 8 rows.

Zigzag Chevron Stripes II
Multiple of 14 sts + 2
Drape: good
Skill: intermediate
Note: This example is worked using a multiple of 14 sts but any multiple of 2 can be added or subtracted to make the zigzags wider or narrower.

1ST ROW (WS): Using A, purl.
2ND ROW: Using A, k1, inc in next st (by knitting into front and back of st), k4, sl 1, k1, psso, k2tog, k4, ✳inc in each of next 2 sts, k4, sl 1, k1, psso, k2tog, k4; rep from ✳ to last 2 sts, inc in next st, k1.
3RD ROW: Using A, purl.
4TH ROW: As 2nd row.
Rep the last 4 rows using B.
Rep these 8 rows.

Butterfly Wings
Multiple of 26 sts
Drape: good
Skill: experienced

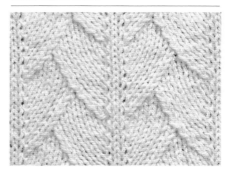

1ST AND EVERY ALT ROW (WS): Purl.
2ND ROW: K1, ✳M1, sl 1, k1, psso, k4, k2tog, k3, M1, k2, M1, k3, sl 1, k1, psso, k4, k2tog, M1, k2; rep from ✳ but ending last rep with k1 instead of k2.
4TH ROW: K1, ✳M1, k1, sl 1, k1, psso, k2, k2tog, k4, M1, k2, M1, k4, sl 1, k1, psso, k2, k2tog, k1, M1, k2; rep from ✳ but ending last rep with k1 instead of k2.
6TH ROW: K1, ✳M1, k2, sl 1, k1, psso, k2tog, k5, M1, k2, M1, k5, sl 1, k1, psso, k2tog, k2, M1, k2; rep from ✳ but ending last rep with k1 instead of k2.
8TH ROW: K1, ✳M1, k3, sl 1, k1, psso, k4, k2tog, M1, k2, M1, sl 1, k1, psso, k4, k2tog, k3, M1, k2; rep from ✳ but ending last rep with k1 instead of k2.
10TH ROW: K1, ✳M1, k4, sl 1, k1, psso, k2, k2tog, k1, M1, k2, M1, k1, sl 1, k1, psso, k2, k2tog, k4, M1, k2; rep from ✳ but ending last rep with k1 instead of k2.
12TH ROW: K1, ✳M1, k5, sl 1, k1, psso, k2tog, [k2, M1] twice, k2, sl 1, k1, psso, k2tog, k5, M1, k2; rep from ✳ but ending last rep with k1 instead of k2. Rep these 12 rows.

Foxgloves
Multiple of 10 sts + 6
Drape: good
Skill: intermediate
Note: Sts should only be counted after the 10th row of pattern.

1ST ROW (RS): P6, ✳yo, k1, p2, k1, yo, p6; rep from ✳ to end.
2ND ROW: P6, ✳yo, p2, k2, p2, yo, p6; rep from ✳ to end.
3RD ROW: P6, ✳yo, k3, p2, k3, yo, p6; rep from ✳ to end.
4TH ROW: P6, ✳yo, p4, k2, p4, yo, p6; rep from ✳ to end.
5TH ROW: P6, ✳k5, p2, k5, p6; rep from ✳ to end.
6TH ROW: P11, ✳k2, p16; rep from ✳ to last 13 sts, k2, p11.
7TH ROW: P6, ✳sl 1, k1, psso, k3, p2, k3, k2tog, p6; rep from ✳ to end.
8TH ROW: P6, ✳p2tog, p2, k2, p2, p2tog tbl, p6; rep from ✳ to end.
9TH ROW: P6, ✳sl 1, k1, psso, k1, p2, k1, k2tog, p6; rep from ✳ to end.
10TH ROW: P6, ✳p2tog, k2, p2tog tbl, p6; rep from ✳ to end.
Rep these 10 rows.

Wigwams
Multiple of 16 sts
Drape: good
Skill: intermediate

1ST ROW (RS): Knit.
2ND ROW: K4, p8, ✳k8, p8; rep from ✳ to last 4 sts, k4.
3RD ROW: P3, k2tog, k3, pick up horizontal strand of yarn lying between stitch just worked and next st and knit into back and front of it (inc 2), k3, sl 1, k1, psso, ✳p6, k2tog, k3, inc 2 as before, k3, sl 1, k1, psso; rep from ✳ to last 3 sts, p3.
4TH ROW: K3, p10, ✳k6, p10; rep from ✳

to last 3 sts, k3.
5TH ROW: P2, k2tog, k3, M1, k2, M1, k3, sl 1, k1, psso, ✳p4, k2tog, k3, M1, k2, M1, k3, sl 1, k1, psso; rep from ✳ to last 2 sts, p2.
6TH ROW: K2, p12, ✳k4, p12; rep from ✳ to last 2 sts, k2.
7TH ROW: P1, k2tog, k3, M1, k4, M1, k3, sl 1, k1, psso, ✳p2, k2tog, k3, M1, k4, M1, k3, sl 1, k1, psso; rep from ✳ to last st, p1.
8TH ROW: K1, p14, ✳k2, p14; rep from ✳ to last st, k1.
9TH ROW: ✳K2tog, k3, M1, k6, M1, k3, sl 1, k1, psso; rep from ✳ to end.
10TH ROW: Purl.
Rep these 10 rows.

heavyweight patterns

The fabrics in this section make warm garments—jackets and cardigans, or pullovers—to wear outdoors on a cool fall or spring day. They are also useful for lap rugs and other accessories. Many employ cables, bobbles, or slipped stitches; although these techniques require a little patience, the results are well worth the effort.

textured patterns

Some of the many different ways of creating a highly textured surface are explored in this section—among them, working into the stitch immediately below the next one on the left-hand needle, and forming knots and bobbles (*page 24*). Worked in a bulky yarn, such patterns are useful for thick cardigans and jackets. Or, if knitted in baby yarn, they could make a soft, warm blanket for a baby. Some of them work well in slightly fluffy yarns.

Staggered Brioche Rib
Multiple of 2 sts + 1
Drape: fair
Skill: intermediate

FOUNDATION ROW (WS): Knit.
Commence Pattern
1ST ROW: K1, ✳K1B, k1; rep from ✳ to end.
Rep the 1st row 3 times more.
5TH ROW: K2, K1B, ✳k1, K1B; rep from ✳ to last 2 sts, k2.
Rep the 5th row 3 times more.
Rep the last 8 rows.

Knot Pattern
Multiple of 6 sts + 5
Drape: fair
Skill: experienced

Special Abbreviation
MK (Make Knot) = p3tog leaving sts on left-hand needle, now knit them tog, then purl them tog again, slipping sts off needle at end.
Commence Pattern
Work 2 rows in St st, starting knit.
3RD ROW (RS): K1, ✳MK (see Special Abbreviation), k3; rep from ✳ to last 4 sts, MK, k1.
Work 3 rows in St st, starting purl.
7TH ROW: K4, ✳MK, k3; rep from ✳ to last st, k1.
8TH ROW: Purl.
Rep these 8 rows.

Rice Stitch
Multiple of 2 sts + 1
Drape: fair
Skill: intermediate

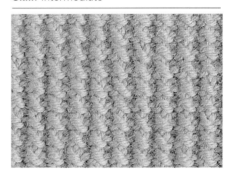

1ST ROW (RS): P1, ✳k1 tbl, p1; rep from ✳ to end.
2ND ROW: Knit.
Rep these 2 rows.

Turkish Rib I (slanting left)
Multiple of 2 sts
Drape: fair
Skill: experienced

Special Abbreviation
PR (Purl Reverse) = purl 1 st, return it to left-hand needle, insert right-hand needle through the st beyond and lift this st over the purled st and off the needle. Return st to right-hand needle.

COMMENCE PATTERN FOUNDATION ROW (RS): Knit.
1ST ROW: P1, ✱yo, PR (see Special Abbreviation); rep from ✱ to last st, p1.
2ND ROW: K1, ✱sl 1, k1, psso, yo; rep from ✱ to last st, k1. Rep the last 2 rows.

Turkish Rib II (slanting right)
Multiple of 2 sts
Drape: fair
Skill: experienced

COMMENCE PATTERN FOUNDATION ROW (RS): Knit.

1ST ROW: P1, ✱p2tog, yo; rep from ✱ to last st, p1.
2ND ROW: K1, ✱yo, k2tog; rep from ✱ to last st, k1. Rep the last 2 rows.

Cob Nut Stitch
Multiple of 4 sts + 3
Drape: good
Skill: experienced
Note: Sts should only be counted after the 4th, 5th, 6th, 10th, 11th, or 12th rows of this pattern.

Special Abbreviation
CN1 (Make 1 Cob Nut) = knit 1 without slipping st off left-hand needle, yo, then k1 once more into same st.

1ST ROW (RS): P3, ✱CN1 (see Special Abbreviation), p3; rep from ✱ to end.
2ND ROW: K3, ✱p3, k3; rep from ✱ to end.
3RD ROW: P3, ✱k3, p3; rep from ✱ to end.
4TH ROW: K3, ✱p3tog, k3; rep from ✱ to end.
5TH ROW: Purl.
6TH ROW: Knit.
7TH ROW: P1, ✱CN1, p3; rep from ✱ to last 2 sts, CN1, p1.
8TH ROW: K1, ✱p3, k3; rep from ✱ to last 4 sts, p3, k1.
9TH ROW: P1, ✱k3, p3; rep from ✱ to last 4 sts, k3, p1.
10TH ROW: K1, ✱p3tog, k3; rep from ✱ to last 4 sts, p3tog, k1.
11TH ROW: Purl.
12TH ROW: Knit. Rep these 12 rows.

Diagonal Knot Stitch I
Multiple of 3 sts + 1
Drape: fair
Skill: experienced

Special Abbreviation
MK (Make Knot) = p3tog leaving sts on needle, yo, then purl same 3 sts together.

1ST AND EVERY ALT ROW (RS): Knit.
2ND ROW: ✱MK (see Special Abbreviation); rep from ✱ to last st, p1.
4TH ROW: P2, ✱MK; rep from ✱ to last 2 sts, p2.
6TH ROW: P1, ✱MK; rep from ✱ to end. Rep these 6 rows.

Diagonal Knot Stitch II
Multiple of 4 sts + 1
Drape: fair
Skill: experienced

Special Abbreviation
MK (Make Knot) = k3tog leaving sts on needle, yo, then knit same 3 sts together again.

1ST ROW (RS): K4, p1, ❋k3, p1; rep from ❋ to last 4 sts, k4.

2ND ROW: P4, k1, ❋p3, k1; rep from ❋ to last 4 sts, p4.

3RD ROW: P1, ❋MK (see Special Abbreviation), p1; rep from ❋ to end.

4TH ROW: As 2nd row.

5TH ROW: K2, p1, ❋k3, p1; rep from ❋ to last 2 sts, k2.

6TH ROW: P2, k1, ❋p3, k1; rep from ❋ to last 2 sts, p2.

7TH ROW: K2, p1, ❋MK, p1; rep from ❋ to last 2 sts, k2.

8TH ROW: As 6th row.
Rep these 8 rows.

Bud Stitch

Multiple of 6 sts + 5
Drape: fair
Skill: intermediate
Note: Sts should only be counted after the 6th and 12th rows.

1ST ROW (RS): P5, ❋k1, yo, p5; rep from ❋ to end.

2ND ROW: K5, ❋p2, k5; rep from ❋ to end.

3RD ROW: P5, ❋k2, p5; rep from ❋ to end. Rep the last 2 rows once more.

6TH ROW: K5, ❋p2tog, k5; rep from ❋ to end.

7TH ROW: P2, ❋k1, yo, p5; rep from ❋ to last 3 sts, k1, yo, p2.

8TH ROW: K2, ❋p2, k5; rep from ❋ to last 4 sts, p2, k2.

9TH ROW: P2, ❋k2, p5; rep from ❋ to last 4 sts, k2, p2.
Rep the last 2 rows once more.

12TH ROW: K2, ❋p2tog, k5; rep from ❋ to last 4 sts, p2tog, k2.
Rep these 12 rows.

Whelk Pattern

Multiple of 4 sts + 3
Drape: fair
Skill: intermediate

1ST ROW (RS): K3, ❋sl 1 purlwise, k3; rep from ❋ to end.

2ND ROW: K3, ❋yo, sl 1 purlwise, yb, k3; rep from ❋ to end.

3RD ROW: K1, ❋sl 1 purlwise, k3; rep from ❋ to last 2 sts, sl 1 purlwise, k1.

4TH ROW: P1, sl 1 purlwise, ❋p3, sl 1 purlwise; rep from ❋ to last st, p1.
Rep these 4 rows.

Rosehip Stitch

Multiple of 4 sts + 3
Drape: fair
Skill: intermediate

1ST ROW (RS): K3, ❋sl 1 purlwise, k3; rep from ❋ to end.

2ND ROW: K3, ❋yf, sl 1 purlwise, yb, k3; rep from ❋ to end.

3RD ROW: K1, ❋sl 1 purlwise, k3; rep from ❋ to last 2 sts, sl 1 purlwise, k1.

4TH ROW: K1, ❋yf, sl 1 purlwise, yb, k3; rep from ❋ to last 2 sts, yf, sl 1 purlwise, yb, k1.
Rep these 4 rows.

Berry Stitch

Multiple of 4 sts + 3
Drape: fair
Skill: experienced
Note: Sts should only be counted after the 2nd and 4th rows.

1ST ROW (RS): K1, [k1, k1 tbl, k1] into next st, ❋p3, [k1, k1 tbl, k1] into next st; rep from ❋ to last st, k1.

2ND ROW: K4, p3tog, ❋k3, p3tog; rep from ❋ to last 4 sts, k4.

3RD ROW: K1, p3, ❋[k1, k1 tbl, k1] into next st, p3; rep from ❋ to last st, k1.

4TH ROW: K1, p3tog, ❋k3, p3tog; rep from ❋ to last st, k1.
Rep these 4 rows.

Flagon Stitch

Multiple of 6 sts + 4
Drape: fair
Skill: experienced
Note: Slip all sts purlwise.

1ST ROW (WS): K1, ✳p2, k1; rep from ✳ to end.

2ND ROW: P1, k2, p1, ✳sl 1, p1, yo, psso the p1 and the yo, p1, k2, p1; rep from ✳ to end.

Rep the last 2 rows 3 times more, then the 1st row again.

10TH ROW: P1, sl 1, p1, yo, psso the p1 and the yo, p1, ✳k2, p1, sl 1, p1, yo, psso the p1 and the yo, p1; rep from ✳ to end.

11TH ROW: As 1st row.

Rep the last 2 rows twice more, then the 10th row again.

Rep these 16 rows.

Hindu Pillar Stitch

Multiple of 4 sts + 1
Drape: fair
Skill: experienced

1ST ROW (RS): K1, ✳p3tog without slipping sts from left-hand needle, knit them tog then purl them tog, k1; rep from ✳ to end.

2ND ROW: Purl.
Rep these 2 rows.

Textured Acorn Stitch

Multiple of 6 sts + 3
Drape: fair
Skill: experienced
Note: Sts should only be counted after 1st, 2nd, 7th, and 8th rows.

Special Abbreviation

M3 (MAKE 3) = knit into front, back, and front of next st.

1ST ROW (RS): P3, ✳k3, p3; rep from ✳ to end.

2ND ROW: K3, ✳p3, k3; rep from ✳ to end.

3RD ROW: P1, M3 (see Special Abbreviation), p1, ✳sl 1, k2tog, psso, p1, M3, p1; rep from ✳ to end.

4TH ROW: K1, p3, ✳k3, p3; rep from ✳ to last st, k1.

5TH ROW: P1, k3, ✳p3, k3; rep from ✳ to last st, p1.

6TH ROW: As 4th row.

7TH ROW: P1, sl 1, k2tog, psso, p1, ✳M3, p1, sl 1, k2tog, psso, p1; rep from ✳ to end.

8TH ROW: As 2nd row.
Rep these 8 rows.

Piqué Squares

Multiple of 12 sts + 8
Drape: good
Skill: experienced

1ST ROW (RS): K7, [p2, slip these sts onto left-hand needle, yb, slip the 2 sts back onto right-hand needle] 3 times, ✳k6, [p2, slip these sts onto left-hand needle, yb, slip the 2 sts back onto right-hand needle] 3 times; rep from ✳ to last 7 sts, k7.

2ND ROW: Purl.
Rep these 2 rows twice more.

7TH ROW: K1, [p2, slip these sts onto left-hand needle, yb, slip the 2 sts back onto right-hand needle] 3 times, ✳k6, [p2, slip these sts onto left-hand needle, yb, slip the 2 sts back onto right-hand needle] 3 times; rep from ✳ to last st, k1.

8TH ROW: Purl.
Rep these 2 rows twice more.
Rep these 12 rows.

Ridge Stitch

Any number of sts
Drape: good
Skill: intermediate

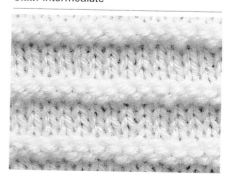

Work 3 rows in St st, starting purl (1st row is wrong side).

4TH ROW: Knit into front and back of each st (thus doubling the number of sts).
5TH ROW: ✳K2tog; rep from ✳ to end (original number of sts restored).
6TH ROW: Knit.
Rep these 6 rows.

Granite Stitch

Multiple of 2 sts
Drape: fair
Skill: intermediate

1ST ROW (RS): Knit.
2ND ROW: ✳K2tog; rep from ✳ to end.
3RD ROW: ✳[K1, p1] into each st; rep from ✳ to end.
4TH ROW: Purl.
Rep these 4 rows.

Bobble and Ridge Stitch

Multiple of 6 sts + 5
Drape: fair
Skill: experienced

Special Abbreviation

MB (Make Bobble) = knit into front, back, and front of next st, turn and p3, turn and k3, turn and p3, turn and sl 1, k2tog, psso (bobble completed).
1ST ROW (RS): Knit.
2ND ROW: Purl.
3RD ROW: K5, ✳MB (see Special Abbreviation), k5; rep from ✳ to end.
4TH ROW: Purl.
5TH ROW: K2, MB, ✳k5, MB; rep from ✳ to last 2 sts, k2.
6TH, 7TH, AND 8TH ROWS: As 2nd, 3rd, and 4th rows.
9TH ROW: Purl.
10TH ROW: Knit.
Rep these 10 rows.

Blanket Moss Stitch

Multiple of 2 sts + 1
Drape: fair
Skill: intermediate
Note: Sts should only be counted after the 2nd and 4th rows.

1ST ROW (RS): Knit into front and back of each st (thus doubling the number of sts).
2ND ROW: K2tog, ✳p2tog, k2tog; rep from ✳ to end (original number of sts restored).
3RD ROW: As 1st row.
4TH ROW: P2tog, ✳k2tog, p2tog; rep from ✳ to end.
Rep these 4 rows.

Pleat Pattern

Multiple of 8 sts + 6
Drape: fair
Skill: experienced

Work 9 rows in St st, starting knit (1st row is right side).
Commence Pattern
1ST ROW (WS): P5, ✳[with right-hand needle pick up loop of next st 7 rows below, place on left-hand needle, then purl together picked-up loop and next st on left-hand needle] 4 times; p4; rep from ✳ to last st, p1.
Work 7 rows in St st, starting knit.
9TH ROW: P1, [pick up loop and purl as before] 4 times, ✳p4, [pick up loop and purl] 4 times, rep from ✳ to last st, p1.
Work 7 rows in St st, starting knit.
Rep the last 16 rows.

Wheat Field Pattern

Multiple of 6 sts + 3
Drape: good
Skill: intermediate
Note: Slip sts purlwise with yarn at back.

FOUNDATION ROW: K1, p1, ✳k2, p1; rep from ✳ to last st, k1.
Commence Pattern
1ST ROW (RS): K1, sl 1, ✳k2, sl 1; rep from ✳ to last st, k1.
2ND ROW: K1, p1, ✳k2, p1; rep from ✳ to last st, k1. Rep the last 2 rows once more.
5TH ROW: K1, sl 1, ✳k5, sl 1; rep from ✳ to last st, k1.
6TH ROW: K1, p1, ✳k5, p1; rep from ✳ to

last st, k1.
Rep the last 2 rows once more.
9TH AND 10TH ROWS: As 1st and 2nd rows.
Rep the last 2 rows once more.
13TH ROW: K4, sl 1, ✳k5, sl 1; rep from ✳ to last 4 sts, k4.
14TH ROW: K4, p1, ✳k5, p1; rep from ✳ to last 4 sts, k4.
Rep the last 2 rows once more.
Rep the last 16 rows.

Mock Rib Checks I

Multiple of 2 sts
Drape: good
Skill: easy

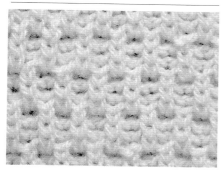

FOUNDATION ROW: Purl.
Commence Pattern
1ST ROW (WS): ✳K1, K1B; rep from ✳ to last 2 sts, k2.
Rep this row 5 times more.
7TH ROW: K2, ✳K1B, k1; rep from ✳ to end. Rep this row 5 times more.
Rep the last 12 rows.

Mock Rib Checks II

Multiple of 2 sts
Drape: good
Skill: easy

Worked as Mock Rib Checks I, using reverse side as right side.

Loop Pattern

Multiple of 2 sts
Drape: fair
Skill: easy
Note: Slip all sts purlwise.

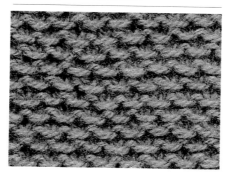

1ST ROW (RS): Knit.
2ND ROW: ✳K1, sl 1; rep from ✳ to last 2 sts, k2.
3RD ROW: Knit.
4TH ROW: K2, ✳sl 1, k1, rep from ✳ to end.
Rep these 4 rows.

Texture Stitch

Multiple of 2 sts + 1
Drape: good
Skill: easy

1ST ROW (RS): Purl.
2ND ROW: K1, ✳yf, sl 1 purlwise, yb, k1; rep from ✳ to end. Rep these 2 rows.

Bobble Twists

Multiple of 8 sts + 6

1ST ROW (RS): P2, ✳C2B, p2; rep from ✳ to end.
2ND AND EVERY ALT ROW: K2, ✳p2, k2; rep from ✳ to end.
3RD ROW: P2, k1, MB (make bobble) as follows: [k1, yo, k1, yo, k1] into next st, turn, p5, turn, k5, turn, p2tog, p1, p2tog, turn,
sl 1, k2tog, psso (bobble completed), p2, ✳C2B, p2, k1, MB, p2; rep from ✳ to end.
5TH ROW: As 1st row.
7TH ROW: P2, C2B, p2, ✳k1, MB, p2, C2B, p2; rep from ✳ to end.
8TH ROW: As 2nd row. Rep these 8 rows.

single color and multicolor patterns

This section shows the different effects produced by using more than one color. The patterns employ a variety of techniques. When using more than one color, it is important to get the balance right: a combination that looks good up close may not work well when viewed from a distance. Buy one ball of yarn in each color you have chosen, plus one or two alternatives. Then knit a large gauge swatch in your first-choice color combination to see the effect.

Bee Stitch I
Multiple of 2 sts + 1
Drape: fair
Skill: intermediate

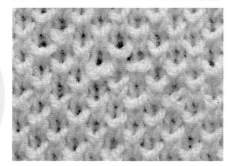

1ST ROW (WS): Knit.
2ND ROW: K1, ✳K1B, k1; rep from ✳ to end.
3RD ROW: Knit.
4TH ROW: K2, K1B, ✳k1, K1B; rep from ✳ to last 2 sts, k2.
Rep these 4 rows.

Bee Stitch II
Multiple of 2 sts + 1
Drape: fair
Skill: intermediate

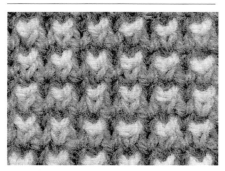

1ST FOUNDATION ROW (RS): Using A, knit.
2ND FOUNDATION ROW: Using A, knit.
Commence Pattern
1ST ROW: Using B, k1, ✳K1B, k1; rep from ✳ to end.
2ND ROW: Using B, knit.
3RD ROW: Using A, k2, K1B, ✳k1, K1B; rep from ✳ to last 2 sts, k2.
4TH ROW: Using A, knit.
Rep the last 4 rows.

Speckle Rib I
Multiple of 2 sts + 1
Drape: fair
Skill: intermediate

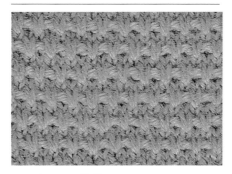

1ST ROW (RS): Knit.
2ND ROW: Purl.
3RD ROW: K1, ✳sl 1 purlwise, k1; rep from ✳ to end.
4TH ROW: K1, ✳yf, sl 1 purlwise, yb, k1; rep from ✳ to end.
5TH ROW: Knit.
6TH ROW: Purl.
7TH ROW: K2, ✳sl 1 purlwise, k1; rep from ✳ to last st, k1.
8TH ROW: K2, ✳yf, sl 1 purlwise, yb, k1; rep from ✳ to last st, k1.
Rep these 8 rows.

Speckle Rib II
Multiple of 2 sts + 1
Drape: fair
Skill: intermediate

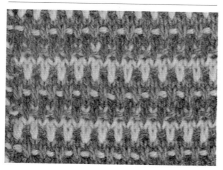

Worked as Speckle Rib I.
Beginning with the 1st row, 2 rows worked in color A, 2 rows in B, and 2 rows in C throughout.

Stockinette Stitch Ridge I
Multiple of 2 sts
Drape: fair
Skill: intermediate
Note: Sts should not be counted after the 2nd row.

1ST ROW (RS): Knit.
2ND ROW: P1, ✳k2tog; rep from ✳ to last st, p1.
3RD ROW: K1, ✳knit into front and back of next st; rep from ✳ to last st, k1.
4TH ROW: Purl.
Rep these 4 rows.

Stockinette Stitch Ridge II
Multiple of 2 sts
Drape: fair
Skill: intermediate

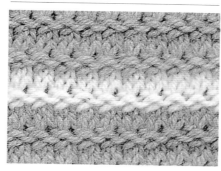

Worked as Stockinette Stitch Ridge I.
Worked in stripes of 4 rows in color A, 4 rows in B, and 4 rows in C throughout.

Star Stitch Pattern I
Multiple of 4 sts + 1
Drape: fair
Skill: experienced

Special Abbreviation
Make Star = p3tog leaving sts on needle, yo, then purl the same 3 sts together again.
1ST ROW (RS): Knit.
2ND ROW: P1, ✳Make Star (see Special Abbreviation), p1; rep from ✳ to end.
3RD ROW: Knit.
4TH ROW: P3, Make Star, ✳p1, Make Star; rep from ✳ to last 3 sts, p3.
Rep these 4 rows.

Star Stitch Pattern II
Multiple of 4 sts + 1
Drape: fair
Skill: experienced

Special Abbreviation
Make Star = p3tog leaving sts on needle, yo, then purl the same 3 sts together again.
1ST ROW (RS): P1, ✳k1, p1; rep from ✳ to end.
2ND ROW: K1, ✳Make Star (see Special Abbreviation), k1; rep from ✳ to end.
3RD ROW: As 1st row.
4TH ROW: K1, p1, k1, ✳Make Star, k1; rep from ✳ to last 2 sts, p1, k1.
Rep these 4 rows.

Thick Woven Blanket Fabric I
Multiple of 4 sts + 1
Drape: fair
Skill: intermediate
Note: Slip all sts purlwise.

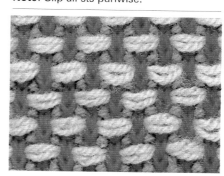

FOUNDATION ROW (WS): Using B, purl.
Commence Pattern
1ST ROW: Using A, k2, sl 1 , ❋k1, sl 1; rep from ❋ to last 2 sts, k2.
2ND ROW: Using A, p1, k1, ❋yf, sl 1, yb, k1, rep from ❋ to last st, p1.
3RD ROW: Using B, k1, ❋sl 1, k1; rep from ❋ to end.
4TH ROW: Using B, p1, ❋sl 1, p1; rep from ❋ to end.
5TH ROW: Using C, k1, yf, sl 1, yb, sl 1, yf, ❋sl 3, yb, sl 1, yf; rep from ❋ to last 2 sts, sl 1, yb, k1.
6TH ROW: Using C, p1, yb, sl 1, yf, sl 1, yb, ❋sl 3, yf, sl 1, yb; rep from ❋ to last 2 sts, sl 1, yf, p1.
Rep the first 4 rows once more.
11TH ROW: Using C, k1, yf, sl 3, yb, ❋sl 1, yf, sl 3, yb; rep from ❋ to last st, k1.
12TH ROW: Using C, p1, yb, sl 3, yf, ❋sl 1, yb, sl 3, yf; rep from ❋ to last st, p1.
Rep the last 12 rows.

Thick Woven Blanket Fabric II
Multiple of 4 sts + 1
Drape: fair
Skill: intermediate

Worked as Thick Woven Blanket Fabric I, but using one color throughout.

Dotted Triple Slip I
Multiple of 6 sts + 5
Drape: fair
Skill: intermediate
Note: Slip all sts purlwise.

1ST ROW (RS): Using A, knit.
2ND ROW: Using A, purl.
3RD ROW: Using B, k1, yf, sl 3, yb, ❋sl 1, k1, sl 1, yf, sl 3, yb; rep from ❋ to last st, k1.
4TH ROW: Using B, p1, yb, sl 3, ❋yf, sl 1, yb, k1, yf, sl 1, yb, sl 3; rep from ❋ to last st, yf, p1.
5TH ROW: As 1st row.
6TH ROW: As 2nd row.
7TH ROW: Using B, [k1, sl 1] twice, ❋yf, sl 3, yb, sl 1, k1, sl 1; rep from ❋ to last st, k1.
8TH ROW: Using B, p1, sl 1, yb, k1, yf, sl 1, ❋yb, sl 3, yf, sl 1, yb, k1, yf, sl 1; rep from ❋ to last st, p1.
Rep these 8 rows.

Dotted Triple Slip II
Multiple of 6 sts + 5
Drape: fair
Skill: intermediate

Work as Dotted Triple Slip I, but using one color throughout.

Aran-style fabrics

These all-over patterns are used for backgrounds and wide panels in Aran knitting (*page 25*) and are shown worked in the traditional cream-colored yarn. One of the most popular, Trinity Stitch (*page 76*), is so-called because it involves alternately making three stitches from one and one from three—symbolic of the Holy Trinity. Note that the stitches are given in order of increasingly large repeats, from 2-row to 16-row repeats.

Speckled Rib
Multiple of 5 sts + 2
Drape: good
Skill: easy

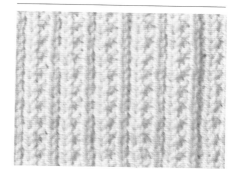

1ST ROW (RS): P2, ✳k3, p2; rep from ✳ to end.
2ND ROW: K2, ✳p1, k1, p1, k2; rep from ✳ to end.
Rep these 2 rows.

Tight Lattice
Multiple of 4 sts + 6
Drape: fair
Skill: intermediate

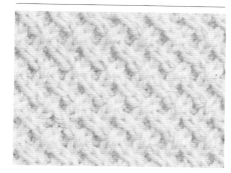

1ST ROW (RS): P1, ✳T2F, T2B; rep from ✳ to last st, p1.
2ND ROW: K2, ✳C2BW, k2; rep from ✳ to end.
3RD ROW: P1, ✳T2B, T2F; rep from ✳ to last st, p1.
4TH ROW: K1, p1, k2, ✳C2FW, k2; rep from ✳ to last 2 sts, p1, k1.
Rep these 4 rows.

Cable and Rib Pattern
Multiple of 9 sts + 5
Drape: fair
Skill: intermediate

1ST ROW (RS): P2, k1 tbl, p2, ✳k4, p2, k1 tbl, p2; rep from ✳ to end.
2ND ROW: K2, p1 tbl, k2, ✳p4, k2, p1 tbl, k2; rep from ✳ to end.
3RD ROW: P2, k1 tbl, p2, ✳C4B, p2, k1 tbl, p2; rep from ✳ to end.
4TH ROW: As 2nd row.
Rep these 4 rows.

Trinity Stitch
Multiple of 4 sts + 2
Drape: fair
Skill: intermediate

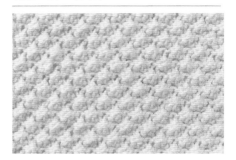

1ST ROW (RS): Purl.
2ND ROW: K1, ✳M3, p3tog; rep from ✳ to last st, k1.
3RD ROW: Purl.
4TH ROW: K1, ✳p3tog, M3; rep from ✳ to last st, k1.
Rep these 4 rows.

Little Cables
Multiple of 6 sts + 2
Drape: fair
Skill: intermediate

1ST ROW (RS): P2, ✳k4, p2; rep from ✳ to end.
2ND ROW: K2, ✳p4, k2; rep from ✳ to end.
3RD ROW: P2, ✳C4B, p2; rep from ✳ to end.
4TH ROW: As 2nd row.
Rep these 4 rows.

Large Cables
Multiple of 7 sts + 2
Drape: good
Skill: intermediate

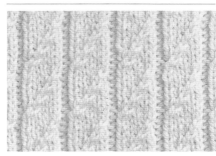

1ST ROW (RS): P2, ✳k3, C2B, p2; rep from ✳ to end.
2ND AND EVERY ALT ROW: K2, ✳p5, k2; rep from ✳ to end.
3RD ROW: P2, ✳k2, C2B, k1, p2; rep from ✳ to end.
5TH ROW: P2, ✳k1, C2B, k2, p2; rep from ✳ to end.
7TH ROW: P2, ✳C2B, k3, p2; rep from ✳ to end.
8TH ROW: As 2nd row.
Rep these 8 rows.

Smocking Pattern
Multiple of 8 sts + 10
Drape: fair
Skill: experienced

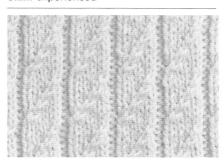

Special Abbreviation
Cluster 6 = k2, p2, k2 from left-hand needle, slip these 6 sts onto a cable needle. Wrap yarn twice anticlockwise

around these 6 sts. Slip sts back onto right-hand needle.
1ST ROW (RS): P2, ✳k2, p2; rep from ✳ to end.
2ND AND EVERY ALT ROW: K2, ✳p2, k2; rep from ✳ to end.
3RD ROW: P2, ✳Cluster 6 (see Special Abbreviation), p2; rep from ✳ to end.
5TH ROW: As 1st row.
7TH ROW: P2, k2, p2, ✳Cluster 6, p2; rep from ✳ to last 4 sts, k2, p2.
8TH ROW: As 2nd row.
Rep these 8 rows.

Honeycomb Pattern I
Multiple of 8 sts + 2
Drape: fair
Skill: intermediate
Note: This is also very effective when worked as a panel with a multiple of 8 sts on a background of reverse St st.

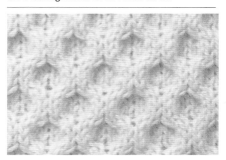

1ST ROW (RS): Knit.
2ND ROW: Purl.
3RD ROW: K1, ✳C4B, C4F; rep from ✳ to last st, k1.
4TH ROW: Purl.
5TH AND 6TH ROWS: As 1st and 2nd rows.
7TH ROW: K1, ✳C4F, C4B; rep from ✳ to last st, k1.
8TH ROW: Purl.
Rep these 8 rows.

Honeycomb Pattern II

Multiple of 6 sts + 2
Drape: fair
Skill: intermediate
Note: This is also very effective when worked as a panel with a multiple of 6 sts on a background of reverse St st.

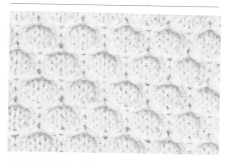

1ST ROW (RS): Knit.
2ND ROW: Purl.
3RD ROW: K1, ✷C3R, C3L; rep from ✷ to last st, k1.
4TH ROW: Purl.
5TH AND 6TH ROWS: As 1st and 2nd rows.
7TH ROW: K1, ✷C3L, C3R; rep from ✷ to last st, k1.
8TH ROW: Purl.
Rep these 8 rows.

Wave Pattern

Multiple of 6 sts + 2
Drape: fair
Skill: intermediate
Note: This is also very effective when worked as a panel of 8 or 14 sts on a background of reverse St st.

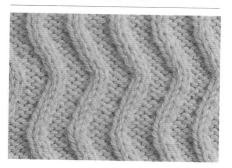

1ST ROW (RS): P4, T3B, ✷p3, T3B; rep from ✷ to last st, p1.
2ND ROW: K2, ✷p2, k4; rep from ✷ to end.
3RD ROW: ✷P3, T3B; rep from ✷ to last 2 sts, p2.
4TH ROW: K3, p2, ✷k4, p2; rep from ✷ to last 3 sts, k3.
5TH ROW: P2, ✷T3B, p3; rep from ✷ to end.
6TH ROW: ✷K4, p2; rep from ✷ to last 2 sts, k2.
7TH ROW: P1, ✷T3B, p3; rep from ✷ to last st, p1.
8TH ROW: K5, p2, ✷k4, p2; rep from ✷ to last st, k1.
9TH ROW: P1, T3F, p3; rep from ✷ to last st, p1.
10TH ROW: As 6th row.
11TH ROW: P2, ✷T3F, p3; rep from ✷ to end.
12TH ROW: As 4th row.
13TH ROW: ✷P3, T3F; rep from ✷ to last 2 sts, p2.
14TH ROW: As 2nd row.
15TH ROW: P4, T3F, ✷P3, T3F; rep from ✷ to last st, p1.
16TH ROW: K1, ✷p2, k4; rep from ✷ to last st, k1.
Rep these 16 rows.

Plaited Cables

Multiple of 16 sts + 8
Drape: fair
Skill: experienced

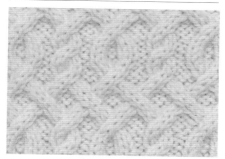

1ST ROW (RS): P2, C4B, ✷p4, C4B; rep from ✷ to last 2 sts, p2.
2ND ROW: K2, p4, ✷k4, p4; rep from ✷ to

last 2 sts, k2.
3RD ROW: P2, k2, ✷T4F, T4B; rep from ✷ to last 4 sts, k2, p2.
4TH ROW: K2, p2, k2, p4, ✷k4, p4; rep from ✷ to last 6 sts, k2, p2, k2.
5TH ROW: P2, k2, p2, C4F, ✷p4, C4F; rep from ✷ to last 6 sts, p2, k2, p2.
6TH ROW: As 4th row.
7TH ROW: P2, k2, ✷T4B, T4F; rep from ✷ to last 4 sts, k2, p2.
8TH ROW: As 2nd row.
9TH AND 10TH ROWS: As 1st and 2nd rows.
11TH ROW: P2, k4, ✷p2, T4B, T4F, p2, k4; rep from ✷ to last 2 sts, p2.
12TH ROW: K2, p4, k2, ✷p2, k4, p2, k2, p4, k2; rep from ✷ to end.
13TH ROW: P2, C4B, p2,✷k2, p4, k2, p2, C4B, p2; rep from ✷ to end.
14TH ROW: As 12th row.
15TH ROW: P2, k4, p2, ✷T4F, T4B, p2, k4, p2; rep from ✷ to end.
16TH ROW: As 2nd row.
Rep these 16 rows.

cable and crossed-stitch fabrics

The versatility of cabling techniques is revealed in these highly textured patterns. Some of them, such as Woven Cables in Relief (*below*), and Bobble Lattice (*page 80*), which also includes bobbles, require considerable skill and patience; but others, such as Forked Cable (*below*), and Dissolving Lattice (*page 81*) can be mastered quite quickly. Experienced knitters might like to try one of these in a glossy cotton yarn, for summer; however, a more pliable wool yarn will make the knitting easier.

(*page 80*) ... (*page 81*)

heavyweight patterns

Forked Cable

Multiple of 8 sts + 2
Drape: fair
Skill: intermediate

1ST ROW (WS): Purl.
2ND ROW: P3, k4, ✳p4, k4; rep from ✳ to last 3 sts, p3.
Rep the last 2 rows twice more then the 1st row again.
8TH ROW: K3, p4, ✳k4, p4; rep from ✳ to last 3 sts, k3.
9TH ROW: Purl.
10TH ROW: K1, ✳C4F, C4B; rep from ✳ to last st, k1.
Rep these 10 rows.

Woven Lattice Pattern

Multiple of 6 sts + 2
Drape: fair
Skill: intermediate

1ST ROW (WS): K3, p4, ✳k2, p4; rep from ✳ to last st, k1.
2ND ROW: P1, C4F, ✳p2, C4F; rep from ✳ to last 3 sts, p3.
3RD ROW: As 1st row.
4TH ROW: P3, ✳k2, T4B; rep from ✳ to last 5 sts, k4, p1.
5TH ROW: K1, p4, ✳k2, p4; rep from ✳ to last 3 sts, k3.
6TH ROW: P3, C4B, ✳p2, C4B; rep from ✳ to last st, p1.
7TH ROW: As 5th row.
8TH ROW: P1, k4, ✳T4F, k2; rep from ✳ to last 3 sts, p3.
Rep these 8 rows.

Woven Cables in Relief

Multiple of 15 sts + 2
Drape: fair
Skill: experienced

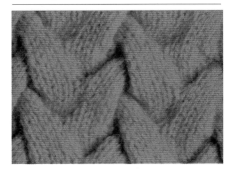

1ST ROW (RS): Knit.
2ND ROW: Purl.
3RD ROW: K1, C10F, ✳k5, C10F; rep from ✳ to last 6 sts, k6.
Work 5 rows in St st, starting purl.
9TH ROW: K6, C10B, ✳k5, C10B; rep from ✳ to last st, k1.
Work 3 rows in St st, starting purl.
Rep these 12 rows.

Medallion Pattern
Multiple of 10 sts + 2
Drape: fair
Skill: experienced
Note: Sts should only be counted after the 1st, 6th, 7th, and 12th rows.

FOUNDATION ROW (RS): K1, p3, k4, ✳p6, k4; rep from ✳ to last 4 sts, p3, k1.
Commence Pattern
1ST ROW: K4, p4, ✳k6, p4; rep from ✳ to last 4 sts, k4.
2ND ROW: K1, p1, T4B, pick up horizontal thread lying between st just worked and next st and [k1, p1] into it (called M2), T4F, ✳p2, T4B, M2, T4F; rep from ✳ to last 2 sts, p1, k1.
3RD ROW: K2, ✳p2, k2; rep from ✳ to end.
4TH ROW: K1, p1, ✳k2, p2; rep from ✳ to last 4 sts, k2, p1, k1.
5TH ROW: As 3rd row.
6TH ROW: K2, ✳sl 1, k1, psso, p6, k2tog, k2; rep from ✳ to end.
7TH ROW: K1, p2, k6, ✳p4, k6; rep from ✳ to last 3 sts, p2, k1.
8TH ROW: K1, M1, T4F, p2, T4B, ✳M2, T4F, p2, T4B; rep from ✳ to last st, M1, k1.
9TH ROW: K1, p1, k2, ✳p2, k2; rep from ✳ to last 2 sts, p1, k1.
10TH ROW: As 3rd row.
11TH ROW: As 9th row.
12TH ROW: K1, p3, k2tog, k2, sl 1, k1, psso, ✳p6, k2tog, k2, sl 1, k1, psso; rep from ✳ to last 4 sts, p3, k1.
Rep these 12 rows.

Slipstitch Twists with Bobbles
Multiple of 9 sts + 1
Drape: fair
Skill: experienced
Note: Sts should only be counted after the 11th and 12th rows.

Special Abbreviation
MB (Make Bobble) = [k1, yo, k1, yo, k1] into next st, turn and k5, turn and p5, turn and k1, sl 1, k2tog, psso, k1, turn and p3tog (bobble completed).
1ST ROW (WS): K4, p1, yo, p1, ✳k7, p1, yo, p1; rep from ✳ to last 4 sts, k4.
2ND ROW: P4, k3, ✳p7, k3; rep from ✳ to last 4 sts, p4.
3RD ROW: K4, p3, ✳k7, p3; rep from ✳ to last 4 sts, k4.
Rep the last 2 rows 3 times, more then the 2nd row again.
11TH ROW: K4, p1, slip next st off left-hand needle and allow it to drop down 10 rows to the made loop, p1, ✳k7, p1, slip next st off needle, p1; rep from ✳ to last 4 sts, k4.
12TH ROW: P4, C2B, ✳p3, MB (see Special Abbreviation), p3, C2B; rep from ✳ to last 4 sts, p4.
Rep these 12 rows.

Cable Fabric
Multiple of 6
Drape: fair
Skill: intermediate

1ST ROW: Knit.
2ND AND EVERY ALT ROW: Purl.
3RD ROW: ✳K2, C4B; rep from ✳ to end.

5TH ROW: Knit.
7TH ROW: ✳C4F, k2; rep from ✳ to end.
8TH ROW: Purl.
Rep these 8 rows.

Flattened Cables
Multiple of 15 sts + 5
Drape: good
Skill: intermediate

1ST ROW (RS): Knit.
2ND AND EVERY ALT ROW: K2, p1, ✳k4, p6, k4, p1; rep from ✳ to last 2 sts, k2.
3RD ROW: Knit.
5TH ROW: K7, C6B, ✳k9, C6B; rep from ✳ to last 7 sts, k7.
7TH ROW: Knit.
9TH ROW: As 5th row.
11TH ROW: Knit.
13TH ROW: As 5th row.
15TH, 17TH, 19TH, 21ST, AND 23RD ROWS: Knit.
24TH ROW: As 2nd row.
Rep these 24 rows.

heavyweight patterns

Square Lattice
Multiple of 14 sts + 2
Drape: fair
Skill: intermediate

1ST ROW (RS): P2, k1, p2, [k2, p2] twice, ✳[k1, p2] twice, [k2, p2] twice; rep from ✳ to last 3 sts, k1, p2.
2ND ROW: K2, p1, k2, [p2, k2] twice, ✳[p1, k2] twice, [p2, k2] twice; rep from ✳ to last 3 sts, p1, k2.
Rep the last 2 rows once more.
5TH ROW: P2, ✳k12, p2; rep from ✳ to end.
6TH ROW: K2, ✳P12, k2; rep from ✳ to end.
7TH ROW: P2, ✳C6B, C6F, p2; rep from ✳ to end.
8TH ROW: As 6th row.
9TH AND 10TH ROWS: As 1st and 2nd rows.
Rep these 10 rows.

Elongated Lattice
Multiple of 8 sts + 4
Drape: fair
Skill: intermediate

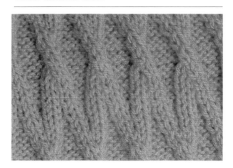

1ST ROW (WS): K1, p2, ✳k6, p2; rep from ✳ to last st, k1.
2ND ROW: P1, ✳C3F, p5; rep from ✳ to last 3 sts, k2, p1.
3RD ROW: K1, p2, ✳k5, p3; rep from ✳ to last st, k1.
4TH ROW: P1, ✳k1, C3F, p4; rep from ✳ to last 3 sts, k2, p1.
5TH ROW: K1, p2, ✳k4, p4; rep from ✳ to last st, k1.
6TH ROW: P1, k2, ✳T3F, p3, k2; rep from ✳ to last st, p1.
7TH ROW: K1, p2, ✳k3, p2, k1, p2; rep from ✳ to last st, k1.
8TH ROW: P1, k2, p1, ✳T3F, p2, k2, p1; rep from ✳ to end.
9TH ROW: K1, p2, ✳k2, p2; rep from ✳ to last st, k1.
10TH ROW: P1, k2, ✳p2, T3F, p1, k2; rep from ✳ to last st, p1.
11TH ROW: [K1, p2] twice, k3, p2, ✳k1, p2, k3, p2; rep from ✳ to last st, k1.
12TH ROW: P1, k2, ✳p3, T3F, k2; rep from ✳ to last st, p1.
13TH ROW: K1, ✳p4, k4; rep from ✳ to last 3 sts, p2, k1.
14TH ROW: P1, k2, ✳p4, T3F, k1; rep from ✳ to last st, p1.
15TH ROW: K1, ✳p3, k5; rep from ✳ to last 3 sts, p2, k1.
16TH ROW: P1, k2, ✳p5, T3F; rep from ✳ to last st, p1.
Rep these 16 rows.

Seed Lattice
Multiple of 12 sts + 8
Drape: fair
Skill: intermediate

1ST ROW (RS): P3, k2, ✳p2, k6, p2, k2; rep from ✳ to last 3 sts, p3.
2ND ROW: K3, p2, ✳k2, p6, k2, p2; rep from ✳ to last 3 sts, k3.
3RD ROW: P3, k2, ✳p4, k2; rep from ✳ to last 3 sts, p3.
4TH ROW: K1, p6, ✳k2, p2, k2, p6; rep from ✳ to last st, k1.
5TH ROW: P1, k6, ✳p2, k2, p2, k6; rep from ✳ to last st, p1.

6TH ROW: As 4th row.
7TH ROW: P1, C6F, ✳p2, k2, p2, C6F; rep from ✳ to last st, p1.
8TH AND 9TH ROWS: As 4th and 5th rows.
10TH ROW: As 4th row.
11TH ROW: As 3rd row.
12TH ROW: As 2nd row.
13TH AND 14TH ROWS: As 1st and 2nd rows.
15TH ROW: P3, k2, ✳p2, C6F, p2, k2; rep from ✳ to last 3 sts, p3.
16TH ROW: As 2nd row.
Rep these 16 rows.

Bobble Lattice
Multiple of 14 sts + 15
Drape: fair
Skill: experienced

Special Abbreviation
MB (Make Bobble) = work [k1, p1, k1, p1, k1, p1, k1] all into next st, then pass 2nd, 3rd, 4th, 5th, 6th, and 7th sts over first st.
1ST ROW (WS): K1, ✳p2, k2, p2, k1; rep from ✳ to end.

2ND ROW: P1, k2, p2, ✳T5L, p2; rep from ✳ to last 3 sts, k2, p1.

3RD ROW: K5, p2, k1, p2, ✳k9, p2, k1, p2; rep from ✳ to last 5 sts, k5.

4TH ROW: P4, T3B, MB (see Special Abbreviation), T3F, ✳p7, T3B, MB, T3F; rep from ✳ to last 4 sts, p4.

5TH ROW: K4, p2, k3, p2, ✳k7, p2, k3, p2; rep from ✳ to last 4 sts, k4.

6TH ROW: P3, T3B, MB, p1, MB, T3F, ✳p5, T3B, MB, p1, MB, T3F; rep from ✳ to last 3 sts, p3.

7TH ROW: K3, p2, ✳k5, p2; rep from ✳ to last 3 sts, k3.

8TH ROW: P2, T3B, MB, [p1, MB] twice, T3F, ✳p3, T3B, MB, [p1, MB] twice, T3F; rep from ✳ to last 2 sts, p2.

9TH ROW: K2, p2, [k1, p2] 3 times, ✳k3, p2, [k1, p2] 3 times; rep from ✳ to last 2 sts, k2.

10TH ROW: P1, ✳T3B, p1, [k2, p1] twice, T3F, p1; rep from ✳ to end.

11TH AND 12TH ROWS: As 1st and 2nd rows.

13TH ROW: K1, p2, k9, ✳p2, k1, p2, k9; rep from ✳ to last 3 sts, p2, k1.

14TH ROW: P1, T3F, p7, T3B, ✳MB, T3F, p7, T3B; rep from ✳ to last st, p1.

15TH ROW: K2, p2, k7, ✳p2, k3, p2, k7; rep from ✳ to last 4 sts, p2, k2.

16TH ROW: P1, MB, T3F, p5, T3B, ✳MB, p1, MB, T3F, p5, T3B; rep from ✳ to last 2 sts, MB, p1.

17TH ROW: As 7th row.

18TH ROW: P2, MB, T3F, p3, T3B, ✳MB, [p1, MB] twice, T3F, p3, T3B; rep from ✳ to last 3 sts, MB, p2.

19TH ROW: [K1, p2] twice, k3, p2, ✳[k1, p2] 3 times, k3, p2; rep from ✳ to last 4 sts, k1, p2, k1.

20TH ROW: P1, k2, p1, T3F, p1, T3B, p1, ✳[k2, p1] twice, T3F, p1, T3B, p1; rep from ✳ to last 3 sts, k2, p1.

Rep these 20 rows.

Dissolving Lattice

Multiple of 12 sts + 2
Drape: fair
Skill: intermediate

1ST ROW (RS): Knit.

2ND AND EVERY ALT ROW: Purl.

3RD ROW: K1, ✳C4B, k4, C4F; rep from ✳ to last st, k1.

5TH ROW: Knit.

7TH ROW: K3, C4F, C4B, ✳k4, C4F, C4B; rep from ✳ to last 3 sts, k3.

8TH ROW: Purl.

Rep these 8 rows.

Cable and Garter Pattern

Multiple of 10 sts + 8
Drape: good
Skill: intermediate

1ST ROW (RS): Knit.

2ND ROW: P7, ✳k4, p6; rep from ✳ to last st, p1.

Rep the last 2 rows twice more.

7TH ROW: K1, C6F, ✳k4, C6F; rep from ✳ to last st, k1.

8TH ROW: As 2nd row.

9TH ROW: Knit.

Rep the last 2 rows twice more.

14TH ROW: P2, k4, ✳p6, k4; rep from ✳ to

last 2 sts, p2.

15TH ROW: Knit.

Rep the last 2 rows once more, then 14th row again.

19TH ROW: K6, ✳C6B, k4; rep from ✳ to last 2 sts, k2.

20TH ROW: As 14th row.

21ST ROW: Knit.

Rep the last 2 rows once more, then 14th row again.

Rep these 24 rows.

Seeded Cables

Multiple of 20 sts + 12
Drape: good
Skill: intermediate

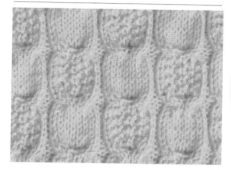

1ST ROW (RS): P2, k8, p2, ✳[k1, p1] 3 times, k2, p2, k8, p2; rep from ✳ to end.

2ND ROW: K2, p8, k2, ✳[p1, k1] 3 times, p2, k2, p8, k2; rep from ✳ to end.

Rep the last 2 rows 3 times more.

9TH ROW: P2, ✳C4B, C4F, p2; rep from ✳ to end.

10TH ROW: K2, [p1, k1] 3 times, p2, k2, ✳p8, k2, [p1, k1] 3 times, p2, k2; rep from ✳ to end.

11TH ROW: P2, [k1, p1] 3 times, k2, p2, ✳k8, p2, [k1, p1] 3 times, k2, p2; rep from ✳ to end.

Rep the last 2 rows 3 times more, then 10th row again.

19TH ROW: As 9th row.

20TH ROW: As 2nd row.

Rep these 20 rows.

Rippling Cables

Multiple of 24 sts + 2
Drape: fair
Skill: intermediate

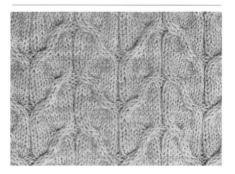

1ST ROW (RS): P2, ✳k10, p2; rep from ✳ to end.
2ND AND EVERY ALT ROW: K2, ✳p10, k2; rep from ✳ to end.
3RD ROW: As 1st row.
5TH ROW: P2, ✳C6R, k4, p2, k4, C6L, p2; rep from ✳ to end.
7TH AND 9TH ROWS: As 1st row.
11TH ROW: P2, ✳k4, C6R, p2, C6L, k4, p2; rep from ✳ to end.
12TH ROW: As 2nd row.
Rep these 12 rows.

V-line Cables

Multiple of 14 sts + 2
Drape: fair
Skill: intermediate

1ST ROW (RS): K2, ✳p4, k4, p4, k2; rep from ✳ to end.

2ND ROW: P2, ✳k4, p4, k4, p2; rep from ✳ to end.
3RD ROW: K2, ✳p4, C4B, p4, k2; rep from ✳ to end.
4TH ROW: As 2nd row.
5TH ROW: K2, ✳p3, T3B, T3F, p3, k2; rep from ✳ to end.
6TH ROW: P2, k3, p2, k2, p2, ✳[k3, p2] twice, k2, p2; rep from ✳ to last 5 sts, k3, p2.
7TH ROW: K2, ✳p2, T3B, p2, T3F, p2, k2; rep from ✳ to end.
8TH ROW: P2, k2, p2, k4, ✳[p2, k2] twice, p2, k4; rep from ✳ to last 6 sts, p2, k2, p2.
9TH ROW: K2, ✳p1, T3B, p4, T3F, p1, k2; rep from ✳ to end.
10TH ROW: [P2, k1] twice, p4, k1, ✳[p2, k1] 3 times, p4, k1; rep from ✳ to last 5 sts, p2, k1, p2.
Rep these 10 rows.

Elongated Ovals

Multiple of 20 sts + 12
Drape: fair
Skill: experienced

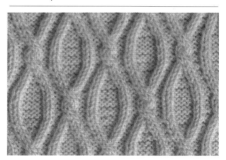

1ST ROW (RS): P1, k2, p6, k2, ✳p3, k4, p3, k2, p6, k2; rep from ✳ to last st, p1.
2ND ROW: K1, p2, k6, p2, ✳k3, p4, k3, p2, k6, p2; rep from ✳ to last st, k1.
3RD ROW: P1, k2, p6, k2, ✳p3, C4F, p3, k2, p6, k2; rep from ✳ to last st, p1.
4TH ROW: As 2nd row.
5TH ROW: P1, T3F, p4, T3B, ✳p2, T3B, T3F, p2, T3F, p4, T3B; rep from ✳ to last st, p1.
6TH ROW: K2, p2, k4, p2, ✳k3, p2, k2, p2, k3, p2, k4, p2; rep from ✳ to last 2 sts, k2.
7TH ROW: P2, T3F, ✳[p2, T3B] twice,

[p2, T3F] twice; rep from ✳ to last 7 sts, p2, T3B, p2.
8TH ROW: K3, p2, k2, p2, k3, ✳p2, k4, p2, k3, p2, k2, p2, k3; rep from ✳ to end.
9TH ROW: P3, T3F, T3B, ✳p2, T3B, p4, T3F, p2, T3F, T3B; rep from ✳ to last 3 sts, p3.
10TH, 12TH, 14TH AND 16TH ROWS: K4, p4, ✳k3, p2, k6, p2, k3, p4; rep from ✳ to last 4 sts, k4.
11TH ROW: P4, C4F, ✳p3, k2, p6, k2, p3, C4F; rep from ✳ to last 4 sts, p4.
13TH ROW: P4, k4, ✳p3, k2, p6, k2, p3, k4; rep from ✳ to last 4 sts, p4.
15TH ROW: As 11th row.
17TH ROW: P3, T3B, T3F, ✳p2, T3F, p4, T3B, p2, T3B, T3F; rep from ✳ to last 3 sts, p3.
18TH ROW: As 8th row.
19TH ROW: P2, T3B, p2, ✳[T3F, p2] twice, [T3B, p2] twice; rep from ✳ to last 5 sts, T3F, p2.
20TH ROW: As 6th row.
21ST ROW: P1, T3B, p4, T3F, ✳p2, T3F, T3B, p2, T3B, p4, T3F; rep from ✳ to last st, p1.
22ND AND 23RD ROWS: As 2nd and 3rd rows.
24TH ROW: As 2nd row.
Rep these 24 rows.

slipstitch color patterns

These mosaic patterns, as they are also called, are an easy way of producing great multicolored effects. Using this technique, you can create wonderful tweed and checked fabrics, as well as striped, zigzag, and lattice patterns. Even where a pattern uses three or four colors, only one color is used for the knitting in any given row. The fabric produced is relatively thick, and thus well-suited for jackets and other warm items.

Simple Grille Pattern
Multiple of 3 sts + 3
Drape: fair
Skill: intermediate

1ST ROW (RS): Using A, knit.
2ND ROW: Using A, purl.
3RD AND 4TH ROWS: Using B, k1, sl 1, ✳k2, sl 1; rep from ✳ to last st, k1.
Rep these 4 rows.

Knot Ridges I
Multiple of 2 sts + 1
Drape: fair
Skill: intermediate

Using A, work 4 rows in St st, starting knit (right side).
5TH ROW: Using B, k1, [k1, yo, k1] into next st, ✳sl 1, [k1, yo, k1] into next st; rep from ✳ to last st, k1.
6TH ROW: Using B, k1, k3tog tbl, ✳sl 1, k3tog tbl; rep from ✳ to last st, k1.
Rep these 6 rows.

Knot Ridges II
Multiple of 2 sts + 1
Drape: fair
Skill: intermediate

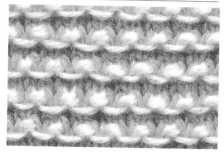

1ST ROW (RS): Using A, knit.
2ND ROW: Using A, purl.
3RD ROW: Using B, k1, [k1, yo, k1] into next st, ✳sl 1, [k1, yo, k1] into next st; rep from ✳ to last st, k1.
4TH ROW: Using B, k1, k3tog tbl, ✳sl 1, k3tog tbl; rep from ✳ to last st, k1.
5TH ROW: Using A, knit.
6TH ROW: Using A, purl.
7TH ROW: Using B, k2, [k1, yo, k1] into next st, ✳sl 1, [k1, yo, k1] into next st; rep from ✳ to last 2 sts, k2.
8TH ROW: Using B, p2, k3tog tbl, ✳sl 1, k3tog tbl; rep from ✳ to last 2 sts, p2.
Rep these 8 rows.

Knot Ridges with Twists

Multiple of 8 sts + 5
Drape: fair
Skill: intermediate
Note: Slip all sts purlwise.

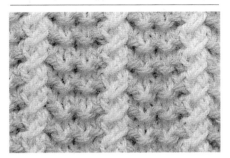

1ST ROW (RS): Using A, k5, ✳C3R, k5; rep from ✳ to end.
2ND ROW: Using A, purl.
3RD ROW: Using B, [k1, sl 1] twice, k1, ✳sl 3, [k1, sl 1] twice, k1; rep from ✳ to end.
4TH ROW: Using B, [k1, sl 1] twice, k1, ✳yf, sl 3, yb, [k1, sl 1] twice, k1; rep from ✳ to end. Rep these 4 rows.

Flecked Tweed

Multiple of 4 sts + 3
Drape: fair
Skill: intermediate
Note: Slip all sts purlwise.

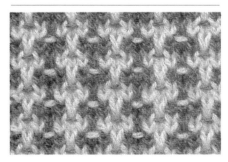

1ST ROW (WS): Using A, p1, yb, sl 1, yf, ✳p3, yb, sl 1, yf; rep from ✳ to last st, p1.
2ND ROW: Using A, k1, sl 1, ✳k3, sl 1; rep from ✳ to last st, k1.
3RD ROW: Using B, p3, ✳yb, sl 1, yf, p3; rep from ✳ to end.

4TH ROW: Using B, k3, ✳sl 1, k3; rep from ✳ to end. Rep these 4 rows.

3-Color Flecked Tweed

Multiple of 4 sts + 3
Drape: fair
Skill: intermediate

Worked as Flecked Tweed.
Beginning with the 1st row, work 2 rows in A, 2 rows in B, and 2 rows in C throughout.

3-Color Scottie Tweed

Multiple of 3 sts + 2
Drape: fair
Skill: intermediate
Note: Slip all sts purlwise.

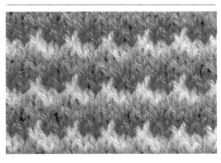

1ST ROW (WS): Using A, purl.
2ND ROW: Using B, k2, ✳sl 1, k2; rep from ✳ to end.
3RD ROW: Using B, purl.
4TH ROW: Using C, k1, sl 1, ✳k2, sl 1; rep from ✳ to last 3 sts, k3.
5TH ROW: Using C, purl.

6TH ROW: Using A, k3, sl 1, ✳k2, sl 1; rep from ✳ to last st, k1. Rep these 6 rows.

4-Color Tweed

Multiple of 6 sts + 2
Drape: fair
Skill: intermediate

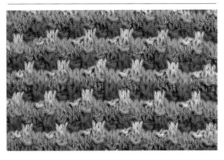

FOUNDATION ROW: Using A, purl.
Commence Pattern
1ST ROW (RS): Using B, k1, ✳sl 2, k4; rep from ✳ to last st, k1.
2ND ROW: Using B, p1, k2, p2, sl 2, ✳k2, p2, sl 2; rep from ✳ to last st, p1.
3RD ROW: Using C, k3, sl 2, ✳k4, sl 2; rep from ✳ to last 3 sts, k3.
4TH ROW: Using C, p3, sl 2, k2, ✳p2, sl 2, k2; rep from ✳ to last st, p1.
5TH ROW: Using D, k5, sl 2, ✳k4, sl 2; rep from ✳ to last st, k1.
6TH ROW: Using D, p1, ✳sl 2, k2, p2; rep from ✳ to last st, p1.
7TH AND 8TH ROWS: As 1st and 2nd rows, but using A instead of B.
9TH AND 10TH ROWS: As 3rd and 4th rows, but using B instead of C.
11TH AND 12TH ROWS: As 5th and 6th rows, but using C instead of D.
13TH AND 14TH ROWS: As 1st and 2nd rows, but using D instead of B.
15TH AND 16TH ROWS: As 3rd and 4th rows, but using A instead of C.
17TH AND 18TH ROWS: As 5th and 6th rows, but using B instead of D.
19TH AND 20TH ROWS: As 1st and 2nd rows, but using C instead of B.
21ST AND 22ND ROWS: As 3rd and 4th rows, but using D instead of C.

23RD AND 24TH ROWS: As 5th and 6th rows, but using A instead of D.
Rep the last 24 rows.

Moroccan Pattern

Multiple of 6 sts + 5
Drape: fair
Skill: experienced
Note: Slip all sts purlwise.

FOUNDATION ROW (WS): Using A, purl.
Commence Pattern
1ST ROW: Using B, k6, sl 1, ✳k5, sl 1; rep from ✳ to last 4 sts, k4.
2ND ROW: Using B, k4, yf, sl 1, yb, ✳k5, yf, sl 1, yb; rep from ✳ to last 6 sts, k6.
3RD ROW: Using A, k3, sl 1, k1, ✳sl 1, k3, sl 1, k1; rep from ✳ to end.
4TH ROW: Using A, k1, yf, sl 1, yb, k3, ✳yf, sl 1, yb, k1, yf, sl 1, yb, k3; rep from ✳ to end.
5TH ROW: Using B, k2, sl 1, ✳k5, sl 1; rep from ✳ to last 2 sts, k2.
6TH ROW: Using B, k2, yf, sl 1, yb, ✳k5, yf, sl 1, yb; rep from ✳ to last 2 sts, k2.
7TH ROW: Using A, [k1, sl 1] twice, ✳k3, sl 1, k1, sl 1; rep from ✳ to last st, k1.
8TH ROW: Using A, [k1, yf, sl 1, yb] twice, ✳k3, yf, sl 1, yb, k1, yf, sl 1, yb; rep from ✳ to last st, k1.
9TH ROW: Using B, k4, sl 1, ✳k5, sl 1; rep from ✳ to last 6 sts, k6.
10TH ROW: Using B, k6, yf, sl 1, yb, ✳k5, yf, sl 1, yb; rep from ✳ to last 4 sts, k4.

11TH ROW: Using A, k1, sl 1, k3, ✳sl 1, k1, sl 1, k3; rep from ✳ to end.
12TH ROW: Using A, k3, yf, sl 1, yb, k1, ✳yf, sl 1, yb, k3, yf, sl 1, yb, k1; rep from ✳ to end. Rep the last 12 rows.

Dots and Dashes

Multiple of 10 sts + 7
Drape: fair
Skill: intermediate

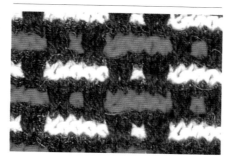

1ST ROW (RS): Using A, knit.
2ND ROW: Using A, purl.
3RD AND 4TH ROWS: Using B, k6, ✳sl 2, k1, sl 2, k5; rep from ✳ to last st, k1.
5TH AND 6TH ROWS: As 1st and 2nd rows.
7TH AND 8TH ROWS: Using C, [k1, sl 2] twice, ✳k5, sl 2, k1, sl 2; rep from ✳ to last st, k1.
Rep these 8 rows.

Whitecaps

Multiple of 10 sts + 7
Drape: fair
Skill: experienced

1ST ROW (RS): Using A, knit.
2ND ROW: Using A, purl.
3RD ROW: Using B, knit.
4TH ROW: Using B, k2, p3, ✳k7, p3; rep from ✳ to last 2 sts, k2.
5TH ROW: Using A, k2, sl 3, ✳k7, sl 3; rep from ✳ to last 2 sts, k2.
6TH ROW: Using A, p2, sl 3, ✳p7, sl 3; rep from ✳ to last 2 sts, p2.
Rep the last 2 rows once more.

9TH ROW: Using A, k1, C2R, k1, C2L ✳k5, C2R, k1, C2L; rep from ✳ to last st, k1.
Using A work 3 rows in St st, starting purl.
13TH ROW: Using B, knit.
14TH ROW: Using B, k7, ✳p3, k7; rep from ✳ to end.
15TH ROW: Using A, k7, ✳sl 3, k7; rep from ✳ to end.
16TH ROW: Using A, p7, ✳sl 3, p7; rep from ✳ to end.
Rep the last 2 rows once more.
19TH ROW: Using A, k6, ✳C2R, k1, C2L, k5; rep from ✳ to last st, k1.
20TH ROW: Using A, purl.
Rep these 20 rows.

Greek Key Pattern

Multiple of 6 sts + 2
Drape: fair
Skill: intermediate

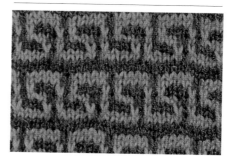

1ST ROW (RS): Using A, knit.
2ND ROW: Using A, purl.
3RD ROW: Using B, k6, sl 1, ✳k5, sl 1; rep from ✳ to last st, k1.
4TH ROW: Using B, p1, ✳sl 1, p5; rep from ✳ to last st, p1.

5TH ROW: Using A, ❊k1, sl 1, k3, sl 1; rep from ❊ to last 2 sts, k2.

6TH ROW: Using A, p2, sl 1, p3, sl 1, ❊p1, sl 1, p3, sl 1; rep from ❊ to last st, p1.

7TH ROW: Using B, k4, sl 1, k1, sl 1, ❊k3, sl 1, k1, sl 1; rep from ❊ to last st, k1.

8TH ROW: Using B, p1, ❊sl 1, p1, sl 1, p3; rep from ❊ to last st, p1.

9TH ROW: Using A, ❊k3, sl 1, k1, sl 1; rep from ❊ to last 2 sts, k2.

10TH ROW: Using A, p2, ❊sl 1, p1, sl 1, p3; rep from ❊ to end.

11TH ROW: Using B, k4, sl 1, ❊k5, sl 1; rep from ❊ to last 3 sts, k3.

12TH ROW: Using B, p3, sl 1, ❊p5, sl 1; rep from ❊ to last 4 sts, p4.

Rep these 12 rows.

2-Color Loop Pattern

Multiple of 2 sts + 1
Drape: fair
Skill: intermediate
Note: All slip sts should be slipped purlwise.

1ST ROW (RS): Using A, knit.
2ND ROW: Using A, purl.
3RD ROW: Using B, k1, ❊sl 1, k1; rep from ❊ to end.
4TH ROW: As 3rd row.
5TH ROW: Using B, knit.
6TH ROW: Using B, purl.
7TH ROW: Using A, k2, sl 1, ❊k1, sl 1; rep from ❊ to last 2 sts, k2.
8TH ROW: Using A, p1, k1, ❊sl 1, k1; rep from ❊ to last st, p1.
Rep these 8 rows.

2-Color Loop Pattern Variation

Multiple of 4 sts + 1
Drape: fair
Skill: intermediate
Note: All slip sts should be slipped purlwise.

1ST ROW (RS): Using A, knit.
2ND ROW: Using A, purl.
3RD ROW: Using B, k1, ❊sl 3, k1; rep from ❊ to end.
4TH ROW: As 3rd row.
5TH ROW: Using B, knit.
6TH ROW: Using B, purl.
7TH ROW: Using A, k3, sl 3, ❊k1, sl 3; rep from ❊ to last 3 sts, k3.
8TH ROW: Using A, p2, k1, ❊sl 3, k1; rep from ❊ to last 2 sts, p2.
Rep these 8 rows.

3-Color Loop Pattern

Multiple of 2 sts + 1
Drape: fair
Skill: intermediate

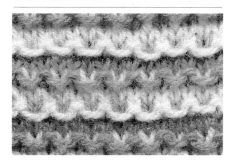

1ST ROW (RS): Using A, knit.
2ND ROW: Using A, purl.

3RD ROW: Using B, k1, ❊sl 1, k1; rep from ❊ to end.
4TH ROW: As 3rd row.
5TH ROW: Using B, knit.
6TH ROW: Using B, purl.
7TH AND 8TH ROWS: As 3rd row, but using A instead of B.
9TH ROW: Using A, knit.
10TH ROW: Using A, purl.
11TH AND 12TH ROWS: As 3rd row, but using C instead of B.
13TH ROW: Using C, knit.
14TH ROW: Using C, purl.
15TH AND 16TH ROWS: As 3rd row, but using A instead of B.
Rep these 16 rows.

Simulated Basketweave

Multiple of 10 sts + 5
Drape: fair
Skill: intermediate
Note: Slip all sts purlwise.

FOUNDATION ROW (WS): Using A, purl.
Commence Pattern
1ST ROW: Using B, k4, sl 2, ❊k8, sl 2; rep from ❊ to last 9 sts, k9.
2ND ROW: Using B, p9, sl 2, ❊p8, sl 2; rep from ❊ to last 4 sts, p4.
3RD ROW: Using A, [k1, sl 1] twice, ❊k2, sl 1, k1, sl 1; rep from ❊ to last st, k1.
4TH ROW: Using A, [p1, sl 1] twice, ❊p2, sl 1, p1, sl 1; rep from ❊ to last st, p1.
5TH ROW: Using B, k9, sl 2, ❊k8, sl 2; rep from ❊ to last 4 sts, k4.
6TH ROW: Using B, p4, sl 2, ❊p8, sl 2; rep from ❊ to last 9 sts, p9.
7TH ROW: Using A, k1, sl 1, ❊k6, sl 1, k2,

sl 1; rep from ✳ to last 3 sts, k3.
8TH ROW: Using A, p3, sl 1, ✳p2, sl 1, p6, sl 1; rep from ✳ to last st, p1.
9TH ROW: As 5th row.
10TH ROW: As 6th row.
11TH ROW: As 3rd row.
12TH ROW: As 4th row.
13TH ROW: As 1st row.
14TH ROW: As 2nd row.
15TH ROW: Using A, k3, sl 1, ✳k2, sl 1, k6, sl 1; rep from ✳ to last st, k1.
16TH ROW: Using A, p1, sl 1, ✳p6, sl 1, p2, sl 1; rep from ✳ to last 3 sts, p3.
Rep the last 16 rows.

3-Color Ladders

Multiple of 4 sts + 3
Drape: fair
Skill: intermediate
Note: Slip all sts purlwise.

FOUNDATION ROW (WS): Using A purl.
Commence Pattern
1ST ROW: Using B, k3, ✳sl 1, k3; rep from ✳ to end.
2ND ROW: Using B, k3, ✳yf, sl 1, yb, k3; rep from ✳ to end.
3RD ROW: Using A, k1, sl 1, ✳k3, sl 1; rep from ✳ to last st, k1.
4TH ROW: Using A, p1, sl 1, ✳p3, sl 1; rep from ✳ to last st, p1.
5TH ROW: Using C, as 1st row.
6TH ROW: Using C, as 2nd row.
7TH ROW: As 3rd row.
8TH ROW: As 4th row.
Rep the last 8 rows.

2-Color Ladders with Twists

Multiple of 6 sts
Drape: fair
Skill: intermediate
Note: Slip all sts purlwise.

1ST FOUNDATION ROW (RS): Using A, knit.
2ND FOUNDATION ROW: Using A, purl.
Commence Pattern
1ST ROW: Using B, k2, sl 2, ✳k4, sl 2; rep from ✳ to last 2 sts, k2.
2ND ROW: Using B, k1, p1, sl 2, p1, ✳k2, p1, sl 2, p1; rep from ✳ to last st, k1.
3RD ROW: Using A, k1, C2B, C2F, ✳k2, C2B, C2F; rep from ✳ to last st, k1.
4TH ROW: Using A, purl.
Rep the last 4 rows.

3-Color Honeycomb

Multiple of 8 sts + 4
Drape: fair
Skill: intermediate
Note: Slip all sts purlwise.

1ST AND 2ND ROWS: Using A, knit (1st row is right side).
3RD ROW: Using B, k1, sl 2, ✳k6, sl 2; rep

from ✳ to last st, k1.
4TH ROW: Using B, p1, sl 2, ✳p6, sl 2; rep from ✳ to last st, p1.
Rep the last 2 rows twice more.
9TH AND 10TH ROWS: Using A knit.
11TH ROW: Using C, k5, sl 2, ✳k6, sl 2; rep from ✳ to last 5 sts, k5.
12TH ROW: Using C, p5, sl 2, ✳p6, sl 2; rep from ✳ to last 5 sts, p5.
Rep the last 2 rows twice more.
Rep these 16 rows.

Brick Pattern

Multiple of 16 sts + 7
Drape: fair
Skill: experienced
Note: Slip all sts purlwise.

1ST ROW (RS): Using A, knit.
2ND ROW: Using A, purl.
3RD ROW: Using B, k2, sl 3, ✳k13, sl 3; rep from ✳ to last 2 sts, k2.
4TH ROW: Using B, k2, yf, sl 3, yb, ✳k13, yf, sl 3, yb; rep from ✳ to last 2 sts, k2.
5TH ROW: Using B, p2, yb, sl 3, yf, ✳p13, yb, sl 3, yf; rep from ✳ to last 2 sts, p2.
Rep the last 2 rows twice more, then 4th row again.
Using A, work 4 rows in St st, starting knit.
15TH ROW: Using B, k10, sl 3, ✳k13, sl 3; rep from ✳ to last 10 sts, k10.
16TH ROW: Using B, k10, yf, sl 3, yb, ✳k13, yf, sl 3, yb; rep from ✳ to last 10 sts, k10.
17TH ROW: Using B, p10, yb, sl 3, yf, ✳p13, yb, sl 3, yf; rep from ✳ to last 10 sts, p10.
Rep the last 2 rows twice more, then 16th row again.

23RD ROW: Using A, knit.
24TH ROW: Using A, purl.
Rep these 24 rows.

Surface Quilting Stitch

Multiple of 10 sts + 7
Drape: fair
Skill: experienced
Note: Slip all sts purlwise.

Cast on with A and purl 1 row.
FOUNDATION ROW (RS): Using B, k6, yf, sl 5, yb, ✳k5, yf, sl 5, yb; rep from ✳ to last 6 sts, k6.
Commence pattern
1ST ROW: Using B, k6, sl 5, ✳k5, sl 5; rep from ✳ to last 6 sts, k6.
Using A work 4 rows in St st, starting knit.
6TH ROW: Using B k1, yf, sl 5, yb, ✳k2, insert point of right-hand needle upward under loose strands in B in front of the slip sts 4 and 5 rows down, place on to left-hand needle and knit these loops together with next st on left-hand needle tbl (called pull-up loops), k2, yf, sl 5, yb; rep from ✳ to last st, k1.
7TH ROW: Using B, k1, sl 5, ✳k5, sl 5; rep from ✳ to last st, k1.
Using A work 4 rows in St st, starting knit.
12TH ROW: Using B, k3, pull up the loops, ✳k2, yf, sl 5, yb, k2, pull up loops; rep from ✳ to last 3 sts, k3.
Rep the last 12 rows.

Hexagons

Multiple of 12 sts + 3
Drape: fair
Skill: intermediate

1ST ROW (RS): Using A, knit.
2ND ROW: Using A, knit.
3RD AND 4TH ROWS: Using B, k7, sl 1, ✳k11, sl 1; rep from ✳ to last 7 sts, k7.
5TH AND 6TH ROWS: Using A, k6, sl 1, k1, sl 1, ✳k9, sl 1, k1, sl 1; rep from ✳ to last 6 sts, k6.
7TH AND 8TH ROWS: Using B, k5, [sl 1, k1] twice, sl 1, ✳k7, [sl 1, k1] twice, sl 1; rep from ✳ to last 5 sts, k5.
9TH AND 10TH ROWS: As 5th and 6th rows.
11TH AND 12TH ROWS: As 3rd and 4th rows.
13TH AND 14TH ROWS: As 1st and 2nd rows.
15TH AND 16TH ROWS: Using B, k1, sl 1, ✳k11, sl 1; rep from ✳ to last st, k1.
17TH AND 18TH ROWS: Using A, k2, sl 1, k9, ✳sl 1, k1, sl 1, k9; rep from ✳ to last 3 sts, sl 1, k2.
19TH AND 20TH ROWS: Using B, [k1, sl 1] twice, k7, ✳[sl 1, k1] twice, sl 1, k7; rep from ✳ to last 4 sts, [sl 1, k1] twice.
21ST AND 22ND ROWS: As 17th and 18th rows.
23RD AND 24TH ROWS: As 15th and 16th rows. Rep these 24 rows.

Linking Checks

Multiple of 8 sts + 2
Drape: fair
Skill: intermediate

FOUNDATION ROW (WS): Using B, knit.
Commence pattern
1ST AND 2ND ROWS: Using A, k3, sl 1, k2, sl 1, ✳k4, sl 1, k2, sl 1; rep from ✳ to last 3 sts, k3.
3RD AND 4TH ROWS: Using B, k1, sl 1, k2, ✳sl 2, k2; rep from ✳ to last 2 sts, sl 1, k1.
5TH AND 6TH ROWS: As 1st and 2nd rows.
7TH AND 8TH ROWS: Using B, k2, ✳sl 1, k4, sl 1, k2; rep from ✳ to end.
9TH AND 10TH ROWS: As 3rd and 4th rows but using A instead of B.
11TH AND 12TH ROWS: As 7th and 8th rows. Rep the last 12 rows.

Daisy Petals

Multiple of 8 sts + 7
Drape: fair
Skill: intermediate

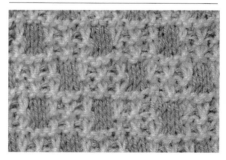

1ST ROW (RS): Using A, knit.
2ND ROW: Using A, knit.
3RD ROW: Using B, k1, sl 1, k3, ✳sl 1, [k1, sl 1] twice, k3; rep from ✳ to last 2 sts, sl 1, k1.
4TH ROW: Using B, k1, sl 1, p3, ✳sl 1, [k1, sl 1] twice, p3; rep from ✳ to last

2 sts, sl 1, k1.

5TH AND 6TH ROWS: Using A, k2, sl 3, ✳k5, sl 3; rep from ✳ to last 2 sts, k2.

7TH AND 8TH ROWS: As 3rd and 4th rows.

9TH AND 10TH ROWS: Using A, knit.

11TH ROW: Using B, [k1, sl 1] 3 times, ✳k3, sl 1, [k1, sl 1] twice; rep from ✳ to last st, k1.

12TH ROW: Using B, [k1, sl 1] 3 times, ✳p3, sl 1, [k1, sl 1] twice; rep from ✳ to last st, k1.

13TH AND 14TH ROWS: Using A, k6, ✳sl 3, k5; rep from ✳ to last st, k1.

15TH AND 16TH ROWS: As 11th and 12th rows.

Rep these 16 rows.

Fenced Squares

Multiple of 8 sts + 1
Drape: fair
Skill: intermediate

1ST ROW (RS): Using A, knit.

2ND ROW: Using A, knit.

3RD AND 4TH ROWS: Using B k1, ✳sl 1, k1; rep from ✳ to end.

5TH AND 6TH ROWS: As 1st and 2nd rows.

7TH AND 8TH ROWS: Using B, k1, ✳sl 1, k5, sl 1, k1; rep from ✳ to end.

9TH AND 10TH ROWS: Using A, k2, sl 1, ✳k3, sl 1; rep from ✳ to last 2 sts, k2.

11TH AND 12TH ROWS: As 3rd and 4th rows.

13TH AND 14TH ROWS: As 9th and 10th rows.

15TH AND 16TH ROWS: As 7th and 8th rows.

Rep these 16 rows.

Minicheck Pattern

Multiple of 4 sts + 2
Drape: fair
Skill: intermediate

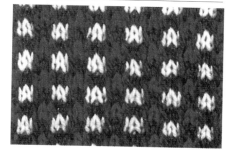

1ST ROW (RS): Using A, knit.

2ND ROW: Using B p1, ✳sl 2, p2; rep from ✳ to last st, p1.

3RD ROW: Using B, k3, sl 2, ✳k2, sl 2; rep from ✳ to last st, k1.

4TH ROW: Using A, purl.

5TH ROW: Using C, k1, ✳sl 2, k2; rep from ✳ to last st, k1.

6TH ROW: Using C, p3, sl 2, ✳p2, sl 2; rep from ✳ to last st, p1.

Rep these 6 rows.

Field of Crosses

Multiple of 16 sts + 5
Drape: fair
Skill: experienced

FOUNDATION ROW (WS): Using A, knit.
Commence pattern

1ST AND 2ND ROWS: Using B, k4, ✳sl 1, [k1, sl 1] twice, k3; rep from ✳ to last st, k1.

3RD AND 4TH ROWS: Using A, k9, sl 1, k1, sl 1, ✳k13, sl 1, k1, sl 1; rep from ✳ to last 9 sts, k9.

5TH AND 6TH ROWS: Using B, k2, sl 1, ✳ k1, sl 1; rep from ✳ to last 2 sts, k2.

7TH AND 8TH ROWS: As 3rd and 4th rows.

9TH AND 10TH ROWS: Using B, k2, sl 1, k1, [sl 1, k5] twice, ✳sl 1, [k1, sl 1] twice, k5, sl 1, k5; rep from ✳ to last 5 sts, sl 1, k1, sl 1, k2.

11TH AND 12TH ROWS: Using A, k5, ✳sl 1, k9, sl 1, k5; rep from ✳ to end.

13TH AND 14TH ROWS: As 9th and 10th rows.

15TH, 16TH, 17TH AND 18TH ROWS: As 3rd, 4th, 5th, and 6th rows.

19TH AND 20TH ROWS: As 3rd and 4th rows.

21ST AND 22ND ROWS: As 1st and 2nd rows.

23RD AND 24TH ROWS: Using A, [k1, sl 1] twice, ✳k13, sl 1, k1, sl 1; rep from ✳ to last st, k1.

25TH AND 26TH ROWS: As 5th and 6th rows.

27TH AND 28TH ROWS: As 23rd and 24th rows.

29TH AND 30TH ROWS: Using B, k2, sl 1, ✳k5, sl 1, [k1, sl 1] twice, k5, sl 1; rep from ✳ to last 2 sts, k2.

31ST AND 32ND ROWS: Using A, k7, sl 1, k5, sl 1, ✳k9, sl 1, k5, sl 1; rep from ✳ to last 7 sts, k7.

33RD AND 34TH ROWS: As 29th and 30th rows.

35TH AND 36TH ROWS: As 23rd and 24th rows.

37TH AND 38TH ROWS: As 5th and 6th rows.

39TH AND 40TH ROWS: As 23rd and 24th rows.

Rep the last 40 rows.

Narrow Chevron Stripes
Multiple of 24 sts + 3
Drape: fair
Skill: intermediate

FOUNDATION ROW (WS): Using A, purl.
Commence pattern
1ST AND 2ND ROWS: Using B, k1, sl 1, ✳k2, sl 1; rep from ✳ to last st, k1.
3RD AND 4TH ROWS: Using A, [k2, sl 1] 4 times, k3, sl 1, [k2, sl 1] 3 times, ✳k1, sl 1, [k2, sl 1] 3 times, k3, sl 1, [k2, sl 1] 3 times; rep from ✳ to last 2 sts, k2.
5TH AND 6TH ROWS: Using B, k3, ✳[sl 1, k2] 3 times, sl 1, k1, sl 1, [k2, sl 1] 3 times, k3; rep from ✳ to end.
7TH AND 8TH ROWS: As 1st and 2nd rows, using A instead of B.
9TH AND 10TH ROWS: As 3rd and 4th rows, using B instead of A.
11TH AND 12TH ROWS: As 5th and 6th rows, using A instead of B. Rep the last 12 rows.

Steep Diagonal Stripes
Multiple of 3 sts + 2
Drape: fair
Skill: intermediate

FOUNDATION ROW: Using A, purl.
Commence pattern
1ST ROW (RS): Using B, k3, sl 1, ✳k2, sl 1; rep from ✳ to last st, k1.
2ND ROW: Using B, p1, ✳sl 1, p2; rep from ✳ to last st, p1.
3RD ROW: Using A, k1, ✳sl 1, k2; rep from ✳ to last st, k1.
4TH ROW: Using A, p3, sl 1, ✳p2, sl 1; rep from ✳ to last st, p1.

5TH ROW: Using B, k2, ✳sl 1, k2; rep from ✳ to end.
6TH ROW: Using B, p2, ✳sl 1, p2; rep from ✳ to end.
7TH AND 8TH ROWS: As 1st and 2nd rows, but using A instead of B.
9TH AND 10TH ROWS: As 3rd and 4th rows, but using B instead of A.
11TH AND 12TH ROWS: As 5th and 6th rows, but using A instead of B.
Rep the last 12 rows.

Narrow Crosses
Multiple of 4 sts + 3
Drape: fair
Skill: intermediate

FOUNDATION ROW: Using A, purl.
Commence pattern
1ST ROW (RS): Using B, k2, ✳[sl 1, k1] twice; rep from ✳ to last st, k1.
2ND ROW: Using B, p2, ✳[sl 1, p1] twice; rep from ✳ to last st, p1.
3RD ROW: Using A, k3, ✳sl 1, k3; rep from ✳ to end.
4TH ROW: Using A, p3, ✳sl 1, p3; rep from ✳ to end.

5TH ROW: Using B, k1, sl 1, ✳k3, sl 1; rep from ✳ to last st, k1.
6TH ROW: Using B, p1, sl 1, ✳k3, sl 1; rep from ✳ to last st, p1.
7TH AND 8TH ROWS: As 3rd and 4th rows.
9TH AND 10TH ROWS: As 1st and 2nd rows.
11TH ROW: As 5th row, but using A instead of B.
12TH ROW: Using A, p1, sl 1, ✳p3, sl 1; rep from ✳ to last st, p1.
13TH ROW: As 3rd row, using B instead of A.
14TH ROWS: Using B, p1, k2, sl 1, ✳k3, sl 1; rep from ✳ to last 3 sts, k2, p1.
15TH AND 16TH ROW: As 11th and 12th rows. Rep the last 16 rows.

Little Dashes
Multiple of 6 sts + 4
Drape: fair
Skill: intermediate

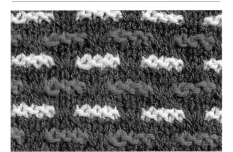

1ST ROW (RS): Using A, knit.
2ND ROW: Using A, purl.
3RD AND 4TH ROWS: Using B, k4, ✳sl 2, k4; rep from ✳ to end.
5TH ROW: Using A, knit.
6TH ROW: Using A, purl.
7TH AND 8TH ROWS: Using C, k1, sl 2, ✳k4, sl 2; rep from ✳ to last st, k1.
Rep these 8 rows.

Flecked Lattice Pattern
Multiple of 16 sts + 3
Drape: fair
Skill: experienced

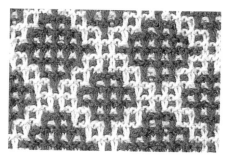

FOUNDATION ROW (WS): Using A, knit.
Commence pattern
1ST AND 2ND ROWS: Using B, [k1, sl 1]
3 times, k7, ✷sl 1, [k1, sl 1]4 times, k7;
rep from ✷ to last 6 sts, [sl 1, k1] 3 times.
3RD AND 4TH ROWS: Using A, k6, sl 1,
[k1, sl 1] 3 times, ✷k9, sl 1, [k1, sl 1] 3
times; rep from ✷ to last 6 sts, k6.
5TH AND 6TH ROWS: Using B, [k1, sl 1]
twice, k5, sl 1, k5, ✷sl 1, [k1, sl 1] twice,
k5, sl 1, k5; rep from ✷ to last 4 sts,
[sl 1, k1] twice.
7TH AND 8TH ROWS: Using A, k4, sl 1, k1,
sl 1, ✷k5, sl 1, k1, sl 1; rep from ✷ to last
4 sts, k4.
9TH AND 10TH ROWS: Using B, k1, sl 1,
✷k5, sl 1, [k1, sl 1] twice, k5, sl 1; rep
from ✷ to last st, k1.
11TH AND 12TH ROWS: Using A, k2, sl 1,
k1, sl 1, k9, ✷sl 1, [k1, sl 1] 3 times, k9;
rep from ✷ to last 5 sts, sl 1, k1, sl 1, k2.
13TH AND 14TH ROWS: Using B, k5, sl 1,
[k1, sl 1] 4 times, ✷k7, sl 1, [k1, sl 1]
4 times; rep from ✷ to last 5 sts, k5.
15TH AND 16TH ROWS: Using A, k2, sl 1,
k13, ✷sl 1, k1, sl 1, k13; rep from ✷ to
last 3 sts, sl 1, k2.
17TH AND 18TH ROWS: As 13th and 14th
rows.
19TH AND 20TH ROWS: As 11th and 12th
rows.
21ST AND 22ND ROWS: As 9th and 10th
rows.
23RD AND 24TH ROWS: As 7th and 8th rows.
25TH AND 26TH ROWS: As 5th and 6th
rows.
27TH AND 28TH ROWS: As 3rd and 4th
rows. Rep the last 28 rows.

Patchwork Squares
Multiple of 12 sts + 7
Drape: fair
Skill: experienced

1ST ROW (RS): Using A, knit.
2ND ROW: Using A, p1, ✷k5, p1; rep from
✷ to end.
3RD ROW: Using B, k2, sl 1, [k1, sl 1] twice,
k5, ✷sl 1, [k1, sl 1] 3 times, k5; rep from
✷ to last 7 sts, sl 1, [k1, sl 1] twice, k2.
4TH ROW: Using B, p2, sl 1, [p1, sl 1] twice,
k5, ✷sl 1, [p1, sl 1] 3 times, k5; rep from
✷ to last 7 sts, sl 1, [p1, sl 1] twice, p2.
5TH ROW: Using A, [k1, sl 1] 3 times, ✷k7,
sl 1, [k1, sl 1] twice; rep from ✷ to last st,
k1.
6TH ROW: Using A, [p1, sl 1] 3 times, p1,
✷k5, p1, [sl 1, p1] 3 times; rep from ✷ to
end. Rep the last 4 rows once more.
11TH ROW: As 3rd row.
12TH ROW: As 4th row.
13TH ROW: As 1st row.
14TH ROW: As 2nd row.
15TH ROW: Using B, k6, sl 1, [k1, sl 1]
3 times, ✷k5, sl 1, [k1, sl 1] 3 times; rep
from ✷ to last 6 sts, k6.
16TH ROW: Using B, p1, k5, ✷sl 1, [p1, sl
1] 3 times, k5; rep from ✷ to last st, p1.
17TH ROW: Using A, k7, ✷sl 1, [k1, sl 1]
twice, k7; rep from ✷ to end.
18TH ROW: Using A, p1, k5, p1, ✷[sl 1, p1]
3 times, k5, p1; rep from ✷ to end. Rep
the last 4 rows once more.
23RD ROW: As 15th row.
24TH ROW: As 16th row.
Rep these 24 rows.

Ladder Lattice
Multiple of 10 sts + 8
Drape: fair
Skill: intermediate

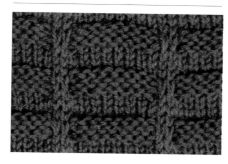

1ST ROW (RS): Using A, knit.
2ND ROW: Using A, purl.
Rep the last 2 rows once more.
5TH AND 6TH ROWS: Using B k8, ✷sl 2, k8;
rep from ✷ to end.
7TH ROW: Using B, p8, ✷sl 2, p8; rep from
✷ to end.
8TH ROW: As 6th row.
Rep these 8 rows.

Domino Lattice
Multiple of 8 sts + 5
Drape: fair
Skill: experienced

1ST ROW (RS): Using A, knit.
2ND ROW: Using A, knit.
3RD AND 4TH ROWS: Using B, [k1, sl 1]
twice, ✷k5, sl 1, k1, sl 1; rep from ✷ to
last st, k1.
5TH AND 6TH ROWS: Using A, k4, ✷sl 1,

k3; rep from ✳ to last st, k1.
Rep the last 4 rows twice more.
15TH AND 16TH ROWS: As 3rd and 4th rows.
17TH AND 18TH ROWS: As 1st and 2nd rows.
19TH AND 20TH ROWS: As 3rd and 4th rows.
21ST AND 22ND ROWS: Using A, k4, ✳sl 1, [k1, sl 1] twice, k3; rep from ✳ to last st, k1.
23RD AND 24TH ROWS: As 3rd and 4th rows. Rep the last 4 rows twice more.
Rep these 32 rows.

Scattered Flecks
Multiple of 6 sts + 2
Drape: fair
Skill: intermediate

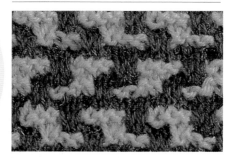

1ST ROW (RS): Using A, knit.
2ND ROW: Using A, purl.
3RD AND 4TH ROWS: Using B, k3, sl 2, ✳k4, sl 2; rep from ✳ to last 3 sts, k3.
5TH ROW: Using A, k1, ✳sl 2, k4; rep from ✳ to last st, k1.
6TH ROW: Using A, p5, sl 2, ✳p4, sl 2; rep from ✳ to last st, p1.
7TH ROW: Using B, k5, sl 2, ✳k4, sl 2; rep from ✳ to last st, k1.
8TH ROW: Using B, k1, ✳sl 2, k4; rep from ✳ to last st, k1.
9TH AND 10TH ROWS: As 1st and 2nd rows.
11TH ROW: Using B, k2, ✳sl 2, k4; rep from ✳ to end.
12TH ROW: Using B, ✳k4, sl 2; rep from ✳ to last 2 sts, k2.
13TH ROW: Using A, ✳k4, sl 2; rep ✳ from to last 2 sts, k2.
14TH ROW: Using A, p2, ✳sl 2, p4; rep

from ✳ to end.
15TH AND 16TH ROWS: Using B k1, sl 1, k4, ✳sl 2, k4; rep from ✳ to last 2 sts, sl 1, k1.
Rep these 16 rows.

Linking Crosses
Multiple of 12 sts + 3
Drape: fair
Skill: experienced

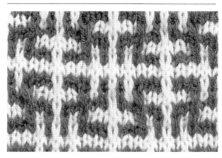

1ST ROW (RS): Using B, knit.
2ND ROW: Using B, purl.
3RD ROW: Using A, k1, sl 1, ✳k3, [sl 1, k1] twice, sl 1, k3, sl 1; rep from ✳ to last st, k1.
4TH ROW: Using A, p1, sl 1, ✳p3, [sl 1, p1] twice, sl 1, p3, sl 1; rep from ✳ to last st, p1.
5TH ROW: Using B, k4, [sl 1, k1] 3 times, sl 1, ✳k5, [sl 1, k1] 3 times, sl 1; rep from ✳ to last 4 sts, k4.
6TH ROW: Using B, p4, [sl 1, p1] 3 times, sl 1, ✳p5, [sl 1, p1] 3 times, sl 1; rep from ✳ to last 4 sts, p4.
7TH ROW: Using A, k1, sl 1, ✳k5, sl 1; rep from ✳ to last st, k1.
8TH ROW: Using A, p1, sl 1, ✳p5, sl 1; rep from ✳ to last st, p1.
9TH ROW: Using B, k2, sl 1, k1, sl 1, k5, ✳[sl 1, k1] 3 times, sl 1, k5; rep from ✳ to last 5 sts, sl 1, k1, sl 1, k2.
10TH ROW: Using B, p2, sl 1, p1, sl 1, p5, ✳[sl 1, p1] 3 times, sl 1, p5; rep from ✳ to last 5 sts, sl 1, p1, sl 1, p2.
11TH ROW: Using A, [k1, sl 1] twice, k3, sl 1, k3, ✳[sl 1, k1] twice, [sl 1, k3] twice; rep from ✳ to last 4 sts, [sl 1, k1] twice.
12TH ROW: Using A, [p1, sl 1] twice, p3, sl 1, p3, ✳[sl 1, p1] twice, [sl 1, p3] twice; rep from ✳ to last 4 sts, [sl 1, p1] twice.

13TH AND 14TH ROWS: As 1st and 2nd rows.
15TH AND 16TH ROWS: As 11th and 12th rows.
17TH AND 18TH ROWS: As 9th and 10th rows.
19TH AND 20TH ROWS: As 7th and 8th rows.
21ST AND 22ND ROWS: As 5th and 6th rows.
23RD AND 24TH ROWS: As 3rd and 4th rows.
Rep these 24 rows.

Snowflakes
Multiple of 8 sts + 5
Drape: fair
Skill: intermediate

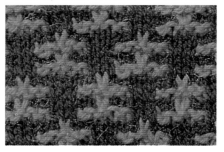

1ST ROW (WS): Using A, purl.
2ND AND 3RD ROWS: Using B, k1, sl 3, ✳k5, sl 3; rep from ✳ to last st, k1.
4TH ROW: Using A, k6, sl 1, ✳k7, sl 1; rep from ✳ to last 6 sts, k6.
5TH ROW: Using A, p6, sl 1, ✳p7, sl 1; rep from ✳ to last 6 sts, p6.
6TH, 7TH, AND 8TH ROWS: As 2nd, 3rd, and 4th rows.
9TH ROW: Using A, purl.
10TH ROW: Using B, k5, ✳sl 3, k5; rep from ✳ to end.
11TH ROW: Using B, p1, k4, sl 3, ✳k5, sl 3; rep from ✳ to last 5 sts, k4, p1.
12TH ROW: Using A, k2, sl 1, ✳k7, sl 1; rep from ✳ to last 2 sts, k2.
13TH ROW: Using A, p2, sl 1, ✳p7, sl 1; rep from ✳ to last 2 sts, p2.
14TH, 15TH, AND 16TH ROWS: As 10th, 11th, and 12th rows.
Rep these 16 rows.

Maze of Crosses
Multiple of 16 sts + 3
Drape: fair
Skill: experienced

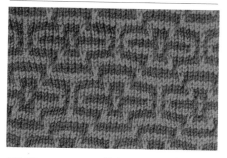

FOUNDATION ROW: Using A, purl.
Commence pattern
1ST ROW (RS): Using B, k5, sl 1, ✳k7, sl 1; rep from ✳ to last 5 sts, k5.
2ND ROW: Using B, p5, sl 1, ✳p7, sl 1; rep from ✳ to last 5 sts, p5.
3RD ROW: Using A, k6, sl 1, k5, sl 1, ✳k9, sl 1, k5, sl 1; rep from ✳ to last 6 sts, k6.
4TH ROW: Using A, p6, sl 1, p5, sl 1, ✳p9, sl 1, p5, sl 1; rep from ✳ to last 6 sts, p6.
5TH ROW: Using B, k1, sl 1, ✳k5, sl 1, k3, sl 1, k5, sl 1; rep from ✳ to last st, k1.
6TH ROW: Using B, p1, sl 1, ✳p5, sl 1, p3, sl 1, p5, sl 1; rep from ✳ to last st, p1.
7TH ROW: Using A, k2, sl 1, k5, ✳sl 1, k1, sl 1, k5; rep from ✳ to last 3 sts, sl 1, k2.
8TH ROW: Using A, p2, sl 1, p5, ✳sl 1, p1, sl 1, p5; rep from ✳ to last 3 sts, sl 1, p2.
9TH ROW: Using B, [k1, sl 1] twice, k5, sl 1, k5, ✳[sl 1, k1] twice, [sl 1, k5] twice; rep from ✳ to last 4 sts, [sl 1, k1] twice.
10TH ROW: Using B, [p1, sl 1] twice, p5, sl 1, p5, ✳[sl 1, p1] twice, [sl 1, p5] twice; rep from ✳ to last 4 sts, [sl 1, p1] twice.
11TH AND 12TH ROWS: As 7th and 8th rows.
13TH AND 14TH ROWS: As 5th and 6th rows.
15TH AND 16TH ROWS: As 3rd and 4th rows.
17TH AND 18TH ROWS: As 1st and 2nd rows.
19TH ROW: Using A, k4, sl 1, k9, sl 1, ✳k5, sl 1, k9, sl 1; rep from ✳ to last 4 sts, k4.
20TH ROW: Using A, p4, sl 1, p9, sl 1, ✳p5, sl 1, p9, sl 1; rep from ✳ to last 4 sts, p4.
21ST ROW: Using B, k3, ✳[sl 1, k5 twice, sl 1, k3; rep from ✳ to end.
22ND ROW: Using B, p3, ✳[sl 1, p5] twice,

sl 1, p3; rep from ✳ to end.
23RD AND 24TH ROWS: As 7th and 8th rows.
25TH ROW: Using B, k1, sl 1, ✳k5, [sl 1, k1] twice, sl 1, k5, sl 1; rep from ✳ to last st, k1.
26TH ROW: Using B, p1, sl 1, ✳p5, [sl 1, p1] twice, sl 1, p5, sl 1, rep from ✳ to last st, p1.
27TH AND 28TH ROWS: As 7th and 8th rows.
29TH AND 30TH ROWS: As 21st and 22nd rows.
31ST AND 32ND ROWS: As 19th and 20th rows.
Rep the last 32 rows.

Ziggurat Pattern
Multiple of 12 sts + 5
Drape: fair
Skill: intermediate

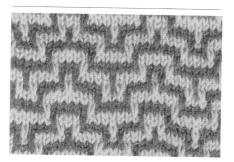

FOUNDATION ROW: Using A, purl.
Commence pattern
1ST ROW (RS): Using B, k4, ✳sl 1, k7, sl 1, k3; rep from ✳ to last st, k1.
2ND ROW: Using B, p4, ✳sl 1, p7, sl 1, p3; rep from ✳ to last st, p1.
3RD ROW: Using A, k5, ✳sl 1, k5; rep from ✳ to end.
4TH ROW: Using A, p5, ✳sl 1, p5; rep from ✳ to end.
5TH ROW: Using B, k6, sl 1, k3, sl 1, ✳k7, sl 1, k3, sl 1; rep from ✳ to last 6 sts, k6.
6TH ROW: Using B, p6, sl 1, p3, sl 1, ✳p7, sl 1, p3, sl 1; rep from ✳ to last 6 sts, p6.
7TH ROW: Using A, k2, sl 1, k4, sl 1, k1, sl 1, ✳[k4, sl 1] twice, k1, sl 1; rep from ✳ to last 7 sts, k4, sl 1, k2.
8TH ROW: Using A, p2, sl 1, ✳p4, sl 1, p1, sl 1, p4, sl 1; rep from ✳ to last 2 sts, p2.
9TH ROW: Using B, [k1, sl 1] twice, ✳[k4,

sl 1 twice, k1, sl 1; rep from ✳ to last st, k1.
10TH ROW: Using B, [p1, sl 1] twice, ✳[p4, sl 1] twice, p1, sl 1; rep from ✳ to last st, p1.
11TH AND 12TH ROWS: As 1st and 2nd rows but using A instead of B.
13TH AND 14TH ROWS: As 3rd and 4th rows but using B instead of A.
15TH AND 16TH ROWS: As 5th and 6th rows but using A instead of B.
17TH AND 18TH ROWS: As 7th and 8th rows but using B instead of A.
19TH AND 20TH ROWS: As 9th and 10th rows, but using A instead of B.
Rep the last 20 rows.

Gathered Stripes
Multiple of 21 sts + 11
Drape: fair
Skill: intermediate

FOUNDATION ROW: Using A, purl.
Commence pattern
1ST ROW (RS): Using B, [k1, sl 1] 5 times, ✳k12, sl 1, [k1, sl 1] 4 times; rep from ✳ to last st, k1.
2ND ROW: Using B, [p1, sl 1] 5 times, ✳p12, sl 1, [p1, sl 1] 4 times; rep from ✳ to last st, p1.
3RD ROW: Using A, k2, sl 1, [k1, sl 1] 3 times, ✳k14, sl 1, [k1, sl 1] 3 times; rep from ✳ to last 2 sts, k2.
4TH ROW: Using A, p2, sl 1, [p1, sl 1] 3 times, ✳p14, sl 1, [p1, sl 1] 3 times; rep from ✳ to last 2 sts, p2.
Rep the last 4 rows.

slipped and elongated stitches

The technique of slipping stitches (*page 14*) can be combined with that of winding the yarn once or twice around the needle to produce other interesting textures in one or more colors. Cabling too (*pages 22–23*) can be employed, creating a lattice effect on the surface of the fabric. These elongated stitches are somewhat vulnerable to snagging. Practice with some spare yarn to ensure an even gauge in the finished work.

Arrow Darts
Multiple of 6 sts + 2
Drape: fair
Skill: intermediate

Special Abbreviation
PW2 = p1 wrapping yarn twice around needle.
1ST ROW (WS): P1, PW2 (see Special Abbreviation), p4, ✳[PW2] twice, p4; rep from ✳ to last 2 sts, PW2, p1.
2ND ROW: K1, sl 1, k4, ✳sl 2, k4; rep from ✳ to last 2 sts, sl 1, k1.
3RD ROW: P1, sl 1, p4, ✳sl 2, p4; rep from ✳ to last 2 sts, sl 1, p1.
Rep the last 2 rows once more.
6TH ROW: K1, ✳C3L, C3R; rep from ✳ to last st, k1.
Rep these 6 rows.

Slipstitch Crosses
Multiple of 6 sts
Drape: fair
Skill: intermediate
Note: Slip all sts purlwise.

1ST FOUNDATION ROW (RS): Using A, knit.
2ND FOUNDATION ROW: Using A, purl.
Commence Pattern
1ST ROW: Using B, k2, ✳sl 2, k4; rep from ✳ to last 4 sts, sl 2, k2.
2ND ROW: Using B, p2, ✳sl 2, p4; rep from ✳ to last 4 sts, sl 2, p2.
3RD ROW: Using A, k1, C2B, C2F, ✳k2, C2B, C2F; rep from ✳ to last st, k1.
4TH ROW: Using A, purl.
5TH ROW: Using B, k5, sl 2, ✳k4, sl 2; rep from ✳ to last 5 sts, k5.
6TH ROW: Using B, p5, ✳sl 2, p4; rep from ✳ to last 7 sts, sl 2, p5.
7TH ROW: Using A, k4, C2B, C2F, ✳k2, C2B, C2F; rep from ✳ to last 4 sts, k4.
8TH ROW: Using A, purl.
Rep the last 8 rows.

Slipstitch Zigzags
Multiple of 4 sts + 1
Drape: fair
Skill: intermediate

1ST ROW (RS): Using A, k1, ✳sl 1 purlwise, k3; rep from ✳ to end.
2ND ROW: Using A, ✳p3, sl 1 purlwise; rep from ✳ to last st, p1.
3RD ROW: Using B, k1, ✳C3L, k1; rep from ✳ to end.
4TH ROW: Using B, purl.
5TH ROW: Using A, k5, ✳sl 1, k3; rep from ✳ to end.
6TH ROW: Using A, ✳p3, sl 1; rep from ✳ to last 5 sts, p5.
7TH ROW: Using B, k3, ✳C3R, k1; rep from ✳ to last 2 sts, k2.
8TH ROW: Using B, purl.
Rep these 8 rows.

Little Cable Fabric

Multiple of 4 sts + 1
Drape: fair
Skill: experienced

1ST ROW (RS): K1, ✳sl 1 purlwise, k3; rep from ✳ to end.

2ND ROW: ✳P3, sl 1 purlwise; rep from ✳ to last st, p1.

3RD ROW: K1, ✳C3L, k1; rep from ✳ to end.

4TH ROW: Purl.

5TH ROW: K5, ✳sl 1, k3; rep from ✳ to end.

6TH ROW: ✳P3, sl 1; rep from ✳ to last 5 sts, p5.

7TH ROW: K3, ✳C3R, k1; rep from ✳ to last 2 sts, k2.

8TH ROW: Purl.
Rep these 8 rows.

Brick Stitch

Multiple of 4 sts + 1
Drape: fair
Skill: experienced

1ST ROW (RS): K4, ✳k1 winding yarn twice

around needle, k3; rep from ✳ to last st, k1.

2ND ROW: P4, ✳sl 1 purlwise dropping extra loop, p3; rep from ✳ to last st, p1.

3RD ROW: K4, ✳sl 1 purlwise, k3; rep from ✳ to last st, k1.

4TH ROW: K4, ✳yf, sl 1 purlwise, yb, k3; rep from ✳ to last st, k1.
Rep the last 4 rows once more.

9TH ROW: K2, ✳k1 winding yarn twice around needle, k3; rep from ✳ to last 3 sts, k1 winding yarn twice around needle, k2.

10TH ROW: P2, ✳sl 1 purlwise dropping extra loop, p3; rep from ✳ to last 3 sts, sl 1 purlwise, p2.

11TH ROW: K2, ✳sl 1 purlwise, k3; rep from ✳ to last 3 sts, sl 1 purlwise, k2.

12TH ROW: K2, ✳yf, sl 1 purlwise, yb, k3; rep from ✳ to last 3 sts, yf, sl 1 purlwise, yb, k2. Rep the last 4 rows once more.
Rep these 16 rows.

Snowballs

Multiple of 5 sts + 1
Drape: fair
Skill: experienced
Note: Sts should not be counted after 4th, 5th, and 6th rows.

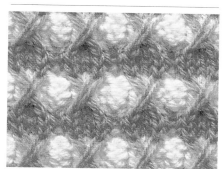

1ST ROW (WS): Using A, purl.
2ND ROW: Using A, knit.
3RD ROW: Using A, p1, ✳p1 wrapping yarn twice around needle, p2, p1 wrapping yarn twice around needle, p1; rep from ✳ to end.

4TH ROW: Using B, k1, sl 1 (dropping extra loop), k2, sl 1 (dropping extra loop), ✳[k1,

yo, k1, yo, k1] into next st, sl 1 (dropping extra loop), k2, sl 1 (dropping extra loop); rep from ✳ to last st, k1.

5TH ROW: Using B, p1, sl 1, p2, sl 1, ✳yb, k5, yf, sl 1, p2, sl 1; rep from ✳ to last st, p1.

6TH ROW: Using B, k1, sl 1, k2, sl 1, ✳yf, p5, yb, sl 1, k2, sl 1; rep from ✳ to last st, k1.

7TH ROW: Using B, p1, sl 1, p2, sl 1, ✳yb, k2tog, k3tog, pass k2tog st over k3tog st, yf, sl 1, p2, sl 1; rep from ✳ to last st, p1.

8TH ROW: Using A, k1, ✳drop first elongated st off needle, with yb sl 2, drop next elongated st off needle, with left-hand needle pick up first elongated st, pass the slipped sts from right-hand needle back to left-hand needle, then pick up second elongated st on left-hand needle, k5; rep from ✳ to end.
Rep these 8 rows.

Slipstitch Plaid

Multiple of 8 sts + 6
Drape: fair
Skill: experienced
Note: Slip all sts purlwise.

Special Abbreviation
KW = k1 wrapping yarn twice around needle.
Using A, work 2 rows in Garter st (1st row is right side).

3RD ROW: Using B, k1, sl 1, k2, sl 1, ✳k4, sl 1, k2, sl 1; rep from ✳ to last st, k1.

4TH ROW: Using B, p1, sl 1, p2, sl 1, ✳p4, sl 1, p2, sl 1; rep from ✳ to last st, p1.

5TH ROW: Using A, knit.

6TH ROW: Using A, k1, KW (see Special Abbreviation), k2, KW, ✳k4, KW, k2, KW; rep from ✳ to last st, k1.

7TH ROW: Using B, k1, sl 1, k2, sl 1, ✳k4, sl 1, k2, sl 1; rep from ✳ to last st, k1 (dropping extra loops off needle when slipping sts).

8TH ROW: As 4th row.

9TH ROW: As 3rd row.

Rep the last 2 rows once more, then 4th row again. Rep these 12 rows.

2-Color Herringbone Twists

Multiple of 8 sts + 2
Drape: fair
Skill: experienced
Note: Slip all sts purlwise.

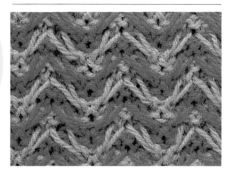

1ST FOUNDATION ROW (WS): Using A, k4, p2 wrapping yarn twice around needle for each st, ✳k6, p2 wrapping yarn twice around needle for each st; rep from ✳ to last 4 sts, k4.

2ND FOUNDATION ROW: Using A, k4, sl 2 dropping extra loops, ✳k6, sl 2 as before; rep from ✳ to last 4 sts, k4.

Commence Pattern

1ST ROW: Using A, k4, yf, sl 2, yb, ✳k6, yf, sl 2, yb; rep from ✳ to last 4 sts, k4.

2ND ROW: Using A, k4, sl 2, ✳k6, sl 2; rep from ✳ to last 4 sts, k4.

3RD ROW: Using A, k3, p1 wrapping yarn twice around needle (PW1), sl 2, PW1, ✳k4, PW1, sl 2, PW1; rep from ✳ to last 3 sts, k3.

4TH ROW: Using B, k1, ✳slip next 3 sts onto

cable needle dropping extra loop and hold at back of work, knit next st from left-hand needle, then k2 and sl 1 from cable needle, slip next st onto cable needle and hold at front of work, sl 1 dropping extra loop, k2 from left-hand needle, then knit st from cable needle; rep from ✳ to last st, k1.

5TH ROW: As 1st row, but using B.

6TH ROW: As 2nd row, but using B.

7TH ROW: As 3rd row, but using B.

8TH ROW: As 4th row, but using A.

Rep the last 8 rows.

Herringbone Twists

Multiple of 8 sts + 2
Drape: fair
Skill: experienced

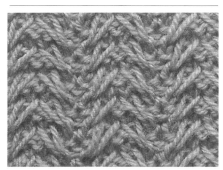

Worked as given for 2-Color Herringbone Twists, but using one color only throughout.

Diamonds

Multiple of 6 sts + 2
Drape: fair
Skill: experienced

Special Abbreviation

PW2 = p1 wrapping yarn twice around needle.

1ST ROW (WS): P1, PW2 (see Special Abbreviation), p4, ✳[PW2] twice, p4; rep from ✳ to last 2 sts, PW2, p1.

2ND ROW: k1, sl 1, k4, ✳sl 2, k4; rep from ✳ to last 2 sts, sl 1, k1.

3RD ROW: P1, sl 1, p4, ✳sl 2, p4; rep from ✳ to last 2 sts, sl 1, p1.

Rep the last 2 rows once more.

6TH ROW: K1, ✳C3L, C3R; rep from ✳ to last st, k1.

7TH ROW: P3, [PW2] twice, ✳p4, [PW2] twice; rep from ✳ to last 3 sts, p3.

8TH ROW: K3, sl 2, ✳k4, sl 2; rep from ✳ to last 3 sts, k3.

9TH ROW: P3, sl 2, ✳p4, sl 2; rep from ✳ to last 3 sts, p3.

Rep the last 2 rows once more.

12TH ROW: K1, ✳C3R, C3L; rep from ✳ to last st, k1.

Rep these 12 rows.

thick fabrics

With the use of a circular needle or a pair of double-pointed needles (*page 9*), it is possible to produce reversible knitted fabrics. Fur stitch (*below*) is another kind of thick fabric, made by forming loops with the yarn. Clearly, these techniques are for experienced knitters, but with a little practice and patience, you should be able to master them. Try a reversible fabric for a small item, such as a scarf, or use Fur Stitch for the top of a cushion cover.

Reversible Stockinette Stitch
Multiple of 2 sts
Drape: fair
Skill: experienced
Note: This must be worked on a circular needle or two double-pointed needles, as the work is not turned at the end of rows 1 and 3.
When turning work, make sure yarns are crossed around each other.
Slip all sts purlwise.

1ST ROW: Using A, ✳k1, yf, sl 1, yb; rep from ✳ to end. Return to beg of row without turning work.
2ND ROW: Using B, ✳yb, sl 1, yf, p1; rep from ✳ to end, turn work.
3RD ROW: Using B, as 1st row.
4TH ROW: Using A, as 2nd row.
Rep these 4 rows.

Reversible Checks
Multiple of 16 sts + 8
Drape: fair
Skill: experienced
Note: Work on a circular needle or two double-pointed needles, as the work is not turned on 1st and following alt rows.
When turning work ensure yarns cross around each other. Slip all sts purlwise.

1ST ROW: Using A, [yb, k1, yf, sl 1] 4 times, ✳[yb, sl 1, yf, p1] 4 times, ✳[yb, k1, yf, sl 1] 4 times; rep from ✳ to end. Return to beg of row without turning work.
2ND ROW: Using B, [yb, sl 1, yf, p1] 4 times, ✳[yb, k1, yf, sl 1] 4 times, [yb, sl 1, yf, p1] 4 times; rep from ✳ to end. Turn work.
3RD ROW: Using B, as 1st row.
4TH ROW: Using A, as 2nd row. Rep last 4 rows again.
9TH ROW: Using B, as 1st row.
10TH ROW: Using A, as 2nd row.
11TH ROW: As 1st row.
12TH ROW: As 2nd row. Rep the last 4 rows once more.
Rep these 16 rows.

Fur Stitch
Multiple of 2 sts
Drape: fair
Skill: experienced

1ST ROW (WS): Knit.
2ND ROW: ✳K1, k1, keeping st on left-hand needle, bring yf, pass yarn over left thumb to make a loop (approx 1½in, 4cm), yb and knit this st again, slipping st off the needle, yo and pass the 2 sts just worked over this loop (1 loop made = ML); rep from ✳ to last 2 sts, k2.
3RD ROW: Knit.
4TH ROW: K2, ✳ML, k1; rep from ✳ to end.
Rep these 4 rows.

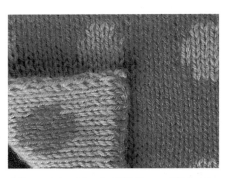

Reversible Triangles

Multiple of 12 sts + 10

Drape: fair

Skill: experienced

Note: This must be worked on a circular needle or two double-pointed needles, as the work is not turned on 1st and following alt rows.

When turning work, make sure yarns are crossed around each other.

Slip all sts purlwise.

1ST ROW: Using A, [yb, k1, yf, sl 1] 5 times, ✳yb, sl 1, yf, p1, [yb, k1, yf, sl 1] 5 times; rep from ✳ to end. Return to beg of row without turning work.

2ND ROW: Using B, [yb, sl 1, yf, p1] 5 times, ✳yb, k1, yf, sl 1, [yb, sl 1, yf, p1] 5 times; rep from ✳ to end. Turn work.

3RD ROW: Using B, as 1st row.

4TH ROW: Using A, as 2nd row.

5TH ROW: Using A, yb, sl 1, yf, p1, [yb, k1, yf, sl 1] 3 times, ✳[yb, sl 1, yf, p1] 3 times, [yb, k1, yf, sl 1] 3 times; rep from ✳ to last 2 sts, yb, sl 1, yf, p1. Do not turn.

6TH ROW: Using B, yb, k1, yf, sl 1, [yb, sl 1, yf, p1] 3 times, ✳[yb, k1, yf, sl 1] 3 times, [yb, sl 1, yf, p1] 3 times; rep from ✳ to last 2 sts, yb, k1, yf, sl 1, turn.

7TH ROW: Using B, as 5th row.

8TH ROW: Using A, as 6th row.

9TH ROW: Using A, [yb, sl 1, yf, p1] twice, yb, k1, yf, sl 1, ✳[yb, sl 1, yf, p1] 5 times, yb, k1, yf, sl 1; rep from ✳ to last 4 sts, [yb, sl 1, yf, p1] twice. Do not turn work.

10TH ROW: Using B, [yb, k1, yf, sl 1] twice, ✳yb, sl 1, yf, p1, [yb, k1, yf, sl 1] 5 times, yb, sl 1, yf, p1; rep from ✳ to last 4 sts, [yb, k1, yf, sl 1] twice, turn.

11TH ROW: Using B, as 9th row.

12TH ROW: Using A, as 10th row.

13TH ROW: Using A, as 10th row, but do not turn work at end of row.

14TH ROW: Using B, as 9th row, but turn work at end of row.

15TH ROW: Using B, as 10th row, but do not turn work at end of row.

16TH ROW: Using A, as 9th row, but turn work at end of row.

17TH ROW: Using A, as 6th row, but do not turn work at end of row.

18TH ROW: Using B, as 5th row, but turn work at end of row.

19TH ROW: As 6th row, but do not turn work at end of row.

20TH ROW: As 5th row, but turn work at end of row.

21ST ROW: Using A, as 2nd row, but do not turn work at end of row.

22ND ROW: Using B, as 1st row, but turn work at end of row.

23RD ROW: Using B, as 2nd row, but do not turn work at end of row.

24TH ROW: Using A, as 1st row, but turn work at end of row.

Rep these 24 rows.

Reversible Motif

Multiple of 22 sts

Drape: fair

Skill: experienced

Note: This must be worked on a circular needle or two double-pointed needles, as the work is not turned on 1st and following alt rows.

When turning work, make sure yarns are crossed around each other.

Slip all sts purlwise.

1ST ROW: Using A, ✳yb, k1, yf, sl 1; rep from ✳ to end. Return to beg of row without turning work.

2ND ROW: Using B, ✳yb, sl 1, yf, p1; rep from ✳ to end. Turn work.

3RD ROW: Using B, as 1st row.

4TH ROW: Using A, as 2nd row.

Rep the last 4 rows twice more.

13TH ROW: Using A, [yb, k1, yf, sl 1] 4 times, [yb, sl 1, yf, p1] 3 times, ✳[yb, k1, yf, sl 1] 8 times, [yb, sl 1, yf, p1] 3 times; rep from ✳ to last 8 sts, [yb, k1, yf, sl 1] 4 times. Do not turn.

14TH ROW: Using B, [yb, sl 1, yf, p1] 4 times, [yb, k1, yf, sl 1] 3 times, ✳[yb, sl 1, yf, p1] 8 times, [yb, k1, yf, sl 1] 3 times; rep from ✳ to last 8 sts, [yb, sl 1, yf, p1] 4 times. Turn.

15TH ROW: Using B, as 13th row.

16TH ROW: Using A, as 14th row.

17TH ROW: Using A, [yb, k1, yf, sl 1] 3 times, [yb, sl 1, yf, p1] 5 times, ✳[yb, k1, yf, sl 1] 6 times, [yb, sl 1, yf, p1] 5 times; rep from ✳ to last 6 sts, [yb, k1, yf, sl 1] 3 times. Do not turn.

18TH ROW: Using B, [yb, sl 1, yf, p1] 3 times, [yb, k1, yf, sl 1] 5 times, ✳[yb, sl 1, yf, p1] 6 times, [yb, k1, yf, sl 1] 5 times; rep from ✳ to last 6 sts, [yb, sl 1, yf, p1] 3 times. Turn.

19TH ROW: Using B, as 17th row.

20TH ROW: Using A, as 18th row.

Rep the last 4 rows once more.

25TH ROW: As 13th row.

26TH ROW: As 14th row.

27TH ROW: As 15th row.

28TH ROW: As 16th row.

29TH ROW: As 1st row.

30TH ROW: As 2nd row.

31ST ROW: As 3rd row.

32ND ROW: As 4th row.

Rep the last 4 rows twice more.

Rep these 40 rows.

lace patterns

Lace and other openwork stitch patterns are the "glamour queens" of knitting. Some of them are quite spectacular, composed of intricate, delicate motifs suggesting flowers, vines, and other natural forms. Fortunately, they are, for the most part, easier to work than they look. Once you have worked a few, you should find that the knitting proceeds quite smoothly.

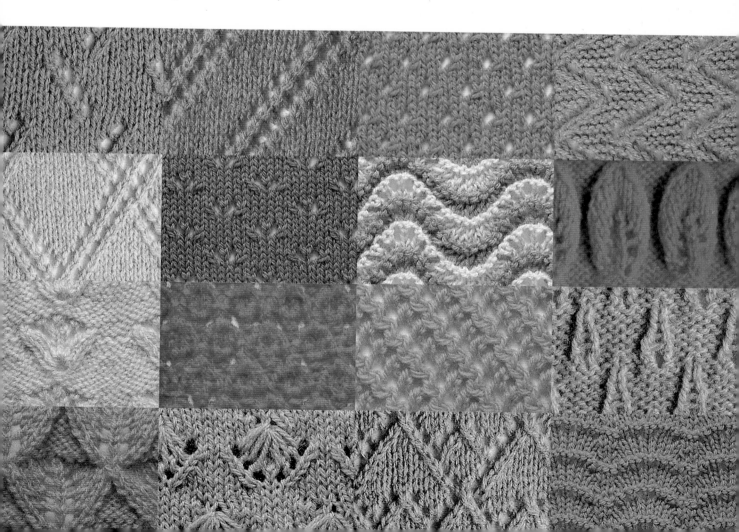

simple eyelet patterns

The basic "building block" of lace knitting is a hole, or eyelet. This is produced by pairing an eyelet, or yarn-over increase, with a decrease at specified places across a row (*pages 19–20*). For your first attempt at lace, try one of these simple eyelet patterns. They can be used for all sorts of garments. You could easily substitute one of these stitches for Stockinette stitch in a commercial pattern, although you might need to adjust the number of cast-on stitches.

Little Flowers
Multiple of 6 sts + 3
Drape: good
Skill: intermediate

1ST ROW (RS): Knit.
2ND AND EVERY ALT ROW: Purl.
3RD ROW: Knit.
5TH ROW: ✳K4, yo, sl 1, k1, psso; rep from ✳ to last 3 sts, k3.
7TH ROW: K2, k2tog, yo, k1, yo, sl 1, k1, psso, ✳k1, k2tog, yo, k1, yo, sl 1, k1, psso; rep from ✳ to last 2 sts, k2.
9TH AND 11TH ROWS: Knit.
13TH ROW: K1, yo, sl 1, k1, psso, ✳k4, yo, sl 1, k1, psso; rep from ✳ to end.
15TH ROW: K2, yo, sl 1, k1, psso, k1, k2tog, yo, ✳k1, yo, sl 1, k1, psso, k1, k2tog, yo; rep from ✳ to last 2 sts, k2.
16TH ROW: Purl.
Rep these 16 rows.

Eyelet V-Stitch
Multiple of 12 sts + 1
Drape: good
Skill: intermediate

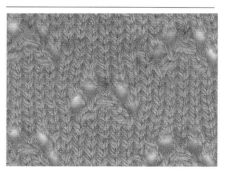

1ST ROW (RS): Knit.
2ND AND EVERY ALT ROW: Purl.
3RD ROW: K4, yo, sl 1, k1, psso, k1, k2tog, yo, ✳k7, yo, sl 1, k1, psso, k1, k2tog, yo; rep from ✳ to last 4 sts, k4.
5TH ROW: K5, yo, sl 1, k2tog, psso, yo, ✳k9, yo, sl 1, k2tog, psso, yo; rep from ✳ to last 5 sts, k5.
7TH ROW: Knit.
9TH ROW: K1, ✳k2tog, yo, k7, yo, sl 1, k1, psso, k1; rep from ✳ to end.
11TH ROW: k2tog, yo, k9, ✳yo, sl 1, k2tog, psso, yo, k9; rep from ✳ to last 2 sts, yo, sl 1, k1, psso.
12TH ROW: Purl.
Rep these 12 rows.

Zigzag Eyelets
Multiple of 9 sts
Drape: good
Skill: intermediate

1ST ROW (RS): K4, ✳yo, sl 1, k1, psso, k7; rep from ✳ to last 5 sts, yo, sl 1, k1, psso, k3.
2ND AND EVERY ALT ROW: Purl.
3RD ROW: K5, ✳yo, sl 1, k1, psso, k7; rep from ✳ to last 4 sts, yo, sl 1, k1, psso, k2.
5TH ROW: K6, ✳yo, sl 1, k1, psso, k7; rep from ✳ to last 3 sts, yo, sl 1, k1, psso, k1.
7TH ROW: ✳K7, yo, sl 1, k1, psso; rep from ✳ to end.
9TH ROW: K3, ✳k2tog, yo, k7; rep from ✳ to last 6 sts, k2tog, yo, k4.
11TH ROW: K2, ✳k2tog, yo, k7; rep from ✳ to last 7 sts, k2tog, yo, k5.
13TH ROW: K1, ✳k2tog, yo, k7; rep from ✳ to last 8 sts, k2tog, yo, k6.
15TH ROW: ✳K2tog, yo, k7; rep from ✳ to end.
16TH ROW: Purl.
Rep these 16 rows.

All-over Eyelets
Multiple of 10 sts + 1
Drape: good
Skill: intermediate

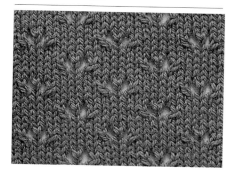

1ST ROW (RS): Knit.
2ND AND EVERY ALT ROW: Purl.
3RD ROW: K3, ✳k2tog, yo, k1, yo, sl 1, k1, psso, k5; rep from ✳ to last 8 sts, k2tog, yo, k1, yo, sl 1, k1, psso, k3.
5TH ROW: Knit.
7TH ROW: K1, ✳yo, sl 1, k1, psso, k5, k2tog, yo, k1; rep from ✳ to end.
8TH ROW: Purl.
Rep these 8 rows.

Eyelet Diamonds
Multiple of 8 sts + 7
Drape: good
Skill: intermediate

1ST ROW (RS): Knit.
2ND ROW AND EVERY ALT ROW: Purl.
3RD ROW: K3, ✳yo, sl 1, k1, psso, k6; rep from ✳ to last 4 sts, yo, sl 1, k1, psso, k2.

5TH ROW: K2, ✳yo, sl 1, k2tog, psso, yo, k5; rep from ✳ to last 5 sts, yo, sl 1, k2tog, psso, yo, k2.
7TH ROW: As 3rd row.
9TH ROW: Knit.
11TH ROW: K7, ✳yo, sl 1, k1, psso, k6; rep from ✳ to end.
13TH ROW: K6, ✳yo, sl 1, k2tog, psso, yo, k5, rep from ✳ to last st, k1.
15TH ROW: As 11th row.
16TH ROW: Purl.
Rep these 16 rows.

Staggered Eyelets
Multiple of 4 sts + 3
Drape: good
Skill: intermediate

Work 2 rows in St st, starting knt.
3RD ROW (RS): ✳K2, k2tog, yo; rep from ✳ to last 3 sts, k3.
Work 3 rows in St st, starting purl.
7TH ROW: ✳K2tog, yo, k2; rep from ✳ to last 3 sts, k2tog, yo, k1.
8TH ROW: Purl.
Rep these 8 rows.

Pine Cone Pattern
Multiple of 10 sts + 1
Drape: good
Skill: intermediate

1ST ROW (RS): Knit.
2ND AND EVERY ALT ROW: Purl.
3RD ROW: K3, k2tog, yo, k1, yo, sl 1, k1,

psso, ✳k5, k2tog, yo, k1, yo, sl 1, k1, psso; rep from to last 3 sts, k3.
5TH ROW: K2, k2tog, yo, k3, yo, sl 1, k1, psso, ✳k3 k2tog, yo, k3, yo, sl 1, k1, psso; rep from ✳ to last 3 sts, k2.
7TH AND 9TH ROWS: As 3rd row.
11TH ROW: Knit.
13TH ROW: K1, ✳yo, sl 1, k1, psso, k5, k2tog, yo, k1; rep from ✳ to end.
15TH ROW: K2, yo, sl 1, k1, psso, k3, k2tog, yo, ✳k3, yo, sl 1, k1, psso, k3, k2tog, yo; rep from ✳ to last 2 sts, k2.
17TH AND 19TH ROWS: As 13th row.
20TH ROW: Purl.
Rep these 20 rows.

mesh patterns

These patterns employ a variety of techniques, from the basic eyelet increase to more complex maneuvers, such as winding the yarn twice around the needle (*see Mesh Zigzag Stitch, page 103*). The fabrics have a very soft drape and are well-suited to scarves and shawls. Knitted in a fine silk or synthetic yarn, they are slinky and flowing. A slightly fuzzy, but still fine, yarn will produce a strikingly different effect. Try different needle sizes to see the effects you can achieve.

lace patterns

Filet Net
Multiple of 3 sts
Drape: excellent
Skill: intermediate

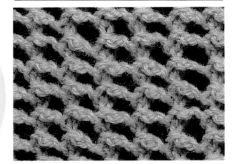

1ST ROW (RS): K2, ✷sl 2, pass 1st slipped st over 2nd and off needle, sl 1, pass 2nd slipped st over 3rd and off needle, slip the 3rd slipped st back onto left-hand needle, yo twice (to make 2 sts), knit the 3rd slipped st in usual way; rep from ✷ to last st, k1 (original number of sts retained).
2ND ROW: K3, ✷p1, k2; rep from ✷ to end.
Rep these 2 rows.

Cell Stitch
Multiple of 4 sts + 3
Drape: excellent
Skill: intermediate

1ST ROW (RS): K2, ✷yo, sl 1, k2tog, psso, yo, k1; rep from ✷ to last st, k1.
2ND ROW: Purl.
3RD ROW: K1, k2tog, yo, k1, ✷yo, sl 1, k2tog, psso, yo, k1; rep from ✷ to last 3 sts, yo, sl 1, k1, psso, k1.
4TH ROW: Purl.
Rep these 4 rows.

Diagonal Openwork
Multiple of 4 sts + 2
Drape: excellent
Skill: intermediate

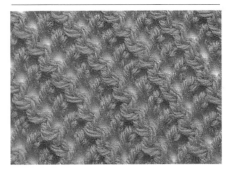

1ST ROW (RS): ✷K1, yo, sl 1, k2tog, psso, yo; rep from ✷ to last 2 sts, k2.
2ND AND EVERY ALT ROW: Purl.
3RD ROW: K2, ✷yo, sl 1, k2tog, psso, yo, k1; rep from ✷ to end.
5TH ROW: K2tog, yo, k1, yo, ✷sl 1, k2tog, psso, yo, k1, yo; rep from ✷ to last 3 sts, sl 1, k1, psso, k1.
7TH ROW: K1, k2tog, yo, k1, yo, ✷sl 1, k2tog, psso, yo, k1, yo; rep from ✷ to last 2 sts, sl 1, k1, psso.
8TH ROW: Purl.
Rep these 8 rows.

Mesh Zigzag Stitch
Multiple of 11 sts
Drape: excellent
Skill: experienced

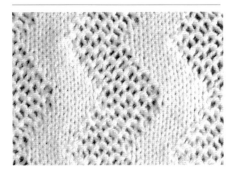

Special Abbreviation
KW5 = knit 5 sts wrapping yarn twice around needle for each st.

1ST ROW (RS): K1, KW5 (see Special Abbreviation), ✳k6, KW5; rep from ✳ to last 5 sts, k5.
2ND ROW: P5, k5 dropping extra loops, ✳p6, k5 dropping extra loops; rep from ✳ to last st, p1.
3RD ROW: K2, KW5, ✳k6, KW5; rep from ✳ to last 4 sts, k4.
4TH ROW: P4, k5 dropping extra loops, ✳p6, k5 dropping extra loops; rep from ✳ to last 2 sts, p2.
5TH ROW: K3, KW5, ✳k6, KW5; rep from ✳ to last 3 sts, k3.
6TH ROW: P3, k5 dropping extra loops, ✳p6, k5 dropping extra loops; rep from ✳ to last 3 sts, p3.
7TH ROW: K4, KW5, ✳k6, KW5; rep from ✳ to last 2 sts, k2.
8TH ROW: P2, k5 dropping extra loops, ✳p6, k5 dropping extra loops; rep from ✳ to last 4 sts, p4.
9TH ROW: K5, KW5, ✳k6, KW5; rep from ✳ to last st, k1.
10TH ROW: P1, k5 dropping extra loops, ✳p6, k5 dropping extra loops; rep from ✳ to last 5 sts, p5.
11TH ROW: As 7th row.
12TH ROW: As 8th row.
13TH ROW: As 5th row.
14TH ROW: As 6th row.
15TH ROW: As 3rd row.
16TH ROW: As 4th row.
17TH ROW: As 1st row.
18TH ROW: As 2nd row. Rep these 18 rows.

Lacy Rib
Multiple of 3 sts + 1
Drape: excellent
Skill: intermediate

1ST ROW (RS): K1, ✳k2tog, yo, p1; rep from ✳ to last 3 sts, k2tog, yo, k1.
2ND ROW: P3, ✳k1, p2; rep from ✳ to last 4 sts, k1, p3.
3RD ROW: K1, yo, sl 1, k1, psso, ✳p1, sl 1, yo, k1, psso; rep from ✳ to last st, k1.
4TH ROW: As 2nd row.
Rep these 4 rows.

Fancy Openwork
Multiple of 4 sts
Drape: excellent
Skill: intermediate
Note: Sts should only be counted after the 2nd and 4th rows.

1ST ROW (RS): K2, ✳yo, k4; rep from ✳ to last 2 sts, yo, k2.
2ND ROW: P2tog, ✳[k1, p1] into the yo of previous row, [p2tog] twice; rep from ✳ to last 3 sts, [k1, p1] into the yo, p2tog.
3RD ROW: K4, ✳yo, k4; rep from ✳ to end.
4TH ROW: P2, p2tog, ✳[k1, p1] into the yo of previous row, [p2tog] twice; rep from ✳ to last 5 sts, [k1, p1] into the yo, p2tog, p2
Rep these 4 rows.

Ridged Openwork
Multiple of 2 sts + 1
Drape: excellent
Skill: intermediate
Note: Sts should only be counted after the 1st, 3rd, or 4th rows of this pattern.

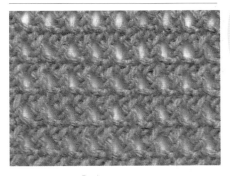

1ST ROW (RS): Purl.
2ND ROW: ✳P2tog; rep from ✳ to last st, P1.
3RD ROW: P1, ✳purl through horizontal strand of yarn lying between stitch just worked and next st, p1; rep from ✳ to end.
4TH ROW: P1, ✳yo, p2tog; rep from ✳ to end.
Rep these 4 rows.

small-scale lace patterns

More ambitious than eyelet patterns (*pages 100–101*), these stitches are more open and also more textured—the texture being produced by the numerous decreases, which raise the surface of the knitting. The multiples (*page 17*) are still quite small, which makes these patterns easy to design with. Before planning your design, make a gauge swatch and then block the swatch (*page 29*) in order to make accurate calculations for the finished pieces.

Lacy Lattice Stitch
Multiple of 6 sts + 1
Drape: excellent
Skill: intermediate

1ST ROW (RS): K1, ✳yo, p1, p3tog, p1, yo, k1; rep from ✳ to end.
2ND AND EVERY ALT ROW: Purl.
3RD ROW: K2, yo, sl 1, k2tog, psso, yo, ✳k3, yo, sl 1, k2tog, psso, yo; rep from ✳ to last 2 sts, k2.
5TH ROW: P2tog, p1, yo, k1, yo, p1, ✳p3tog, p1, yo, k1, yo, p1; rep from ✳ to last 2 sts, p2tog.
7TH ROW: K2tog, yo, k3, yo, ✳sl 1, k2tog, psso, yo, k3, yo; rep from ✳ to last 2 sts, sl 1, k1, psso.
8TH ROW: Purl.
Rep these 8 rows.

Lattice Lace
Multiple of 7 sts + 2
Drape: excellent
Skill: intermediate

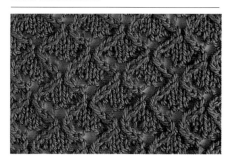

1ST ROW (RS): K3, ✳k2tog, yo, k5; rep from ✳ to last 6 sts, k2tog, yo, k4.
2ND ROW: P2, ✳p2tog tbl, yo, p1, yo, p2tog, p2; rep from ✳ to end.
3RD ROW: K1, ✳k2tog, yo, k3, yo, sl 1, k1, psso; rep from ✳ to last st, k1.
4TH ROW: Purl.
5TH ROW: K1, ✳yo, sl 1, k1, psso, k5; rep from ✳ to last st, k1.
6TH ROW: ✳P1, yo, p2tog, p2, p2tog tbl, yo; rep from ✳ to last 2 sts, p2.
7TH ROW: ✳K3, yo, sl 1, k1, psso, k2tog, yo; rep from ✳ to last 2 sts, k2.
8TH ROW: Purl.
Rep these 8 rows.

Snowflakes I
Multiple of 8 sts + 7
Drape: excellent
Skill: intermediate

1ST AND EVERY ALT ROW (WS): Purl.
2ND ROW: k5, sl 1, k1, psso, yo, k1, yo, k2tog, ✳k3, sl 1, k1, psso, yo, k1, yo, k2tog; rep from ✳ to last 5 sts, k5.
4TH ROW: K6, yo, sl 2, k1, p2sso, yo, ✳k5, yo, sl 2, k1, p2sso, yo; rep from ✳ to last 6 sts, k6.
6TH ROW: As 2nd row.
8TH ROW: K1, sl 1, k1, psso, yo, k1, yo, k2tog, ✳k3, sl 1, k1, psso, yo, k1, yo, k2tog; rep from ✳ to last st, k1.
10TH ROW: K2, yo, sl 2, k1, p2sso, yo, ✳k5, yo, sl 2, k1, p2sso, yo; rep from ✳ to last 2 sts, k2.
12TH ROW: As 8th row.
Rep these 12 rows.

Little Shell Pattern
Multiple of 7 sts + 2
Drape: excellent
Skill: intermediate

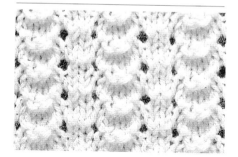

1ST ROW (RS): Knit.
2ND ROW: Purl.
3RD ROW: K2, ✳yo, p1, p3tog, p1, yo, k2;
rep from ✳ to end.
4TH ROW: Purl.
Rep these 4 rows.

Snowflakes II
Multiple of 6 sts + 1
Drape: excellent
Skill: intermediate
Note: Sts should not be counted after
3rd, 4th, 9th, and 10th rows.

1ST ROW (RS): K1, ✳yo, sl 1, k1, psso, k1,
k2tog, yo, k1; rep from ✳ to end.
2ND AND EVERY ALT TWO: Purl.
3RD ROW: K2, yo, ✳k3, yo; rep from ✳ to
last 2 sts, k2.
5TH ROW: K2tog, yo, sl 1, k1, psso, k1,
k2tog, yo, ✳sl 1, k2tog, psso, yo, sl 1, k1,
psso, k1, k2tog, yo; rep from ✳ to last

2 sts, sl 1, k1, psso.
7TH ROW: K1, ✳k2tog, yo, k1, yo, sl 1, k1,
psso, k1; rep from ✳ to end.
9TH ROW: As 3rd row.
11TH ROW: K1, ✳k2tog, yo, sl 1, k2tog,
psso, yo, sl 1, k1, psso, k1; rep from ✳ to
end.
12TH ROW: Purl.
Rep these 12 rows.

Feather Lace
Multiple of 6 sts + 1
Drape: excellent
Skill: intermediate

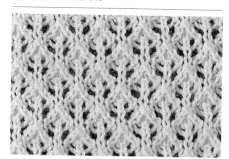

1ST ROW (RS): K1, ✳yo, k2tog tbl, k1,
k2tog, yo, k1; rep from ✳ to end.
2ND AND EVERY ALT ROW: Purl.
3RD ROW: K1, ✳yo, k1, sl 1, k2tog, psso,
k1, yo, k1; rep from ✳ to end.
5TH ROW: K1, ✳k2tog, yo, k1, yo, k2tog
tbl, k1; rep from ✳ to end.
7TH ROW: K2tog, ✳[k1, yo] twice, k1, sl 1,
k2tog, psso; rep from ✳ to last 5 sts,
[k1, yo] twice, k1, k2tog tbl.
8TH ROW: Purl.
Rep these 8 rows.

Eyelet Check
Multiple of 8 sts + 7
Drape: excellent
Skill: intermediate

1ST ROW (RS): K2, ✳p3, k5; rep from ✳ to
last 5 sts, p3, k2.
2ND ROW: P2, ✳k3, p5; rep from ✳ to last

5 sts, k3, p2.
3RD ROW: K2, ✳p1, yo, p2tog, k5; rep
from ✳ to last 5 sts, p1, yo, p2tog, k2.
4TH ROW: As 2nd row.
5TH ROW: As 1st row.
6TH ROW: Purl.
7TH ROW: K6, ✳p3, k5; rep from ✳ to last
9 sts, p3, k6.
8TH ROW: P6, ✳k3, p5; rep from ✳ to last
9 sts, k3, p6.
9TH ROW: K6, ✳p1, yo, p2tog, k5; rep from
✳ to last 9 sts, p1, yo, p2tog, k6.
10TH ROW: As 8th row.
11TH ROW: K6, ✳p3, k5; rep from ✳ to
last 9 sts, p3, k6.
12TH ROW: Purl.
Rep these 12 rows.

Lacy Checks
Multiple of 6 sts + 5
Drape: excellent
Skill: intermediate

1ST ROW (RS): K1, ✳yo, sl 1, k2tog, psso,
yo, k3; rep from ✳ to last 4 sts, yo, sl 1,
k2tog, psso, yo, k1.
2ND AND EVERY ALT ROW: Purl.

3RD ROW: As 1st row.
5TH ROW: Knit.
7TH ROW: K4, ✳yo, sl 1, k2tog, psso, yo, k3; rep from ✳ to last st, k1.
9TH ROW: As 7th row.
11TH ROW: Knit.
12TH ROW: Purl.
Rep these 12 rows.

Horizontal Leaf Pattern

Multiple of 3 sts
Drape: excellent
Skill: intermediate

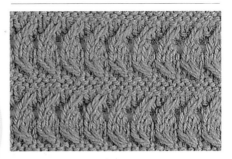

1ST ROW (RS): K2, ✳sl 1 purlwise, k2; rep from ✳ to last st, k1.
2ND ROW: P3, ✳sl 1 purlwse, p2; rep from ✳ to end.
3RD ROW: K2, ✳C3L; rep from ✳ to last st, k1.
4TH ROW: Purl.
5TH ROW: K2, ✳yo, k2tog, k1; rep from ✳ to last st, k1.
6TH ROW: Purl.
7TH ROW: K4, ✳sl 1 purlwise, k2; rep from ✳ to last 2 sts, sl 1 purlwise, k1.
8TH ROW: P1, ✳sl 1 purlwise, p2; rep from ✳ to last 2 sts, p2.
9TH ROW: K2, ✳C3R; rep from ✳ to last st, k1.
10TH ROW: Knit.
11TH ROW: Purl.
12TH ROW: Purl.
Rep these 12 rows.

Twisted Openwork Pattern I

Multiple of 4 sts + 1
Drape: excellent
Skill: intermediate

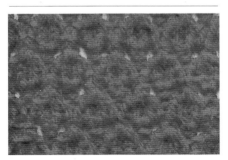

1ST ROW (RS): P1, ✳k3, p1; rep from ✳ to end.
2ND ROW: K1, ✳p3, k1; rep from ✳ to end.
3RD ROW: As 1st row.
4TH ROW: K1, ✳yo, p3tog, yo, k1; rep from ✳ to end.
5TH ROW: K2, p1, ✳k3, p1; rep from ✳ to last 2 sts, k2.
6TH ROW: P2, k1, ✳p3, k1; rep from ✳ to last 2 sts, p2.
7TH ROW: As 5th row.
8TH ROW: P2tog, yo, k1, yo, ✳p3tog, yo, k1, yo; rep from ✳ to last 2 sts, p2tog.
Rep these 8 rows.

Twisted Openwork Pattern II

Multiple of 4 sts + 1
Drape: excellent
Skill: intermediate

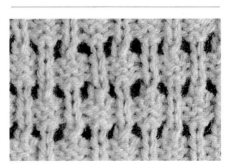

Worked as Twisted Openwork Pattern I, using reverse side as right side.

Trellis Lace

Multiple of 6 sts + 5
Drape: excellent
Skill: intermediate

1ST ROW (RS): K4, ✳yo, sl 1, k2tog, psso, yo, k3; rep from ✳ to last st, k1.
2ND ROW: Purl.
3RD ROW: K1, ✳yo, sl 1, k2tog, psso, yo, k3; rep from ✳ to last 4 sts, yo, sl 1, k2tog, psso, yo, k1.
4TH ROW: Purl.
Rep these 4 rows.

Bell Lace

Multiple of 8 sts + 3
Drape: excellent
Skill: intermediate

1ST ROW (RS): K1, p1, k1, ✳p1, yo, sl 1, k2tog, psso, yo, [p1, k1] twice; rep from ✳ to end.

2ND ROW: P1, k1, p1, ✳k1, p3, [k1, p1] twice; rep from ✳ to end.
Rep last 2 rows twice more.

7TH ROW: K1, k2tog, ✳yo, [p1, k1] twice, p1, yo, sl 1, k2tog, psso; rep from ✳ to last 8 sts, yo, [p1, k1] twice, p1, yo, sl 1, k1, psso, k1.

8TH ROW: P3, ✳[k1, p1] twice, k1, p3; rep from ✳ to end. Rep the last 2 rows twice more. Rep these 12 rows.

Canterbury Bells
Multiple of 5 sts
Drape: excellent
Skill: intermediate
Note: Sts should only be counted after the 1st, 2nd, and 10th rows.

1ST ROW (RS): P2, k1 tbl, ✳p4, k1 tbl; rep from ✳ to last 2 sts, p2.

2ND ROW: K2, p1 tbl, ✳k4, p1 tbl; rep from ✳ to last 2 sts, k2.

3RD ROW: P2, k1 tbl, ✳p2, turn, cast on 8 sts cable method (see page 13), turn, p2, k1 tbl; rep from ✳ to last 2 sts, p2.

4TH ROW: K2, p1 tbl, ✳k2, p8, k2, p1 tbl; rep from ✳ to last 2 sts, k2.

5TH ROW: P2, k1 tbl, ✳p2, k8, p2, k1 tbl; rep from ✳ to last 2 sts, p2.

6TH ROW: As 4th row.

7TH ROW: P2, k1 tbl, ✳p2, yb, sl 1, k1, psso, k4, k2tog, p2, k1 tbl; rep from ✳ to last 2 sts, p2.

8TH ROW: K2, p1 tbl, ✳k2, p2tog, p2, p2tog tbl, k2, p1 tbl; rep from ✳ to last 2 sts, k2.

9TH ROW: P2, k1 tbl, ✳p2, yb, sl 1, k1, psso, k2tog, p2, k1 tbl; rep from ✳ to last 2 sts, p2.

10TH ROW: K2, p1 tbl, ✳k1, sl 1, k1, psso, k2tog, k1, p1 tbl; rep from ✳ to last 2 sts, k2. Rep these 10 rows.

Raindrops
Multiple of 6 sts + 5
Drape: excellent
Skill: intermediate

1ST ROW (RS): P5, ✳yo, p2tog, p4; rep from ✳ to end.

2ND ROW: K5, ✳p1, k5; rep from ✳ to end.

3RD ROW: P5, ✳k1, p5; rep from ✳ to end.
Rep the last 2 rows once more, then the 2nd row again.

7TH ROW: P2, yo, p2tog, ✳p4, yo, p2tog; rep from ✳ to last st, p1.

8TH ROW: K2, p1, ✳k5, p1; rep from ✳ to last 2 sts, k2.

9TH ROW: P2, k1, ✳p5, k1; rep from ✳ to last 2 sts, p2.
Rep the last 2 rows once more, then the 8th row again.
Rep these 12 rows.

Snowdrop Lace
Multiple of 8 sts + 5
Drape: excellent
Skill: intermediate

1ST ROW (RS): K1, ✳yo, sl 1 purlwise, k2tog, psso, yo, k5; rep from ✳ to last 4 sts, yo, sl 1 purlwise, k2tog, psso, yo, k1.

2ND AND EVERY ALT ROW: Purl.

3RD ROW: As 1st row.

5TH ROW: K4, ✳yo, sl 1 purlwise, k1, psso, k1, k2tog, yo, k3; rep from ✳ to last st, k1.

7TH ROW: K1, ✳yo, sl 1 purlwise, k2tog, psso, yo, k1; rep from ✳ to end.

8TH ROW: Purl.
Rep these 8 rows.

Alternating Lace
Multiple of 6 sts + 5
Drape: excellent
Skill: intermediate

1ST ROW (RS): K1, ✳yo, sl 1, k2tog, psso, yo, k3; rep from ✳ to last 4 sts, yo, sl 1, k2tog, psso, yo, k1.

2ND ROW: Purl.
Rep the last 2 rows 3 times more.

9TH ROW: K4, ✳yo, sl 1, k2tog, psso, yo, k3; rep from ✳ to last st, k1.

10TH ROW: Purl.
Rep the last 2 rows 3 times more.
Rep these 16 rows.

Trellis Pattern

Multiple of 4 sts + 2
Drape: excellent
Skill: intermediate

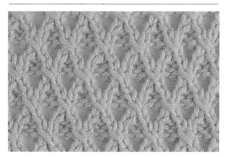

1ST ROW (RS): K1, yo, ✳sl 1, k1, psso, k2tog, yo twice (2 sts made); rep from ✳ to last 5 sts, sl 1, k1, psso, k2tog, yo, k1.
2ND ROW: K2, p2, ✳k into front of first loop of double yo, then k into back of 2nd loop, p2; rep from ✳ to last 2 sts, k2.
3RD ROW: K1, p1, ✳C2F, p2; rep from ✳ to last 4 sts, C2F, p1 , k1.
4TH ROW: K2, ✳p2, k2; rep from ✳ to end.
5TH ROW: K1, k2tog, ✳ yo twice, sl 1, k1, psso, k2tog; rep from ✳ to last 3 sts, yo twice, sl 1, k1, psso, k1.
6TH ROW: K1, p1, k into front of first loop of double yo, then k into back of 2nd loop, ✳p2, work into double yo as before; rep from ✳ to last 2 sts, p1, k1.
7TH ROW: K2, ✳p2, C2F; rep from ✳ to last 4 sts, p2, k2.
8TH ROW: K1, p1, k2, ✳p2, k2; rep from ✳ to last 2 sts, p1, k1.
Rep these 8 rows.

Eyelet Panes

Multiple of 6 sts + 3
Drape: excellent
Skill: intermediate
Note: Sts should not be counted after the 3rd, 4th, 9th, and 10th rows.

1ST ROW (RS): K2, ✳yo, sl 1, k1, psso, k1, k2tog, yo, k1; rep from ✳ to last st, k1.
2ND AND EVERY ALT ROW: Purl.
3RD ROW: K3, ✳yo, k3; rep from ✳ to end.

5TH ROW: K1, k2tog, ✳yo, sl 1, k1, psso, k1, k2tog, yo, sl 1, k2tog, psso; rep from ✳ to last 8 sts, yo, sl 1, k1, psso, k1, k2tog, yo, sl 1, k1, psso, k1.
7TH ROW: K2, ✳k2tog, yo, k1, yo, sl 1, k1, psso, k1; rep from ✳ to last st, k1.
9TH ROW: As 3rd row.
11TH ROW: K2, ✳k2tog, yo, sl 1, k2tog, psso, yo, sl 1, k1, psso, k1; rep from ✳ to last st, k1.
12TH ROW: Purl.
Rep these 12 rows.

Diamond Lace

Multiple of 6 sts + 3
Drape: excellent
Skill: intermediate

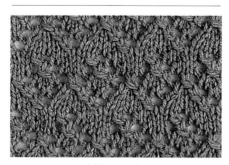

1ST ROW (RS): ✳K4, yo, sl 1, k1, psso; rep from ✳ to last 3 sts, k3.
2ND AND EVERY ALT ROW: Purl.
3RD ROW: K2, ✳k2tog, yo, k1, yo, sl 1, k1, psso, k1; rep from ✳ to last st, k1.
5TH ROW: K1, k2tog, yo, ✳k3, yo, sl 1, k2tog, psso, yo; rep from ✳ to last 6 sts, k3, yo, sl 1, k1, psso, k1.
7TH ROW: K3, ✳yo, sl 1, k2tog, psso, yo,

k3; rep from ✳ to end.
9TH ROW: As 1st row.
11TH ROW: K1, ✳yo, sl 1, k1, psso, k4; rep from ✳ to last 2 sts, yo, sl 1, k1, psso.
13TH ROW: K2, ✳yo, sl 1, k1, psso, k1, k2tog, yo, k1; rep from ✳ to last st, k1.
15TH ROW: As 7th row.
17TH ROW: As 5th row.
19TH ROW: As 11th row.
20TH ROW: Purl.
Rep these 20 rows.

Lacy Diamonds

Multiple of 6 sts + 1
Drape: excellent
Skill: intermediate

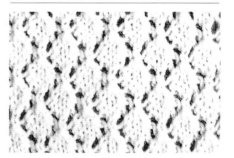

1ST ROW (RS): ✳K1, k2tog, yo, k1, yo, k2tog tbl; rep from ✳ to last st, k1.
2ND AND EVERY ALT ROW: Purl.
3RD ROW: K2tog, ✳yo, k3, yo, [sl 1] twice, k1, p2sso; rep from ✳ to last 5 sts, yo, k3, yo, k2tog tbl.
5TH ROW: ✳K1, yo, k2tog tbl, k1, k2tog, yo; rep from ✳ to last st, k1.
7TH ROW: K2, ✳yo, [sl 1] twice, k1, p2sso, yo, k3; rep from ✳ to last 5 sts, yo, [sl 1] twice, k1, p2sso, yo, k2.
8TH ROW: Purl.
Rep these 8 rows.

vertical and diagonal lace patterns

Some lace patterns have a directional quality which gives them a slightly more formal aspect than other lace stitches. Relatively solid patterns, such as Chevron and Feather (*page 113*), might be substituted for Stockinette stitch on the front and back of a plain pullover, giving it a little extra zing. (The number of stitches to cast on for these sections would need to be calculated: *see page 16*.) A few of the patterns incorporate cabling techniques, which give them additional textural interest.

Fishtail Lace
Multiple of 8 sts + 1
Drape: excellent
Skill: intermediate

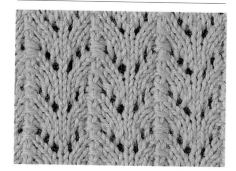

1ST ROW (RS): K1, ✳yo, k2, sl 1, k2tog, psso, k2, yo, k1; rep from ✳ to end.
2ND ROW: Purl.
3RD ROW: K2, ✳yo, k1, sl 1, k2tog, psso, k1, yo, k3; rep from ✳ to last 7 sts, yo, k1, sl 1, k2tog, psso, k1, yo, k2.
4TH ROW: Purl.
5TH ROW: K3, ✳yo, sl 1, k2tog, psso, yo, k5; rep from ✳ to last 6 sts, yo, sl 1, k2tog, psso, yo, k3.
6TH ROW: Purl.
Rep these 6 rows.

Herringbone Lace Rib
Multiple of 7 sts + 1
Drape: excellent
Skill: intermediate

1ST ROW (RS): K1, ✳p1, k1, yo, p2tog, k1, p1, k1; rep from ✳ to end.
2ND ROW: P1, ✳k2, yo, p2tog, k2, p1; rep from ✳ to end.
Rep these 2 rows.

Single Lace Rib
Multiple of 4 sts + 1
Drape: excellent
Skill: easy

1ST ROW (RS): K1, ✳yo, k2tog, p1, k1; rep from ✳ to end.
2ND ROW: P1, ✳yo, p2tog, k1, p1; rep from ✳ to end.
Rep these 2 rows.

lace patterns

Double Lace Rib

Multiple of 6 sts + 2
Drape: excellent
Skill: intermediate

1ST ROW (RS): K2, ✳p1, yo, k2tog tb11, p1, k2; rep from ✳ to end.
2ND ROW: P2, ✳k1, p2; rep from ✳ to end.
3RD ROW: K2, ✳p1, k2tog, yo, p1, k2; rep from ✳ to end.
4TH ROW: As 2nd row.
Rep these 4 rows.

Leafy Lace

Multiple of 10 sts + 1
Drape: excellent
Skill: intermediate

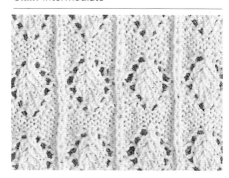

1ST ROW (RS): K1 tbl, ✳p9, k1 tbl; rep from ✳ to end.
2ND ROW: P1, ✳k9, p1; rep from ✳ to end.
Rep the last 2 rows once more.
5TH ROW: K1 tbl, ✳p2, p2tog, yo, k1 tbl,

yo, p2tog, p2, k1 tbl; rep from ✳ to end.
6TH ROW: P1, ✳k4, p1 tbl, k4, p1; rep from ✳ to end.
7TH ROW: K1 tbl, ✳p1, p2tog, yo, [k1 tbl] 3 times, yo, p2tog, p1, k1 tbl; rep from ✳ to end.
8TH ROW: P1, ✳k3, [p1 tbl] 3 times, k3, p1; rep from ✳ to end.
9TH ROW: K1 tbl, ✳p2tog, yo, [k1 tbl] 5 times, yo, p2tog, k1 tbl; rep from ✳ to end.
10TH ROW: P1, ✳k2, [p1 tbl] 5 times, k2, p1; rep from ✳ to end.
11TH ROW: K1 tbl, ✳p1, yo, [k1 tbl] twice, sl 1, k2tog, psso, [k1 tbl] twice, yo, p1, k1 tbl; rep from ✳ to end.
12TH ROW: As 10th row.
13TH ROW: K1 tbl, ✳p2, yo, k1 tbl, sl 1, k2tog, psso, k1 tbl, yo, p2, k1 tbl; rep from ✳ to end.
14TH ROW: As 8th row.
15TH ROW: K1 tbl, ✳p3, yo, sl 1, k2tog, psso, yo, p3, k1 tbl; rep from ✳ to end.
16TH ROW: As 6th row.
Rep these 16 rows.

Bluebell Ribs

Multiple of 5 sts + 2
Drape: excellent
Skill: intermediate

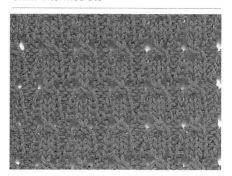

1ST ROW (RS): P2, ✳k3, p2; rep from ✳ to end.
2ND ROW: K2, ✳p3, k2; rep from ✳ to end.
Rep the last 2 rows once more.
5TH ROW: P2, ✳yo, sl 1, k2tog, psso, yo, p2; rep from ✳ to end.

6TH ROW: As 2nd row. Rep these 6 rows.

Little Fountain Pattern

Multiple of 4 sts + 1
Drape: excellent
Skill: intermediate
Note: Sts should only be counted after the 3rd and 4th rows.

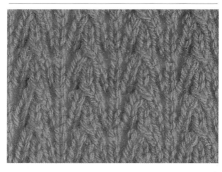

1ST ROW (RS): K1, ✳yo, k3, yo, k1; rep from ✳ to end.
2ND ROW: Purl.
3RD ROW: K2, sl 1, k2tog, psso, ✳k3, sl 1, k2tog, psso; rep from ✳ to last 2 sts, k2.
4TH ROW: Purl. Rep these 4 rows.

Diamond Rib

Multiple of 9 sts + 2
Drape: excellent
Skill: intermediate

1ST ROW (RS): P2, ✳k2tog, [k1, yo] twice, k1, sl 1, k1, psso, p2; rep from ✳ to end.

lace patterns

2ND AND EVERY ALT ROW: K2, ✳p7, k2; rep from ✳ to end.
3RD ROW: P2, ✳k2tog, yo, k3, yo, sl 1, k1, psso, p2; rep from ✳ to end.
5TH ROW: P2, ✳k1, yo, sl 1, k1, psso, k1, k2tog, yo, k1, p2; rep from ✳ to end.
7TH ROW: P2, ✳k2, yo, sl 1, k2tog, psso, yo, k2, p2; rep from ✳ to end.
8TH ROW: As 2nd row.
Rep these 8 rows.

Ridged Lace
Multiple of 2 sts
Drape: excellent
Skill: intermediate

1ST ROW (RS): K1, ✳yo, k2tog tbl; rep from ✳ to last st, k1.
2ND ROW: P1, ✳yo, p2tog; rep from ✳ to last st, p1.
Rep these 2 rows.

Waterfall Pattern
Multiple of 6 sts + 3
Drape: excellent
Skill: intermediate
Note: Sts should only be counted after the 4th, 5th, and 6th rows.

1ST ROW (RS): P3, ✳k3, yo, p3; rep from ✳ to end.
2ND ROW: K3, ✳p4, k3; rep from ✳ to end.
3RD ROW: P3, ✳k1, k2tog, yo, k1, p3; rep from ✳ to end.
4TH ROW: K3, ✳p2, p2tog, k3; rep from ✳

to end.
5TH ROW: P3, ✳k1, yo, k2tog, p3; rep from ✳ to end.
6TH ROW: K3, ✳p3, k3; rep from ✳ to end.
Rep these 6 rows.

Chevron Rib
Multiple of 7 sts + 2
Drape: excellent
Skill: intermediate

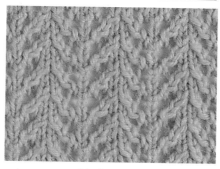

1ST ROW (RS): K2, ✳k2tog, yo, k1, yo, sl 1, k1, psso, k2; rep from ✳ to end.
2ND ROW: Purl.
3RD ROW: K1, ✳k2tog, yo, k3, yo, sl 1, k1, psso; rep from ✳ to last st, k1.
4TH ROW: Purl.
Rep these 4 rows.

Fuchsia Stitch
Multiple of 6 sts
Drape: good
Skill: intermediate

Note: Sts should only be counted after the 11th and 12th rows.

1ST ROW (RS): P2, ✳k2, yo, p4; rep from ✳ to last 4 sts, k2, yo, p2.
2ND ROW: K2, ✳p3, K4; rep from ✳ to last 5 sts, p3, k2.
3RD ROW: P2, ✳k3, yo, p4; rep from ✳ to last 5 sts, k3, yo, p2.
4TH ROW: K2, ✳p4, k4; rep from ✳ to last 6 sts, p4, k2.
5TH ROW: P2, ✳k4, yo, p4; rep from ✳ to last 6 sts, k4, yo, p2.
6TH ROW: K2, ✳p5, k4; rep from ✳ to last 7 sts, p5, k2.
7TH ROW: P2, ✳k3, k2tog, p4; rep from ✳ to last 7 sts, k3, k2tog, p2.
8TH ROW: As 4th row.
9TH ROW: P2, ✳k2, k2tog, p4; rep from ✳ to last 6 sts, k2, k2tog, p2.
10TH ROW: As 2nd row.
11TH ROW: P2, ✳k1, k2tog, p4; rep from ✳ to last 5 sts, k1, k2tog, p2.
12TH ROW: K2, ✳p2, k4; rep from ✳ to last 4 sts, p2, k2.
Rep these 12 rows.

Fern Lace
Multiple of 9 sts + 4
Drape: excellent
Skill: intermediate

1ST ROW (WS): Purl.
2ND ROW: K3, ✳yo, k2, sl 1, k1, psso, k2tog, k2, yo, k1; rep from ✳ to last st, k1.
3RD ROW: Purl.
4TH ROW: K2, ✳yo, k2, sl 1, k1, psso, k2tog, k2, yo, k1; rep from ✳ to last 2 sts,

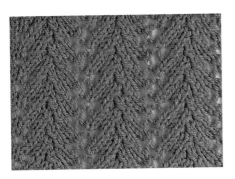

k2. Rep these 4 rows.

Lacy Zigzag
Multiple of 6 sts + 1
Drape: excellent
Skill: intermediate

1ST ROW (RS): ❋Sl 1, k1, psso, k2, yo, k2; rep from ❋ to last st, k1.
2ND ROW: Purl.
Rep the last 2 rows twice more.
7TH ROW: K3, ❋yo, k2, k2tog, k2; rep from ❋ to last 4 sts, yo, k2, k2tog.
8TH ROW: Purl.
Rep the last 2 rows twice more.
Rep these 12 rows.

Arrowhead Lace
Multiple of 10 sts + 1
Drape: excellent
Skill: intermediate

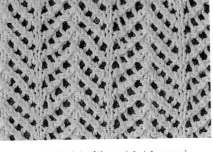

1ST ROW (RS): k1, ❋[yo, sl 1, k1, psso] twice, k1, [k2tog, yo] twice, k1; rep from ❋ to end.
2ND ROW: Purl.
3RD ROW: K2, ❋yo, sl 1, k1, psso, yo, sl 1, k2tog, psso, yo, k2tog, yo, k3; rep from ❋ to last 9 sts, yo, sl 1, k1, psso, yo, sl 1, k2tog, psso, yo, k2tog, yo, k2.
4TH ROW: Purl.
Rep these 4 rows.

Little Arrowhead
Multiple of 6 sts + 1
Drape: excellent
Skill: intermediate

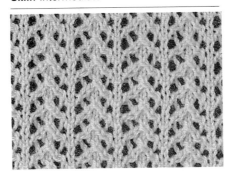

1ST ROW (RS): K1, ❋yo, sl 1, k1, psso, k1, k2tog, yo, k1; rep from ❋ to end.
2ND ROW: Purl.
3RD ROW: K2, ❋yo, sl 1, k2tog, psso, yo, k3; rep from ❋ to last 5 sts, yo, sl 1, k2tog, psso, yo, k2.
4TH ROW: Purl. Rep these 4 rows.

Purse Stitch
Multiple of 2 sts
Drape: excellent
Skill: easy

1ST ROW: P1, ❋yo, p2tog; rep from ❋ to last st, p1.
Rep this row.

Feather Openwork
Multiple of 5 sts + 2
Drape: excellent
Skill: easy

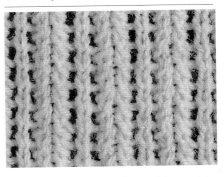

1ST ROW (RS): K1, ❋k2tog, yo, k1, yo, sl 1, k1, psso; rep from ❋ to last st, k1.
2ND ROW: Purl.
Rep these 2 rows.

Lacy Openwork
Multiple of 4 sts + 1
Drape: excellent
Skill: intermediate

1ST ROW: K1, ✳yo, p3tog, yo, k1; rep from
✳ to end.
2ND ROW: P2tog, yo, k1, yo, ✳p3tog,
yo, k1, yo; rep from ✳ to last 2 sts,
p2tog.
Rep these 2 rows.

Chevron and Feather
Multiple of 13 sts + 1
Drape: excellent
Skill: easy

1ST ROW (RS): ✳K1, yo, k4, k2tog, sl 1, k1,
psso, k4, yo; rep from ✳ to last st, k1.
2ND ROW: Purl.
Rep these 2 rows.

Alternating Feather Openwork
Multiple of 6 sts + 1
Drape: excellent
Skill: intermediate

1ST ROW (RS): K1, ✳k2tog, yo, k1, yo, sl 1,

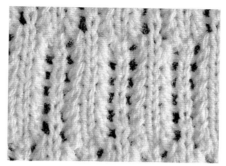

k1, psso, k1; rep from ✳ to end.
2ND ROW: Purl.
Rep these 2 rows 5 times more.
13TH ROW: K1, ✳yo, sl 1, k1, psso, k1,
k2tog, yo, k1; rep from ✳ to end.
14TH ROW: Purl.
Rep the last 2 rows 5 times more.
Rep these 24 rows.

Gate and Ladder Pattern
Multiple of 9 sts + 3
Drape: excellent
Skill: intermediate

FOUNDATION ROW (WS): Purl.
Commence Pattern
1ST ROW: K1, k2tog, k3, yo twice, k3,
✳k3tog, k3, yo twice, k3; rep from ✳ to
last 3 sts, k2tog, k1.
2ND ROW: P6, k1, ✳p8, k1; rep from ✳ to
last 5 sts, p5.
Rep the last 2 rows.

Bead Stitch
Multiple of 7 sts
Drape: good
Skill: intermediate

1ST ROW (RS): K1, k2tog, yo, k1, yo, sl 1,
k1, psso, ✳k2, k2tog, yo, k1, yo, sl 1, k1,
psso; rep from ✳ to last st, k1.
2ND ROW: ✳P2tog tbl, yo, p3, yo, p2tog;
rep from ✳ to end.
3RD ROW: K1, yo, sl 1, k1, psso, k1, k2tog,
yo, ✳k2, yo, sl 1, k1, psso, k1, k2tog, yo;
rep from ✳ to last st, k1.
4TH ROW: P2, yo, p3tog, yo, ✳p4, yo,
p3tog, yo; rep from ✳ to last 2 sts, p2.
Rep these 4 rows.

Lace and Cables
Multiple of 11 sts + 7
Drape: excellent
Skill: intermediate

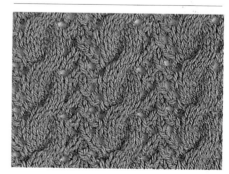

1ST ROW (RS): K1, ✳yo, sl 1, k1, psso, k1,
k2tog, yo, k6; rep from ✳ to last 6 sts, yo,
sl 1, k1, psso, k1, k2tog, yo, k1.

2ND AND EVERY ALT ROW: Purl.

3RD ROW: K2, ✳yo, sl 1, k2tog, psso, yo, k8; rep from ✳ to last 5 sts, yo, sl 1, k2tog, psso, yo, k2.

5TH ROW: As 1st row.

7TH ROW: K2, ✳yo, sl 1, k2tog, psso, yo, k1, C6B, k1; rep from ✳ to last 5 sts, yo, sl 1, k2tog, psso, yo, k2.

8TH ROW: Purl.

Rep these 8 rows.

Vertical Ripple Stripes

Multiple of 4 sts + 3
Drape: excellent
Skill: experienced
Note: Do not count yo and sts resulting from yo as a stitch.

1ST FOUNDATION ROW (RS): K3, ✳yo, k4; rep from ✳ to end.

2ND, 3RD AND 4TH FOUNDATION ROWS: Work 3 rows in St st, starting purl.

Commence Pattern

1ST ROW: ✳K5, yo; rep from ✳ to last 3 sts, k3.

2ND AND EVERY ALT ROW: Purl.

3RD ROW: K3, ✳slip next st off left-hand needle and allow it to drop down to the loop made 6 rows below, k5; rep from ✳ to end.

5TH ROW: K3, ✳yo, k5; rep from ✳ to end.

7TH ROW: ✳K5, slip next st off left-hand needle as before; rep from ✳ to last 3 sts, k3.

8TH ROW: Purl.

Rep the last 8 rows.

Snowshoe Pattern

Multiple of 8 sts + 4
Drape: excellent
Skill: experienced
Note: Sts should only be counted after the 8th, 9th, 10th, 18th, 19th, and 20th rows.

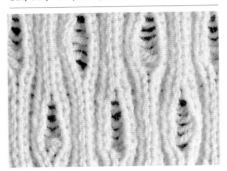

1ST ROW (RS): K2, M1, ✳k1, p2, k2, p2, k1, M1; rep from ✳ to last 2 sts, k2.

2ND ROW: P4, k2, p2, k2, ✳p3, k2, p2, k2; rep from ✳ to last 4 sts, p4.

3RD ROW: K4, p2, k2, p2, ✳k3, p2, k2, p2; rep from ✳ to last 4 sts, k4.

Rep the last 2 rows twice more.

8TH ROW: P2, drop next st down 7 rows, ✳p1, k2, p2, k2, p1, drop next st down 7 rows; rep from ✳ to last 2 sts, p2.

9TH ROW: K3, p2, ✳k2, p2; rep from ✳ to last 3 sts, k3.

10TH ROW: P3, k2, ✳p2, k2; rep from ✳ to last 3 sts, p3.

11TH ROW: K3, p2, k1, M1, k1, p2, ✳k2, p2, k1, M1, k1, p2; rep from ✳ to last 3 sts, k3.

12TH ROW: P3, k2, p3, k2, ✳p2, k2, p3, k2; rep from ✳ to last 3 sts, p3.

13TH ROW: K3, p2, k3, p2, ✳k2, p2, k3, p2; rep from ✳ to last 3 sts, k3.

Rep the last 2 rows twice more.

18TH ROW: P3, k2, p1, drop next st down 7 rows, p1, k2, ✳p2, k2, p1, drop next st down 7 rows, p1, k2; rep from ✳ to last 3 sts, p3.

19TH ROW: K3, p2, ✳k2, p2; rep from ✳ to last 3 sts, k3.

20TH ROW: P3, k2, ✳p2, k2; rep from ✳ to last 3 sts, p3.

Rep these 20 rows.

Twist Cable and Ladder Lace

Multiple of 7 sts + 6
Drape: excellent
Skill: experienced

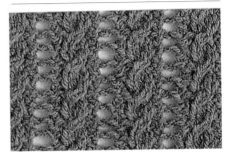

1ST ROW (RS): K1, ✳k2tog, yo twice, sl 1, k1, psso, k3; rep from ✳ to last 5 sts, k2tog, yo twice, sl 1, k1, psso, k1.

2ND ROW: K2, ✳[k1 tbl, k1] into double yo of previous row, k1, p3, k1; rep from ✳ to last 4 sts, [k1 tbl, k1] into double yo of previous row, k2.

3RD ROW: K1, ✳k2tog, yo twice, sl 1, k1, psso, knit into 3rd st on left-hand needle, then knit into 2nd st, then knit into 1st st, slipping all 3 sts on to right-hand needle tog; rep from ✳ to last 5 sts, k2tog, yo twice, sl 1, k1, psso, k1.

4TH ROW: As 2nd row.

Rep these 4 rows.

String of Beads

Multiple of 10 sts + 1
Drape: excellent
Skill: intermediate

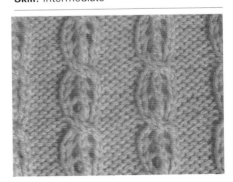

Special Abbreviation

C5F (CROSS 5 FRONT) = slip next 2 sts onto cable needle and hold at front of work, knit next 3 sts from left-hand needle, then knit sts from cable needle.

1ST AND EVERY ALT ROW (WS): K3, p5, ✳k5, p5; rep from ✳ to last 3 sts, k3.

2ND ROW: P3, C5F (see Special Abbreviation), ✳p5, C5F; rep from ✳ to last 3 sts, p3.

4TH, 6TH AND 8TH ROWS: P3, k1, yo, sl 2 tog knitwise, k1, p2sso, yo, k1, ✳p5, k1, yo, sl 2 tog knitwise, k1, p2sso, yo, k1; rep from ✳ to last 3 sts, p3.

Rep these 8 rows.

Lacy Chains

Multiple of 8 sts + 2
Drape: excellent
Skill: experienced

1ST AND EVERY ALT ROW (WS): K2, ✳p6, k2; rep from ✳ to end.

2ND ROW: P2, ✳k6, p2; rep from ✳ to end.

4TH ROW: P2, ✳C6B, p2; rep from ✳ to end.

6TH ROW: As 2nd row.

8TH ROW: P2, ✳k1, yo, k2tog, k3, p2; rep from ✳ to end.

10TH ROW: P2, ✳sl 1, k1, psso, yo, k4, p2; rep from ✳ to end.

12TH ROW: As 8th row.

14TH ROW: As 2nd row.

16TH ROW: As 4th row.

18TH ROW: As 2nd row.

20TH ROW: P2, ✳k3, sl 1, k1, psso, yo, k1, p2; rep from ✳ to end.

22ND ROW: P2, ✳k4, yo, k2tog, p2; rep from ✳ to end.

24TH ROW: As 20th row.
Rep these 24 rows.

Lacy Diagonals

Multiple of 10 sts + 2
Drape: excellent
Skill: intermediate

1ST ROW (RS): K7, sl 1, k1, psso, yo, k2tog, yo, ✳k6, sl 1, k1; psso, yo, k2tog, yo; rep from ✳ to last st, k1.

2ND AND EVERY ALT ROW: Purl.

3RD ROW: ✳K6, sl 1, k1, psso, yo, k2tog, yo; rep from ✳ to last 2 sts, k2.

5TH ROW: K5, sl 1, k1, psso, yo, k2tog, yo, ✳k6, sl 1, k1, psso, yo, k2tog, yo; rep from ✳ to last 3 sts, k3.

7TH ROW: K4, sl 1, k1, psso, yo, k2tog, yo, ✳k6, sl 1, k1, psso, yo, k2tog, yo; rep from ✳ to last 4 sts, k4.

9TH ROW: K3, sl 1, k1, psso, yo, k2tog, yo, ✳k6, sl 1, k1, psso, yo, k2tog, yo; rep from ✳ to last 5 sts, k5.

11TH ROW: K2, ✳sl 1, k1, psso, yo, k2tog, yo, k6; rep from ✳ to end.

13TH ROW: K1, sl 1, k1, psso, yo, k2tog, yo, ✳k6, sl 1, k1, psso, yo, k2tog, yo; rep from ✳ to last 7 sts, k7.

15TH ROW: Sl 1, k1, psso, yo, k2tog, yo, ✳k6, sl 1, k1, psso, yo, k2tog, yo; rep from ✳ to last 8 sts, k8.

17TH ROW: K1, ✳k2tog, yo, k6, sl 1, k1, psso, yo; rep from ✳ to last st, k1.

19TH ROW: ✳K2tog, yo, k6, sl 1, k1, psso, yo; rep from ✳ to last 2 sts, k2.

20TH ROW: Purl. Rep these 20 rows.

Slanting Eyelets

Multiple of 8 sts + 2
Drape: excellent
Skill: intermediate

1ST ROW (RS): K1, ✳yo, p2tog, k1, p2tog, yo, k3; rep from ✳ to last st, k1.

2ND ROW: K6, ✳p2tog, yo, k6; rep from ✳ to last 4 sts, p2tog, yo, k2.

3RD ROW: K3, ✳yo, p2tog, k1, p2tog, yo, k3; rep from ✳ to last 7 sts, yo, p2tog, k1, p2tog, yo, k2.

4TH ROW: K4, ✳p2tog, yo, k6; rep from ✳ to last 6 sts, p2tog, yo, k4.

5TH ROW: ✳P2tog, yo, k3, yo, p2tog, k1; rep from ✳ to last 2 sts, k2.

6TH ROW: K2, ✳p2tog, yo, k6; rep from ✳ to end.

7TH ROW: K2, ✳p2tog, yo, k3, yo, p2tog, k1; rep from ✳ to end.

8TH ROW: ✳P2tog, yo, k6; rep from ✳ to last 2 sts, k2.

Rep these 8 rows.

Diagonal Lace

Multiple of 8 sts + 4
Drape: excellent
Skill: intermediate

1ST ROW (RS): K2, ✳yo, sl 1, k1, psso, k1, k2tog, yo, k3; rep from ✳ to last 2 sts, k2.

2ND ROW: P7, ✳p2tog tbl, yo, p6; rep from ✳ to last 5 sts, p2tog tbl, yo, p3.

3RD ROW: K4, ✳yo, sl 1, k1, psso, k1, k2tog, yo, k3; rep from ✳ to end.

4TH ROW: P5, ✳p2tog tbl, yo, p6; rep from ✳ to last 7 sts, p2tog tbl, yo, p5.

lace patterns

5TH ROW: K1, ✳k2tog, yo, k3, yo, sl 1, k1, psso, k1; rep from ✳ to last 3 sts, k2tog, yo, k1.
6TH ROW: P3, ✳p2tog tbl, yo, p6; rep from ✳ to last st, p1.
7TH ROW: K3, ✳k2tog, yo, k3, yo, sl 1, k1, psso, k1; rep from ✳ to last st, k1.
8TH ROW: P1, ✳p2tog tbl, yo, p6; rep from ✳ to last 3 sts, p2tog tbl, yo, p1.
Rep these 8 rows.

Eyelet Chevron
Multiple of 12 sts + 1
Drape: excellent
Skill: intermediate

1ST ROW (RS): K4, ✳k2tog, yo, k1, yo, sl 1, k1, psso, k7; rep from ✳ to last 9 sts, k2tog, yo, k1, yo, sl 1, k1, psso, k4.
2ND AND EVERY ALT ROW: Purl.
3RD ROW: K3, ✳k2tog, yo, k3, yo, sl 1, k1, psso, k5; rep from ✳ to last 10 sts, k2tog, yo, k3, yo, sl 1, k1, psso, k3.
5TH ROW: K2, ✳k2tog, yo, k5, yo, sl 1, k1, psso, k3; rep from ✳ to last 11 sts, k2tog,

yo, k5, yo, sl 1, k1, psso, k2.
7TH ROW: K1, ✳k2tog, yo, k7, yo, sl 1, k1, psso, k1; rep from ✳ to end.
9TH ROW: K2tog, yo, k9, ✳yo, sl 1, k2tog, psso, yo, k9; rep from ✳ to last 2 sts, yo, sl 1, k1, psso.
10TH ROW: Purl.
Rep these 10 rows.

Diagonal Ridges
Multiple of 5 sts + 2
Drape: excellent
Skill: intermediate

1ST ROW (RS): K2tog, yo, ✳k3, k2tog, yo; rep from ✳ to last 5 sts, k5.
2ND ROW: P2, ✳k3, p2; rep from ✳ to end.
3RD ROW: K4, k2tog, yo, ✳k3, k2tog, yo; rep from ✳ to last st, k1.
4TH ROW: K1, ✳p2, k3; rep from ✳ to last st, st, p1.
5TH ROW: ✳K3, k2tog, yo; rep from ✳ to last 2 sts, k2.
6TH ROW: K2, ✳p2, k3; rep from ✳ to end.
7TH ROW: K2, ✳k2tog, yo, k3; rep from ✳ to end.
8TH ROW: ✳K3, p2; rep from ✳ to last 2 sts, k2.
9TH ROW: K1, k2tog, yo, ✳k3, k2tog, yo; rep from ✳ to last 4 sts, k4.
10TH ROW: P1, ✳k3, p2; rep from ✳ to last st, k1.
Rep these 10 rows.

Snakes and Ladders
Multiple of 8 sts + 2
Drape: excellent
Skill: intermediate

1ST ROW (RS): K7, ✳k2tog, yo, k6; rep from ✳ to last 3 sts, k2tog, yo, k1.
2ND ROW: K2, ✳yo, p2tog, k6; rep from ✳ to end.
3RD ROW: K5, ✳k2tog, yo, k6; rep from ✳ to last 5 sts, k2tog, yo, k3.
4TH ROW: K4, ✳yo, p2tog, k6; rep from ✳ to last 6 sts, yo, p2tog, K4.
5TH ROW: K3, ✳k2tog, yo, k6; rep from ✳ to last 7 sts, k2tog, yo, k5.
6TH ROW: ✳K6, yo, p2tog; rep from ✳ to last 2 sts, k2.
7TH ROW: K1, ✳k2tog, yo, k6; rep from ✳ to last st, k1.
8TH ROW: K7, ✳p2tog tbl, yo, k6; rep from ✳ to last 3 sts, p2tog tbl, yo, k1.
9TH ROW: K2, ✳yo, k2tog tbl, k6; rep from ✳ to end.
10TH ROW: K5, ✳p2tog tbl, yo, k6; rep from ✳ to last 5 sts, p2tog tbl, yo, k3.
11TH ROW: K4, ✳yo, k2tog tbl, k6; rep from ✳ to last 6 sts, yo, k2tog tbl, k4.
12TH ROW: K3, ✳p2tog tbl, yo, k6; rep from ✳ to last 7 sts, p2tog tbl, yo, k5.
13TH ROW: ✳K6, yo, k2tog tbl; rep from ✳ to last 2 sts, k2.
14TH ROW: K1, ✳p2tog tbl, yo, k6; rep from ✳ to last st, k1.
Rep these 14 rows.

lace patterns

large lace patterns

This section includes some traditional favorites from the repertoire of lace knitting, such as Fancy Horseshoe Print (*page 126*) and Crowns of Glory (*page 129*). Make some samples first, using fine yarn to enhance their delicacy. Then try the same stitches in a thicker yarn, such as a lightweight cotton, or even a slightly fluffy yarn. Although the latter will obscure the pattern somewhat, the effect can often be pleasingly soft and subtle, and the resulting fabric perfect for a warm shawl.

Diamond and Eyelet Pattern
Multiple of 6 sts + 3
Drape: excellent
Skill: intermediate

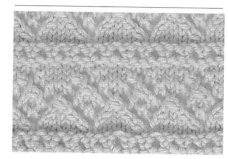

1ST ROW (WS): Knit.
2ND ROW: p1, ✳yo, p2tog; rep from ✳ to end.
3RD AND 4TH ROWS: Knit.
5TH ROW AND EVERY WS ROW TO 15TH ROW: Purl.
6TH ROW: ✳K4, yo, sl 1, k1, psso; rep from ✳ to last 3 sts, k3.
8TH ROW: K2, ✳k2tog, yo, k1, yo, sl 1, k1, psso, k1; rep from ✳ to last st, k1.
10TH ROW: K1, k2tog, yo, ✳k3, yo, sl 1, k2tog, psso, yo; rep from ✳ to last 6 sts, k3, yo, sl 1, k1, psso, k1.
12TH ROW: K3, ✳yo, sl 1, k2tog, psso, yo, k3; rep from ✳ to end.
14TH ROW: As 6th row.
16TH ROW: Knit.
Rep these 16 rows.

Large Lattice Lace
Multiple of 6 sts + 2
Drape: excellent
Skill: intermediate

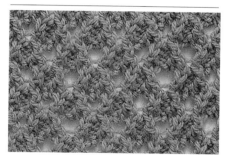

1ST ROW (RS): K1, p1, ✳yo, k2tog tbl, k2tog, yo, p2; rep from ✳ to last 6 sts, yo, k2tog tbl, k2tog, yo, p1, k1.
2ND ROW: K2, ✳p4, k2; rep from ✳ to end.
3RD ROW: K1, p1, ✳k2tog, yo twice, k2tog tbl, p2; rep from ✳ to last 6 sts, k2tog, yo twice, k2tog tbl, p1, k1.
4TH ROW: K2, ✳p1, [k1, p1] into double yo of previous row, p1, k2; rep from ✳ to end.
5TH ROW: K1, ✳k2tog, yo, p2, yo, k2tog tbl; rep from ✳ to last st, k1.
6TH ROW: K1, p2, ✳k2, p4; rep from ✳ to last 5 sts, k2, p2, k1.
7TH ROW: K1, yo, ✳k2tog tbl, p2, k2tog, yo twice; rep from ✳ to last 7 sts, k2tog tbl, p2, k2tog, yo, k1.
8TH ROW: K1, p2, k2, p1, ✳[k1, p1] into double yo of previous row, p1, k2, p1; rep from ✳ to last 2 sts, p1, k1.
Rep these 8 rows.

Flower Buds
Multiple of 8 sts + 5
Drape: excellent
Skill: intermediate

1ST ROW (RS): K3, ✳yo, k2, p3tog, k2, yo, k1; rep from ✳ to last 2 sts, k2.
2ND ROW: Purl.
Rep the last 2 rows twice more.
7TH ROW: K2, p2tog, ✳k2, yo, k1, yo, k2, p3tog; rep from ✳ to last 9 sts, k2, yo, k1, yo, k2, p2tog, k2.
8TH ROW: Purl.
Rep the last 2 rows twice more.
Rep these 12 rows.

Falling Leaves
Multiple of 10 sts + 3
Drape: excellent
Skill: experienced

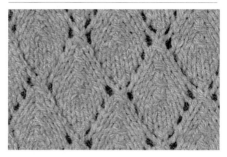

1ST ROW (RS): K1, k2tog, k3, ✳yo, k1, yo, k3, sl 1, k2tog, psso, k3; rep from ✳ to last 7 sts, yo, k1, yo, k3, sl 1, k1, psso, k1.
2ND AND EVERY ALT ROW: Purl.
3RD ROW: K1, k2tog, k2, ✳yo, k3, yo, k2, sl 1, k2tog, psso, k2; rep from ✳ to last 8 sts, yo, k3, yo, k2, sl 1, k1, psso, k1.
5TH ROW: K1, k2tog, k1, ✳yo, k5, yo, k1, sl 1, k2tog, psso, k1; rep from ✳ to last 9 sts, yo, k5, yo, k1, sl 1, k1, psso, k1.
7TH ROW: K1, k2tog, yo, k7, ✳yo, sl 1, k2tog, psso, yo, k7; rep from ✳ to last 3 sts, yo, sl 1, k1, psso, k1.
9TH ROW: K2, yo, k3, ✳sl 1, k2tog, psso, k3, yo, k1, yo, k3; rep from ✳ to last 8 sts, sl 1, k2tog, psso, k3, yo, k2.
11TH ROW: K3, yo, k2, ✳sl 1, k2tog, psso, k2, yo, k3, yo, k2; rep from ✳ to last 8 sts, sl 1, k2tog, psso, k2, yo, k3.
13TH ROW: K4, yo, k1, ✳sl 1, k2tog, psso, k1, yo, k5, yo, k1; rep from ✳ to last 8 sts, sl 1, k2tog, psso, k1, yo, k4.
15TH ROW: K5, ✳yo, sl 1, k2tog, psso, yo, k7; rep from ✳ to last 8 sts, yo, sl 1, k2tog, psso, yo, k5.
16TH ROW: Purl. Rep these 16 rows.

Loose Lattice Lace
Multiple of 8 sts + 3
Drape: excellent
Skill: intermediate
Note: Sts should only be counted after the 5th, 6th, 11th, and 12th rows.

1ST ROW (RS): K1, ✳k2tog, k1, yo, k1, sl 1, k1, psso, k2; rep from ✳ to last 2 sts, k2.
2ND AND EVERY ALT ROW: Purl.
3RD ROW: ✳K2tog, k1, [yo, k1] twice, sl 1, k1, psso; rep from ✳ to last 3 sts, k3.
5TH ROW: K2, ✳yo, k3, yo, k1, sl 1, k1, psso, k1; rep from ✳ to last st, k1.
7TH ROW: K4, ✳k2tog, k1, yo, k1, sl 1, k1, psso, k2; rep from ✳ to last 7 sts, k2tog, k1, yo, k1, sl 1, k1, psso, k1.
9TH ROW: K3, ✳k2tog, k1, [yo, k1] twice, sl 1, k1, psso; rep from ✳ to end.
11TH ROW: K2, ✳k2tog, k1, yo, k3, yo, k1; rep from ✳ to last st, k1.
12TH ROW: Purl.
Rep these 12 rows.

Wheatear Stitch
Multiple of 8 sts + 6
Drape: excellent
Skill: intermediate

1ST ROW (RS): P5, ✳k2, yo, sl 1, k1, psso, p4; rep from ✳ to last st, p1.
2ND ROW: K5, ✳p2, yo, p2tog, k4; rep from ✳ to last st, k1.
Rep the last 2 rows 3 times more.

9TH ROW: P1, ✳k2, yo, sl 1, k1, psso, p4; rep from ✳ to last 5 sts, k2, yo, sl 1, k1, psso, p1.
10TH ROW: K1, ✳p2, yo, p2tog, k4; rep from ✳ to last 5 sts, p2, yo, p2tog, k1.
Rep the last 2 rows 3 times more.
Rep these 16 rows.

Garter Stitch Lacy Diamonds
Multiple of 10 sts + 1
Drape: excellent
Skill: intermediate

1ST AND EVERY ALT ROW (RS): Knit.
2ND ROW: K3, ✳k2tog, yo, k1, yo, k2tog, k5; rep from ✳ to last 8 sts, k2tog, yo, k1, yo, k2tog, k3.
4TH ROW: K2, ✳k2tog, yo, k3, yo, k2tog, k3; rep from ✳ to last 9 sts, k2tog, yo, k3, yo, k2tog, k2.
6TH ROW: K1, ✳k2tog, yo, k5, yo, k2tog, k1; rep from ✳ to end.
8TH ROW: K1, ✳yo, k2tog, k5, k2tog, yo, k1; rep from ✳ to end.
10TH ROW: K2, ✳yo, k2tog, k3, k2tog, yo, k3; rep from ✳ to last 9 sts, yo, k2tog, k3, k2tog, yo, k2.
12TH ROW: K3, ✳yo, k2tog, k1, k2tog, yo, k5; rep from ✳ to last 8 sts, yo, k2tog, k1, k2tog, yo, k3.
Rep these 12 rows.

Moss Lace Diamonds

Multiple of 8 sts + 1
Drape: excellent
Skill: intermediate

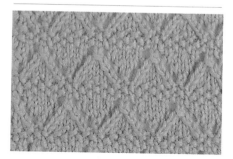

1ST ROW (RS): K1, ✳p1, k1; rep from ✳ to end.
2ND ROW: K1, ✳p1, k1; rep from ✳ to end.
Rep the last 2 rows once more.
5TH ROW: k1, ✳yo, sl 1, k1, psso, k3, k2tog, yo, k1; rep from ✳ to end.
6TH ROW: Purl.
7TH ROW: K2, ✳yo, sl 1, k1, psso, k1, k2tog, yo, k3; rep from ✳ to last 7 sts, yo, sl 1, k1, psso, k1, k2tog, yo, k2.
8TH ROW: Purl.
9TH ROW: K3, ✳yo, sl 1, k2tog, psso, yo, k5; rep from ✳ to last 6 sts, yo, sl 1, k2tog, psso, yo, k3.
10TH ROW: Purl.
11TH ROW: K1, ✳p1, k1; rep from ✳ to end.
Rep the last row 3 times more.
15TH ROW: K2, ✳k2tog, yo, k1, yo, sl 1, k1, psso, k3; rep from ✳ to last 7 sts, k2tog, yo, k1, yo, sl 1, k1, psso, k2.
16TH ROW: Purl.
17TH ROW: K1, ✳k2tog, yo, k3, yo, sl 1, k1, psso, k1; rep from ✳ to end.
18TH ROW: Purl.
19TH ROW: K2tog, ✳yo, k5, yo, sl 1, k2tog, psso; rep from ✳ to last 7 sts, yo, k5, yo, sl 1, k1, psso.
20TH ROW: Purl.
Rep these 20 rows.

Scallop Pattern

Multiple of 13 sts + 2
Drape: excellent
Skill: intermediate
Note: Sts should only be counted after the 5th and 6th rows.

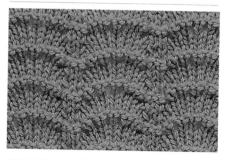

1ST ROW (RS): K1, ✳sl 1, k1, psso, k9, k2tog; rep from ✳ to last st, k1.
2ND ROW: Purl.
3RD ROW: K1, ✳sl 1, k1, psso, k7, k2tog; rep from ✳ to last st, k1.
4TH ROW: Purl.
5TH ROW: K1, ✳sl 1, k1, psso, yo, [k1, yo] 5 times, k2tog; rep from ✳ to last st, k1.
6TH ROW: Knit.
Rep these 6 rows.

Traveling Vine

Multiple of 8 sts + 2
Drape: excellent
Skill: intermediate
Note: Sts should only be counted after wrong-side rows.

1ST ROW (RS): K1, ✳yo, k1 tbl, yo, k2tog tbl, k5; rep from ✳ to last st, k1.

2ND ROW: P5, ✳p2tog tbl, p7; rep from ✳ to last 6 sts, p2tog tbl, p4.
3RD ROW: K1, ✳yo, k1 tbl, yo, k2, k2tog tbl, k3; rep from ✳ to last st, k1.
4TH ROW: P3, ✳p2tog tbl, p7; rep from ✳ to last 8 sts, p2tog tbl, p6.
5TH ROW: K1, ✳k1 tbl, yo, k4, k2tog tbl, k1, yo; rep from ✳ to last st, k1.
6TH ROW: P2, ✳p2tog tbl, p7; rep from ✳ to end.
7TH ROW: K6, ✳k2tog, yo, k1 tbl, yo, k5; rep from ✳ to last 4 sts, k2tog, yo, k1 tbl, yo, k1.
8TH ROW: P4, ✳p2tog, p7; rep from ✳ to last 7 sts, p2tog, p5.
9TH ROW: K4, ✳k2tog, k2, yo, k1 tbl, yo, k3; rep from ✳ to last 6 sts, k2tog, k2, yo, k1 tbl, yo, k1.
10TH ROW: P6, ✳p2tog, p7; rep from ✳ to last 5 sts, p2tog, p3.
11TH ROW: K1, ✳yo, k1, k2tog, k4, yo, k1 tbl; rep from ✳ to last st, k1.
12TH ROW: ✳P7, p2tog; rep from ✳ to last 2 sts, p2. Rep these 12 rows.

Wavy Cable Lace

Multiple of 14 sts + 1
Drape: excellent
Skill: experienced

1ST ROW (RS): K1, ✳yo, k2, p3, p3tog, p3, k2, yo, k1; rep from ✳ to end.
2ND ROW: P4, ✳k7, p7; rep from ✳ to last 11 sts, k7, p4.
3RD ROW: K2, ✳yo, k2, p2, p3tog, p2, k2, yo, k3; rep from ✳ to last 13 sts, yo, k2, p2, p3tog, p2, k2, yo, k2.
4TH ROW: P5, ✳k5, p9; rep from ✳ to last

10 sts, k5, p5.

5TH ROW: K3, ✳yo, k2, p1, p3tog, p1, k2, yo, k5; rep from ✳ to last 12 sts, yo, k2, p1, p3tog, p1, k2, yo, k3.

6TH ROW: P6, ✳k3, p11; rep from ✳ to last 9 sts, k3, p6.

7TH ROW: K4, ✳yo, k2, p3tog, k2, yo, k7; rep from ✳ to last 11 sts, yo, k2, p3tog, k2, yo, k4.

8TH ROW: P7, ✳k1, p13; rep from ✳ to last 8 sts, k1, p7.

9TH ROW: P2tog, ✳p3, k2, yo, k1, yo, k2, p3, p3tog; rep from ✳ to last 13 sts, p3, k2, yo, k1, yo, k2, p3, p2tog.

10TH ROW: K4, ✳p7, k7; rep from ✳ to last 11 sts, p7, k4.

11TH ROW: P2tog, ✳p2, k2, yo, k3, yo, k2, p2, p3tog; rep from ✳ to last 13 sts, p2, k2, yo, k3, yo, k2, p2, p2tog.

12TH ROW: K3, ✳p9, k5; rep from ✳ to last 12 sts, p9, k3.

13TH ROW: P2tog, ✳p1, k2, yo, k5, yo, k2, p1, p3tog; rep from ✳ to last 13 sts, p1, k2, yo, k5, yo, k2, p1, p2tog.

14TH ROW: K2, ✳p11, k3; rep from ✳ to last 13 sts, p11, k2.

15TH ROW: P2tog, ✳k2, yo, k7, yo, k2, p3tog; rep from ✳ to last 13 sts, k2, yo, k7, yo, k2, p2tog.

16TH ROW: K1, ✳p13, k1; rep from ✳ to end.
Rep these 16 rows.

Gothic Windows

Multiple of 8 sts + 2
Drape: excellent
Skill: experienced
Note: Sts should not be counted after the 3rd, 7th, 9th, and 11th rows.

1ST ROW (RS): P4, ✳k2, p6; rep from ✳ to last 6 sts, k2, p4.

2ND ROW: K4, ✳p2, k6; rep from ✳ to last 6 sts, p2, k4.

3RD ROW: P3, ✳k2tog, yo, sl 1, k1, psso, p4; rep from ✳ to last 7 sts, k2tog, yo, sl 1, k1, psso, p3.

4TH ROW: K3, ✳p1, knit into back then front of next st, p1, k4; rep from ✳ to last 6 sts,

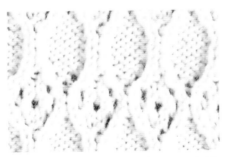

p1, knit into back then front of next st, p1, k3.

5TH ROW: P2, ✳k2tog, yo, k2, yo, sl 1, k1, psso, p2; rep from ✳ to end.

6TH ROW: K2, ✳p6, k2; rep from ✳ to end.

7TH ROW: K1, ✳k2tog, yo, k2tog, [yo, sl 1, k1, psso] twice; rep from ✳ to last st, k1.

8TH ROW: P4, ✳knit into front then back of next st, p6; rep from ✳ to last 5 sts, knit into front then back of next st, p4.

9TH ROW: K1, ✳[yo, sl 1, k1, psso] twice, k2tog, yo, k2tog; rep from ✳ to last st, yo, k1.

10TH ROW: K1, k1 tbl, ✳p6, k into back then front of next st; rep from ✳ to last 8 sts, p6, k1 tbl, k1.

11TH ROW: P2, ✳yo, k3tog tbl, yo, k3tog, yo, p2; rep from ✳ to end.

12TH ROW: K2, ✳k1 tbl, p1, knit into back then front of next st, p1, k1 tbl, k2; rep from ✳ to end.

13TH ROW: P3, ✳yo, sl 1, k1, psso, k2tog, yo, p4; rep from ✳ to last 7 sts, yo, sl 1, k1, psso, k2tog, yo, p3.

14TH ROW: K3, ✳k1 tbl, p2, k1 tbl, k4; rep from ✳ to last 7 sts, k1 tbl, p2, k1 tbl, k3.
Rep these 14 rows.

Florette Pattern

Multiple of 12 sts + 7
Drape: excellent
Skill: intermediate

1ST ROW (RS): K1, ✳p2tog, yo, k1, yo, p2tog, k7; rep from ✳ to last 6 sts, p2tog, yo, k1, yo, p2tog, k1.

2ND AND EVERY ALT ROW: Purl.

3RD ROW: K1, ✳yo, p2tog, k1, p2tog, yo, k7; rep from ✳ to last 6 sts, yo, p2tog, k1,

p2tog, yo, k1.

5TH ROW: As 3rd row.

7TH ROW: As 1st row.

9TH ROW: K7, ✳p2tog, yo, k1, yo, p2tog, k7; rep from ✳ to end.

11TH ROW: K7, ✳yo, p2tog, k1, p2tog, yo, k7; rep from ✳ to end.

13TH ROW: As 11th row.

15TH ROW: As 9th row.

16TH ROW: Purl.
Rep these 16 rows.

Wavy Eyelet Rib

Multiple of 7 sts + 2
Drape: excellent
Skill: intermediate

1ST ROW (RS): ✳P2, yo, sl 1, k1, psso, k1, k2tog, yo; rep from ✳ to last 2 sts, p2.

2ND ROW: K2, ✳p5, k2; rep from ✳ to end.
Rep the last 2 rows twice more.

7TH ROW: ✳P2, k5; rep from ✳ to last 2 sts, p2.

8TH ROW: As 2nd row.

9TH ROW: ✳P2, k2tog, yo, k1, yo, sl 1, k1, psso; rep from ✳ to last 2 sts, p2.

10TH ROW: As 2nd row.
Rep the last 2 rows twice more.
15TH ROW: As 7th row.
16TH ROW: As 2nd row.
Rep these 16 rows.

Fir Cone
Multiple of 10 sts + 1
Drape: excellent
Skill: intermediate

1ST ROW (WS): Purl.
2ND ROW: K1, ✳yo, k3, sl 1, k2tog, psso, k3, yo, k1; rep from ✳ to end.
Rep the last 2 rows 3 times more.
9TH ROW: Purl.
10TH ROW: K2tog, ✳k3, yo, k1, yo, k3, sl 1, k2tog, psso; rep from ✳ to last 9 sts, k3, yo, k1, yo, k3, sl 1, k1, psso.
Rep the last 2 rows 3 times more.
Rep these 16 rows.

Fern Diamonds
Multiple of 10 sts + 1
Drape: excellent
Skill: intermediate

1ST ROW (RS): K3, ✳k2tog, yo, k1, yo, sl 1, k1, psso, k5; rep from ✳ to last 8 sts, k2tog, yo, k1, yo, sl 1, k1, psso, k3.
2ND AND EVERY ALT ROW: Purl.
3RD ROW: K2, ✳k2tog, [k1, yo] twice, k1, sl 1, k1, psso, k3; rep from ✳ to last 9 sts, k2tog, [k1, yo] twice, k1, sl 1, k1, psso, k2.
5TH ROW: K1, ✳k2tog, k2, yo, k1, yo, k2, sl 1, k1, psso, k1; rep from ✳ to end.

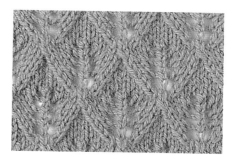

7TH ROW: K2tog, ✳k3, yo, k1, yo, k3, sl 1, k2tog, psso; rep from ✳ to last 9 sts, k3, yo, k1, yo, k3, sl 1, k1, psso.
9TH ROW: k1, ✳yo, sl 1, k1, psso, k5, k2tog, yo, k1; rep from ✳ to end.
11TH ROW: K1, ✳yo, k1, sl 1, k1, psso, k3, k2tog, k1, yo, k1; rep from ✳ to end.
13TH ROW: K1, ✳yo, k2, sl 1, k1, psso, k1, k2tog, k2, yo, k1; rep from ✳ to end.
15TH ROW: K1, ✳yo, k3, sl 1, k2tog, psso, k3, yo, k1; rep from ✳ to end.
16TH ROW: Purl.
Rep these 16 rows.

Foaming Waves
Multiple of 12 sts + 1
Drape: excellent
Skill: intermediate

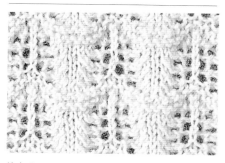

Knit 4 rows.
5TH ROW (RS): K1, ✳[k2tog] twice, [yo, k1] 3 times, yo, [sl 1, k1, psso] twice, k1; rep from ✳ to end.
6TH ROW: Purl.
Rep the last 2 rows 3 times more.
Rep these 12 rows.

Garter Stitch Eyelet Chevron
Multiple of 9 sts + 1
Drape: excellent
Skill: intermediate

1ST ROW (RS): K1, ✳yo, sl 1, k1, psso, k4, k2tog, yo, k1; rep from ✳ to end.
2ND ROW: P2, ✳k6, p3; rep from ✳ to last 8 sts, k6, p2.
3RD ROW: K2, ✳yo, sl 1, k1, psso, k2, k2tog, yo, k3; rep from ✳ to last 8 sts, yo, sl 1, k1, psso, k2, k2tog, yo, k2.
4TH ROW: P3, ✳k4, p5; rep from ✳ to last 7 sts, k4, p3.
5TH ROW: K3, ✳yo, sl 1, k1, psso, k2tog, yo, k5; rep from ✳ to last 7 sts, yo, sl 1, k1, psso, k2tog, yo, k3.
6TH ROW: P4, ✳k2, p7; rep from ✳ to last 6 sts, k2, p4.
Rep these 6 rows.

Eyelet Diamonds
Multiple of 16 sts + 11
Drape: excellent
Skill: intermediate

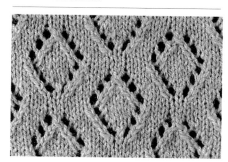

lace patterns

1ST ROW (RS): K10, yo, sl 1, k1, psso, k3, k2tog, yo, ✳k9, yo, sl 1, k1, psso, k3, k2tog, yo; rep from ✳ to last 10 sts, k10.

2ND AND EVERY ALT ROW: Purl.

3RD ROW: K3, k2tog, yo, k1, yo, sl 1, k1, psso, ✳k3, yo, sl 1, k1, psso, k1, k2tog, yo, k3, k2tog, yo, k1, yo, sl 1, k1, psso; rep from ✳ to last 3 sts, k3.

5TH ROW: K2, k2tog, yo, k3, yo, sl 1, k1, psso, ✳k3, yo, sl 1, k2tog, psso, yo, k3, k2tog, yo, k3, yo, sl 1, k1, psso; rep from ✳ to last 2 sts, k2.

7TH ROW: K1, k2tog, yo, k5, yo, sl 1, k1, psso, ✳k7, k2tog, yo, k5, yo, sl 1, k1, psso; rep from ✳ to last st, k1.

9TH ROW: K2, yo, sl 1, k1, psso, k3, k2tog, yo, ✳k9, yo, sl 1, k1, psso, k3, k2tog, yo; rep from ✳ to last 2 sts, k2.

11TH ROW: K3, yo, sl 1, k1, psso, k1, k2tog, yo, k3, ✳k2tog, yo, k1, yo, sl 1, k1, psso, k3, yo, sl 1, k1, psso, k1, k2tog, yo, k3; rep from ✳ to end.

13TH ROW: K4, yo, sl 1, k2tog, psso, yo, ✳k3, k2tog, yo, k3, yo, sl 1, k1, psso, k3, yo, sl 1, k2tog, psso, yo; rep from ✳ to last 4 sts, k4.

15TH ROW: K9, k2tog, yo, k5, yo, sl 1, k1, psso, ✳k7, k2tog, yo, k5, yo, sl 1, k1, psso; rep from ✳ to last 9 sts, k9.

16TH ROW: Purl. Rep these 16 rows.

Fish Hooks

Multiple of 8 sts + 1
Drape: excellent
Skill: intermediate

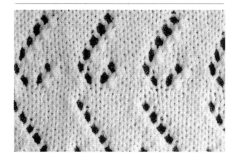

1ST AND EVERY ALT ROW (WS): Purl.
2ND ROW: Knit.

4TH ROW: K2, sl 1, k1, psso, yo, k1, yo, k2tog, ✳k3, sl 1, k1, psso, yo, k1, yo, k2tog; rep from ✳ to last 2 sts, k2.

6TH ROW: K1, ✳sl 1, k1, psso, yo, k3, yo, k2tog, k1; rep from ✳ to end.

8TH ROW: K4, sl 1, k1, psso, yo, ✳k6, sl 1, k1, psso, yo; rep from ✳ to last 3 sts, k3.

10TH ROW: K3, sl 1, k1, psso, yo, ✳k6, sl 1, k1, psso, yo; rep from ✳ to last 4 sts, k4.

12TH ROW: K2, sl 1, k1, psso, yo, ✳k6, sl 1, k1, psso, yo; rep from ✳ to last 5 sts, k5.

14TH ROW: K1, ✳sl 1, k1, psso, yo, k6; rep from ✳ to end.

16TH ROW: Knit.

18TH ROW: As 4th row.

20TH ROW: As 6th row.

22ND ROW: K3, yo, k2tog, ✳k6, yo, k2tog; rep from ✳ to last 4 sts, k4.

24TH ROW: K4, yo, k2tog, ✳k6, yo, k2tog; rep from ✳ to last 3 sts, k3.

26TH ROW: K5, yo, k2tog, ✳k6, yo, k2tog; rep from ✳ to last 2 sts, k2.

28TH ROW: ✳K6, yo, k2tog; rep from ✳ to last st, k1.
Rep these 28 rows.

Swinging Triangles

Multiple of 12 sts + 1
Drape: excellent
Skill: intermediate

1ST AND EVERY ALT ROW (WS): Purl.
2ND ROW: ✳K10, sl 1, k1, psso, yo; rep from ✳ to last st, k1.
4TH ROW: K9, sl 1, k1, psso, yo, ✳k10, sl 1, k1, psso, yo; rep from ✳ to last 2 sts, k2.

6TH ROW: ✳K8, [sl 1, k1, psso, yo] twice; rep from ✳ to last st, k1.

8TH ROW: K7, [sl 1, k1, psso, yo] twice, ✳k8, [sl 1, k1, psso, yo] twice; rep from ✳ to last 2 sts, k2.

10TH ROW: ✳K6, [sl 1, k1, psso, yo] 3 times; rep from ✳ to last st, k1.

12TH ROW: K5, [sl 1, k1, psso, yo] 3 times, ✳k6, [sl 1, k1, psso, yo] 3 times; rep from ✳ to last 2 sts, k2.

14TH ROW: ✳K4, [sl 1, k1, psso, yo] 4 times; rep from ✳ to last st, k1.

16TH ROW: K1, ✳yo, k2tog, k10; rep from ✳ to end.

18TH ROW: K2, yo, k2tog, ✳k10, yo, k2tog; rep from ✳ to last 9 sts, k9.

20TH ROW: K1, ✳[yo, k2tog] twice, k8; rep from ✳ to end.

22ND ROW: K2, [yo, k2tog] twice, ✳k8, [yo, k2tog] twice; rep from ✳ to last 7 sts, k7.

24TH ROW: K1, ✳[yo, k2tog] 3 times, k6; rep from ✳ to end.

26TH ROW: K2, [yo, k2tog] 3 times, ✳k6, [yo, k2tog] 3 times; rep from ✳ to last 5 sts, k5.

28TH ROW: K1, ✳[yo, k2tog] 4 times, k4; rep from ✳ to end. Rep these 28 rows.

Inverted Hearts

Multiple of 14 sts + 1
Drape: excellent
Skill: intermediate

1ST ROW (RS): P2tog, yo, k11, ✳yo, p3tog, yo, k11; rep from ✳ to last 2 sts, yo, p2tog.

2ND ROW: K1, ✳p13, k1; rep from ✳ to end.

3RD ROW: P2, yo, sl 1, k1, psso, k7, ✳k2tog, yo, p3, yo, sl 1, k1, psso, k7; rep from ✳ to last 4 sts, k2tog, yo, p2.

4TH ROW: K2, p11, ✳k3, p11; rep from ✳ to last 2 sts, k2.

5TH ROW: P3, yo, sl 1, k1, psso, k5, k2tog, yo, ✳p5, yo, sl 1, k1, psso, k5, k2tog, yo; rep from ✳ to last 3 sts, p3.

6TH ROW: K3, p9, ✳k5, p9; rep from ✳ to last 3 sts, k3.

7TH ROW: P4, yo, sl 1, k1, psso, k3, k2tog, yo, ✳p7, yo, sl 1, k1, psso, k3, k2tog, yo; rep from ✳ to last 4 sts, p4.

8TH ROW: K4, p7, ✳k7, p7; rep from ✳ to last 4 sts, k4.

9TH ROW: P2, p2tog, yo, k1, yo, sl 1, k1, psso, k1, k2tog, yo, k1, yo, p2tog, ✳p3, p2tog, yo, k1, yo, sl 1, k1, psso, k1, k2tog, yo, k1, yo, p2tog; rep from ✳ to last 2 sts, p2.

10TH ROW: As 6th row.

11TH ROW: P1, ✳p2tog, yo, k3, yo, sl 1, k2tog, psso, yo, k3, yo, p2tog, p1; rep from ✳ to end.

12TH ROW: As 4th row.
Rep these 12 rows.

Cogwheel Eyelets
Multiple of 8 sts + 1
Drape: excellent
Skill: experienced

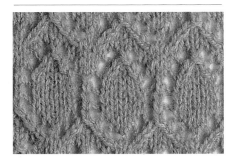

1ST ROW (RS): K2, k2tog, yo, k1, yo, sl 1, k1, psso, ✳k3, k2tog, yo, k1, yo, sl 1, k1, psso; rep from ✳ to last 2 sts, k2.

2ND AND EVERY ALT ROW: Purl.

3RD ROW: K1, ✳k2tog, yo, k3, yo, sl 1, k1, psso, k1; rep from ✳ to end.

5TH ROW: K2tog, yo, k5, ✳yo, sl 1, k2tog, psso, yo, k5; rep from ✳ to last 2 sts, yo, sl 1, k1, psso.

7TH ROW: Sl 1, k1, psso, yo, k5, ✳yo, sl 2tog knitwise, k1, p2sso, yo, k5; rep from ✳ to last 2 sts, yo, k2tog.

9TH ROW: As 7th row.

11TH ROW: K2, yo, sl 1, k1, psso, k1, k2tog, yo, ✳k3, yo, sl 1, k1, psso, k1, k2tog, yo; rep from ✳ to last 2 sts, k2.

13TH ROW: K3, yo, sl 1, k2tog, psso, yo, ✳k5, yo, sl 1, k2tog, psso, yo; rep from ✳ to last 3 sts, k3.

15TH ROW: K1, ✳yo, sl 1, k1, psso, k3, k2tog, yo, k1; rep from ✳ to end.

17TH ROW: As 11th row.

19TH ROW: As 13th row.

21ST ROW: K3, yo, sl 2tog knitwise, k1, p2sso, yo, ✳k5, yo, sl 2tog knitwise, k1, p2sso, yo; rep from ✳ to last 3 sts, k3.

23RD ROW: As 21st row.

25TH ROW: As 3rd row.

27TH ROW: As 5th row.

28TH ROW: Purl.
Rep these 28 rows.

Diamond Trellis
Multiple of 16 sts + 1
Drape: excellent
Skill: experienced

1ST ROW (RS): K2tog, yo, k12, ✳[k2tog, yo] twice, k12; rep from ✳ to last 3 sts, k2tog, yo, k1.

2ND AND EVERY ALT ROW: Purl.

3RD ROW: K2, yo, sl 1, k1, psso, k9, ✳[k2tog, yo] twice, k1, yo, sl 1, k1, psso, k9; rep from ✳ to last 4 sts, k2tog, yo, k2.

5TH ROW: K1, ✳[yo, sl 1, k1, psso] twice, k7, [k2tog, yo] twice, k1; rep from ✳ to end.

7TH ROW: K2, [yo, sl 1, k1, psso] twice, k5, [k2tog, yo] twice, ✳k3, [yo, sl 1, k1, psso] twice, k5, [k2tog, yo] twice; rep from ✳ to last 2 sts, k2.

9TH ROW: K3, [yo, sl 1, k1, psso] twice, k3, [k2tog, yo] twice, ✳k5, [yo, sl 1, k1, psso] twice, k3, [k2tog, yo] twice; rep from ✳ to last 3 sts, k3.

11TH ROW: K4, [yo, sl 1, k1, psso] twice, k1, [k2tog, yo] twice, ✳k7, [yo, sl 1, k1, psso] twice, k1, [k2tog, yo] twice; rep from ✳ to last 4 sts, k4.

13TH ROW: K5, yo, sl 1, k1, psso, yo, k3tog, yo, k2tog, yo, ✳k9, yo, sl 1, k1, psso, yo, k3tog, yo, k2tog, yo; rep from ✳ to last 5 sts, k6.

15TH ROW: K6, yo, k3tog, yo, k2tog, yo, ✳k11, yo, k3tog, yo, k2tog, yo; rep from ✳ to last 6 sts, k6.

17TH ROW: K6, [k2tog, yo] twice, ✳k12, [k2tog, yo] twice; rep from ✳ to last 7 sts, k7.

19TH ROW: K5, [k2tog, yo] twice, k1, yo, sl 1, k1, psso, ✳k9, [k2tog, yo] twice, k1, yo, sl 1, k1, psso; rep from ✳ to last 5 sts, k5.

21ST ROW: K4, [k2tog, yo] twice, k1, [yo, sl 1, k1, psso] twice, ✳k7, [k2tog, yo] twice, k1, [yo, sl 1, k1, psso] twice; rep from ✳ to last 4 sts, k4.

23RD ROW: K3, [k2tog, yo] twice, k3, [yo, sl 1, k1, psso] twice, ✳k5, [k2tog, yo] twice, k3, [yo, sl 1, k1, psso] twice; rep from ✳ to last 3 sts, k3.

25TH ROW: K2, [k2tog, yo] twice, k5, [yo, sl 1, k1, psso] twice, ✳k3, [k2tog, yo] twice, k5, [yo, sl 1, k1, psso] twice; rep from ✳ to last 2 sts, k2.

27TH ROW: ✳K1, [k2tog, yo] twice, k7, [yo, sl 1, k1, psso] twice; rep from ✳ to last st, k1.

29TH ROW: [k2tog, yo] twice, k9, ✳yo, sl 1, k1, psso, yo, k3tog, yo, k2tog, yo, k9; rep from ✳ to last 4 sts, [yo, sl 1, k1, psso] twice.

31ST ROW: K1, k2tog, yo, k11, ✳yo, k3tog, yo, k2tog, yo, k11; rep from ✳ to last 3 sts, yo, k2tog, k1.

32ND ROW: Purl. Rep these 32 rows.

Eyelet Boxes
Multiple of 14 sts + 11
Drape: excellent
Skill: experienced

1ST ROW (RS): K2, p7, ✳k3, yo, sl 1, k1, psso, k2, p7; rep from ✳ to last 2 sts, k2.
2ND, 4TH, 6TH, 8TH, AND 10TH ROWS: P2, k7, ✳p7, k7; rep from ✳ to last 2 sts, p2.
3RD ROW: K2, p7, ✳k1, k2tog, yo, k1, yo, sl 1, k1, psso, k1, p7; rep from ✳ to last 2 sts, k2.
5TH ROW: K2, p7, ✳k2tog, yo, k3, yo, sl 1, k1, psso, p7; rep from ✳ to last 2 sts, k2.
7TH ROW: K2, p7, ✳k2, yo, sl 1, k2tog, psso, yo, k2, p7; rep from ✳ to last 2 sts, k2.
9TH ROW: As 1st row.
11TH ROW: P2, k3, yo, sl 1, k1, psso, k2, ✳p7, k3, yo, sl 1, k1, psso, k2; rep from ✳ to last 2 sts, p2.
12TH, 14TH, 16TH, AND 18TH ROWS: K2, p7, ✳k7, p7; rep from ✳ to last 2 sts, k2.
13TH ROW: P2, k1, k2tog, yo, k1, yo, sl 1, k1, psso, k1, ✳p7, k1, k2tog, yo, k1, yo, sl 1, k1, psso, k1; rep from ✳ to last 2 sts, p2.
15TH ROW: P2, k2tog, yo, k3, yo, sl 1, k1, psso, ✳p7, k2tog, yo, k3, yo, sl 1, k1, psso; rep from ✳ to last 2 sts, p2.
17TH ROW: P2, k2, yo, sl 1, k2tog, psso, yo, k2, ✳p7, k2, yo, sl 1, k2tog, psso, yo, k2; rep from ✳ to last 2 sts, p2.
19TH ROW: As 11th row.
20TH ROW: K2, p7, ✳k7, p7; rep from ✳ to last 2 sts, k2. Rep these 20 rows.

Shadow Triangles
Multiple of 10 sts + 3
Drape: excellent
Skill: experienced

1ST ROW (RS): K2, yo, sl 1, k1, psso, k5, k2tog, yo, ✳k1, yo, sl 1, k1, psso, k5, k2tog, yo; rep from ✳ to last 2 sts, k2.
2ND ROW: P4, k5, ✳p5, k5; rep from ✳ to last 4 sts, p4.
3RD ROW: K3, ✳yo, sl 1, k1, psso, k3, k2tog, yo, k3; rep from ✳ to end.
4TH ROW: P5, k3, ✳p7, k3; rep from ✳ to last 5 sts, p5.
5TH ROW: K4, yo, sl 1, k1, psso, k1, k2tog, yo, ✳k5, yo, sl 1, k1, psso, k1, k2tog, yo; rep from ✳ to last 4 sts, k4.
6TH ROW: P6, k1, ✳p9, k1; rep from ✳ to last 6 sts, p6.
7TH ROW: K5, yo, sl 1, k2tog, psso, yo, ✳k7, yo, sl 1, k2tog, psso, yo; rep from ✳ to last 5 sts, k5.
8TH ROW: Purl.
9TH ROW: K4, k2tog, yo, k1, yo, sl 1, k1, psso, ✳k5, k2tog, yo, k1, yo, sl 1, k1, psso; rep from ✳ to last 4 sts, k4.
10TH ROW: K4, p5, ✳k5, p5; rep from ✳ to last 4 sts, k4.
11TH ROW: K3, ✳k2tog, yo, k3, yo, sl 1, k1, psso, k3; rep from ✳ to end.
12TH ROW: K3, ✳p7, k3; rep from ✳ to end.
13TH ROW: K2, k2tog, yo, k5, yo, sl 1, k1, psso, ✳k1, k2tog, yo, k5, yo, sl 1, k1, psso; rep from ✳ to last 2 sts, k2.
14TH ROW: P1, k1, ✳p9, k1; rep from ✳ to last st, p1.
15TH ROW: K1, k2tog, yo, k7, ✳yo, sl 1, k2tog, psso, yo, k7; rep from ✳ to last 3 sts, yo, sl 1, k1, psso, k1.
16TH ROW: Purl.
Rep these 16 rows.

Little and Large Diamonds
Multiple of 12 sts + 1
Drape: excellent
Skill: experienced

1ST ROW (RS): K1, ✳yo, sl 1, k1, psso, k7, k2tog, yo, k1; rep from ✳ to end.
2ND AND EVERY ALT ROW: Purl.
3RD ROW: K2, yo, sl 1, k1, psso, k5, ✳k2tog, yo, k3, yo, sl 1, k1, psso, k5; rep from ✳ to last 4 sts, k2tog, yo, k2.
5TH ROW: K3, yo, sl 1, k1, psso, k3, ✳k2tog, yo, k5, yo, sl 1, k1, psso, k3; rep from ✳ to last 5 sts, k2tog, yo, k3.
7TH ROW: ✳K1, k2tog, yo, k1, yo, sl 1, k1, psso; rep from ✳ to last st, k1.
9TH ROW: K2tog, yo, k3, ✳yo, sl 1, k2tog, psso, yo, k3; rep from ✳ to last 2 sts, yo, sl 1, k1, psso.
11TH ROW: K4, k2tog, yo, k1, yo, sl 1, k1, psso, ✳k7, k2tog, yo, k1, yo, sl 1, k1, psso; rep from ✳ to last 4 sts, k4.
13TH ROW: K3, k2tog, yo, k3, yo, sl 1, k1, psso, ✳k5, k2tog, yo, k3, yo, sl 1, k1, psso; rep from ✳ to last 3 sts, k3.
15TH ROW: K2, k2tog, yo, k5, yo, sl 1, k1, psso, ✳k3, k2tog, yo, k5, yo, sl 1, k1, psso; rep from ✳ to last 2 sts, k2.
17TH ROW: As 7th row.
19TH ROW: As 9th row.
20TH ROW: Purl.
Rep these 20 rows.

Feather and Fan
Multiple of 18 sts + 2
Drape: excellent
Skill: intermediate

lace patterns

1ST ROW (RS): Knit.
2ND ROW: Purl.
3RD ROW: K1, ✳[k2tog] 3 times, [yo, k1] 6 times, [k2tog] 3 times; rep from ✳ to last st, k1.
4TH ROW: Knit. Rep these 4 rows.

2-Colored Feather and Fan
Multiple of 18 sts + 2
Drape: excellent
Skill: intermediate

Worked as Feather and Fan.
Work 4 rows in color A, and 4 rows in color B throughout.

Creeping Vines
Multiple of 22 sts + 3
Drape: excellent
Skill: intermediate

1ST ROW (RS): K4, k2tog, k3, [yo, k2tog] twice, ✳yo, k13, k2tog, k3, [yo, k2tog] twice; rep from ✳ to last 12 sts, yo, k12.
2ND AND EVERY ALT ROW: Purl.

3RD ROW: K3, ✳k2tog, k3, yo, k1, yo, [sl 1, k1, psso, yo] twice, k3, sl 1, k1, psso, k7; rep from ✳ to end.
5TH ROW: K2, k2tog, [k3, yo] twice, [sl 1, k1, psso, yo] twice, k3, sl 1, k1, psso, ✳k5, k2tog, [k3, yo] twice, [sl 1, k1, psso, yo] twice, k3, sl 1, k1, psso; rep from ✳ to last 6 sts, k6.
7TH ROW: K1, k2tog, k3, yo, k5, yo, [sl 1, k1, psso, yo] twice, k3, sl 1, k1, psso, ✳k3, k2tog, k3, yo, k5, yo, [sl 1, k1, psso, yo] twice, k3, sl 1, k1, psso; rep from ✳ to last 5 sts, k5.
9TH ROW: K12, yo, [sl 1, k1, psso, yo] twice, k3, sl 1, k1, psso, ✳k13, yo, [sl 1, k1, psso, yo] twice, k3, sl 1, k1, psso; rep from ✳ to last 4 sts, k4.
11TH ROW: K7, k2tog, k3, [yo, k2tog] twice, yo, k1, yo, k3, sl 1, k1, psso; rep from ✳ to last 3 sts, k3.
13TH ROW: K6, k2tog, k3, [yo, k2tog] twice, [yo, k3] twice, sl 1, k1, psso, ✳k5, k2tog, k3, [yo, k2tog] twice, [yo, k3] twice, sl 1, k1, psso; rep from ✳ to last 2 sts, k2.
15TH ROW: K5, k2tog, k3, [yo, k2tog] twice, yo, k5, yo, k3, sl 1, k1, psso, ✳k3, k2tog, k3, [yo, k2tog] twice, yo, k5, yo, k3, sl 1, k1, psso; rep from ✳ to last st, k1.
16TH ROW: Purl. Rep these 16 rows.

Ears of Wheat
Multiple of 12 sts + 2
Drape: excellent
Skill: intermediate

1ST ROW (RS): Knit.
2ND ROW: Purl.
3RD ROW: K4, k2tog, k1, yo, ✳k9, k2tog,

k1, yo; rep from ✳ to last 7 sts, k7.
4TH ROW: P8, yo, p1, p2tog, ✳p9, yo, p1, p2tog; rep from ✳ to last 3 sts, p3.
5TH ROW: K2, ✳k2tog, k1, yo, k9; rep from ✳ to end.
6TH ROW: P10, yo, p1, p2tog, ✳p9, yo, p1, p2tog; rep from ✳ to last st, p1.
Work 2 rows in St st, starting knit.
9TH ROW: K7, yo, k1, sl 1, k1, psso, ✳k9, yo, k1, sl 1, k1, psso; rep from ✳ to last 4 sts, k4.
10TH ROW: P3, p2tog tbl, p1, yo, ✳p9, p2tog tbl, p1, yo; rep from ✳ to last 8 sts, p8.
11TH ROW: ✳K9, yo, k1, sl 1, k1, psso; rep from ✳ to last 2 sts, k2.
12TH ROW: P1, p2tog tbl, p1, yo, ✳p9, p2tog tbl, p1, yo; rep from ✳ to last 10 sts, p10. Rep these 12 rows.

Horseshoe Print
Multiple of 10 sts + 1
Drape: excellent
Skill: intermediate

1ST ROW (WS): Purl.
2ND ROW: K1, ✳yo, k3, sl 1, k2tog, psso,

k3, yo, k1; rep from ✳ to end.

3RD ROW: Purl.

4TH ROW: P1, ✳k1, yo, k2, sl 1, k2tog, psso, k2, yo, k1, p1; rep from ✳ to end.

5TH ROW: K1, ✳p9, k1; rep from ✳ to end.

6TH ROW: P1, ✳k2, yo, k1, sl 1, k2tog, psso, k1, yo, k2, p1; rep from ✳ to end.

7TH ROW: As 5th row.

8TH ROW: P1, ✳k3, yo, sl 1, k2tog, psso, yo, k3, p1; rep from ✳ to end.
Rep these 8 rows.

Fancy Horseshoe Print
Multiple of 10 sts + 1
Drape: excellent
Skill: intermediate

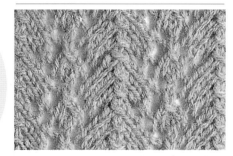

1ST ROW (RS): K1, ✳yo, k3, sl 1, k2tog, psso, k3, yo, k1; rep from ✳ to end.

2ND AND EVERY ALT ROW: Purl.

3RD ROW: K2, yo, k2, sl 1, k2tog, psso, k2, ✳yo, k3, yo, k2, sl 1, k2tog, psso, k2; rep from ✳ to last 2 sts, yo, k2.

5TH ROW: K2tog, [yo, k1] twice, ✳sl 1, k2tog, psso, [k1, yo] twice, sl 1, k2tog, psso, [yo, k1] twice; rep from ✳ to last 7 sts, sl 1, k2tog, psso, [k1, yo] twice, sl 1, k1, psso.

6TH ROW: Purl. Rep these 6 rows.

Flickering Flames
Multiple of 10 sts + 1
Drape: excellent
Skill: intermediate

1ST ROW (RS): K1, ✳yo, k3, sl 1, k2tog,

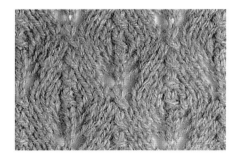

psso, k3, yo, k1; rep from ✳ to end.

2ND ROW: Purl.
Rep the last 2 rows 3 times more.

9TH ROW: K2tog, k3, yo, k1, yo, k3, ✳sl 1, k2tog, psso, k3, yo, k1, yo, k3; rep from ✳ to last 2 sts, sl 1, k1, psso.

10TH ROW: Purl.
Rep the last 2 rows 3 times more.
Rep these 16 rows.

Tracery Pattern
Multiple of 12 sts + 1
Drape: excellent
Skill: intermediate

1ST ROW (RS): K1, ✳yo, k2tog, yo, sl 1, k1, psso, k3, k2tog, yo, k3; rep from ✳ to end.

2ND AND EVERY ALT ROW: P1, ✳yo, p2tog, p10; rep from ✳ to end.

3RD ROW: K1, ✳yo, k2tog, yo, k1, sl 1, k1, psso, k1, k2tog, k1, yo, k3; rep from ✳ to end.

5TH ROW: K1, ✳yo, k2tog, k1, k2tog, yo, k1, yo, sl 1, k1, psso, k4; rep from ✳ to end.

7TH ROW: K1, ✳yo, [k2tog] twice, k1, [yo, k1] twice, sl 1, k1, psso, k3; rep from ✳ to end.

8TH ROW: As 2nd row. Rep these 8 rows.

Rhombus Lace
Multiple of 8 sts + 2
Drape: excellent
Skill: intermediate

1ST ROW (RS): K1, [k2tog, yo] twice, ✳k4, [k2tog, yo] twice; rep from ✳ to last 5 sts, k5.

2ND AND EVERY ALT ROW: Purl.

3RD ROW: [K2tog, yo] twice, ✳k4, [k2tog, yo] twice; rep from ✳ to last 6 sts, k6.

5TH ROW: K1, k2tog, yo, k4, ✳[k2tog, yo] twice, k4; rep from ✳ to last 3 sts, k2tog, yo, k1.

7TH ROW: K3, [k2tog, yo] twice, ✳k4, [k2tog, yo] twice; rep from ✳ to last 3 sts, k3.

9TH ROW: K2, ✳[k2tog, yo] twice, k4; rep from ✳ to end.

11TH ROW: As 1st row.

13TH ROW: K5, [k2tog, yo] twice, ✳k4, [k2tog, yo] twice; rep from ✳ to last st, k1.

15TH ROW: ✳K4, [k2tog, yo] twice; rep from ✳ to last 2 sts, k2.

17TH ROW: As 7th row.

19TH ROW: As 5th row.

21ST ROW: K2tog, yo, k4, ✳[k2tog, yo] twice, k4; rep from ✳ to last 4 sts, k2tog, yo, k2.

23RD ROW: As 13th row.

24TH ROW: Purl.
Rep these 24 rows.

Chalice Pattern

Multiple of 10 sts + 3
Drape: excellent
Skill: intermediate

1ST ROW (RS): K2, yo, k1, sl 1, k1, psso, k3, k2tog, k1, ✳[yo, k1] twice, sl 1, k1, psso, k3, k2tog, k1; rep from ✳ to last 2 sts, yo, k2.
2ND AND EVERY ALT ROW: Purl.
3RD ROW: K3, ✳yo, k1, sl 1, k1, psso, k1, k2tog, k1, yo, k3; rep from ✳ to end.
5TH ROW: K4, yo, k1, sl 1, k2tog, psso, k1, yo, ✳k5, yo, k1, sl 1, k2tog, psso, k1, yo; rep from ✳ to last 4 sts, k4.
7TH ROW: K2, k2tog, k1, yo, k3, yo, k1, sl 1, k1, psso, ✳k1, k2tog, k1, yo, k3, yo, k1, sl 1, k1, psso; rep from ✳ to last 2 sts, k2.
9TH ROW: K1, sl 1, k1, psso, k2, yo, k3, yo, k2, ✳sl 1, k2tog, psso, k2, yo, k3, yo, k2; rep from ✳ to last 3 sts, k2tog, k1.
11TH ROW: K3, ✳k2tog, k1, [yo, k1] twice, sl 1, k1, psso, k3; rep from ✳ to end.
13TH ROW: K2, k2tog, k1, yo, k3, yo, k1, sl 1, k1, psso, ✳k1, k2tog, k1, yo, k3, yo, k1, sl 1, k1, psso; rep from ✳ to last 2 sts, k2.
15TH ROW: K1, sl 1, k1, psso, k1, yo, k5, yo, k1, ✳sl 1, k2tog, psso, k1, yo, k5, yo, k1; rep from ✳ to last 3 sts, k2tog, k1.
17TH ROW: K3, ✳yo, k1, sl 1, k1, psso, k1, k2tog, k1, yo, k3; rep from ✳ to end.
19TH ROW: K3, ✳yo, k2, sl 1, k2tog, psso, k2, yo, k3; rep from ✳ to end.
20TH ROW: Purl. Rep these 20 rows.

Clover Pattern

Multiple of 12 sts + 1
Drape: excellent
Skill: intermediate

1ST ROW (RS): K2tog, k4, yo, k1, yo, k4, ✳sl 1, k2tog, psso, k4, yo, k1, yo, k4; rep from ✳ to last 2 sts, sl 1, k1, psso.
2ND AND EVERY ALT ROW: Purl.
3RD ROW: K2tog, k3, [yo, k3] twice, ✳sl 1, k2tog, psso, k3, [yo, k3] twice; rep from ✳ to last 2 sts, sl 1, k1, psso.
5TH ROW: K2tog, k2, yo, k5, yo, k2, ✳sl 1, k2tog, psso, k2, yo, k5, yo, k2; rep from ✳ to last 2 sts, sl 1, k1, psso.
7TH ROW: K1, ✳yo, k4, sl 1, k2tog, psso, k4, yo, k1; rep from ✳ to end.
9TH ROW: K2, yo, k3, sl 1, k2tog, psso, k3, ✳[yo, k3] twice, sl 1, k2tog, psso, k3; rep from ✳ to last 2 sts, yo, k2.
11TH ROW: K3, yo, k2, sl 1, k2tog, psso, k2, ✳yo, k5, yo, k2, sl 1, k2tog, psso, k2; rep from ✳ to last 3 sts, yo, k3.
12TH ROW: Purl.
Rep these 12 rows.

Goblet Lace

Multiple of 10 sts + 1
Drape: excellent
Skill: intermediate

1ST ROW (RS): K1, ✳yo, sl 1, k1, psso,
k2tog, yo, k1; rep from ✳ to end.
2ND AND EVERY ALT ROW: Purl.
Rep the last 2 rows twice more.
7TH ROW: K1, ✳yo, sl 1, k1, psso, k5, k2tog, yo, k1; rep from ✳ to end.
9TH ROW: K2, yo, sl 1, k1, psso, k3, k2tog, yo, ✳k3, yo, sl 1, k1, psso, k3, k2tog, yo; rep from ✳ to last 2 sts, k2.
11TH ROW: K3, yo, sl 1, k1, psso, k1, k2tog, yo, ✳k5, yo, sl 1, k1, psso, k1, k2tog, yo; rep from ✳ to last 3 sts, k3.
13TH ROW: K4, yo, sl 1, k2tog, psso, yo, ✳k7, yo, sl 1, k2tog, psso, yo; rep from ✳ to last 4 sts, k4.
14TH ROW: Purl.
Rep these 14 rows.

Ornamental Arrow Pattern

Multiple of 12 sts + 1
Drape: excellent
Skill: intermediate

1ST ROW (RS): K1, ✳sl 1, k1, psso, k3, yo, k1, yo, k3, k2tog, k1; rep from ✳ to end.
2ND ROW: P1, ✳p2tog, p2, yo, p3, yo, p2, p2tog tbl, p1; rep from ✳ to end.
3RD ROW: K1, ✳sl 1, k1, psso, k1, yo, k5, yo, k1, k2tog, k1; rep from ✳ to end.
4TH ROW: P1, ✳yo, p2tog, p7, p2tog tbl, yo, p1; rep from ✳ to end.
5TH ROW: K1, ✳yo, k3, k2tog, k1, sl 1, k1, psso, k3, yo, k1; rep from ✳ to end.
6TH ROW: P2, yo, p2, p2tog tbl, p1, p2tog, p2, yo, ✳p3, yo, p2, p2tog tbl, p1, p2tog, p2, yo; rep from ✳ to last 2 sts, p2.
7TH ROW: K3, yo, k1, k2tog, k1, sl 1, k1, psso, k1, yo, ✳k5, yo, k1,

k2tog, k1, sl 1, k1, psso, k1, yo; rep from ✳ to last 3 sts, k3.

8TH ROW: P4, p2tog tbl, yo, p1, yo, p2tog, ✳p7, p2tog tbl, yo, p1, yo, p2tog; rep from ✳ to last 4 sts, p4.

Rep these 8 rows.

Triangles and Lace

Multiple of 12 sts + 1
Drape: excellent
Skill: experienced

1ST ROW (RS): K1, ✳yo, sl 1, k1, psso, p7, k2tog, yo, k1; rep from ✳ to end.

2ND ROW: P3, k7, ✳p5, k7; rep from ✳ to last 3 sts, p3.

3RD ROW: K1, ✳yo, k1, sl 1, k1, psso, p5, k2tog, k1, yo, k1; rep from ✳ to end.

4TH ROW: P4, k5, ✳p7, k5; rep from ✳ to last 4 sts, p4.

5TH ROW: K1, ✳yo, k2, sl 1, k1, psso, p3, k2tog, k2, yo, k1; rep from ✳ to end.

6TH ROW: P5, k3, ✳p9, k3; rep from ✳ to last 5 sts, p5.

7TH ROW: K1, ✳yo, k3, sl 1, k1, psso, p1, k2tog, k3, yo, k1; rep from ✳ to end.

8TH ROW: P6, k1, ✳p11, k1; rep from ✳ to last 6 sts, p6.

9TH ROW: K1, ✳yo, k4, sl 1, k2tog, psso, k4, yo, k1; rep from ✳ to end.

10TH ROW: Purl.

11TH ROW: P4, k2tog, yo, k1, yo, sl 1, k1, psso, ✳p7, k2tog, yo, k1, yo, sl 1, k1, psso; rep from ✳ to last 4 sts, p4.

12TH ROW: K4, p5, ✳k7, p5; rep from ✳ to last 4 sts, k4.

13TH ROW: P3, k2tog, k1, [yo, k1] twice, sl 1, k1, psso, ✳p5, k2tog, k1, [yo, k1] twice,

sl 1, k1, psso; rep from ✳ to last 3 sts, p3.

14TH ROW: K3, p7, ✳k5, p7; rep from ✳ to last 3 sts, k3.

15TH ROW: P2, k2tog, k2, yo, k1, yo, k2, sl 1, k1, psso, ✳p3, k2tog, k2, yo, k1, yo, k2, sl 1, k1, psso; rep from ✳ to last 2 sts, p2.

16TH ROW: K2, p9, ✳k3, p9; rep from ✳ to last 2 sts, k2.

17TH ROW: P1, ✳k2tog, k3, yo, k1, yo, k3, sl 1, k1, psso, p1; rep from ✳ to end.

18TH ROW: K1, ✳p11, k1; rep from ✳ to end.

19TH ROW: K2tog, k4, yo, k1, yo, k4, ✳sl 1, k2tog, psso, k4, yo, k1, yo, k4; rep from ✳ to last 2 sts, sl 1, k1, psso.

20TH ROW: Purl.

Rep these 20 rows.

Plumes

Multiple of 11 sts + 2
Drape: excellent
Skill: intermediate

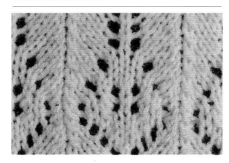

1ST ROW (RS): K1, ✳k2tog, k3, yo, k1, yo, k3, sl 1, k1, psso; rep from ✳ to last st, k1.

2ND AND EVERY ALT ROW: Purl.

3RD AND 5TH ROWS: As 1st row.

7TH ROW: K1, ✳k2tog, k2, yo, k3, yo, k2, sl 1, k1, psso; rep from ✳ to last st, k1.

9TH ROW: K1, ✳k2tog, k1, yo, k5, yo, k1, sl 1, k1, psso; rep from ✳ to last st, k1.

11TH ROW: K1, ✳[k2tog, yo, k1] twice, yo, sl 1, k1, psso, k1, yo, sl 1, k1, psso; rep from ✳ to last st, k1.

13TH ROW: As 11th row.

15TH ROW: As 9th row.

17TH ROW: As 7th row.

18TH ROW: Purl.

Rep these 18 rows.

Filigree Lace

Multiple of 16 sts + 2
Drape: excellent
Skill: experienced

1ST FOUNDATION ROW (RS): K6, k2tog, yo, k2, yo, sl 1, k1, psso, ✳k10, k2tog, yo, k2, yo, sl 1, k1, psso; rep from ✳ to last 6 sts, k6.

2ND FOUNDATION ROW: P5, p2tog tbl, yo, p4, yo, p2tog, ✳p8, p2tog tbl, yo, p4, yo, p2tog; rep from ✳ to last 5 sts, p5.

3RD FOUNDATION ROW: K4, k2tog, yo, k6, yo, sl 1, k1, psso, ✳k6, k2tog, yo, k6, yo, sl 1, k1, psso; rep from ✳ to last 4 sts, k4.

4TH FOUNDATION ROW: P3, p2tog tbl, yo, p4, yo, p2tog, p2, yo, p2tog, ✳p4, p2tog tbl, yo, p4, yo, p2tog, p2, yo, p2tog; rep from ✳ to last 3 sts, p3.

Commence Pattern

1ST ROW: K2, ✳k2tog, yo, k5, yo, sl 1, k1, psso, k3, yo, sl 1, k1, psso, k2; rep from ✳ to end.

2ND ROW: P1, ✳p2tog tbl, yo, p6, yo, p2tog, p4, yo, p2tog; rep from ✳ to last st, p1.

3RD ROW: K1, sl 1 purlwise, k1, yo, sl 1, k1, psso, k4, yo, sl 1, k1, psso, k2, k2tog, yo, k1, ✳[sl 1 purlwise] twice, k1, yo, sl 1, k1, psso, k4, yo, sl 1, k1, psso, k2, k2tog, yo, k1; rep from ✳ to last 2 sts, sl 1 purlwise, k1.

4TH ROW: P4, yo, p2tog, p3, yo, p2tog, p1, p2tog tbl, ✳yo, p6, yo, p2tog, p3,

---

yo, p2tog, p1, p2tog tbl; rep from ✳ to last 4 sts, yo, p4.

5TH ROW: K1, yo, sl 1, k1, psso, k2, yo, sl 1, k1, psso, k4, k2tog, ✳yo, k4, yo, sl 1, k1, psso, k2, yo, sl 1, k1, psso, k4, k2tog; rep from ✳ to last 5 sts, yo, k5.

6TH ROW: P1, yo, p2tog, p3, yo, p2tog, p2, p2tog tbl, ✳yo, p5, yo, p2tog, p3, yo, p2tog, p2, p2tog tbl; rep from ✳ to last 6 sts, yo, p6.

7TH ROW: K1, yo, sl 1, k1, psso, k4, yo, sl 1, k1, psso, k2tog, ✳yo, k6, yo, sl 1, k1, psso, k4, yo, sl 1, k1, psso, k2tog; rep from ✳ to last 7 sts, yo, k7.

8TH ROW: P1, yo, p2tog, p2, p2tog tbl, yo, p1, [sl 1 purlwise] twice, p1, yo, p2tog, ✳p4, yo, p2tog, p2, p2tog tbl, yo, p1, [sl 1 purlwise] twice, p1, yo, p2tog; rep from ✳ to last 5 sts, p5.

9TH ROW: K1, yo, sl 1, k1, psso, k1, k2tog, yo, k2, C2B, k2, yo, sl 1, k1, psso, ✳k3, yo, sl 1, k1, psso, k1, k2tog, yo, k2, C2B, k2, yo, sl 1, k1, psso; rep from ✳ to last 4 sts, k4.

10TH ROW: P3, p2tog tbl, yo, p4, yo, p2tog, p2, yo, p2tog, ✳p4, p2tog tbl, yo, p4, yo, p2tog, p2, yo, p2tog; rep from ✳ to last 3 sts, p3. Rep the last 10 rows.

Crowns of Glory (Cat's Paw)
Multiple of 14 sts + 1
Drape: excellent
Skill: intermediate
Note: Sts should only be counted after the 7th, 8th, 9th, 10th, 11th, and 12th rows.

1ST ROW (RS): K1, ✳sl 1, k1, psso, k9, k2tog, k1; rep from ✳ to end.

2ND ROW: P1, ✳p2tog, p7, p2tog tbl, p1; rep from ✳ to end.

3RD ROW: K1, ✳sl 1, k1, psso, k2, yo 3 times, k3, k2tog, k1; rep from ✳ to end.

4TH ROW: P1, ✳p2tog, p2, [k1, p1, k1, p1, k1] into yo 3 times making 5 sts, p1, p2tog tbl, p1; rep from ✳ to end.

5TH ROW: K1, ✳sl 1, k1, psso, k6, k2tog, k1; rep from ✳ to end.

6TH ROW: P1, ✳p2tog, p7; rep from ✳ to end.

7TH ROW: K2, [yo, k1] 5 times, yo, ✳k3, [yo, k1] 5 times, yo; rep from ✳ to last 2 sts, k2.

8TH ROW: Purl.

9TH AND 10TH ROWS: Knit.

11TH ROW: Purl.

12TH ROW: Knit.

Rep these 12 rows.

Ornamental Tulip Pattern
Multiple of 13 sts
Drape: excellent
Skill: experienced
Note: Sts should only be counted after the 1st, 2nd, 9th, and 10th rows.

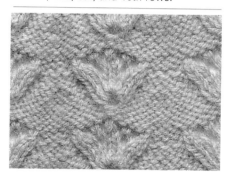

1ST ROW (RS): Purl.

2ND ROW: Knit.

3RD ROW: P6, [p1, k1] 3 times into next st, ✳p12, [p1, k1] 3 times into next st; rep from ✳ to last 6 sts, p6.

4TH ROW: K6, p6, ✳k12, p6; rep from ✳ to last 6 sts, k6.

5TH ROW: P6, k6, ✳p12, k6; rep from ✳ to last 6 sts, p6.

6TH ROW: As 4th row.

7TH ROW: [P2tog] twice, p2, [k2, yo] twice, k2, ✳p2, [p2tog] 4 times, p2, [k2, yo] twice, k2; rep from ✳ to last 6 sts, p2, [p2tog] twice.

8TH ROW: K4, p8, ✳k8, p8; rep from ✳ to last 4 sts, k4.

9TH ROW: [P2tog] twice, [k2tog, yo, k1, yo] twice, k2tog, ✳[p2tog] 4 times, [k2tog, yo, k1, yo] twice, k2tog; rep from ✳ to last 4 sts, [p2tog] twice.

10TH ROW: K2, p9, ✳k4, p9; rep from ✳ to last 2 sts, k2.

Rep these 10 rows.

Embossed Leaf Pattern
Multiple of 7 sts + 6
Drape: good
Skill: intermediate
Note: Sts should only be counted after the 15th and 16th rows.

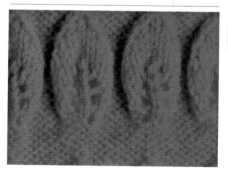

1ST ROW (RS): P6, ✳yo, k1, yo, p6; rep from ✳ to end.

2ND ROW: K6, ✳p3, k6; rep from ✳ to end.

3RD ROW: P6, ✳[k1, yo] twice, k1, p6; rep from ✳ to end.

4TH ROW: K6, ✳p5, k6; rep from ✳ to end.

5TH ROW: P6, ✳k2, yo, k1, yo, k2, p6; rep from ✳ to end.

6TH ROW: K6, ✳p7, k6; rep from ✳ to end.

7TH ROW: P6, ✳k3, yo, k1, yo, k3, p6; rep from ✳ to end.

8TH ROW: K6, ✳p9, k6; rep from ✳ to end.

9TH ROW: P6, ✳sl 1, k1, psso, k5, k2tog, p6; rep from ✳ to end.

10TH ROW: K6, ✳p7, k6; rep from ✳ to end.

11TH ROW: P6, ✳sl 1, k1, psso, k3, k2tog, p6; rep from ✳ to end.

12TH ROW: K6, ✳p5, k6; rep from ✳ to end.

13TH ROW: P6, ✳sl 1, k1, psso, k1, k2tog, p6; rep from ✳ to end.

14TH ROW: K6, ✳p3, k6; rep from ✳ to end.

15TH ROW: P6, ✳sl 1, k2tog, psso, p6; rep from ✳ to end.

16TH ROW: Knit.

17TH ROW: Purl.

Rep the last 2 rows once more, then the 16th row again.

Rep these 20 rows.

Lattice Twist with Eyelets

Multiple of 8 sts + 3
Drape: excellent
Skill: intermediate

1ST ROW (RS): K3, ✳k2tog, yo, k1, yo, sl 1, k1, psso, k3; rep from ✳ to end.

2ND AND EVERY ALT ROW: Purl.

3RD ROW: K2, C2B, k3, C2F, ✳k1, C2B, k3, C2F; rep from ✳ to last 2 sts, k2.

5TH ROW: K1, C2B, k5, ✳C3R, k5; rep from ✳ to last 3 sts, C2F, k1.

7TH ROW: K2, yo, sl 1, k1, psso, k3, k2tog, yo, ✳k1, yo, sl 1, k1, psso, k3, k2tog, yo; rep from ✳ to last 2 sts, k2.

9TH ROW: K3, ✳C2F, k1, C2B, k3; rep from ✳ to end.

11TH ROW: K4, C3R, ✳k5, C3R; rep from ✳ to last 4 sts, k4.

12TH ROW: Purl.

Rep these 12 rows.

Puff Stitch Check

Multiple of 10 sts + 7
Drape: good
Skill: experienced

Special Abbreviation

K5W = knit next 5 sts wrapping yarn twice around needle for each st.

1ST ROW (WS): P6, k5W (see Special Abbreviation), ✳p5, k5W; rep from ✳ to last 6 sts, p6.

2ND ROW: K6, p5 dropping extra loops, ✳k5, p5 dropping extra loops; rep from ✳ to last 6 sts, k6.

Rep the last 2 rows 3 times more.

9TH ROW: P1, k5W, ✳p5, k5W; rep from ✳ to last st, p1.

10TH ROW: K1, p5 dropping extra loops, ✳k5, p5 dropping extra loops; rep from ✳ to last st, k1.

Rep the last 2 rows 3 times more.

Rep these 16 rows.

Open Diamonds with Bobbles

Multiple of 10 + 1
Drape: excellent
Skill: experienced

1ST ROW (RS): P1, ✳yo, sl 1, k1, psso, p5, k2tog, yo, p1; rep from ✳ to end.

2ND ROW: K2, ✳p1, k5, p1, k3; rep from ✳ to last 9 sts, p1, k5, p1, k2.

3RD ROW: P2, ✳yo, sl 1, k1, psso, p3, k2tog, yo, p3; rep from ✳ to last 9 sts, yo, sl 1, k1, psso, p3, k2tog, yo, p2.

4TH ROW: K3, ✳p1, k3, p1, k5; rep from ✳ to last 8 sts, p1, k3, p1, k3.

5TH ROW: P3, ✳yo, sl 1, k1, psso, p1,

k2tog, yo, p5; rep from ✳ to last 8 sts, yo, sl 1, k1, psso, p1, k2tog, yo, p3.

6TH ROW: K4, ✳p1, k1, p1, k7; rep from ✳ to last 7 sts, p1, k1, p1, k4.

7TH ROW: P4, ✳yo, sl 1, k2tog, psso, yo, p3, make bobble (MB) as follows: [k1, p1, k1, p1, k1] into next st, turn and k5, turn and p5, turn and sl 1, k1, psso, k1, k2tog, turn and p3tog, (bobble completed), p3; rep from ✳ to last 7 sts, yo, sl 1, k2tog, psso, yo, p4.

8TH ROW: K4, ✳p3, k3, p1 tbl, k3; rep from ✳ to last 7 sts, p3, k4.

9TH ROW: P3, ✳k2tog, yo, p1, yo, sl 1, k1, psso, p5; rep from ✳ to last 8 sts, k2tog, yo, p1, yo, sl 1, k1, psso, p3.

10TH ROW: K3, ✳p1, k3, p1, k5; rep from ✳ to last 8 sts, p1, k3, p1, k3.

11TH ROW: P2, ✳k2tog, yo, p3, yo, sl 1, k1, psso, p3; rep from ✳ to last 9 sts, k2tog, yo, p3, yo, sl 1, k1, psso, p2.

12TH ROW: K2, ✳p1, k5, p1, k3; rep from ✳ to last 9 sts, p1, k5, p1, k2.

13TH ROW: P1, ✳k2tog, yo, p5, yo, sl 1, k1, psso, p1; rep from ✳ to end.

14TH ROW: K1, ✳p1, k7, p1, k1; rep from ✳ to end.

15TH ROW: K2tog, ✳yo, p3, MB, p3, yo, sl 1, k2tog, psso; rep from ✳ to last 9 sts, yo, p3, MB, p3, yo, sl 1, k1, psso.

16TH ROW: P2, ✳k3, p1 tbl, k3, p3; rep from ✳ to last 9 sts, k3, p1 tbl, k3, p2.

Rep these 16 rows.

Peacock Plumes

Multiple of 16 sts + 1
Drape: excellent
Skill: experienced

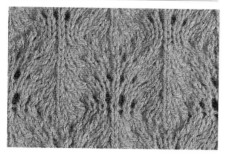

1ST AND 3RD ROWS (WS): Purl.
2ND ROW: Knit.
4TH ROW: [K1, yo] 3 times, [sl 1, k1, psso] twice, sl 2, k1, p2sso, [k2tog] twice, ❋yo, [k1, yo] 5 times, [sl 1, k1, psso] twice, sl 2, k1, p2sso, [k2tog] twice; rep from ❋ to last 3 sts, [yo, k1] 3 times.
Rep the last 4 rows 3 times more.
17TH AND 19TH ROWS: Purl.
18TH ROW: Knit.
20TH ROW: [K2tog] 3 times, ❋yo, [sl 1, k1, psso] twice, sl 2, k1, p2sso, [k2tog] twice, [yo, k1] 5 times; rep from ❋ to last 6 sts, yo, [sl 1, k1, psso] 3 times. Rep the last 4 rows 3 times more.
Rep these 32 rows.

Corona Pattern Stitch

Multiple of 10 sts + 1
Drape: good
Skill: experienced

1ST ROW (RS): K3, k2tog, yo, k1, yo, sl 1, k1, psso, ❋k5, k2tog, yo, k1, yo, sl 1, k1, psso; rep from ❋ to last 3 sts, k3.
2ND, 4TH, 6TH AND 8TH ROWS: Purl.
3RD ROW: K2, k2tog, yo, k3, yo, sl 1, k1, psso, ❋k3, k2tog, yo, k3, yo, sl 1, k1, psso; rep from ❋ to last 2 sts, k2.
5TH ROW: K1, ❋k2tog, yo, k5, yo, sl 1, k1, psso, k1; rep from ❋ to end.
7TH ROW: Knit.
9TH ROW: K6, ❋insert right-hand needle in first space of 5th row, wrap yarn around tip of needle and draw through to make a long loop which is kept on needle; rep from ❋ into each of remaining 5 spaces of leaf from right to left, k10; rep from ❋ to last 5 sts, take up a long loop as before in next 6 spaces, knit to end.
10TH ROW: P5, purl tog the 6 long loops with the next st, ❋p9, purl tog the 6 long loops with the next st; rep from ❋ to last 5 sts, p5.
11TH ROW: Knit.
12TH, 14TH, 16TH, 18TH, AND 20TH ROWS: Purl.
13TH ROW: K1, ❋yo, sl 1, k1, psso, k5, k2tog, yo, k1; rep from ❋ to end.
15TH ROW: K2, yo, sl 1, k1, psso, k3, k2tog, yo, ❋k3, yo, sl 1, k1, psso, k3, k2tog, yo; rep from ❋ to last 2 sts, k2.
17TH ROW: K3, yo, sl 1, k1, psso, k1, k2tog, yo, ❋k5, yo, sl 1, k1, psso, k1, k2tog, yo; rep from ❋ to last 3 sts, k3.
19TH ROW: Knit.
21ST ROW: K1, take up a long loop as before in next 3 spaces, k10, ❋take up a long loop in each of next 6 spaces, k10; rep from ❋ to last st, take up a long loop in each of next 3 spaces.
22ND ROW: Purl tog the first 3 long loops with the next st, p9, ❋purl tog the 6 long loops with the next st, p9; rep from ❋ to last st, purl tog the last 3 long loops with the last st.
23RD ROW: Knit.
24TH ROW: Purl.
Rep these 24 rows.

Filigree Cables Pattern

Multiple of 12 sts + 8
Drape: excellent
Skill: experienced

1ST ROW (RS): P2, ❋k2, yo, k2tog, p2; rep from ❋ to end.
2ND ROW: K2, ❋p2, yo, p2tog, k2; rep from ❋ to end.
Rep the last 2 rows twice more.
7TH ROW: P2, k2, yo, k2tog, p2, ❋C4F, p2, k2, yo, k2tog, p2; rep from ❋ to end.
8TH ROW: As 2nd row.
Rep the 1st and 2nd rows 3 times more.
15TH ROW: P2, C4F, p2, ❋k2, yo, k2tog, p2, C4F, p2; rep from ❋ to end.
16TH ROW: As 2nd row.
Rep these 16 rows.

panel patterns

The easiest way to give a distinctive touch to a simple Stockinette stitch or reverse Stockinette stitch garment is by adding a panel pattern. This can be placed in the front center or asymmetrically on a pullover or down each side on a cardigan. Often, you can simply subtract the number of stitches in the panel from those across the width of the garment, and insert the panel stitches at the appropriate place.

cable panels

Cables are magical. Even a simple ropelike cable beguiles the eye with its sinuous twisting, and elaborate interlaced effects, such as Celtic Plait (*page 138*), have an almost mystical quality. When combined, as in traditional Aran designs, they are quite spectacular; but even a single cable panel, such as Yoked Cable (*page 145*), would make a striking feature. A smooth yarn will best display the cable, and in most cases reverse Stockinette stitch will provide the best background.

Slipped 3-Stitch Cable
Skill: intermediate

Slipped to the left
1ST ROW (RS): Sl 1 purlwise, k2.
2ND ROW: P2, sl 1 purlwise.
3RD ROW: C3L.
4TH ROW: Purl.
Rep these 4 rows.

Slipped to the right
1ST ROW (RS): K2, sl 1 purlwise.
2ND ROW: Sl 1 purlwise, p2.
3RD ROW: C3R.
4TH ROW: Purl.
Rep these 4 rows.

12-Stitch Plait
Skill: intermediate

DOWNWARD PLAIT
1ST ROW (RS): Knit.
2ND AND EVERY ALT ROW: Purl.
3RD ROW: C8F, k4.
5TH AND 7TH ROWS: Knit.
9TH ROW: K4, C8B.
11TH ROW: Knit.
12TH ROW: Purl.
Rep these 12 rows.

UPWARD PLAIT
1ST ROW (RS): Knit.
2ND ROW AND EVERY ALT ROW: Purl.
3RD ROW: C8B, k4.
5TH AND 7TH ROWS: Knit.
9TH ROW: K4, C8F.
11TH ROW: Knit.
12TH ROW: Purl.
Rep these 12 rows.

6-Stitch Slipped Double Cable
Skill: intermediate

DOWNWARD CABLE
1ST ROW (RS): Sl 1 purlwise, k4, sl 1 purlwise.
2ND ROW: Sl 1 purlwise, p4, sl 1 purlwise.
Rep the last 2 rows once more.
5TH ROW: C3L, C3R.
6TH ROW: Purl.
Rep these 6 rows.

UPWARD CABLE
1ST ROW (RS): K2, [sl 1 purlwise] twice, k2.
2ND ROW: P2, [sl 1 purlwise] twice, p2.
Rep the last 2 rows once more.
5TH ROW: C3R, C3L.
6TH ROW: Purl.
Rep these 6 rows.

panel patterns

4-Stitch Cable
Skill: intermediate

1ST ROW (RS): Knit.
2ND ROW: Purl.
Rep the last 2 rows once more.
5TH ROW: C4B.
6TH ROW: Purl.
Rep these 6 rows.
The cable as given above twists to the right. To work the 4 st cable twisted to the left, work C4F instead of C4B in the 5th row.

Wide Cable Panel
Worked over 20 sts on a background of reversed St st
Skill: intermediate

1ST AND EVERY ALT ROW (WS): Purl.
2ND ROW: K6, C4B, C4F, k6.
4TH ROW: K4, C4B, k4, C4F, k4.
6TH ROW: K2, C4B, k8, C4F, k2.
8TH ROW: C4B, k12, C4F.
Rep these 8 rows.

Double Cable
Worked over 12 sts on a background of reverse St st
Skill: intermediate

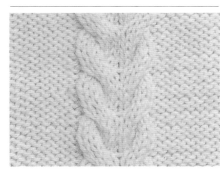

1ST ROW (RS): K12.
2ND ROW: P12.
3RD ROW: C6B, C6F.
4TH ROW: P12.
5TH AND 6TH ROWS: As 1st and 2nd rows.
Rep these 6 rows.

Fishtails
Worked over 9 sts
Skill: intermediate
Fishtails (on left of photograph): panel of 9 sts on a background of reverse St st.
Fishtails (on right of photograph): work as for left-hand panel, but working RC4 in place of LC4, and LC4 in place of RC4.

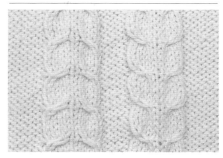

Special Abbreviations
RC4 (Right Cable 4) = slip next 3 sts onto cable needle and hold at back of work, knit next st from left-hand needle, then knit sts from cable needle.

LC4 (Left Cable 4) = slip next st onto cable needle and hold at front of work, knit next 3 sts from left-hand needle, then knit st from cable needle.
1ST ROW (RS): K9.
2ND ROW: P9.
3RD ROW: LC4 (see Special Abbreviations), k1, RC4 (see Special Abbreviations).
4TH ROW: P9.
5TH AND 6TH ROWS: As 1st and 2nd rows.
Rep these 6 rows.

Knotted Cable
Panel with a multiple of 4 sts + 6
Skill: intermediate

Example shown is worked over 10 sts on a background of reverse St st.
1ST ROW (RS): K2, ✳C4F; rep from ✳ to end.
2ND ROW: Purl.
3RD ROW: ✳C4B; rep from ✳ to last 2 sts, k2.
4TH ROW: Purl.
Rep these 4 rows.

Triple Cable
Panel with a multiple of 6 sts + 9
Example shown is worked over 15 sts on a background of reverse St st.
Skill: intermediate

1ST ROW (RS): Knit.
2ND ROW: Purl.
3RD ROW: K3, ✳C6F; rep from ✳ to end.
4TH ROW: Purl.

5TH AND 6TH ROWS: As 1st and 2nd rows.
7TH ROW: ✳C6B; rep from ✳ to last 3 sts, k3.
8TH ROW: Purl.
Rep these 8 rows.

Arrow Cable
Panel of 24 sts on a background of reverse St st
Skill: experienced

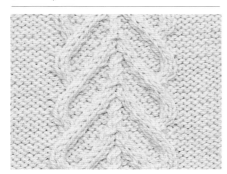

1ST ROW (RS): k2, p4, T4F, p1, C2B, p1, T4B, p4, k2.
2ND ROW: P2, k6, [p2, k1] twice, p2, k6, p2.
3RD ROW: T4F, p4, T4F, T4B, p4, T4B.
4TH ROW: K2, p2, k6, p4, k6, p2, k2.
5TH ROW: P2, C4F, p4, T2F, T2B, p4, C4B, p2.
6TH ROW: K2, p4, k5, p2, k5, p4, k2.
7TH ROW: T4B, T4F, p3, C2B, p3, T4B, T4F.
8TH ROW: P2, k4, [p2, k3] twice, p2, k4, p2.
Rep these 8 rows.

Ribbed Cable
Panel of 11 sts on a background of reverse St st
Skill: intermediate

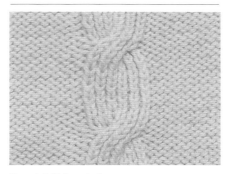

Special Abbreviation
T11B RIB (Twist 11 Back Rib) = slip next 6 sts onto cable needle and hold at back of work, k1, [p1, k1] twice from left-hand needle, then [p1, k1] 3 times from cable needle.
1ST ROW (RS): K1, [p1, k1] 5 times.
2ND ROW: p1 tbl, [k1, p1 tbl] 5 times.
3RD ROW: T11B Rib (see Special Abbreviation).
4TH ROW: As 2nd row.
5TH TO 14TH ROWS: Rep 1st and 2nd rows 5 times. Rep these 14 rows.

Ribbed Double Cable
Panel of 16 sts on a background of reverse St st
Skill: intermediate

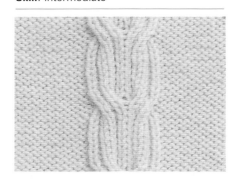

Special Abbreviations
T8B RIB (Twist 8 Back Rib) = slip next 4 sts onto cable needle and hold at back of work, k1, p2, k1 from left-hand needle, then k1, p2, k1 from cable needle.
T8F RIB (Twist 8 Front Rib) = slip next 4 sts onto cable needle and hold at front of work, k1, p2, k1 from left-hand needle, then k1, p2, k1 from cable needle.
1ST ROW (RS): K1, p2, [k2, p2] 3 times, k1.
2ND ROW: P1, k2, [p2, k2] 3 times, p1.
3RD ROW: T8B Rib, T8F Rib (see Special Abbreviations for both).
4TH ROW: As 2nd row.
5TH TO 12TH ROWS: Rep 1st and 2nd rows 4 times. Rep these 12 rows.

Figure-of-Eight
Panel of 10 sts on a background of reverse St st
Skill: intermediate

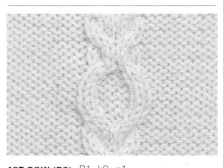

1ST ROW (RS): P1, k8, p1.
2ND ROW: K1, p8, k1.
3RD ROW: P1, C4B, C4F, p1.
4TH ROW: As 2nd row.
5TH AND 6TH ROWS: As 1st and 2nd rows.
7TH ROW: P1, T4B, T4F, p1.
8TH ROW: K1, p2, k4, p2, k1.
9TH ROW: T3B, p4, T3F.
10TH ROW: P2, k6, p2.
11TH ROW: K2, p6, k2.
12TH ROW: P2, k6, p2.
13TH ROW: T3F, p4, T3B.
14TH ROW: As 8th row.
15TH ROW: P1, C4F, C4B, p1.
16TH ROW: K1, p8, k1. Rep these 16 rows.

panel patterns

Twisted Cable

Panel of 6 sts on a background of reverse St st
Skill: intermediate

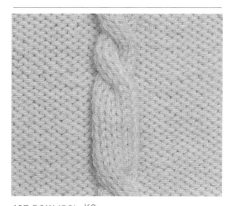

1ST ROW (RS): K6.
2ND ROW: P6.
3RD ROW: C6F.
4TH ROW: P6.
5TH TO 10TH ROWS: Rep 1st and 2nd rows once, then rep 1st to 4th rows once.
11TH TO 20TH ROWS: Rep 1st and 2nd rows 5 times. Rep these 20 rows.

Framed Double Moss Stitch

Panel of 16 sts on a background of reverse St st
Skill: intermediate

1ST ROW (RS): P4, C4R, T4L, p4.
2ND ROW: K4, p3, k1, p4, k4.
3RD ROW: P3, C4R, p1, k1, T4L, p3.
4TH ROW: K3, p3, k1, p1, k1, p4, k3.

5TH ROW: p2, C4R, [p1, k1] twice, T4L, p2.
6TH ROW: K2, p3, [p1, k1] twice, p4, k2.
7TH ROW: P1, C4R, [p1, k1] 3 times, T4L, p1.
8TH ROW: K1, p3, k1, [p1, k1] 3 times, p4, k1.
9TH ROW: C4R, [p1, k1] 4 times, T4L.
10TH ROW: P3, k1, [p1, k1] 4 times, p4.
11TH ROW: T4L [k1, p1] 4 times, T4R.
12TH ROW: As 8th row.
13TH ROW: P1, T4L, [k1, p1] 3 times, T4R, p1.
14TH ROW: As 6th row.
15TH ROW: P2, T4L, [k1, p1] twice, T4R, p2.
16TH ROW: As 4th row.
17TH ROW: P3, T4L, k1, p1, T4R, p3.
18TH ROW: As 2nd row.
19TH ROW: P4, T4L, T4R, p4.
20TH ROW: K5, p6, k5.
21ST ROW: P5, C6B, p5.
22ND ROW: K5, p6, k5.
Rep these 22 rows.

Branched Cable

Worked over 10 sts on a background of reversed St st
Skill: intermediate
The cable as given below crosses to the left. To work the cable crossed to the right, work C4B instead of C4F in the 1st row.

1ST ROW (RS): P3, C4F, p3.
2ND ROW: K3, p4, k3.
3RD ROW: P2, C3B, C3F, p2.
4TH ROW: K2, p6, k2.
5TH ROW: P1, C3B, k2, C3F, p1.
6TH ROW: K1, p8, k1.
7TH ROW: C3B, k4, C3F.
8TH ROW: Purl. Rep these 8 rows.

Interlocking Twist

Worked over 27 sts
Skill: experienced

1ST ROW (RS): K5, p1, k6, p3, k6, p1, k5.
2ND ROW: P5, k1, p6, k3, p6, k1, p5.
3RD ROW: K5, p1, C6B, p3, C6F, p1, k5.
4TH ROW: As 2nd row.
Rep the last 4 rows once more, then 1st and 2nd rows again.
11TH ROW: C12F, p3, C12B.
12TH ROW: P6, k1, p5, k3, p5, k1, p6.
13TH ROW: K6, p1, k5, p3, k5, p1, k6.
14TH ROW: As 12th row.
15TH ROW: C6F, p1, k5, p3, k5, p1, C6B.
16TH ROW: As 12th row.
Rep the last 4 rows 3 times more, then 13th and 14th rows again.
31ST ROW: C12B, p3, C12F.
32ND ROW: As 2nd row.
33RD TO 36TH ROWS: As 1st to 4th rows inclusive. Rep these 4 rows once more. Rep these 40 rows.

Woven Cable

Worked over a multiple of 8 sts + 4 on a background of reversed St st (min. 20 sts).
Skill: intermediate
The example shown (page 137) is worked over 28 sts.

1ST ROW (RS): Knit.
2ND AND EVERY ALT ROW: K2, purl to 2 sts

before end of panel, k2.
3RD ROW: Knit.
5TH ROW: K2, ✳C8B; rep from ✳ to 2 sts before end of panel, k2.
7TH ROW: Knit.
9TH ROW: Knit.
11TH ROW: K6, ✳C8F; rep from ✳ to 6 sts before end of panel, k6.
12TH ROW: As 2nd row. Rep these 12 rows.

Cupped Cable
Worked over 15 sts on a background of reversed St st
Skill: intermediate

Special Abbreviation
T5L (TWIST 5 LEFT) = slip next 2 sts onto cable needle and hold at front of work, K2, p1 from left-hand needle, then K2 from cable needle.
1ST ROW (RS): P5, T5L (see Special Abbreviation), p5.
2ND ROW: K5, p2, k1, p2, k5.
3RD ROW: P4, T3B, k1, T3F, p4.
4TH ROW: K4, p2, k1, p1, k1, p2, k4.

5TH ROW: P3, T3B, k1, p1, k1, T3F, p3.
6TH ROW: K3, p2, [k1, p1] twice, k1, p2, k3.
7TH ROW: P2, T3B, [k1, p1] twice, k1, T3F, p2.
8TH ROW: K2, p2, [k1, p1] 3 times, k1, p2, k2.
9TH ROW: P1, T3B, [k1, p1] 3 times, k1, T3F, p1.
10TH ROW: K1, p2, [k1, p1] 4 times, k1, p2, k1.
11TH ROW: T3B, [k1, p1] 4 times, k1, T3F.
12TH ROW: P2, [k1, p1] 5 times, k1, p2.
Rep these 12 rows.

9-Stitch Cable with Bobbles
Worked over 9 sts on a background of reverse St st
Skill: intermediate

1ST ROW (RS): Knit.
2ND ROW: Purl.
Rep the last 2 rows once more.
5TH ROW: C9F.
6TH ROW: Purl.
7TH ROW: K4, [k1, yo, k1, yo, k1] into next st, turn and k5, turn and p5, turn and sl 1, k1, psso, k1, k2tog, turn and p3tog (1 bobble completed), k4.
8TH ROW: Purl. Rep 1st and 2nd rows twice more. Rep these 12 rows.

Small Moss Stitch Cable
Worked over 5 sts on a background of reverse St st
Skill: intermediate

1ST ROW (WS): [P1, k1] twice, p1.
2ND ROW: K2, p1, k2.

Rep the last 2 rows once more, then the 1st row again.
6TH ROW: Slip next st onto cable needle and hold at front of work, slip next 3 sts onto 2nd cable needle and hold at back of work, knit next st from left-hand needle, knit the 3 sts from 2nd cable needle, then knit st from 1st cable needle.
Work 5 rows in St st, starting purl.
12TH ROW: As 6th row.
Work 1st and 2nd rows twice more.
Rep these 16 rows.

Climbing Vine
Worked over 14 sts on a background of reverse St st
Skill: experienced

Special Abbreviations
C2BP OR C2FP (Cross 2 Back or Cross 2 Front Purlwise) = slip next st onto cable needle and hold at back (or front) of work, purl next st from left-hand needle, then purl st from cable needle.
1ST ROW (WS): P3, k3, p4, C2BP (see

Special Abbreviations), k2.
2ND ROW: P1, C2B, k1, T2B, k2, p3, T2F, k1.
3RD ROW: P2, k4, p2, k1, p3, C2BP.
4TH ROW: K3, T2B, p1, k1, C2F, p3, T2F.
5TH ROW: K4, C2FP, p2, k2, p4.
6TH ROW: K2, T2B, p2, k1, [C2F] twice, p3.
7TH ROW: K2, C2FP, p4, k3, p3.
8TH ROW: K1, T2B, p3, k2, T2F, k1, C2F, p1.
9TH ROW: C2FP, p3, k1, p2, k4, p2.
10TH ROW: T2B, p3, C2B, k1, p1, T2F, k3.
11TH ROW: P4, k2, p2, C2BP, k4.
12TH ROW: P3, [C2B] twice, k1, p2, T2F, k2.
Rep these 12 rows.

Double Chain
Worked over 18 sts on a background of reverse St st
Skill: experienced

1ST ROW (RS): P3, k3, [p1, k1] twice, p1, k4, p3.
2ND ROW: K3, p3, [k1, p1] twice, k1, p4, k3.
Rep the last 2 rows once more.
5TH ROW: P3, slip next 3 sts onto cable needle and hold at back of work, k1, p1, k1 from left-hand needle, then k3 from cable needle, slip next 3 sts onto cable needle and hold at front of work, knit the next 3 sts from left-hand needle, then p1, k1, p1 from cable needle, p3.
6TH ROW: K3, p1, k1, p7, k1, p1, k4.
7TH ROW: P3, k1, p1, k7, p1, k1, p4.
Rep the last 2 rows 3 times more, then work 6th row again.
15TH ROW: P3, slip next 3 sts onto cable needle and leave at front of work, knit next 3 sts from left-hand needle, then

p1, k1, p1 from cable needle, slip next 3 sts onto cable needle and leave at back of work, k1, p1, k1 from left-hand needle, then k3 from cable needle, p3.
16TH ROW: As 2nd row.
17TH ROW: As 1st row.
Rep the last 2 rows 3 times more, then work 16th row again. Rep these 24 rows.

Cable and Bobble Panel
Panel of 6 sts on a background of reverse St st
Skill: intermediate

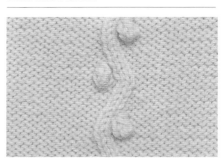

1ST ROW (RS): P1, MB#2, p1, T3B.
2ND ROW: K1, p2, k3.
3RD ROW: P2, T3B, p1.
4TH ROW: K2, p2, k2.
5TH ROW: P1, T3B, p2.
6TH ROW: K3, p2, k1.
7TH ROW: T3B, p3.
8TH ROW: K4, p2.
9TH ROW: T3F, p1, MB#2, p1.
10TH ROW: K3, p2, k1.
11TH ROW: P1, T3F, p2.
12TH ROW: K2, p2, k2.
13TH ROW: P2, T3F, p1.
14TH ROW: K1, p2, k3.
15TH ROW: P3, T3F.
16TH ROW: P2, k4.
Rep these 16 rows.

Celtic Plait
Panel of 24 sts on a background of reverse St st
Skill: experienced

1ST ROW (RS): P2, C4B, [p4,C4B] twice, p2.
2ND ROW: K2, p4, [k4, p4] twice, k2.
3RD ROW: P1, T3B, [T4F, T4B] twice, T3F, p1.
4TH ROW: K1, p2, k3, p4, 4, p4, k3, p2, k1, k.
5TH ROW: T3B, p3, C4F, p4, C4F, p3, T3F.
6TH ROW: P2, k4, [p4, k4] twice, p2.
7TH ROW: K2, p3, T3B, T4F, T4B, T3F, p3, k2.
8TH ROW: [P2, k3] twice, p4, [k3, p2] twice.
9TH ROW: [K2, p3] twice, C4B, [p3, k2] twice.
10TH ROW: As 8th row.
11TH ROW: K2, p3, T3F, T4B, T4F, T3B, p3, k2.
12TH ROW: As 6th row.
13TH ROW: T3F, p3, C4F, p4, C4F, p3, T3B.
14TH ROW: As 4th row.
15TH ROW: P1, T3F, [T4B, T4F] twice, T3B, p1.
16TH ROW: As 2nd row. Rep these 16 rows.

Pinched Cable
Panel of 9 sts on a background of reverse St st
Skill: experienced

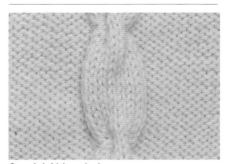

Special Abbreviation
C9X (Cable 9X) = slip next 3 sts onto a cable needle and hold at back of work, slip following 3 sts onto 2nd cable needle and

hold at front of work, knit next 3 sts from left-hand needle, knit the 3 sts from 2nd cable needle, then the 3 sts from 1st cable needle.

1ST ROW (RS): K9.
2ND ROW: P9.
Rep the last 2 rows once more.
5TH ROW: C9X (see Special Abbreviation).
6TH ROW: P9.
7TH TO 16TH ROWS: Rep 1st and 2nd rows 5 times. Rep these 16 rows.

Noughts and Crosses
Panel of 12 sts on a background of reverse St st
Skill: intermediate

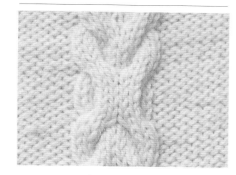

1ST ROW (RS): K12.
2ND ROW: P12.
3RD ROW: C6B, C6F.
4TH ROW: P12.
5TH TO 8TH ROWS: Rep 1st and 2nd rows twice.
9TH AND 10TH ROWS: As 3rd and 4th rows.
11TH TO 14TH ROWS: Rep 1st and 2nd rows twice.
15TH ROW: C6F, C6B.
16TH ROW: P12.
17TH AND 20TH ROWS: Rep 1st and 2nd rows twice.
21ST AND 22ND ROWS: As 15th and 16th rows.
23RD AND 24TH ROWS: As 1st and 2nd rows. Rep these 24 rows.

Crossing Lines
Panel of 16 sts on a background of reverse St st
Skill: experienced

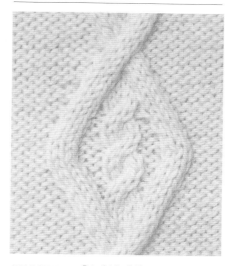

1ST ROW (RS): P4, C4R, C4L, p4.
2ND ROW: K4, p8, k4.
3RD ROW: P3, C4R, k2, C4L, p3.
4TH ROW: K3, p10, k3.
5TH ROW: P2, T4R, k4, T4L, p2.
6TH ROW: K2, p3, k1, p4, k1, p3, k2.
7TH ROW: P1, T4R, p1, C4B, p1, T4L, p1.
8TH ROW: K1, p3, k2, p4, k2, p3, k1.
9TH ROW: T4R, p2, k4, p2, T4L.
10TH ROW: P3, k3, p4, k3, p3.
11TH ROW: K3, p3, C4B, p3, k3.
12TH ROW: As 10th row.
13TH ROW: T4L, p2, k4, p2, T4R.
14TH ROW: As 8th row.
15TH ROW: P1, T4L, p1, C4B, p1, T4R, p1.
16TH ROW: As 6th row.
17TH ROW: P2, T4L, k4, T4R, p2.
18TH ROW: K3, p10, k3.
19TH ROW: P3, T4L, k2, T4R, p3.
20TH ROW: K4, p8, k4.
21ST ROW: P4, T4L, T4R, p4.
22ND ROW: K5, p6, k5.
23RD ROW: P5, C6B, p5.
24TH ROW: K5, p6, k5.
Rep these 24 rows.

Cabled Arrows
Worked over 14 sts on a background of reverse St st
Skill: intermediate

1ST ROW (RS): K4, p2, k2, p2, k4.
2ND ROW: P4, k2, p2, k2, p4.
Rep these 2 rows 3 times more.
9TH ROW: C4F, p2, K2, p2, C4B.
10TH ROW: As 2nd row.
11TH ROW: K2, C4F, k2, C4B, k2.
12TH ROW: Purl.
13TH ROW: K4, p1, T2F, T2B, p1, k4.
14TH ROW: As 2nd row.
15TH ROW: As 1st row.
16TH ROW: As 2nd row. Rep these 16 rows.

Bobbles and Waves
Worked over 26 sts on a background of reversed St st
Skill: experienced

1ST ROW (RS): P2, T3B, p5, C6B, p5, T3F, p2.

2ND ROW: K2, p2, k6, p6, k6, p2, k2.
3RD ROW: P1, T3B, p4, T5B, T5F, p4, T3F, p1.
4TH ROW: K1, p2, k5, p3, k4, p3, k5, p2, k1.
5TH ROW: T3B, p3, T5B, p4, T5F, p3, T3F.
6TH ROW: P2, k1, Make Bobble as follows: knit into front, back, and front of next st, [turn and knit these 3 sts] 3 times, then turn and sl 1, k2tog, psso (bobble completed), k2, p3, k8, p3, k2, Make Bobble as before, k1, p2.
7TH ROW: T3F, p3, k3, p8, k3, p3, T3B.
8TH ROW: K1, p2, k3, p3, k8, p3, k3, p2, k1.
9TH ROW: P1, T3F, p2, T5F, p4, T5B, p2, T3B, p1.
10TH ROW: K2, p2, [k4, p3] twice, k4, p2, k2.
11TH ROW: P2, T3F, p3, T5F, T5B, p3, T3B, p2.
12TH ROW: K1, Make Bobble as before, k1, p2, k5, p6, k5, p2, k1, Make Bobble, k1.
Rep these 12 rows.

Sloping Diamonds
Worked over 10 sts
Skill: intermediate

Slope to the right
1ST ROW (RS): K2, p5, C3B.
2ND ROW: P3, k5, p2.
3RD ROW: K2, p4, C3B, k1.
4TH ROW: P4, k4, p2.
5TH ROW: K2, p3, T3B, k2.
6TH ROW: P2, k1, p2, k3, p2.
7TH ROW: K2, p2, T3B, p1, k2.
8TH ROW: P2, [k2, p2] twice.
9TH ROW: K2, p1, T3B, p2, k2.

10TH ROW: P2, k3, p2, k1, p2.
11TH ROW: K2, T3B, p3, k2.
12TH ROW: P2, k4, p4.
13TH ROW: K1, T3B, p4, k2.
14TH ROW: P2, k5, p3.
15TH ROW: T3B, p5, k2.
16TH ROW: P2, k6, p2.
Rep these 16 rows.

Slope to the left
1ST ROW (RS): C3F, p5, k2.
2ND ROW: P2, k5, p3.
3RD ROW: K1, C3F, p4, k2.
4TH ROW: P2, k4, p4.
5TH ROW: K2, T3F, p3, k2.
6TH ROW: P2, k3, p2, k1, p2.
7TH ROW: K2, p1, T3F, p2, k2.
8TH ROW: P2, [k2, p2] twice.
9TH ROW: K2, p2, T3F, p1, k2.
10TH ROW: P2, k1, p2, k3, p2.
11TH ROW: K2, p3, T3F, k2.
12TH ROW: P4, k4, p2.
13TH ROW: K2, p4, T3F, k1.
14TH ROW: P3, k5, p2.
15TH ROW: K2, p5, T3F.
16TH ROW: P2, k6, p2.
Rep these 16 rows.

Fancy Cross and Cable Panel
Worked over 24 sts on a background of reverse St st
Skill: experienced

1ST ROW (WS): [K2, p2] 3 times, [p2, k2] 3 times.
2ND ROW: P2, C2B, p2, T4F, C4F, T4B, p2, C2B, p2.

3RD ROW: K2, p2, k4, p8, k4, p2, k2.
4TH ROW: P2, k2, p4, [C4B] twice, p4, k2, p2.
5TH ROW: As 3rd row.
6TH ROW: P2, C2B, p2, T4B, C4F, T4F, p2, C2B, p2.
7TH ROW: [K2, p2] twice, k2, p4, [k2, p2] twice, k2.
8TH ROW: P2, [k2, p2] twice, k4, p2, [k2, p2] twice.
9TH ROW: K2, [p4, k4] twice, p4, k2.
10TH ROW: P2, [k4, p4] twice, k4, p2.
11TH ROW: As 9th row.
12TH ROW: P2, k4, p4, C4F, p4, k4, p2.
13TH ROW: As 9th row.
14TH ROW: As 10th row.
15TH ROW: As 9th row.
16TH ROW: P2, k2, T4F, p2, k4, p2, T4B, k2, p2.
Rep these 16 rows.

Knotted Cable
Worked over 6 sts on a background of reverse St st
Skill: intermediate

1ST ROW (RS): K2, P2, k2.
2ND AND EVERY ALT ROW: P2, k2, p2.
3RD ROW: C6.
5TH, 7TH, AND 9TH ROWS: K2, p2, k2.
10TH ROW: As 2nd row.
Rep these 10 rows.

Cable Gate

Worked over 16 sts on a background of reverse St st
Skill: experienced
Note: Increases should be made by purling into front and back of next st.

Special Abbreviations

T4BR (Twist 4 Back Right) = slip next st onto cable needle and hold at back of work, knit next 3 sts from left-hand needle, then purl st from cable needle.

C5RI (Cross 5 Right Increase) = slip next st onto cable needle and hold at back of work, knit next 4 sts from left-hand needle, then knit into front and back of st on cable needle.

1ST ROW (RS): P2, [k5, p2] twice.
2ND ROW: K2, [p5, k2] twice.
3RD ROW: P1, inc in next st, k4, sl 1, k1, psso, k2tog, k4, inc in next st, p1.
4TH ROW: K3, p10, k3.
5TH ROW: P2, inc in next st, k2, sl 1, k1, psso, C5RI (see Special Abbreviations), T2F, p2.
6TH ROW: K2, p1, k2, p7, k4.
7TH ROW: P3, inc in next st, k2, sl 1, k1, psso, T3B, p2, T2F, p1.
8TH ROW: K1, p1, k4, p5, k5.
9TH ROW: P5, T4BR (see Special Abbreviations), T2F, p3, T2F.
10TH ROW: P1, k4, p1, k2, p3, k5.
11TH ROW: P4, T4BR, p2, T2F, p2, T2B.
12TH ROW: K1, p1, k2, p1, k4, p3, k4.
13TH ROW: P3, T3B, T2F, p3, T2F, T2B, p1.
14TH ROW: K2, p2, k4, p1, k2, p2, k3.
15TH ROW: P2, T3B, p2, T2F, p2, T3B, p2.
16TH ROW: K3, p2, k2, p1, k4, p2, k2.
17TH ROW: P1, T2B, T2F, p3, T2F, T3B, p3.
18TH ROW: K4, p3, k4, p1, k2, p1, k1.
19TH ROW: T2B, p2, T2F, p2, T4BR, p4.
20TH ROW: K5, p3, k2, p1, k4, p1.
21ST ROW: T2F, p3, T2F, T4BR, p5.
22ND ROW: K6, p4, k4, p1, k1.
23RD ROW: P1, T2F, p2, C5RI, k1, p2tog, p3.
24TH ROW: K4, p7, k2, p1, k2.
25TH ROW: P2, T2F, C5RI, k3, p2tog, p2.
26TH ROW: K3, p10, k3.
27TH ROW: P1, p2tog, k5, purl into front and back of loop lying between stitch just worked and next stitch, k5, p2tog, p1.
28TH ROW: As 2nd row.
Rep these 28 rows.

Lattice Cable

Worked across 24 sts on a background of reverse St st
Skill: intermediate

1ST ROW (RS): K2, p8, C4B, p8, k2.
2ND ROW: P2, k8, p4, k8, p2.
3RD ROW: T4F, p4, T4B, T4F, p4, T4B.
4TH ROW: K2, [p2, k4] 3 times, p2, k2.
5TH ROW: P2, T4F, T4B, p4, T4F, T4B, p2.
6TH ROW: K4, p4, k8, p4, k4.
7TH ROW: P4, C4B, p8, C4F, p4.
8TH ROW: As 6th row.
9TH ROW: P2, T4B, T4F, p4, T4B, T4F, p2.
10TH ROW: As 4th row.
11TH ROW: T4B, p4, T4F, T4B, p4, T4F.
12TH ROW: As 2nd row.
Rep these 12 rows.

Garter and Stocking Stitch Cable

Worked over 8 sts on a background of reverse St st
Skill: intermediate

1ST ROW (RS): Knit.
2ND ROW: P4, k4.
Rep the last 2 rows twice more.
7TH ROW: C8B.
8TH ROW: K4, p4.
9TH ROW: Knit.
Rep the last 2 rows 4 times more, then the 8th row again.
19TH ROW: C8B.
20TH ROW: As 2nd row.
21ST ROW: Knit.
Rep the last 2 rows once more, then the 20th row again.
Rep these 24 rows.

Criss-cross Cable with Twists

Worked over 16 sts on a background of reverse St st
Skill: experienced

1ST ROW (RS): P2, C4F, p4, C4F, p2.
2ND ROW: K2, p4, k4, p4, k2.
3RD ROW: P2, k4, p4, k4, p2.
4TH ROW: As 2nd row.
5TH ROW: As 1st row.
6TH ROW: As 2nd row.
7TH ROW: [T4B, T4F] twice.
8TH ROW: As 3rd row.
9TH ROW: K2, p4, C4F, p4, k2.
10TH ROW: As 3rd row.
11TH ROW: As 2nd row.
12TH ROW: As 3rd row.
13TH ROW: As 9th row.
Rep the last 4 rows twice more.
22ND ROW: As 3rd row.
23RD ROW: [T4F, T4B] twice.
24TH ROW: As 2nd row.
Rep these 24 rows.

Ribbed Arrows
Panel of 18 sts on a background of reverse St st
Skill: experienced

1ST ROW (RS): K1 tbl, p1, T2B, p3, C2B, C2F, p3, T2F, p1, k1 tbl.
2ND ROW: P1 tbl, k1, p1, k4, p1, [p1 tbl] twice, p1, k4, p1, k1, p1 tbl.
3RD ROW: K1 tbl, T2B, p3, T2B, [k1 tbl] twice, T2F, p3, T2F, k1 tbl.
4TH ROW: P2, k4, p1, k1, [p1 tbl] twice, k1, p1, k4, p2.
5TH ROW: T2B, p3, C2B, p1, [k1 tbl] twice, p1, C2F, p3, T2F.
6TH ROW: K5, p1, p1 tbl, k1, [p1 tbl] twice, k1, p1 tbl, p1, k5.
7TH ROW: P4, T2B, k1 tbl, p1, [k1 tbl]

twice, p1, k1 tbl, T2F, p4.
8TH ROW: K4, p1, k1, p1 tbl, k1, [p1 tbl] twice, k1, p1 tbl, k1, p1, k4.
9TH ROW: P3, C2B, p1, k1 tbl, p1, [k1 tbl] twice, p1, k1 tbl, p1, C2F, p3.
10TH ROW: K3, p1, [p1 tbl, k1] twice, [p1 tbl] twice, [k1, p1 tbl] twice, p1, k3.
11TH ROW: P2, T2B, [k1 tbl, p1] twice, [k1 tbl] twice, [p1, k1 tbl] twice, T2F, p2.
12TH ROW: K2, p1, k1, [p1 tbl, k1] twice, [p1 tbl] twice, k1, [p1 tbl, k1] twice, p1, k2.
13TH ROW: P1, C2B, p1, [k1 tbl, p1] twice, [k1 tbl] twice, [p1, k1 tbl] twice, p1, C2F, p1.
14TH ROW: K1, p1, [p1 tbl, k1] 3 times, [p1 tbl] twice, [k1, p1 tbl] 3 times, p1, k1.
15TH ROW: T2B, [k1 tbl, p1] twice, k1 tbl, C2B, C2F, k1 tbl, [p1, k1 tbl] twice, T2F.
16TH ROW: [P1 tbl, k1] 3 times, p6, [k1, p1 tbl] 3 times.
17TH ROW: [K1 tbl, p1] 3 times, T2B, k2, T2F, [p1, k1 tbl] 3 times.
18TH ROW: [P1 tbl, k1] 3 times, p1, k1, p2, k1, p1, [k1, p1 tbl] 3 times.
19TH ROW: K1 tbl, [p1, k1 tbl] twice, T2B, p1, C2B, p1, T2F, k1 tbl, [p1, k1 tbl] twice.
20TH ROW: [P1 tbl, k1] twice, p2, [k2, p2] twice, [k1, p1 tbl] twice.
21ST ROW: [K1 tbl, p1] twice, T2B, p2, k2, p2, T2F, [p1, k1 tbl] twice.
22ND ROW: [P1 tbl, k1] twice, p1, k3, p2, k3, p1, [k1, p1 tbl] twice.
23RD ROW: K1 tbl, p1, k1 tbl, T2B, p3, C2B, p3, T2F, k1 tbl, p1, k1 tbl.
24TH ROW: P1 tbl, k1, p2, [k4, p2] twice, k1, p1 tbl. Rep these 24 rows.

Bobble Points—right
Panel of 12 sts on a background of reverse St st
Skill: experienced

1ST ROW (RS): K2, [p1, k1] 5 times.
2ND ROW: [P1, k1] 5 times, p2.
3RD ROW: T4F, [p1, k1] 4 times.
4TH ROW: [P1, k1] 4 times, p2, k2.
5TH ROW: P2, T4F, [p1, k1] 3 times.
6TH ROW: [P1, k1] 3 times, p2, k4.
7TH ROW: P4, T4F, [p1, k1] twice.

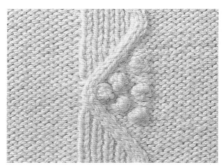

8TH ROW: [P1, k1] twice, p2, k6.
9TH ROW: P1, MB#8, p4, T4F, p1, k1.
10TH ROW: P1, k1, p2, k8.
11TH ROW: P4, MB#8, p3, T4F.
12TH ROW: P2, k10.
13TH ROW: P1, MB#8, p5, MB#8, p2, k2.
14TH ROW: P2, k10.
15TH ROW: P4, MB#8, p3, T4BP.
16TH ROW: As 10th row.
17TH ROW: P1, MB#8, p4, T4BP, p1, k1.
18TH ROW: As 8th row.
19TH ROW: P4, T4BP, [p1, k1] twice.
20TH ROW: As 6th row.
21ST ROW: P2, T4BP, [p1, k1] 3 times.
22ND ROW: As 4th row.
23RD ROW: T4BP, [p1, k1] 4 times.
24TH ROW: As 2nd row. Rep these 24 rows.

Bobble Points—left
Panel of 12 sts on a background of reverse St st
Skill: experienced

1ST ROW (RS): [K1, p1] 5 times, k2.
2ND ROW: P2, [k1, p1] 5 times.

3RD ROW: [K1, p1] 4 times, T4B.
4TH ROW: K2, p2, [k1, p1] 4 times.
5TH ROW: [K1, p1] 3 times, T4B, p2.
6TH ROW: K4, p2, [k1, p1] 3 times.
7TH ROW: [K1, p1] twice, T4B, p4.
8TH ROW: K6, p2, [k1, p1] twice.
9TH ROW: K1, p1, T4B, p4, MB#8, p1.
10TH ROW: K8, p2, k1, p1.
11TH ROW: T4B, p3, MB#8, p4.
12TH ROW: K10, p2.
13TH ROW: K2, p2, MB#8, p5, MB#8, p1.
14TH ROW: K10, p2.
15TH ROW: T4FP, p3, MB#8, p4.
16TH ROW: As 10th row.
17TH ROW: K1, p1, T4FP, p4, MB#8, p1.
18TH ROW: As 8th row.
19TH ROW: [K1, p1] twice, T4FP, p4.
20TH ROW: As 6th row.
21ST ROW: [K1, p1] 3 times, T4FP, p2.
22ND ROW: As 4th row.
23RD ROW: [K1, p1] 4 times, T4FP.
24TH ROW: P2, [k1, p1] 5 times.
Rep these 24 rows.

Enclosed Ribs
Panel of 13 sts on a background of reverse St st
Skill: experienced

1ST ROW (RS): P3, C3B, p1, C3F, p3.
2ND ROW: K3, p3, k1, p3, k3.
3RD ROW: P2, T3B, k1 tbl, p1, k1 tbl, T3F, p2.
4TH ROW: K2, p2, k1, [p1, k1] twice, p2, k2.
5TH ROW: P1, C3B, p1, [k1 tbl, p1] twice, C3F, p1.
6TH ROW: K1, p3, k1, [p1, k1] twice, p3, k1.
7TH ROW: T3B, k1 tbl, [p1, k1 tbl] 3 times, T3F.

8TH ROW: P2, k1, [p1, k1] 4 times, p2.
9TH ROW: T3F, k1 tbl, [p1, k1 tbl] 3 times, T3B.
10TH ROW: As 6th row.
11TH ROW: P1, T3F, p1, [k1 tbl, p1] twice, T3B, p1.
12TH ROW: As 4th row.
13TH ROW: P2, T3F, k1 tbl, p1, k1 tbl, T3B, p2.
14TH ROW: As 2nd row.
15TH ROW: P3, T3F, p1, T3B, p3.
16TH ROW: K4, p2, k1, p2, k4.
17TH ROW: P4, T5BP, p4.
18TH ROW: As 16th row.
19TH ROW: P3, T3B, p1, T3F, p3.
20TH ROW: K3, [p2, k3] twice.
21ST ROW: P2, T3B, p3, T3F, p2.
22ND ROW: K2, p2, k5, p2, k2.
23RD ROW: P2, T3F, p3, T3B, p2.
24TH ROW: As 20th row.
25TH TO 28TH ROWS: As 15th to 18th rows.
Rep these 28 rows.

Long and Short Cables
Panel of 8 sts on a background of reverse St st
Skill: intermediate

1ST ROW (WS): P8.
2ND ROW: C8F.
3RD ROW: P8.
4TH ROW: C4B, k4.
5TH ROW: P8.
6TH ROW: K8.
Rep the last 4 rows twice more, then 3rd, 4th, and 5th rows again.
18TH ROW: C8F.
19TH ROW: P8.
20TH ROW: K4, C4B.

21ST ROW: P8.
22ND ROW: K8.
Rep the last 4 rows twice more, then 19th and 20th rows again.
Rep these 32 rows.

Seed Cable
Panel of 16 sts on a background of Garter st
Skill: intermediate

1ST ROW (RS): K4, p3, k2, p3, k4.
2ND ROW: P4, k3, p2, k3, p4.
Rep the last 2 rows 4 times more.
11TH ROW: C8F, C8B.
12TH ROW: P16. Rep these 12 rows.

Chain Mail
Panel of 14 sts on a background of reverse St st
Skill: experienced

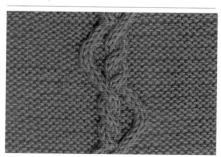

1ST ROW (WS): K4, p6, k4.
2ND ROW: P4, C4B, T4F, p2.

3RD ROW: K2, p2, k2, p4, k4.
4TH ROW: P4, k4, p2, T4F.
5TH AND 7TH ROWS: P2, k4, p4, k4.
6TH ROW: P4, C4B, p4, k2.
8TH ROW: P4, k4, p2, T4B.
9TH ROW: K2, p2, k2, p4, k4.
10TH ROW: P4, C4B, T4B, p2.
11TH ROW: As 1st row.
12TH ROW: P2, T4B, C4F, p4.
13TH ROW: K4, p4, k2, p2, k2.
14TH ROW: T4B, p2, k4, p4.
15TH AND 17TH ROWS: K4, p4, k4, p2.
16TH ROW: K2, p4, C4F, p4.
18TH ROW: T4F, p2, k4, p4.
19TH ROW: As 13th row.
20TH ROW: P2, T4F, C4F, p4.
Rep these 20 rows.

Twine Cable
Panel of 14 sts on a background of reverse St st
Skill: experienced

Special Abbreviation
C8RL (Cross 8 Right/Left) = slip next 4 sts onto cable needle and hold at back of work, knit next 2 sts from left-hand needle, knit first 2 sts from cable needle and hold remaining 2 sts at front of work, knit next 2 sts from left-hand needle, then knit sts from cable needle.
1ST AND EVERY ALT ROW (WS): P1 tbl, k2, [p1 tbl] twice, p4, [p1 tbl] twice, k2, p1 tbl.
2ND ROW: K1 tbl, p2, [k1 tbl] twice, k4, [k1 tbl] twice, p2, k1 tbl.
4TH ROW: K1 tbl, p2, [k1 tbl] twice, C4B, [k1 tbl] twice, p2, k1 tbl.

6TH AND 8TH ROWS: As 2nd row.
10TH ROW: K1 tbl, p2, C8RL (see Special Abbreviation), p2, k1 tbl. Rep these 10 rows.

Snakes and Ladders
Panel of 19 sts on a background of reverse St st
Skill: experienced

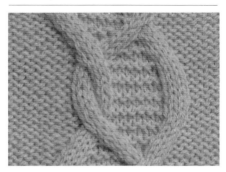

Special Abbreviations
Cr5BR (Cross 5 Back Right) = slip next 2 sts onto cable needle and hold at back of work, knit next 3 sts from left-hand needle, then knit sts from cable needle.
Cr5FL (Cross 5 Front Left) = slip next 3 sts onto cable needle and hold at front of work, knit next 2 sts from left-hand needle, then knit sts from cable needle.
1ST ROW (WS): K3, p6, k6, p3, k1.
2ND ROW: P1, T4L, k3, Cr5BR (see Special Abbreviations), C4L, p2.
3RD ROW: K2, p3, [k3, p3] twice, k2.
4TH ROW: P2, T4L, Cr5BR, k3, C4L, p1.
5TH ROW: K1, p3, k6, p6, k3.
6TH ROW: P3, C6B, k6, C4L.
7TH ROW: P3, k7, p6, k3.
8TH ROW: P3, k16.
Rep the last 2 rows twice more, then 7th row again.
14TH ROW: P3, C6B, k6, T4R.
15TH ROW: As 5th row.
16TH ROW: P2, C4R, Cr5FL (see Special Abbreviations), k3, T4R, p1.
17TH ROW: As 3rd row.
18TH ROW: P1, C4R, k3, Cr5FL, T4R, p2.
19TH ROW: As 1st row.
20TH ROW: C4R, k6, C6F, p3.

21ST ROW: K3, p6, k7, p3.
22ND ROW: K16, p3.
Rep the last 2 rows twice more, then 21st row again.
28TH ROW: T4L, k6, C6F, p3. Rep these 28 rows.

Bobble and Twine
Panel of 16 sts on a background of reverse St st
Skill: intermediate

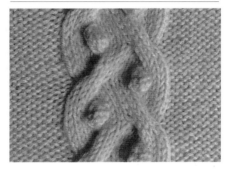

Special Abbreviation
MB (Make Bobble) = [k1, yo, k1, yo, k1] all into next st, turn and k5, turn and p5, turn and k5, turn and sl 2, k3tog, p2sso. Work 4 rows in St st, starting knit (1st row is right side).
5TH ROW: C8F, k3, MB (See Special Abbreviation), k4.
Work 5 rows in St st, starting purl.
11TH ROW: K4, MB, k3, C8B.
12TH ROW: P16. Rep these 12 rows.

Soft Plait
Panel of 26 sts on a background of reverse St st
Skill: intermediate

1ST ROW (RS): C2B, p2, k18, p2, C2L.
2ND AND EVERY ALT ROW: P2, k2, k18, k2, p2.
3RD ROW: C2B, p2, C12F, k6, p2, C2F.
5TH AND 7TH ROWS: As 1st row.
9TH ROW: C2B, p2, k6, C12B, p2, C2F.
11TH ROW: As 1st row.
12TH ROW: As 2nd row.
Rep these 12 rows.

Yoked Cable

Panel of 28 sts on a background of reverse St st
Skill: intermediate

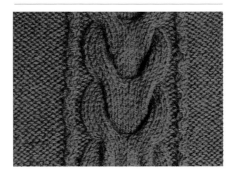

1ST ROW (RS): C2F, p2, k20, p2, C2F.
2ND AND EVERY ALT ROW: P2, k2, p20, k2, p2.
3RD ROW: C2B, p2, k20, p2, C2B.
5TH ROW: As 1st row.
7TH ROW: C2B, p2, C10B, C10F, p2, C2B.
9TH ROW: As 1st row.
11TH ROW: As 3rd row.
12TH ROW: As 2nd row.
Rep these 12 rows.

Intricate Cable

Panel of 22 sts on a background of reverse St st
Skill: intermediate

Special Abbreviation

Cluster 6 = k2, p2, k2, slip the last 6 sts just

worked onto cable needle and wrap yarn counterclockwise 4 times around these 6 sts, then slip sts back onto right-hand needle.
Note: Slip sts purlwise with yarn at back of work (wrong side).
1ST ROW (WS): P1, k4, [p4, k4] twice, p1.
2ND ROW: Sl 1, p4, C4B, p4, C4F, p4, sl 1.
3RD ROW: As 1st row.
4TH ROW: Sl 1, p3, T3B, T3F, p2, T3B, T3F, p3, sl 1.
5TH ROW: P1, k3, p2, [k2, p2] 3 times, k3, p1.
6TH ROW: Sl 1, p2, [T3B, p2, T3F] twice, p2, sl 1.
7TH ROW: P1, k2, p2, k4, p4, k4, p2, k2, p1.
8TH ROW: Sl 1, p2, k2, p4, C4B, p4, k2, p2, sl 1.
9TH ROW: As 7th row.
10TH ROW: Sl 1, p2, k2, p4, k4, p4, k2, p2, sl 1.
11TH AND 12TH ROWS: As 7th and 8th rows.
13TH ROW: As 7th row.
14TH ROW: Sl 1, p2, [T3F, p2, T3B] twice, p2, sl 1.
15TH ROW: As 5th row.
16TH ROW: Sl 1, p3, T3F, T3B, p2, T3F, T3B, p3, sl 1.
17TH AND 18TH ROWS: As 1st and 2nd rows.
19TH ROW: As 1st row.
20TH AND 21ST ROWS: As 4th and 5th rows.
22ND ROW: Sl 1, p3, k2, p2, Cluster 6 (see Special Abbreviation), p2, k2, p3, sl 1.
23RD ROW: As 5th row.
24TH ROW: As 16th row.
Rep these 24 rows.

Staked Cables

Panel of 12 sts on a background of reverse St st
Skill: intermediate

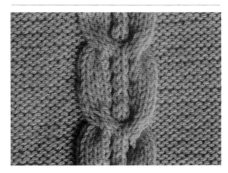

1ST AND EVERY ALT ROW (WS): P12.
2ND ROW: C6B, C6F.
4TH, 6TH, 8TH, AND 10TH ROWS: K4, yo, k2tog, sl 1, k1, psso, yo, k4.
12TH ROW: K12.
Rep these 12 rows.

Wrapped Cables

Panel of 20 sts on a background of reverse St st
Skill: experienced

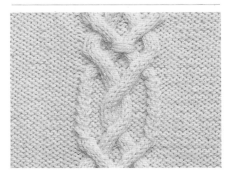

Special Abbreviations

Cluster 6 = knit next 6 sts and slip them onto cable needle. Wrap yarn 4 times counterclockwise around these 6 sts. Slip sts back onto right-hand needle.
Bind 3 = slip 1 st with yarn at back of work, k1, yo, k1, pass slipped st over the k1, yo, k1.

1ST ROW (RS): Bind 3, p4, k6, p4, Bind 3.
2ND ROW: P3, k4, p6, k4, p3.
3RD ROW: Bind 3, p4, C6B, p4, Bind 3.
4TH ROW: As 2nd row.
5TH ROW: Bind 3, p3, T4R, T4L, p3, Bind 3.
6TH ROW: P3, k3, p3, k2, p3, k3, p3.
7TH ROW: T5L, T4R, p2, T4L, T5R.
8TH ROW: K2, p6, k4, p6, k2.
9TH ROW: P2, C6B, p4, C6F, p2.
10TH ROW: As 8th row.
11TH ROW: [T5R, T5L] twice.
12TH ROW: As 2nd row.
13TH ROW: K3, p4, Cluster 6, p4, k3.
14TH ROW: As 2nd row.
15TH ROW: [T5L, T5R] twice.
16TH TO 18TH ROWS: As 8th to 10th rows.
19TH ROW: T5R, T4L, p2, T4R, T5L.
20TH ROW: As 6th row.
21ST ROW: Bind 3, p3, T4L, T4R, p3, Bind 3.
22ND TO 24TH ROWS: As 2nd to 4th rows.
25TH TO 28TH ROWS: Rep 1st and 2nd rows twice.
Rep these 28 rows.

Pleated Diamonds I
Panel of 16 sts on a background of reverse St st
Skill: experienced

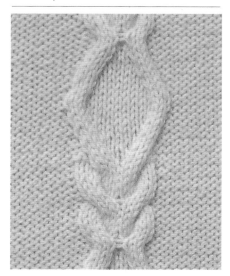

1ST ROW (RS): P4, C4R, C4L, p4.
2ND ROW: K4, p8, k4.
3RD ROW: P3, C4R, k2, C4L, p3.
4TH ROW: K3, p10, k3.
5TH ROW: P2, C4R, k4, C4L, p2.
6TH ROW: K2, p12, k2.
7TH ROW: P1, C4R, k6, C4L, p1.
8TH ROW: K1, p14, k1.
9TH ROW: C4R, k8, C4L.
10TH ROW: P16.
11TH ROW: T4L, k8, T4R.
12TH ROW: K1, p14, k1.
13TH ROW: P1, T4L, k6, T4R, p1.
14TH ROW: K2, p12, k2.
15TH ROW: P2, T4L, k4, T4R, p2.
16TH ROW: K3, p10, k3.
17TH ROW: P3, T4L, k2, T4R, p3.
18TH ROW: K4, p8, k4.
19TH ROW: P4, T4L, T4R, p4.
20TH ROW: K5, p6, k5.
21ST ROW: P2, C6B, C6F, p2.
22ND ROW: K2, p12, k2.
23RD ROW: P2, k12, p2.
24TH TO 26TH ROWS: Rep the last 2 rows once more, then 22nd row again.
27TH TO 32ND ROWS: As 21st to 26th rows. Rep these 32 rows.

Pleated Diamonds II
Panel of 17 sts on a background of reverse St st
Skill: experienced

1ST ROW (RS): P5, k7, p5.
2ND ROW: K5, p7, k5.
3RD ROW: P5, C7B, p5.
4TH ROW: K5, p7, k5.
5TH ROW: P4, T4R, k1 tbl, T4L, p4.
6TH ROW: K4, p3, k1, p1, k1, p3, k4.
7TH ROW: P3, C4R, p1, k1 tbl, p1, C4L, p3.
8TH ROW: K3, p4, k1, p1, k1, p4, k3.
9TH ROW: P2, T4R, k1 tbl, [p1, k1 tbl] twice, T4L, p2.
10TH ROW: K2, p3, k1, [p1, k1] 3 times, p3, k2.
11TH ROW: P1, C4R, p1, [k1 tbl, p1] 3 times, C4L, p1.
12TH ROW: K1, p4, k1, [p1, k1] 3 times, p4, k1.

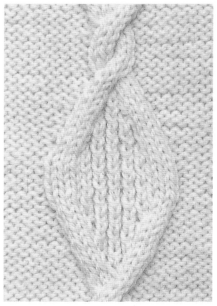

13TH ROW: T4R, k1 tbl, [p1, k1 tbl] 4 times, T4L.
14TH ROW: P3, k1, [p1, k1] 5 times, p3.
15TH ROW: K3, p1, [k1 tbl, p1] 5 times, k3.
16TH TO 18TH ROWS: Rep the last 2 rows once more, then 14th row again.
19TH ROW: T4L, k1 tbl, [p1, k1 tbl] 4 times, T4R.
20TH ROW: As 12th row.
21ST ROW: P1, T4L, p1, [k1 tbl, p1] 3 times, T4R, p1.
22ND ROW: As 10th row.
23RD ROW: P2, T4L, k1 tbl, [p1, k1 tbl] twice, T4R, p2.
24TH ROW: As 8th row.
25TH ROW: P3, T4L, p1, k1 tbl, p1, T4R, p3.
26TH ROW: As 6th row.
27TH ROW: P4, T4L, k1 tbl, T4R, p4.
28TH TO 30TH ROWS: As 2nd to 4th rows.
31ST AND 32ND ROWS: As 1st and 2nd rows. Rep these 32 rows.

Interweaving Cables I
Panel of 26 sts on a background of reverse St st
Skill: experienced

1ST ROW (RS): P1, T4L, T4R, p8, T4L, T4R, p1.

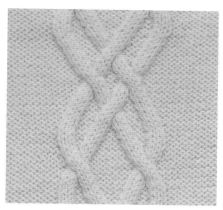

2ND ROW: K2, p6, k10, p6, k2.
3RD ROW: P2, C6F, p10, C6F, p2.
4TH ROW: As 2nd row.
5TH ROW: P1, T4R, T4L, p8, T4R, T4L, p1.
6TH ROW: K1, p3, k2, p3, k8, p3, k2, p3, k1.
7TH ROW: T4R, p2, T4L, p6, T4R, p2, T4L.
8TH ROW: P3, k4, p3, k6, p3, k4, p3.
9TH ROW: K3, p4, T4L, p4, T4R, p4, k3.
10TH ROW: P3, k5, p3, k4, p3, k5, p3.
11TH ROW: T4L, p4, T4L, p2, T4R, p4, T4R.
12TH ROW: K1, p3, k5, p3, k2, p3, k5, p3, k1.
13TH ROW: P1, T4L, p4, T4L, T4R, p4, T4R, p1.
14TH ROW: K2, p3, k5, p6, k5, p3, k2.
15TH ROW: P2, T4L, p4, C6B, p4, T4R, p2.
16TH ROW: K3, p3, k4, p6, k4, p3, k3.
17TH ROW: P3, [T4L, p2, T4R] twice, p3.
18TH ROW: K4, p3, [k2, p3] 3 times, k4.
19TH ROW: P4, T4L, T4R, p2, T4L, T4R, p4.
20TH ROW: K5, p6, k4, p6, k5.
21ST ROW: P5, C6F, p4, C6F, p5.
22ND ROW: As 20th row.
23RD ROW: P4, T4R, T4L, p2, T4R, T4L, p4.
24TH ROW: As 18th row.
25TH ROW: P3, [T4R, p2, T4L] twice, p3.
26TH ROW: As 16th row.
27TH ROW: P2, T4R, p4, C6B, p4, T4L, p2.
28TH ROW: As 14th row.
29TH ROW: P1, T4R, p4, T4R, T4L, p4, T4L, p1.
30TH ROW: As 12th row.
31ST ROW: T4R, p4, T4R, p2, T4L, p4, T4L.
32ND ROW: As 10th row.
33RD ROW: K3, p4, T4R, p4, T4L, p4, k3.
34TH ROW: As 8th row.
35TH ROW: T4L, p2, T4R, p6, T4L, p2, T4R.
36TH ROW: As 6th row. Rep these 36 rows.

Interweaving Cables II
Panel of 16 sts on a background of reverse St st
Skill: experienced

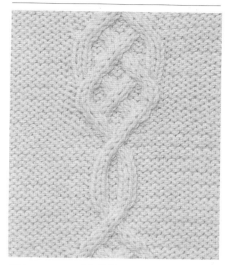

1ST ROW (RS): P6, C4B, p6.
2ND ROW: K6, p4, k6.
3RD ROW: P4, T4B, T4F, p4.
4TH ROW: K4, [p2, k4] twice.
5TH ROW: P2, C4B, p4, C4F, p2.
6TH ROW: K2, p4, k4, p4, k2.
7TH ROW: [T4B, T4F] twice.
8TH ROW: P2, k4, p4, k4, p2.
9TH ROW: K2, p4, C4B, p4, k2.
10TH ROW: As 8th row.
11TH ROW: C4F, T4B, T4F, C4B.
12TH ROW: P6, k4, p6.
13TH ROW: K2, T4F, p4, T4B, k2.
14TH ROW: P2, k2, p2, k4, p2, k2, p2.
15TH ROW: K2, p2, T4F, T4B, p2, k2.
16TH TO 18TH ROWS: As 8th to 10th rows.
19TH ROW: [T4F, T4B] twice.
20TH ROW: As 6th row.
21ST ROW: P2, T4F, p4, T4B, p2.
22ND ROW: As 4th row.
23RD ROW: P4, T4F, T4B, p4.
24TH ROW: K6, p4, k6.
25TH TO 28TH ROWS: As 1st to 4th rows.
29TH ROW: P4, [k2, p4] twice.
30TH ROW: As 4th row.
31ST TO 34TH ROWS: Rep the last 2 rows twice more.

35TH ROW: As 23rd row.
36TH ROW: K6, p4, k6. Rep these 36 rows.

Zigzag Ribbon
Panel of 12 sts on a background of reverse St st
Skill: experienced

1ST ROW (WS): P12.
2ND ROW: C2F, k8, T2B.
3RD ROW: K1, T2PR, p6, C2PL, p1.
4TH ROW: K2, C2F, k4, T2B, p2.
5TH ROW: K3, T2PR, p2, C2PL, p3.
6TH ROW: K4, C2F, T2B, p4.
7TH ROW: K5, C2PL, p5.
8TH ROW: K6, C2F, p4.
9TH ROW: K3, C2PL, p7.
10TH ROW: K8, C2L, p2.
11TH ROW: K1, C2PL, p9.
12TH ROW: K10, C2L.
13TH ROW: P12.
14TH ROW: T2F, k8, C2B.
15TH ROW: P1, C2PR, p6, T2PL, k1.
16TH ROW: P2, T2F, k4, C2B, k2.
17TH ROW: P3, C2PR, p2, T2PL, k3.
18TH ROW: P4, T2F, C2B, k4.
19TH ROW: P5, C2PR, k5.
20TH ROW: P4, C2B, k6.
21ST ROW: P7, C2PR, k3.
22ND ROW: P2, C2B, k8.
23RD ROW: P9, C2PR, k1.
24TH ROW: C2B, k10. Rep these 24 rows.

knit and purl panels

Simple knit and purl panels were traditionally used on the yokes of fishermen's pullovers on the island of Guernsey, in the English Channel, and so are called guernseys. You can also use these panels singly or in pairs to embellish a plain garment. The gauge is virtually the same as for Stockinette stitch, so no adjustment to the total number of stitches is needed. The patterns show up best in a smooth yarn, and would not lend themselves to mohair or a fashion yarn.

Latin Star
Worked over 19 sts on a background of St st
Skill: intermediate

1ST ROW (WS): Purl.
2ND ROW: Knit.
3RD ROW: P9, k1, p9.
4TH ROW: K8, p1, k1, p1, k8.
5TH ROW: P1, k1, [p7, k1] twice, p1.
6TH ROW: K2, p1, k5, p1, k1, p1, k5, p1, k2.
7TH ROW: [P1, k1] twice, p5, k1, p5, [k1, p1] twice.
8TH ROW: K2, [p1, k1, p1, k3] twice, p1, k1, p1, k2.
9TH ROW: P3, k1, p1, [k1, p3] twice, k1, p1, k1, p3.
10TH ROW: K4, [p1, k1] 5 times, p1, k4.
11TH ROW: P5, [k1, p1] 4 times, k1, p5.
12TH ROW: K6, p1, k5, p1, k6.
13TH ROW: [P1, k1] 3 times, p2, k1, p1, k1, p2, [k1, p1] 3 times.
14TH ROW: [P1, k1] 3 times, p1, [k2, p1] twice, [k1, p1] 3 times.
Work in reverse order from 13th row to 2nd row inclusive.
Rep these 26 rows.

Marriage Lines
Worked over 17 sts on a background of St st
Skill: easy

1ST ROW (RS): P3, k6, p1, k2, p1, k1, p3.
2ND ROW: K1, p1, [k1, p2] twice, k1, p5, k1, p1, k1.
3RD ROW: P3, k4, p1, k2, p1, k3, p3.
4TH ROW: K1, p1, k1, p4, k1, p2, k1, p3, k1, p1, k1.
5TH ROW: P3, [k2, p1] twice, k5, p3.
6TH ROW: K1, p1, k1, p6, k1, p2, [k1, p1] twice, k1.
7TH ROW: As 5th row.
8TH ROW: As 4th row.
9TH ROW: As 3rd row.
10TH ROW: As 2nd row.
Rep these 10 rows.

Flying Wedge
Worked over 18 sts on a background of St st
Skill: intermediate

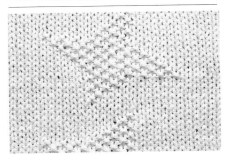

1ST ROW (WS): Purl.
2ND ROW: K11, p1, k6.
3RD ROW: P7, k1, p10.
4TH ROW: K9, p1, k1, p1, k6.
5TH ROW: P7, k1, p1, k1, p8.
6TH ROW: K7, [p1, k1] twice, p1, k6.
7TH ROW: P7, [k1, p1] 5 times, k1.
8TH ROW: [K1, p1] 6 times, k6.
9TH ROW: P5, [k1, p1] 5 times, k1, p2.
10TH ROW: K3, [p1, k1] 5 times, p1, k4.
11TH ROW: P3, [k1, p1] 5 times, k1, p4.
12TH ROW: K5, [p1, k1] 5 times, p1, k2.
13TH ROW: [P1, k1] 6 times, p6.
14TH ROW: K7, [p1, k1] 5 times, p1.
15TH ROW: P7, [k1, p1] twice, k1, p6.
16TH ROW: K7, p1, k1, p1, k8.
17TH ROW: P9, k1, p1, k1, p6.
18TH ROW: K7, p1, k10.
19TH ROW: P11, k1, p6.
20TH ROW: Knit.
Rep these 20 rows.

Ridge and Furrow

Worked over 23 sts on a background of St st

Skill: easy

1ST ROW (RS): P4, k7, p1, k7, p4.

2ND ROW: K1, p2, k1, p5, [k1, p1] twice, k1, p5, k1, p2, k1.

3RD ROW: P4, k4, [p1, k2] twice, p1, k4, p4.

4TH ROW: K1, p2, [k1, p3] 4 times, k1, p2, k1.

5TH ROW: P4, k2, [p1, k4] twice, p1, k2, p4.

6TH ROW: K1, p2, k1, p1, [k1, p5] twice, k1, p1, k1, p2, k1.

Rep these 6 rows.

Tree of Life

Worked over 23 sts on a background of St st

Skill: intermediate

1ST ROW (RS): P4, k7, p1, k7, p4.

2ND ROW: K1, p2, k1, p6, k1, p1, k1, p6, k1, p2, k1.

3RD ROW: P4, k5, p1, k3, p1, k5, p4.

4TH ROW: K1, p2, k1, p4, [k1, p2] twice, k1, p4, k1, p2, k1.

5TH ROW: P4, k3, p1, k2, p1, k1, p1, k2, p1, k3, p4.

6TH ROW: [K1, p2] 3 times, k1, p3, [k1, p2] 3 times, k1.

7TH ROW: P4, k1, [p1, k2] 4 times, p1, k1, p4.

8TH ROW: K1, p2, k1, p3, k1, p2, k1, p1, k1, p2, k1, p3, k1, p2, k1.

9TH ROW: P4, [k2, p1] twice, k3, [p1, k2] twice, p4.

10TH ROW: As 4th row.

11TH ROW: As 5th row.

12TH ROW: K1, p2, k1, p5, k1, p3, k1, p5, k1, p2, k1.

13TH ROW: P4, k4, [p1, k2] twice, p1, k4, p4.

14TH ROW: As 2nd row.

15TH ROW: As 3rd row.

16TH ROW: K1, p2, k1, [p7, k1] twice, p2, k1.

17TH ROW: P4, k6, p1, k1, p1, k6, p4.

18TH ROW: K1, p2, k1, p15, k1, p2, k1.

19TH ROW: As 1st row.

20TH ROW: As 18th row.

Rep these 20 rows.

Anchor

Worked over 17 sts on a background of St st

Skill: intermediate

1ST ROW (RS): P3, k11, p3.

2ND ROW: K1, p1, [k1, p5] twice, k1, p1, k1.

3RD ROW: P3, k4, p1, k1, p1, k4, p3.

4TH ROW: K1, p1, k1, p3, [k1, p1] twice, k1, p3, k1, p1, k1.

5TH ROW: P3, k2, p1, k5, p1, k2, p3.

6TH ROW: [K1, p1] twice, [k1, p3] twice, [k1, p1] twice, k1.

7TH ROW: P3, k1, p1, k7, p1, k1, p3.

8TH ROW: K1, p1, [k1, p5] twice, k1, p1, k1.

9TH ROW: As 1st row.

Rep the last 2 rows once more.

12TH ROW: K1, p1, k1, p3, k5, p3, k1, p1, k1.

13TH ROW: P3, k3, p5, k3, p3.

14TH ROW: As 12th row.

15TH ROW: As 1st row.

16TH ROW: As 8th row.

Rep the last 2 rows once more.

19TH ROW: As 3rd row.

20TH ROW: K1, p1, [k1, p3] 3 times, k1, p1, k1.

21ST ROW: As 3rd row.

22ND ROW: As 2nd row.

23RD ROW: As 1st row.

24TH ROW: K1, p1, k1, p11, k1, p1, k1.

Rep these 24 rows.

Triple Wave

Worked over 14 sts on a background of St st

Skill: easy

1ST ROW (RS): P3, k8, p3.

2ND ROW: [K1, p1] twice, k2, p2, k2, [p1, k1] twice.

3RD ROW: P3, k3, p2, k3, p3.

4TH ROW: K1, p1, k1, p8, k1, p1, k1.

5TH ROW: P3, k1, p2, k2, p2, k1, p3.

6TH ROW: K1, p1, k1, p3, k2, p3, k1, p1, k1.

Rep these 6 rows.

panel patterns

lace panels

A lace panel will give a little glamour to a simple pullover or cardigan in a fraction of the time required to knit a whole lace garment. Insert a line of Lozenge Lace Panel (*below*) down each front of a cardigan; or use a panel of graceful Spiral and Eyelet (*page 163*), to embellish the front of a pullover. As a rule, lace patterns are suited to a relatively fine, smooth yarn, but some patterns acquire a lovely softness, without losing their definition, when knitted in a fine, slightly fuzzy yarn. Experiment to see the effect.

Lozenge Lace Panel
Worked over 11 sts on a background of St st
Skill: easy

1ST ROW (RS): K1, yo, sl 1, k1, psso, k5, k2tog, yo, k1.
2ND AND EVERY ALT ROW: Purl.
3RD ROW: K2, yo, sl 1, k1, psso, k3, k2tog, yo, k2.
5TH ROW: K3, yo, sl 1, k1, psso, k1, k2tog, yo, k3.
7TH ROW: K4, yo, sl 1, k2tog, psso, yo, k4.
9TH ROW: K3, k2tog, yo, k1, yo, sl 1, k1, psso, k3.
11TH ROW: K2, k2tog, yo, k3, yo, sl 1, k1, psso, k2.
13TH ROW: K1, k2tog, yo, k5, yo, sl 1, k1, psso, k1.
15TH ROW: K2tog, yo, k7, yo, sl 1, k1, psso.
16TH ROW: Purl.
Rep these 16 rows.

Arch Lace Panel
Worked over 11 sts on a background of St st
Skill: easy

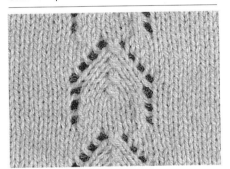

1ST ROW (RS): K1, yo, k2tog, k5, sl 1, k1, psso, yo, k1.
2ND AND EVERY ALT ROW: Purl.
3RD ROW: As 1st row.
5TH ROW: As 1st row.
7TH ROW: K1, yo, k3, sl 1, k2tog, psso, k3, yo, k1.
9TH ROW: K2, yo, k2, sl 1, k2tog, psso, k2, yo, k2.
11TH ROW: K3, yo, k1, sl 1, k2tog, psso, k1, yo, k3.
13TH ROW: K4, yo, sl 1, k2tog, psso, yo, k4.
14TH ROW: Purl.
Rep these 14 rows.

Lace Rib Panel
Worked over 7 sts on a background of reversed St st
Skill: easy

1ST ROW (RS): P1, yo, sl 1, k1, psso, k1, k2tog, yo, p1.
2ND ROW: K1, p5, k1.
3RD ROW: P1, k1, yo, sl 1, k2tog, psso, yo, k1, p1.
4TH ROW: K1, p5, k1.
Rep these 4 rows.

Zigzag Insertion
Worked over 5 sts on a background of reverse St st
Skill: easy

1ST ROW: Knit.
2ND AND EVERY ALT ROW: Purl.
3RD ROW: K1, k2tog, yo, k2.
5TH ROW: K2tog, yo, k3.
7TH ROW: Knit.
9TH ROW: K2, yo, sl 1, k1, psso, k1.
11TH ROW: K3, yo, sl 1, k1, psso.
12TH ROW: Purl.
Rep these 12 rows.

Eyelet Twist Panel
Worked over 13 sts on a background of St st
Skill: intermediate

1ST AND EVERY ALT ROW (WS): Purl.
2ND ROW: K1, [yo, sl 1, k1, psso] twice, k3, [k2tog, yo] twice, k1.
4TH ROW: K2, [yo, sl 1, k1, psso] twice, k1, [k2tog, yo] twice, k2.

6TH ROW: K3, yo, sl 1, k1, psso, yo, sl 1, k2tog, psso, yo, k2tog, yo, k3.
8TH ROW: K4, yo, sl 1, k2tog, psso, yo, k2tog, yo, k4.
10TH ROW: K4, [k2tog, yo] twice, k5.
12TH ROW: K3, [k2tog, yo] twice, k1, yo, sl 1, k1, psso, k3.
14TH ROW: K2, [k2tog, yo] twice, k1, [yo, sl 1, k1, psso] twice, k2.
16TH ROW: K1, [k2tog, yo] twice, k3, [yo, sl 1, k1, psso] twice, k1.
18TH ROW: [K2tog, yo] twice, k5, [yo, sl 1, k1, psso] twice.
Rep these 18 rows.

Fish Scale Lace Panel
Worked over 17 sts on a background of St st
Skill: intermediate

1ST ROW (RS): K1, yo, k3, sl 1, k1, psso, p5, k2tog, k3, yo, k1.
2ND ROW: P6, k5, p6.
3RD ROW: K2, yo, k3, sl 1, k1, psso, p3, k2tog, k3, yo, k2.
4TH ROW: P7, k3, p7.
5TH ROW: K3, yo, k3, sl 1, k1, psso, p1, k2tog, k3, yo, k3.
6TH ROW: P8, k1, p8.
7TH ROW: K4, yo, k3, sl 1, k2tog, psso, k3, yo, k4.
8TH ROW: Purl.
Rep these 8 rows.

Eyelet Twigs
Worked over 14 sts on a background of St st
Skill: intermediate

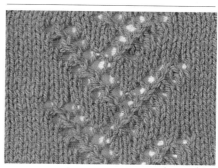

1ST ROW (RS): K1, yo, k3tog, yo, k3, yo, sl 1, k2tog, psso, yo, k4.
2ND AND EVERY ALT ROW: Purl.
3RD ROW: Yo, k3tog, yo, k5, yo, sl 1, k2tog, psso, yo, k3.
5TH ROW: K5, yo, k3tog, yo, k1, yo, sl 1, k2tog, psso, yo, k2.
7TH ROW: K4, yo, k3tog, yo, k3, yo, sl 1, k2tog, psso, yo, k1.
9TH ROW: K3, yo, k3tog, yo, k5, yo, sl 1, k2tog, psso, yo.
11TH ROW: K2, yo, k3tog, yo, k1, yo, sl 1, k2tog, psso, yo, k5.
12TH ROW: Purl.
Rep these 12 rows.

Eyelet Twigs and Bobbles
Worked over 16 sts on a background of St st
Skill: intermediate

1ST ROW (RS): K2, yo, k3tog, yo, k3, yo, sl 1, k2tog, psso, yo, k5.
2ND AND EVERY ALT ROW: Purl.
3RD ROW: K1, yo, k3tog, yo, k5, yo, sl 1, k2tog, psso, yo, k4.
5TH ROW: MB, k5, yo, k3tog, yo, k1, yo, sl 1, k2tog, psso, yo, k3.
7TH ROW: K5, yo, k3tog, yo, k3, yo, sl 1, k2tog, psso, yo, k2.
9TH ROW: K4, yo, k3tog, yo, k5, yo, sl 1, k2tog, psso, yo, MB.
11TH ROW: K3, yo, k3tog, yo, k1, yo, sl 1, k2tog, psso, yo, k6.
12TH ROW: Purl.
Rep these 12 rows.

Candelabra Panel
Worked over 13 sts on a background of St st
Skill: intermediate

1ST ROW (RS): Knit.
2ND AND EVERY ALT ROW: Purl.
3RD ROW: Knit.
5TH ROW: K4, k2tog, yo, k1, yo, sl 1, k1, psso, k4.
7TH ROW: K3, k2tog, yo, k3, yo, sl 1, k1, psso, k3.
9TH ROW: K2, [k2tog, yo] twice, k1, [yo, sl 1, k1, psso] twice, k2.
11TH ROW: K1, [k2tog, yo] twice, k3, [yo, sl 1, k1, psso] twice, k1.
13TH ROW: [K2tog, yo] 3 times, k1, [yo, sl 1, k1, psso] 3 times.
14TH ROW: Purl.
Rep these 14 rows.

Faggoted Panel
Worked over 9 sts on a St st background
Skill: intermediate

1ST ROW (RS): P1, k1, k2tog, yo, k1, yo, k2tog tbl, k1, p1.
2ND ROW: K1, p7, k1.
3RD ROW: P1, k2tog, yo, k3, yo, k2tog tbl, p1.
4TH ROW: As 2nd row. Rep these 4 rows.

Diamond Panel
Worked over 11 sts on a background of St st
Skill: intermediate

1ST ROW (RS): P2, k2tog, [k1, yo] twice, k1, sl 1, k1, psso, p2.
2ND AND EVERY ALT ROW: K2, p7, k2.
3RD ROW: P2, k2tog, yo, k3, yo, sl 1, k1, psso, p2.
5TH ROW: P2, k1, yo, sl 1, k1, psso, k1, k2tog, yo, k1, p2.
7TH ROW: P2, k2, yo, sl 1, k2tog, psso, yo, k2, p2.

8TH ROW: As 2nd row.
Rep these 8 rows.

Parasol Stitch
Worked over 17 sts on a background of St st
Skill: intermediate
Note: Sts should only be counted after the 11th and 12th rows.

1ST ROW (RS): Yo, k1, [p3, k1] 4 times, yo.
2ND AND EVERY ALT ROW: Purl.
3RD ROW: K1, yo, k1, [p3, k1] 4 times, yo, k1.
5TH ROW: K2, yo, k1, [p3, k1] 4 times, yo, k2.
7TH ROW: K3, yo, k1, [p2tog, p1, k1] 4 times, yo, k3.
9TH ROW: K4, yo, k1, [p2tog, k1] 4 times, yo, k4.
11TH ROW: K5, yo, k1, [k3tog, k1] twice, yo, k5.
12TH ROW: Purl. Rep these 12 rows.

Fishtail Lace Panel
Worked over 11 sts on a background of St st
Skill: intermediate

1ST ROW (RS): P1, k1, yo, k2, sl 1, k2tog, psso, k2, yo, k1, p1.
2ND ROW: K1, p9, k1.
3RD ROW: P1, k2, yo, k1, sl 1, k2tog, psso, k1, yo, k2, p1.
4TH ROW: As 2nd row.
5TH ROW: P1, k3, yo, sl 1, k2tog, psso, yo, k3, p1.
6TH ROW: As 2nd row.

Rep these 6 rows.

Bear Paw Panel
Worked over 23 sts on a background of St st
Skill: intermediate

1ST ROW (RS): K2, [p4, k1] 3 times, p4, k2.
2ND ROW: P2, [k4, p1] 3 times, k4, p2.
3RD ROW: K1, yo, k1, p2, p2tog, [k1, p4] twice, k1, p2tog, p2, k1, yo, k1.
4TH ROW: P3, k2, p2, k4, p1, k4, p2, k2, p3.
5TH ROW: K2, yo, k1, p3, k1, p2, p2tog, k1, p2tog, p2, k1, p3, k1, yo, k2.
6TH ROW: P4, k3, p1, k2, p3, k2, p1, k3, p4.
7TH ROW: K3, yo, k1, p1, p2tog, [k1, p3] twice, k1, p2tog, p1, k1, yo, k3.
8TH ROW: P5, k1, p2, k3, p1, k3, p2, k1, p5.
9TH ROW: K4, yo, k1, p2, k1, p1, p2tog, k1, p2tog, p1, k1, p2, k1, yo, k4.
10TH ROW: P6, k2, p1, k1, p3, k1, p1, k2, p6.
11TH ROW: K5, yo, k1, p2tog, [k1, p2] twice, k1, p2tog, k1, yo, k5.
12TH ROW: P9, k2, p1, k2, p9.
13TH ROW: K6, yo, k1, p1, k1, [p2tog, k1]

twice, p1, k1, yo, k6.
14TH ROW: P8, k1, p5, k1, p8.
Rep these 14 rows.

Lace and Cable Pattern
Worked over 21 sts on a St st background
Skill: experienced

Special Abbreviation
CB4F OR CB4B (Cable-Back 4 Front or Back) = slip next 2 sts onto a cable needle and hold at front (or back) of work, knit into the back of next 2 sts on left-hand needle, then knit into the back of sts on cable needle.
1ST ROW (RS): P2, [k1 tbl] 4 times, k1, yo, k2tog tbl, k3, k2tog, yo, k1, [k1 tbl] 4 times, p2.
2ND AND EVERY ALT ROW: K2, [p1 tbl] 4 times, k1, p7, k1, [p1 tbl] 4 times, k2.
3RD ROW: P2, [k1 tbl] 4 times, k2, yo, k2tog tbl, k1, k2tog, yo, k2, [k1 tbl] 4 times, p2.
5TH ROW: P2, CB4F (see Special Abbreviation), k3, yo, sl 1, k2tog, psso, yo, k3, CB4B, p2.
7TH ROW: P2, [k1 tbl] 4 times, k9, [k1 tbl] 4 times, p2.
8TH ROW: As 2nd row. Rep these 8 rows.

Fan Lace Panel
Worked over 11 sts on a background of St st
Skill: intermediate

1ST ROW (RS): Sl 1, k1, psso, [k1 tbl] 3 times, yo, k1, yo, [k1 tbl] 3 times, k2tog.

2ND AND EVERY ALT ROW: Purl.
3RD ROW: Sl 1, k1, psso, [k1 tbl] twice, yo, k1, yo, sl 1, k1, psso, yo, [k1 tbl] twice, k2tog.
5TH ROW: Sl 1, k1, psso, k1 tbl, yo, k1, [yo, sl 1, k1, psso] twice, yo, k1 tbl, k2tog.
7TH ROW: Sl 1, k1, psso, yo, k1, [yo, sl 1, k1, psso] 3 times, yo, k2tog.
8TH ROW: Purl. Rep these 8 rows.

Lace Chain Panel
Worked over 10 sts on a background of St st
Skill: intermediate

1ST ROW (RS): K2, k2tog, yo, k2tog but do not slip from needle, knit the first of these 2 sts again, then slip both sts from needle together, yo, sl 1, k1, psso, k2.
2ND ROW: Purl.
3RD ROW: K1, k2tog, yo, k4, yo, sl 1, k1, psso, k1.
4TH ROW: Purl.
5TH ROW: K2tog, yo, k1, k2tog, yo twice, sl 1, k1, psso, k1, yo, sl 1, k1, psso.
6TH ROW: P4, k1 into first yo, p1 into 2nd yo, p4.

7TH ROW: K2, yo, sl 1, k1, psso, k2, k2tog, yo, k2.
8TH ROW: Purl.
9TH ROW: K3, yo, sl 1, k1, psso, k2tog, yo, k3.
10TH ROW: Purl.
Rep these 10 rows.

Quatrefoil Panel

Worked over 15 sts on a background of St st
Skill: intermediate
Note: Stitches should not be counted after the 6th, 7th, 8th, and 9th rows.

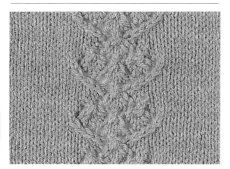

1ST ROW (RS): K5, k2tog, yo, k1, yo, sl 1, k1, psso, k5.
2ND ROW: P4, p2tog tbl, yo, p3, yo, p2tog, p4.
3RD ROW: K3, k2tog, yo, k5, yo, sl 1, k1, psso, k3.
4TH ROW: P2, p2tog tbl, yo, p1, yo, p2tog, p1, p2tog tbl, yo, p1, yo, p2tog, p2.
5TH ROW: K1, k2tog, yo, k3, yo, k3tog, yo, k3, yo, sl 1, k1, psso, k1.
6TH ROW: P2, yo, p5, yo, p1, yo, p5, yo, p2.
7TH ROW: [K3, yo, sl 1, k1, psso, k1, k2tog, yo] twice, k3.
8TH ROW: P4, p3tog, yo, p5, yo, p3tog, p4.
9TH ROW: K6, yo, sl 1, k1, psso, k1, k2tog, yo, k6.
10TH ROW: P3, p2tog tbl, p2, yo, p3tog, yo, p2, p2tog, p3.
Rep these 10 rows.

Openweave Panel

Worked over 11 sts on a background of St st
Skill: intermediate

1ST ROW (RS): P2, yb, sl 1, k1, psso, yo, k3, yo, k2tog, p2.
2ND ROW: K2, p7, k2.
3RD ROW: P2, k2, yo, sl 1, k2tog, psso, yo, k2, p2.
4TH ROW: K2, p7, k2.
Rep these 4 rows.

Little Lace Panel

Worked on 5 sts on a background of St st
Skill: intermediate
Note: Sts should not be counted after the 1st and 2nd rows.

1ST ROW (RS): K1, yo, k3, yo, k1.
2ND ROW: Purl.
3RD ROW: K2, sl 1, k2tog, psso, k2.
4TH ROW: Purl.
Rep these 4 rows.

Tulip Bud Panel

Worked over 33 sts on a background of garter st
Skill: intermediate

1ST ROW (WS): K16, p1, k16.
2ND ROW: K14, k2tog, yo, k1, yo, sl 1, k1, psso, k14.
3RD ROW: K14, p5, k14.
4TH ROW: K13, k2tog, yo, k3, yo, sl 1, k1, psso, k13.
5TH ROW: K13, p7, k13.
6TH ROW: K12, [k2tog, yo] twice, k1, [yo, sl 1, k1, psso twice, k12.
7TH ROW: K12, p9, k12.
8TH ROW: K11, [k2tog, yo] twice, k3, [yo, sl 1, k1, psso] twice, k11.
9TH ROW: K11, p4, k1, p1, k1, p4, k11.
10TH ROW: k10, [k2tog, yo] twice, k5, [yo, sl 1, k1, psso] twice, k10.
11TH ROW: K10, p4, k2, p1, k2, p4, k10.
12TH ROW: K9, [k2tog, yo] twice, k3, yo, k1, yo, k3, [yo, sl 1, k1, psso] twice, k9. (35 sts.)
13TH ROW: K9, p4, k3, p3, k3, p4, k9.
14TH ROW: K1, yo, sl 1, k1, psso, k5, [k2tog, yo] twice, k5, yo, k1, yo, k5, [yo, sl 1, k1, psso] twice, k5, k2tog, yo, k1. (37 sts.)
15TH ROW: K1, p2, k5, p4, k4, p5, k4, p4, k5, p2, k1.
16TH ROW: K2, yo, sl 1, k1, psso, k3, [k2tog, yo] twice, k7, yo, k1, yo, k7, [yo, sl 1, k1, psso] twice, k3, k2tog, yo, k2. (39 sts.)
17TH ROW: K2, p2, k3, p4, k5, p7, k5, p4, k3, p2, k2.
18TH ROW: K3, yo, sl 1, k1, psso, k1, [k2tog, yo] twice, k9, yo, k1, yo, k9, [yo, sl 1, k1, psso] twice, k1, k2tog, yo, k3. (41 sts.)
19TH ROW: K3, p2, k1, p4, k6, p9, k6, p4, k1, p2, k3.

20TH ROW: K4, yo, sl 1, k2tog, psso, yo, k2tog, yo, k7, sl 1, k1, psso, k5, k2tog, k7, yo, sl 1, k1, psso, yo, k3tog, yo, k4. (39 sts.)
21ST ROW: K4, p5, k7, p7, k7, p5, k4.
22ND ROW: K16, sl 1, k1, psso, k3, k2tog, k16. (37 sts.)
23RD ROW: K16, p5, k16.
24TH ROW: K16, sl 1, k1, psso, k1, k2tog, k16. (35 sts.)
25TH ROW: K16, p3, k16.
26TH ROW: K16, sl 1, k2tog, psso, k16. (33 sts.)
27TH ROW: As 1st row.

Twin Leaf Lace Panel

Worked over 23 sts on a background of St st
Skill: experienced

1ST ROW (RS): K8, k2tog, yo, k1, p1, k1, yo, sl 1, k1, psso, k8.
2ND ROW: P7, p2tog tbl, p2, yo, k1, yo, p2, p2tog, p7.
3RD ROW: K6, k2tog, k1, yo, k2, p1, k2, yo, k1, sl 1, k1, psso, k6.
4TH ROW: P5, p2tog tbl, p3, yo, p1, k1, p1, yo, p3, p2tog, p5.
5TH ROW: K4, k2tog, k2, yo, k3, p1, k3, yo, k2, sl 1, k1, psso, k4.
6TH ROW: P3, p2tog tbl, p4, yo, p2, k1, p2, yo, p4, p2tog, p3.
7TH ROW: K2, k2tog, k3, yo, k4, p1, k4, yo, k3, sl 1, k1, psso, k2.
8TH ROW: P1, p2tog tbl, p5, yo, p3, k1, p3, yo, p5, p2tog, p1.
9TH ROW: K2tog, k4, yo, k5, p1, k5, yo, k4, sl 1, k1, psso.
10TH ROW: P11, k1, p1.

11TH ROW: K11, p1, k1.
12TH ROW: P11, k1, p1.
Rep these 12 rows.

Shetland Fern Panel

Worked over 13 sts on a background of St st
Skill: experienced

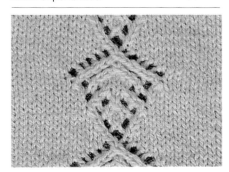

1ST ROW (RS): K6, yo, sl 1, k1, psso, k5.
2ND ROW: Purl.
3RD ROW: K4, k2tog, yo, k1, yo, sl 1, k1, psso, k4.
4TH ROW: Purl.
5TH ROW: K3, k2tog, yo, k3, yo, sl 1, k1, psso, k3.
6TH ROW: Purl.
7TH ROW: K3, yo, sl 1, k1, psso, yo, sl 1, k2tog, psso, yo, k2tog, yo, k3.
8TH ROW: Purl.
9TH ROW: K1, k2tog, yo, k1, yo, sl 1, k1, psso, k1, k2tog, yo, k1, yo, sl 1, k1, psso, k1.
10TH ROW: Purl.
11TH ROW: K1, [yo, sl 1, k1, psso] twice, k3, [k2tog, yo] twice, k1.
12TH ROW: P2, [yo, p2tog] twice, p1, [p2tog tbl, yo] twice, p2.
13TH ROW: K3, yo, sl 1, k1, psso, yo, sl 1, k2tog, psso, yo, k2tog, yo, k3.
14TH ROW: P4, yo, p2tog, p1, p2tog tbl, yo, p4.
15TH ROW: K5, yo, sl 1, k2tog, psso, yo, k5.
16TH ROW: Purl.
Rep these 16 rows.

Pyramid Lace Panel

Worked over 25 sts on a background of St st
Skill: intermediate

1ST ROW (RS): Purl.
2ND ROW: Knit.
3RD ROW: K3, yo, k8, sl 1, k2tog, psso, k8, yo, k3.
4TH AND EVERY FOLLOWING ALT ROW TO 18TH ROW: Purl.
5TH ROW: K4 , yo, k7, sl 1, k2tog, psso, k7, yo, k4.
7TH ROW: K2, k2tog, yo, k1, yo, k6, sl 1, k2tog, psso, k6, yo, k1, yo, sl 1, k1, psso, k2.
9TH ROW: K6, yo, k5, sl 1, k2tog, psso, k5, yo, k6.
11TH ROW: K3, yo, sl 1, k2tog, psso, yo, k1, yo, k4, sl 1, k2tog, psso, k4, yo, k1, yo, sl 1, k2tog, psso, yo, k3.
13TH ROW: K8, yo, k3, sl 1, k2tog, psso, k3, yo, k8.
15TH ROW: K2, k2tog, yo, k1, yo, sl 1, k2tog, psso, yo, k1, yo, k2, sl 1, k2tog, psso, k2, yo, k1, yo, sl 1, k2tog, psso, yo, k1, yo, sl 1, k1, psso, k2.
17TH ROW: K10, yo, k1, sl 1, k2tog, psso, k1, yo, k10.
19TH ROW: K3, [yo, sl 1, k2tog, psso, yo, k1] 4 times, yo, sl 1, k2tog, psso, yo, k3.
20TH ROW: Knit.
Rep these 20 rows.

Lacy Chain

Worked over 16 sts on a background of St st

Skill: intermediate

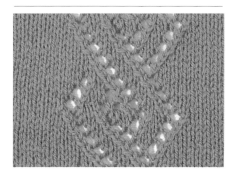

1ST ROW (RS): K5, yo, sl 1, k1, psso, k2, yo, sl 1, k1, psso, k5.

2ND AND EVERY ALT ROW: Purl.

3RD ROW: K3, k2tog, yo, k1, yo, sl 1, k1, psso, k2, yo, sl 1, k1, psso, k4.

5TH ROW: K2, k2tog, yo, k3, yo, sl 1, k1, psso, k2, yo, sl 1, k1, psso, k3.

7TH ROW: K1, k2tog, yo, k2, k2tog, yo, k1, yo, sl 1, k1, psso, k2, yo, sl 1, k1, psso, k2.

9TH ROW: K2tog, yo, k2, k2tog, yo, k3, yo, sl 1, k1, psso, k2, yo, sl 1, k1, psso, k1.

11TH ROW: K2, yo, sl 1, k1, psso, k2, yo, sl 1, k1, psso, yo, k2tog, yo, k2, k2tog, yo, k2tog.

13TH ROW: K3, yo, sl 1, k1, psso, k2, yo, sl 1, k2tog, psso, yo, k2, k2tog, yo, k2.

15TH ROW: K4, yo, sl 1, k1, psso, k2, yo, sl 1, k1, psso, k1, k2tog, yo, k3.

16TH ROW: Purl. Rep these 16 rows.

Diamond and Bobble Panel

Worked over 11 sts on a background of reversed St st

Skill: experienced

1ST ROW (RS): P1, yo, sl 1, k1, psso, p5, k2tog, yo, p1.

2ND ROW: K2, p1, k5, p1, k2.

3RD ROW: P2, yo, sl 1, k1, psso, p3, k2tog, yo, p2.

4TH ROW: K3, [p1, k3] twice.

5TH ROW: P3, yo, sl 1, k1, psso, p1, k2tog,

yo, p3.

6TH ROW: K4, p1, k1, p1, k4.

7TH ROW: P4, yo, sl 1, k2tog, psso, yo, p4.

8TH ROW: K5, p1, k5.

9TH ROW: P3, k2tog, yo, p1, yo, sl 1, k1, psso, p3.

10TH ROW: As 4th row.

11TH ROW: P2, k2tog, yo, p3, yo, sl 1, k1, psso, p2.

12TH ROW: As 2nd row.

13TH ROW: P1, k2tog, yo, p5, yo, sl 1, k1, psso, p1.

14TH ROW: K1, p1, k7, p1, k1.

15TH ROW: K2tog, yo, p3, make bobble as follows: into next st work [k1, yo, k1, yo, k1], turn, p5, turn, k5, turn, p2tog, p1, p2tog tbl, turn, sl 1, k2tog, psso, p3, yo, sl 1, k1, psso.

16TH ROW: K1, p1, k3, k1 tbl, k3, p1, k1. Rep these 16 rows.

Staggered Fern Lace Panel

Worked over 20 sts on a background of St st

Skill: intermediate

1ST ROW (RS): P2, k9, yo, k1, yo, k3, sl 1, k2tog, psso, p2.

2ND AND EVERY ALT ROW: Purl.

3RD ROW: P2, k10, yo, k1, yo, k2, sl 1, k2tog, psso, p2.

5TH ROW: P2, k3tog, k4, yo, k1, yo, k3, [yo, k1] twice, sl 1, k2tog, psso, p2.

7TH ROW: P2, k3tog, k3, yo, k1, yo, k9, p2.

9TH ROW: P2, k3tog, k2, yo, k1, yo, k10, p2.

11TH ROW: P2, k3tog, [k1, yo] twice, k3, yo, k1, yo, k4, sl 1, k2tog, psso, p2.

12TH ROW: Purl. Rep these 12 rows.

Chalice Cup Panel

Worked over 13 sts on a background of St st

Skill: intermediate

Note: Sts should not be counted after the 7th, 8th, 15th, and 16th rows.

1ST ROW (RS): P1, k3, k2tog, yo, k1, yo, sl 1, k1, psso, k3, p1.

2ND ROW: K1, p11, k1.

3RD ROW: P1, k2, k2tog, yo, k3, yo, sl 1, k1, psso, k2, p1.

4TH ROW: As 2nd row.

5TH ROW: P1, k1, k2tog, yo, k1, yo, sl 1, k2tog, psso, yo, k1, yo, sl 1, k1, psso, k1, p1.

6TH ROW: As 2nd row.

7TH ROW: P1, k2tog, yo, k3, yo, k1, yo, k3, yo, sl 1, k1, psso, p1.

8TH ROW: K1, p13, k1.

9TH ROW: P1, k2tog, yo, sl 1, k1, psso, k5, k2tog, yo, sl 1, k1, psso, p1.

10TH ROW: As 2nd row.

11TH ROW: P1, k2tog, yo, k1, yo, sl 1, k1, psso, k1, k2tog, yo, k1, yo, sl 1, k1, psso, p1.

12TH ROW: As 2nd row.
Rep the last 2 rows once more.
15TH ROW: P1, k1, yo, k3, yo, sl 1, k2tog, psso, yo, k3, yo, k1, p1.
16TH ROW: As 8th row.
17TH ROW: P1, k3, k2tog, yo, sl 1, k2tog, psso, yo, sl 1, k1, psso, k3, p1.
18TH ROW: As 2nd row. Rep these 18 rows.

Bluebell Insertion
Worked over 8 sts on a background of reversed St st
Skill: intermediate

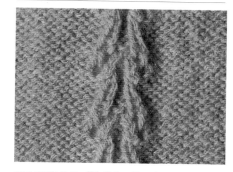

1ST ROW (RS): P2, [k1, p2] twice.
2ND ROW: K2, [p1, k2] twice.
Rep the last 2 rows once more.
5TH ROW: P1, yo, sl 1, k1, psso, p2, k2tog, yo, p1.
6TH ROW: K1, p2, k2, p2, k1.
7TH ROW: P2, yo, sl 1, k1, psso, k2tog, yo, p2.
8TH ROW: K2, p4, k2.
Rep these 8 rows.

Lyre Panel
Worked over 21 sts on a background of St st
Skill: intermediate

1ST AND EVERY ALT ROW (WS): Purl.
2ND ROW: K1, yo, k2tog, k5, k2tog, yo, k1, yo, sl 1, k1, psso, k5, sl 1, k1, psso, yo, k1.
4TH ROW: K1, yo, k2tog, k4, k2tog, yo, k3, yo, sl 1, k1, psso, k4, sl 1, k1, psso, yo, k1.

6TH ROW: K1, yo, k2tog, k3, k2tog, yo, k5, yo, sl 1, k1, psso, k3, sl 1, k1, psso, yo, k1.
8TH ROW: K1, yo, k2tog, k2, [k2tog, yo] twice, k3, [yo, sl 1, k1, psso] twice, k2, sl 1, k1, psso, yo, k1.
10TH, 12TH, 14TH, 16TH, AND 18TH ROWS: K1, yo, k2tog, k3, yo, k2tog, yo, sl 1, k1, psso, k1, k2tog, yo, sl 1, k1, psso, yo, k3, sl 1, k1, psso, yo, k1.
20TH ROW: K1, yo, k2tog, k1, k2tog, yo, k9, yo, sl 1, k1, psso, k1, sl 1, k1, psso, yo, k1. Rep these 20 rows.

Little Shell Insertion
Worked over 7 sts on a background of St st
Skill: intermediate

1ST ROW (RS): Knit.
2ND ROW: Purl.
3RD ROW: K1, yo, p1, p3tog, p1, yo, k1.
4TH ROW: Purl.
Rep these 4 rows.

Eyelet Lattice Insertion
Worked over 8 sts on a background of St st
Skill: intermediate

1ST ROW (RS): K1, [k2tog, yo] 3 times, k1.
2ND ROW: Purl.
3RD ROW: K2, [k2tog, yo] twice, k2.
4TH ROW: Purl.
Rep these 4 rows.

Eyelet Fan Panel
Worked over 13 sts on a background of St st
Skill: intermediate

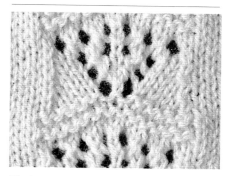

Work 4 rows in garter st (1st row is right side).
5TH ROW: Sl 1, k1, psso, k4, yo, k1, yo, k4, k2tog.
6TH 8TH, 10TH AND 12TH ROWS: Purl.
7TH ROW: Sl 1, k1, psso, [k3, yo] twice, k3, k2tog.
9TH ROW: Sl 1, k1, psso, k2, yo, k2tog, yo, k1, yo, sl 1, k1, psso, yo, k2, k2tog.

11TH ROW: Sl 1, k1, psso, k1, yo, k2tog, yo, k3, yo, sl 1, k1, psso, yo, k1, k2tog.
13TH ROW: Sl 1, k1, psso, [yo, k2tog] twice, yo, k1, [yo, sl 1, k1, psso] twice, yo, k2tog.
14TH ROW: Purl.
Rep these 14 rows.

Ribbed Diamond Panel

Worked over 17 sts on a background of St st
Skill: intermediate

1ST ROW (RS): K6, k2tog, yo, k1, yo, sl 1, k1, psso, k6.
2ND ROW: P7, k1, p1, k1, p7.
3RD ROW: K5, k2tog, yo, p1, k1, p1, yo, sl 1, k1, psso, k5.
4TH ROW: As 2nd row.
5TH ROW: K4, k2tog, yo, [k1, p1] twice, k1, yo, sl 1, k1, psso, k4.
6TH ROW: P5, k1, [p1, k1] 3 times, p5.
7TH ROW: K3, k2tog, yo, [p1, k1] 3 times, p1, yo, sl 1, k1, psso, k3.
8TH ROW: As 6th row.
9TH ROW: K2, k2tog, yo, [k1, p1] 4 times, k1, yo, sl 1, k1, psso, k2.
10TH ROW: P3, k1, [p1, k1] 5 times, p3.
11TH ROW: K1, k2tog, yo, [p1, k1] 5 times, p1, yo, sl 1, k1, psso, k1.
12TH ROW: As 10th row.
13TH ROW: K1, yo, sl 1, k1, psso, [p1, k1] 5 times, p1, k2tog, yo, k1.
14TH ROW: As 10th row.
15TH ROW: K2, yo, sl 1, k1, psso, [k1, p1] 4 times, k1, k2tog, yo, k2.
16TH ROW: As 6th row.
17TH ROW: K3, yo, sl 1, k1, psso, [p1, k1]

3 times, p1, k2tog, yo, k3.
18TH ROW: As 6th row.
19TH ROW: K4, yo, sl 1, k1, psso, [k1, p1] twice, k1, k2tog, yo, k4.
20TH ROW: As 2nd row.
21ST ROW: K5, yo, sl 1, k1, psso, p1, k1, p1, k2tog, yo, k5.
22ND ROW: As 2nd row.
23RD ROW: K6, yo, sl 1, k1, psso, k1, k2tog, yo, k6.
24TH ROW: Purl.
Rep these 24 rows.

Double-Moss Stitch Diamond Panel

Worked over 19 sts on a background of St st
Skill: experienced

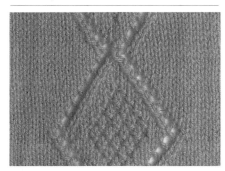

1ST ROW (RS): K8, yo, sl 1, k2tog, psso, yo, k8.
2ND, 4TH, 6TH AND 8TH ROWS: Purl.
3RD ROW: K7, k2tog, yo, k1, yo, sl 1, k1, psso, k7.
5TH ROW: K6, k2tog, yo, k3, yo, sl 1, k1, psso, k6.
7TH ROW: K5, k2tog, yo, k5, yo, sl 1, k1, psso, k5.
9TH ROW: K4, k2tog, yo, k3, p1, k3, yo, sl 1, k1, psso, k4.
10TH ROW: P9, k1, p9.
11TH ROW: K3, k2tog, yo, k3, p1, k1, p1, k3, yo, sl 1, k1, psso, k3.
12TH ROW: P8, k1, p1, k1, p8.
13TH ROW: K2, k2tog, yo, k3, [p1, k1] twice, p1, k3, yo, sl 1, k1, psso, k2.

14TH ROW: P7, [k1, p1] twice, k1, p7.
15TH ROW: K1, k2tog, yo, k3, [p1, k1] 3 times, p1, k3, yo, sl 1, k1, psso, k1.
16TH ROW: P6, [k1, p1] 3 times, k1, p6.
17TH ROW: K2tog, yo, k3, [p1, k1] 4 times, p1, k3, yo, sl 1, k1, psso.
18TH ROW: P5, [k1, p1] 4 times, k1, p5.
19TH ROW: K2, yo, sl 1, k1, psso, k2, [p1, k1] 3 times, p1, k2, k2tog, yo, k2.
20TH ROW: As 16th row.
21ST ROW: K3, yo, sl 1, k1, psso, k2, [p1, k1] twice, p1, k2, k2tog, yo, k3.
22ND ROW: As 14th row.
23RD ROW: K4, yo, sl 1, k1, psso, k2, p1, k1, p1, k2, k2tog, yo, k4.
24TH ROW: As 12th row.
25TH ROW: K5, yo, sl 1, k1, psso, k2, p1, k2, k2tog, yo, k5.
26TH ROW: As 10th row.
27TH ROW: K6, yo, sl 1, k1, psso, k3, k2tog, yo, k6.
28TH ROW: Purl.
29TH ROW: K7, yo, sl 1, k1, psso, k1, k2tog, yo, k7.
30TH ROW: Purl. Rep these 30 rows.

Ascending Arrow Panel

Worked over 13 sts on a background of reverse St st
Skill: intermediate

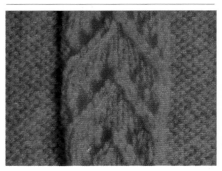

1ST ROW (RS): P2, yo, sl 1, k1, psso, k5, k2tog, yo, p2.
2ND AND EVERY ALT ROW: K2, p9, k2.
3RD ROW: P2, k1, yo, sl 1, k1, psso, k3, k2tog, yo, k1, p2.
5TH ROW: P2, k2, yo, sl 1, k1, psso, k1,

k2tog, yo, k2, p2.
7TH ROW: P2, k3, yo, sl 1, k2tog, psso, yo, k3, p2.
8TH ROW: K2, p9, k2.
Rep these 8 rows.

Vertical Arrow Panel
Worked over 13 sts on a background of St st
Skill: intermediate

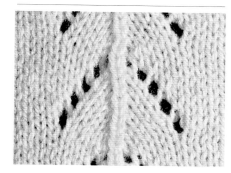

1ST ROW (RS): K1, yo, k4, sl 2tog, k1, p2sso, k4, yo, k1.
2ND AND EVERY ALT ROW: Purl.
3RD ROW: K2, yo, k3, sl 2tog, k1, p2sso, k3, yo, k2.
5TH ROW: K3, yo, k2, sl 2tog, k1, p2sso, k2, yo, k3.
7TH ROW: K4, yo, k1, sl 2tog, k1, p2sso, k1, yo, k4.
9TH ROW: K5, yo, sl 2tog, k1, p2sso, yo, k5.
10TH ROW: Purl.
Rep these 10 rows.

Twig and Leaf Insertion
Worked over 13 sts on a background of St st
Skill: intermediate

1ST AND EVERY ALT ROW (WS): Purl.
2ND ROW: [K1, yo] twice, sl 1, k2tog, psso, k3, k3tog, [yo, k1] twice.
4TH ROW: K1, yo, k3, yo, sl 1, k1, psso, k1, k2tog, yo, k3, yo, k1. (15 sts.)

6TH ROW: K1, yo, sl 1, k1, psso, k1, k2tog, yo, sl 1, k2tog, psso, yo, sl 1, k1, psso, k1, k2tog, yo, k1. (13 sts.)
8TH ROW: K1, [yo, sl 1, k1, psso, k1, k2tog, yo, k1] twice.
10TH ROW: As 8th row. Rep these 10 rows.

Fishtails
Worked over 15 sts on a background of St st
Skill: intermediate

1ST ROW (RS): K6, yo, sl 1, k2tog, psso, yo, k6.
2ND AND EVERY ALT ROW: Purl.
Rep these 2 rows 3 times more.
9TH ROW: [K1, yo] twice, sl 1, k1, psso, k2, sl 1, k2tog, psso, k2, k2tog, [yo, k1] twice.
11TH ROW: K2, yo, k1, yo, sl 1, k1, psso, k1, sl 1, k2tog, psso, k1, k2tog, yo, k1, yo, k2.
13TH ROW: K3, yo, k1, yo, sl 1, k1, psso, sl 1, k2tog, psso, k2tog, yo, k1, yo, k3.
15TH ROW: K4, yo, sl 1, k1, psso, yo, sl 1, k2tog, psso, yo, k2tog, yo, k4.
16TH ROW: Purl.
Rep these 16 rows.

Fountains Panel
Worked over 16 sts on a background of St st
Skill: intermediate

1ST ROW (RS): K1, yo, k1, sl 1, k1, psso, p1, k2tog, k1, yo, p1, yb, sl 1, k1, psso, p1, k2tog, [yo, k1] twice.
2ND ROW: P5, k1, p1, k1, p3, k1, p4.
3RD ROW: K1, yo, k1, sl 1, k1, psso, p1, k2tog, k1, p1, yb, sl 1, k2tog, psso, yo, k3, yo, k1. (15 sts.)
4TH ROW: P7, k1, p2, k1, p4.
5TH ROW: [K1, yo] twice, sl 1, k1, psso, p1, [k2tog] twice, yo, k5, yo, k1. (16 sts.)
6TH ROW: P8, k1, p1, k1, p5.
7TH ROW: K1, yo, k3, yo, sl 1, k2tog, psso, p1, yo, k1, sl 1, k1, psso, p1, k2tog, k1, yo, k1.
8TH ROW: P4, k1, p3, k1, p7.
9TH ROW: K1, yo, k5, yo, sl 1, k1, psso, k1, sl 1, k1, psso, p1, k2tog, k1, yo, k1.
10TH ROW: P4, k1, p2, k1, p8.
Rep these 10 rows.

Comb Panel
Worked over 8 sts on a background of reverse St st
Skill: intermediate

1ST ROW (WS): K1, p6, k1.
2ND ROW: P1, yb, sl 1, k1, psso, k4, yo, p1.
3RD ROW: K1, p1, yo, p3, p2tog tbl, k1.
4TH ROW: P1, yb, sl 1, k1, psso, k2, yo, k2, p1.
5TH ROW: K1, p3, yo, p1, p2tog tbl, k1.
6TH ROW: P1, yb, sl 1, k1, psso, yo, k4, p1.
7TH ROW: As 1st row.

8TH ROW: P1, yo, k4, k2tog, p1.
9TH ROW: K1, p2tog, p3, yo, p1, k1.
10TH ROW: P1, k2, yo, k2, k2tog, p1.
11TH ROW: K1, p2tog, p1, yo, p3, k1.
12TH ROW: P1, k4, yo, k2tog, p1.
Rep these 12 rows.

Butterfly Panel
Worked over 15 sts on a background of reverse St st
Skill: intermediate

1ST ROW (RS): Yb, sl 1, k1, psso, k4, yo, k3, yo, k4, k2tog.
2ND ROW: P2tog, p3, yo, p5, yo, p3, p2tog tbl.
3RD ROW: Yb, sl 1, k1, psso, k2, yo, k7, yo, k2, k2tog.
4TH ROW: P2tog, p1, yo, p9, yo, p1, p2tog tbl.
5TH ROW: Yb, sl 1, k1, psso, yo, k11, yo, k2tog.
6TH ROW: P1, yo, p4, p2tog, k1, p2tog tbl, p4, yo, p1.
7TH ROW: K2, yo, k3, sl 1, k1, psso, p1,

k2tog, k3, yo, k2.
8TH ROW: P3, yo, p2, p2tog, k1, p2tog tbl, p2, yo, p3.
9TH ROW: K4, yo, k1, sl 1, k1, psso, p1, k2tog, k1, yo, k4.
10TH ROW: P5, yo, p2tog, k1, p2tog tbl, yo, p5.
Rep these 10 rows.

Ostrich Plume Panel
Worked over 13 sts on a background of reverse St st
Skill: intermediate

1ST ROW (RS): Knit.
2ND ROW: Purl.
3RD ROW: K4tog, [yo, k1] 5 times, yo, k4tog.
4TH ROW: Purl.
Rep these 4 rows.

Cockleshells
Worked over 19 sts on a background of garter stitch
Skill: experienced

1ST ROW (RS): Knit.
2ND ROW: Knit.
3RD ROW: K1, yo twice, p2tog tbl, k13, p2tog, yo twice, k1. (21 sts.)
4TH ROW: K2, p1, k15, p1, k2.
5TH AND 6TH ROWS: Knit.
7TH ROW: K1, yo twice, p2tog tbl, yo twice, p2tog tbl, k11, p2tog, yo twice, p2tog, yo twice, k1. (25 sts.)

8TH ROW: [K2, p1] twice, k13, [p1, k2] twice.
9TH ROW: Knit.
10TH ROW: K5, k15 wrapping yarn 3 times around needle for each st, k5.
11TH ROW: K1, yo twice, p2tog tbl, yo twice, p2tog tbl, yo twice, pass next 15 sts to right-hand needle dropping extra loops, pass same 15 sts back to left-hand needle and purl all 15 sts tog, yo twice, p2tog, yo twice, p2tog, yo twice, k1. (19 sts.)
12TH ROW: K1, p1, [k2, p1] twice, k3, [p1, k2] twice, p1, k1. Rep these 12 rows.

Gardenia Lace Panel
Worked over 12 sts on a background of St st
Skill: intermediate
Note: Sts should not be counted after 1st row.

1ST ROW (RS): K3, [k2tog, yo] twice, sl 1, k1, psso, k3.
2ND ROW: P2, p2tog tbl, yo, p1, inc 1 in

next st, p1, yo, p2tog, p2.

3RD ROW: K1, k2tog, yo, k6, yo, sl 1, k1, psso, k1.

4TH ROW: P2tog tbl, yo, p8, yo, p2tog.

5TH ROW: K1, yo, k3, k2tog, sl 1, k1, psso, k3, yo, k1.

6TH ROW: P2, yo, p2, p2tog tbl, p2tog, p2, yo, p2.

7TH ROW: K3, yo, k1, k2tog, sl 1, k1, psso, k1, yo, k3.

8TH ROW: P4, yo, p2tog tbl, p2tog, yo, p4. Rep these 8 rows.

Embossed Rosebud Panel

Worked over 9 sts on a background of reverse St st

Skill: experienced

1ST ROW (WS): K3, p3, k3.

2ND ROW: P3, slip next st onto cable needle and hold at front of work, k1, [k1, yo, k1, yo, k1] into next st on left-hand needle, then knit st from cable needle, p3. (13 sts.)

3RD ROW: K3, p1, [k1 tbl] 5 times, p1, k3.

4TH ROW: P3, [k1, yo] 6 times, k1, p3. (19 sts.)

5TH ROW: K3, p13, k3.

6TH ROW: P3, k13, p3.

7TH ROW: K3, p2tog, p9, p2tog tbl, k3. (17 sts.)

8TH ROW: P3, yb, sl 1, k1, psso, k7, k2tog, p3. (15 sts.)

9TH ROW: K3, p2tog, p5, p2tog tbl, k3. (13 sts.)

10TH ROW: P3, yb, sl 1, k1, psso, k3, k2tog, p3. (11 sts.)

11TH ROW: K3, p2tog, p1, p2tog tbl, k3. (9 sts.)

12TH ROW: P3, k3, p3. Rep these 12 rows.

Branch Panel

Worked over 12 sts on a background of reverse St st

Skill: intermediate

1ST ROW (RS): K2tog, k5, yo, k1, yo, k2, sl 1, k1, psso.

2ND AND EVERY ALT ROW: Purl.

3RD ROW: K2tog, k4, yo, k3, yo, k1, sl 1, k1, psso.

5TH ROW: K2tog, k3, yo, k5, yo, sl 1, k1, psso.

7TH ROW: K2tog, k2, yo, k1, yo, k5, sl 1, k1, psso.

9TH ROW: K2tog, k1, yo, k3, yo, k4, sl 1, k1, psso.

11TH ROW: K2tog, yo, k5, yo, k3, sl 1, k1, psso.

12TH ROW: Purl. Rep these 12 rows.

Zigzag Panel

Worked over 9 sts on a background of St st

Skill: easy

1ST ROW (RS): K3, sl 1, k1, psso, yo, k2tog, yo, k2.

2ND AND EVERY ALT ROW: Purl.

3RD ROW: K2, sl 1, k1, psso, yo, k2tog, yo, k3.

5TH ROW: K1, sl 1, k1, psso, yo, k2tog, yo, k4.

7TH ROW: Sl 1, k1, psso, yo, k2tog, yo, k5.

9TH ROW: K2, yo, sl 1, k1, psso, yo, k2tog, k3.

11TH ROW: K3, yo, sl 1, k1, psso, yo, k2tog, k2.

13TH ROW: K4, yo, sl 1, k1, psso, yo, k2tog, k1.

15TH ROW: K5, yo, sl 1, k1, psso, yo, k2tog.

16TH ROW: Purl. Rep these 16 rows.

Zigzag Panel with Diamonds

Worked over 9 sts on a background of St st

Skill: intermediate

1ST ROW (RS): K2, yo, sl 1, k1, psso, k5.

2ND AND EVERY ALT ROW: Purl.

3RD ROW: K3, yo, sl 1, k1, psso, k4.

5TH ROW: K4, yo, sl 1, k1, psso, k3.

7TH ROW: K5, yo, sl 1, k1, psso, k2.

9TH ROW: K2, yo, sl 1, k1, psso, k2, yo, sl 1, k1, psso, k1.

11TH ROW: K1, [yo, sl 1, k1, psso] twice, k2, yo, sl 1, k1, psso.

13TH ROW: K2, yo, sl 1, k1, psso, k2, k2tog, yo, k1.

15TH ROW: K5, k2tog, yo, k2.

17TH ROW: K4, k2tog, yo, k3.

19TH ROW: K3, k2tog, yo, k4.

21ST ROW: K2, k2tog, yo, k5.

23RD ROW: K1, k2tog, yo, k3, yo, sl 1, k1, psso, k1.
25TH ROW: K2tog, yo, k3, [yo, sl 1, k1, psso] twice.
27TH ROW: K1, yo, sl 1, k1, psso, k3, yo, sl 1, k1, psso, k1.
28TH ROW: Purl.
Rep these 28 rows.

Braided Lace Panel
Worked over 20 sts on a background of St st
Skill: experienced

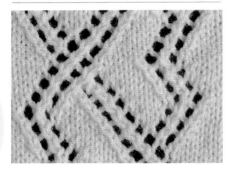

1ST AND EVERY ALT ROW (WS): Purl.
2ND ROW: K4, [yo, sl 1, k1, psso] twice, k3, [k2tog, yo] twice, k5.
4TH ROW: K2, [k2tog, yo] twice, k4, [k2tog, yo] twice, k1, yo, sl 1, k1, psso, k3.
6TH ROW: K1, [k2tog, yo] twice, k4, [k2tog, yo] twice, k1, [yo, sl 1, k1, psso] twice, k2.
8TH ROW: [K2tog, yo] twice, k4, [k2tog, yo] twice, k3, [yo, sl 1, k1, psso] twice, k1.
10TH ROW: K2, [yo, sl 1, k1, psso] twice, k1, [k2tog, yo] twice, k5, [yo, sl 1, k1, psso] twice.
12TH ROW: K3, yo, sl 1, k1, psso, yo, sl 1, k2tog, psso, yo, k2tog, yo, k4, [k2tog, yo] twice, k2.
14TH ROW: K4, yo, sl 1, k1, psso, yo, sl 1, k2tog, psso, yo, k4, [k2tog, yo] twice, k3.
16TH ROW: K5, [yo, sl 1, k1, psso] twice, k3, [k2tog, yo] twice, k4.
18TH ROW: K3, k2tog, yo, k1, [yo, sl 1, k1, psso] twice, k4, [yo, sl 1, k1, psso] twice, k2.
20TH ROW: K2, [k2tog, yo] twice, k1, [yo, sl 1, k1, psso] twice, k4, [yo, sl 1, k1, psso]

twice, k1.
22ND ROW: K1, [k2tog, yo] twice, k3, [yo, sl 1, k1, psso] twice, k4, [yo, sl 1, k1, psso] twice.
24TH ROW: [K2tog, yo] twice, k5, [yo, sl 1, k1, psso] twice, k1, [k2tog, yo] twice, k2.
26TH ROW: K2, [yo, sl 1, k1, psso] twice, k4, yo, sl 1, k1, psso, yo, k3tog, yo, k2tog, yo, k3.
28TH ROW: K3, [yo, sl 1, k1, psso] twice, k4, yo, k3tog, yo, k2tog, yo, k4. Rep these 28 rows.

Pyramid Panel
Worked over 17 sts on a background of St st
Skill: intermediate

1ST ROW (RS): [K1, yo, sl 1, k1, psso] twice, p5, [k2tog, yo, k1] twice.
2ND ROW: P6, k5, p6.
3RD ROW: K2, yo, sl 1, k1, psso, k1, yo, sl 1, k1, psso, p3, k2tog, yo, k1, k2tog, yo, k2.
4TH ROW: P7, k3, p7.
5TH ROW: K3, yo, sl 1, k1, psso, k1, yo, sl 1, k1, psso, p1, k2tog, yo, k1, k2tog, yo, k3.
6TH ROW: P8, k1, p8.
7TH ROW: K4, yo, sl 1, k1, psso, k1, yo, sl 1, k2tog, psso, yo, k1, k2tog, yo, k4.
8TH AND EVERY ALT ROW: Purl.
9TH ROW: K5, yo, sl 1, k1, psso, k3, k2tog, yo, k5.
11TH ROW: K6, yo, sl 1, k1, psso, k1, k2tog, yo, k6.
13TH ROW: K7, yo, sl 1, k2tog, psso, yo, k7.
14TH ROW: Purl.
Rep these 14 rows.

Lace Loops
Worked over 20 sts on a background of St st
Skill: intermediate

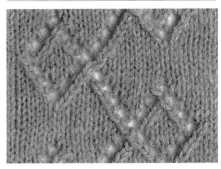

1ST AND EVERY ALT ROW (WS): Purl.
2ND ROW: K2, yo, sl 1, k1, psso, k1, k2tog, yo, k1, yo, sl 1, k1, psso, k10.
4TH ROW: K3, yo, sl 1, k2tog, psso, yo, k3, yo, sl 1, k1, psso, k3, k2tog, yo, k4.
6TH ROW: K4, yo, sl 1, k1, psso, k4, yo, sl 1, k1, psso, k1, k2tog, yo, k1, yo, sl 1, k1, psso, k2.
8TH ROW: K11, yo, k3tog, yo, k3, yo, sl 1, k1, psso, k1.
10TH ROW: K11, k2tog, yo, k5, yo, sl 1, k1, psso.
12TH ROW: K10, k2tog, yo, k1, yo, sl 1, k1, psso, k1, k2tog, yo, k2.
14TH ROW: K4, yo, sl 1, k1, psso, k3, k2tog, yo, k3, yo, k3tog, yo, k3.
16TH ROW: K2, k2tog, yo, k1, yo, sl 1, k1, psso, k1, k2tog, yo, k4, k2tog, yo, k4.
18TH ROW: K1, k2tog, yo, k3, yo, sl 1, k2tog, yo, k11.
20TH ROW: K2tog, yo, k5, yo, sl 1, k1, psso, k11. Rep these 20 rows.

Vandyke Lace Panel I
Worked over 17 sts on a background of St st
Skill: easy

1ST ROW (RS): ✳K2tog, yo, k1, yo, sl 1, k1, psso✳, k3, yo, sl 1, k1, psso, k2, rep from ✳ to ✳ once more.
2ND ROW: Purl.

3RD ROW: [K2tog, yo, k1, yo, sl 1, k1, psso, k1] twice, k2tog, yo, k1, yo, sl 1, k1, psso.
4TH ROW: Purl.
5TH ROW: ✳K2tog, yo, k1, yo, sl 1, k1, psso✳, k2tog, yo, k3, yo, sl 1, k1, psso, rep from ✳ to ✳ once more.
6TH ROW: Purl.
Rep these 6 rows.

Vandyke Lace Panel II
Worked over 9 sts on a background of St st
Skill: easy

1ST ROW (RS): K4, yo, sl 1, k1, psso, k3.
2ND AND EVERY ALT ROW: Purl.
3RD ROW: K2, k2tog, yo, k1, yo, sl 1, k1, psso, k2.
5TH ROW: K1, k2tog, yo, k3, yo, sl 1, k1, psso, k1.
7TH ROW: K2tog, yo, k5, yo, sl 1, k1, psso.
8TH ROW: Purl.
Rep these 8 rows.

Cascading Leaves
Worked over 16 sts on a background of reverse St st
Skill: intermediate

1ST ROW (RS): P1, k3, k2tog, k1, yo, p2, yo, k1, sl 1, k1, psso, k3, p1.
2ND AND EVERY ALT ROW: K1, p6, k2, p6, k1.
3RD ROW: P1, k2, k2tog, k1, yo, k1, p2, k1, yo, k1, sl 1, k1, psso, k2, p1.
5TH ROW: P1, k1, k2tog, k1, yo, k2, p2, k2, yo, k1, sl 1, k1, psso, k1, p1.
7TH ROW: P1, k2tog, k1, yo, k3, p2, k3, yo, k1, sl 1, k1, psso, p1.
8TH ROW: K1, p6, k2, p6, k1.
Rep these 8 rows.

Raised Tire Track Panel
Worked over 10 sts on a background of St st
Skill: intermediate

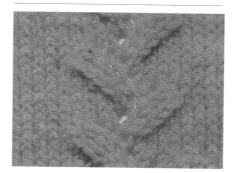

1ST ROW (RS): K4, yo, k1, sl 1, k1, psso, k3.
2ND ROW: P2, p2tog tbl, p1, yo, p5.
3RD ROW: K6, yo, k1, sl 1, k1, psso, k1.

4TH ROW: P2tog tbl, p1, yo, p7.
5TH ROW: K3, k2tog, k1, yo, k4.
6TH ROW: P5, yo, p1, p2tog, p2.
7TH ROW: K1, k2tog, k1, yo, k6.
8TH ROW: P7, yo, p1, p2tog.
Rep these 8 rows.

Leaf Panel
Worked over 24 sts on a background of St st
Skill: intermediate

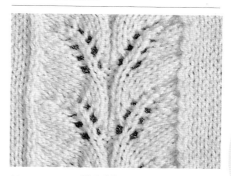

1ST ROW (RS): Sl 1, k2tog, psso, k7, yo, k1, yo, p2, yo, k1, yo, k7, k3tog.
2ND AND EVERY ALT ROW: P11, k2, p11.
3RD ROW: Sl 1, k2tog, psso, k6 [yo, k1] twice, p2, [k1, yo] twice, k6, k3tog.
5TH ROW: Sl 1, k2tog, psso, k5, yo, k1, yo, k2, p2, k2, yo, k1, yo, k5, k3tog.
7TH ROW: Sl 1, k2tog, psso, k4, yo, k1, yo, k3, p2, k3, yo, k1, yo, k4, k3tog.
9TH ROW: Sl 1, k2tog, psso, k3, yo, k1, yo, k4, p2, k4, yo, k1, yo, k3, k3tog.
10TH ROW: As 2nd row. Rep these 10 rows.

Spiral and Eyelet Panel
Worked over 24 sts on a background of reverse St st
Skill: intermediate

1ST ROW (RS): K3, k2tog, k4, yo, p2, yo, k2tog, p2, yo, k4, sl 1, k1, psso, k3.
2ND AND EVERY ALT ROW: P9, k2, p2, k2, p9.
3RD ROW: K2, k2tog, k4, yo, k1, p2, k2tog, yo, p2, k1, yo, k4, sl 1, k1, psso, k2.

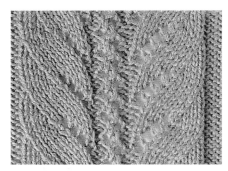

5TH ROW: K1, k2tog, k4, yo, k2, p2, yo, k2tog, p2, k2, yo, k4, sl 1, k1, psso, k1.
7TH ROW: K2tog, k4, yo, k3, p2, k2tog, yo, p2, k3, yo, k4, sl 1, k1, psso.
8TH ROW: P9, k2, p2, k2, p9.
Rep these 8 rows.

Arched Windows

Worked over 13 sts on a background of reverse St st
Skill: intermediate
Note: Stitches should not be counted after the 3rd, 4th, 7th, or 8th rows.

Special Abbreviation

T5R (Twist 5 Right) = slip next 3 sts onto cable needle and hold at back of work, knit next 2 sts from left-hand needle, then p1, k2 from cable needle.
1ST ROW (RS): K2, p2, k2tog, yo, k1, yo, sl 1, k1, psso, p2, k2.
2ND ROW: P2, k2, p5, k2, p2.
3RD ROW: K2, p2, k1, yo, k3, yo, k1, p2, k2.
4TH ROW: P2, k2, p7, k2, p2.
5TH ROW: K2, p2, yb, sl 1, k1, psso, yo, sl

1, k2tog, psso, yo, k2tog, p2, k2.
6TH ROW: As 2nd row.
7TH ROW: T3F, p1, k1, yo, k3, yo, k1, p1, T3B.
8TH ROW: K1, p2, k1, p7, k1, p2, k1.
9TH ROW: P1, T3F, sl 1, k1, psso, yo, sl 1, k2tog, psso, yo, k2tog, T3B, p1.
10TH ROW: K2, p9, k2.
11TH ROW: P2, T3F, p3, T3B, p2.
12TH ROW: [K3, p2] twice, k3.
13TH ROW: P3, T3F, p1, T3B, p3.
14TH ROW: K4, p2, k1, p2, k4.
15TH ROW: P4, T5R (see Special Abbreviation), p4.
16TH ROW: Knit.
Rep these 16 rows.

Catherine Wheels

Worked over 13 sts on a background of St st
Skill: intermediate

Special Abbreviations

inc 1 (increase 1) = knit into front and back of next st.
inc 2 (increase 2) = knit into front, back and front of next st.
work 5tog = sl 1, k1, psso, k3tog, pass the stitch resulting from sl 1, k1, psso over the stitch resulting from k3tog.
1ST AND EVERY ALT ROW (WS): Purl.
2ND ROW: K5, sl 3, yo, pass same slipped sts back to left-hand needle, yb, knit 3 slipped sts, k5.
4TH ROW: K3, k3tog, yo, inc 2 (see Special Abbreviations), yo, k3tog tbl, k3.
6TH ROW: K1, k3tog, yo, k2tog, yo, Inc 2, yo, sl 1, k1, psso, yo, k3tog tbl, k1.

8TH ROW: [K2tog, yo] 3 times, k1 tbl, [yo, sl 1, k1, psso] 3 times.
10TH ROW: K1, [yo, k2tog] twice, yo, sl 1, k2tog, psso, [yo, sl 1, k1, psso] twice, yo, k1.
12TH ROW: [Sl 1, k1, psso, yo] 3 times, k1 tbl [yo, k2tog] 3 times.
14TH ROW: K1, inc 1 (see Special Abbreviations), yo, sl 1, k1, psso, yo, work 5tog (see Special Abbreviations), yo, k2tog, yo, Inc 1, k1.
16TH ROW: K3, inc 1, yo, work 5tog, yo, inc 1, k3.
Rep these 16 rows.

Lace Cable Pattern I

Worked over 8 sts on a background of reversed St st.
Skill: intermediate

1ST ROW (RS): K2, yo, sl 1, k1, psso, k4.
2ND AND EVERY ALT ROW: Purl.
3RD ROW: K3, yo, sl 1, k1, psso, k3.
5TH ROW: K4, yo, sl 1, k1, psso, k2.
7TH ROW: K5, yo, sl 1, k1, psso, k1.
9TH ROW: C6B, yo, sl 1, k1, psso.
10TH ROW: Purl.
Rep these 10 rows.

---

ribs and edgings

The edges of a piece of knitting can be finished in many different ways. Although ribbing is the usual choice, especially for pullovers, a few rows of Seed Stitch (*page 33*) or Garter Stitch (*page 176*) can be very effective where a snug fit is not required. For evening wear, baby clothes and accessories, a lacy border may be a good choice for one or more edges.

rib patterns

The most frequently used rib edging is the basic Single Rib (*page 167*), which is very elastic and simple enough to use with almost any fabric stitch. For a double rib, work 2 knit and 2 purl stitches alternately; for a flatter, less elastic rib, work more knit stitches between the purl stitches. Many rib patterns can be used for the main fabric—among them, the classic Brioche Rib and Fisherman's Rib (*both page 167*) and more elaborate patterns, such as Feather Rib (*below*).

ribs and edgings

Seeded Rib
Multiple of 4 sts + 1
Drape: fair
Skill: easy

1ST ROW (RS): P1, ✳k3, p1; rep from ✳ to end.
2ND ROW: K2, p1, ✳k3, p1; rep from ✳ to last 2 sts, k2.
Rep these 2 rows.

Feather Rib
Multiple of 5 sts + 2
Drape: fair
Skill: intermediate

1ST ROW (RS): P2, ✳yo, k2tog tbl, k1, p2; rep from ✳ to end.
2ND ROW: K2, ✳yo, k2tog tbl, p1, k2; rep from ✳ to end.
Rep these 2 rows.

Blanket Rib
Multiple of 2 sts + 1
Drape: fair
Skill: intermediate

1ST ROW (RS): Knit into front and back of each st (thus doubling the number of sts).
2ND ROW: K2tog, ✳p2tog, k2tog; rep from ✳ to end (original number of sts restored).
Rep these 2 rows.

Brioche Rib
Multiple of 2 sts
Drape: fair
Skill: easy

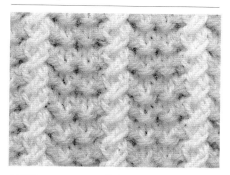

FOUNDATION ROW: Knit.
Commence Pattern
1ST ROW: ✳K1, K1B; rep from ✳ to last 2 sts, k2.
Rep 1st row throughout.

Single Rib (k1, p1)
Multiple of 2 sts
Drape: fair
Skill: easy

1ST ROW: ✳K1, P1; rep to end.
2ND ROW: ✳P1, K1; rep to end.
Rep these 2 rows.

Fisherman's Rib
Multiple of 2 (or 3) sts + 1
Drape: fair
Skill: intermediate
Note: Each set of instructions gives the same appearance but a different "feel." For example (C) is a firmer fabric than (A).

(A) Multiple of 2 sts + 1
FOUNDATION ROW: Knit.
Commence pattern
1ST ROW (RS): Sl 1, ✳K1B, p1; rep from ✳ to end.
2ND ROW: Sl 1, ✳p1, K1B; rep from ✳ to last 2 sts, p1, k1.
Rep the last 2 rows only.

(B) Multiple of 2 sts + 1
FOUNDATION ROW: Knit.
Commence pattern
1ST ROW (RS): Sl 1, ✳K1B, k1; rep from ✳ to end.
2ND ROW: Sl 1, ✳k1, K1B; rep from ✳ to last 2 sts, k2.
Rep the last 2 rows only.

(C) Multiple of 3 sts + 1
1ST ROW (RS): Sl 1, ✳k2tog, yo, sl 1 purlwise; rep from ✳ to last 3 sts, k2tog, k1.
2ND ROW: Sl 1, ✳yo, sl 1 purlwise, k2tog (the yo and sl 1 of previous row); rep from ✳ to last 2 sts, yo, sl 1 purlwise, k1.
Rep the last 2 rows.

Faggotted Rib
Multiple of 4 sts + 2
Drape: fair
Skill: intermediate

1ST ROW: K3, ✳yo, sl 1, k1, psso, k2; rep from ✳ to last 3 sts, yo, sl 1, k1, psso, k1.
2ND ROW: P3, ✳yo, p2tog, p2; rep from ✳ to last 3 sts, yo, p2tog, p1.
Rep these 2 rows.

Mock Cable—to the right
Multiple of 4 sts + 2
Drape: fair
Skill: intermediate

1ST ROW (RS): P2, ✳k2, p2; rep from ✳ to end.
2ND ROW: K2, ✳p2, k2; rep from ✳ to end.
3RD ROW: P2, ✳C2B, p2; rep from ✳ to end.
4TH ROW: As 2nd row.
Rep these 4 rows.

Mock Cable—to the left
Multiple of 4 sts + 2
Drape: fair
Skill: intermediate

1ST ROW (RS): P2, ❉k2, p2; rep from ❉ to end.
2ND ROW: K2, ❉p2, k2; rep from ❉ to end.
3RD ROW: P2, ❉C2F, p2; rep from ❉ to end.
4TH ROW: As 2nd row.
Rep these 4 rows.

Little Hourglass Ribbing
Multiple of 4 sts + 2
Drape: fair
Skill: intermediate
Note: Sts should not be counted after 3rd row.

1ST ROW (WS): K2, ❉p2, k2; rep from ❉ to end.
2ND ROW: P2, ❉k2tog tbl, then knit same 2 sts tog through front loops, p2; rep from ❉ to end.

3RD ROW: K2, ❉p1, yo, p1, k2; rep from ❉ to end.
4TH ROW: P2, ❉yb, sl 1, k1, psso, k1, p2; rep from ❉ to end. Rep these 4 rows.

Double Eyelet Rib
Multiple of 7 sts + 2
Drape: fair
Skill: intermediate

1ST ROW (RS): P2, ❉k5, p2; rep from ❉ to end.
2ND ROW: K2, ❉p5, k2; rep from ❉ to end.
3RD ROW: P2, ❉k2tog, yo, k1, yo, sl 1, k1, psso, p2; rep from ❉ to end.
4TH ROW: As 2nd row.
Rep these 4 rows.

Shadow Rib
Multiple of 3 sts + 2
Drape: fair
Skill: easy

1ST ROW (RS): Knit.

2ND ROW: P2, ❉k1 tbl, p2; rep from ❉ to end. Rep these 2 rows.

Harris Tweed Ribbing
Multiple of 4 sts + 2
Drape: fair
Skill: easy

1ST ROW (RS): K2, ❉p2, k2; rep from ❉ to end.
2ND ROW: P2, ❉k2, p2; rep from ❉ to end.
3RD ROW: Knit.
4TH ROW: Purl.
5TH ROW: As 1st row.
6TH ROW: As 2nd row.
7TH ROW: Purl.
8TH ROW: Knit. Rep these 8 rows.

Slipped Stitch Ribbing
Multiple of 8 sts + 3
Drape: fair
Skill: intermediate
Note: Slip all sts purlwise.

1ST ROW (RS): P3, ✳k1 wrapping yarn twice around needle, p3, k1, p3; rep from ✳ to end.
2ND ROW: K3, ✳p1, k3, yf, sl 1 dropping extra loop, yb, k3; rep from ✳ to end.
3RD ROW: P3, ✳yb, sl 1, yf, p3, k1, p3; rep from ✳ to end.
4TH ROW: K3, ✳p1, k3, yf, sl 1, yb, k3; rep from ✳ to end.
Rep these 4 rows.

Mock Cable Rib
Multiple of 7 sts + 2
Drape: fair
Skill: intermediate

1ST ROW (RS): P2, ✳C2F, k3, p2; rep from ✳ to end.
2ND AND EVERY ALT ROW: K2, ✳p5, k2; rep from ✳ to end.
3RD ROW: P2, ✳k1, C2F, k2, p2; rep from ✳ to end.
5TH ROW: P2, ✳k2, C2F, k1, p2; rep from ✳ to end.
7TH ROW: P2, ✳k3, C2F, p2; rep from ✳ to end.
8TH ROW: K2, ✳p5, k2; rep from ✳ to end.
Rep these 8 rows.

Chain Stitch Rib
Multiple of 3 sts + 2
Drape: fair
Skill: experienced

1ST ROW (WS): K2, gp1, k2; rep from g to end.
2ND ROW: P2, ✳k1, p2; rep from ✳ to end.
3RD ROW: As 1st row.
4TH ROW: P2, ✳yb, insert needle through center of st 3 rows below next st on needle and knit this in the usual way, slipping st above off needle at the same time, p2; rep from ✳ to end.
Rep these 4 rows.

Spiral Rib
Multiple of 6 sts + 3
Drape: fair
Skill: easy

1ST ROW (RS): K3, ✳p3, k3; rep from ✳ to end.
2ND ROW: P3, ✳k3, p3; rep from ✳ to end.
3RD ROW: As 1st row.

4TH ROW: K1, ✳p3, k3; rep from ✳ to last 2 sts, p2.
5TH ROW: K2, ✳p3, k3; rep from ✳ to last st, p1.
6TH ROW: As 4th row.
7TH ROW: As 4th row.
8TH ROW: As 5th row.
9TH ROW: As 4th row.
10TH ROW: K3, ✳p3, k3; rep from ✳ to end.
11TH ROW: As 2nd row.
12TH ROW: As 10th row.
13TH ROW: P2, ✳k3, p3; rep from ✳ to last st, k1.
14TH ROW: P1, ✳k3, p3; rep from ✳ to last 2 sts, k2.
15TH ROW: As 13th row.
16TH ROW: As 13th row.
17TH ROW: As 14th row.
18TH ROW: As 13th row.
Rep these 18 rows.

Slipped Rib
Multiple of 2 sts + 1
Drape: fair
Skill: intermediate

1ST ROW (RS): K1, ✳yo, sl 1 purlwise, yb, k1; rep from ✳ to end.
2ND ROW: Purl.
Rep these 2 rows.

Chunky Rib Pattern
Multiple of 8 sts + 6
Drape: fair
Skill: easy

1ST ROW (RS): P6, ✳k2, k6; rep from ✳ to end.
2ND ROW: K6, ✳p2, k6; rep from ✳ to end. Rep the last 2 rows twice more.
7TH ROW: P2, ✳k2, p2; rep from ✳ to end.
8TH ROW: K2, ✳p2, k2; rep from ✳ to end. Rep the last 2 rows twice more.
13TH ROW: P2, k2, ✳p6, p2; rep from ✳ to last 2 sts, p2.
14TH ROW: K2, p2, ✳k6, p2; rep from ✳ to last 2 sts, k2. Rep the last 2 rows twice more.
19TH ROW: As 7th row.
20TH ROW: As 8th row. Rep the last 2 rows twice more. Rep these 24 rows.

Cluster Rib
Multiple of 3 sts + 1
Drape: fair
Skill: intermediate

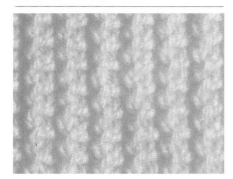

1ST ROW (RS): P1, ✳k2, p1; rep from ✳ to end.
2ND ROW: K1, ✳yo, k2, slip the yo over the 2 knit sts, k1; rep from ✳ to end. Rep these 2 rows.

Cable and Eyelet Rib I
Multiple of 7 sts + 3
Drape: fair
Skill: intermediate

1ST ROW (RS): P3, ✳k4, p3; rep from ✳ to end.
2ND ROW: K1, yo, k2tog, ✳p4, k1, yo, k2tog; rep from ✳ to end.
3RD ROW: P3, ✳C4B, p3; rep from ✳ to end.
4TH ROW: As 2nd row.
5TH ROW: As 1st row.
6TH ROW: As 2nd row.
Rep the last 6 rows.

Cable and Eyelet Rib II
Multiple of 10 sts + 4
Drape: fair
Skill: intermediate

1ST ROW (RS): P1, k2tog, yo, ✳p2, k4, p2, k2tog, yo; rep from ✳ to last st, p1.
2ND AND EVERY ALT ROW: K1, p2, ✳k2, p4, k2, p2; rep from ✳ to last st, k1.
3RD ROW: P1, yo, sl 1, k1, psso, ✳p2, C4F, p2, yo, sl 1, k1, psso; rep from ✳ to last st, p1.
5TH ROW: As 1st row.
7TH ROW: P1, yo, sl 1, k1, psso, ✳p2, k4,

p2, yo, sl 1, k1, psso; rep from ✳ to last st, p1.
8TH ROW: As 2nd row.
Rep these 8 rows.

Little Bobble Rib
Multiple of 8 sts + 3
Drape: fair
Skill: intermediate

1ST ROW (RS): K3, ✳p2, [p1, k1] twice into next st, then slip 2nd, 3rd and 4th sts of this group over first st (bobble completed), p2, k3; rep from ✳ to end.
2ND ROW: P3, ✳k5, p3; rep from ✳ to end.
3RD ROW: K3, ✳p5, k3; rep from ✳ to end.
4TH ROW: As 2nd row.
Rep these 4 rows.

edgings worked across

These edgings are worked parallel to the edge of the main fabric, and the first two examples are worked as part of it. Picot Edging (*below*) is useful where a garment requires a hem. Before knitting the finished edging, make a small sample (you may prefer to use needles one or two sizes smaller than those used for the main fabric), and measure the stitch gauge (*page 16*). Once you know the number of stitches per inch (centimeter), you can calculate the number to cast on.

Picot Edging

Multiple of 2 sts + 1
Drape: as main fabric
Skill: easy
Note: This method can be used on either the cast-on or bind-off edge of fabric.

Work 4 rows in St st, starting knit.
5TH ROW: K1, ✳yo, k2tog; rep from ✳ to end.
Work 4 rows in St st, starting purl.
These 9 rows form the edging.
To finish: Fold back edging along picot row and slipstitch in place.

Picot Point Bind-Off

Multiple (in edge to be bound off) of 3 sts + 2
Drape: as main fabric
Skill: easy

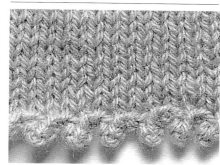

Bind off 2 sts, ✳slip remaining st on right-hand needle onto left-hand needle, cast on 2 sts, bind off 4 sts; rep from ✳ to end and fasten off remaining st.

Scallop Edging

Multiple of 13 sts + 2
Drape: good
Skill: intermediate

1ST ROW (RS): K3, ✳sl 1, k1, psso, sl 2, k3tog, p2sso, k2tog, k4; rep from ✳ to last 12 sts, sl 1, k1, psso, sl 2, k3tog, p2sso, k2tog, k3.
2ND ROW: P4, ✳yo, p1, yo, p6; rep from ✳ to last 5 sts, yo, p1, yo, p4.
3RD ROW: K1, yo, ✳k2, sl 1, k1, psso, k1, k2tog, k2, yo; rep from ✳ to last st, k1.
4TH ROW: P2, ✳yo, p2, yo, p3, yo, p2, yo, p1; rep from ✳ to last st, p1.
5TH ROW: K2, yo, k1, ✳yo, sl 1, k1, psso, k1, sl 1, k2tog, psso, k1, k2tog, [yo, k1] 3 times; rep from ✳ to last 12 sts, yo, sl 1, k1, psso, k1, sl 1, k2tog, psso, k1, k2tog, yo, k1, yo, k2.
6TH ROW: Purl.
7TH ROW: K5, ✳yo, sl 2, k3tog, p2sso, yo, k7; rep from ✳ to last 10 sts, yo, sl 2, k3tog, p2sso, yo, k5.
Work 4 rows in Garter st (every row knit).

Crown Edging

Multiple of 5 sts
Drape: good
Skill: experienced
Note: Bind on using cable method.

1ST ROW: Knit.
2ND ROW: Bind off first 2 sts, ✳slip st remaining on right-hand needle onto left-hand needle, [bind on 2 sts, bind off next 2 sts, slip remaining st onto left-hand needle as before] 3 times, bind on 2 sts, bind off 6 sts; rep from ✳ to end and fasten off remaining st.
These 2 rows form the edging.

Point Edging

Drape: good
Skill: intermediate
Note: Each point is worked separately.

Bind on 2 sts.
1ST ROW: K2.
2ND ROW: Yo (to make a stitch), k2.
3RD ROW: Yo, k3.

4TH ROW: Yo, k4.
5TH ROW: Yo, k5.
6TH ROW: Yo, k6.
7TH ROW: Yo, k7.
8TH ROW: Yo, k8.
9TH ROW: Yo, k9.
10TH ROW: Yo, k10.
11TH ROW: Yo, k11.
12TH ROW: Yo, k12.
Rows 1 to 12 form one point. Break yarn and leave finished point on needle. On the same needle bind on 2 sts and work 2nd point.
Continue in this way until there are as many points as desired. Do not break yarn after completing the last one, but turn and knit across all points on needle. Work 9 rows in Garter st.
To finish: Sew back ends.

Bell Edging I

Multiple of 12 sts + 3
Drape: good
Skill: intermediate
Note: 2 sts are decreased for every repeat on 3rd and following alt rows.

1ST ROW (RS): P3, ✳k9, p3; rep from ✳ to end.
2ND ROW: K3, ✳p9, k3; rep from ✳ to end.
3RD ROW: P3, ✳yb, sl 1, k1, psso, k5, k2tog, p3; rep from ✳ to end.
4TH ROW: K3, ✳p7, k3; rep from ✳ to end.
5TH ROW: P3, ✳yb, sl 1, k1, psso, k3, k2tog, p3; rep from ✳ to end.
6TH ROW: K3, ✳p5, k3; rep from ✳ to end.

7TH ROW: P3, ✳yb, sl 1, k1, psso, k1, k2tog, p3; rep from ✳ to end.
8TH ROW: K3, ✳p3, k3; rep from ✳ to end.
9TH ROW: P3, ✳yb, sl 1, k2tog, psso, p3; rep from ✳ to end.
10TH ROW: K3, ✳p1, k3; rep from ✳ to end.
11TH ROW: P3, ✳k1, p3; rep from ✳ to end.
12TH ROW: As 10th row.
These 12 rows form the edging.

Bell Edging II

Multiple of 8 sts + 7
Drape: good
Skill: intermediate
Note: 2 sts are increased for each repeat on 3rd and following alt rows.

1ST ROW (RS): P7, ✳k1, p7; rep from ✳ to end.
2ND ROW: K7, ✳p1, k7; rep from ✳ to end.
3RD ROW: P7, ✳yo, k1, yo, p7; rep from ✳ to end.
4TH ROW: K7, ✳p3, k7; rep from ✳ to end.
5TH ROW: P7, ✳yo, k3, yo, p7; rep from ✳ to end.
6TH ROW: K7, ✳p5, k7; rep from ✳ to end.
7TH ROW: P7, ✳yo, k5, yo, p7; rep from ✳ to end.
8TH ROW: K7, ✳p7, k7; rep from ✳ to end.
9TH ROW: P7, ✳yo, k7, yo, p7; rep from ✳ to end.
10TH ROW: K7, ✳p9, k7; rep from ✳ to end.
11TH ROW: P7, ✳yo, k9, yo, p7; rep from ✳ to end.

12TH ROW: K7, ✳p11, k7; rep from ✳ to end.
13TH ROW: P7, ✳yo, k11, yo, p7; rep from ✳ to end.
14TH ROW: K7, ✳p13, k7; rep from ✳ to end.
These 14 rows form the edging.

Lace Bells

Bind on multiple of 14 sts + 3 using thumb method
Drape: good
Skill: intermediate
Note: 2 sts are decreased for every repeat on 5th and following alt rows.

Work 2 rows in Garter st (every row knit – 1st row is right side).
3RD ROW: P3, ✳k11, p3; rep from ✳ to end.
4TH ROW: K3, ✳p11, k3; rep from ✳ to end.
5TH ROW: P3, ✳yb, sl 1, k1, psso, k2, yo, sl 1, k2tog, psso, yo, k2, k2tog, p3; rep from ✳ to end.
6TH ROW: K3, ✳p9, k3; rep from ✳ to end.
7TH ROW: P3, ✳yb, sl 1, k1, psso, k1, yo, sl 1, k2tog, psso, yo, k1, k2tog, p3; rep from ✳ to end.
8TH ROW: K3, ✳p7, k3; rep from ✳ to end.
9TH ROW: P3, ✳yb, sl 1, k1, psso, yo, sl 1, k2tog, psso, yo, k2tog, p3; rep from ✳ to end.
10TH ROW: K3, ✳p5, k3; rep from ✳ to end.
11TH ROW: P3, ✳yb, sl 1, k1, psso, k1, k2tog, p3; rep from ✳ to end.
12TH ROW: K3, ✳p3, k3; rep from ✳ to end.
13TH ROW: P3, ✳yb, sl 1, k2tog, psso, p3; rep from ✳ to end.
14TH ROW: K3, ✳p1, k3, rep from ✳ to end.
15TH ROW: P3, ✳k1, p3; rep from ✳ to end.

16TH ROW: As 14th row.
These 16 rows form the edging.

Scalloped Shell Edging I

Multiple of 5 sts + 2
Drape: good
Skill: intermediate
Note: Bind on the required number of sts using the thumb method.

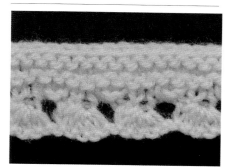

1ST ROW (RS): K1, yo, ✳k5, slip successively the 2nd, 3rd, 4th and 5th sts just worked over the 1st and off needle, yo; rep from ✳ to last st, k1.
2ND ROW: P1, ✳[p1, yo, k1 tbl] into next st, p1; rep from ✳ to end.
3RD ROW: K2, k1 tbl, ✳k3, k1 tbl; rep from ✳ to last 2 sts, k2.
Work 3 rows in Garter st.
These 6 rows form the edging.

Scalloped Shell Edging II

Multiple of 11 sts + 2
Drape: good
Skill: intermediate.
Note: Bind on the required number of sts using the thumb method.

1ST ROW (RS): Purl.
2ND ROW: K2, ✳k1, slip this st back onto left-hand needle, lift the next 8 sts on left-hand needle over this st and off needle, yo twice, knit the first st again, k2; rep from ✳ to end.
3RD ROW: K1, ✳p2tog, drop loop of 2 sts

made in previous row and [k1, k1 tbl] twice into it, p1; rep from ✳ to last st, k1.
Work 5 rows in Garter st (every row knit).
These 8 rows form the edging.

Cobweb Ruffle

Multiple of 3 sts + 1
Drape: excellent
Skill: experienced

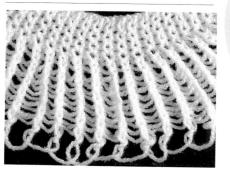

1ST ROW: k1 tbl, ✳p2, k1 tbl; rep from ✳ to end.
2ND ROW: P1, ✳k1 tbl, k1, p1; rep from ✳ to end.
Rep the last 2 rows 5 times more.
13TH ROW: k1 tbl, ✳slip next st off needle and allow it to drop to bind-on edge, p1, k1 tbl; rep from ✳ to end.
14TH ROW: P1, ✳k1 tbl, p1; rep from ✳ to end.
15TH ROW: k1 tbl, ✳p1, k1 tbl; rep from ✳ to end.
Rep the last 2 rows twice more.
These 19 rows form the edging.

edgings worked lengthways

Most of the edgings shown here use openwork increases (*page 25*), which result in some lovely lacy textures. The practical advantage of working an edging lengthwise is that you can keep knitting until the edging is the required length. Try to finish at a point in the pattern that relates well visually to the starting point, even if this makes the edging slightly too long or too short; the length can be adjusted in the blocking process.

Picot Point Chain
Worked over 5 sts
Drape: fair
Skill: easy
Note: Cast on using cable method.

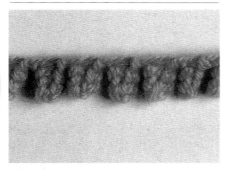

Bind on 5 sts. ✳Bind off 4 sts, slip remaining st on right-hand needle onto left-hand needle, cast on 4 sts; rep from ✳ until chain is of required length.

Butterfly Edging
Worked over 8 sts
Drape: fair
Skill: intermediate

Cast on 8 sts.
1ST ROW (RS): Sl 1, k2, yo, k2tog, yo twice (to make 2 sts), k2tog, k1. (9 sts.)
2ND ROW: K3, p1, k2, yo, k2tog, k1.
3RD ROW: Sl 1, k2, yo, k2tog, k1, yo twice, k2tog, k1. (10 sts.)
4TH ROW: K3, p1, k3, yo, k2tog, k1.
5TH ROW: Sl 1, k2, yo, k2tog, k2, yo twice, k2tog, k1. (11 sts.)
6TH ROW: K3, p1, k4, yo, k2tog, k1.
7TH ROW: Sl 1, k2, yo, k2tog, k6.
8TH ROW: Bind off 3 sts (1 st on right-hand needle), k4, yo, k2tog, k1. (8 sts.)
Rep these 8 rows.

Castle Edging
Worked over 7 sts
Drape: good
Skill: easy
Note: Cast on using cable method.

Cast on 7 sts. Work 3 rows in Garter st (every row knit—1st row is right side).
4TH ROW: Cast on 3 sts, knit across all sts. (10 sts.)
Work 3 rows in Garter st.
8TH ROW: Cast on 3 sts, knit across all sts. (13 sts.)
9TH ROW: K1, ✳p1, k1; rep from ✳ to end.
10TH ROW: P1, ✳k1, p1; rep from ✳ to end.
Rep the last 2 rows twice more, then the 9th row again.
16TH ROW: Bind off 3 sts knitwise, knit to end. (10 sts.)
Work 3 rows in Garter st.
20TH ROW: Bind off 3 sts knitwise, knit to end. (7 sts.)
Rep these 20 rows.

Scalloped Edging in Garter Stitch

Worked over 15 sts
Drape: good
Skill: intermediate
Note: Increase by knitting into front and back of next st.

Cast on 15 sts.
FOUNDATION ROW: Knit.
Commence Pattern
1ST ROW: K4, inc in next st, k2. (8 sts.)
2ND ROW: K1, inc in next st, k6. (9 sts.)
3RD ROW: K6, inc in next st, k2. (10 sts.)
4TH ROW: K1, inc in next st, k8. (11 sts.)
5TH ROW: K8, inc in next st, k2. (12 sts.)
6TH ROW: K1, inc in next st, k10. (13 sts.)
7TH ROW: K10, inc in next st, k2. (14 sts.)
8TH ROW: K1, inc in next st, k12. (15 sts.)
9TH ROW: K12, k2tog, k1. (14 sts.)
10TH ROW: K1, k2tog tbl, k11. (13 sts.)
11TH ROW: K10, k2tog, k1. (12 sts.)
12TH ROW: K1, k2tog tbl, k9. (11 sts.)
13TH ROW: K8, k2tog, k1. (10 sts.)
14TH ROW: K1, k2tog tbl, k7. (9 sts.)
15TH ROW: K6, k2tog, k1. (8 sts.)
16TH ROW: K1, k2tog tbl, k5. (7 sts.)
Rep the last 16 rows.

Laburnum Edging

Worked over 13 sts
Drape: good
Skill: experienced

Cast on 13 sts.
1ST ROW (RS): K2, yo, p2tog, k1, [yo, sl 1, k1, psso] 3 times, yo twice (to make 2 sts),

k2tog. (14 sts).
2ND ROW: Yo (to make 1 st), k2tog, p9, yo, p2tog, k1.
3RD ROW: K2, yo, p2tog, k2, [yo, sl 1, k1, psso] 3 times, yo twice, k2tog. (15 sts.)
4TH ROW: Yo, k2tog, p10, yo, p2tog, k1.
5TH ROW: K2, yo, p2tog, k3, [yo, sl 1, k1, psso] 3 times, yo twice, k2tog. (16 sts.)
6TH ROW: Yo, k2tog, p11, yo, p2tog, k1.
7TH ROW: K2, yo, p2tog, k4, [yo, sl 1, k1, psso] 3 times, yo twice, k2tog. (17 sts.)
8TH ROW: Yo, k2tog, p12, yo, p2tog, k1.
9TH ROW: K2, yo, p2tog, k5, [yo, sl 1, k1, psso] 3 times, yo twice, k2tog. (18 sts.)
10TH ROW: Yo, k2tog, p13, yo, p2tog, k1.
11TH ROW: K2, yo, p2tog, k6, [yo, sl 1, k1, psso] 3 times, yo twice, k2tog. (19 sts.)
12TH ROW: Yo, k2tog, p14, yo, p2tog, k1.
13TH ROW: K2, yo, p2tog, k7, [yo, sl 1, k1, psso] 3 times, yo twice, k2tog. (20 sts.)
14TH ROW: Yo, k2tog, p15, yo, p2tog, k1.
15TH ROW: K2, yo, p2tog, k8, yo, k1, slip last st worked back onto left-hand needle and with point of right-hand needle lift next 7 sts over this st and off needle, then slip st back onto right-hand needle. (14 sts.)
16TH ROW: P2tog, p9, yo, p2tog, k1. (13 sts.)
Rep these 16 rows.

Double Beaded Edge

Worked over 13 sts
Drape: good
Skill: intermediate

Cast on 13 sts.
1ST ROW (RS): Sl 1, k1, ✳yo, p2tog, [k1, p1, k1] into next st; rep from ✳ once more. (12 sts.)
2ND ROW: [K3, yo, p2tog] twice, k2.
3RD ROW: Sl 1, k1, [yo, p2tog, k3] twice.
4TH ROW: Bind off 2 sts knitwise (1 st remains on right-hand needle), yo, p2tog, bind off next 2 sts knitwise (4 sts on right-hand needle), yo, p2tog, k2.
Rep these 4 rows.

Ornamental Diamond Edging

Worked over 17 sts
Drape: good
Skill: experienced

Cast on 17 sts.
1ST FOUNDATION ROW (RS): K1, yo, sl 1, k1, psso, k1, k2tog, yo, k7, yo, k2tog, k2.
2ND FOUNDATION ROW: P3, yo, p2tog, p12.
Commence Pattern

1ST ROW: K1, yo, k2tog, yo, k3, yo, sl 1, k1, psso, k5, yo, k2tog, k2. (18 sts.)
2ND ROW: P3, yo, p2tog, p13.
3RD ROW: K1, yo, k2tog, yo, k5, yo, sl 1, k1, psso, k4, yo, k2tog, k2. (19 sts.)
4TH ROW: P3, yo, p2tog, p14.
5TH ROW: K1, yo, k2tog, yo, k3, yo, sl 1, k1, psso, k2, yo, sl 1, k1, psso, k3, yo, k2tog, k2. (20 sts.)
6TH ROW: P3, yo, p2tog, p15.
7TH ROW: K1, yo, k2tog, yo, k3, [yo, sl 1, k1, psso] twice, k2, yo, sl 1, k1, psso, k2, yo, k2tog, k2. (21 sts.)
8TH ROW: P3, yo, p2tog, p16.
9TH ROW: K1, yo, k2tog, yo, k3, [yo, sl 1, k1, psso] 3 times, k2, yo, sl 1, k1, psso, k1, yo, k2tog, k2. (22 sts.)
10TH ROW: P3, yo, p2tog, p17.
11TH ROW: Sl 1, k1, psso, [yo, sl 1, k1, psso] twice, k2, [yo, sl 1, k1, psso] twice, k1, k2tog, yo, k3, yo, k2tog, k2. (21 sts.)
12TH ROW: P3, yo, p2tog, p16.
13TH ROW: Sl 1, k1, psso, [yo, sl 1, k1, psso] twice, k2, yo, sl 1, k1, psso, k1, k2tog, yo, k4, yo, k2tog, k2. (20 sts.)
14TH ROW: P3, yo, p2tog, p15.
15TH ROW: Sl 1, k1, psso, [yo, sl 1, k1, psso] twice, k3, k2tog, yo, k5, yo, k2tog, k2. (19 sts.)
16TH ROW: P3, yo, p2tog, p14.
17TH ROW: Sl 1, k1, psso, [yo, sl 1, k1, psso] twice, k1, k2tog, yo, k6, yo, k2tog, k2. (18 sts.)
18TH ROW: P3, yo, p2tog, p13.
19TH ROW: Sl 1, k1, psso, yo, sl 1, k1, psso, k1, k2tog, yo, k7, yo, k2tog, k2. (17 sts.)
20TH ROW: P3, yo, p2tog, p12.
Rep the last 20 rows.

Double Diamond Edging

Worked over 9 sts
Drape: good
Skill: intermediate
Note: Sts should only be counted after the 1st and 12th rows.

Cast on 9 sts.
1ST AND EVERY ALT ROW (RS): Knit.
2ND ROW: K3, k2tog, yo, k2tog, [yo, k1] twice.
4TH ROW: K2, [k2tog, yo] twice, k3, yo, k1.

6TH ROW: K1, [k2tog, yo] twice, k5, yo, k1.
8TH ROW: K3, [yo, k2tog] twice, k1, k2tog, yo, k2tog.
10TH ROW: K4, yo, k2tog, yo, k3tog, yo, k2tog.
12TH ROW: K5, yo, k3tog, yo, k2tog.
Rep these 12 rows.

Diamond Edging

Worked over 12 sts
Drape: good
Skill: intermediate
Note: Sts should only be counted after the 1st and 12th rows.

Cast on 12 sts.
1ST AND EVERY ALT ROW (RS): K1, yo, p2tog, knit to end.
2ND ROW: K2, yo, k3, yo, sl 1, k1, psso, k2, yo, p2tog, k1.
4TH ROW: K2, yo, k5, yo, sl 1, k1, psso, k1, yo, p2tog, k1.
6TH ROW: K2, yo, k3, yo, sl 1, k1, psso, k2, yt, sl 1, k1, psso, yo, p2tog, k1.
8TH ROW: K1, k2tog, yo, sl 1, k1, psso, k3, k2tog, yo, k2, yo, p2tog, k1.
10TH ROW: K1, k2tog, yo, sl 1, k1, psso, k1,

k2tog, yo, k3, yo, p2tog, k1.
12TH ROW: K1, k2tog, yo, sl 1, k2tog, psso, yo, k4, yo, p2tog, k1.
Rep these 12 rows.

Garter Stitch Edging

Worked over 10 sts
Drape: good
Skill: intermediate
Note: Sts should only be counted after the 8th row.

Cast on 10 sts.
1ST ROW (RS): K3, [yo, k2tog] twice, yo twice, k2tog, k1.
2ND ROW: K3, p1, k2, [yo, k2tog] twice, k1.
3RD ROW: K3, [yo, k2tog] twice, k1, yo twice, k2tog, k1.
4TH ROW: K3, p1, k3, [yo, k2tog] twice, k1.
5TH ROW: K3, [yo, k2tog] twice, k2, yo twice, k2tog, k1.
6TH ROW: K3, p1, k4, [yo, k2tog] twice, k1.
7TH ROW: K3, [yo, k2tog] twice, k6.
8TH ROW: Bind off 3 sts, k4 (not including st already on needle after binding off), [yo, k2tog] twice, k1. Rep these 8 rows.

Diagonal Rib and Scallop

Worked over 8 sts
Drape: good
Skill: experienced

Cast on 8 sts.
1ST FOUNDATION ROW (RS): K6, knit into front and back of next st, yo twice, sl 1 purlwise. 9 sts.

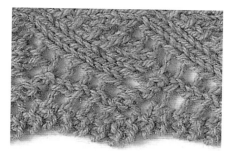

2ND FOUNDATION ROW: k1 tbl, k1, [yo, sl 1, k1, psso, k1] twice, yo, sl 1 purlwise. (9 sts.)

1ST ROW: K1 tbl, knit to last st, knit into front and back of last st, turn and cast on 2 sts. (12 sts.)

2ND ROW: K1, knit into front and back of next st, k2, [yo, sl 1, k1, psso, k1] twice, yo, k1, yo, sl 1 purlwise. (14 sts.)

3RD ROW: K1 tbl, knit to last 2 sts, knit into front and back of next st, yo, sl 1 purlwise. (15 sts.)

4TH ROW: K1 tbl, knit to last 2 sts, knit into front and back of next st, k2, [yo, sl 1, k1, psso, k1] 3 times, k1, yo, sl 1 purlwise. (16 sts.)

5TH ROW: K1 tbl, knit to last 2 sts, k2tog. (15 sts.)

6TH ROW: Sl 1 purlwise, k1, psso, sl 1, k1, psso, k4, [yo, sl 1, k1, psso, k1] twice, yo, sl 1 purlwise. (13 sts.)

7TH ROW: K1 tbl, knit to last 2 sts, k2tog. (12 sts.)

8TH ROW: Bind off 3 sts (1 st on right-hand needle), k2, yo, sl 1, k1, yo, sl 1, k1, psso, yo, sl 1 purlwise. (9 sts.)
Rep these 8 rows.

Fan Edging

Worked over 14 sts
Drape: fair
Skill: experienced
Note: Sts should only be counted after the 19th and 20th rows.

Cast on 14 sts.
1ST ROW (WS): K2, yo, k2tog, k5, yo, k2tog, yo, k3.
2ND AND EVERY ALT ROW: K1, yo, k2tog, knit to end.

3RD ROW: K2, yo, k2tog, k4, [yo, k2tog] twice, yo, k3.
5TH ROW: K2, yo, k2tog, k3, [yo, k2tog] 3 times, yo, k3.
7TH ROW: K2, yo, k2tog, k2, [yo, k2tog] 4 times, yo, k3.
9TH ROW: K2, yo, k2tog, k1, [yo, k2tog] 5 times, yo, k3.
11TH ROW: K2, yo, k2tog, k1, k2tog, [yo, k2tog] 5 times, k2.
13TH ROW: K2, yo, k2tog, k2, k2tog, [yo, k2tog] 4 times, k2.
15TH ROW: K2, yo, k2tog, k3, k2tog, [yo, k2tog] 3 times, k2.
17TH ROW: K2, yo, k2tog, k4, k2tog, [yo, k2tog] twice, k2.
19TH ROW: K2, yo, k2tog, k5, k2tog, yo, k2tog, k2.
20TH ROW: K1, yo, k2tog, knit to end.
Rep these 20 rows.

Wavy Border

Worked over 13 sts
Drape: good
Skill: experienced
Note: Sts should only be counted after the 1st, 4th, 5th, and 14th rows.

Cast on 13 sts.
1ST AND EVERY ALT ROW (WS): K2, purl to last 2 sts, k2.
2ND ROW: Sl 1, k3, yo, k5, yo, k2tog, yo, k2.
4TH ROW: Sl 1, k4, sl 1, k2tog, psso, k2, [yo, k2tog] twice, k1.
6TH ROW: Sl 1, k3, sl 1, k1, psso, k2, [yo, k2tog] twice, k1.
8TH ROW: S1 1, k2, sl 1, k1, psso, k2, [yo, k2tog] twice, k1.

10TH ROW: Sl 1, k1, sl 1, k1, psso, k2, [yo, k2tog] twice, k1.
12TH ROW: K1, sl 1, k1, psso, k2, yo, k1, yo, k2tog, yo, k2.
14TH ROW: Sl 1, [k3, yo] twice, k2tog, yo, k2. Rep these 14 rows.

Leaf Edging

Worked over 8 sts
Drape: fair
Skill: experienced
Note: Sts should only be counted after the 18th row.

Cast on 8 sts.
1ST ROW (RS): K5, yo, k1, yo, k2.
2ND ROW: P6, inc in next st by knitting into front and back of it, k3
3RD ROW: K4, p1, k2, yo, k1, yo, k3.
4TH ROW: P8, inc in next st, k4.
5TH ROW: K4, p2, k3, yo, k1, yo, k4.
6TH ROW: P10, inc in next st, k5.
7TH ROW: K4, p3, k4, yo, k1, yo, k5.
8TH ROW: P12, inc in next st, k6.
9TH ROW: K4, p4, yb, sl 1, k1, psso, k7, k2tog, k1.
10TH ROW: P10, inc in next st, k7.

11TH ROW: K4, p5, yb, sl 1, k1, psso, k5, k2tog, k1.

12TH ROW: P8, inc in next st, k2, p1, k5.

13TH ROW: K4, p1, k1, p4, yb, sl 1, k1, psso, k3, k2tog, k1.

14TH ROW: P6, inc in next st, k3, p1, k5.

15TH ROW: K4, p1, k1, p5, yb, sl 1, k1, psso, k1, k2tog, k1.

16TH ROW: P4, inc in next st, k4, p1, k5.

17TH ROW: K4, p1, k1, p6, yb, sl 1, k2tog, psso, k1.

18TH ROW: P2tog, bind off 5 sts using p2tog as first of these sts (1 st on right-hand needle), k1, p1, k5. Rep these 18 rows.

Bird's-eye Edging
Worked over 7 sts
Drape: good
Skill: intermediate
Note: Sts should only be counted after the 4th row.

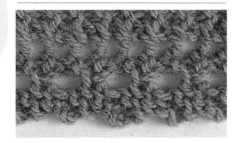

Cast on 7 sts.

1ST ROW (RS): K1, k2tog, yo twice, k2tog, yo twice, k2.

2ND ROW: K3, [p1, k2] twice.

3RD ROW: K1, k2tog, yo twice, k2tog, k4.

4TH ROW: Bind off 2 sts, k3 (not including st already on needle after binding off), p1, k2. Rep these 4 rows.

Willow Edging
Worked over 10 sts
Drape: good
Skill: intermediate
Note: Sts should only be counted after the 8th row.

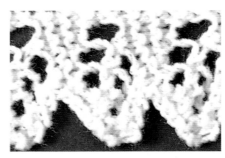

Cast on 10 sts.

1ST ROW (RS): Sl 1, k2, yo, k2tog, ✳yo twice, k2tog; rep from ✳ once more, k1.

2ND ROW: K3, [p1, k2] twice, yo, k2tog, k1.

3RD ROW: Sl 1, k2, yo, k2tog, k2, ✳yo twice, k2tog; rep from ✳ once more, k1.

4TH ROW: K3, p1, k2, p1, k4, yo, k2tog, k1.

5TH ROW: Sl 1, k2, yo, k2tog, k4, ✳yo twice, k2tog; rep from ✳ once more, k1.

6TH ROW: K3, p1, k2, p1, k6, yo, k2tog, k1.

7TH ROW: Sl 1, k2, yo, k2tog, k11.

8TH ROW: Bind off 6 sts, k6 (not including st already on needle after binding off), yo, k2tog, k1.
Rep these 8 rows.

Moss and Faggot
Worked over 17 sts
Drape: good
Skill: experienced
Note: Sts should only be counted after the 12th row.

Cast on 17 sts.

1ST ROW (RS): K2, yo, k3, yo, k2tog, [p1, k1] 5 times.

2ND ROW: Yo (to make 1 st), k2tog, [k1, p1] 3 times, k1, k2tog, yo, k5, yo, k2.

3RD ROW: K2, yo, k1, k2tog, yo, k1, yo, k2tog, k1, yo, k2tog, [p1, k1] 4 times.

4TH ROW: Yo (to make 1 st), k2tog, [k1, p1] twice, k1, [k2tog, yo, k1] twice, k2, yo, k2tog, k1, yo, k2.

5TH ROW: K2, yo, k1, k2tog, yo, k5, yo, k2tog, k1, yo, k2tog, [p1, k1] 3 times.

6TH ROW: Yo (to make 1 st), k2tog, k1, p1, k1, [k2tog, yo, k1] twice, k6, yo, k2tog, k1, yo, k2.

7TH ROW: [K2tog, k1, yo] twice, k2tog, k3, [k2tog, yo, k1] twice, [p1, k1] 3 times.

8TH ROW: Yo (to make 1 st), k2tog, [k1, p1] 3 times, yo, k2tog, k1, yo, k2tog, [k1, k2tog, yo] twice, k1, k2tog.

9TH ROW: [K2tog, k1, yo] twice, k3tog, yo, k1, k2tog, yo, [k1, p1] 4 times, k1.

10TH ROW: Yo (to make 1 st), k2tog, [k1, p1] 4 times, yo, k2tog, k3, yo, k2tog, k1, k2tog.

11TH ROW: K2tog, k1, yo, k2tog, k1, k2tog, yo, [k1, p1] 5 times, k1.

12TH ROW: Yo (to make 1 st), k2tog, [k1, p1] 5 times, yo, k3tog, yo, k1, k2tog.
Rep these 12 rows.

Antique Edging
Cast on 13 sts. Worked over 13 sts
Drape: good
Skill: experienced

Cast on 13 sts.

1ST ROW (WS): K2, yo, sl 1, k1, psso, yo, k1, yo, sl 1, k2tog, psso, yo, k3, yo, k2. (15 sts.)

2ND ROW: K4, [k1, p1] 3 times into next st, p2, k1, p3, k4. (20 sts.)

3RD ROW: K2, yo, sl 1, k1, psso, [k1, p1]

3 times into next st, yb, sl 1, k1, psso, p1, k2tog, bind off next 5 sts, knit to last 2 sts, yo, k2. (19 sts.)

4TH ROW: K5, yo, [k1, p1] twice, bind off next 5 sts, knit to end. (15 sts.)

5TH ROW: K2, yo, sl 1, k1, psso, yo, k1, yo, sl 1, k2tog, psso, yo, k3, yo, k2tog, yo, k2. (17 sts.)

6TH ROW: K6, [k1, p1] 3 times into next st, p2, k1, p3, k4. (22 sts.)

7TH ROW: K2, yo, sl 1, k1, psso, [k1, p1] 3 times into next st, yb, sl 1, k1, psso, p1, k2tog, bind off next 5 sts, knit to last 4 sts, yo, k2tog, yo, k2. (21 sts.)

8TH ROW: Bind off 4 sts (1 st on right-hand needle after binding off), k2, yo, p2, k1, p1, bind off next 5 sts, knit to end. (13 sts.) Rep these 8 rows.

Zigzag Filigree Edging
Worked over 20 sts
Drape: good
Skill: experienced

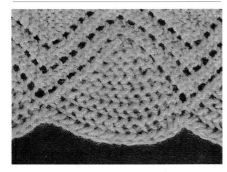

Cast on 20 sts.

1ST ROW (RS): K9, [k2tog, yo, k1] 3 times, yo, sl 1, k1, psso.

2ND ROW: Yo (to make 1 st), sl 1, k1, psso, k18.

3RD ROW: K8, [k2tog, yo, k1] 3 times, yo, k1, yo, sl 1, k1, psso. (21 sts.)

4TH ROW: Yo, sl 1, k1, psso, yo, sl 1, k1, psso, k17.

5TH ROW: K7, [k2tog, yo, k1] 3 times, yo, k1, [yo, sl 1, k1, psso] twice. (22 sts.)

6TH ROW: Yo, sl 1, k1, psso, [yo, sl 1, k1, psso] twice, k16.

7TH ROW: K6, [k2tog, yo, k1] 3 times, yo, k1, [yo, sl 1, k1, psso] 3 times. (23 sts.)

8TH ROW: Yo, sl 1, k1, psso, [yo, sl 1, k1, psso] 3 times, k15.

9TH ROW: K5, [k2tog, yo, k1] 3 times, yo, k1, [yo, sl 1, k1, psso] 4 times. (24 sts.)

10TH ROW: Yo, sl 1, k1, psso, [yo, sl 1, k1, psso] 4 times, k14.

11TH ROW: K4, [k2tog, yo, k1] 3 times, yo, k1, [yo, sl 1, k1, psso] 5 times. (25 sts.)

12TH ROW: Yo, sl 1, k1, psso, [yo, sl 1, k1, psso] 5 times, k13.

13TH ROW: K3, [k2tog, yo, k1] 3 times, yo, k1, [yo, sl 1, k1, psso] 6 times. (26 sts.)

14TH ROW: Yo, sl 1, k1, psso, [yo, sl 1, k1, psso] 6 times, k12.

15TH ROW: K2, [k2tog, yo, k1] 3 times, yo, k1, [yo, sl 1, k1, psso] 7 times. (27 sts.)

16TH ROW: Yo, sl 1, k1, psso, [yo, sl 1, k1, psso] 7 times, k11.

17TH ROW: K4, yo, [k2tog, k1, yo] twice, sl 1, k2tog, psso, [yo, sl 1, k1, psso] 7 times. (26 sts.)

18TH ROW: Yo, sl 1, k1, psso, [yo, sl 1, k1, psso] 6 times, k12.

19TH ROW: K5, yo, [k2tog, k1, yo] twice, sl 1, k2tog, psso, [yo, sl 1, k1, psso] 6 times. (25 sts.)

20TH ROW: Yo, sl 1, k1, psso, [yo, sl 1, k1, psso] 5 times, k13.

21ST ROW: K6, yo, [k2tog, k1, yo] twice, sl 1, k2tog, psso, [yo, sl 1, k1, psso] 5 times. (24 sts.)

22ND ROW: Yo, sl 1, k1, psso, [yo, sl 1, k1, psso] 4 times, k14.

23RD ROW: K7, yo, [k2tog, k1, yo] twice, sl 1, k2tog, psso, [yo, sl 1, k1, psso] 4 times. (23 sts.)

24TH ROW: Yo, sl 1, k1, psso, [yo, sl 1, k1, psso] 3 times, k15.

25TH ROW: K8, yo, [k2tog, k1, yo] twice, sl 1, k2tog, psso, [yo, sl 1, k1, psso] 3 times. (22 sts.)

26TH ROW: Yo, sl 1, k1, psso, [yo, sl 1, k1, psso] twice, k16.

27TH ROW: K9, yo, [k2tog, k1, yo] twice, sl 1, k2tog, psso, [yo, sl 1, k1, psso] twice. (21 sts.)

28TH ROW: Yo, sl 1, k1, psso, yo, sl 1, k1, psso, k17.

29TH ROW: K10, yo, [k2tog, k1, yo] twice, sl 1, k2tog, psso, yo, sl 1, k1, psso. (20 sts.)

30TH ROW: Yo, sl 1, k1, psso, k18. Rep these 30 rows.

Fern and Bobble Edging
Worked over 21 sts
Drape: good
Skill: experienced

Cast on 21 sts.

1ST ROW (RS): K2, k2tog, yo twice (to make 2 sts), k2tog twice, yo twice, k2tog, k2, yo twice, k2tog, k7. (22 sts.)

2ND ROW: K9, p1, k4, [p1, k3] twice.

3RD ROW: K2, k2tog, yo twice, k2tog twice, yo twice, k2tog, k1, MB, k2, yo twice, k2tog, k6. (23 sts.)

4TH ROW: K8, p1, k6, [p1, k3] twice.

5TH ROW: K2, k2tog, yo twice, k2tog twice, yo twice, k2tog, k3, MB, k2, yo twice, k2tog, k5. (24 sts.)

6TH ROW: K7, p1, k8, [p1, k3] twice.

7TH ROW: K2, k2tog, yo twice, k2tog twice, yo twice, k2tog, k5, MB, k2, yo twice, k2tog, k4. (25 sts.)

8TH ROW: K6, p1, k1O, [p1, k3] twice.

9TH ROW: K2, k2tog, yo twice, k2tog twice, yo twice, k2tog, k7, MB, k2, yo twice, k2tog, k3. (26 sts.)

10TH ROW: K5, p1, k12, [p1, k3] twice.

11TH ROW: K2, k2tog, yo twice, k2tog twice, yo twice, k2tog, k9, MB, k2, yo twice, k2tog, k2. (27 sts.)

12TH ROW: K4, p1, k14, [p1, k3] twice.

13TH ROW: K2, k2tog, yo twice, k2tog twice, yo twice, k2tog, k11, MB, k2, yo twice, k2tog, k1. (28 sts.)

14TH ROW: K3, p1, k16, [p1, k3] twice.

15TH ROW: K2, k2tog, yo twice, k2tog

twice, yo twice, k2tog, k18. (28 sts.)

16TH ROW: Bind off 7 sts, knit until there are 13 sts on right-hand needle, [p1, k3] twice. (21 sts).
Rep these 16 rows.

Puffball Cluster Edging
Worked over 13 sts
Drape: good
Skill: experienced

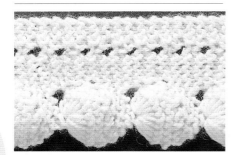

Special Abbreviation
YO2 = yarn over twice to make 2 sts.
Cast on 13 sts.
1ST ROW (RS): K2, k2tog, YO2 (see Special Abbreviation), k2tog, k7.
2ND ROW: K9, p1, k3.
3RD AND 4TH ROWS: Knit.
5TH ROW: K2, k2tog, YO2, k2tog, k2, [YO2, k1] 3 times, YO2, k2. (21 sts.)
6TH ROW: K3, [p1, k2] 3 times, p1, k4, p1, k3.
7TH AND 8TH ROWS: Knit.
9TH ROW: K2, k2tog, YO2, k2tog, k15.
10TH ROW: Knit 12 sts wrapping yarn twice around needle for each st, YO2, k5, p1, k3. (23 sts.)
11TH ROW: K10, [p1, k1] into next st, slip next 12 sts to right-hand needle dropping extra loops; return sts to left-hand needle then k12tog. (13 sts.)
12TH ROW: Knit. Rep these 12 rows.

Scalloped Eyelet Edging
Worked over 11 sts
Drape: good
Skill: intermediate

Cast on 11 sts.
1ST ROW (RS): Sl 1, k2, yo, p2tog, yo, sl 1, k1, psso, [yo, sl 1, k1, psso] twice.
2ND ROW: Yo (to make 1 st), ✳p1, [k1, p1] into next st (made st of previous row); rep from ✳ twice more, p2, yo, p2tog, k1 tbl. (15 sts.)
3RD ROW: Sl 1, k2, yo, p2tog, k10.
4TH ROW: Sl 1, p11, yo, p2tog, k1 tbl.
5TH ROW: Sl 1, k2, yo, p2tog, k10.
6TH ROW: Bind off 4 sts purlwise (1 st remains on right-hand needle), p7, yo, p2tog, k1 tbl. (11 sts). Rep these 6 rows.

Lacy Arrow Edging
Worked over 21 sts
Drape: fair
Skill: intermediate

Cast on 21 sts.
1ST ROW (RS): K3, yo, k2tog, p2, yo, sl 1, k1, psso, k3, k2tog, yo, p2, k1, yo, k2tog, k2.

2ND AND EVERY ALT ROW: K3, yo, k2tog tbl, k2, p7, k3, yo, k2tog tbl, k2.
3RD ROW: K3, yo, k2tog, p2, k1, yo, sl 1, k1, psso, k1, k2tog, yo, k1, p2, k1, yo, k2tog, k2.
5TH ROW: K3, yo, k2tog, p2, k2, yo, sl 1, k2tog, psso, yo, k2, p2, k1, yo, k2tog, k2.
6TH ROW: As 2nd row. Rep these 6 rows.

Fancy Leaf Edging
Worked over 17 sts
Drape: good
Skill: intermediate

Cast on 17 sts.
1ST ROW (RS): K3, yo, p2tog, yo, p2tog, yo, k1 tbl, k2tog, p1, yb, sl 1, k1, psso, k1 tbl, yo, k3.
2ND ROW: K3, p3, k1, p3, k2, yo, p2tog, yo, p2tog, k1.
Rep the last 2 rows once more.
5TH ROW: K3, yo, p2tog, yo, p2tog, yo, k1 tbl, yo, k2tog, p1, yb, sl 1, k1, psso, yo, k4. (18 sts.)
6TH ROW: K4, p2, k1, p4, k2, yo, p2tog, yo, p2tog, k1.
7TH ROW: K3, yo, p2tog, yo, p2tog, yo, k1 tbl, k1, k1 tbl, yo, sl 1, k2tog, psso, yo, k5. (19 sts.)
8TH ROW: K5, p7, k2, yo, p2tog, yo, p2tog, k1.
9TH ROW: K3, yo, p2tog, yo, p2tog, yo, k1 tbl, k3, k1 tbl, yo, k7. (21 sts.)
10TH ROW: Bind off 4 sts (1 st remains on right-hand needle), k2, p7, k2, yo, p2tog, yo, p2tog, k1. (17 sts.) Rep these 10 rows.

CROCHET CONTENTS

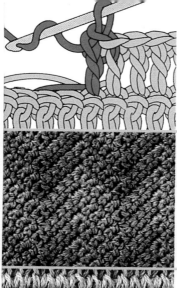

techniques 182

Basic stitches, working in rows, working in rounds, changing color, joining motifs, groups of stitches, stitch variations, filet crochet, Tunisian crochet, Irish-style crochet, abbreviations.

medium-weight patterns 198

Suited to a wide range of garments for adults and children and for home accessories, such as placemats.

• **simple stitch patterns 199** • **complex stitch pattens 206**

heavyweight patterns 223

Suited to jackets, coats, afghans, cushion covers and other homeware, purses and bags, children's toys.

• **assorted patterns 224** • **highly-textured stitches 235**
• **Tunisian crochet 241**

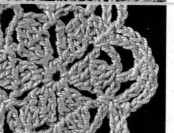

openwork patterns 251

Suited to summer-weight wraps, shawls, and scarves, delicate home accessories and baby clothes.

• **filet crochet 252** • **trellis-type patterns 262** • **dense lace patterns 266** • **mesh-type patterns 287**

crochet motifs 291

Suited to afghans, bedspreads, tablecloths and other household items, and for embellishing articles of woven fabric.

• **Irish motifs 292** • **assorted motifs 299**

edgings 307

Suited to collars, cuffs, waistbands, and button panels.

• **edgings worked on fabric 308** • **edgings worked separately 309**

crochet techniques

Holding the Hook and Yarn

Everyone has their own personal way of holding the hook and controlling the yarn in crochet. Most crocheters hold the hook as shown below, as if it were a pencil, with the thumb and forefinger over the flat section of the hook.

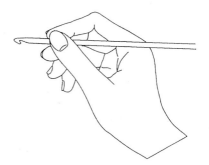

The other hand holds the work and at the same time controls the yarn supply. If you prefer, the index finger can be used to manipulate the yarn, while the middle finger helps to hold the work.

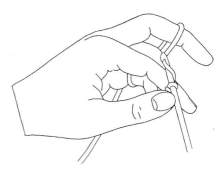

TIP FOR LEFT-HANDERS: *Prop the book up next to a mirro so you can see the illustrations in "mirror image" while still reading the text from the original page.*

Basic Stitches

Almost all crochet starts with a base (or foundation) chain. This is the equivalent of "casting on" in knitting. The base chain is a series of chain stitches which normally begin with a loop secured by a slip knot.

Slip Knot

1. Make a loop; hook another loop through it.
2. Tighten gently and slide the knot up to the hook.

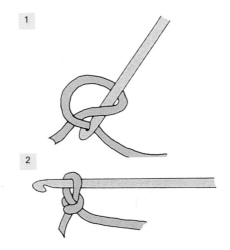

Chain Stitch (ch)

1. Wrap the yarn over the hook in an counterclockwise direction (or hold the yarn still and maneuvre the hook).
2. Draw the yarn through to form a new loop without tightening the previous one.
NOTE: *Unless otherwise instructed, always wrap the yarn this way around.*
Repeat steps 1 and 2 to make as many chains as specified for the pattern.
HINT: *Keep shifting your yarn-hand position up close to the hook every couple of stitches or so; this is easy if you use the fingers of the other hand to hold down the loop on the hook while you do so.*

To count chains correctly as you make them, do not count the initial slip loop as a chain. To count them afterwards, first make sure that they are not twisted and that you are looking at the "front"; then count back, without counting the loop still on the hook.

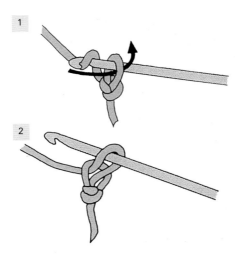

Slip Stitch (sl st)

Also sometimes called Bosnian stitch, the slip stitch is the shortest of the basic stitches. It is used mainly to join two pieces of crochet, to close a ring *(see "Working in Rounds" page 186)*, and to work along the top edge of the work, bringing the hook to a new position in order to narrow the fabric.

For simplicity, slip stitch is illustrated here being worked into a base chain; however, you will find it easier to work over some other stitches, such as the ones shown on the following pages.

Slip stitch (sl st)

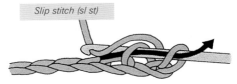

Single Crochet (sc)

1. Insert the hook into the work (or second chain from hook), wrap the yarn over the hook and draw the yarn through the work only.
2. Wrap the yarn again and draw it through both loops.
3. 1 sc made.

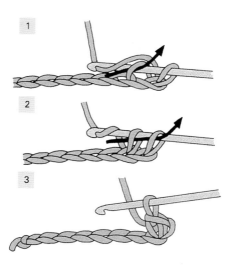

Half Double (hdc)

1. Wrap the yarn over the hook and insert the hook into the work (or third chain from hook).

2. Wrap the yarn over the hook, draw through the work only and wrap the yarn again.

3. Draw through all three loops on the hook.

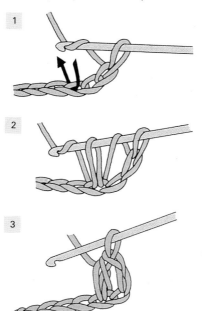

Double (dc)

1. Wrap the yarn over the hook and insert the hook into the work (or fourth chain from hook).

2. Wrap the yarn over the hook, draw through the work only and wrap the yarn again.

3. Draw through the first two loops only and wrap the yarn again.

4. Draw through the last two loops on the hook.

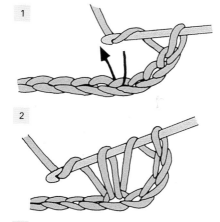

Treble (tr)

1. Wrap the yarn over the hook twice and insert the hook into the work (or fifth chain from hook).

2. Wrap the yarn over the hook, draw through the work and wrap again.

3. Draw through the first 2 loops only and wrap the yarn again.

4. Draw through the next two loops only and wrap the yarn again; draw through the last two loops.

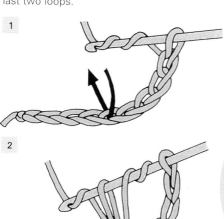

techniques

Double Treble (dtr)

1. Wrap the yarn over the hook 3 times and insert the hook into the work (or sixth chain from hook).

2. Wrap the yarn over the hook and draw it through 2 loops.

3. Repeat step 2 three times to complete the triple treble. (Note that every crochet stitch begins and ends with one loop on the hook.)

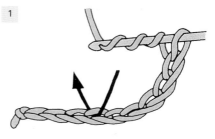

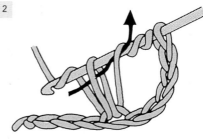

Longer Basic Stitches

Longer basic stitches—for example, Triple Treble (ttr), Quadruple Treble (quad tr), Quintuple Treble (quin tr), etc.—are made by wrapping the yarn three, four, five, etc. times over the hook at the beginning and by wrapping and drawing it

through two loops as often as required to complete the stitch.

Gauge

In crochet, as in knitting, the gauge of the work—the number of stitches and rows obtained over a given measurement—is of crucial importance. If you are following a published pattern or substituting a different stitch for the one used, you must obtain the same gauge as that obtained by the designer in order for the item to be the correct size. Determining the gauge is also a crucial stage in designing your own work. The instructions given for knitting gauge on pages 15—16 apply equally to crochet and should be followed.

Pattern Repeats or Multiples

Most crochet stitch patterns consist of a set of stitches, the multiple, which are repeated across the row. The patterns given in this book specify the multiple along with the number of starting chains. To understand how to use multiples in designing, see page 17.

Working in Rows

To work to and fro in rows, make a base chain *(see page 182)* to begin.

TIP: *To avoid reaching the end of a first row and finding there are too few chains in the base chain to complete it, leave a generous end of yarn when making the slip knot; then you can remove your hook temporarily from the working loop, insert it through the end of the base chain, and use the spare end of yarn to add the necessary chains.*

1. The first row of the fabric is made by working across the base chain as shown in the preceeding stitch diagrams. (Right-handers work from right to left; left-handers work from left to right.) Insert the hook under either one or two of the three threads that make up each individual chain. (Choose which you find suits you best, and then be consistent.)

At the very beginning of the first row, one or more of the base chains is "skipped" in order to allow the first stitch to stand to its

proper height. The skipped chains then stand up alongside the stitches. Together they look like and may often count as the first stitch in the row. The number of chains skipped depends upon the height of the stitch they are to match as follows: double crochet = 1 or 2 chains skipped; half treble = 2 chains skipped; treble = 3 chains skipped; double treble = 4 chains skipped; triple treble = 5 chains skipped. Thus, you must make a larger number of chains for the base chain than there are stitches required in the base row.

2. At the end of each row turn the work so that another row can be worked across the top of the previous one.

Before the new row can begin, a "turning chain" (one or more single chains) must be worked to bring the hook up to the height of the stitches in the new row. The number of chains for turning depends upon the height of the stitch they are to match, as follows: single crochet = 1 chain; half double = 2 chains; double = 3 chains; treble = 4 chains; double treble = 5 chains. *(These numbers are a guideline only; in some circumstances more or fewer chains may give a better result.)*

3. The turning chain may also count as the first stitch in the new row. In this case, skip the first stitch in the previous row.

4. and 5. Work a stitch into the top of the previous turning chain when you reach the end of the row. However, if the turning chain does not count as a stitch, work into the first stitch at the beginning of the row, but not into the top of the previous turning chain at the end.

To make each stitch, insert the hook under the two top loops of each stitch in the previous row (unless instructed otherwise.)

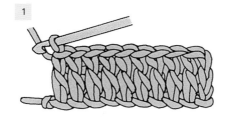

techniques

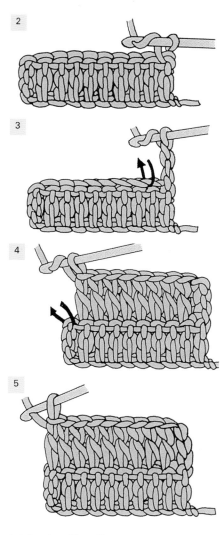

"yarn over" to complete a stitch, simply drop the old yarn, make a loop with the new one, pick this up and draw through to complete. Hold down both short ends temporarily until you have worked the next stitch. A knot or splice is unnecessary.

If you are making a solid fabric (single crochet is shown here), work as follows:
2. Lay the new yarn in advance across the tops of the stitches ahead and work over it.
3. After the change, work over the end of the old yarn for a few stitches. Trim both ends close to the fabric.

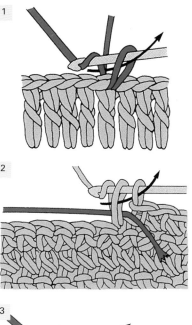

Changing Color

When you are joining in a new color or changing from one yarn to another for reasons of color, work as follows:
1. Work the last stitch (double is shown here) only up to the penultimate step, so that two loops remain on the hook. Then pick up the new color and use this to complete the stitch.
2. Work the next stitch in the new color. Note that the top of this stitch will be in the new color, whereas if the previous stitch had been completed in the old color, that color would have encroached on the area of new color.

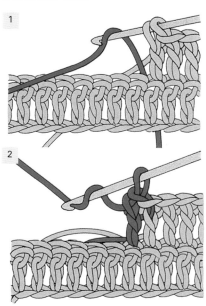

Joining in a New Yarn

To join in new yarn because the pattern has involved fastening off in one place and rejoining in another or to begin an edging:
1. Insert the hook into the appropriate place, loop the yarn over, draw through and make 1 chain. Or make the first loop with a slip knot as though for starting a base chain.

You will often need to join a new ball in the middle of the work, when the old ball runs out. Then just as you make the final

Fastening Off

To fasten off working yarn permanently, make one chain, cut the yarn about 2 in (5 cm) away (longer if you need to sew pieces together), draw the end through the chain and tighten.

When you are working whole rows in different colors, make the change during the last stitch in the row so the color for the next row is used for the turning chain.

Do not cut off any yarns that will be needed again later at the same edge, but rejoin them as required, leaving an unbroken "float" thread up the side.

If, at the end of a row, the pattern requires you to return to the beginning of the same row without turning and to work another row in another color in the same direction, complete the first row in the old color and fasten off by lengthening the final loop on the hook, passing the whole ball through it and gently tightening again. That yarn is now available if you need to rejoin it later at this edge (if not, cut it).

When you are changing color during a row—for instance, when following a chart or other multicolor pattern, it is important not only to change color just before you complete the previous stitch, but also to be very aware which is the right and wrong side of your fabric at all times. After every color change and before continuing, make sure all yarns that are not for the time being used are taken to the wrong side. When they are rejoined later, allow them to form loose "float" threads on the wrong side. In some circumstances, notably with solid stitch patterns on right-side rows, you can avoid "floats" by working over any yarns you need to carry along, or by winding off short lengths of yarn into separate balls. These can then be introduced at different points along the row. Your precise treatment will depend upon the stitch pattern, the nature of the article, the character of the yarn, and your personal preferences.

Working in Rounds

Crochet motifs (see pages 299—306) are worked in rounds, from the center outwards.
1. Make three or more chains (the exact number depends on the design) and join them into a ring by inserting the hook into the first of them and making a slip stitch.
2. To begin each round, make a "starting chain" (the equivalent of a "turning chain"—see p.184) to match the height of the stitches of the round. Always insert the hook into the center of the base chain ring to work the stitches of the first round.
3. On second and subsequent rows, after working the starting chain, insert the hook under the top two loops of the stitches in the previous round, unless otherwise instructed.
4. When each round is complete, insert the hook into the top of the starting chain and make a slip stitch to join the round.

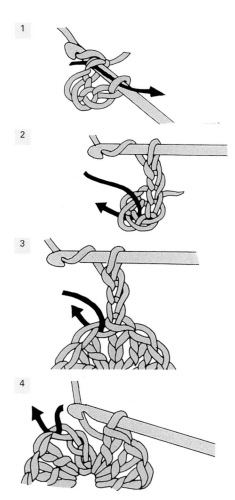

NOTE: *Unless otherwise stated, do not turn the work between rounds, but continue with the same side facing and treat this as the right side of the fabric.*

To fasten off after making the slip stitch that completes a round, do not make another chain, but cut the yarn and draw the end through to the front; then insert the hook again from the back through the place in the fabric where the slip stitch was worked (but not through the slip stitch loop itself) and draw the end of the yarn once again through to the back. Tighten gently.

Joining Motifs

Depending upon their shape, some motifs, such as squares, hexagons, etc., fit together exactly. Others leave interesting spaces along the edges that touch after they are joined with sewing or crochet. Large spaces may then be partially filled with smaller round motifs, made and joined in while the last round is being worked.
1. Motifs that fit exactly can be joined on the wrong side with whip stitch, using a wool needle and matching yarn (contrasting yarn is shown for clarity).
2. Alternatively, the motifs can be joined with crochet, using slip stitch or single crochet. Place the motifs together with right sides facing and work through the single outer or inner loop of each edge, depending on the desired effect.
3. If spaces must be left between motifs, they can be joined with a series of chain arches and bridges anchored with slip stitches or single crochets.
4. Some designs, particularly those with picots or chain arches around their edges, can be joined to previously worked motifs during the course of their final rounds. This is done by interrupting the picots or arches at midpoint and slip stitching to the corresponding places on the adjacent motifs.

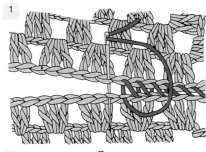

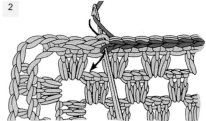

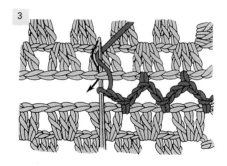

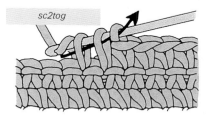

Groups

For decoration

A *"group"*: several complete stitches worked in one place—may consist of more than one kind of stitch. A group of five double stitches is sometimes called a "shell."

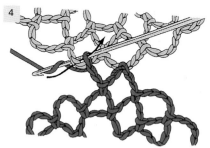

For decoration

For Increasing (making the fabric wider by adding stitches to it)

In a fabric made of solid, basic stitches, such as single or double crochet, working two or more stitches into one stitch at the end of a row is usually the best way of increasing smoothly.

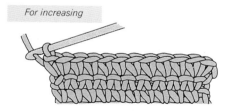

For increasing

Clusters

For Decoration

A *"cluster"*: two or more stitches joined together at the top—may consist of more than one kind of basic, or special, stitch. Any combination of stitches may be joined into a cluster by leaving the last loop of each temporarily on the hook and taking them all off together at the end.

For Decreasing

Clusters of single and double crochet stitches in simple arrangements are used for decreasing as well as for pattern interest.

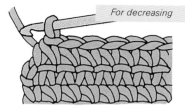

For decreasing

To work two single crochet stitches together (sc2tog)

Insert the hook into the next stitch (or as required), wrap the yarn round the hook, draw a loop through; repeat this step into the next stitch (3 loops on the hook); wrap the yarn and draw through all the loops on the hook to complete.

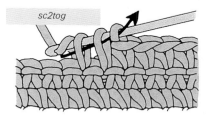

sc2tog

To work three single crochet stitches together (sc3tog)

Work as for sc2tog until there are 3 loops on the hook; insert the hook into a third stitch, wrap the yarn and draw through a loop (4 loops on the hook); wrap the yarn and draw through all the loops

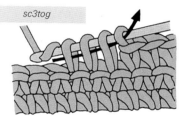

sc3tog

To work two or more double crochet stitches together (dc2tog, dc3tog, etc.)

1. Wrap the yarn over the hook, insert the hook into the next stitch (or as instructed), wrap the yarn, draw a loop through, wrap the yarn and draw through 2 of the loops on the hook (2 loops left on the hook). Repeat this step into the next stitch (3 loops on the hook).
For dc2tog wrap yarn and draw it through all loops to complete cluster.
2. For dc3tog repeat the first stage of step 1 again, so that there are 4 loops on the hook. Wrap yarn over hook and draw through all loops to complete cluster.

For larger clusters repeat as required *(see "Summary of Basic Clusters" page 188).*

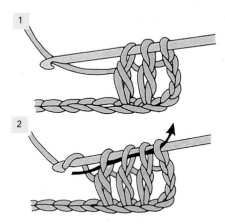

TIP: *It is important to be sure exactly how and where the hook is to be inserted for each "leg" of a cluster. The legs may be worked over adjacent stitches, or stitches may be skipped between legs. To make Bobbles or Puff Stitches (see pages 190—191) all legs are worked into the same stitch.*

techniques

Summary of Basic Clusters

In each case repeat from * to * for each "leg" of the cluster, ending yo, and draw through all loops on hook.

sc2(3)tog: *insert hook as indicated, yo, draw loop through* = 3(4) loops on hook.

hdc2(3/4)tog: *yo, insert hook as indicated, yo, draw loop through* = 5(7/9) loops on hook.

dc2(3/4/5)tog: *yo, insert hook as indicated, yo, draw loop through, yo, draw through 2 loops* = 3(4/5/6) loops on hook.

tr2(3/4/5)tog: yo twice, insert hook as indicated, yo, draw loop through, (yo, draw through 2 loops) twice* = 3(4/5/6) loops on hook.

dtr2(3/4/5/etc)tog: *yo 3 times, insert hook as indicated, yo, draw loop through, (yo, draw through 2 loops) 3 times* = 3(4/5/6/etc) loops on hook.

Working Between Stitches

Inserting the hook between the stems of stitches and beneath the bundle of threads that joins them at the top opens up a solid fabric *(see Wide Double Crochet stitch pattern, page 202)*.

Working Under One Loop Only

Inserting the hook under one top loop only (either the back loop or the front loop) leaves the other loop exposed as a horizontal bar. Depending upon which stitches are picked out in this way, horizontal

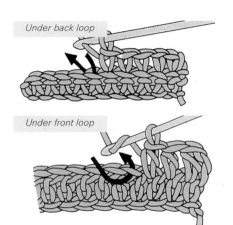

Under back loop

Under front loop

ridges or woven effects can be created. The fabric also tends to become more elastic.

Spikes

"Spikes" are made by inserting the hook farther down into the fabric than usual, either below the next stitch, or to one side.
1. Insert the hook into the work where specified by the pattern and draw a loop up to the height of the current row.
2. Complete the stitch normally. (The illustration shows double crochet being worked.)

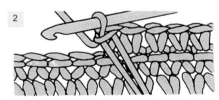

Spikes can be worked singly, in sequences, or in clusters, by inserting the hook in different places, drawing a loop through each and finishing by drawing a loop through all the loops collected. They add interest to fabric texture, but are most dramatic when worked in a contrasting color.
NOTE: *It is important to work spike loops loosely enough to avoid squashing the fabric, but with sufficient gauge to maintain the stability of the fabric. When a whole sequence of stitches is "spiked," it may help to work each one as a twin cluster together with a stitch worked normally under the top two loops of the stitch above as follows:*
Insert the hook as indicated for the spike, wrap the yarn around the hook and draw a loop through and up to the height of the current row; insert the hook under the top 2 loops of the next stitch, wrap the yarn and draw a loop through (3 loops on the hook);

wrap the yarn and draw through all the loops on the hook to complete the stitch.

Post (Relief) Stitches

Inserting the hook around the whole stem of a stitch creates raised or relief effects.

To work a raised double crochet at the front (1dc/rf) (also called "working around the post").
1. Wrap the yarn around the hook, insert the hook from in front and from right to left around the stem of the appropriate stitch.
2.–3. Complete the stitch normally.

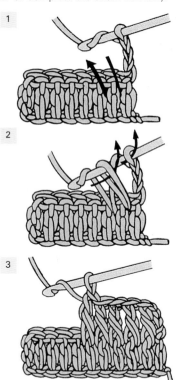

To work a raised double crochet at the back of the fabric (1dc/rb)
1. Wrap the yarn around the hook, insert the hook from behind and from right to left around the stem of the appropriate stitch.
2.–3. Complete the stitch normally.

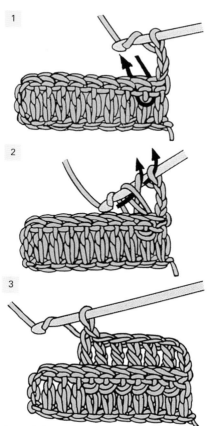

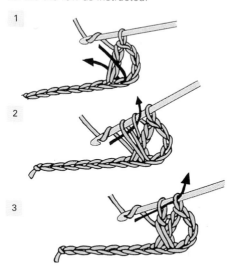

2. and 3. Work another double crochet into the skipped stitch. Repeat these steps across the row as instructed.

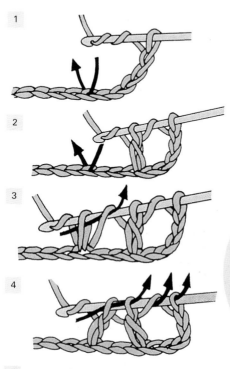

hand side, and draw a loop through; wrap the yarn and draw through 2 loops; repeat this last step to complete the "X."

Any stitch can be worked in this way, singly or in a group or cluster. A raised stitch may also be worked as a twin cluster together with a stitch worked normally under the top two loops of a stitch above.

Crossed Stitch

The simplest form of crossed stitch is made by inserting the hook into a previous stitch, wrapping the yarn and bringing a loop through and forward again in order to be able to complete the stitch normally. The threads of the new stitch thus made not only cross over but also sandwich previous stitches.

To work 2 crossed double crochet stitches (2Cdc)

1. Skip one stitch, then work on 1 double crochet into the next stitch. Insert the hook into the skipped stitch.

Branched Shapes

In lacy stitch patterns long stitches are sometimes made into "X" and "λ" shapes without being crossed.

To make a Treble "λ" and "X" shape

Wrap the yarn around the hook twice and insert the hook in the position for the first "leg."

2. Wrap the yarn, draw a loop through, wrap the yarn and draw through 2 loops (3 loops on the hook, lower part of first leg completed); wrap the yarn once more and insert the hook again where instructed for the second leg.

3. Wrap yarn, draw a loop through, wrap the yarn and draw through 2 loops—both legs completed.

4. Wrap the yarn and draw through 2 loops; repeat this last step twice.

5. This completes a " λ" shape. If an "X" shape is required, work as follows:
Make chains as required to the position of the second "arm," wrap the yarn once, insert the hook into the center of the cluster just made, picking up 2 threads at the left-

Working into Chain Spaces

Many openwork crochet patterns involve working into the chain spaces that were left between groups of stitches in the previous row. To do this, simply insert the hook under the chain and work the stitches as usual, filling the space.

Note, however, that in other cases you must work one or more stitches into a particular chain. Read the pattern instructions carefully and count the chains, so as to ensure that the work is positioned correctly.

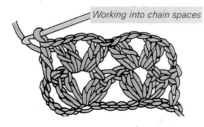

Working into chain spaces

Solomon's Knot

A Solomon's Knot is a lengthened chain stitch locked with a single crochet stitch worked into its back loop.

Each knot is begun by lengthening the loop left on the hook to the required size. *(See full Solomon's Knot instructions on page 285.)* The technique requires a little practice, but the resulting fabric is very attractive. Try working it in bright-colored string (the kind used for macramé) for a handy shopping bag or in fine crochet cotton to make a delicate shawl.

1. Make 1 chain and lengthen the loop as required.
2. Wrap the yarn over the hook.
3. Draw through the loop on the hook, keeping the single back thread of this long chain separate from the 2 front threads.
4. Insert the hook under this single back thread and wrap the yarn again.

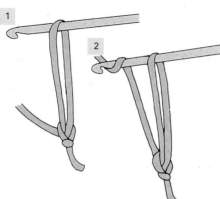

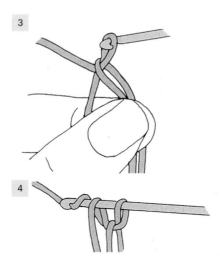

5. Draw a loop through and wrap again.
6. Draw through both loops on the hook to complete the knot.
7. To begin a new row, skip the knot on the hook and the next 2 knots, and work a knot into the center of the 3rd knot as shown and into every alternate knot thereafter. The loops on the second and subsequent rows should be about half again as long as those on the base row.

Popcorn

A popcorn is a group of complete stitches, usually worked into the same place, folded and closed at the top. The number and type of stitches included varies.

To make a popcorn with 4 double crochet stitches

1. Work 4 double crochet stitches into one stitch normally; take the hook out of the working loop, insert it under the top 2 loops of the first double crochet in the group just made.
2. Pick up the working loop again. Draw through to close up the group of stitches. The popcorn projects toward the front.

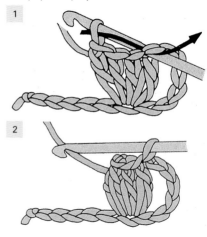

NOTE: *On a wrong-side row insert the hook from behind and close the group so that it projects toward the right side of the fabric.*

Bobble

A bobble is a cluster of stitches (usually three to five) joined together at the top (unlike popcorn, where they are separated) and also worked into the same place. Bobbles are thrown into relief most effectively when the stitches before and after are shorter and worked on wrong-side rows.

To make a bobble of 3 double crochet stitches

1. Work 3 double crochets, always inserting the hook into the same stitch and leaving

the last loop of each on the hook as for a dc3tog cluster *(see page 188)*; wrap the yarn over the hook and draw through all the loops on the hook to complete.
2. It often helps, particularly with the bulkier bobble clusters, to work an extra chain stitch to close them firmly.

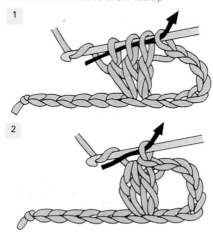

Puff Stitch

A puff stitch is a cluster of half double crochet stitches (usually three to five), worked into the same place, to make a soft lump.

To make a puff stitch of 3 half double crochet stitches

1. Wrap the yarn over the hook, insert the hook, wrap the yarn again and draw a loop through (3 loops on the hook).
2. Repeat this step twice, inserting the hook into the same stitch (7 loops on the hook); wrap the yarn and draw through all the loops on the hook.
3. Work an extra chain stitch to close the puff stitch firmly.

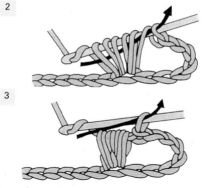

Bullion Stitch

Wrap the yarn over the hook as many times as specified (usually seven to ten times); insert the hook where instructed; wrap the yarn once again and draw a loop through; wrap the yarn again and draw through all the loops on the hook, picking them off one at a time, if necessary; work a chain to complete the bullion stitch.

Loop (Fur) Stitch

Loop stitch is a variation of single crochet and is usually worked on wrong-side rows because the loops form at the back of the fabric.

1. Insert the hook into the stitch below as usual. Using a finger of the free hand, pull up the yarn to form a loop of the required size. Pick up both strands of the loop and draw them through.
2. Wrap the supply yarn over the hook.

3. Draw the yarn through all 3 loops.
NOTE: *When each loop is cut afterward the texture of the fabric resembles fur.*

Crab Stitch or Reversed Single Crochet

Crab stitch is used as a decorative texture (Corded Rib) or edging (Corded Edge). Also known as reversed single crochet, it consists of working single crochet stitches in the "wrong" direction—i.e. from left to right for right-handers.

The stitch is worked on the right side of the fabric. After completing the previous right-side row, do not turn as usual, but work as follows:

1. Starting with the hook downwards insert the hook back into the next stitch to the right. Pull the yarn through, twisting the hook to face upward at the same time.
2. Wrap the yarn and draw through to finish off the single crochet as usual.
3. Insert hook ready for next stitch. The direction of working causes the stitches to twist and create the decorative effect.

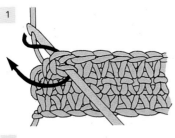

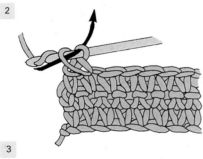

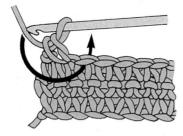

Tunisian Crochet

Tunisian crochet—also called afghan stitch —is worked with a long hook that is available in the same range of thicknesses as ordinary crochet hooks. The hooks are longer than crochet hooks because they are required to hold the loops created on the first (Forward) half of the row before working them off on the Return half.

The fabric produced by this technique can be dense and thick. It is important to use a suitable size of hook in relation to the yarn. This is usually at least two sizes larger than would be used when working ordinary crochet with the same yarn.

Each row is worked in two parts. The first, or "Forward," part of the row involves working from right to left and pulling up loops or stitches on to the hook. On the second, or "Return," part of the row these loops are worked off again as the hook travels back from left to right. Tunisian crochet is nearly always made without turning; therefore the right side is always facing.

Starting Chain

Make the number of chains needed to correspond to the number of stitches required in the first row.

TIP: *When working a large piece it is sensible to start with more chains than necessary, as it is simple to undo the extra chains if you have miscounted.* Although there are exceptions, Tunisian stitch patterns usually begin with the same initial Forward and Return row—referred to as Basic Forward and Return row.

Forward

1. Working into back loop only of each chain, insert hook into second chain from hook, yarn over, draw loop through and leave on hook.
2. Insert hook into next chain, yarn over, draw loop through and leave on hook.
Repeat this in each chain to end. Do not turn.

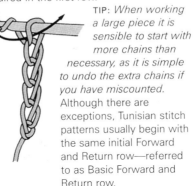

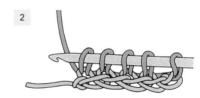

The number of loops on hook should equal the number of stitches required for the first row.

NOTE: *Because the fabric produced in Tunis-ian crochet is usually firmer than in ordinary crochet, we recommend that the hook be inserted into the back loop only of the starting chain, as this produces a firmer edge.*

Return

1. Yarn over, draw through one loop. (This chain forms the edge stitch.)
2. Yarn over, and draw through 2 loops.
3. Repeat step 2 until one loop remains on hook. Do not turn. The loop left on the hook is the first stitch of the next row.

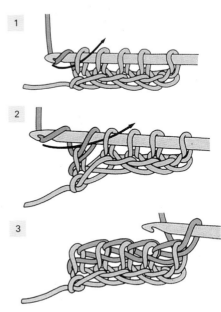

The Basic Stitches

These are produced by varying the technique of picking up loops on the Forward row. (See Tunisian Crochet, pages 241—250).

Tunisian Simple Stitch (Tss):
1. Insert hook from right to left behind single vertical thread.
2. Yarn over hook.
3. Draw loop through and leave on hook.

Unless otherwise stated, the hook is always inserted in this way. For example, Tunisian half double crochet, double crochet, etc. are worked from this position.

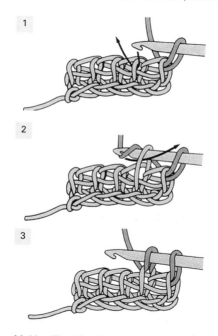

Making Tunisian Fabric

It is important to understand how to produce basic Tunisian fabric before attempting pattern stitches.

Make chain as required and work a Basic Forward and Return row. Generally, the single loop on the hook at the end of each Return row counts as the first stitch in the next Forward row, and so the first stitch is skipped. (See step 1 for Tunisian Simple Stitch, above.)

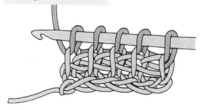

Making Tunisian fabric

Next row: Pick up loop in each stitch (Tss or as required) including edge stitch.

If you require a firmer edge at this end of the row you can work through two loops of the last stitch.

Return as Basic Return row.

Repeat Forward and Return row as required.

Finishing Off

It is possible simply to finish with a Return row, cutting the yarn and threading it through the remaining stitch to secure it. However, the following method leaves a neater edge and is useful where the Tunisian fabric is complete in itself—as for a mat or rug, for example.
1. Finish with a Return row. Insert hook into next stitch, yarn over.
2. Draw through 2 loops.

Repeat steps 1 and 2 to end. Fasten off remaining loop.
NOTE: *The hook can be inserted as if working Tunisian simple, Tunisian knit or Tunisian purl stitch so that stitches can be finished off in pattern.*

Tunisian Knit Stitch (Tks):
1. Insert hook from front to back through fabric and below chains formed by previous Return row, to right of front vertical thread but to left of corresponding back thread.
2. Yarn over, draw loop through and leave on hook.
3. Repeat steps 1 and 2 into each stitch to end. At the last stitch of each Forward row work under 2 loops; return as Basic Return row.

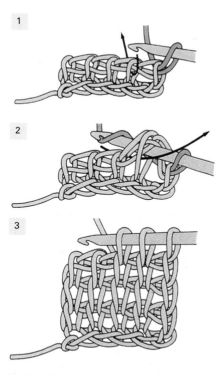

Tunisian Purl Stitch (Tps):
1. Bring yarn to front, insert hook as for Tunisian Simple stitch.
2. Take yarn to back of work and over hook (yo). Draw loop through and leave on hook.
3. Repeat steps 1 and 2 in each stitch to end, return as Basic Return row.

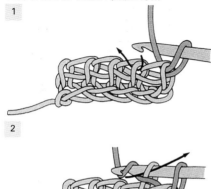

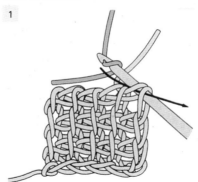

3

Increasing
Inc 1Tss:
1. To increase one stitch on a Forward row, insert hook under the back loop between 2 stitches, yarn over and draw loop through.
2. Work next stitch in the normal way. Two loops are to be worked off on Return row.

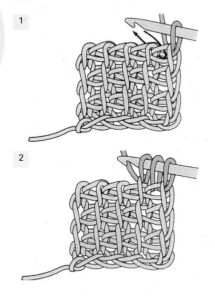

1

2

Decreasing
Tss2tog:
1. To decrease one stitch on a Forward row, insert hook through 2 stitches.
2. Yarn over hook and draw through 2 loops. One loop to be worked off on the Return row

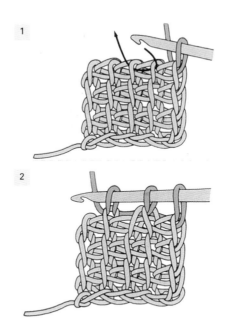

1

2

Tss3tog:
To decrease 2 stitches on a Forward row work as Tss2tog but insert hook through next 3 stitches.

Changing Color
1. When a color change is required at the beginning of a Forward row, work the yarn over in the new color when 2 loops remain on the hook at the end of previous Return row.
2. Draw through both loops.
   To change color at the beginning of a Return row, change yarn and continue to work as normal.

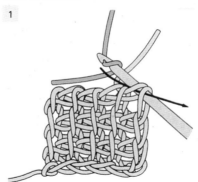

1

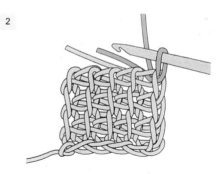

2

Stitch Variations
Ordinary crochet stitches, such as double crochet, half double crochet and treble, can be adapted for Tunisian crochet. The following instructions show how to work a Tunisian double crochet; other stitches use the same basic method, combined with the basic crochet method for that stitch.

Tunisian double crochet (Tdc):
1. Make two chains for the first stitch at beginning of the row. Yarn over and insert hook into the next stitch as if working a Tunisian simple stitch.
2. Yarn over and draw loop through.

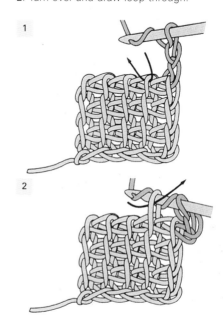

1

2

3. Yarn over and draw through two loops on hook.
4. Leave remaining loop on hook.
5. Double crochet is completed when Return row is worked.

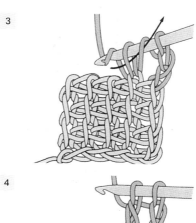

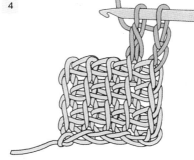

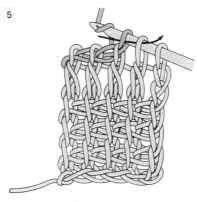

Working between stitches
1. Insert hook between vertical loops that form stitches.
2. Yarn over and draw loop through.
Thdc, Tdc, etc, can also be worked this way.

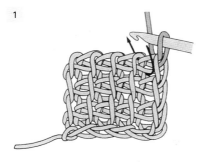

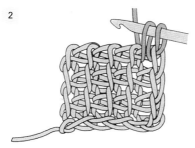

Tunisian Slipped Stitch (Tsl st):
1. Insert hook into stitch as for Tunisian Simple stitch but do not pull yarn through.
2. Continue, leaving slipped stitch on hook.

Twisted Tunisian Simple Stitch (Tw Tss):
1. Insert hook into stitch from left to right.
2. Yarn over and draw loop through.
3. Finish stitch with Basic Return row.

Filet Crochet
Filet crochet is based on a simple network, or "ground," with a regular, square grid, made of double crochet and chain stitches. Pattern instructions are therefore usually presented in the form of squared charts, in which the vertical lines represent treble stitches and the horizontal lines (the tops of the rows) chain stitches. Designs of all kinds—flowers, geometric patterns, lettering, and even whole scenes—are created by filling in some of the squares, or spaces, with double crochet stitches.

Filet charts are read from the bottom to the top, right-side rows from right to left and wrong-side rows from left to right. Each open square represents an open space, whereas a filled-in square represents a block of stitches. Every row starts with three chains (count as one treble), bringing the work to the correct height and balancing the pattern.

Ideally each space or block should be square, but this is hard to achieve because of variations in gauge. Small variations to the ratio between height and width can be made by changing the way you hold the yarn or hook. To test your gauge, first work a swatch based on the Greek Key pattern on page 252.

Like all the patterns in that section, apart from Lacets and Bars (see below), this uses a three-stitch grid consisting of one double crochet and two chain, with two double crochets substituting for the chain to form blocks. Every block or group of blocks includes one extra double crochet, which is actually the first stitch of the following space. Thus, one block has four double crochets, two blocks have seven, three blocks have ten, and so on.

If the grid in your sample is not square, or nearly square, try adjusting the way you work -- e.g. by lengthening the double crochet slightly if the grid is squat or shortening them if it is elongated vertically. If this does not work, you may need to reduce or increase the number of chains, or change the double crochet to a treble. However, as you can see by comparing the charts with the completed samples, the latter are not perfectly square. The most important thing is that the work be regular, with the lines crossing at right angles.

Lacets and Bars
A somewhat more elaborate form of filet crochet, Lacets and Bars *(see page 253)* is based on a grid two double crochets high and six stitches wide, partially filled with a "V" shape of chain. The instructions with the pattern are for the basic network only, but this can be combined with blocks of double crochets to form designs.

Increasing and Decreasing
In filet crochet increases are usually made in whole squares rather than stitches. If increases are made at the beginning of rows and decreases at the ends of rows,

no special techniques are required as the following stitch diagram shows.

When increases are needed at the end of a row or decreases at the beginning of a row, the following techniques should be used.

To increase a space at the end of a row
1. Work 2 chains, then work a double treble into same place as previous double crochet.
2. The double treble makes the outer edges of the increased space.

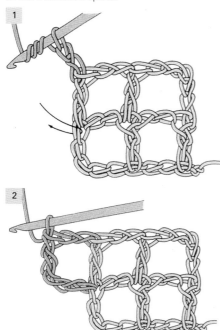

To increase a block at the end of a row
1. Work a treble into same place as previous double crochet.
2. Then work [a treble into bottom segment of previous treble] twice.
3. This produces one increased block.

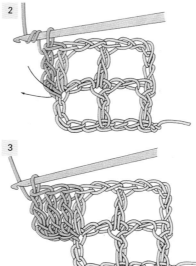

To decrease at the beginning of a row
In decreasing on a filet crochet fabric the method is the same whether the decrease is worked over a block or over a space, as shown in the diagrams below.
1. Turn the work. Slip-stitch into top of last double crochet worked, then into each of next 2 chains (or top of double crochet if a block) and into top of next double crochet.
2. Hook is in position to commence row.

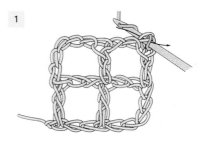

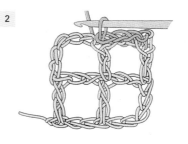

Irish Crochet
True Irish crochet is made by first working motifs and then creating a net or mesh background incorporating the motifs and forming the fabric that holds them in position. This is done by first placing the motifs in the required position face down on paper or a scrap of fabric and temporarily securing them to this. The background, or filling, is then worked progressively joining in the motifs. After the work is completed the paper or fabric is carefully removed.

Irish crochet reaches levels of complexity and delicacy not seen in other styles of crochet work and has its own stitches and techniques. The use of padding threads that are held at the edge of the work so that subsequent rows or rounds can be worked over them to give a three-dimensional effect, a distinguishing feature of this style of crochet.

Padding Threads
Padding threads are used to give a three-dimensional quality to some Irish crochet motifs. The thread used is normally the same as the thread used for the motif, and

the number of threads worked over determines the amount of padding. The motifs in this book are worked over three threads.

The example is for padding threads at the beginning of a motif, but they can also be used in other areas of motifs.

1. Make the required number of chains and join with a slip stitch.
2. Wind a length of thread 3 or 4 times around the end of a pencil or finger and hold against the chain.
3. The stitches are then worked over the chain and padding threads.

When the motif is complete, the ends of the padding thread are pulled through several stitches and cut.

The instructions for individual patterns indicate where it is appropriate to use padding threads.

Working into Base of Stitch
Insert the hook under 2 strands at the base of the stitch. The diagram below shows the work viewed from the back.

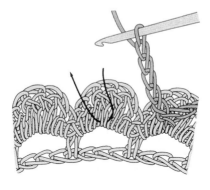

Finishing Crocheted Fabrics
Crochet fabrics vary considerably in the kind of treatment they require before being made up. Solid medium-weight and heavy-weight fabrics may need little or no press-ing, particularly if they are worked in wool or another type of knitting yarn; check the ball band for the recommended treatment and care of the finished work. If in doubt, try the treatment on the gauge swatch you made before starting the project.

Lacy fabrics, especially those worked in cotton crochet threads, require special treatment. Cotton yarns benefit from being wetted or thoroughly steamed. If you are starching the item using ordinary household starch, as opposed to spray starch, you can either immerse the work in it or dab the wet starch onto the fabric after pinning it out to shape. Otherwise, either immerse the work in water or spray it with water or spray starch after pinning it out as follows.

Pin the crochet to a well padded ironing board or other flat surface, placing pins at close intervals along the edges. In the case of filet crochet, make sure that the mesh is straight, with horizontal and vertical lines lying at right angles to each other. If the pattern has picots, bobbles or other embellishments, position these carefully and pin them in place.

Place a pressing cloth over the dampened crochet and press it gently with a hot, dry iron. Do not allow the full weight of the iron to rest on the work, especially where interesting textures are involved. Remove the pins and, if necessary, make fine adjustments to the edges of the material to ensure that they are straight. Now leave the work to dry thoroughly. In the case of Irish crochet, leave the pins in until the work is completely dry.

Joining Seams
To join the seams of a crocheted garment, you can use one of the methods for joining motifs shown on page 186. Or, for a decorative effect, work a double crochet seam on the right side of the work, using a contrasting yarn or thread.

To join an edging to a piece of woven fabric, first turn under the fabric edges and hem them in place. Then, using fine thread and a sewing needle, whipstitch the crochet edge to the lower edge of the fabric.

General Crochet Abbreviations
alt = alternate
approx = approximate(ly)
beg = begin(ning)
ch(s) = chain(s)

ch sp = chain space
cm = centimeter(s)
cont = continue
dc = double crochet
dtr = double treble
folls = follows
hdc = half double crochet
quad tr = quadruple treble
quin tr = quintuple treble
rem = remaining
rep = repeat
sc = single crochet
sext tr = sextuple treble
sl st = slip stitch
st(s) = stitch(es)
stch = starting chain
tch = turning chain
tog = together
tr = treble
dtr = double treble

Cl = cluster
dec = decrease
gr = group
inc = increase
in = inch(es)
yo = yarn over

Tunisian Crochet Abbreviations
beg = beginning
ch = chain
dec = decrease
inc = increase
rep = repeat
sp = space
st(s) = stitch(es)
tog = together
Tdc = Tunisian double crochet
Tdtr = Tunisian double treble
Thdc = Tunisian half double crochet
Tks = Tunisian knit stitch
Tps = Tunisian purl stitch
Tsl st = Tunisian slipped stitch
Tss = Tunisian simple stitch
Ttr = Tunisian treble
Tttr = Tunisian triple treble
TwTss = Twisted Tunisian simple stitch
yo = yarn over
yf = yarn forward
yb = yarn back

techniques

medium-weight patterns

Some of the most useful crochet stitch patterns are to be found in this section. They range from the basic single and double stitches to fairly complex patterns. Although the fabrics produced are heavier than medium-weight knitting stitch patterns, a great variation of weight can be achieved with different yarns and also with different hook sizes.

simple stitch patterns

The patterns in these seven pages include the "workhorses" of the crochet repertoire. They all produce a relatively smooth fabric, suitable for sweaters, cardigans, and other garments. It is often possible to substitute one for another in a commercial pattern, as the multiples are small. Stripes can be used to create interesting effects, as can be seen in Simple Chevron II (*below*), where three colors have been used to accentuate the zigzag effect.

Basic Single Crochet
Starting chain: any number of sts + 1
Drape: good
Skill: easy

1ST ROW: Skip 2ch (count as 1sc), 1sc into next and each ch to end, turn.
2ND ROW: 1ch (counts as 1sc), skip 1 st, 1sc into next and each st to end working last st into tch, turn.
Rep 2nd row.
HINT: In some patterns the turning chain does not count as a stitch when working single crochet. In these cases the first sc is worked into the second ch from hook on the first row, and thereafter into the first sc of the previous row.

Simple Chevron I
Starting chain: multiple of 16 sts + 2
Drape: good
Skill: easy

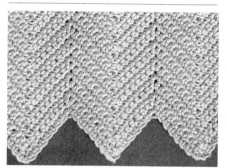

1ST ROW (RS): Work 2sc into 2nd ch from hook, ✳1sc into each of next 7ch, skip 1ch, 1sc into each of next 7ch, 3sc into next ch; rep from ✳ to end omitting 1sc at end of last rep, turn.
2ND ROW: 1ch, work 2sc into 1st sc, ✳1sc into each of next 7sc, skip 2sc, 1sc into each of next 7sc, 3sc into next sc; rep from ✳ to end omitting 1sc at end of last rep, turn.
Rep 2nd row only.

Simple Chevron II
Starting chain: multiple of 16 sts + 2
Drape: good
Skill: easy

Work as given for Simple Chevron I but working 1 row each in colors A, B and C throughout.

199

Basic Half Double Crochet
Starting chain: any number of sts + 1
Drape: good
Skill: easy

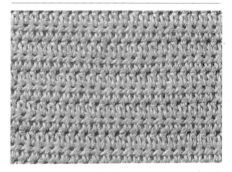

1ST ROW: Skip 2ch (count as 1hdc), 1hdc into next and each ch to end, turn.
2ND ROW: 2ch (count as 1hdc), skip 1 st, 1hdc into next and each st to end working last st into top of tch, turn.
Rep 2nd row.

Basic Double Crochet
Starting chain: any number of sts + 2
Drape: good
Skill: easy

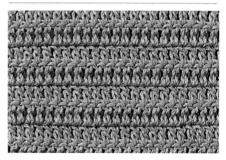

1ST ROW: Skip 3ch (count as 1dc), 1dc into next and each ch to end, turn.
2ND ROW: 3ch (count as 1dc), skip 1 st, 1dc into next and each st to end working last st into top of tch, turn.
Rep 2nd row.

Basic Treble Crochet
Starting chain: any number of sts + 3
Drape: good
Skill: easy

1ST ROW: Skip 4ch (count as 1tr), 1tr into next and each ch to end, turn.
2ND ROW: 4ch (count as 1tr), skip 1 st, 1tr into next and each st to end, working last st into top of tch, turn.
Rep 2nd row.

Peephole Chevron Stitch
Starting chain: multiple of 10 sts + 2
Drape: excellent
Skill: easy

1ST ROW: Skip 2ch (count as 1dc), 1dc into each of next 4ch, ✳skip 2ch, 1dc into each of next 4ch, 2dc into each of next 4ch; rep from ✳ to last 6ch, skip 2ch, 1dc into each of next 3ch, 2dc into last ch, turn.
2ND ROW: 3ch (count as 1dc), 1dc into 1st st, 1dc into each of next 3 sts, ✳skip 2 sts, 1dc into each of next 3 sts, [1dc, 2ch,

1dc] into 2ch sp, 1dc into each of next 3 sts; rep from ✳ to last 6 sts, skip 2 sts, 1dc into each of next 3 sts, 2dc into top of tch, turn. Rep 2nd row.

Back Loop Single Crochet
Starting chain: any number of sts + 1
Drape: good
Skill: easy

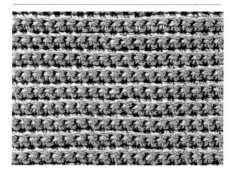

Worked as Basic Single Crochet, except from 2nd row insert hook into back loop only of each st.

Front Loop Single Crochet
Starting chain: any number of sts + 1
Drape: good
Skill: easy

Worked as Basic Single Crochet, except from 2nd row insert hook into front loop only of each st.

Back and Front Loop Single Crochet

Starting chain: multiple of 2 sts + 1
Drape: good
Skill: easy

1ST ROW: Skip 2ch (count as 1sc), 1sc into next and each ch to end, turn.
2ND ROW: 1ch (counts as 1sc), skip 1 st, ✳1sc into back loop only of next st, 1sc into front loop only of next st; rep from ✳ ending 1sc into top of tch, turn.
Rep 2nd row.

Corded Ridge Stitch

Starting chain: any number of sts + 2
Drape: good
Skill: easy
Note: Work all rows with right side facing, i.e. work even numbered rows from left to right. See also page 191 (Corded or Reversed Single Crochet).

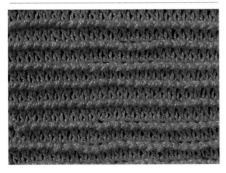

1ST ROW (RS): Skip 3ch (count as 1dc), 1dc into next and each ch to end. Do not turn.

2ND ROW: 1ch, 1sc into front loop only of last dc made, ✳1sc into front loop only of next dc to right; rep from ✳ ending sl st into top of tch at beginning of row. Do not turn.
3RD ROW: 3ch (count as 1dc), skip 1 st, 1dc into back loop only of next and each st of last-but-one row to end. Do not turn.
Rep 2nd and 3rd rows.

Shallow Single Crochet

Starting chain: any number of sts + 1
Drape: good
Skill: easy

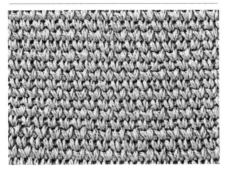

Worked as Basic Single Crochet except from 2nd row insert hook low into body of each st below 3 horizontal loops and between 2 vertical threads.

Close Chevron Stitch

Starting chain: multiple of 11 sts + 2
Drape: good
Skill: easy

Work 4 rows each in colors A and B alternately throughout.
1ST ROW (RS): 2sc into 2nd ch from hook, ✳1sc into each of next 4ch, skip 2ch, 1sc into each of next 4ch, 3sc into next ch; rep from ✳ ending last rep with 2sc only into last ch, turn.
2ND ROW: 1ch, 2sc into 1st st, ✳1sc into each of next 4 sts, skip 2 sts, 1sc into each of next 4 sts, 3sc into next st; rep

from ✳ ending last rep with 2sc only into last st, skip tch, turn. Rep 2nd row.

Back Loop Half Double Crochet

Starting chain: any number of sts + 1
Drape: good
Skill: easy

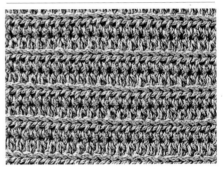

Worked as Basic Half Double Crochet except from 2nd row insert hook into back loop only of each st.

Back and Front Loop Half Double Crochet

Starting chain: multiple of 2 sts + 1
Drape: good
Skill: easy

1ST ROW: Skip 2ch (count as 1hdc), 1hdc into next and each ch to end, turn.
2ND ROW: 2ch (count as 1hdc), skip 1 st, ✳1hdc into back loop only of next st, 1hdc into front loop only of next st; rep from ✳

ending 1hdc into top of tch, turn.
Rep 2nd row.

Linked Half Double Crochets

Starting chain: any number of sts + 1
Drape: good
Skill: intermediate
Note: To make 1st Lhdc at beg of row treat
2nd ch from hook as a single vertical thread.

Special Abbreviation

Lhdc (Linked Half Double Crochet) = insert
hook into single vertical thread at left-hand
side of previous st, yo, draw loop through,
insert hook normally into next st, yo, draw
loop through st, yo, draw through all
3 loops on hook.
1ST ROW: 1Lhdc (see Special Abbreviation)
into 3rd ch from hook (picking up loop
through 2nd ch from hook), 1Lhdc into next
and each ch to end, turn.
2ND ROW: 2ch (count as 1hdc), skip 1 st,
1Lhdc into next and each st to end,
working last st into top of tch, turn.
Rep 2nd row.

Herringbone Half Double

Starting chain: any number of sts + 1
Drape: good
Skill: easy

Special Abbreviation

HBhdc (Herringbone Half Double Crochet) = yo,
insert hook, yo, draw through st and 1st loop
on hook yo, draw through both loops on hook.
1ST ROW: Skip 2ch (count as 1hdc),
1HBhdc into next and each ch to end, turn.
2ND ROW: 2ch (count as 1hdc), skip 1 st,
1HBhdc (see Special Abbreviation) into next
and each st to end work last st into top of
tch, turn. Rep 2nd row.

Wide Double Crochet

Starting chain: any number of sts + 2
Drape: good
Skill: easy
Note: Base chain should be worked
loosely to accommodate extra width.

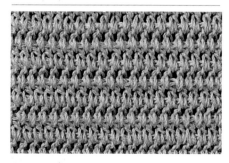

Worked as Basic Double Crochet but after
1st row insert hook between stems and
below all horizontal threads connecting sts

Herringbone Double Crochet

Starting chain: any number of sts + 2
Drape: good
Skill: easy

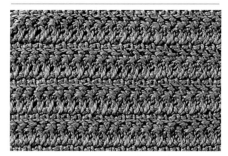

Special Abbreviation

HBdc (Herringbone Double Crochet) = yo,
insert hook, yo, draw through st and 1st
loop on hook, yo, draw through 1 loop, yo,
draw through both loops on hook.
1ST ROW: Skip 3ch (count as 1dc), 1HBdc
(see Special Abbreviation) into next and
each ch to end, turn.
2ND ROW: 3ch (count as 1dc), skip 1 st,
1HBdc into next and each st to end,
working last st into top of tch, turn.
Rep 2nd row.

Sharp Chevron Stitch

Starting chain: multiple of 14 sts + 2
Drape: good
Skill: easy
Note: For description of dc3tog see page
187 (Clusters).

1ST ROW: Skip 2ch (count as 1dc), 2dc into
next ch, ✳1dc into each of next 3ch,

medium-weight patterns

[over next 3ch work dc3tog] twice, 1dc into each of next 3ch, [3dc into next st] twice; rep from ✳ ending last rep with 3dc once only into last ch, turn.

2ND ROW: 3ch (count as 1dc), 2dc into 1st st, ✳1dc into each of next 3 sts, [over next 3 sts work dc3tog] twice, 1dc into each of next 3 sts, [3dc into next st] twice; rep from ✳ ending last rep with 3dc once only into top of tch, turn.
Rep 2nd row.

Ridged Chevron Stitch
Starting chain: multiple of 12 sts + 3
Drape: good
Skill: easy
Note: For description of dc2tog see page 187 (Clusters).

1ST ROW: Skip 3ch (count as 1dc), 1dc into next ch, ✳1dc into each of next 3ch, [over next 2ch work dc2tog] twice, 1dc into each of next 3ch, [2dc into next ch] twice; rep from ✳ ending last rep with 2dc once only into last ch, turn.

2ND ROW: 3ch (count as 1dc), 1dc into 1st st, always inserting hook into back loop only of each st ✳1dc into each of next 3 sts, [over next 2 sts work dc2tog] twice, 1dc into each of next 3 sts, [2dc into next st] twice; rep from ✳ ending last rep with 2dc once only into top of tch, turn.
Rep 2nd row.

Alternative Double Crochets
Starting chain: any number of sts + 2
Drape: good
Skill: easy

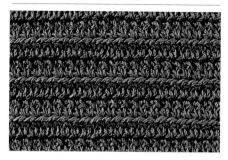

Special Abbreviation
Alt dc (Alternative Double Crochet) = yo, insert hook, yo, draw loop through, yo, draw through 1 loop only, yo, draw through all 3 loops on hook.
1ST ROW: Skip 3ch (count as 1dc), 1dc into next and each ch to end, turn.
2ND ROW: 3ch (count as 1dc), skip 1 st, work 1 Alt dc (see Special Abbreviation) into next and each st to end, work last st into top of tch, turn. Rep 2nd row.

Linked Treble Crochet
Starting chain: any number of sts + 3
Drape: good
Skill: easy
Note: to make 1st Lddc (at beg of row), treat 2nd and 4th chs from hook as upper and lower horizontal loops.

Special Abbreviation
Ltr (Linked Treble Crochet) = insert hook

down through upper of 2 horizontal loops round stem of last st made, yo, draw loop through, insert hook down through lower horizontal loop of same st, yo, draw loop through, insert hook normally into next st, yo, draw loop through st, (4 loops on hook), [yo, draw through 2 loops] 3 times.
1ST ROW: 1Ltr (see Special Abbreviation) into 5th ch from hook (picking up loops through 2nd and 4th chs from hook), 1Ltr into next and each ch to end, turn.
2ND ROW: 4ch (count as 1tr), skip 1 st, 1Ltr into next and each st to end, working last st into top of tch, turn.
Rep 2nd row.

Singles and Double Crochets
Starting chain: any number of sts + 1
Drape: good
Skill: easy

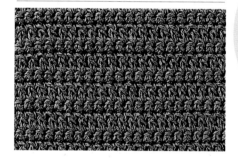

1ST ROW (WS): Skip 2ch (count as 1sc), 1sc into next and each ch to end, turn.
2ND ROW: 3ch (counts as 1dc), skip 1 st, 1dc into next and each st to end, working last st into top of tch, turn.
3RD ROW: 1ch (counts as 1sc), skip 1 st, 1sc into next and each st to end, working last st into top of tch, turn.
Rep 2nd and 3rd rows.
HINT: This is one of the simplest and most effective combination stitch patterns. It is also one of the easiest to get wrong! Concentration is required as you work the ends of the rows to avoid increasing or decreasing, or working two rows running of the same stitch by mistake.

medium-weight patterns

Track Stitch

Starting chain: any number of sts + 1
Drape: good
Skill: easy

1ST ROW (WS): Skip 2ch (count as 1sc), 1sc into next and each ch to end, turn.
2ND ROW: 5ch (count as 1dtr), skip 1 st, 1dtr into next and each st to end working last st into top of tch, turn.
3RD, 4TH AND 5TH ROWS: 1ch (counts as 1sc), skip 1 st, 1sc into next and each st to end, working last st into top of tch, turn. Rep 2nd to 5th rows.

Shallow Chevron Stitch

Starting chain: multiple of 10 sts + 3
Drape: good
Skill: easy
Note: For description of dc3tog see page 187 (Clusters).

1ST ROW: Skip 2ch (count as 1dc), 1dc into next ch, ✳1dc into each of next 3ch, over next 3ch work dc3tog, 1dc into each of next 3ch, 3dc into next ch; rep from ✳ ending last rep with 2dc into last ch, turn.

2ND ROW: 3ch (count as 1dc), 1dc into 1st st, ✳1dc into each of next 3dc, over next 3 sts work dc3tog, 1dc into each of next 3dc, 3dc into next dc; rep from ✳ ending last rep with 2dc into top of tch, turn. Rep 2nd row.

Half Double Crochet Cluster Stitch I

Starting chain: any number of sts + 1
Drape: good
Skill: easy
Note: For description of hdc2tog see page 191 (Puff Stitch).

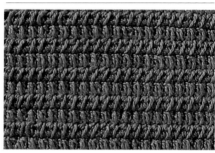

1ST ROW: Skip 2ch (count as 1hdc), ✳hdc2tog all into next ch; rep from ✳ to end, turn.
2ND ROW: 2ch (count as 1hdc), skip 1 st, hdc2tog all into next and each st, ending with hdc2tog into top of tch, turn. Rep 2nd row.

Half Double Crochet Cluster Stitch II

Starting chain: any number of sts + 2
Drape: good
Skill: easy
Note: For description of hdc2tog see pages 187–188 (Clusters).

1ST ROW: Skip 2ch (count as 1hdc), hdc2tog inserting hook into each of next 2ch, ✳hdc2tog inserting hook first into same ch as previous Cluster then into next ch; rep from ✳ until 1ch remains, 1hdc into last ch, turn.
2ND ROW: 2ch (count as 1hdc), hdc2tog inserting hook 1st into first st then into next st, ✳hdc2tog inserting hook first into same

st as previous Cluster then into next st; rep from ✳ ending 1hdc into top of tch, turn. Rep 2nd row.

Half Double Crochet Cluster Stitch III

Starting chain: multiple of 2 sts + 1
Drape: good
Skill: easy
Note: For description of hdc2tog see pages 187–188 (Clusters).

1ST ROW: Skip 2ch (count as 1hdc), ✳hdc2tog inserting hook into each of next 2ch, 1ch; rep from ✳ ending 1hdc into last ch, turn.
2ND ROW: 2ch (count as 1hdc), skip 1 st, ✳hdc2tog inserting hook into next ch sp then into next st, 1ch; rep from ✳ ending 1hdc into top of tch, turn. Rep 2nd row.

Forked Cluster Stitch

Starting chain: any number of sts + 2
Drape: good
Skill: intermediate

Special Abbreviation

FC (Forked Cluster) = [yo, insert hook into ch or st as indicated, yo, draw loop through] twice (5 loops on hook), [yo, draw through 3 loops] twice.

1ST ROW: Skip 2ch (count as 1dc), work 1FC (see Special Abbreviation) inserting hook into each of next 2ch, ✳work 1FC inserting hook into same ch as previous FC then into next ch; rep from ✳ until 1ch remains, 1dc into last ch, turn.
2ND ROW: 3ch (count as 1dc), 1FC inserting hook into each of first 2 sts, ✳1FC inserting hook into same st as previous FC then into next st; rep from ✳ ending 1dc into top of tch, turn. Rep 2nd row.

Odd Forked Cluster Stitch

Starting chain: any number of sts + 2
Drape: good
Skill: intermediate

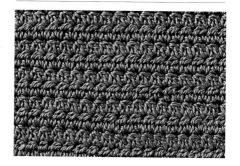

Special Abbreviation

OFC (Odd Forked Cluster) = yo, insert hook into ch or st as indicated, yo, draw loop through, yo, draw through 2 loops, insert hook into next ch or st, yo, draw loop through, yo, draw through all 3 loops on hook.

1ST ROW: Skip 2ch (count as 1hdc), 1OFC (see Special Abbreviation) inserting hook first into 3rd then 4th ch from hook, ✳1OFC inserting hook first into same ch as previous OFC then into next ch; rep from ✳ until 1ch remains, 1hdc into last ch, turn.
2ND ROW: 2ch (count as 1hdc), 1OFC inserting hook into 1st st then into next st, ✳1OFC inserting hook into same st as previous OFC then into next st; rep from ✳ ending 1hdc into top of tch, turn. Rep 2nd row.

Mixed Cluster Stitch

Starting chain: multiple of 2 sts + 2
Drape: good
Skill: intermediate

Special Abbreviation

MC (Mixed Cluster) = yo, insert hook into 1st st as indicated, yo, draw loop through, yo, draw through 2 loops, skip 1 st, [yo, insert hook into next st, yo, draw loop through] twice all into same st, (6 loops on hook), yo, draw through all loops on hook.

1ST ROW (WS): Skip 2ch (count as 1sc), 1sc into next and each ch to end, turn.
2ND ROW: 2ch (count as 1hdc),1MC (see Special Abbreviation) inserting hook into 1st then 3rd st, ✳1ch, 1MC inserting hook first into same st as previous MC; rep from ✳ ending last rep in top of

tch, 1hdc into same place, turn.
3RD ROW: 1ch (counts as 1sc), skip 1 st, 1sc into next and each st to end, working last st into top of tch, turn.
Rep 2nd and 3rd rows.

Double Crochet Cluster Stitch I

Starting chain: multiple of 2 sts + 2
Drape: good
Skill: intermediate

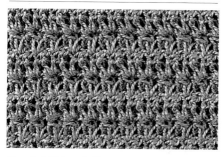

Special Abbreviation

DcC (Double Crochet Cluster) = ✳yo, insert hook into ch or st as indicated, yo, draw loop through, yo, draw through 2 loops✳, skip 1 ch or st, rep from ✳ to ✳ into next st, yo, draw through all 3 loops on hook.

1ST ROW: Skip 2ch (count as 1dc), work 1DcC (see Special Abbreviation) inserting hook first into 3rd ch, 1ch, ✳work 1DcC inserting hook first into same ch as previous DcC, 1ch; rep from ✳ ending 1dc into last ch, turn.
2ND ROW: 3ch (counts as 1dc), 1DcC inserting hook first into 1st st, 1ch, ✳1dcC inserting hook first into same st as previous DcC, 1ch; rep from ✳ ending 1dc into top of tch, turn. Rep 2nd row.

complex stitch patterns

Wonderfully intriguing effects can be produced in crochet by techniques such as varying the height of the stitches, as in Long Wave Stitch (*page 209*); crossing stitches, as in the first two stitches below; and working clusters, as in the Catherine Wheel patterns (*pages 207 and 208*). The technique of working spikes (*page 188*) can produce dramatic color contrasts. The long strands on the surface are vulnerable to snagging, so should be used on low-risk items.

Crossed Double Crochet Stitch
Starting chain: multiple of 2 sts + 2
Drape: excellent
Skill: intermediate

Special Abbreviation
2Cdc (2 Crossed Double Crochets) = skip next st, 1dc into next st, 1dc into skipped st working over previous dc.
1ST ROW (RS): Skip 3ch (count as 1dc), ✳2Cdc (see Special Abbreviation) over next 2ch; rep from ✳ ending 1dc into last ch, turn.
2ND ROW: 1ch (counts as 1sc), skip 1 st, 1sc into next and each st to end, working last st into top of tch, turn.
3RD ROW: 3ch (count as 1dc), skip 1 st, ✳work 2Cdc over next 2 sts; rep from ✳ ending 1dc into tch, turn.
Rep 2nd and 3rd rows.

Crossbill Stitch
Starting chain: multiple of 4 sts + 3
Drape: excellent
Skill: intermediate

Special Abbreviation
2Cdc (2 Crossed Double Crochets) = skip 2 sts, 1dc into next st, 1ch, 1dc into 1st of 2 sts just skipped working back over last dc made.
1ST ROW: Skip 3ch (count as 1dc), ✳work 2Cdc (see Special Abbreviation) over next 3ch, 1dc into next ch; rep from ✳ to end, turn.
2ND ROW: 3ch (count as 1dc), 1dc into 1st st, skip 1dc, ✳1dc into next ch, work 2Cdc over next 3dc, rep from ✳ ending 1dc into last ch, skip 1dc, 2dc into top of tch, turn.
3RD ROW: 3ch (count as 1dc), skip 1 st, ✳work 2Cdc over next 3dc, 1dc into next ch; rep from ✳ ending last rep into top of tch, turn.
Rep 2nd and 3rd rows.

Twin V Stitch
Starting chain: multiple of 4 sts + 4
Drape: good
Skill: easy

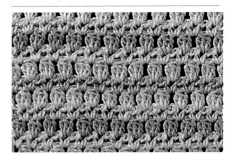

1ST ROW (RS): 2dc into 5th ch from hook, 2dc into next ch, ✳skip 2ch, 2dc into each of next 2ch; rep from ✳ to last 2ch, skip 1ch, 1dc into last ch, turn.

2ND ROW: 3ch, ✳skip 2 sts, 2dc into each of next 2 sts; rep from ✳ to last 2 sts, skip 1 st, 1dc into tch, turn.
Rep 2nd row.

medium-weight patterns

Crossed Cluster Stitch

Starting chain: multiple of 8 sts + 5
Drape: good
Skill: intermediate

Special Abbreviation

2CC (2 Crossed Clusters) = skip 1 st, into next st work ✻[yo, insert hook, yo, draw loop through] twice, yo, draw through all 5 loops on hook; rep from ✻ into st just skipped working over previous Cluster.

1ST ROW (WS): Skip 2ch (count as 1sc), 1sc into next and each ch to end, turn.

2ND ROW: 3ch (count as 1dc), skip 1 st, ✻2CC (see Special Abbreviation) over next 2 sts, 1dc into each of next 6 sts, rep from ✻ to last 3 sts, 2CC over next 2 sts, 1dc into tch, turn.

3RD ROW: 1ch (counts as 1sc), skip 1 st, 1sc into next and each st to end, working last st into top of tch, turn.

4TH ROW: 3ch (counts as 1dc), skip 1 st, 1dc into each of next 4 sts, ✻2CC over next 2 sts, 1dc into each of next 6 sts; rep from ✻ to last 7 sts, 2CC over next 2 sts, 1dc into each of last 5 sts, working last st into tch, turn.

5TH ROW: As 3rd row.
Rep 2nd, 3rd, 4th and 5th rows.

Hexagon Stitch

Starting chain: multiple of 8 sts + 5
Drape: good
Skill: experienced

Special Abbreviations

CL (Cluster) = work [yo, insert hook, yo, draw loop through loosely] over number

and position of sts indicated, ending yo, draw through all loops, 1ch tightly to close Cluster. See also page 187 (Clusters).
PICOT = 5ch, 1sc into 2nd ch from hook, 1sc into each of next 3ch.

1ST ROW (WS): 1sc into 2nd ch from hook, 1sc into each of next 3ch (counts as Picot —see Special Abbreviations), skip 3ch, 3dc into next ch, skip 3ch, 1sc into next ch, ✻skip 3ch, into next ch work [3dc, 1 Picot, 3dc], skip 3ch, 1sc into next ch; rep from ✻ to end, turn.

2ND ROW: 4ch (count as 1tr), 1CL (see Special Abbreviations) over each of first 8 sts, 3ch, 1sc into top of Picot, ✻3ch, 1CL over next 15 sts inserting hook into underside of each of 4ch of Picot, into next 3dc, 1sc, 3dc and 4sc of next Picot, then 3ch, 1sc into top of Picot; rep from ✻ to end, turn.

3RD ROW: 1ch, 1sc into 1st st, ✻skip 3ch, into loop which closed next CL work [3dc, 1 Picot, 3dc], skip 3ch, 1sc into next sc; rep from ✻ ending skip 3ch, 4dc into loop which closed last CL, skip 1ch, turn.

4TH ROW: 7ch (count as 1tr and 3ch), starting into 5th ch from hook work 1CL over next 15 sts as before, ✻3ch, 1sc into top of Picot, 3ch, 1CL over next 15 sts; rep from ✻ ending last rep with 1CL over last 8 sts, skip tch, turn.

5TH ROW: 8ch, 1sc into 2nd ch from hook, 1sc into each of next 3ch (counts as 1dc and 1 Picot), 3dc into 1st st, skip 3ch, 1sc into next sc, ✻skip 3ch, into loop which closed next CL work [3dc, 1 Picot, 3dc], skip 3ch, 1sc into next sc; rep from ✻ ending last rep with 1sc into 4th ch of tch, turn. Rep 2nd, 3rd, 4th and 5th rows.

Catherine Wheel I

Starting chain: multiple of 10 sts + 7
Drape: good
Skill: experienced

Special Abbreviation

CL (Cluster) = work [yo, insert hook, yo, draw loop through, yo, draw through 2 loops] over the number of sts indicated, yo, draw through all loops on hook. See also page 187 (Clusters).

1ST ROW (WS): 1sc into 2nd ch from hook, 1sc into next ch ✻skip 3ch, 7dc into next ch, skip 3ch, 1sc into each of next 3ch; rep from ✻ to last 4 ch, skip 3 ch, 4dc into last ch, turn.

2ND ROW: 1ch, 1sc into 1st st, 1sc into next st, ✻3ch, 1CL over next 7 sts, 3ch, 1sc into each of next 3 sts; rep from ✻ to last 4 sts, 3ch, 1CL over last 4 sts, skip tch, turn.

3RD ROW: 3ch (count as 1dc), 3dc into 1st st, ✻skip 3ch, 1sc into each of next 3sc, skip 3ch, 7dc into loop which closed next CL; rep from ✻ to end finishing with skip 3ch, 1sc into each of last 2sc, skip tch, turn.

4TH ROW: 3ch (count as 1dc) skip 1st st, 1CL over next 3 sts, ✻3ch, 1sc into each of next 3 sts, 3ch, 1CL over next 7 sts; rep from ✻ finishing with 3ch, 1sc into next st, 1sc into top of tch, turn.

5TH ROW: 1ch, 1sc into each of 1st 2sc, ✻skip 3ch, 7dc into loop which closed next CL, skip 3ch, 1sc into each of next 3sc; rep from ✻ ending skip 3ch, 4dc into top of tch, turn.
Rep 2nd, 3rd, 4th and 5th rows.

Catherine Wheel II
Starting chain: multiple of 10 sts + 7
Drape: good
Skill: experienced

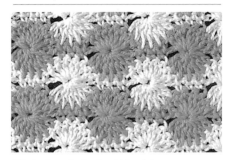

Worked as Catherine Wheel I.
Make base chain and work 1st row in color A. Thereafter work 2 rows each in color B and color A.

Catherine Wheel III
Starting chain: multiple of 10 sts + 7
Drape: good
Skill: experienced

Worked as Catherine Wheel I.
Work 1 row each in colors A, B and C throughout.

Catherine Wheel IV
Starting chain: multiple of 8 sts + 2
Drape: good
Skill: experienced

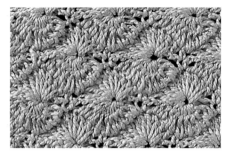

Special Abbreviation
CL (Cluster) = worked as Catherine Wheel I.
1ST ROW (RS): 1sc into 2nd ch from hook, ✳skip 3ch, 9dc into next ch, skip 3ch, 1sc into next ch; rep from ✳ to end, turn.
2ND ROW: 3ch (count as 1dc), skip 1st st, 1CL (see Special Abbreviation) over next 4 sts, ✳3ch, 1sc into next st, 3ch, 1CL over next 9 sts; rep from ✳ ending last rep with 1CL over last 5 sts, skip tch, turn.
3RD ROW: 3ch (count as 1dc), 4dc into 1st st, ✳skip 3ch, 1sc into next sc, skip 3ch, 9dc into loop which closed next CL; rep from ✳ ending last rep with 5dc into top of tch, turn.
4TH ROW: 1ch, 1sc into 1st st, ✳3ch, 1CL over next 9 sts, 3ch, 1sc into next st; rep from ✳ ending last rep with 1sc into top of tch, turn.
5TH ROW: 1ch, 1sc into 1st st, ✳skip 3ch, 9dc into loop which closed next CL, skip 3ch, 1sc into next sc; rep from ✳ to end, skip tch, turn.
Rep 2nd, 3rd, 4th and 5th rows.

Wedge Stitch I
Starting chain: multiple of 6 sts + 2
Drape: good
Skill: intermediate

Special Abbreviation
WP (Wedge Picot) = work 6ch, 1sc into 2nd ch from hook, 1hdc into next ch, 1dc into next ch, 1tr into next ch, 1dtr into next ch.
1ST ROW (WS): 1sc into 2nd ch from hook, ✳1WP (see Special Abbreviation), skip 5ch, 1sc into next ch; rep from ✳ to end, turn.

2ND ROW: 5ch (count as 1dtr), ✳1sc into top of WP, over next 5ch at underside of WP work 1sc into next ch, 1hdc into next ch, 1dc into next ch, 1tr into next ch, 1dtr into next ch, skip next sc; rep from ✳ omitting 1dtr at end of last rep when 2 sts remain, ✳✳[yo] 3 times, insert hook into last ch at underside of WP, yo, draw loop through, [yo, draw through 2 loops] 3 times, rep from ✳✳ into next sc, yo, draw through all 3 loops on hook, skip tch, turn.
3RD ROW: 1ch, 1sc into 1st st, ✳1WP, skip next 5 sts, 1sc into next st; rep from ✳ ending last rep with 1sc into top of tch, turn.
Rep 2nd and 3rd rows.

Wedge Stitch II
Starting chain: multiple of 6 sts + 2
Drape: good
Skill: intermediate

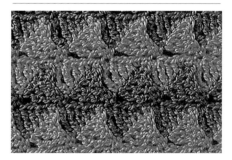

Worked as Wedge Stitch I.
Make base chain and work 1st row in color A. Thereafter work 2 rows each in color B and color A.

Wavy Shell Stitch I
Starting chain: multiple of 14 sts + 3
Drape: good
Skill: intermediate

1ST ROW (RS): Skip 2ch (count as 1dc), 3dc into next ch, ✳skip 3ch, 1sc into each of next 7ch, skip 3ch, 7dc into next ch; rep from ✳ ending last rep with 4dc into last ch, turn.
2ND ROW: 1ch,1sc into 1st st, 1sc into each st to end, finishing with 1sc into top of tch, turn.
3RD ROW: 1ch, 1sc into each of 1st 4 sts, ✳skip 3 sts, 7dc into next st, skip 3 sts, 1sc into each of next 7 sts; rep from ✳ to last 11 sts, skip 3 sts, 7dc into next st, skip 3 sts, 1sc into each of last 4 sc, skip tch, turn.
4TH ROW: 1ch, 1sc into 1st st, 1sc into next and each st to end, skip tch, turn.
5TH ROW: 3ch (count as 1dc), 3dc into first st, ✳skip 3 sts, 1sc into each of next 7 sts, skip 3 sts, 7dc into next st; rep from ✳ ending last rep with 4dc into last sc, skip tch, turn.
Rep 2nd, 3rd, 4th and 5th rows.

Wavy Shell Stitch II
Starting chain: multiple of 14 sts + 4
Drape: good
Skill: intermediate

Worked as Wavy Shell Stitch I.
Work 1 row each in colors A, B and C throughout.

Crosshatch Stitch I
Starting chain: multiple of 7 sts + 7
Drape: excellent
Skill: easy

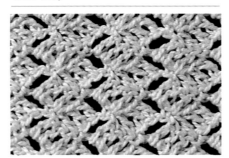

1ST ROW: Skip 2ch (count as 1dc), 2dc into next ch, ✳skip 3ch, 1sc into next ch, 3ch, 1dc into each of next 3ch; rep from ✳ to last 4ch, skip 3ch, 1sc into last ch, turn.
2ND ROW: 3ch (count as 1dc), 2dc into 1st sc, ✳skip 3dc, 1sc into 1st of 3ch, 3ch, 1dc into each of next 2ch, 1dc into next sc; rep from ✳ ending skip 2dc, 1sc into top of tch, turn.
Rep 2nd row.

Crosshatch Stitch II
Starting chain: multiple of 7 sts + 7
Drape: excellent
Skill: easy

Worked as Crosshatch Stitch I.
Work 1 row each in colors A, B and C throughout.

Long Wave Stitch
Starting chain: multiple of 14 sts + 2
Drape: good
Skill: intermediate

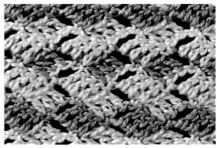

Special Abbreviations
Gr (Group) (worked over 14 sts) = 1sc into next st, [1hdc into next st] twice, [1dc into next st] twice, [1tr into next st] 3 times, [1dc into next st] twice, [1hdc into next st] twice, [1sc into next st] twice.
Rev Gr (Reverse Group) (worked over 14 sts) = 1tr into next st, [1dc into next st] twice, [1hdc into next st] twice, [1sc into next st] 3 times, [1hdc into next st] twice, [1dc into next st] twice, [1tr into next st] twice.
Work 2 rows each in colors A and B alternately throughout.
1ST ROW (RS): Skip 2ch (count as 1sc), ✳1Gr (see Special Abbreviations) over next 14ch; rep from ✳ to end, turn.
2ND ROW: 1ch (counts as 1sc), skip 1st st, 1sc into next and each st to end working last st into top of tch, turn.
3RD ROW: 4ch (count as 1tr), skip 1st st, ✳1 Rev Gr (see Special Abbreviations) over

next 14 sts; rep from ✳ ending last rep in tch, turn.
4TH ROW: As 2nd row.
5TH ROW: 1ch (counts as 1sc), skip 1st st, ✳1Gr over next 14 sts; rep from ✳ ending last rep in tch, turn.
6TH ROW: As 2nd row.
Rep 3rd, 4th, 5th and 6th rows.

Smooth Wave Stitch

Starting chain: multiple of 8 sts + 5
Drape: good
Skill: intermediate

Work 2 rows each in colors A and B alternately throughout.
1ST ROW (RS): Skip 2ch (count as 1sc), 1sc into each of next 3ch, ✳1dc into each of next 4ch, 1sc into each of next 4ch; rep from ✳ to end, turn.
2ND ROW: 1ch (counts as 1sc), skip 1st st, 1sc into each of next 3 sts, ✳1dc into each of next 4 sts, 1sc into each of next 4 sts; rep from ✳ to end working last st into top of tch, turn.
3RD ROW: 3ch (count as 1dc), skip 1st st, 1dc into each of next 3 sts, ✳1sc into each of next 4 sts, 1dc into each of next 4 sts; rep from ✳ to end working last st into top of tch, turn.
4TH ROW: As 3rd row.
5TH AND 6TH ROWS: As 2nd row.
Rep 3rd, 4th, 5th and 6th rows.

Wave and Chevron Stitch

Starting chain: multiple of 6 sts + 2
Drape: good
Skill: intermediate
Note: For description of sc2tog, sc3tog, tr2tog and tr3tog see pages 187–188 (Clusters).

Work 2 rows each in colors A, B, C and D throughout.
BASE ROW (RS): Skip 2ch (count as 1sc), 1sc into next and each ch to end, turn.

Commence Pattern

1ST ROW: 1ch (counts as 1sc), skip 1 st, ✳1hdc into next st, 1dc into next st, 3tr into next st, 1dc into next st, 1hdc into next st, 1sc into next st; rep from ✳ to end, turn.
2ND ROW: 1ch, skip 1 st, 1sc into next st (counts as sc2tog), 1sc into each of next 2 sts, ✳3sc into next st, 1sc into each of next 2 sts, over next 3 sts work sc3tog, 1sc into each of next 2 sts; rep from ✳ to last 5 sts, 3sc into next st, 1sc into each of next 2 sts, over last 2 sts work sc2tog, skip tch, turn.
3RD ROW: As 2nd row.
4TH ROW: 4ch, skip 1 st, 1tr into next st (counts as tr2tog), ✳1dc into next st, 1hdc into next st, 1sc into next st, 1hdc into next st, 1dc into next st✳✳, over next 3 sts work tr3tog; rep from ✳ ending last rep at ✳✳, over last 2 sts work tr2tog, skip tch, turn.
5TH ROW: 1ch (counts as 1sc), skip 1 st, 1sc into next and each st to end, turn.
6TH ROW: As 5th row.
Rep these 6 rows.

Interlocking Block Stitch I

Starting chain: multiple of 6 sts + 5
Drape: good
Skill: intermediate

Special Abbreviation

Sdc (Spike double crochet) = work dc over ch sp by inserting hook into top of next row below (or base chain). Work 1 row each in colors A, B and C throughout.
1ST ROW: Skip 3ch (count as 1dc), 1dc into each of next 2ch, ✳3ch, skip 3ch, 1dc into each of next 3ch; rep from ✳ to end, turn.
2ND ROW: ✳3ch, skip 3 sts, 1Sdc (see Special Abbreviation) over each of next 3 sts; rep from ✳ to last 3 sts, 2ch, skip 2 sts, sl st into top of tch, turn.
3RD ROW: 3ch (count as 1Sdc), skip 1 st, 1Sdc over each of next 2 sts, ✳3ch, skip 3 sts, 1Sdc over each of next 3 sts; rep from ✳ to end, turn. Rep 2nd and 3rd rows.

Interlocking Block Stitch II

Starting chain: multiple of 6 sts + 5
Drape: good
Skill: intermediate

Worked as Interlocking Block Stitch I. Work 1 row each in colors A and B alternately throughout. Do not break yarn when changing color, but begin row at same end as color.

Diagonal Spike Stitch

Starting chain: multiple of 4 sts + 4
Drape: good
Skill: intermediate

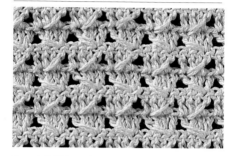

Special Abbreviation
Sdc (Spike double crochet) = yo, insert hook into same place that 1st dc of previous 3dc block was worked, yo, draw loop through and up so as not to crush 3dc block, [yo, draw through 2 loops] twice.
1ST ROW: Skip 3ch (count as 1dc), ✳1dc into each of next 3ch, skip next ch and work 1Sdc (see Special Abbreviation) over it instead; rep from ✳ ending 1dc into last ch, turn.
2ND ROW: 3ch (count as 1dc), skip 1 st, ✳1dc into each of next 3 sts, skip next st and work 1Sdc over it instead; rep from ✳ end 1dc into top of tch, turn. Rep 2nd row.

Alternating Spike Stitch I

Starting chain: multiple of 2 sts + 1
Drape: good
Skill: intermediate

Special Abbreviation
Ssc (Spike single crochet) = insert hook below next st 1 row down (i.e. into same place as that st was worked), yo, draw

loop through and up to height of present row, yo, draw through both loops on hook. See also page 188 (Spikes).
1ST ROW: Skip 2ch (count as 1sc), 1sc into next and each ch to end, turn.
2ND ROW: 1ch (count as 1sc), skip 1 st, ✳1sc into next st, 1Ssc (see Special Abbreviation) over next st; rep from ✳ ending 1sc into tch, turn. Rep 2nd row.

Alternating Spike Stitch II

Starting chain: multiple of 2 sts + 1
Drape: good
Skill: intermediate

Worked as Alternating Spike Stitch I. Work 1 row each in colors A, B and C throughout.

Arrowhead Spike Stitch

Starting chain: multiple of 6 sts + 3
Drape: good
Skill: experienced

Special Abbreviation
Ssc (Spike single crochet) = insert hook below next st 1 or more rows down (indicated thus: Ssc1, Ssc2, Ssc3, etc), yo, draw loop through and up to height of current row, yo, draw through both loops on hook. See also page 188. (Spikes). Work 6 rows each in colors A and B alternately throughout.
BASE ROW (RS): Using A 1sc into 2nd ch from hook, 1sc into each ch to end, turn.
Commence pattern
1ST ROW: 1ch, 1sc into 1st and each st to end, skip tch, turn. Work 4 rows as 1st row.
6TH ROW: Using B 1ch, 1sc into 1st st, ✳1sc into next st, 1Ssc1 (see Special Abbreviation) over next st, 1Ssc2 over next st, 1Ssc3 over next st, 1Ssc4 over next st, 1Ssc5 over next st; rep from ✳ ending 1sc into last st, skip tch, turn.
Work 5 rows as 1st row.
12TH ROW: Using A 1ch, 1sc into 1st st, ✳1Ssc5 over next st, 1Ssc4 over next st, 1Ssc3 over next st, 1Ssc2 over next st, 1Ssc1 over next st, 1sc into next st; rep from ✳ ending 1sc into last st, skip tch, turn. Rep these 12 rows.

Spiked Squares

Starting chain: multiple of 10 sts + 2
Drape: good
Skill: experienced

Special Abbreviation
Ssc (Spike single crochet) = worked as under Arrowhead Spike Stitch. Note: When working Sscs over previous Sscs, be careful to insert hook in centers of

previous Sscs.

Work 2 rows each in colors A, B and C throughout.

BASE ROW (RS): 1sc into 2nd ch from hook, 1sc into next and each ch to end, turn.

Commence Pattern

1ST ROW: 1ch, 1sc into first and each st to end, skip tch, turn.

2ND ROW: 1ch, 1sc into first st, ✳1Ssc2 (see Special Abbreviation) over each of next 5 sts, 1sc into each of next 5 sts; rep from ✳ ending 1sc into last sc, skip tch, turn.

Rep the last 2 rows 3 times more.

9TH ROW: As 1st row.

10TH ROW: 1ch, 1sc into first st, ✳1sc into each of next 5 sts, 1Ssc2 over each of next 5 sts; rep from ✳ ending 1sc into last sc, skip tch, turn.

Rep the last 2 rows 3 times more.

Rep these 16 rows.

Spike Cluster Stitch

Starting chain: multiple of 8 sts + 6
Drape: good
Skill: experienced

Special Abbreviation

SPC (Spike Cluster) = over next st pick up 5 spike loops by inserting hook as follows: 2 sts to right of next st and 1 row down; 1 st to right and 2 rows down; directly below and 3 rows down; 1 st to left and 2 rows down; 2 sts to left and 1 row down, (6 loops on hook); now insert hook into top of next st itself, yo, draw loop through, yo, draw through all 7 loops on hook. (See also page 188.)

Work 4 rows each in colors A and B alternately throughout.

BASE ROW (RS): 1sc into 2nd ch from hook, 1sc into each ch to end, turn.

Commence Pattern

1ST ROW: 1ch, 1sc into 1st and each st to end, skip tch, turn.

2ND AND 3RD ROWS: As 1st row.

4TH ROW: 1ch, 1sc into each of 1st 4 sts, ✳1SPC (see Special Abbreviation) over next st, 1sc into each of next 7 sts (Hint: be careful not to pick up any of the spikes of the previous SPC); rep from ✳ ending 1sc into last st, skip tch, turn.

5TH, 6TH AND 7TH ROWS: As 1st row.

8TH ROW: 1ch, 1sc into each of 1st 8 sts, ✳1SPC over next st, 1sc into each of next 7 sts; rep from ✳ to last 5 sts, 1SPC over next st, 1sc into each of last 4 sts, skip tch, turn. Rep these 8 rows.

5-Star Marguerite Stitch

Starting chain: multiple of 2 sts + 2
Drape: good
Skill: intermediate

Special Abbreviation

M5C (Marguerite Cluster with 5 Spike Loops) = pick up spike loops (i.e.: yo and draw through) inserting hook as follows: into loop which closed previous M5C, under 2 threads of last spike loop of same M5C, into same place that last spike loop of same M5C was worked, into each of next 2 sts (6 loops on hook), yo, draw through all loops on hook.

1ST ROW (WS): 1sc into 2nd ch from hook, 1sc into next and each ch to end, turn.

2ND ROW: 3ch, 1M5C (see Special Abbreviation) inserting hook into 2nd and 3rd chs from hook and then 1st 3 sts to pick up 5 spike loops, ✳1ch, 1M5C; rep from ✳ to end, skip tch, turn.

3RD ROW: 1ch, 1sc into loop which closed last M5C, ✳1sc into next ch, 1sc into loop which closed next M5C; rep from ✳ ending 1sc into each of next 2ch of tch, turn.

Rep 2nd and 3rd rows.

Simple Marguerite Stitch

Starting chain: multiple of 2 sts + 3
Drape: good
Skill: intermediate

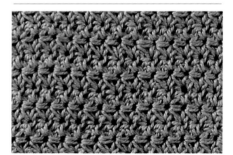

Special Abbreviation

M3C (Marguerite Cluster with 3 Spike Loops) = see text below and also page 188 (Spikes).

1ST ROW: Make a spike loop (i.e. yo and draw through) into 2nd, 3rd and 5th chs from hook, yo and through all 4 loops (1M3C made—see Special Abbreviation), ✳1ch, make 1M3C picking up 1 loop in ch which closed previous M3C, 2nd loop in same place as last spike of previous M3C, skip 1ch, then last loop in next ch, yo and through all 4 loops; rep from ✳ to end, turn.

2ND ROW: 3ch, make 1M3C picking up loops in 2nd and 3rd ch from hook and in ch which closed 2nd M3C on previous row, ✳1ch, work 1M3C picking up 1st loop in ch which closed previous M3C, 2nd loop in same place as last spike of previous M3C and last loop in ch which closed next M3C on previous row; rep from ✳ to end, picking up final loop in top of ch at beg of previous row.
Rep 2nd row.

Caterpillar Stripe
Starting chain: multiple of 4 sts + 4
Drape: good
Skill: intermediate

1ST ROW (RS): Using A, work 1dc into 4th ch from hook, 1dc into each ch to end, turn.
2ND ROW: Using A, 1ch, work 1sc into each dc to end working last sc into top of 3ch, turn.
3RD ROW: Using B, 3ch (count as 1dc), skip first sc, 1dc into next sc, ✳2ch, skip 2sc, 1dc into each of next 2sc; rep from ✳ to end, turn.
4TH ROW: Using B, 1ch, work 1sc into each of 2dc, ✳2ch, 1sc into each of next 2dc; rep from ✳ to end working last sc into 3rd of 3ch at beg of previous row, turn.
5TH ROW: Using C, 1ch, 1sc into each of 1st 2sc, ✳1tr into each of the 2 skipped sc 3 rows below, 1sc into each of next 2sc; rep from ✳ to end, turn.
6TH ROW: Using C, 1ch, 1sc into each sc

and each tr to end, turn.
7TH ROW: Using A, 3ch, skip first sc, 1dc into each sc to end, turn.
8TH ROW: Using A, 1ch, 1sc into each dc to end working last sc into 3rd of 3ch at beg of previous row, turn.
Rep 3rd to 8th rows.

Encroaching Stripes
Starting chain: multiple of 8 sts + 7
Drape: good
Skill: intermediate

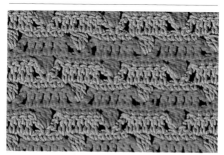

Special Abbreviation
Bobble = work 3dc into next sc until last loop of each dc remains on hook, yo and through all 4 loops.
Note: Count each sc, ch sp and Bobble as 1 st throughout.
1ST ROW (WS): Using A work 1dc into 4th ch from hook, 1dc into each of next 3ch, ✳3ch, skip 1ch, 1sc into next ch, 3ch, skip 1ch, 1dc into each of next 5ch; rep from ✳ to end, turn.
2ND ROW: Using B, 1ch, work 1sc into each of 1st 5dc, ✳1ch, 1 Bobble (see Special Abbreviation) into next sc, 1ch, 1sc into each of next 5dc; rep from ✳ to end placing last sc into top of 3ch, turn.
3RD ROW: Using B, 6ch (count as 1dc, 3ch), skip 1st 2sc, 1sc into next sc, 3ch, ✳skip 1sc, 1dc into each of next 5 sts (see note above), 3ch, skip 1sc, 1sc into next sc, 3ch; rep from ✳ to last 2sc, skip 1sc, 1dc into last sc, turn.
4TH ROW: Using A, 1ch, work 1sc into 1st dc, 1ch, 1 Bobble into next sc, 1ch, ✳1sc into each of next 5dc, 1ch, 1 Bobble into

next sc, 1ch; rep from ✳ to last dc, 1sc into 3rd of 6ch at beg of previous row, turn.
5TH ROW: Using A, 3ch (count as 1dc), skip 1st sc, 1dc into each of next 4 sts, ✳3ch, skip 1sc, 1sc into next sc, 3ch, skip 1sc, 1dc into each of next 5 sts; rep from ✳ to end, turn.
Rep 2nd to 5th rows.

Embossed Circles
Starting chain: multiple of 10 sts + 12
Drape: good
Skill: experienced

Special Abbreviation
1 Circle = rotating work as required work 6dc down and around stem of next dc 1 row below, then work 6dc up and around stem of previous dc 1 row below.
1ST ROW (RS): Work 1dc into 4th ch from hook, 1dc into each ch to end, turn.
2ND ROW: 3ch (count as 1dc), skip 1st dc, work 1dc into each dc to end working last dc into 3rd of 3ch at beg of previous row, turn.
3RD ROW: 3ch, skip 1st dc, work 1dc into each of next 4dc, ✳work 1 Circle (see Special Abbreviation), working behind Circle work 1dc into each of next 10dc; rep from ✳ to end omitting 5dc at end of last rep and working last dc into 3rd of 3ch at beg of previous row, turn.
4TH, 5TH AND 6TH ROWS: 3ch, skip 1st dc, work 1dc into each dc to end working last dc into 3rd of 3ch at beg of previous row, turn.
7TH ROW: 3ch, skip 1st dc, work 1dc into each of next 9dc, ✳work 1 Circle, 1dc into

each of next 10dc; rep from ✳ to end working last dc into 3rd of 3ch, turn.
8TH AND 9TH ROWS: 3ch, skip 1st dc, work 1dc into each dc to end working last dc into 3rd of 3ch, turn. Rep 2nd to 9th rows.

Embossed Pockets

Starting chain: multiple of 3 sts + 3
Drape: good
Skill: intermediate

Special Abbreviation
Pgr (Pocket Group) = work [1sc, 1hdc, 3dc] round stem of indicated st.
1ST ROW: (WS): Skip 3ch (count as 1dc), 1dc into each ch to end, turn.
2ND ROW: 1Pgr (see Special Abbreviation) round 1st st, skip 2 sts, sl st into top of next st, ✳1Pgr round same st as sl st, skip 2 sts, sl st into top of next st; rep from ✳ to end, turn.
3RD ROW: 3ch (count as 1dc), skip 1 st, 1dc into each st to end, turn.
Rep 2nd and 3rd rows.

Aligned Puff Stitch

Starting chain: multiple of 2 sts + 2
Drape: good
Skill: intermediate
Note: For description of htr4tog see page 191 (Puff Stitch).

1ST ROW (RS): 1sc into 2nd ch from hook, ✳1ch, skip 1ch, 1sc into next ch; rep from ✳ to end, turn.
2ND ROW: 2ch (count as 1hdc), skip 1st st, ✳htr4tog all into next ch sp, 1ch, skip 1sc; rep from ✳ ending htr4tog into last ch sp, 1hdc into last sc, skip tch, turn.
3RD ROW: 1ch, 1sc into 1st st, ✳1ch, skip 1 st, 1sc into next ch sp; rep from ✳ ending in top of tch, turn.
Rep 2nd and 3rd rows.

Little Wave Stitch

Starting chain: multiple of 4 sts + 2
Drape: good
Skill: intermediate

Work 2 rows each in colors A and B alternately.
1ST ROW (RS): 1sc into 2nd ch from hook, ✳1hdc into next ch, 1dc into next ch, 1hdc into next ch, 1sc into next ch; rep from ✳ to end, turn.
2ND ROW: 1ch, 1sc into 1st st, ✳1hdc into next hdc, 1dc into next dc, 1hdc into next hdc, 1sc into next sc; rep from ✳ to end, skip tch, turn.

3RD ROW: 3ch (count as 1dc), skip 1st st, ✳1hdc into next hdc, 1sc into next dc, 1hdc into next hdc, 1dc into next sc; rep from ✳ to end, skip tch, turn.
4TH ROW: 3ch (count as 1dc), skip 1st st, ✳1hdc into next hdc, 1sc into next sc, 1hdc into next hdc, 1dc into next dc; rep from ✳ ending last rep in top of tch, turn.
5TH ROW: 1ch, 1sc into 1st st, ✳1hdc into next hdc, 1dc into next sc, 1hdc into next hdc, 1sc into next dc; rep from ✳ ending last rep in top of tch, turn.
Rep 2nd, 3rd, 4th and 5th rows.

Interlocking Diamond Stitch

Starting chain: multiple of 6 sts + 2
Drape: good
Skill: intermediate

Work 1st row in color A, then 2 rows each in colors B and A alternately throughout.
1ST ROW (WS): Sl st into 2 and ch from hook, ✳3ch, skip 2ch, 1dc into next ch, 3ch, skip 2ch, sl st into next ch; rep from ✳ to end, turn.
2ND ROW: 4ch (count as 1dc and 1ch), 1dc into sl st, ✳skip 3ch, sl st into next dc✳✳, skip 3ch, work [1dc, 1ch, 1dc, 1ch, 1dc] into next sl st; rep from ✳ ending last rep at ✳✳ in last dc, skip 3ch, work [1dc, 1ch, 1dc] into last sl st, turn.
3RD ROW: 6ch (count as 1dc and 3ch), skip [1st st, 1ch and 1dc], ✳sl st into next sl st✳✳, 3ch, skip 1dc and 1ch, 1dc into next dc 3ch, skip 1ch and 1dc; rep from ✳ ending last rep at ✳✳ in last sl st, 3ch, skip 1dc and 1ch, 1dc into next ch of tch, turn.
4TH ROW: Sl st into 1st st, ✳skip 3ch,

[1dc, 1ch, 1dc, 1ch, 1dc] all into next sl st, skip 3ch, sl st into next dc; rep from ✳ ending in 3rd ch of tch loop, turn.

5TH ROW: ✳3ch, skip 1dc and 1ch, 1dc into next dc, 3ch, skip 1ch and 1dc, sl st into next sl st; rep from ✳ to end, turn. Rep 2nd, 3rd, 4th and 5th rows.

Zigzag Pip Stitch

Starting chain: multiple of 4 sts + 2
Drape: good
Skill: intermediate
Note: For description of dc2tog see page 187 (Clusters).

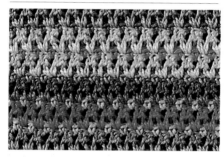

Work 1 row each in colors A, B, C, D and E throughout.

1ST ROW (RS): 1sc into 2nd ch from hook, ✳1ch, skip 1ch, 1sc into next ch; rep from ✳ to end, turn.

2ND ROW: 3ch, 1dc into next ch sp (counts as dc2tog), ✳1ch, dc2tog inserting hook into same sp as previous st for 1st leg and into next sp for 2nd leg; rep from ✳ to last sp, ending 1ch, dc2tog over same sp and last sc, skip tch, turn.

3RD ROW: 1ch, 1sc into 1st st, ✳1sc into next sp, 1ch, skip next cluster; rep from ✳ ending 1sc into last sp, 1sc into last st, skip tch, turn.

4TH ROW: 3ch (count as 1dc), dc2tog inserting hook into 1st st for 1st leg and into next sp for 2nd leg, ✳1ch, dc2tog inserting hook into same sp as previous st for 1st leg and into next sp for 2nd leg; rep from ✳ ending with 2nd leg of last cluster in last sc, 1dc into same place, skip tch, turn.

5TH ROW: 1ch, 1sc into 1st st, ✳1ch, skip

next cluster, 1sc into next sp; rep from ✳ working last sc into top of tch, turn. Rep 2nd, 3rd, 4th and 5th rows.

Shadow Tracery Stitch

Starting chain: multiple of 6 sts + 2
Drape: good
Skill: experienced
Note: For description of hdc5tog see page 191 (Puff Stitch).

Special Abbreviation

Puff St = work hdc5tog all into same place ending with 1ch drawn tightly to close. Work 1 row each in colors A and B alternately throughout. Do not break yarn when changing color, but fasten off temporarily and begin row at same end as new color.

1ST ROW (RS IN A): 1sc into 2nd ch from hook, ✳3ch, skip 2ch, Puff St (see Special Abbreviation) into next ch, 3ch, skip 2ch, 1sc into next ch; rep from ✳ to end. Do not turn.

2ND ROW (RS IN B): Join yarn into 1st st, 1ch, 1sc into 1st st, ✳3ch, skip 3ch, 1sc into next Puff St, 3ch, skip 3ch, 1sc into next sc; rep from ✳ to end, turn.

3RD ROW (WS IN A): 6ch (count as 1dc and 3ch), skip 1st st and 3ch, 1sc into next sc, ✳3ch, skip 3ch, Puff St into next sc, 3ch, skip 3ch, 1sc into next sc; rep from ✳ ending 3ch, skip 3ch, 1dc into last sc. Do not turn.

4TH ROW (WS IN B): Pick up yarn in 3rd ch of tch, 1ch, 1sc into same place, ✳3ch, skip 3ch, 1sc into next sc, 3ch, skip 3ch, 1sc into next st; rep from ✳ to end, turn.

5TH ROW (RS IN A): 1ch, 1sc into 1st st, ✳3ch, skip 3ch, Puff St into next sc, 3ch, skip 3ch, 1sc into next sc; rep from ✳ to end. Do not turn.
Rep 2nd, 3rd, 4th and 5th rows.

Fleur de Lys Stitch

Starting chain: multiple of 6 sts + 3
Drape: good
Skill: experienced
Note: For description of dc/rf and dc/rb see page 188 (Raised Stitches).

Special Abbreviations

FC/rf (Fleur Cluster raised at front) = leaving last loop of each st on hook work 1dc/rf round next dc, skip 1ch, 1dc into top of next sc, skip 1ch, 1dc/rf round next dc, (4 loops on hook), yo, draw through all loops.

FC/rb (Fleur Cluster raised at back) = as for FC/rf except insert hook at back for first and 3rd legs.

Work 1 row each in colors A and B alternately throughout. Do not break yarn when changing color, but fasten off temporarily and begin row at same end as new color.

1ST ROW (RS IN A): Skip 2ch (count as 1dc), 1dc into next ch, ✳1ch, skip 2ch, 1sc into next ch, 1ch, skip 2ch✳✳, 3dc into next ch; rep from ✳ ending last rep at ✳✳, 2dc into last ch. Do not turn.

2ND ROW (RS IN B): Join new yarn into top of tch, 1ch, 1sc into same place, ✳2ch, FC/rb (see Special Abbreviations), 2ch, 1sc into next dc; rep from ✳ to end, turn.

3RD ROW (WS IN A): 3ch (count as 1dc), 1dc into 1st st, ✳1ch, skip 2ch, 1sc into next cluster, 1ch, skip 2ch✳✳, 3dc into next sc; rep from ✳ ending last rep at ✳✳, 2dc into last sc. Do not turn.

4TH ROW (WS IN B): Rejoin new yarn at top of 3ch, 1ch, 1sc into same place, ✳2ch, FC/rf (see Special Abbreviations), 2ch, 1sc into next dc; rep from ✳ to end, turn.

5TH ROW (RS IN A): 3ch (count as 1dc), 1dc into 1st st, ✳1ch, skip 2ch, 1sc into next cluster, 1ch, skip 2ch✳✳, 3dc into next sc; rep from ✳ ending last rep at ✳✳, 2dc into last sc. Do not turn.

Rep 2nd, 3rd, 4th and 5th rows.

Zigzag Lozenge Stitch

Starting chain: multiple of 2 sts + 3
Drape: good
Skill: intermediate
Note: For description of dc2tog and dc3tog see page 190 (Bobble).

Work 1 row each in colors A, B and C alternately throughout.

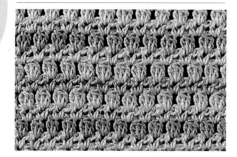

1ST ROW (WS): Skip 2ch (count as 1hdc), 1hdc into next ch, ✳skip 1ch, [1hdc, 1ch, 1hdc] into next ch; rep from ✳ to last 2 ch, skip 1ch, 2hdc into last ch, turn.

2ND ROW: 3ch, 1dc into 1st st (counts as dc2tog), ✳1ch, work dc3tog into next ch sp; rep from ✳ to last sp, ending 1ch, dc2tog into top of tch, turn.

3RD ROW: 2ch (count as 1hdc), skip 1st st, ✳work [1hdc, 1ch, 1hdc] into next ch sp; rep from ✳ ending 1hdc into top of tch, turn.

4TH ROW: 3ch (count as 1dc), skip 1st st, ✳work dc3tog into next sp, 1ch; rep from

✳ ending 1dc into top of tch, turn.

5TH ROW: 2ch (count as 1hdc), 1hdc into 1st st, ✳work [1hdc, 1ch, 1hdc] into next ch sp; rep from ✳ ending 2hdc into top of tch, turn.

Rep 2nd, 3rd, 4th and 5th rows.

Multicolored Parquet Stitch

Starting chain: multiple of 3 sts + 2
Drape: good
Skill: intermediate

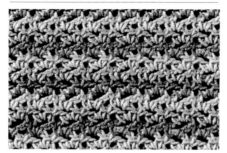

Work 1 row each in colors A, B and C alternately throughout.

1ST ROW (RS): 1sc into 2nd ch from hook, ✳3ch, 1dc into same place as previous sc, skip 2ch, 1sc into next ch; rep from ✳ to end, turn.

2ND ROW: 3ch (count as 1dc), 1dc into 1st st, 1sc into next 3ch arch, ✳3ch, 1dc into same 3ch arch, 1sc into next 3ch arch; rep from ✳ ending 2ch, 1dc into last sc, skip tch, turn.

3RD ROW: 1ch, 1sc into 1st st, 3ch, 1dc into next 2ch sp, ✳work [1sc, 3ch, 1dc] into next 3ch arch; rep from ✳ ending 1sc into top of tch, turn.

Rep 2nd and 3rd rows.

Shell and V Stitch

Starting chain: multiple of 8 sts + 3
Drape: good
Skill: easy

1ST ROW (RS): Skip 2ch (count as 1dc), 2dc into next ch, ✳skip 3ch, work a V st of [1dc, 1ch, 1dc] into next ch, skip 3ch✳✳, 5dc into next ch; rep from ✳ ending last rep at ✳✳, 3dc into last ch, turn.

2ND ROW: 3ch (count as 1dc), 1dc into 1st st, ✳5dc into sp at center of next V st✳✳, V st into 3rd of next 5dc; rep from ✳ ending last rep at ✳✳, 2dc into top of tch, turn.

Rep 2nd row.

Lozenge Mosaic I

Starting chain: multiple of 12 sts + 11
Drape: good
Skill: experienced

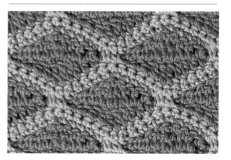

1ST ROW (RS): Using A, work 1sc into 2nd ch from hook, 1sc into each ch to end, turn.

2ND ROW: Using A, 1ch, work 1sc into each sc to end, turn.

3RD ROW: Using B, 3ch (count as 1dc), skip 1st sc, 1dc into next sc, 1hdc into next sc, 1sc into next sc, ✳2ch, skip 2sc, 1sc into next sc, 1hdc into next sc, 1dc into each of next 2sc, 1tr into each of next 2sc, 1dc into each of next 2sc, 1hdc into next sc, 1sc into next sc; rep from ✳ to last 6sc, 2ch, skip 2sc, 1sc into next sc, 1hdc into next sc, 1dc into each of last 2sc, turn.

4TH ROW: Using B, 3ch, skip 1st dc, work 1dc into next dc, 1hdc into next hdc, 1sc into next sc, ✳2ch, 1sc into next sc, 1hdc into next hdc, 1dc into each of next 2dc, 1tr into each of next 2tr, 1dc into each of next 2dc, 1hdc into next hdc, 1sc into next sc; rep from ✳ to last 6 sts, 2ch, 1sc into next sc, 1hdc into next hdc, 1dc into next dc, 1dc into 3rd of 3ch at beg of previous row, turn.

5TH ROW: Using A, 1ch, work 1sc into each of 1st 4 sts, [inserting hook from front of work, work 1sc into each of 2 free sc in A 3 rows below], ✳1sc into each of next 10 sts on previous row, work 2sc 3 rows below as before; rep from ✳ to last 4 sts, 1sc into each of next 3 sts, 1sc into 3rd of 3ch at beg of previous row, turn.

6TH ROW: Using A, 1ch, work 1sc into each sc to end, turn,

7TH ROW: Using B, 1ch, ✳work 1sc into 1st sc, 1hdc into next sc, 1dc into each of next 2sc, 1tr into each of next 2sc, 1dc into each of next 2sc, 1hdc into next sc, 1sc into next sc, 2ch, skip 2sc; rep from ✳ to end omitting 2ch at end of last rep, turn.

8TH ROW: Using B, 1ch, ✳work 1sc into next sc, 1hdc into next hdc, 1dc into each of next 2dc, 1tr into each of next 2tr, 1dc into each of next 2dc, 1hdc into next hdc, 1sc into next sc, 2ch; rep from ✳ to end omitting 2ch at end of last rep, turn.

9TH ROW: Using A, 1ch, ✳1sc into each of next 10 sts, inserting hook from front of work, work 1sc into each of 2 free sc in A 3 rows below; rep from ✳ to end omitting 2sc at end of last rep, turn.
Rep 2nd to 9th rows.

Lozenge Mosaic II

Starting chain: multiple of 12 sts + 11
Drape: good
Skill: experienced

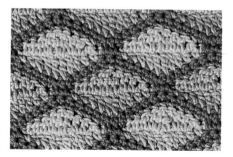

Work as given for Lozenge Mosaic I but working 2 rows in A, 2 rows in B, 2 rows in A and 2 rows in C throughout.
Rep 2nd to 9th rows.

Goblet Pattern

Starting chain: multiple of 4 sts + 2
Drape: good
Skill: experienced

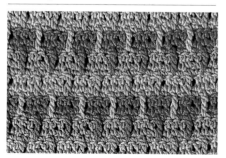

1ST ROW (RS): Using A, work 1sc into 2nd ch from hook, 1sc into next ch, ✳1ch, skip 1ch, 1sc into each of next 3ch; rep from ✳ to end omitting 1sc at end of last rep, turn.
2ND ROW: Using A, 3ch (count as 1dc), skip 1st sc, work 1dc into next sc, ✳1ch, skip 1ch, 1dc into each of next 3sc; rep from ✳ to end omitting 1dc at end of last rep, turn.
3RD ROW: Using B, 1ch, work 1sc into each of 1st 2dc, 1tr into 1st skipped starting ch, ✳1sc into next dc, 1ch, skip 1dc, 1sc into next dc, 1tr into next skipped starting ch; rep from ✳ to last 2dc, 1sc into next dc, 1sc into 3rd of 3ch at beg of previous row, turn.
4TH ROW: Using B, 3ch, skip 1st sc, work

1dc into each of next 3 sts, ✳1ch, skip 1ch, 1dc into each of next 3 sts; rep from ✳ to last sc, 1dc into last sc, turn.
5TH ROW: Using C, 1ch, work 1sc into each of 1st 2dc, ✳1ch, skip 1dc, 1sc into next dc, 1tr into next skipped dc 3 rows below, 1sc into next dc; rep from ✳ to last 3dc, 1ch, skip 1dc, 1sc into next dc, 1sc into 3rd of 3ch at beg of previous row, turn.
6TH ROW: Using C, 3ch, skip 1st sc, 1dc into next sc, ✳1ch, skip 1ch, 1dc into each of next 3 sts; rep from ✳ to end omitting 1dc at end of last rep, turn.
7TH ROW: Using A, 1ch, 1sc into each of 1st 2dc, 1tr into next skipped dc 3 rows below, ✳1sc into next dc, 1ch, skip 1dc, 1sc into next dc, 1tr into next skipped dc 3 rows below; rep from ✳ to last 2dc, 1sc into each of last 2dc, turn.
8TH ROW: As 4th row but using A instead of B.
Rep 5th to 8th rows continuing to work 2 rows each in colors B, C and A as set.

Flying Shell Stitch

Starting chain: multiple of 4 sts + 2
Drape: good
Skill: intermediate
Note: For description of dc2tog see page 187 (Clusters).

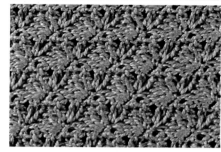

1ST ROW (RS): Work a Flying Shell (called FS) of [1sc, 3ch, 3dc] into 2nd ch from hook, ✳skip 3ch, 1FS into next ch; rep from ✳ to last 4ch, skip 3ch, 1sc into last ch, turn.
2ND ROW: 3ch, 1dc into 1st st, ✳skip 3

sts, 1sc into top of 3ch✳✳, work a V st of [1dc, 1ch, 1dc] into next sc; rep from ✳ ending last rep at ✳✳, 2dc into last sc, skip tch, turn.

3RD ROW: 3ch, 3dc into 1st st, skip next st, ✳1FS into next sc, skip next V st; rep from ✳ ending 1sc into last sc, 3ch, dc2tog over last dc and top of tch, turn.

4TH ROW: 1ch (counts as 1sc), ✳V st into next sc, skip 3 sts, 1sc into top of 3ch; rep from ✳ to end, turn.

5TH ROW: 1ch, FS into 1st st, ✳skip next V st, FS into next sc; rep from ✳ ending skip last V st, 1sc into tch, turn.

Rep 2nd, 3rd, 4th and 5th rows.

Fancy Picot Stitch

Starting chain: multiple of 10 sts + 3
Drape: good
Skill: intermediate

1ST ROW (RS): Skip 3ch (count as 1dc), ✳1dc into each of next 2ch, work a Picot of [3ch, insert hook down through top of last st made and sl st to close], [1ch, skip 1ch, 1dc into next ch, Picot] twice, 1ch, skip 1ch, 1dc into each of next 2ch✳✳, 1ch, skip 1ch; rep from ✳ ending last rep at ✳✳, 1dc into last ch, turn.

2ND ROW: 3ch (count as 1dc), skip 1st st, ✳1dc into each of next 2 sts, [Picot, 1ch, skip next ch and picot, 1dc into next dc] 3 times, 1dc into next dc✳✳, 1ch, skip 1ch; rep from ✳ ending last rep at ✳✳, 1dc into top of tch, turn.

Rep 2nd row.

Crossed Garters I

Starting chain: multiple of 10 sts + 1
Drape: good
Skill: experienced

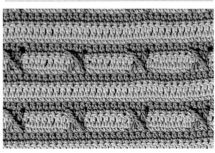

Using A make the required number of chain.

1ST ROW (RS): Using A, work 1sc into 2nd ch from hook, 1sc into each ch to end, turn.

2ND ROW: Using A, 3ch (count as 1dc), skip 1st sc, work 1dc into each sc to end, turn.

3RD ROW: Using B, 1ch, work 1sc into each dc to end placing last sc into 3rd of 3ch at beg of previous row, turn.

4TH ROW: Using B, 1ch, work 1sc into each sc to end, turn.

5TH ROW: Using A, 1ch, work 1sc into each of 1st 3sc, ✳1ch, skip 1sc, 1sc into each of next 2sc, 1ch, skip 1sc, 1sc into each of next 6sc; rep from ✳ to end omitting 3sc at end of last rep, turn.

6TH ROW: Using A, 3ch (count as 1dc), skip first sc, 1dc into each sc and into each ch to end, turn.

On 6th row work dc into ch not ch space. (Rep 2nd to 9th rows.)

7TH ROW: Using B, 1ch, 1sc into each of 1st 3dc, ✳work 1dtr into 2nd skipped sc 3 rows below, skip 1dc, 1sc into each of next 2dc, 1dtr into 1st skipped sc 3 rows below (thus crossing 2dtr), skip 1dc, 1sc into each of next 6dc; rep from ✳ to end omitting 3sc at end of last rep and placing last sc into 3rd of 3ch at beg of previous row, turn.

8TH ROW: Using B, 1ch, work 1sc into each st to end, turn.

9TH ROW: Using A, 1ch, work 1sc into each sc to end, turn. Rep 2nd to 9th rows.

Crossed Garters II

Starting chain: multiple of 4 sts + 3
Drape: good
Skill: experienced

Using A make the required number of chain.

1ST ROW (RS): Using A, work 1sc into 2nd ch from hook, 1sc into each ch to end, turn.

2ND ROW: Using A, 3ch (count as 1dc), skip 1st sc, work 1dc into each sc to end, turn.

3RD ROW: Using B, 1ch, 1sc into each of 1st 4dc, 1ch, skip 1dc, ✳1sc into each of next 3dc, 1ch, skip 1dc; rep from ✳ to last dc, 1sc into 3rd of 3ch at beg of previous row, turn.

4TH ROW: Using B, 3ch, skip 1st sc, work 1dc into each ch and each sc to end, turn. (On 4th and 8th rows, work dc into ch, not ch space.)

5TH ROW: Using A, 1ch, 1sc into 1st dc, ✳1dtr into next skipped dc 3 rows below, skip 1dc on 4th row, 1sc into each of next 3dc; rep from ✳ to last dc, 1sc into 3rd of 3ch at beg of previous row.

6TH ROW: Using A, 3ch, skip 1st sc, work 1dc into each sc and each dtr to end, turn.

7TH ROW: Using B, 1ch, work 1sc into 1st dc, ✳1ch, skip 1dc, 1sc into each of next 3dc; rep from ✳ to last dc, 1sc into 3rd of 3ch, turn. (See 4th row.)

8TH ROW: Using B, 3ch, skip 1st sc, work 1dc into each sc and each ch to end, turn.

9TH ROW: Using A, 1ch, 1sc into each of first 4dc, work 1dtr into 1st skipped dc 3 rows below, skip next dc, ✳1sc into each of next 3dc, 1dtr into next skipped dc 3 rows below, skip next dc; rep from ✳ to

last dc, 1sc into 3rd of 3ch, turn.
10TH ROW: Using A, 3ch, skip 1st sc, work 1dc into each dtr and each sc to end, turn. Rep 3rd to 10th rows.

Crossed Garters III

Starting chain: multiple of 10 sts + 1
Drape: good
Skill: experienced

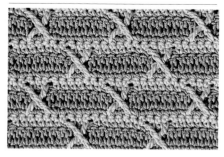

Using A make the required number of chain.
1ST ROW (WS): Using A, work 1sc into 2nd ch from hook, 1sc into each ch to end, turn.
2ND ROW: Using B, 1ch, work 1sc into each of 1st 8sc, ✳1ch, skip 1sc, 1sc into each of next 2sc, 1ch, skip 1sc, 1sc into each of next 6sc; rep from ✳ to last 2sc, 1sc into each sc to end, turn.
3RD ROW: Using B, 3ch (count as 1dc), skip 1st sc, work 1dc into each sc and into each ch to end, turn. On 3rd and 7th rows, work dc into ch, not ch space.
4TH ROW: Using A, 1ch, work 1sc into each of 1st 8dc ✳work 1dtr into 2nd skipped sc 3 rows below, skip 1dc, 1sc into each of next 2dc, 1dtr into 1st skipped sc 3 rows below (thus crossing 2dtr), skip 1dc, 1sc into each of next 6dc; rep from ✳ to last 2dc, 1sc into next dc, 1sc into 3rd of 3ch at beg of previous row, turn.
5TH ROW: Using A, 1ch, work 1sc into each st to end, turn.
6TH ROW: Using B, 1ch, work 1sc into each of 1st 3sc, ✳1ch, skip 1sc, 1sc into each of next 2sc, 1ch, skip 1sc, 1sc into each of next 6sc; rep from ✳ to end omitting 3sc at end of last rep, turn.
7TH ROW: Using B, 3ch, skip 1st sc, 1dc

into each sc and into each ch to end, turn. (See 3rd row.)
8TH ROW: Using A, 1ch, 1sc into each of 1st 3dc, ✳work 1dtr into 2nd skipped sc 3 rows below, skip 1dc, 1sc into each of next 2dc, 1dtr into 1st skipped sc 3 rows below (thus crossing 2dtr), skip 1dc, 1sc into each of next 6dc; rep from ✳ to end omitting 3sc at end of last rep and placing last sc into 3rd of 3ch at beg of previous row, turn.
9TH ROW: Using A, 1ch, work 1sc into each st to end, turn. Rep 2nd to 9th rows.

Dew Drop Pattern

Starting chain: multiple of 4 sts + 6
Drape: good
Skill: intermediate

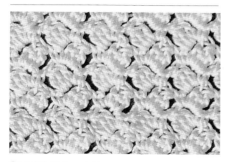

Special Abbreviation

Cluster = work 3dc into next st until 1 loop of each remains on hook, yo and through all 4 loops on hook.
1ST ROW (RS): Work 1 Cluster (see Special Abbreviation) into 5th ch from hook (1dc, 1ch formed at beg of row), 1ch, skip 2ch, 1sc into next ch, ✳3ch, 1 Cluster into next ch, 1ch, skip 2ch, 1sc into next ch; rep from ✳ to last 2ch, 2ch, 1dc into last ch, turn.
2ND ROW: 4ch (count as 1dc, 1ch), 1 Cluster into 1st 2ch sp, 1ch, ✳1sc into next 3ch sp, 3ch, 1 Cluster into same sp as last sc, 1ch; rep from ✳ to last ch sp, 1sc into last ch sp, 2ch, 1dc into 3rd of 4ch at beg of previous row, turn. Rep 2nd row.

Rapids Pattern

Starting chain: multiple of 6 sts + 3
Drape: good
Skill: experienced

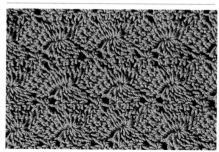

Special Abbreviations

Dc2tog = work 1dc into each of next 2 sts until 1 loop of each remains on hook, yo and through all 3 loops on hook.
Half Cluster = work 1dc into each of next 3 sts until 1 loop of each remains on hook, yo and through all 4 loops on hook.
Cluster = work 1dc into each of next 5 sts until 1 loop of each remains on hook, yo and through all 6 loops on hook.
1ST ROW (RS): Work dc2tog (see Special Abbreviations) working into 4th and 5th ch from hook, ✳3ch, 1sc into next ch, turn, 1ch, 1sc into last sc worked, 3sc into last 3ch sp formed, [turn, 1ch, 1sc into each of the 4sc] 3 times, work 1 Cluster (see Special Abbreviations) over next 5ch; rep from ✳ to end but working Half Cluster (see Special Abbreviations) at end of last rep, turn.
2ND ROW: 4ch (count as 1 tr), work 2tr into top of 1st Half Cluster, skip 3sc, 1sc into next sc, ✳5tr into top of next Cluster, skip 3sc, 1sc into next sc; rep from ✳ to last dc2tog, 3tr into top of 3ch at beg of previous row, turn.
3RD ROW: 3ch (count as 1 dc), skip 1st tr, work dc2tog over next 2tr, ✳3ch, 1sc into next sc, turn, 1ch, 1sc into last sc worked, 3sc into last 3ch sp formed, [turn, 1ch, 1sc into each of the 4sc] 3 times, work 1 Cluster over next 5tr; rep from ✳ to end but working Half Cluster at end of last rep placing last dc of Half Cluster into 4th of 4ch at beg of previous row, turn. Rep 2nd and 3rd rows ending with a 2nd row.

Cobweb Pattern

Starting chain: multiple of 6 sts + 2
Drape: good
Skill: intermediate

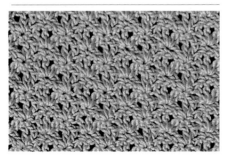

1ST ROW (RS): Work 1sc into 2nd ch from hook, ✳skip 2ch, 1dc into next ch,1ch, into same ch as last dc work [1dc, 1ch, 1dc], skip 2ch, 1sc into next ch; rep from ✳ to end, turn.
2ND ROW: 4ch (count as 1dc, 1ch), 1dc into 1st sc, skip 1dc, 1sc into next dc, ✳1dc into next sc, 1ch, into same st as last dc work [1dc, 1ch, 1dc], skip 1dc, 1sc into next dc; rep from ✳ to last sc, into last sc work [1dc, 1ch, 1 dc], turn.
3RD ROW: 1ch, 1sc into 1st dc, ✳1dc into next sc, 1ch, into same st as last dc work [1dc, 1ch, 1dc], skip 1dc, 1sc into next dc; rep from ✳ to end placing last sc into 3rd of 4ch at beg of previous row, turn.
Rep 2nd and 3rd rows.

Haystack Pattern

Starting chain: multiple of 10 sts + 10
Drape: good
Skill: experienced

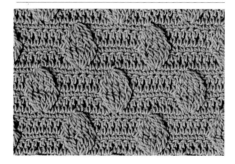

Special Abbreviations

Lower Cluster = work 5tr into next skipped sc 2 rows below.
Upper Cluster = ✳[yo] twice then insert hook from right to left round stem of next tr 2 rows below, work 1tr in usual way until last loop of tr remains on hook; rep from ✳ 4 times more, yo and through all 6 loops.
Note: Count each ch sp as 1 st throughout.
1ST ROW (RS): Work 1sc into 2nd ch from hook, 1sc into each ch to end, turn.
2ND ROW: 3ch (count as 1dc), skip 1st sc, work 1dc into each of next 3sc, ✳1ch, skip 1sc, 1dc into each of next 9 sts; rep from ✳ to end omitting 5dc at end of last rep, turn.
3RD ROW: 1ch, work 1sc into each of 1st 2dc, ✳work Lower Cluster (see Special Abbreviations), skip 5 sts of previous row, 1sc into each of next 5dc; rep from ✳ to end omitting 3sc at end of last rep and placing last sc into 3rd of 3ch at beg of previous row, turn.
4TH ROW: 3ch, skip 1st sc, work 1dc into each st to end, turn.
5TH ROW: 1ch, work 1sc into each of 1st 4dc, ✳work Upper Cluster (see Special Abbreviations) over next 5tr 2 rows below, skip next dc on previous row, 1sc into each of next 9dc; rep from ✳ to end omitting 5sc at end of last rep and placing last sc into 3rd of 3ch at beg of previous row, turn.
6TH ROW: 3ch, skip 1st sc, work 1dc into each of next 8 sts, ✳1ch, skip 1sc, 1dc into each of next 9 sts; rep from ✳ to end.
7TH ROW: 1ch, work 1sc into each of 1st 7dc, ✳work Lower Cluster, skip 5 sts of previous row, 1sc into each of next 5dc; rep from ✳ to last 2dc, 1sc into each of last 2dc, working last sc into 3rd of 3ch at beg of previous row, turn.
8TH ROW: 3ch, skip 1st sc, work 1dc into each st to end, turn.
9TH ROW: 1ch, work 1sc into each of 1st 9dc, ✳work Upper Cluster over next 5tr 2 rows below, skip next dc on previous row, 1sc into each of next 9dc; rep from ✳ to end placing last sc into 3rd of 3ch at beg of previous row, turn. Rep 2nd to 9th rows.

Basket of Fruit

Starting chain: multiple of 20 sts + 25
Drape: good
Skill: experienced

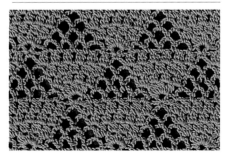

Special Abbreviations

Dc2tog = work 2dc into next st until 1 loop of each remains on hook, yo and through all 3 loops on hook.
Bobble = work 3dc into next st until 1 loop of each remains on hook, yo and through all 4 loops on hook.
1ST ROW (RS): Work 1sc into 7th ch from hook, 5ch, skip 3ch, 1sc into next ch, 1ch, skip 3ch, into next ch work [1 Bobble (see Special Abbreviations), 1ch] 3 times, ✳skip 3ch, 1sc into next ch, [5ch, skip 3ch, 1sc into next ch] 3 times, 1ch, skip 3ch, into next ch work
[1 Bobble, 1ch] 3 times, rep from ✳ to last 10ch, skip 3ch, 1sc into next ch, 5ch, skip 3ch, 1sc into next ch, 2ch, 1dc into last ch, turn.
2ND ROW: 1ch, 1sc into 1st dc, 5ch, 1sc into 1st 5ch arch, 1ch,
[1 Bobble into next ch sp, 1ch] 4 times, ✳1sc into next 5ch arch, [5ch, 1sc into next 5ch arch] twice, 1ch, [1 Bobble into next ch sp, 1ch] 4 times; rep from ✳ to last 2 arches, 1sc into next 5ch arch, 5ch, skip 2ch, 1sc into next ch, turn.
3RD ROW: 5ch (count as 1dc, 2ch), 1sc into 1st 5ch arch, 1ch, [1 Bobble into next ch sp, 1ch] 5 times, ✳1sc into next 5ch arch, 5ch, 1sc into next 5ch arch, 1ch,
[1 Bobble into next ch sp, 1ch] 5 times; rep from ✳ to last arch, 1sc into last arch, 2ch, 1dc into last sc, turn.
4TH ROW: 1ch, 1sc into 1st dc, skip 2ch sp, ✳2ch, [1 Bobble into next ch sp, 2ch]

6 times, 1sc into next 5ch arch; rep from ✳ to end placing last sc into 3rd of 5ch at beg of previous row, turn.

5TH ROW: 5ch (count as 1dc, 2ch), skip 1st 2ch sp, 1sc into next 2ch sp, [5ch, 1sc into next 2ch sp] 4 times,✳1ch, into next sc work [1dc, 1ch] twice, skip next 2ch sp, 1sc into next 2ch sp, [5ch, 1sc into next 2ch sp] 4 times; rep from ✳ to last 2ch sp, 2ch, 1dc into last sc, turn.

6TH ROW: 3ch (count as 1dc), into 1st dc work [1dc, 1ch, 1 Bobble], 1ch, 1sc into next 5ch arch, [5ch, 1sc into next 5ch arch] 3 times, ✳1ch, skip 1ch sp, into next ch sp work [1 Bobble, 1ch] 3 times, 1sc into next 5ch arch, [5ch, 1sc into next 5ch arch] 3 times; rep from ✳ to last sp, 1ch, into 3rd of 5ch at beg of previous row work [1 Bobble, 1ch, dc2tog—see Special Abbreviations], turn.

7TH ROW: 3ch (count as 1dc), [1 Bobble into next ch sp, 1ch] twice, 1sc into 1st 5ch arch, [5ch, 1sc into next 5ch arch] twice, ✳1ch, [1 bobble into next ch sp, 1ch] 4 times, 1sc into next 5ch arch, [5ch, 1sc into next 5ch arch] twice; rep from ✳ to last Bobble, [1ch, 1 Bobble into next ch sp] twice, 1dc into 3rd of 3ch at beg of previous row, turn.

8TH ROW: 3ch, 1dc into 1st dc, 1ch, [1 Bobble into next ch sp, 1ch] twice, 1sc into next 5ch arch, 5ch, 1sc into next 5ch arch, ✳1ch, [1 Bobble into next ch sp, 1ch] 5 times, 1sc into next 5ch arch, 5ch, 1sc into next 5ch arch; rep from ✳ to last 2 bobbles, 1ch, [1 Bobble into next ch sp, 1ch] twice, dc2tog into 3rd of 3ch at beg of previous row, turn.

9TH ROW: 4ch (count as 1dc, 1ch), [1 Bobble into next ch sp, 2ch] 3 times, 1sc into next 5ch arch, ✳2ch, [1 Bobble into next ch sp, 2ch] 6 times, 1sc into next 5ch arch; rep from ✳ to last 2 Bobbles, [2ch, 1 Bobble into next ch sp] 3 times, 1ch, 1dc into 3rd of 3ch at beg of previous row, turn.

10TH ROW: 1ch, 1sc into 1st dc, 5ch, skip 1st ch sp, 1sc into next 2ch sp, 5ch, 1sc into next 2ch sp, 1ch, into next sc work [1dc, 1ch] twice, ✳skip next 2ch sp, 1sc into next 2ch sp, [5ch, 1sc into next 2ch sp] 4 times, 1ch, into next sc work [1dc, 1ch] twice; rep from ✳ to last 3 Bobbles, skip next 2ch sp, [1sc into next 2ch sp, 5ch] twice, 1sc into 3rd of 4ch at beg of previous row, turn.

11TH ROW: 5ch (count as 1dc, 2ch), 1sc into 1st 5ch arch, 5ch, 1sc into next 5ch arch, 1ch, skip 1ch sp, into next ch sp work [1 Bobble, 1ch] 3 times, ✳1sc into next 5ch arch, [5ch, 1sc into next 5ch arch] 3 times, 1ch, skip 1ch sp, into next ch sp work [1 Bobble, 1ch] 3 times; rep from ✳ to last 2 arches, 1sc into next 5ch arch, 5ch, 1sc into next 5ch arch, 2ch, 1dc into last sc, turn. Rep 2nd to 11th rows.

═══════════════════

Ostrich Feather Fan
Starting chain: multiple of 30 sts + 32
Drape: good
Skill: experienced

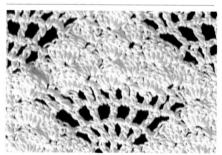

1ST ROW (RS): Work 1sc into 2nd ch from hook, [skip 2ch, 5dc into next ch, skip 2ch, 1sc into next ch] twice, skip 2ch, 1dc into next ch, 1ch, into same ch as last dc work [1dc, 1ch, 1dc], ✳skip 2ch, 1sc into next ch, [skip 2ch, 5dc into next ch, skip 2ch, 1sc into next ch] 4 times, skip 2ch, 1dc into next ch, 1ch, into same ch as last dc work [1dc, 1ch, 1dc]; rep from ✳ to last 15ch, skip 2ch, 1sc into next ch, [skip 2ch, 5dc into next ch, skip 2ch, 1sc into next ch] twice, turn.

2ND ROW: 3ch (count as 1dc), 2dc into 1st sc, skip 2dc, 1sc into next dc, 5dc into next sc, skip 2dc, 1sc into next dc, 1ch, skip 2dc, 1dc into next dc, 1ch, [1dc into

next ch sp, 1ch, 1dc into next dc, 1ch] twice, ✳ skip 2dc, 1sc into next dc, [5dc into next sc, skip 2dc, 1sc into next dc] 3 times, 1ch, skip 2dc, 1dc into next dc, 1ch, [1dc into next ch sp, 1ch, 1dc into next dc, 1ch] twice; rep from ✳ to last 2 groups of 5dc, skip 2dc, 1sc into next dc, 5dc into next sc, skip 2dc, 1sc into next dc, 3dc into last sc, turn.

3RD ROW: 1ch, 1sc into 1st dc, 5dc into 1st sc, skip 2dc, 1sc into next dc, 2ch, skip 2dc, [1dc into next dc, 2ch] 5 times, ✳skip 2dc, 1sc into next dc, [5dc into next sc, skip 2dc, 1sc into next dc] twice, 2ch, skip 2dc, [1dc into next dc, 2ch] 5 times; rep from ✳ to last group of 5dc, skip 2dc, 1sc into next dc, 5dc into next sc, 1sc into 3rd of 3ch at beg of previous row, turn.

4TH ROW: 3ch (count as 1dc), 2dc into 1st sc, skip 2dc, 1sc into next dc, 1ch, 1dc into next 2ch sp, [1ch, 1dc into next dc, 1ch, 1dc into next 2ch sp] 5 times, ✳1ch, skip 2dc, 1sc into next dc, 5dc into next sc, skip 2dc, 1sc into next dc, 1ch, 1dc into next 2ch sp, [1ch, 1dc into next dc, 1ch, 1dc into next 2ch sp] 5 times; rep from ✳ to last group of 5dc, 1ch, skip 2dc, 1sc into next dc, 3dc into last sc, turn.

5TH ROW: 1ch, 1sc into 1st dc, ✳5dc into next sc, skip 1ch sp, 1 sc into next ch sp, [skip 1ch sp, 5dc into next dc, skip 1ch sp, 1sc into next ch sp] 3 times, 5dc into next sc, 1sc into center dc of next group of 5; rep from ✳ to end placing last sc into 3rd of 3ch at beg of previous row, turn.

6TH ROW: 4ch (count as 1dc, 1ch), 1dc into 1st sc, 1sc into center dc of 1st group of 5, [5dc into next sc, 1sc into center dc of next group of 5] 4 times, ✳1dc into next sc, 1ch, into same st as last dc work [1dc, 1ch, 1dc], 1sc into center dc of next group of 5, [5dc into next sc, 1sc into center dc of next group of 5] 4 times; rep from ✳ to last sc, 1dc into last sc work [1dc, 1ch, 1dc], turn.

7TH ROW: 4ch (count as 1dc, 1ch), 1dc into 1st ch sp, 1ch, 1dc into next dc, 1ch, 1sc into center dc of 1st group of 5, [5dc into next sc, 1sc into center dc of next group of 5] 3 times, ✳1ch, skip 2dc, 1dc into next dc, 1ch, [1dc into next ch sp, 1ch, 1dc into next dc, 1ch] twice, 1sc into center dc

of next group of 5, [5dc into next sc, 1sc into center dc of next group of 5] 3 times; rep from ✳ to last 4dc, 1ch, skip 2dc, 1dc into next dc, 1ch, 1dc into last ch sp, 1ch, 1dc into 3rd of 4ch at beg of previous row, turn.
8TH ROW: 5ch (count as 1dc, 2ch), skip 1st dc, [1dc into next dc, 2ch] twice, 1sc into center dc of group of 5, [5dc into next sc, 1sc into center dc of next group of 5] twice, ✳2ch, skip 2dc, [1dc into next dc, 2ch] 5 times, 1sc into center dc of next group of 5, [5dc into next sc, 1sc into center dc of next group of 5] twice; rep from ✳ to last 5dc, 2ch, skip 2dc, [1dc into next dc, 2ch] twice, 1dc into 3rd of 4ch at beg of previous row, turn.
9TH ROW: 4ch (count as 1dc, 1ch), 1dc into 1st 2ch sp, 1ch, [1dc into next dc, 1ch, 1dc into next 2ch sp, 1ch] twice, 1sc into center dc of 1st group of 5, 5dc into next sc, 1sc into center dc of next group of 5, ✳1ch, 1dc into next 2ch sp, 1ch, [1dc into next dc, 1ch, 1dc into next 2ch sp, 1ch] 5 times, 1sc into center dc of next group of 5, 5dc into next sc, 1 sc into center dc of next group of 5; rep from ✳ to last 5dc, 1ch, 1dc into next 2ch sp, 1ch, [1dc into next dc, 1ch, 1dc into next 2ch sp, 1ch] twice, 1dc into 3rd of 5ch at beg of previous row, turn.
10TH ROW: 3ch (count as 1dc), 2dc into 1st dc, skip 1ch sp, 1sc into next ch sp, skip 1ch sp, 5dc into next dc, skip 1ch sp, 1sc into next ch sp, 5dc into next sc, 1sc into center dc of next group of 5, 5dc into next sc, ✳skip 1ch sp, 1sc into next ch sp, [skip 1ch sp, 5dc into next dc, skip 1ch sp, 1sc into next ch sp] 3 times, 5dc into next sc, 1sc into center dc of next group of 5, 5dc into next sc; rep from ✳ to last 6dc, skip 1ch sp, 1sc into next ch sp, skip 1ch sp, 5dc into next dc, skip 1ch sp, 1sc into next ch sp, 3dc into 3rd of 4ch at beg of previous row, turn.
11TH ROW: 1ch, 1sc into 1st dc, [5dc into next sc, 1sc into center dc of next group of 5] twice, 1dc into next sc, 1ch, into same st as last dc work [1dc, 1ch, 1dc], ✳1sc into center dc of next group of 5, [5dc into next sc, 1sc into center dc of next group of 5] 1ch, into same st as last dc

work [1dc, 1ch, 1dc]; rep from ✳ to last 2 groups of 5dc, [1sc into center dc of next group of 5, 5dc into next sc] twice, 1sc into 3rd of 3ch at beg of previous row, turn. Rep 2nd to 11th rows.

Sidesaddle Shell Stitch
Multiple of 6 sts + 1 (add 3 for base chain)
Drape: excellent
Skill: intermediate

Special Abbreviation
Shell = 3dc, 1ch, [1sc, 1hdc, 1dc] all into side of last of 3dc just made.
1ST ROW (WS): Skip 3ch (count as 1dc), 3dc into next ch, skip 2ch, 1sc into next ch, ✳skip 2ch, Shell (see Special Abbreviation) into next ch, skip 2ch, 1sc into next ch; rep from ✳ to last 3ch, skip 2ch, 4dc into last ch, turn.
2ND ROW: 1ch (counts as 1sc), skip 1 st, ✳skip next 3 sts, Shell into next sc, skip 3 sts, 1sc into next ch sp; rep from ✳ ending last rep with 1sc into top of tch, turn.
3RD ROW: 3ch (count as 1dc), 3dc into first st, skip 3 sts, 1sc into next ch sp, ✳skip 3 sts, Shell into next sc, skip 3 sts, 1sc into next ch sp; rep from ✳ ending skip 3 sts, 4dc into tch, turn. Rep 2nd and 3rd rows.

Crossbill Stitch
Multiple of 4 sts + 1 (add 2 for base chain)
Drape: excellent
Skill: intermediate

Special Abbreviation
2Cdc (2 crossed double crochets) = skip 2sts, 1dc into next st, 1ch, 1dc into first of 2sts just skipped working back over last dc made. (See also page 11, Crossed Stitch I)
1ST ROW: Skip 3ch (count as 1dc), ✳ work 2Cdc (see Special Abbreviation) over next 3ch, 1dc into next ch; rep from ✳ to end,turn.
2ND ROW: 3ch (count as 1dc), 1dc into first st, skip 1dc, ✳ 1dc into next ch, work 2Cdc over next 3dc, rep from ✳ ending 1dc into last ch, skip 1dc, 2dc into top of tch, turn.
3RD ROW: 3ch (count as 1dc), skip 1 st, ✳ work 2Cdc over next 3dc, 1dc into next ch; rep from ✳ ending last rep into top of tch, turn. Rep 2nd and 3rd rows.

Crunch Stitch
Multiple of 2 sts (add 1 for base chain)
Drape: good
Skill: intermediate

1ST ROW: Skip 2ch (count as 1hdc), ✳ sl st into next ch, 1hdc into next ch; rep from ✳ ending sl st into last ch, turn.
2ND ROW: 2ch (count as 1hdc), skip 1 st, ✳ sl st into next hdc, 1hdc into next sl st; rep from ✳ ending sl st into top of tch, turn. Rep 2nd row.

heavyweight patterns

Many crochet fabrics are ideally suited to warm garments, such as jackets and coats, and to home accessories such as afghans and pillow covers. A great variety of chunky textures can be achieved through the use of raised stitches, bobbles, and other stitch techniques. Tunisian crochet is a special technique which lends itself especially well to producing heavier fabrics.

assorted patterns

The patterns in this section exploit various crochet effects, such as clusters and shells (*page 187*), to create richly tactile surfaces. The "earthy" quality of some of the fabrics is reflected in their names: Sedge Stitch (*below*), Silt Stitch (*page 226*), and Wattle Stitch (*page 227*), for example. Some use the technique of raised stitches, including Post Stitch (*page 188*), which is employed to striking effect in Basketweave Stitch (*page 231*) and Zigzag Rib (*page 230*).

heavyweight patterns

Solid Shell Stitch
Starting chain: multiple of 6 sts + 2
Drape: fair
Skill: intermediate

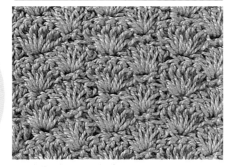

1ST ROW: 1sc into 2nd ch from hook, ✳skip 2ch, 5dc into next ch, skip 2ch, 1sc into next ch; rep from ✳ to end, turn.
2ND ROW: 3ch (count as 1dc), 2dc into 1st st, ✳skip 2dc, 1sc into next dc, skip 2dc, 5dc into next sc; rep from ✳ ending last rep with 3dc into last sc, skip tch, turn.
3RD ROW: 1ch, 1sc into 1st st, ✳skip 2dc, 5dc into next sc, skip 2dc, 1sc into next dc; rep from ✳ ending last rep with 1sc into top of tch, turn.
Rep 2nd and 3rd rows.

Sedge Stitch I
Starting chain: multiple of 3 sts + 3
Drape: good
Skill: easy

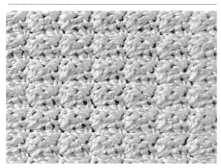

1ST ROW: Skip 2ch (count as 1sc), work [1hdc] 1dc] into next ch, ✳skip 2ch, work [1sc, 1hdc] 1dc] into next ch; rep from ✳ to last 3ch, skip 2ch, 1sc into last ch, turn.
2ND ROW: 1ch (counts as 1sc), work [1hdc] 1dc] into first st, ✳skip [1dc and 1hdc], work [1sc, 1hdc] 1dc] into next sc; rep from ✳ to last 3 sts, skip [1dc and 1hdc], 1sc into top of tch, turn.
Rep 2nd row.

Sedge Stitch II
Multiple of 3 sts + 3
Drape: good
Skill: easy

1ST ROW: Skip 2ch (count as 1sc), 2dc into next ch, ✳skip 2ch, [1sc, 2dc] into next ch; rep from ✳ to last 3ch, skip 2ch, 1sc into last ch, turn.
2ND ROW: 1ch (counts as 1 sc), 2dc into 1st st, ✳skip 2dc [1sc, 2dc] into next sc; rep from ✳ to last 3 sts, skip 2dc, 1sc into top of tch, turn.
Rep 2nd row.

Trinity Stitch I

Starting chain: multiple of 2 sts + 2
Drape: good
Skill: intermediate
Note: For description of sc3tog see page 187 (Clusters).

1ST ROW: 1sc into 2nd ch from hook, sc3tog inserting hook first into same ch as previous sc, then into each of next 2ch, ✳1ch, sc3tog inserting hook first into same ch as 3rd leg of previous cluster, then into each of next 2ch; rep from ✳ to last ch, 1sc into same ch as 3rd leg of previous cluster, turn.
2ND ROW: 1ch, 1sc into 1st st, sc3tog inserting hook first into same place as previous sc, then into top of next cluster, then into next ch sp, ✳1ch, sc3tog inserting hook first into same ch sp as 3rd leg of previous cluster, then into top of next cluster, then into next ch sp; rep from ✳ to end working 3rd leg of last cluster into last sc, 1sc into same place, skip tch, turn.
Rep 2nd row.

Trinity Stitch II

Starting chain: multiple of 2 sts + 2
Drape: good
Skill: intermediate

Worked as Trinity Stitch I.
Work 1 row each in colors A, B and C throughout.
HINT: Normally, the maximum number of stitches that may be worked together into a single crochet cluster is 3. (Longer stitches may have more.) Remember that working stitches together into clusters is often the best way to decrease.

Single Crochet Cluster Stitch I

Starting chain: multiple of 2 sts + 2
Drape: good
Skill: intermediate
Note: For description of sc2tog see page 187 (Clusters).

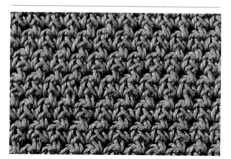

1ST ROW (WS): 1sc into 2nd ch from hook, ✳1ch, skip 1ch, 1sc into next ch; rep from ✳ to end, turn.
2ND ROW: 1ch, 1sc into 1st st, 1ch, sc2tog inserting hook into each of next 2 ch sps, 1 ch, ✳sc2tog inserting hook first into same ch sp as previous st, then into next ch sp, 1ch; rep from ✳ ending 1sc into last st, skip tch, turn.
3RD ROW: 1ch, 1sc into 1st st, ✳1ch, skip 1ch, 1sc into next st; rep from ✳ to end, skip tch, turn.
Rep 2nd and 3rd rows.

Single Crochet Cluster Stitch II

Starting chain: multiple of 2 sts + 2
Drape: good
Skill: intermediate
Note: For description of sc2tog see page 187 (Clusters).

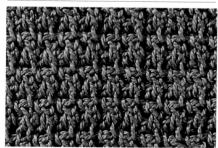

1ST ROW: Skip 1ch, ✳sc2tog inserting hook into each of next 2ch, 1ch; rep from ✳ ending 1sc into last ch, turn.
2ND ROW: 1ch, sc2tog inserting hook into 1st st then into next ch sp, 1ch, ✳sc2tog inserting hook first before and then after the vertical thread between the next 2 clusters, 1ch; rep from ✳ ending 1sc into last sc, skip tch, turn.
Rep 2nd row.

Single Crochet Cluster Stitch III

Starting chain: multiple of 2 sts + 1
Drape: good
Skill: intermediate
Note: For description of sc2tog see page 187 (Clusters).

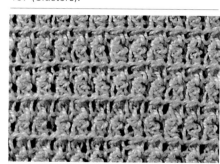

225

1ST ROW: Skip 2ch (count as 1hdc), ✳sc2tog inserting hook into each of next 2ch, 1ch; rep from ✳ ending with 1hdc into last ch, turn.

2ND ROW: 2ch (count as 1hdc), skip 1 st, ✳sc2tog inserting hook into back loop only of next ch then into back loop only of next st, 1ch; rep from ✳ ending with 1hdc into top of tch, turn. Rep 2nd row.

Single Crochet Cluster Stitch IV

Starting chain: multiple of 2 sts + 2
Drape: good
Skill: intermediate

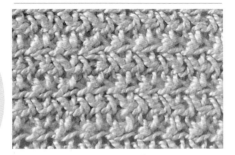

Special Abbreviation

SC (Slip Cluster) = insert hook into ch or st as indicated, yo, draw loop through, insert hook again as indicated, yo, draw loop through st and through next loop on hook, yo, draw through last 2 loops on hook.

1ST ROW: 1SC (see Special Abbreviation) inserting hook into 2nd and then 3rd ch from hook, 1ch; ✳1SC inserting hook into each of next 2ch, 1ch; rep from ✳ ending 1sc into last ch, turn.

2ND ROW: 1ch (counts as 1sc), skip 1 st, ✳1SC inserting hook into front loop only of next ch then front loop only of next st, 1ch; rep from ✳ ending 1sc into top of tch, turn. Rep 2nd row.

Crunch Stitch

Starting chain: multiple of 2 sts + 1
Drape: good
Skill: easy

1ST ROW: Skip 2ch (count as 1hdc), ✳sl st into next ch, 1hdc into next ch; rep from ✳ ending sl st into last ch, turn.

2ND ROW: 2ch (count as 1hdc), skip 1 st, ✳sl st into next hdc) 1hdc into next sl st; rep from ✳ ending sl st into top of tch, turn. Rep 2nd row.

Silt Stitch

Starting chain: multiple of 3 sts + 3
Drape: good
Skill: easy

1ST ROW (RS): Skip 3ch (count as 1dc), 1dc into next and each ch to end, turn.

2ND ROW: 1ch (counts as 1sc), 2dc into 1st st, ✳skip 2 sts, work [1sc, 2dc] into next st; rep from ✳ to last 3 sts, skip 2 sts, 1sc into top of tch, turn.

3RD ROW: 3ch (count as 1dc), skip 1 st, 1dc into next and each st to end, working last st into top of tch, turn.
Rep 2nd and 3rd rows.

Griddle Stitch

Starting chain: multiple of 2 sts + 2
Drape: good
Skill: easy

1ST ROW: Skip 3ch (count as 1dc), ✳1sc into next ch, 1dc into next ch; rep from ✳ ending sc into last ch, turn.

2ND ROW: 3ch (count as 1dc), skip 1 st, ✳1sc into next dc) 1dc into next sc; rep from ✳ ending 1sc into top of tch, turn. Rep 2nd row.

Crumpled Griddle Stitch

Starting chain: multiple of 2 sts + 3
Drape: good
Skill: easy

1ST ROW: Skip 3ch (count as 1dc), ✳1sc into next ch, 1dc into next ch; rep from ✳ to end, turn.

2ND ROW: 3ch (count as 1dc), skip 1 st, ✳1sc into next sc, 1dc into next dc; rep from ✳ ending last rep into top of tch, turn. Rep 2nd row.

Grit Stitch I
Starting chain: multiple of 2 sts + 3
Drape: good
Skill: easy

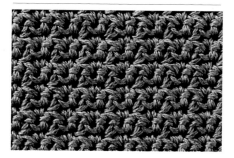

1ST ROW: Skip 2ch (count as 1sc), 1sc into next ch, ✻skip 1ch, 2sc into next ch; rep from ✻ to last 2ch, skip 1ch, 1sc into last ch, turn.
2ND ROW: 1ch (counts as 1sc), 1sc into 1st st, ✻skip 1sc, 2sc into next sc; rep from ✻ to last 2 sts, skip 1sc, 1sc into top of tch, turn.
Rep 2nd row.

Grit Stitch II
Starting chain: multiple of 2 sts + 3
Drape: good
Skill: easy

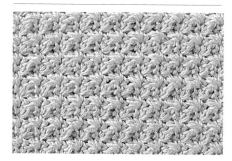

1ST ROW: Skip 2ch (count as 1sc), 1dc into next ch, ✻skip 1ch, work [1sc and 1dc] into next ch; rep from ✻ to last 2ch, skip 1ch, 1sc into last ch, turn.
2ND ROW: 1ch (counts as 1sc), 1dc into 1st st, ✻skip 1dc) work [1sc and 1dc] into next sc; rep from ✻ to last 2 sts, skip 1dc) 1sc

into top of tch, turn.
Rep 2nd row.

Wattle Stitch
Starting chain: multiple of 3 sts + 3
Drape: good
Skill: easy

1ST ROW: Skip 2ch (count as 1sc), ✻work [1sc, 1ch, 1dc] into next ch, skip 2ch; rep from ✻ ending 1sc into last ch, turn.
2ND ROW: 1ch (counts as 1sc), skip 1st sc and next dc) ✻work [1sc, 1ch, 1dc] into next ch sp, skip 1sc and 1dc; rep from ✻ ending with [1sc, 1ch, 1dc] into last ch sp, skip next sc, 1sc into top of tch, turn.
Rep 2nd row.

Crunchy Chevron Stitch
Starting chain: multiple of 8 sts + 1
Drape: good
Skill: intermediate
Note: For description of hdc2tog see page 191 (Puff Stitch with 1 step repeated once).

Work 1 row each in colors A, B, C, D and E throughout.
1ST ROW: 1sc into 2nd ch from hook, 1sc into each of next 3ch, ✻hdc2tog all into each of next 4ch, 1sc into each of next 4ch; rep from ✻ to last 4ch, hdc2tog all into each of last 4ch, turn.
2ND ROW: 1ch, then starting in 1st st, ✻1sc into each of next 4 sts, hdc2tog all into each of next 4sc, rep from ✻ to end, skip tch, turn. Rep 2nd row.

Textured Wave Stitch
Starting chain: multiple of 20 sts + 1
Drape: good
Skill: intermediate

Special Abbreviation
2Cdc (2 Crossed Doubles) = skip next st, 1dc into next st, 1dc into skipped st working over previous dc. See also page 189 (Crossed Stitch).
Work 2 rows each in colors A and B alternately throughout.
1ST BASE ROW (RS): Skip 2ch (count as 1sc), 1sc into next and each ch to end, turn.
2ND BASE ROW: 1ch (counts as 1sc), skip 1 st, 1sc into next and each st to end working last st into tch, turn.
Commence Pattern
1ST ROW: 3ch (count as 1dc), skip 1 st, over next 4 sts work [2Cdc] twice, ✻1sc into each of next 10 sts, over next 10 sts work [2Cdc— see Special Abbreviation] 5 times; rep from ✻ to last 15 sts, 1sc into each of next 10 sts, over next 4 sts work [2Cdc] twice, 1dc into tch, turn.
2ND ROW: As 1st row.

3RD AND 4TH ROWS: As 2nd base row.

5TH ROW: 1ch (counts as 1sc), skip 1 st, 1sc into each of next 4 sts, ✳over next 10 sts work [2Cdc] 5 times, 1sc into each of next 10 sts; rep from ✳ to last 15 sts, over next 10 sts work [2Cdc] 5 times, 1sc into each of last 5 sts working last st into tch, turn.

6TH ROW: As 5th row.

7TH AND 8TH ROWS: As 2nd base row.
Rep these 8 rows.

Woven Shell Stitch

Starting chain: multiple of 6 sts + 3
Drape: fair
Skill: intermediate

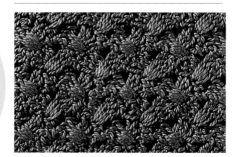

Special Abbreviation

CGr (Crossed Group) = skip 3dc and next st, 3dc into 2nd of next 3dc) 3ch, 3dc into 2nd of 3dc just skipped working back over last 3dc made.

1ST ROW: Skip 3ch (count as 1dc), ✳skip next 3ch, 3dc into next ch, 3ch, 3dc into 2nd of 3ch just skipped working back over last 3dc made, skip 1ch, 1dc into next ch; rep from ✳ to end, turn.

2ND ROW: 3ch (count as 1dc), 3dc into 1st st, 1sc into next 3ch arch, ✳1CGr (see Special Abbreviation), 1sc into next 3ch arch; rep from ✳ ending 4dc into top of tch, turn.

3RD ROW: 3ch (count as 1dc), skip 1 st, 1CGr, ✳1sc into next 3ch loop, 1CGr; rep from ✳ ending 1dc into top of tch, turn.
Rep 2nd and 3rd rows.

Sidesaddle Cluster Stitch

Starting chain: multiple of 5 sts + 2
Drape: fair
Skill: intermediate
Note: For description of dc4tog see page 187 (Clusters).

1ST ROW: 1sc into 2nd ch from hook, ✳3ch, dc4tog over next 4ch, 1ch, 1sc into next ch; rep from ✳ to end, turn.

2ND ROW: 5ch, 1sc into next CL, ✳3ch, dc4tog all into next 3ch arch, 1ch, 1sc into next CL; rep from ✳ ending 3ch, dc4tog all into next 3ch arch, 1dc into last sc, skip tch, turn.

3RD ROW: 1ch, skip 1 st, 1sc into next CL, ✳3ch, 1CL into next 3ch arch, 1ch, 1de into next CL; rep from ✳ ending last rep with 1sc into tch arch, turn.
Rep 2nd and 3rd rows.

Diagonal Shell Stitch

Starting chain: multiple of 4 sts + 2
Drape: good
Skill: intermediate
Note: For description of dc2tog see page 187 (Clusters).

Special Abbreviation

Shell = [1sc, 3ch, 4dc] all into same st.

1ST ROW (RS): Work 1 Shell (see Special Abbreviation) into 2nd ch from hook, ✳skip 3ch, 1 Shell into next ch; rep from ✳ to last 4ch, skip 3ch, 1sc into last ch, turn.

2ND ROW: 3ch (count as 1dc), skip 1 st, ✳skip 1dc) over next 2 sts work dc2tog, 3ch, skip 1dc) 1sc into top of 3ch; rep

from ✳ to end, turn.

3RD ROW: 1ch, 1 Shell into 1st st, ✳skip 3ch and next st, 1 Shell into next sc; rep from ✳ ending skip 3ch and next st, 1sc into top of tch, turn.
Rep 2nd and 3rd rows.

Sidesaddle Shell Stitch

Starting chain: multiple of 6 sts + 4
Drape: good
Skill: intermediate

Special Abbreviation

Shell = 3dc) 1ch, [1sc, 1hdc] 1dc] all into side of last of 3dc just made.

1ST ROW (WS): Skip 3ch (count as 1dc), 3dc into next ch, skip 2ch, 1sc into next ch, ✳skip 2ch, Shell (see Special Abbreviation) into next ch, skip 2ch, 1sc into next ch; rep from ✳ to last 3ch, skip 2ch, 4dc into last ch, turn.

2ND ROW: 1ch (counts as 1sc), skip 1 st, ✳skip next 3 sts, Shell into next sc, skip 3 sts, 1sc into next ch sp; rep from ✳ ending last rep with 1sc into top of tch, turn.

3RD ROW: 3ch (count as 1dc), 3dc into first

st, skip 3 sts, 1sc into next ch sp, ✳skip 3 sts, Shell into next sc, skip 3 sts, 1sc into next ch sp; rep from ✳ ending skip 3 sts, 4dc into tch, turn.
Rep 2nd and 3rd rows.

Gothic Arches I

Starting chain: multiple of 4 sts + 4
Drape: fair
Skill: experienced

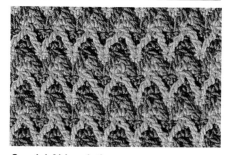

Special Abbreviation

Tr2tog 3 rows below = work 1tr into same st as last tr until last loop of tr remains on hook, skip 3 sts, work 1 tr into next skipped st 3 rows below until last loop of tr remains on hook, yo and through all 3 loops.
Work dc into actual stitch of ch on wrong side rows, not into ch sp.
Note: Sts either side of tr2tog must be worked behind tr2tog.
Using A make required number of chain.
1ST ROW (RS): Using A, work 1sc into 2nd ch from hook, 1sc into each of next 2ch, ✳1ch, skip 1ch, 1sc into each of next 3ch; rep from ✳ to end, turn.
2ND ROW: Using A, 3ch (count as 1dc), skip 1st sc, work 1dc into each st to end (working into actual st of each ch, not into ch sp), turn.
3RD ROW: Using B, 1ch, 1sc into 1st dc) 1tr into 1st skipped starting ch, skip 1dc on 2nd row, 1sc into next dc) 1ch, skip 1dc) 1sc into next dc) ✳tr2tog 3 rows below (see Special Abbreviation) (into skipped starting ch), skip 1dc on 2nd row, 1sc into next dc) 1ch, skip 1dc) 1sc into next dc; rep from ✳ to last 2dc) 1tr into same ch as

2nd leg of last tr2tog, skip 1dc) 1sc into 3rd of 3ch at beg of previous row, turn.
4TH ROW: Using B, 3ch, skip 1st sc, work 1dc into each st to end, turn.
5TH ROW: Using A, 1ch, 1sc into 1st dc) 1tr into next skipped dc 3 rows below, skip 1dc on previous row, 1sc into next dc) 1ch, skip 1dc) 1sc into next dc) ✳tr2tog 3 rows below, skip 1dc on previous row, 1sc into next dc) 1ch, skip 1dc) 1sc into next dc; rep from ✳ to last 2dc) 1tr into same dc as 2nd leg of last tr2tog, skip 1dc) 1sc into 3rd of 3ch at beg of previous row, turn.
6TH ROW: As 4th row but using A instead of B.
7TH ROW: As 5th row but using B instead of A.
Rep 4th to 7th rows.

Gothic Arches II

Starting chain: multiple of 4 sts + 4
Drape: fair
Skill: experienced

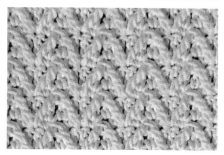

Work as given for Gothic Arches I, but using one color throughout.

Granule Stitch

Starting chain: multiple of 4 sts + 2
Drape: fair
Skill: intermediate

Special Abbreviation

Psc (Picot single crochet) = insert hook, yo, draw loop through, [yo, draw through 1 loop] 3 times to make 3ch, yo, draw through both loops on hook.
Note: draw picot chain loops to the back

(right side) of fabric.
1ST ROW (RS): 1sc into 2nd ch from hook, 1sc into each ch to end, turn.
2ND ROW: 1ch, 1sc into 1st st, ✳1Psc (see Special Abbreviation) into next st, 1sc into next st; rep from ✳ to end, skip tch, turn.
3RD ROW: 1ch, 1sc into 1st and each st to end, skip tch, turn.
Hint: hold down the picot chains at the front and you will see the top 2 loops of the Psc where you are to insert the hook.
4TH ROW: 1ch, 1sc into each of first 2 sts, ✳1Psc into next st, 1sc into next st; rep from ✳ to last st, 1sc into last st, skip tch, turn.
5TH ROW: As 3rd row.
Rep 2nd, 3rd, 4th and 5th rows.

Relief Arch Stitch

Starting chain: multiple of 8 sts + 2
Drape: good
Skill: intermediate

1ST ROW (WS): 1sc into 2nd ch from hook, 1sc into each of next 2ch, ✳7ch, skip 3ch, 1sc into each of next 5ch; rep from ✳ to last 6ch, 7ch, skip 3ch, 1sc into each of last 3ch, turn.

2ND ROW: 3ch (count as 1dc), skip 1 st, 1dc into each of next 2 sts, ✳going behind 7ch loop work 1tr into each of next 3 base ch✳✳, 1dc into each of next 5sc; rep from ✳ ending last rep at ✳✳ when 3 sts remain, 1dc into each of last 3 sts, skip tch, turn.

3RD ROW: 1ch, 1sc into 1st st, ✳7ch, skip 3 sts, 1sc into next st at same time catching in center of 7ch loop of last-but-one row, 7ch, skip 3 sts, 1sc into next st; rep from ✳ to end, turn.

4TH ROW: 3ch (count as 1dc), skip 1 st, ✳going behind 7ch loop of last row work 1 tr into each of next 3 sts of last-but-one row, 1dc into next sc; rep from ✳ to end, skip tch, turn.

5TH ROW: 1ch, 1sc into each of 1st 2 sts, ✳1sc into next st at same time catching in center of 7ch loop of last-but-one row, 7ch, skip 3 sts, 1sc into next st at same time catching in center of 7ch loop of last-but-one row✳✳, 1sc into each of next 3 sts; rep from ✳ ending last rep at ✳✳ when 2 sts remain, 1sc into each of last 2 sts, turn.

6TH ROW: As 2nd row working trs into last-but-one row.

Rep 3rd, 4th, 5th and 6th rows.

Single Rib

Starting chain: multiple of 2 sts + 2
Drape: good
Skill: easy
Note: For description of dc/rf and dc/rb see page 188 (Raised Stitches).

1ST ROW (WS): Skip 3ch (count as 1dc), 1dc into next and each ch to end, turn.

2ND ROW: 2ch (count as 1dc), skip 1st st, ✳1dc/rf round next st, 1dc/rb round next st; rep from ✳ ending 1dc into top of tch, turn. Rep 2nd row.

Raised Rib

Starting chain: multiple of 3 sts + 3
Drape: good
Skill: intermediate

Special Abbreviation

1dc/rf = work 1dc around stem of next st 2 rows below inserting hook round stem from right to left to draw up loops.

1ST ROW (RS): Work 1sc into 2nd ch from hook, 1sc into each ch to end, turn.

2ND ROW: 1ch, work 1sc into each sc to end, turn.

3RD ROW: 1ch, work 1sc into each of 1st 2sc, ✳1dc/rf (see Special Abbreviation) round next sc 2 row below, 1sc into each of next 2sc; rep from ✳ to end, turn.

4TH ROW: 1ch, work 1sc into each st to end, turn.

5TH ROW: 1ch, work 1sc into each of 1st 2sc, ✳1dc/rf round stem of next dc/rf 2 rows below, 1sc into each of next 2sc; rep from ✳ to end, turn.

Rep 4th and 5th rows.

Zigzag Rib

Starting chain: multiple of 4 sts + 4
Drape: fair
Skill: intermediate

Note: For description of dc/rf and dc/rb see page 188 (Raised Stitches).

BASE ROW (WS): Skip 3ch (count as 1dc), 1dc into next and each ch to end, turn.

Commence Pattern

1ST ROW: 2ch (count as 1dc), skip 1st st, ✳1dc/rf round each of next 2 sts, 1dc/rb round each of next 2 sts; rep from ✳ ending 1dc into top of tch, turn.

2ND ROW: 2ch (count as 1dc), skip 1st st, 1dc/rb round next st, ✳1dc/rf round each of next 2 sts✳✳, 1dc/rb round each of next 2 sts; rep from ✳ ending last rep at ✳✳ when 2 sts remain, 1dc/rb round next st, 1dc into top of tch, turn.

3RD ROW: 2ch (count as 1dc), skip 1st st, ✳1dc/rb round each of next 2sts, 1dc/rf round each of next 2 sts; rep from ✳ ending 1dc into top of tch, turn.

4TH ROW: 2ch (count as 1dc), skip 1st st, 1dc/rf round next st, ✳1dc/rb round each of next 2 sts✳✳, 1dc/rf round each of next 2 sts; rep from ✳ ending last rep at ✳✳ when 2 sts remain, 1dc/rf round next st, 1dc into top of tch, turn.

5TH ROW: As 3rd row.
6TH ROW: As 2nd row.
7TH ROW: As 1st row.
8TH ROW: As 4th row.
Rep these 8 rows.

Ripple Stitch I

Starting chain: multiple of 2 sts + 3
Drape: fair
Skill: intermediate
Note: For description of tr/rf see page 188 (Raised Stitches).

1ST ROW (RS): Skip 3ch (count as 1dc), 1dc into each ch to end, turn.
2ND ROW: 1ch (counts as 1sc), skip 1st st, 1sc into each st to end, working last st into top of tch, turn.
3RD ROW: 3ch (count as 1dc), skip 1st st, ✳1tr/rf round dc below next st, 1dc into next st; rep from ✳ to end, turn.
4TH ROW: As 2nd row.
5TH ROW: 3ch (count as 1dc), skip first st, ✳1dc into next st, 1 tr/rf round dc below next st; rep from ✳ to last 2 sts, 1dc into each of last 2 sts, turn.
Rep 2nd, 3rd, 4th and 5th rows.

Ripple Stitch II

Starting chain: multiple of 2 sts + 3
Drape: fair
Skill: intermediate

Worked as Ripple Stitch I.
Work 2 rows each in colors A and B alternately throughout.

Basketweave Stitch

Starting chain: multiple of 8 sts + 4
Drape: fair
Skill: intermediate
Note: For description of dc/rf and dc/rb see page 188 (Raised Stitches).

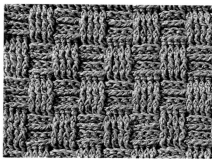

BASE ROW (WS): Skip 3ch (count as 1dc), 1dc into next and each ch to end, turn.
Commence Pattern
1ST ROW: 2ch (count as 1dc), skip 1st st, ✳1dc/rf round each of next 4 sts, 1dc/rb round each of next 4 sts; rep from ✳ ending 1dc into top of tch, turn.
Rep the last row 3 times.
5TH ROW: 2ch (count as 1dc), skip 1st st, ✳1dc/rb round each of next 4 sts, 1dc/rf round each of next 4 sts; rep from ✳ ending 1dc into top of tch, turn.
Rep the last row 3 times.
Rep these 8 rows.

Crinkle Stitch I

Starting chain: multiple of 2 sts + 1
Drape: fair
Skill: intermediate
Note: For description of sc/rf and sc/rb see page 188 (Raised Stitches).

1ST ROW (WS): Skip 2ch (count as 1hdc), 1hdc into each ch to end, turn.
2ND ROW: 1ch, 1sc into 1st st, ✳1sc/rf round next st, 1sc/rb round next st; rep from ✳ ending 1sc into top of tch, turn.
3RD ROW: 2ch (count as 1hdc), skip 1st st, 1hdc into next and each st to end, skip tch, turn.

4TH ROW: 1ch, 1sc into 1st st, ✳1sc/rb round next st, 1sc/rf round next st; rep from ✳ ending 1sc into top of tch, turn.
5TH ROW: As 3rd row.
Rep 2nd, 3rd, 4th and 5th rows.

Crinkle Stitch II

Starting chain: multiple of 3 sts + 3
Drape: fair
Skill: intermediate

Worked as Crinkle Stitch I, but using wrong side of fabric as right side.

Crossed Ripple Stitch

Starting chain: multiple of 3 sts + 3
Drape: fair
Skill: intermediate
Note: For description of dc/rf see page 188 (Raised Stitches).

1ST BASE ROW (WS): 1sc into 2nd ch from hook, 1sc into each ch to end, turn.
2ND BASE ROW: 3ch (count as 1dc), skip

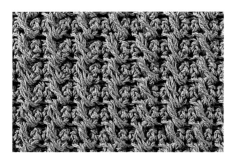

1st st, ❋skip next 2 sts, 1dc into next st, 1ch, 1dc back into 1st of 2 sts just skipped (called Crossed Pair); rep from ❋ ending 1dc into last st, skip tch, turn.

Commence Pattern

1ST ROW: 1ch, 1sc into 1st st, 1sc into next and each st and each ch sp to end working last st into top of tch, turn.

2ND ROW: As 2nd base row, except as 2nd st of each Crossed Pair work 1dc/rf loosely round 1st st of corresponding Crossed Pair 2 rows below. Rep these 2 rows.

Leafhopper Stitch

Starting chain: multiple of 4 sts + 3
Drape: fair
Skill: experienced

Special Abbreviation

LCL (Leafhopper Cluster) = ❋[yo, insert hook at front and from right to left behind stem of st before next st, yo, draw loop through and up to height of hdc] twice, yo, draw through 4 loops❋❋, skip next st, rep from ❋ to ❋❋ round stem of next st, ending yo, draw through all 3 loops on hook.

1ST ROW (WS): Skip 3ch (count as 1dc), 1dc into next and each ch to end, turn.
2ND ROW: 3ch (count as 1dc), skip 1st st, 1dc into next st, ❋1LCL (see Special Abbreviation) over next st, 1dc into each of next 3 sts; rep from ❋ omitting 1dc from end of last rep, turn.
3RD ROW: 3ch (count as 1dc), skip 1st st, 1dc into next and each st to end, working last st into top of tch, turn.
4TH ROW: 3ch (count as 1dc), skip 1st st, ❋1dc into each of next 3 sts, 1LCL over next st; rep from ❋ end 1dc into each of last 4 sts, work last st into top of tch, turn.
5TH ROW: As 3rd row.
Rep 2nd, 3rd, 4th and 5th rows.

Dots and Diamonds

Starting chain: multiple of 4 sts + 4
Drape: good
Skill: experienced

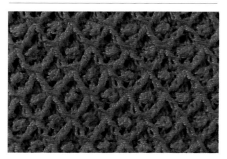

Note: For description of tr/rf see page 188 (Raised Stitches). For tr2tog see page 187 (Clusters).

Special Abbreviation

Psc (Picot single crochet) = insert hook, yo, draw loop through, [yo, draw through 1 loop] 3 times, yo, draw through both loops on hook. Note: Draw picot ch loops to front (right side) of fabric.
BASE ROW (RS): 1sc into 2nd ch from hook, 1sc into each of next 2ch, ❋Psc into next ch, 1sc into each of next 3ch; rep from ❋ to end, turn.

Commence Pattern

1ST ROW: 3ch (count as 1dc), skip 1st st, 1dc into each st to end, skip tch, turn.

2ND ROW: 1ch, 1sc into 1st st, ❋Psc (see Special Abbreviation) into next st, 1sc into next st❋❋, tr/rf2tog over next st inserting hook round 2nd sc in last-but-one row for 1st leg and round following 4th sc for 2nd leg (skipping 3 sts between), 1sc into next st; rep from ❋ ending last rep at ❋❋ in top of tch, turn.

3RD ROW: As 1st row.
4TH ROW: 1ch, 1sc into 1st st, 1tr/rf over next st inserting hook round top of 1st raised Cluster 2 rows below, ❋1sc into next st, Psc into next st, 1sc into next st❋❋, tr/rf2tog over next st inserting hook round same Cluster as last raised st for 1st leg and round top of next raised Cluster for 2nd leg; rep from ❋ ending last rep at ❋❋ when 2 sts remain, 1tr/rf over next st inserting hook round top of same Cluster as last raised st, 1sc into top of tch, turn.
5TH ROW: As 1st row.
6TH ROW: As 2nd row, except to make new raised Clusters insert hook round previous raised Clusters instead of scs. Rep 3rd, 4th, 5th and 6th rows.

Boxed Puff Stitch

Starting chain: multiple of 3 sts + 5
Drape: good
Skill: intermediate
Note: For description of Puff Stitch see page 191.

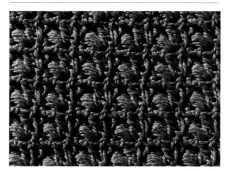

Special Abbreviation

Puff Stitch = hdc4tog all into same st and closed with 1ch drawn tightly.
1ST ROW (RS): Puff St (see Special

Abbreviation) into 5th ch from hook, ✳skip 2ch, [1dc) 2ch, Puff St] all into next ch; rep from ✳ ending skip 2ch, 1dc into last ch, turn.

2ND ROW: 1ch, skip 1st st, ✳work 1dc loosely over next row into first of 2 skipped sts in row below, 1sc into Puff St, 1sc into next 2ch sp; rep from ✳ ending 1sc into 3rd ch of tch, turn.

3RD ROW: 5ch (count as 1dc and 2ch), Puff St into 1st st, ✳skip 2sc, [1dc) 2ch, Puff St] all into next dc; rep from ✳ ending skip 2sc, 1dc into last dc) skip tch, turn.
Rep 2nd and 3rd rows.

Aligned Cobble Stitch
Starting chain: multiple of 2 sts + 2
Drape: good
Skill: easy

1ST ROW (RS): 1sc into 2nd ch from hook, 1sc into each ch to end, turn.

2ND ROW: 1ch, 1sc into 1st st, ✳1tr into next st, 1sc into next st; rep from ✳ to end, skip tch, turn.

3RD ROW: 1ch, 1sc into 1st st, 1sc into next and each st to end, skip tch, turn.
Rep 2nd and 3rd rows.

Wavy Puff Stitch Sprays
Starting chain: multiple of 17 sts + 2
Drape: good
Skill: intermediate
Note: For description of dc2tog and hdc4tog see pages 187–188 (Clusters) and page 181 (Puff Stitch).

1ST ROW (RS): 1dc into 4th ch from hook (counts as dc2tog), [dc2tog over next 2ch] twice, ✳[1ch, work hdc4tog into next ch] 5 times, 1ch✳✳, [dc2tog over next 2ch] 6 times; rep from ✳ ending last rep at ✳✳ when 6ch remain, [dc2tog over next 2ch] 3 times, turn.

2ND ROW: 1ch, 1sc into 1st st and then into each st and each ch sp to end excluding tch, turn.

3RD ROW: 3ch, skip 1st st, 1dc into next st (counts as dc2tog), [dc2tog over next 2 sts] twice, ✳[1ch, work hdc4tog into next st] 5 times, 1ch✳✳, [dc2tog over next 2 sts] 6 times; rep from ✳ ending last rep at ✳✳ when 6 sts remain, [dc2tog over next 2 sts] 3 times, skip tch, turn.
Rep 2nd and 3rd rows.

Interweave Stitch
Starting chain: multiple of 2 sts + 3
Drape: good
Skill: intermediate
Note: For description of tr/rf see page 188.

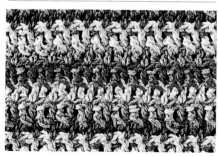

Work 1 row each in colors A, B and C throughout.

1ST ROW (RS): Skip 3 ch (count as 1dc), 1dc into next and each ch to end, turn.

2ND ROW: 3ch (count as 1dc), skip 1st st, ✳1tr/rf round next st, 1dc into next st; rep from ✳ ending last rep in top of tch, turn.
Rep 2nd row.

Interlocking Shell Stitch
Starting chain: multiple of 6 sts + 3
Drape: good
Skill: intermediate
Note: For description of dc5tog see pages 187–188 (Clusters).

Work 1 row each in colors A and B alternately; fasten off each color at end of each row.

1ST ROW (RS): Skip 2ch (count as 1dc), 2dc into next ch, skip 2ch, 1sc into next ch, ✳skip 2ch, 5dc into next ch, skip 2ch, 1sc into next ch; rep from ✳ to last 3ch, skip 2ch, 3dc into last ch, turn.

2ND ROW: 1ch, 1sc into 1st st, ✳2ch, dc5tog over next 5 sts, 2ch, 1sc into next st; rep from ✳ ending last rep in top of tch, turn.

3RD ROW: 3ch (count as 1dc), 2dc into 1st st, skip 2ch, 1sc into next Cluster, ✳skip 2ch, 5dc into next sc, skip 2ch, 1sc into next Cluster; rep from ✳ to last Cluster, skip 2ch, 3dc into last sc, skip tch, turn.
Rep 2nd and 3rd rows.

Aligned Railing Stitch

Starting chain: multiple of 2 sts + 3
Drape: good
Skill: intermediate
Note: For description of Raised Stitches see page 187.

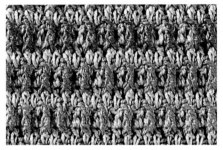

On a background of basic trebles in color M work raised rows; one row each in colors A, B, and C throughout.
Work 2 rows basic trebles in M.

Commence Pattern

1ST ROW (RS): Put working loop temporarily on a stitch holder or safety pin, draw loop of contrast color through top of last background st completed, 1ch, work 1tr/rf round stem of 2nd st in last-but-one row, ✷1ch, skip 1 st, 1tr/rf round stem of next st in last-but-one row; rep from ✷ ending sl st into top of tch at beg of last background row worked. Fasten off but do not turn work.

2ND ROW: Replace hook in working loop of M. 3ch, work 1dc inserting hook through top of raised st and background st at the same time, ✷work 1dc inserting hook under condcast color ch and top of next st in background color at the same time, work 1dc inserting hook under top of next raised st and background st as before; rep from ✷ to end.
Work 1 row in basic trebles.
Rep these 3 rows.

Relief Squares

Starting chain: multiple of 10 sts + 5
Drape: fair
Skill: intermediate
Note: For description of Raised Stitches see page 188.

1ST BASE ROW (RS): Using A, 1sc into 2nd ch from hook, 1sc into next and each ch to end, turn.
2ND BASE ROW: 1 ch, 1sc into 1st and each st to end, skip tch, turn.

Commence Pattern

Change to B and rep the 2nd base row twice.
Change to C and rep the 2nd base row 4 times.
7TH ROW: Using B, 1 ch, 1sc into each of 1st 3 sts, ✷[1dtr/rf round st corresponding to next st 5 rows below, i.e. last row worked in B] twice, 1sc into each of next 4 sts, [1dtr/rf round st corresponding to next st 5 rows below] twice, 1sc into each of next 2 sts; rep from ✷ ending 1sc into last st, skip tch, turn.
8TH ROW: Using B rep 2nd base row.
9TH ROW: Using A, 1 ch, 1sc into 1st st, ✷[1quintr/rf round st corresponding to next st 9 rows below, i.e. last row worked in A] twice, 1sc into each of next 8 sts; rep from ✷ to last 3 sts, [1quintr/rf round st corresponding to next st 9 rows below] twice, 1sc into last st, skip tch, turn.
10TH ROW: Using A rep 2nd base row.
Rep these 10 rows.

Cats' Eyes

Starting chain: multiple of 8 sts + 2
Drape: good
Skill: intermediate

Special Abbreviations

Cr3R (Cross 3 Right) = skip 2sc, work 1tr into next sc, working behind last tr work 1dc into each of 2 skipped sc.
Cr3L (Cross 3 Left) = skip 1sc, work 1dc into each of next 2sc, working in front of last 2dc work 1tr into skipped sc.
1ST ROW (WS): Work 1sc into 2nd ch from hook, 1sc into each ch to end, turn.
2ND ROW: 3ch (count as 1dc), skip 1st sc, ✷Cr3R (see Special Abbreviations), 1dc into next sc, Cr3L (see Special Abbreviations), 1dc into next sc; rep from ✷ to end, turn.
3RD ROW: 1ch, work 1sc into each st to end placing last sc into 3rd of 3ch at beg of previous row, turn.
Rep 2nd and 3rd rows.

highly-textured stitches

These high-relief patterns create heavy fabrics with real impact. Some incorporate popcorns or bobbles (*page 190*). The unusual Astrakhan Stitch (*below*) has a texture formed from loops of chain. Raised Chevron Stitch (*page 238*) alternates crisp zigzags of raised double crochets with vertical rows of clusters. For contrasting textures of rough and smooth, a panel such as Bobble Braid Stitch (*page 239*) or Tulip Cable (*page 238*) would be ideal.

Blackberry Salad Stitch

Starting chain: multiple of 4 sts + 3
Drape: fair
Skill: intermediate
Note: For description of dc5tog see page 190 (Bobble).

1ST ROW (RS): Skip 3ch (count as 1dc), 1dc into each ch to end, turn.
2ND ROW: 1ch, 1sc into each of 1st 2 sts, ✳work dc5tog into next st, 1sc into each of next 3 sts; rep from ✳ to last 3 sts, work dc5tog into next st, 1sc into each of last
2 sts (including top of tch), turn.
3RD ROW: 3ch (count as 1dc), skip 1st st, 1dc into each st to end, skip tch, turn.
4TH ROW: 1ch, 1sc into each of 1st 4 sts, ✳work dc5tog into next st, 1sc into each of next 3 sts; rep from ✳ ending 1sc into top of tch, turn.
5TH ROW: As 3rd row.
Rep 2nd, 3rd, 4th and 5th rows.

Astrakhan Stitch

Starting chain: any number of sts + 2
Drape: fair
Skill: intermediate
Note: Work all rows with right side facing, i.e. work even-numbered rows from left to right.

1ST ROW (RS): Skip 3ch (count as 1dc), 1dc into each ch to end. Do not turn.
2ND ROW: ✳7ch, sl st into front loop only of next dc to right; rep from ✳ ending 7ch, sl st into top of tch at beginning of row. Do not turn.
3RD ROW: 3ch (count as 1dc), skip 1 st, 1dc into back loop only of next and each st of last-but-one row to end. Do not turn.
Rep 2nd and 3rd rows.

Popcorn Waffle Stitch

Multiple of 4 sts + 2
Drape: fair
Skill: intermediate
Note: For description of 5dc Popcorn see page 190, but add 1dc to 4 shown.

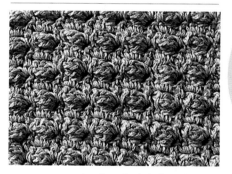

1ST ROW (RS): 1sc into 2nd ch from hook, ✳3ch, 5dc Popcorn into same place as previous sc, skip 3ch, 1sc into next ch; rep from ✳ to end, turn.
2ND ROW: 3ch (count as 1dc), skip 1st st, ✳1sc into each of next 2ch, 1hdc into next ch, 1dc into next sc; rep from ✳ to end, skip tch, turn.
3RD ROW: 1ch, 1sc into 1st st, ✳3ch, 5dc Popcorn into same place as previous sc, skip next 3 sts, 1sc into next dc; rep from ✳ ending last rep in top of tch, turn.
Rep 2nd and 3rd rows.

Ribbed Bobble Pattern

Starting chain: multiple of 8 sts + 2
Drape: fair
Skill: intermediate

Special Abbreviation

Popcorn = work 4dc into next st, drop loop from hook, insert hook from the front into top of first of these dc, pick up dropped loop and draw through dc, 1ch to secure Popcorn.

1ST ROW (RS): Work 1sc into 2nd ch from hook, ✳1ch, skip 3ch, 1dc into next ch, 1ch, into same ch as last dc work [1dc, 1ch, 1dc], 1ch, skip 3ch, 1sc into next ch; rep from ✳ to end, turn.

2ND ROW: 6ch (count as 1dc, 3ch), skip 1dc, 1sc into next dc, ✳3ch, 1 Popcorn (see Special Abbreviation) into next sc, 3ch, skip 1dc, 1sc into next dc; rep from ✳ to last sc, 3ch, 1dc into last sc, turn.

3RD ROW: 1ch, 1sc into 1st dc, ✳1ch, 1dc into next sc, 1ch, into same st as last dc work [1dc, 1ch, 1dc], 1ch, 1sc into top of next Popcorn; rep from ✳ to end, placing last sc into 3rd of 6ch at beg of previous row, turn. Rep 2nd and 3rd rows.

Flower Panels

Starting chain: multiple of 12 sts + 8
Drape: fair
Skill: intermediate

Special Abbreviations

Puff St = ✳yo, insert hook into next st, yo and draw a loop through; rep from ✳ 4 times more inserting hook into same st as before (11 loops on hook), yo and draw

through 10 loops, yo and draw through 2 remaining loops.

1dc/rf = work 1dc around stem of next st 2 rows below inserting hook round stem from right to left to draw up loops.

1ST ROW (RS): Work 1sc into 2nd ch from hook, 1sc into each ch to end, turn.

2ND AND EVERY ALT ROW: 1ch, work 1sc into each st to end, turn.

3RD ROW: 1ch, work 1sc into each of 1st 2sc, 1dc/rf, (see Special Abbreviations) 1sc into next sc, 1dc/rf, ✳1sc into each of next 4sc, 1 Puff St (see Special Abbreviations) into next sc, 1sc into each of next 4sc, 1dc/rf, 1sc into next sc, 1dc/rf; rep from ✳ to last 2sc, 1sc into each of last 2sc, turn.

5TH ROW: 1ch, work 1sc into each of 1st 2sc, 1dc/rf, 1sc into next sc, 1dc/rf, ✳1sc into each of next 2sc, 1 Puff St into next sc, 1sc into each of next 3sc, 1 Puff St into next sc, 1sc into each of next 2sc, 1dc/rf, 1sc into next sc, 1dc/rf; rep from ✳ to last 2sc, 1sc into each of last 2sc, turn.

7TH ROW: As 3rd row.

9TH ROW: 1ch, 1sc into each of 1st 2sc, 1dc/rf, 1sc into next sc, 1dc/rf, ✳1sc into each of next 9sc, 1dc/rf, 1sc into next sc, 1dc/rf; rep from ✳ to last 2sc, 1sc into each of last 2sc, turn. Rep 2nd to 9th rows.

Diamond Bobble Pattern

Starting chain: multiple of 12 sts + 6
Drape: fair
Skill: experienced

Special Abbreviation

Bobble = working in front of work, work 5tr into ch sp 2 rows below until 1 loop of

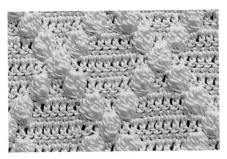

each tr remains on hook, yo and through all 6 loops.

1ST ROW (RS): Work 1sc into 2nd ch from hook, 1sc into next ch, 1ch, skip 1ch, ✳1sc into each of next 11ch, 1ch, skip 1ch; rep from ✳ to last 2ch, 1sc into each of last 2ch, turn.

2ND ROW: 3ch (count as 1dc), skip 1st sc, work 1dc into next sc, 1ch, skip 1ch sp, ✳1dc into each of next 11 sts, 1ch, skip 1ch sp; rep from ✳ to last 2sc, 1dc into each of last 2sc, turn.

3RD ROW: 1ch, work 1sc into each of 1st 2dc, 1 Bobble (see Special Abbreviation) into ch sp 2 rows below, ✳1sc into next dc, 1ch, skip 1dc, 1sc into each of next 7dc, 1ch, skip 1dc, 1sc into next dc, 1 Bobble into next ch sp 2 rows below; rep from ✳ to last 2dc, 1sc into next dc, 1sc into 3rd of 3ch at beg of previous row, turn.

4TH ROW: 3ch, skip 1st sc, 1dc into each of next 3 sts, ✳1ch, skip 1ch sp, 1dc into each of next 7 sts, 1ch, skip 1ch sp, 1dc into each of next 3 sts; rep from ✳ to last sc, 1dc into last sc, turn.

5TH ROW: 1ch, work 1sc into each of first 4dc, ✳1 Bobble into ch sp 2 rows below, 1sc into next dc, 1ch, skip 1dc, 1sc into each of next 3dc, 1ch, skip 1dc, 1sc into next dc, 1 Bobble into ch sp 2 rows below, 1sc into each of next 3dc; rep from ✳ to last st, 1sc into 3rd of 3ch at beg of previous row, turn.

6TH ROW: 3ch, skip 1st sc, work 1dc into each of next 5 sts, ✳1ch, skip 1ch sp, 1dc into each of next 3 sts, 1ch, skip 1ch sp, 1dc into each of next 7 sts; rep from ✳ to end omitting 1dc at end of last rep, turn.

7TH ROW: 1ch, work 1sc into each of first 6dc, ✳1 Bobble into ch sp 2 rows below,

1sc into next dc, 1ch, skip 1dc, 1sc into next dc, 1 Bobble into ch sp 2 rows below, 1sc into each of next 7dc; rep from ✳ to end omitting 1sc at end of last rep, turn.

8TH ROW: 3ch, skip 1st sc, work 1dc into each of next 7 sts, 1ch, skip 1ch sp, ✳1dc into each of next 11 sts, 1ch, skip 1ch sp; rep from ✳ to last 8 sts, 1dc into each of last 8 sts, turn.

9TH ROW: 1ch, work 1sc into each of 1st 6dc, ✳1ch, skip 1dc, 1sc into next dc, 1 Bobble into ch sp 2 rows below, 1sc into next dc, 1ch, skip 1dc, 1sc into each of next 7dc; rep from ✳ to end omitting 1sc at end of last rep, turn.

10TH ROW: As 6th row.

11TH ROW: 1ch, work 1sc into each of 1st 4dc, ✳1ch, skip 1dc, 1sc into next dc, 1 Bobble into ch sp 2 rows below, 1sc into each of next 3dc, 1 Bobble into ch sp 2 rows below, 1sc into next dc, 1ch, skip 1dc, 1sc into each of next 3dc; rep from ✳ to last dc, 1sc into 3rd of 3ch, turn.

12TH ROW: As 4th row.

13TH ROW: 1ch, 1sc into each of 1st 2dc, 1ch, skip 1dc, 1sc into next dc, ✳1 Bobble into ch sp 2 rows below, 1sc into each of next 7dc, 1 Bobble into ch sp 2 rows below, 1sc into next dc, 1ch, skip 1dc, 1sc into next dc; rep from ✳ to last dc, 1sc into 3rd of 3ch, turn. Rep 2nd to 13th rows.

Thistle Pattern

Starting chain: multiple of 10 sts + 2
Drape: fair
Skill: experienced
Note: For description of sc2tog see page 187 (Clusters).

Special Abbreviation

Catch Loop = Catch 10ch loop of Thistle by inserting hook under ch at tip of loop at the same time as under the next st.
BASE ROW (WS): Skip 2ch (count as 1sc), 1sc into each of next 4ch, ✳into next st work a Thistle of 1sc, [10ch, 1sc] 3 times✳✳, 1sc into each of next 9ch; rep from ✳ ending last rep at ✳✳, 1sc into each of last 5sc, turn.

Commence Pattern

NOTE: Hold loops of Thistle down at front of work on right-side rows.

1ST ROW: 1ch (count as 1sc), skip 1sc, 1sc into each of next 4sc, ✳skip 1sc of Thistle, work sc2tog over next 2sc, skip last sc of Thistle✳✳, work 1sc into each of next 9 sts; rep from ✳ ending last rep at ✳✳, 1sc into each of next 4sc, 1sc into tch, turn.

2ND, 4TH, 8TH AND 10TH ROWS: 1ch, skip 1 st, 1sc into each st to end, turn.

3RD ROW: 1ch, skip 1 st, 1sc into next sc, ✳catch first loop (see Special Abbreviation) of Thistle in next sc, 1sc into each of next 5sc, skip center loop of Thistle, catch 3rd loop in next st✳✳, 1sc into each of next 3sc; rep from ✳ ending last rep at ✳✳, 1sc into each of last 2 sts, turn.

5TH ROW: 1ch, skip 1 st, 1sc into each of next 4sc, ✳work 6dc into next sc and at the same time catch center loop✳✳, 1sc into each of next 9sc; rep from ✳ ending last rep at ✳✳, 1sc into each of last 5 sts, turn.

6TH ROW: 1ch, skip 1 st, 1sc into each of 1st 4sc, ✳1ch, skip 6dc, 1sc into each of next 4sc✳✳, work a Thistle into next sc, 1sc into each of next 4sc; rep from ✳ ending last rep at ✳✳, 1sc into last st, turn.

7TH ROW: 1ch, skip 1 st, 1sc into each of next 9 sts, ✳work sc2tog over center 2 of next 4sc, skip 1sc, 1sc into each of next 9 sts; rep from ✳ to last st, 1sc into last st, turn.

9TH ROW: 1ch, skip 1 st, 1sc into each of next 6sc, ✳catch 1st loop into next sc, 1sc into each of next 5sc, catch 3rd loop into next sc✳✳, 1sc into each of next 3sc; rep from ✳ ending last rep at ✳✳, 1sc into each st to end, turn.

11TH ROW: 1ch, skip 1 st, 1sc into each of next 9 sts, ✳work 6dc into next sc and catch center loop at the same time, 1sc into each of next 9sc; rep from ✳ to last st, 1sc in last st, turn.

12TH ROW: 1ch, skip 1 st, 1sc into each of next 4sc, ✳work a Thistle into next sc, 1sc into each of next 4sc✳✳, 1ch, skip 6dc, 1sc into each of next 4sc; rep from ✳ ending last rep at ✳✳, 1sc into last st, turn. Rep these 12 rows.

Embossed Roundels

Starting chain: multiple of 8 sts + 7
Drape: fair
Skill: experienced

Special Abbreviation

ERd (Embossed Roundel) = work [1dc, 2ch] 9 times all into same st, remove hook from working loop, insert hook from back through top of 1st dc of Roundel and, keeping sts of Roundel at back of fabric, pick up working loop again and draw through to close Roundel.

1ST ROW (RS): Skip 3ch (count as 1dc), 1dc into next and each ch to end, turn.

2ND ROW: 3ch (count as 1dc), skip 1 st, 1dc into each of next 3 sts, ✳1ERd (see Special Abbreviation) into next st, 1dc into each of next 7 sts; rep from ✳ ending 1dc into top of tch, turn.

3RD ROW: 3ch (count as 1dc), skip 1 st, 1dc into next and each st to end, working last st into top of tch, turn.

4TH ROW: 3ch (count as 1dc), skip 1 st, ✳1dc into each of next 7 sts, 1ERd into

next st; rep from ✳ to last 4 sts, 1dc into each of last 4 sts, turn.
5TH ROW: As 3rd row.
Rep 2nd, 3rd, 4th and 5th rows.

Raised Chevron Stitch

Starting chain: multiple of 16 sts + 3
Drape: fair
Skill: experienced
Note: For description of dc/rb and dc/rf see page 188 (Raised Stitches). For dc2tog and dc3tog see page 187 (Clusters).

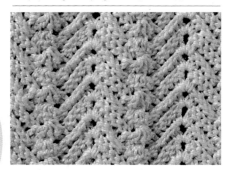

1ST ROW (RS): Skip 3ch, dc2tog over next 2ch (counts as dc3tog), ✳1dc into each of next 5ch, [2dc, 1ch, 2dc] into next ch, 1dc into each of next 5ch✳✳, dc5tog over next 5ch; rep from ✳ ending last rep at ✳✳ when 3ch remain, dc3tog, turn.
2ND ROW: 3ch, skip 1st st, poststB2tog over next 2 sts (all counts as poststB3tog), ✳1dc/rf round each of next 5 sts, [2dc, 1ch, 2dc] into next ch sp, 1dc/rf round each of next 5 sts✳✳, poststB5tog over next 5 sts; rep from ✳ ending last rep at ✳✳ when 3 sts remain, poststB3tog, turn.
3RD ROW: 3ch, skip 1st st, poststF2tog over next 2 sts (all counts as poststF3tog), ✳1dc/rb round each of next 5 sts, [2dc, 1ch, 2dc] into next ch sp, 1dc/rb round each of next 5 sts✳✳, poststF5tog over next 5 sts; rep from ✳ ending last rep at ✳✳ when 3 sts remain, poststF3tog, turn.
Rep 2nd and 3rd rows.

Gwenyth's Cable

Worked over 19 sts on a background of basic double crochets with any number of sts
Skill: experienced
Note: For description of tr/rf and tr/rb see page 188 (Raised Stitches). To "go behind" stitches, take hook behind these stitches and insert it where instructed.

1ST ROW (RS): 1tr/rf round 1st st, 1dc into next st, skip next 3 sts, 1dtr into each of next 3 sts, going behind last 3dtrs work 1dtr into each of 3 sts just skipped, 1dc into next st, 1tr/rf round next st, 1dc into next st, skip next 3 sts, 1dtr into each of next 3 sts, going in front of last 3dtrs but not catching them, work 1dtr into each of 3 sts just skipped, 1dc into next st, 1tr/rf round next st.
2ND ROW: As 1st row, except work 1tr/rb instead of rf over 1st, 10th and 19th sts to keep raised ridges on right side of fabric. Rep 1st and 2nd rows.

Crossed Puff Cables

Worked over 11 sts on a background of basic double crochets with any number of sts
Skill: experienced
Note: For description of tr/rb and tr/rf see page 188 (Raised Stitches); for hdc5tog see page 191 (Puff Stitch).

1ST ROW (RS): 1dc into each st.
2ND ROW: ✳1tr/rb round next st, work a Puff St of hdc5tog all into next st, 1tr/rb round next st✳✳, 1dc into next st; rep

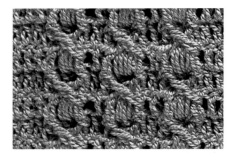

from ✳ once and from ✳ to ✳✳ again.
3RD ROW: ✳Leaving last loop of each st on hook work [1dc into next st, skip Puff St, work 1tr/rf round next st] ending yo, draw through all 3 loops on hook, 1dc into top of Puff St, leaving last loop of each st on hook work [1tr/rf round st before same Puff St and 1dc into top of st after Puff st], ending yo, draw through all 3 loops on hook✳✳, 1dc into next st; rep from ✳ once and from ✳ to ✳✳ again.
4TH ROW: As 2nd row, but make new tr/rbs by inserting hook under raised stems only of previous sts. Rep 3rd and 4th rows.

Tulip Cable

Worked over 15 sts on a background of basic double crochets with any number of sts
Skill: experienced
Note: For description of tr/rf and tr/rb see page 188 (Raised Stitches). For description of hdc5tog see page 191 (Puff Stitch with step 1 repeated 4 times).

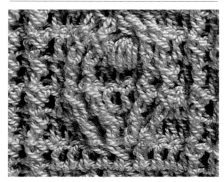

Special Abbreviations

FCL (Forward Cluster) = leaving last loop of each st on hook work 1dc into next st and 1tr/rf or rb (see Note below) round next st after that, ending yo, draw through all 3 loops on hook.

BCL (Backward Cluster) = leaving last loop of each st on hook work 1tr/rf or rb round st below dc just made and 1dc into next st.

NOTE: raised legs of these Clusters are to be worked at front (rf) on right-side rows and at back (rb) on wrong-side rows as indicated in the text thus: FCL/rf, FCL/rb, BCL/rf, BCL/rb.

TCL (Triple Cluster) = leaving last loop of each st on hook work 1tr/rf round st below dc just made, 1dc/rf round next Puff St, and 1tr/rf round next st, ending yo, draw through all 4 loops on hook.

1ST ROW (RS): 1tr/rf round next st, 1dc into next st, 1tr/rf round next st, 1dc into each of next 2 sts, [1FCL/rf—see Special Abbreviations] twice, 1dc into next st, [1BCL/rf—see Special Abbreviations] twice, 1dc into each of next 2 sts, 1tr/rf round next st, 1dc into next st, 1tr/rf round next st.

2ND ROW: [1tr/rb round next st, 1dc into next st] twice, [1FCL/rb] twice, 1dc into each of next 3 sts, [1BCL/rb] twice, [1dc into next st, 1tr/rb round next st] twice.

3RD ROW: [1tr/rf round next st, 1dc into next st] twice, 1tr/rf round each of next 2 sts, 1dc into each of next 3 sts, 1tr/rf round each of next 2 sts, [1dc into next st, 1tr/rf round next st] twice.

4TH ROW: 1tr/rb round next st, 1dc into next st, 1tr/rb round each of next 2 sts, [1BCL/rb] twice, work a Puff St of hdc5tog all into next st, [1FCL/rb] twice, 1dc into each of next 2 sts, 1tr/rb round next st, 1dc into next st, 1tr/rb round next st.

5TH ROW: 1tr/rf round next st, 1dc into next st, 1tr/rf round next st, 1dc into each of next 3 sts, 1BCL/rf, 1TCL (see Special Abbreviations), 1FCL/rf, 1dc into each of next 3 sts, 1tr/rf round next st, 1dc into next st, 1tr/rf round next st.

6TH ROW: ✳1tr/rb round next st, 1dc into next st, 1tr/rb round next st✳✳, 1dc into each of next 9 sts, rep from ✳ to ✳✳. Rep these 6 rows.

Bobble Braid Stitch

Worked over 13 sts on a background of any number of sts worked in basic double crochet on right-side rows and single crochet on wrong-side rows
Skill: experienced
Note: For description of tr/rf see page 188 (Raised Stitches); for dc5tog see page 190 (Bobble).

1ST ROW (RS): 1dc into each of 1st 4 sts, [1ch, skip 1 st, 1dc into next st] 3 times, 1dc into each of last 3 sts.

2ND ROW: 1sc into each of 1st 4 sts, work dc5tog into next ch sp, 1sc into next dc, 1sc into next sp, 1sc into next dc, dc5tog into next sp, 1sc into each of last 4 sts.

3RD ROW: 1tr/rf round 1st st 2 rows below (i.e.: 1st row), 1dc into next st on previous (i.e.: 2nd) row, 1tr/rf round next st 2 rows below, [1ch, skip 1 st, 1dc into next st on previous row] 3 times, 1ch, skip 1 st, 1tr/rf round next st 2 rows below, 1dc into next st on previous row, 1tr/rf round next st 2 rows below.

4TH ROW: 1sc into each of 1st 6 sts, work dc5tog into next st, 1sc into each of last 6 sts.

5TH ROW: [1tr/rf round corresponding raised st 2 rows below, 1dc into next st] twice, [1ch, skip 1 st, 1dc into next st] 3 times, 1tr/rf round corresponding raised st 2 rows below, 1dc into next st, 1tr/rf round corresponding raised st 2 rows below.

Continue as set on 2nd, 3rd, 4th and 5th rows.

Puff Stitch Plaits

Starting chain: multiple of 8 sts + 2
Drape: fair
Skill: intermediate
Note: For description of hdc3tog see page 191 (Puff Stitch).

1ST ROW (RS): Skip 2ch (count as 1hdc), 1hdc into each of next 2ch, ✳1ch, skip 1ch, hdc3tog all into next ch, 1ch, skip 1ch✳✳, 1hdc into each of next 5ch; rep from ✳ ending last rep at ✳✳ when 3ch remain, 1hdc into each of last 3ch, turn.

2ND ROW: 2ch (count as 1hdc), skip 1st st, 1hdc into each of next 2 sts, ✳hdc3tog into next ch sp, 1ch, skip 1 st, hdc3tog into next ch sp✳✳, 1hdc into each of next 5 sts; rep from ✳ ending last rep at ✳✳ when 3 sts remain including tch, 1hdc into each of last 3 sts, turn.

3RD ROW: 2ch (count as 1hdc), skip 1st st, 1hdc into each of next 2 sts, ✳1ch, skip 1 st, hdc3tog into next ch sp, 1ch, skip 1 st✳✳, 1hdc into each of next 5 sts; rep from ✳ ending last rep at ✳✳ when 3 sts remain including tch, 1hdc into each of last 3 sts, turn.

Rep 2nd and 3rd rows.

V-Twin Popcorn Stitch

Starting chain: multiple of 11 sts + 5
Drape: fair
Skill: intermediate
Note: For description of 5dc Popcorn see page 190, adding 1dc; for tr/rb and tr/rf see page 188 (Raised Stitches).

1ST ROW (RS): Skip 3ch (count as 1dc), 1dc into each of next 2ch, ✳2ch, skip 3ch, 5dc Popcorn into next ch, 1ch, 5 dc Popcorn into next ch, 1ch, skip 2ch, 1dc into each of next 3ch; rep from ✳ to end, turn.

2ND ROW: 3ch (count as 1dc), skip 1st st, 1tr/rb round next st, 1dc into next st, ✳3ch, skip 1ch and 1 Popcorn, 2sc into next ch sp, 3ch, skip 1 Popcorn and 2ch, 1dc into next st, 1tr/rb round next st, 1dc into next st; rep from ✳ ending last rep in top of tch, turn.

3RD ROW: 3ch (count as 1dc), skip 1st st, 1tr/rf round next st, 1dc into next st, ✳2ch, skip 3ch, 5dc Popcorn into next sc, 1ch, 5dc Popcorn into next sc, 1ch, skip 3ch, 1dc into next st, 1tr/rf round next st, 1dc into next st; rep from ✳ ending last rep in top of tch, turn.

Rep 2nd and 3rd rows.

Bullion Diagonals

Starting chain: multiple of 6 sts + 3
Drape: fair
Skill: intermediate
Note: For description of Bullion St see page 191. Make Bullion Sts with [yo] 7 times.

1ST ROW (WS): 1sc into 2nd ch from hook, 1ch, skip 1ch, 1sc into next ch, ✳2ch, skip 2ch, 1sc into next ch; rep from ✳ to last 2ch, 1ch, skip 1ch, 1sc into last ch, turn.

2ND ROW: 3ch (count as 1dc), skip 1st st, 1dc into next ch sp, ✳1dc into next sc, 1 Bullion St into each of next 2ch, 1dc into next sc✳✳, 1dc into each of next 2ch; rep

from ✳ ending last rep at ✳✳ when 1 ch sp remains, 1dc into next ch, 1dc into last sc, skip tch, turn.

3RD ROW: 1ch, 1sc into 1st st, 1ch, skip 1 st, 1sc into next st, ✳2ch, skip 2 sts, 1sc into next st; rep from ✳ to last 2 sts, 1ch, skip 1 st, 1sc into top of tch, turn.

4TH ROW: 3ch (count as 1dc), skip 1st st, 1 Bullion St into next ch sp, ✳1dc into next sc, 1dc into each of next 2ch, 1dc into next sc✳✳, 1 Bullion St into each of next 2ch; rep from ✳ ending last rep at ✳✳ when 1ch sp remains, 1 Bullion St into next sp, 1dc into last sc, skip tch, turn.

5TH ROW: As 3rd row.
Rep 2nd, 3rd, 4th and 5th rows.

Diagonal Trip Stitch

Starting chain: multiple of 6 sts + 3
Drape: fair
Skill: intermediate

1ST ROW (RS): 1sc into 2nd ch from hook, 1sc into each ch to end, turn.

2ND ROW: 1ch, 1sc into 1st st, ✳1tr into next st, 1sc into next st, 1tr into next st, 1sc into each of next 3 sts; rep from ✳

ending 1sc into last sc, skip tch, turn.

3RD ROW: 1ch, 1sc into 1st st, 1sc into next and each st to end, skip tch, turn.

4TH ROW: 1ch, 1sc into each of first 2 sts, ✳1tr into next st, 1sc into next st, 1tr into next st, 1sc into each of next 3 sts; rep from ✳ to end, skip tch, turn.

5TH ROW: As 3rd row.

6TH ROW: 1 ch, 1sc into each of 1st 3 sts, ✳1tr into next st, 1sc into next st, 1tr into next st, 1sc into each of next 3 sts; rep from ✳ to end, omitting 1sc at end of last rep, skip tch, turn.

Continue in this way, working the pairs of tr 1 st further to the left on every wrong-side row.

Loop or Fur Stitch

Starting chain: multiple of 8 sts + 2
Drape: fair
Skill: experienced
Note: For description of Loop St see page 191. For plain Loop Stitch do not cut loops.

1ST ROW (RS): Skip 3ch (count as 1dc), 1dc into next and each ch to end, turn.

2ND ROW: 1ch, 1sc into each of 1st 2 sts, ✳1 Loop St into each of next 4 sts✳✳, 1sc into each of next 4 sts; rep from ✳ ending last rep at ✳✳, 1sc into each of last 2 sts including top of tch, turn.

3RD ROW: 3ch (count as 1dc), skip 1 st, 1dc into next and each st to end, skip tch, turn.

Rep 2nd and 3rd rows.

Tunisian crochet

Also known as afghan stitch, Tunisian crochet (*page 8*) typically produces a relatively dense fabric, although some openwork patterns, such as Little Fan Openwork (*page 250*), can also be created. As its alternative name suggests, this technique is well-suited to afghans and other home accessories. These lace patterns are all-over patterns with a larger motif repeat. They are most effective when worked in plain yarns, as fluffy or textured yarns do not show much detail of the pattern.

Tunisian Simple Stitch I
Starting chain: any number of sts
Drape: good
Skill: easy

1ST ROW: As Basic Forward and Return row.
2ND ROW: 1Tss (Tunisian Simple St) into next and each st to end including edge st. Return.
Rep 2nd row.

Tunisian Simple Stitch II
Starting chain: any number of sts
Drape: good
Skill: easy

Worked as for Tunisian Simple Stitch I, except using 2 colors, A and B, as follows:
1ST ROW: Col A.
2ND ROW: Col B.
3RD ROW (FORWARD): ✳4 sts in Col B, 4 sts in Col A, rep from ✳ to end, (REVERSE) ✳4 sts in Col A, 4 sts in Col B; rep from ✳ to end.
9TH ROW: Col A.
10TH ROW: Col B.
11TH ROW (FORWARD): ✳4 sts in Col A, 4 sts in Col B, rep from ✳ to end, (REVERSE) ✳4 sts in Col B, 4 sts in Col A; rep from ✳ to end.
Rep 11th row 5 times.
Rep these 16 rows.
HINT: Remember to change yarn one step before new color is required each time.

Tunisian Knit Stitch
Starting chain: any number of sts
Drape: good
Skill: easy

1ST ROW: As Basic Forward and Return row.
2ND ROW: 1Tks (Tunisian Knit St) into next and each st to end including edge st. Return.
Rep 2nd row.

Tunisian Purl Stitch

Starting chain: any number of sts
Drape: good
Skill: easy

1ST ROW: As Basic Forward and Return row.
2ND ROW: 1Tps (Tunisian Purl St) into next and each st to end including edge st. Return.
Rep 2nd row.

Tunisian Plain Stitch

Starting chain: multiple of 2 sts + 3
Drape: good
Skill: easy

1ST ROW: As Basic Forward and Return row.
2ND ROW: With 1 loop on hook, ✳1Tps into next st, 1Tss into next st; rep from ✳ to end. Return.
3RD ROW: With 1 loop on hook, ✳1Tss into next st, 1Tps into next st; rep from ✳ to last 2 sts, 1Tss into each of last 2 sts.

Return.
Rep 2nd and 3rd rows.

Tunisian Net Stitch

Starting chain: any number of sts
Drape: good
Skill: easy
Note: Check the number of sts after each Forward row. It will be easier to keep the number of sts correct and the edges of the material straight if you take care to alternate the placing of the first Tss, as given on 2nd and 3rd rows.

1ST ROW: As Basic Forward and Return row.
2ND ROW: With 1 loop on hook, work 1Tss into space between 2nd and 3rd sts, 1Tss into each sp to end, 1Tss into last st. Return.
3RD ROW: With 1 loop on hook, work 1Tss into sp between 1st and 2nd sts, 1Tss into each sp to last sp, skip last sp, work 1Tss into last st. Return.
Rep 2nd and 3rd rows.

Ribbed Tunisian Stitch

Starting chain: multiple of 2 sts + 1
Drape: good
Skill: easy

1ST ROW: As Basic Forward and Return row.
2ND ROW: With 1 loop on hook, ✳1TwTss into next st, 1Tss into next st; rep from ✳ to end. Return.
Rep 2nd row.

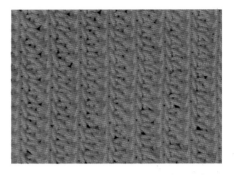

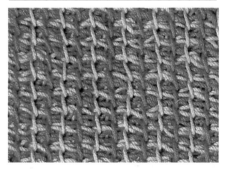

Tunisian Running Stitch

Starting chain: multiple of 2 sts + 3
Drape: fair
Skill: intermediate
Note: Because this pattern incorporates a slipped stitch it should be worked on a hook which is at least two sizes (1 mm) larger than usual.

1ST ROW: Using A, as Basic Forward and Return row, changing to B when 2 loops remain at end of return.
2ND ROW: Using B, with 1 loop on hook, ✳1Tss into next st, 1Tsl st into next st; rep from ✳ to last 2 sts, 1Tss into each of next 2 sts. Return, changing to A when 2 loops remain.
3RD ROW: Using A, with 1 loop on hook, ✳1Tsl st into next st, 1Tss into next st; rep from ✳ to end. Return, changing to B when 2 loops remain.
Rep 2nd and 3rd rows.

heavyweight patterns

Flecked Stripe Stitch

Starting chain: multiple of 4 sts + 3
Drape: fair
Skill: intermediate

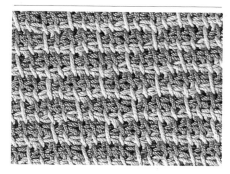

1ST ROW: Using A, as Basic Forward and Return row, changing to B when 2 loops remain.
2ND ROW: Using B, with 1 loop on hook, ✳1Tsl st into next st, work 1Tss into each of next 3 sts; rep from ✳ to last 2 sts, 1Tsl st into next st, work 1Tss into last st. Return, changing to A when 2 loops remain.
3RD ROW: Using A with 1 loop on hook work 1Tss into each st to end. Return, changing to B when 2 loops remain.
4TH ROW: Using B, with 1 loop on hook, work 1Tss into each of next 2 sts, ✳1Tsl st into next st, 1Tss into each of next 3 sts; rep from ✳ to end. Return, changing to A when 2 loops remain.
5TH ROW: As 3rd row.
Rep 2nd to 5th rows.

Bubble Stitch

Starting chain: multiple of 2 sts + 3
Drape: fair
Skill: intermediate
Note: It is recommended that this stitch is worked using a hook one or two sizes (0.5 mm or 1 mm) larger than usual.

Special Abbreviation

sl 1 fwd = yf, insert hook into next st without working it, yb.
1ST ROW: Using A, as Basic Forward and Return row.

2ND ROW: Using B, with 1 loop on hook, ✳sl 1 fwd (see Special Abbreviation), 1Tss into next st; rep from ✳ to end. Return, changing to A when 2 loops remain.
3RD ROW: Using A, with 1 loop on hook, ✳1Tss into next st, sl 1 fwd; rep from ✳ to last 2 sts, 1Tss into each of last 2 sts. Return, changing to B when 2 loops remain.
Rep 2nd and 3rd rows.

Plough Stitch

Starting chain: multiple of 2 sts + 2
Drape: fair
Skill: intermediate

Special Abbreviation

Cross 2 = skip next st, 1Tss into next st, 1Tss into skipped st.
Note: The Crossed Stitches appear 1 row below the row on which the Cross 2 is worked.
1ST ROW: Using A, as Basic Forward and Return row.

2ND ROW: Using A, with 1 loop on hook, 1Tss into each st to end. Return.
3RD ROW: Using B, as 2nd row.
4TH ROW: Using A, with 1 loop on hook, ✳Cross 2;(see Special Abbreviation) rep from ✳ to last st, 1Tss into last st. Return.Rep 2nd to 4th rows.

Tunisian Basketweave Stitch I

Starting chain: multiple of 8 sts + 4
Drape: fair
Skill: intermediate

1ST ROW: As Basic Forward and Return row.
2ND ROW: Tks into each of next 3 sts, ✳Tps into each of next 4 sts, Tks into each of next 4 sts; rep from ✳ to end. Return.
Rep 2nd row 3 times.
5TH ROW: Tps into each of next 3 sts, ✳Tks into each of next 4 sts, Tps into each of next 4 sts; rep from ✳ to end. Return.
Rep 5th row 3 times.
Rep these 8 rows.

Tunisian Basketweave Stitch II

Starting chain: multiple of 14 sts + 7
Drape: fair
Skill: intermediate

1ST ROW: As Basic Forward and Return row.
2ND ROW: With 1 loop on hook, work 1Tss

into each of next 6 sts, ✳work 1Tps into each of next 7 sts, work 1Tss into each of next 7 sts; rep from ✳ to end. Return.

3RD TO 7TH ROWS: Rep 2nd row 5 times more.

8TH ROW: With 1 loop on hook, work 1Tps into each of next 6 sts, ✳work 1Tss into each of next 7 sts, work 1 Tps into each of next 7 sts; rep from ✳ to end. Return.

9TH TO 13TH ROWS: Rep 8th row 5 times more.

Rep 2nd to 13th rows.

Thick Gauze Stitch
Starting chain: multiple of 2 sts + 3
Drape: good
Skill: intermediate

Special Abbreviation
Long Tdc (worked on Forward rows) = loosely work1Tdc into next st 2 rows below.

1ST ROW: As Basic Forward and Return row.
2ND ROW: With 1 loop on hook, work 1Tss into each st to end. Return.

3RD ROW: With 1 loop on hook, ✳1 Long Tdc (see Special Abbreviation), 1Tss into next st; rep from ✳ to end. Return.
4TH ROW: With 1 loop on hook, ✳1Tss into next st, 1 Long Tdc; rep from ✳ to last 2 sts, 1Tss into each of last 2 sts. Return. Rep 3rd and 4th rows.

Chequered Stitch
Starting chain: multiple of 2 sts + 3
Drape: good
Skill: intermediate

Work as Thick Gauze Stitch, but working 1 row each in colors A and B throughout.

Plough and Cable Stitch
Starting chain: multiple of 8 sts + 4
Drape: good
Skill: easy

1ST ROW: As Basic Forward and Return row.
2ND ROW: With 1 loop on hook, work 1Tss into each of next 3 sts, ✳work 1Tps into each of next 4 sts, work 1Tss into each of next 4 sts; rep from ✳ to end. Return. Rep 2nd row.

Thick Gauze Stitch II
Starting chain: multiple of 10 sts + 11
Drape: good
Skill: intermediate

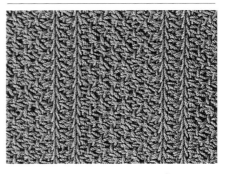

1ST ROW: As Basic Forward and Return row.
2ND ROW: With 1 loop on hook, 1Tps into next st, 1Tss into each of next 2 sts, ✳1TwTss into next st, 1Tss into next st, 1TwTss into next st, 1Tps into next st, [1Tss into next st, 1Tps into next st] twice, 1Tss into each of next 2 sts; rep from ✳ to last 7 sts, 1TwTss into next st, 1Tss into next st, 1TwTss into next st, [1Tps into next st, 1Tss into next st] twice. Return.
3RD ROW: With 1 loop on hook, 1Tss into next st, 1Tps into next st, 1Tss into next st, ✳[1TwTss into next st, 1Tss into next st] twice, [1Tps into next st, 1Tss into next st] 3 times; rep from ✳ to last 7 sts, [1TwTss into next st, 1Tss into next st] twice, 1Tps into next st, 1Tss into next st, 1Tps into last st. Return.
Rep 2nd and 3rd rows.

Frosted Stitch

Starting chain: multiple of 6 sts + 3
Drape: good
Skill: intermediate

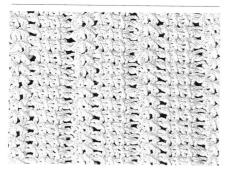

Special Abbreviations

Basic Group 3 = 1st part worked as Basic Forward row, on Return row work 1ch, yo, draw hook through 4 loops, 1ch.

Group 3 = on Forward row insert hook under next ch, yo, draw loop through, insert hook into loop over the Group 3 on previous row, yo, draw loop through, insert hook under next ch, yo, draw loop through. On Return row work 1ch, yo, draw hook through 4 loops, 1ch.

1ST ROW: As Basic Forward row. Return as follows: yo, draw hook through 1 loop, [yo, draw hook through 2 loops] twice, ✳Basic Group 3 (see Special Abbreviations), [yo, draw through 2 loops] 3 times; rep from ✳ to end.

2ND ROW: With 1 loop on hook, work 1Tss into each of next 2 sts, ✳Group 3, (see Special Abbreviations) work 1Tss into each of next 3 sts; rep from ✳ to end. Return as follows: yo, draw hook through 1 loop, [yo, draw hook through 2 loops] twice, ✳Group 3, [yo, draw through 2 loops] 3 times; rep from ✳ to end. Rep 2nd row.

2-Color Ripple Stitch

Starting chain: multiple of 6 sts + 3
Drape: good
Skill: intermediate

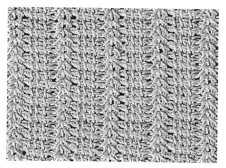

Work as given for Frosted Stitch but working 1 row in A and 1 row in B throughout.

Fan Stitch

Starting chain: multiple of 14 sts + 2
Drape: good
Skill: intermediate

1ST ROW: As Basic Forward and Return row.
Commence Pattern
2ND ROW: Using A, 1Tss into next and each st to end. Return. Rep 2nd row 3 times.
6TH ROW: Using B, 1Tss in each of next 7 sts, skip 3 sts, leaving last loop of each on hook and always inserting hook as for Tks work 7Tdc into next st = (called Fan), skip 3 sts; rep from ✳ ending 1tss into edge st. Return.Using A, rep 2nd row 4 times.
11TH ROW: Using B, ✳skip 3 sts, Fan into next st, skip 3 sts, 1Tss into each of next 7 sts; rep from ✳ ending 1Tss into edge st. Return. Rep 2nd to 11th rows.

Open Cluster Stitch

Starting chain: multiple of 4 sts + 1
Drape: fair
Skill: intermediate

1ST ROW: As Basic Forward. Work return as follows: yo, draw through 2 loops, ✳3ch, yo, draw through 5 loops; rep from ✳ until 4 loops remain, 3ch, yo, draw through last 4 loops.
2ND ROW: Skip 1 Cluster, ✳[insert hook into next ch, yo, draw loop through] 3 times, insert hook under thread which closed next Cluster, yo, draw loop through, rep from ✳ to end. Work return as follows: yo, draw through 2 loops, ✳3ch, yo, draw through 5 loops; rep from ✳ until 4 loops remain, 3ch, yo, draw through last 4 loops. Rep 2nd row.

Corded Stitch

Starting chain: any number of sts
Drape: fair
Skill: easy

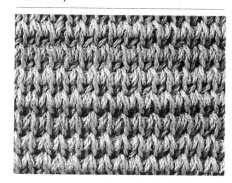

Work one row as a Basic Forward and Return row.

Commence Pattern

1ST ROW: Using B, ✳insert hook into next st as for Tks, yo, draw loop through, yo, draw through 1 loop; rep from ✳ to end including edge st. Return.

2ND ROW: Using C, work as 1st row.

3RD ROW: Using A, work as 1st row. Rep these 3 rows.

Fine Weave Stitch
Starting chain: multiple of 10 sts + 7
Drape: good
Skill: intermediate

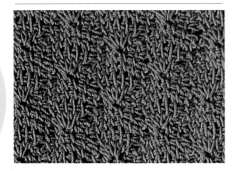

Special Abbreviation

5Tdc Fan = skip next 2 sts, work 5 loose Tdc round stem of next st 3 rows below, skip next 2 sts.

1ST ROW: As Basic Forward and Return row.

2ND ROW: With 1 loop on hook, 1Tss into each st to end. Return.

3RD AND 4TH ROWS: Rep 2nd row twice.

5TH ROW: With 1 loop on hook, work 5Tdc Fan (see Special Abbreviation), ✳1Tss into each of next 5 sts, work 5Tdc Fan; rep from ✳ to last st, 1Tss into last st. Return.

6TH AND 7TH ROWS: Rep 2nd row twice.

8TH ROW: With 1 loop on hook, ✳1Tss into each of next 5 sts, work 5Tdc Fan; rep from ✳ to last 6 sts, 1Tss into each of last 6 sts. Return. Rep 3rd to 8th rows.

Tunisian Bobble Stitch
Starting chain: multiple of 4 sts + 3
Drape: fair
Skill: experienced
Note: For description of tr3tog see page 187.

Work as a Basic Forward and Return row.

Commence Pattern

1ST ROW: 1Tss into each of next 2 sts, ✳inserting hook as for Tks work a Tunisian Bobble of tr3tog all into next st, 1Tss into each of next 3 sts; rep from ✳ to end. Return.

2ND ROW: 1Tss to end. Return.

3RD ROW: Bobble into next st, 1Tss into next 3 sts; rep from ✳ until 2 sts remain, Bobble into next st, 1Tss into last st. Return.

4TH ROW: 1Tss to end. Return. Rep these 4 rows.

Contrasting Bobbles I
Starting chain: multiple of 6 sts + 5
Drape: good
Skill: experienced

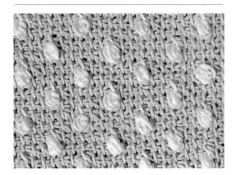

Special Abbreviation

MB (Make Bobble) = using color B [yo, insert hook into next st, yo and draw loop through] 3 times into same st, yo and draw through 6 loops, see Note.

NOTE: Pattern is worked in color A on every row. Color B is used for Bobbles only and is carried loosely across back of work on 2nd and 4th rows. Cut and rejoin color B at beginning of each Bobble row.

1ST ROW: As Basic Forward and Return row.

2ND ROW: With 1 loop on hook, work 1Tss into next st, MB (see Special Abbreviation) into next st, ✳1Tss into each of next 5 sts, MB into next st; rep from ✳ to last 2 sts, 1Tss into each of last 2 sts. Return using A only.

3RD ROW: With 1 loop on hook, 1Tss into each st to end. Return.

4TH ROW: With 1 loop on hook, 1Tss into each of next 4 sts, ✳MB into next st, 1Tss into each of next 5 sts; rep from ✳ to end. Return using A only.

5TH ROW: As 3rd row. Rep 2nd to 5th rows.

Contrasting Bobbles II
Starting chain: multiple of 6 sts + 5
Drape: good
Skill: experienced

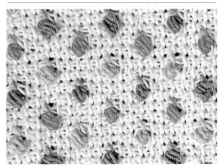

Work as given for Contrasting Bobbles I, but working 1 row of Bobbles each in colors B, C and D.

Bobble and Grid Pattern

Starting chain: multiple of 8 sts + 7
Drape: good
Skill: experienced

Special Abbreviations

Long Tdc (worked on Forward rows) = loosely work 1Tdc into vertical loop above Bobble 3 rows below.

MB (Make Bobble) = [yo, insert hook into next st, yo and draw loop through] 3 times into same st, yo, draw yarn through 6 loops.

1ST ROW: As Basic Forward and Return row.

2ND ROW: With 1 loop on hook, work 1Tss into each of next 2 sts, ✳MB (see Special Abbreviations) into next st, 1Tss into each of next 7 sts; rep from ✳ to last 4 sts, MB, 1Tss into each of last 3 sts. Return.

3RD ROW: With 1 loop on hook, ✳MB into next st, 1Tss into each of next 3 sts; rep from ✳ to last 2 sts, MB, 1Tss into last st. Return.

4TH ROW: As 2nd row.

5TH ROW: With 1 loop on hook work 1Tss into each st to end. Return.

6TH ROW: As 5th row.

7TH ROW: With 1 loop on hook, work 1Tss into each of next 2 sts, ✳work Long Tdc (see Special Abbreviations), 1Tss into each of next 7 sts; rep from ✳ to last 4 sts, work long Tdc, 1Tss into each of last 3 sts. Return.

Rep 2nd to 7th rows.

Spring Bud Pattern

Starting chain: multiple of 2 sts + 3
Drape: fair
Skill: intermediate

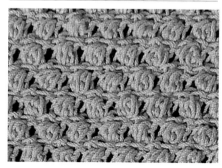

Special Abbreviation

MB (Make Bobble) = work [yo, insert hook into next st, yo and draw loop through] 3 times into same st, yo, draw yarn through 6 loops.

1ST ROW: As Basic Forward and Return row.

2ND ROW: With 1 loop on hook, work 1Tss into next st, ✳MB (see Special Abbreviation) into next st, 1Tss into next st; rep from ✳ to last st, 1Tss into last st. Return.

3RD ROW: With 1 loop on hook, ✳MB into next st, 1Tss into next st; rep from ✳ to end. Return. Rep 2nd and 3rd rows.

Links and Loops

Starting chain: multiple of 3 sts + 3
Drape: fair
Skill: intermediate
Note: Color is changed after each Forward row. Work 1st ch of each Return row in new color.

Special Abbreviation

Cross 2 = skip next st, 1Tss into next st, 1Tss into skipped st. Make chain in color A.

1ST ROW: Using color A as Basic Forward row. Using color B Return.

2ND ROW: Using B, with 1 loop on hook, ✳1Tps into next st, Cross 2; (see Special Abbreviation) rep from ✳ to last 2 sts, 1Tps into next st, 1Tss into last st. Using A Return.

3RD ROW: Using A, with 1 loop on hook, ✳1Tps into next st, Cross 2; rep from ✳ to last 2 sts, 1Tps into next st, 1Tss into last st. Using B Return. Rep 2nd and 3rd rows.

Flowerbed Stitch

Starting chain: multiple of 3 sts + 2
Drape: fair
Skill: intermediate

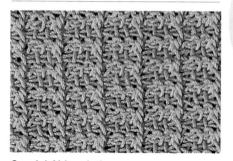

Special Abbreviation

Long Ttr (worked on Forward rows) = loosely work 1 Ttr into vertical loop of next st 2 rows below.

1ST ROW: As Basic Forward and Return row.

2ND ROW: With 1 loop on hook, 1Tps into next st, ✳1Tdc into next st, 1Tss into each of next 2 sts; rep from ✳ to end. Return.

3RD ROW: With 1 loop on hook, work 1Tss into each st to end. Return.

4TH ROW: With 1 loop on hook, 1Tps into next st, ✳work 1 Long Ttr (see Special Abbreviation), 1Tps into each of next 2 sts; rep from ✳ to end. Return. Rep 3rd and 4th rows.

Chunky Mesh Stitch
Starting chain: multiple of 2 sts + 1
Drape: fair
Skill: intermediate

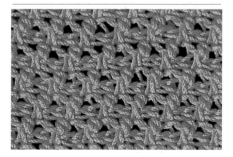

1ST ROW: As Basic Forward and Return row.
2ND ROW: With 1 loop on hook, ✳1Tdc into next st, 1Tps into next st; rep from ✳ to end. Return.
3RD ROW: With 1 loop on hook, ✳work 1Tps into next st, 1Tdc into next st; rep from ✳ to end. Return.
Rep 2nd and 3rd rows.

Crescent Stitch
Starting chain: multiple of 2 sts + 3
Drape: good
Skill: intermediate

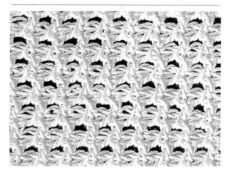

1ST ROW: As Basic Forward and Return row.
2ND ROW: With 1 loop on hook, ✳Tss2tog, yo; rep from ✳ to last 2 sts, 1Tss into each of last 2 sts. Return.
3RD ROW: With 1 loop on hook, ✳1Tss into next vertical loop, 1Tss under ch loop of

next st; rep from ✳ to last 2 sts, 1Tss into each of last 2 sts. Return.
Rep 2nd and 3rd rows.

Tunisian Chevron Stitch I
Starting chain: multiple of 14 sts + 1
Drape: good
Skill: easy

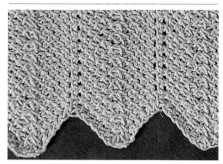

1ST ROW: As Basic Forward and Return row.
2ND ROW: With 1 loop on hook, ✳inc 1Tss, work 1Tss into each of next 4 sts, Tss3tog, work 1Tss into each of next 5 sts, inc 1Tss; rep from ✳ to end. Return.
Rep 2nd row.

Tunisian Chevron Stitch II
Starting chain: multiple of 14 sts + 1
Drape: good
Skill: easy

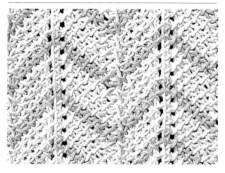

Work as Tunisian Chevron Stitch I, but working 3 rows in color A and 1 row in color B throughout, or work using random colors.

Tunisian Cable Stitch
Starting chain: multiple of 7 sts + 7
Drape: good
Skill: intermediate

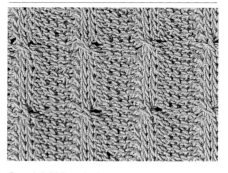

Special Abbreviation
T3st Cable = skip next 2 sts, work 1Tks into 3rd st, work 1Tks into 2nd st, work 1Tks into first st.
1ST ROW: As Basic Forward and Return row.
2ND ROW: With 1 loop on hook 1Tps into next st, ✳1Tks into each of next 3 sts, 1Tps into each of next 4 sts; rep from ✳ to last 5 sts, 1Tks into each of next 3 sts, 1Tps into next st, 1Tss into last st. Return.
3RD AND 4TH ROWS: Rep 2nd row twice.
5TH ROW: With 1 loop on hook 1Tps into next st, ✳T3st Cable (see Special Abbreviation), 1Tps into each of next 4 sts; rep from ✳ to last 5 sts, T3st Cable, 1Tps into next st, 1Tss into last st. Return.
6TH TO 11TH ROWS: Rep 2nd row 6 times.
Rep 5th to 11th rows.

Diagonal Openwork Pattern
Starting chain: multiple of 11 sts + 2
Drape: good
Skill: experienced
Note: When working Tss2tog work

heavyweight patterns

through diagonal loop of yo of previous row where applicable.

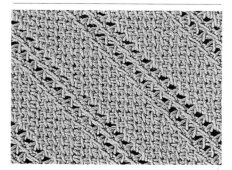

1ST ROW: As Basic Forward and Return row.

2ND ROW: With 1 loop on hook, 1Tss into each of next 3 sts, [yo, Tss2tog] twice, ✳1Tss into each of next 7 sts, [yo, Tss2tog] twice; rep from ✳ to last 5 sts, 1Tss into each of last 5 sts. Return.

3RD ROW: With 1 loop on hook, 1Tss into each of next 3 sts, 1Tss under ch loop of next st, [yo, Tss2tog] twice, ✳1Tss into each of next 6 sts, 1Tss under ch loop of next st, [yo, Tss2tog] twice; rep from ✳ to last 4 sts, 1Tss into each of last 4 sts. Return.

4TH ROW: With 1 loop on hook, 1Tss into each of next 4 sts, 1Tss under ch loop of next st, [yo, Tss2tog] twice, ✳1Tss into each of next 6 sts, 1Tss under ch loop of next st, [yo, Tss2tog] twice; rep from ✳ to last 3 sts, 1Tss into each of last 3 sts. Return.

5TH ROW: With 1 loop on hook, 1Tss into each of next 5 sts, 1Tss under ch loop of next st, [yo, Tss2tog] twice, ✳1Tss into each of next 6 sts, 1Tss under ch loop of next st, [yo, Tss2tog] twice; rep from ✳ to last 2 sts, 1Tss into each of last 2 sts. Return.

6TH ROW: With 1 loop on hook, ✳1Tss into each of next 6 sts, 1Tss under ch loop of next st, [yo, Tss2tog] twice; rep from ✳ to last st, 1Tss into last st. Return.

7TH ROW: With 1 loop on hook, 1Tss into each of next 7 sts, 1Tss under ch loop of next st, ✳[yo, Tss2tog] twice, 1Tss into each of next 6 sts, 1Tss under ch loop of next st; rep from ✳ to last 4 sts, yo, Tss2tog, 1Tss into each of last 2 sts. Return.

8TH ROW: With 1 loop on hook, yo, Tss2tog, 1Tss into each of next 6 sts, 1Tss under ch loop of next st, ✳[yo, Tss2tog] twice, 1Tss into each of next 6 sts, 1Tss under ch loop of next st; rep from ✳ to last 3 sts, yo, Tss2tog, 1Tss into last st. Return.

9TH ROW: With 1 loop on hook, 1Tss under ch loop of next st, yo, Tss2tog, 1Tss into each of next 6 sts, 1Tss under ch loop of next st, ✳[yo, Tss2tog] twice, 1Tss into each of next 6 sts, 1Tss under ch loop of next st; rep from ✳ to last 2 sts, 1Tss into each of last 2 sts. Return.

10TH ROW: With 1 loop on hook, [yo, Tss2tog] twice, ✳1Tss into each of next 6 sts, 1Tss under ch loop of next st, [yo, Tss2tog] twice; rep from ✳ to last 8 sts, 1Tss into each of last 8 sts. Return.

11TH ROW: With 1 loop on hook, ✳1Tss under ch loop of next st, [yo, Tss2tog] twice, 1Tss into each of next 6 sts; rep from ✳ to last st, 1Tss into last st. Return.

12TH ROW: With 1 loop on hook, 1Tss into next st, ✳1Tss under ch loop of next st, [yo, Tss2tog] twice, 1Tss into each of next 6 sts; rep from ✳ to end. Return.

13TH ROW: With 1 loop on hook, 1Tss into each of next 2 sts, 1Tss under ch loop of next st, [yo, Tss2tog] twice, ✳1Tss into each of next 6 sts, 1Tss under ch loop of next st, [yo, Tss2tog] twice; rep from ✳ to last 5 sts, 1Tss into each of last 5 sts. Return.

Rep 3rd to 13th rows.

Two-color Openwork
Starting chain: multiple of 6 sts + 7
Drape: good
Skill: experienced

Special Abbreviation
3 St Triangle = on Forward row work 1Tdc into previous st 2 rows below, work 1Tss into next st, work 1Tdc into next st 2 rows below, yo, draw through 3 loops. Return as

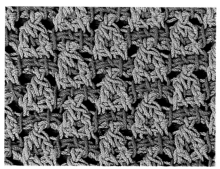

follows: yo, draw through 2 loops.

1ST ROW: Using A, as Basic Forward and Return row.

2ND ROW: Using B, with 1 loop on hook, work 1Tss into next st, ✳skip 1 st, work 1Tss into next st, skip 1 st, work 1Tss into each of next 3 sts; rep from ✳ to last 5 sts, skip next st, work 1Tss into next st, skip next st, work 1Tss into each of last 2 sts. Return as follows: yo, draw hook through 1 loop, yo, draw hook through 2 loops, ✳1ch, yo, draw hook through 2 loops, 1ch, [yo, draw hook through 2 loops] 3 times; rep from ✳ until 4 loops remain on hook, 1ch, yo, draw hook through 2 loops, 1ch, [yo, draw hook through 2 loops] twice.

3RD ROW: Using A, with 1 loop on hook, work 1Tss into next st, skip next sp, work 3 St Triangle (see Special Abbreviation), skip next sp, ✳ work 1Tss into each of next 3 sts, skip next sp, work 3 St Triangle, skip next sp; rep from ✳ to last 2 sts, work 1Tss into each of last 2 sts. Return as follows: yo, draw hook through 1 loop, yo, draw hook through 2 loops, ✳1ch, yo, draw hook through 2 loops, 1ch, [yo, draw hook through 2 loops] 3 times; rep from ✳ until 4 loops remain on hook, 1ch, yo, draw hook through 2 loops, 1ch, [yo, draw hook through 2 loops] twice.

4TH ROW: Using B, with 1 loop on hook, ✳skip next st, 1Tss under ch loop of next st, 1Tss into next st, 1Tss under ch loop of next st, skip 1 st, 1Tss into next st; rep from ✳ to end. Return as follows: yo, draw hook through 1 loop, ✳1ch, [yo, draw hook through 2 loops] 3 times, 1ch, yo, draw hook through 2 loops; rep from ✳ to end.

5TH ROW: Using A, with 1 loop on hook, work 1Tdc into next vertical loop 2 rows below, yo, draw hook through 2 loops, skip next sp, 1Tss into each of next 3 sts, skip next sp, ✳work 3 St Triangle, skip next sp, 1Tss into each of next 3 sts, skip next sp; rep from ✳ to last st, work 1Tdc into previous st 2 rows below, 1Tss into last st, yo and through 2 loops. Return as follows: yo, draw hook through 1 loop, ✳1ch, [yo, draw hook through 2 loops] 3 times, 1ch, yo, draw hook through 2 loops; rep from ✳ to end.

6TH ROW: Using B, with 1 loop on hook, ✳work 1Tss under ch loop of next st, skip next st, 1Tss into next st, skip next st, 1Tss under ch loop of next st, 1Tss into next st; rep from ✳ to end. Return as follows: yo, draw hook through 1 loop, yo, draw hook through 2 loops, ✳1ch, yo, draw hook through 2 loops, 1ch, [yo, draw hook through 2 loops] 3 times; rep from ✳ until 4 loops remain on hook, 1ch, yo, draw hook through 2 loops, 1ch, [yo, draw hook through 2 loops] twice. Rep 3rd to 6th rows always working Tdc into sts 2 rows below.

Tunisian Mesh

Starting chain: multiple of 2 sts + 1
Drape: good
Skill: intermediate

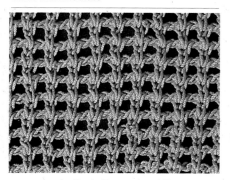

1ST ROW: As Basic Forward and Return row.
2ND ROW: With 1 loop on hook, 2ch, ✳skip next st, yo, 1Tks into next st, 2ch; rep from ✳ to end. Return.

3RD ROW: With 1 loop on hook, 2ch, ✳skip next sp, yo, 1Tks into upper of 2ch of previous Forward row, 2ch; rep from ✳ to end. Return. Rep 3rd row.

Little Fan Openwork

Starting chain: multiple of 3 sts + 2
Drape: good
Skill: intermediate

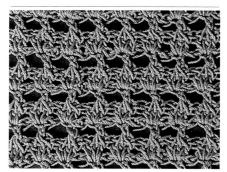

Special Abbreviations

Fan = work 3Tdc into center of upper of 2ch in previous Forward row.

Lace 3tog = insert hook through next 3 vertical loops, yo, draw loop through, 2ch (on Return row 1 ch, yo, draw hook through 2 loops,1ch).

Note: Count sts only after 3rd row.

1ST ROW: As Basic Forward and Return row.
2ND ROW: With 1 loop on hook, 2ch, ✳Lace 3tog (see Special Abbreviations); rep from ✳ to last st, 1Tss into last st, 2ch. Return as follows: yo, draw hook through 1 loop, 1ch, ✳yo, draw hook through 2 loops, 2ch; rep from ✳ until 3 loops remain on hook, yo, draw hook through 2 loops, 1ch, yo, draw hook through 2 loops.
3RD ROW: With 1 loop on hook, 2ch, ✳work 1 Fan (see Special Abbreviations); rep from ✳ to last st, 1Tdc into upper ch of last st. Return.
Rep 2nd and 3rd rows.

openwork patterns

Crocheted lace is one of the most versatile forms of needlework. It can be used for tablecloths, placemats, bedspreads, baby clothes, summer garments, and spectacular evening clothes. Filet crochet is ideally suited to curtains, perhaps for a bathroom or kitchen. Other mesh-type fabrics are used as backgrounds for Irish crochet motifs.

filet crochet

In filet crochet, solid motifs are contrasted with an open rectangular network to produce motifs, edgings, or whole fabrics. The technique is simple (*pages 195–196*) and the effect crisp and appealing. Traditionally, this kind of crochet is usually worked in white or cream, but black or a color could also be attractive. For a simple curtain, work a piece of the required size in the basic network, finishing the lower edge with Greek Key Frieze (*below*). All of these fabrics drape well.

openwork patterns

### Greek Key Frieze	### Alternating Tiles	### Southern Cross
Starting chain: multiple of 36 sts + 9	**Starting chain:** multiple of 24 sts + 6	**Starting chain:** multiple of 45 sts + 18
Pattern repeat: 12 squares	**Pattern repeat:** 8 squares	**Pattern repeat:** 15 squares
Skill: easy	**Skill:** easy	**Skill:** easy

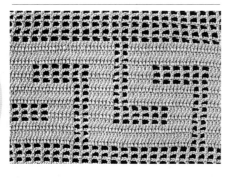 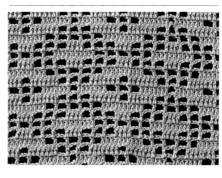 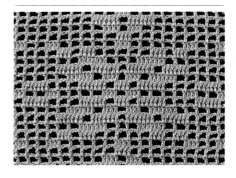

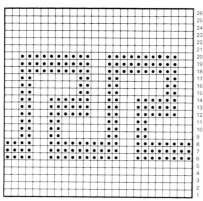 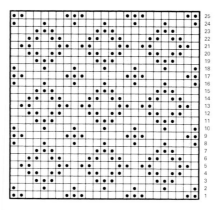 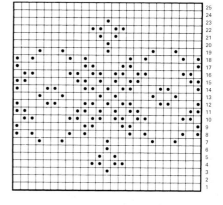

Orchid Blooms

Starting chain: multiple of 3 sts + 1
Pattern repeat: 22 squares
Skill: easy

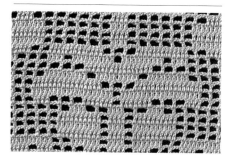

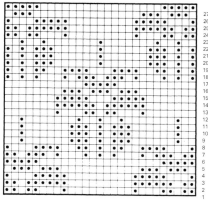

Chequerboard

Starting chain: multiple of 3 sts + 1
Pattern repeat: 2 squares
Skill: easy

Lacets and Bars

Starting chain: multiple of 6 sts + 1
Pattern repeat: 1 square of 2 rows
Skill: intermediate

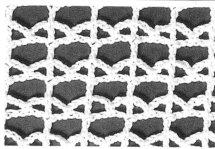

1ST ROW: 1sc into 10th ch from hook, ✳3ch, skip 2ch, 1dc into next ch, 3ch, skip 2ch, 1sc into next ch, rep from ✳ to last 3ch, skip 2ch, 1dc into last ch, turn.
2ND ROW: 8ch (count as 1dc and 5ch sp), 1dc into next dc, ✳5ch, 1dc into next dc, rep from ✳ to end, working last dc into 4th ch from last sc in row below, turn.
3RD ROW: 6ch (count as 1dc and 3ch sp), skip 1st dc and next 2ch, 1sc into next ch (middle chain of 5ch), 3ch, 1dc into next dc, ✳3ch, skip next 2ch, 1sc into next ch, 3ch, 1dc into next dc, rep from ✳ to end, working last dc into into 3rd ch from where last sc was worked in row below, turn.
Rep 2nd and 3rd rows, ending with a 2nd row.

Clover Leaf

Starting chain: multiple of 3 sts + 1
Pattern repeat: 4 squares
Skill: easy

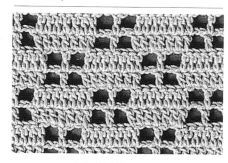

Greek Cross

Starting chain: multiple of 3 sts + 1
Pattern repeat: 12 squares
Skill: easy

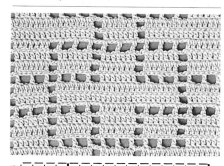

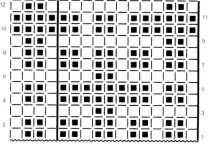

Peony Motif

Starting chain: 90 sts
Pattern: 29 squares
Skill: easy

Poinsettia Motif

Starting chain: 90 sts
Pattern: 29 squares
Skill: easy

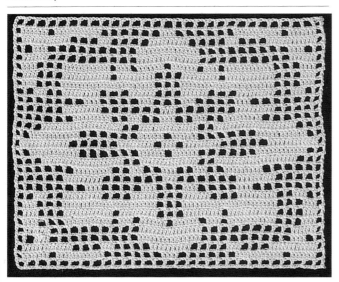

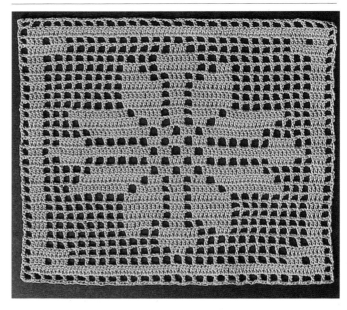

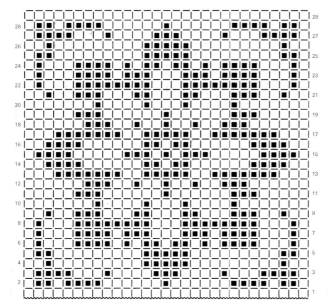

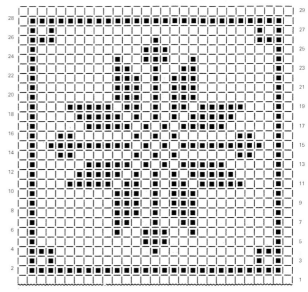

Star Motif
Starting chain: 66 sts
Pattern: 21 squares
Skill: easy

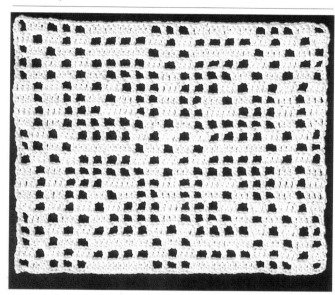

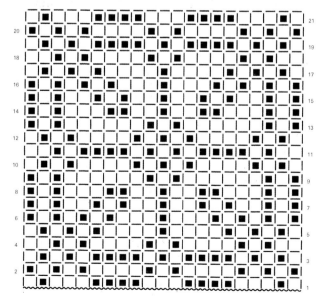

Oak Leaf Motif
Starting chain: 66 sts
Pattern: 29 squares
Skill: easy

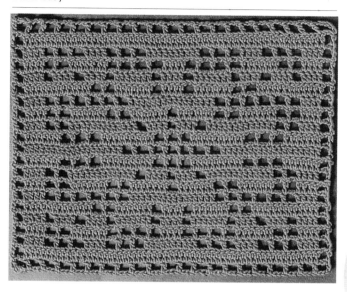

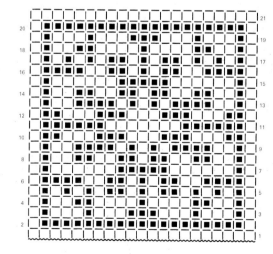

Celtic Cross

Starting chain: 66 sts
Pattern: 21 squares
Skill: easy

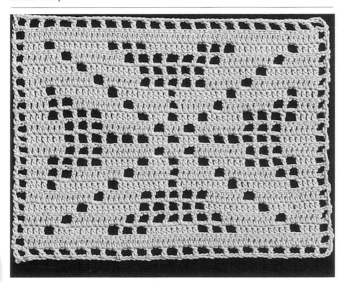

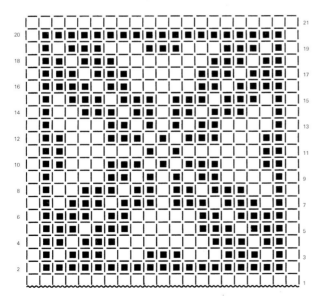

Scalloped Fringe

Starting chain: 54 sts
Pattern repeat: 17 squares and 12 rows
Skill: intermediate

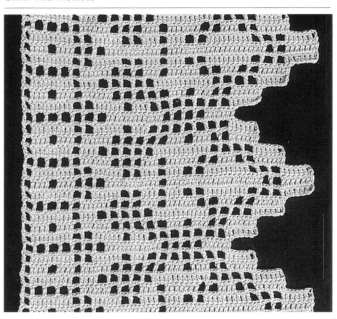

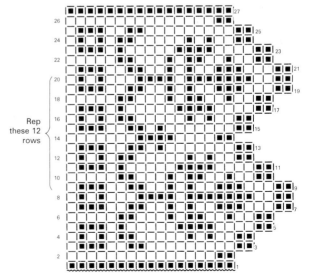

Flowerpots

Starting chain: multiple of 30 sts + 6
Pattern repeat: 10 squares
Skill: easy

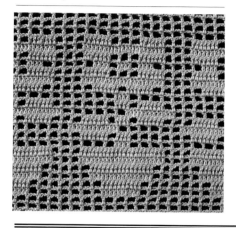

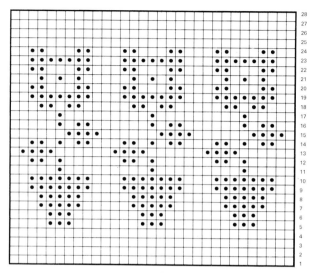

Butterfly

Starting chain: multiple of 93 sts + 3
Pattern repeat: 31 squares
Skill: easy

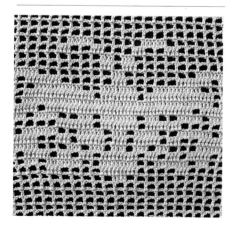

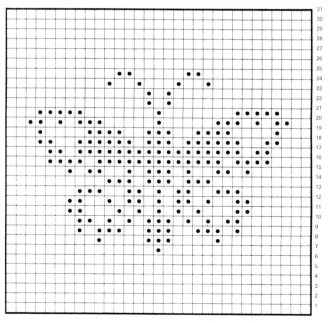

Peace Rose

Starting chain: multiple of 90 sts + 12
Pattern repeat: 30 squares
Skill: intermediate
Note: starting chain allows for a 3-square border at beginning and end of row; for extra spaces add an even multiple of 3 plus 3 chain.

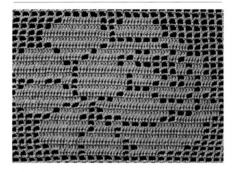

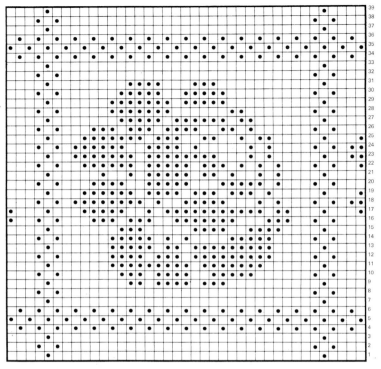

Pokerwork

Starting chain: multiple of 3 sts + 1
Pattern repeat: 24 squares wide by 23 squares deep
Skill: easy

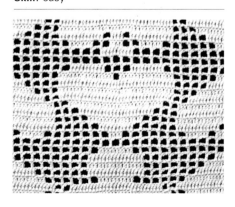

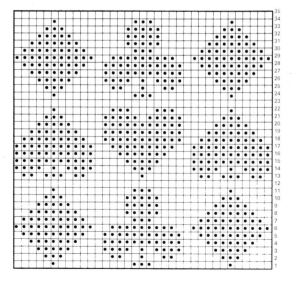

openwork patterns

Letterform

Starting chain: variable (for "A", 69)
Pattern repeat: variable (example shown
here is 22 squares wide by 35 deep)
Skill: easy

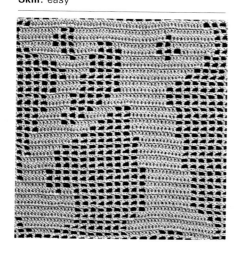

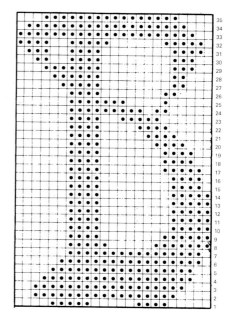

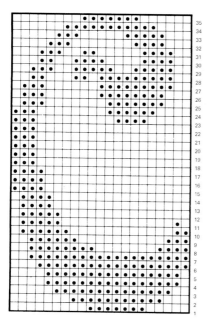

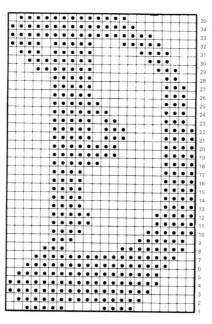

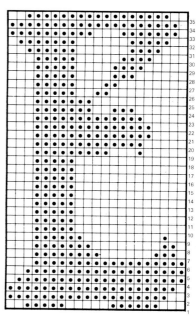

Letterform

Starting chain: multiple of 3 sts + 1
Pattern repeat: variable (example shown
here is 22 squares wide by 35 deep)
Skill: easy

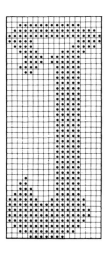

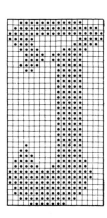

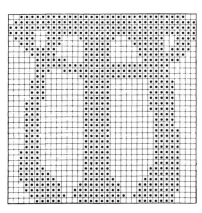

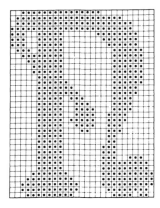

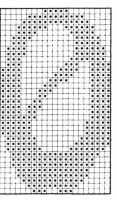

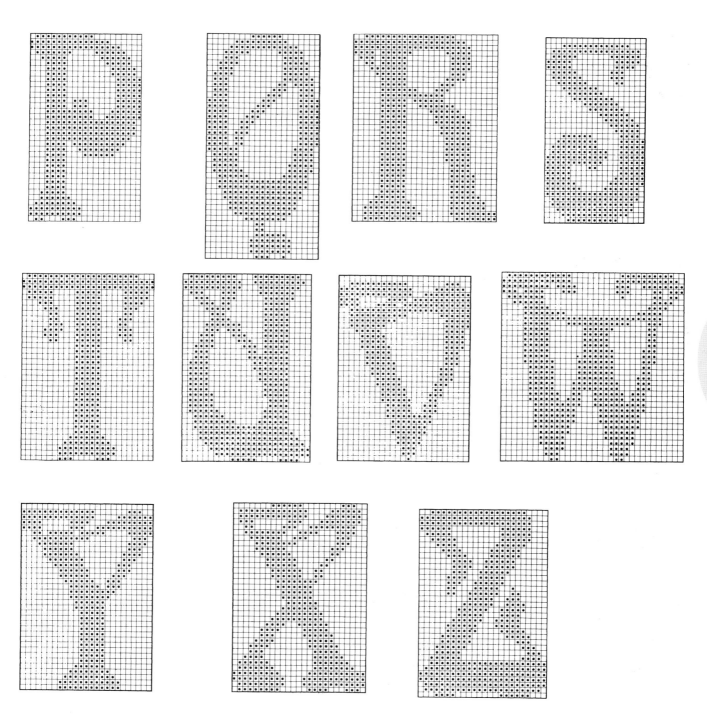

trellis-type patterns

Like filet crochet (*page 252*) these patterns have a network type of structure. Here, however, grouped stitches are used in an all-over repeat, rather than forming motifs, and the groups take various forms. Acrobatic Stitch (*below*) uses groups to form a bold network; this might be worked in cotton string for a hammock. The delicate Floral Trellis Stitch (*page 264*) would be ideal for a shawl—perhaps crocheted in a glossy mercerized cotton—or for the skirt of a christening robe.

Ruled Lattice
Starting chain: multiple of 4 sts + 2
Drape: excellent
Skill: easy

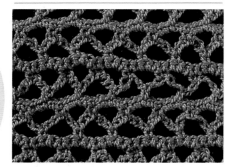

1ST ROW (RS): 1sc into 2nd ch from hook, 1sc into each ch to end, turn.
2ND ROW: 7ch, skip 1st 2 sts, 1sc into next st, ✳7ch, skip 3 sts, 1sc into next st; rep from ✳ to last 2 sts, 3ch, skip 1 st, 1dc into last st, skip tch, turn.
3RD ROW: 1ch, 1sc into 1st st, ✳3ch, 1sc into next 7ch arch; rep from ✳ to end, turn.
4TH ROW: 1ch, 1sc into 1st st, ✳3sc into next 3ch arch, 1sc into next sc; rep from ✳ to end, skip tch, turn.
Rep 2nd, 3rd and 4th rows.

Acrobatic Stitch
Starting chain: multiple of 6 sts + 3
Drape: excellent
Skill: intermediate

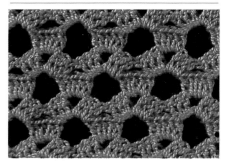

1ST ROW (RS): 2dc into 3rd ch from hook, ✳4ch, skip 5ch, 5dc into next ch; rep from ✳ working only 3dc at end of last rep, turn.
2ND ROW: 2ch (count as 1dc), skip 1st 3 sts, ✳work [3dc, 3ch, 3dc] into next 4ch arch✳✳, skip next 5dc; rep from ✳ ending last rep at ✳✳, skip 2dc, 1dc into top of tch, turn.
3RD ROW: 6ch (count as 1dtr and 1ch), ✳5dc into next 3ch arch✳✳, 4ch; rep from ✳ ending last rep at ✳✳, 1ch, 1dtr into top of tch, turn.
4TH ROW: 5ch (count as 1tr and 1ch), 3dc into next 1ch sp, ✳skip 5dc, work [3dc, 3ch, 3dc] into next 4ch arch; rep from ✳ ending skip 5dc, work [3dc, 1ch, 1tr] into tch, turn.
5TH ROW: 3ch (count as 1dc), 2dc into next 1ch sp, ✳4ch, 5dc into next 3ch arch; rep from ✳ ending 4ch, 3dc into tch, turn.
Rep 2nd, 3rd, 4th and 5th rows.

Block Trellis Stitch
Starting chain: multiple of 8 sts + 6
Drape: excellent
Skill: intermediate

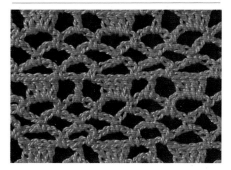

1ST ROW (RS): 1sc into 2nd ch from hook, ✳5ch, skip 3ch, 1sc into next ch; rep from ✳ to end, turn.
2ND ROW: ✳5ch, 1sc into next 5ch arch; rep from ✳ ending 2ch, 1dc into last sc, skip tch, turn.
3RD ROW: 3ch (count as 1dc), 1dc into 1st st, 2ch, 1dc into next 5ch arch, ✳2ch, 4dc into next arch, 2ch, 1dc into next arch; rep from ✳ to end, turn.
4TH ROW: ✳5ch, 1sc into next 2ch sp; rep from ✳ ending 2ch, 1dc into top of tch, turn.
5TH ROW: 1ch, 1sc into 1st st, ✳5ch, 1sc into next 5ch arch; rep from ✳ to end, turn.
Rep 2nd, 3rd, 4th and 5th rows.

Triple-strand Lace

Starting chain: multiple of 8 sts + 2
Drape: excellent
Skill: intermediate

1ST ROW (WS): Work 1sc into 2nd ch from hook, 1sc into each ch to end, turn.
2ND ROW: 1ch, 1sc into each of 1st 3sc, ✳5ch, skip 3sc, 1sc into each of next 5sc; rep from ✳ to end omitting 2sc at end of last rep, turn.
3RD ROW: 1ch, 1sc into each of 1st 2sc, ✳3ch, 1sc into next 5ch arch, 3ch, skip 1sc, 1sc into each of next 3sc; rep from ✳ to end omitting 1sc at end of last rep, turn.
4TH ROW: 1ch, 1sc into 1st sc, ✳3ch, 1sc into next 3ch arch, 1sc into next sc, 1sc into next 3ch arch, 3ch, skip 1sc, 1sc into next sc; rep from ✳ to end, turn.
5TH ROW: 5ch (count as 1dc, 2ch), 1sc into next 3ch arch, 1sc into each of next 3sc, 1sc into next 3ch arch, ✳5ch, 1sc into next 3ch arch, 1sc into each of next 3sc, 1sc into next 3ch arch; rep from ✳ to last sc, 2ch, 1dc into last sc, turn.
6TH ROW: 1ch, 1sc into 1st dc, 3ch, skip 1sc, 1sc into each of next 3sc, ✳3ch, 1sc into next 5ch arch, 3ch, skip 1sc, 1sc into each of next 3sc; rep from ✳ to last 2ch arch, 3ch, 1sc into 3rd of 5ch at beg of previous row, turn.
7TH ROW: 1ch, 1sc into 1st sc, 1sc into 1st 3ch arch, 3ch, skip 1sc, 1sc into next sc, ✳3ch, 1sc into next 3ch arch, 1sc into next sc, 1sc into next 3ch arch, 3ch, skip 1sc, 1sc into next sc; rep from ✳ to last 3ch arch, 3ch, 1sc into 3ch arch, 1sc into last sc, turn.
8TH ROW: 1ch, 1sc into each of 1st 2sc, ✳1sc into next 3ch arch, 5ch, 1sc into

next 3ch arch, 1sc into each of next 3sc; rep from ✳ to end omitting 1sc at end of last rep, turn.
Rep 3rd to 8th rows.

Square-grid Lace

Starting chain: multiple of 18 sts + 8
Drape: excellent
Skill: intermediate

1ST ROW (RS): Work 1dc into 8th ch from hook, ✳2ch, skip 2ch, 1dc into next ch; rep from ✳ to end, turn.
2ND ROW: 5ch (count as 1dc, 2ch), skip 1st dc, 1dc into next dc, ✳4ch, 1tr into each of next 4dc, 4ch, 1dc into next dc, 2ch, 1dc into next dc; rep from ✳ to end placing last dc into 3rd turning ch at beg of previous row, turn.
3RD ROW: 5ch, skip 1st dc, 1dc into next dc, ✳4ch, 1sc into each of next 4tr, 4ch, 1dc into next dc, 2ch, 1dc into next dc; rep from ✳ to end placing last dc into 3rd of 5ch at beg of previous row, turn.
4TH ROW: 5ch, skip 1st dc, 1dc into next dc, ✳4ch, 1sc into each of next 4sc, 4ch, 1dc into next dc, 2ch, 1dc into next dc; rep from ✳ to end placing last dc into 3rd of 5ch at beg of previous row, turn.
5TH ROW: As 4th row.
6TH ROW: 5ch, skip 1st dc, 1dc into next dc, ✳2ch, [1tr into next sc, 2ch] 4 times, 1dc into next dc, 2ch, 1dc into next dc; rep from ✳ to end placing last dc into 3rd of 5ch at beg of previous row, turn.
7TH ROW: 5ch, skip 1st dc, 1dc into next dc, ✳2ch, [1dc into next tr, 2ch] 4 times,

1dc into next dc, 2ch, 1dc into next dc; rep from ✳ to end placing last dc into 3rd of 5ch at beg of previous row, turn.
Rep 2nd to 7th rows.

Interlocking Triangles

Starting chain: multiple of 8 sts + 4
Drape: excellent
Skill: intermediate

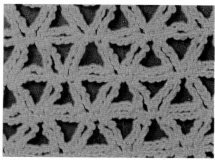

1ST ROW (RS): Work 1sc into 2nd ch from hook, 1sc into next ch, 9ch, 1sc into next ch, 5ch, skip 5ch, 1sc into next ch, ✳[9ch, 1sc into next ch] twice, 5ch, skip 5ch, 1sc into next ch; rep from ✳ to last 2ch, 9ch, 1sc into each of last 2ch, turn.
2ND ROW: 7ch (count as 1tr, 3ch), ✳1sc into next 9ch loop, 1ch, 1sc into next 9ch loop, 5ch; rep from ✳ to end omitting 2ch at end of last rep, 1tr into last sc, turn.
3RD ROW: 1ch, 1sc into 1st tr, 3ch, ✳1sc into next sc, 9ch, 1sc into next ch sp, 9ch, 1sc into next sc, 5ch; rep from ✳ to end omitting 2ch at end of last rep, 1sc into 4th of 7ch at beg of previous row, turn.
4TH ROW: 5ch (count as 1tr, 1ch), ✳1sc into next 9ch loop, 5ch, 1sc into next 9ch loop, 1ch; rep from ✳ to end, 1tr into last sc, turn.
5TH ROW: 1ch, 1sc into 1st tr, 1sc into next ch sp, 9ch, 1sc into next sc, 5ch, ✳1sc into next sc, 9ch, 1sc into next ch sp, 9ch, 1sc into next sc, 5ch; rep from ✳ to last sc, 1sc into last sc, 9ch, 1sc into ch sp, 1sc into 4th of 5ch at beg of previous row, turn. Rep 2nd to 5th rows ending with a 2nd or 4th row.

Shell Trellis Stitch

Starting chain: multiple of 12 sts + 3
Drape: excellent
Skill: intermediate

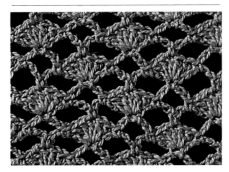

1ST ROW (RS): 2dc into 3rd ch from hook, ✳skip 2ch, 1sc into next ch, 5ch, skip 5ch, 1sc into next ch, skip 2ch, 5dc into next ch; rep from ✳ ending last rep with only 3dc into last ch, turn.

2ND ROW: 1ch, 1sc into 1st st, ✳5ch, 1sc into next 5ch arch, 5ch, 1sc into 3rd dc of next 5dc; rep from ✳ ending last rep with 1sc into top of tch, turn.

3RD ROW: ✳5ch, 1sc into next 5ch arch, 5dc into next sc, 1sc into next arch; rep from ✳ ending 2ch, 1dc into last sc, skip tch, turn.

4TH ROW: 1ch, 1sc into 1st st, ✳5ch, 1sc into 3rd dc of next 5dc, 5ch, 1sc into next 5ch arch; rep from ✳ to end, turn.

5TH ROW: 3ch (count as 1dc), 2dc into first st, ✳1sc into next arch, 5ch, 1 sc into next arch, 5dc into next sc; rep from ✳ ending last rep with only 3dc into last sc, skip tch, turn.

Rep 2nd, 3rd, 4th and 5th rows.

Bullion Trellis Stitch

Starting chain: multiple of 16 sts + 6
Drape: excellent
Skill: experienced
Note: For description of Bullion St see page 191. Make Bullion Sts with [yo] 7 times.

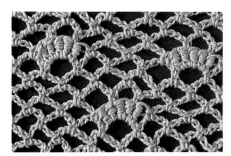

BASE ROW (RS): 1sc into 2nd ch from hook, ✳[5ch, skip 3ch, 1sc into next ch] twice, skip 3ch, work 5 Bullion Sts into next ch, skip 3ch, 1sc into next ch; rep from ✳ to last 4ch, 5ch, skip 3ch, 1sc into last ch, turn.

Commence Pattern

1ST ROW: 5ch, 1sc into next 5ch arch, ✳5ch, 1sc into 2nd of next 5 Bullion Sts, 5ch, 1sc into 4th Bullion St of same group, [5ch, 1sc into next arch] twice; rep from ✳ ending 2ch, 1dc into last sc, skip tch, turn.

2ND ROW: 1ch, 1sc into 1st st, ✳5ch, 1sc into next arch; rep from ✳ to end, turn.

3RD ROW: ✳5ch, 1sc into next arch; rep from ✳ ending 2ch, 1dc into last sc, skip tch, turn.

4TH ROW: 1ch, 1sc into 1st st, skip 2ch sp, ✳5 Bullion Sts into next 5ch arch, 1sc into next arch, [5ch, 1sc into next arch] twice; rep from ✳ ending 5ch, 1sc into tch arch, turn.

5TH ROW: 5ch, 1sc into next 5ch arch, ✳[5ch, 1sc into next arch] twice, 5ch, 1sc into 2nd of next 5 Bullion Sts, 5ch, 1sc into 4th Bullion St of same group; rep from ✳ ending 2ch, 1dc into last sc, skip tch, turn.

6TH ROW: As 2nd row.

7TH ROW: As 3rd row.

8TH ROW: 1ch, 1sc into 1st st, [5ch, 1sc into next 5ch arch] twice, 5 Bullion Sts into next arch, 1sc into next arch; rep from ✳ ending 5ch, 1sc into tch arch, turn.

Rep these 8 rows.

Floral Trellis Stitch

Any number of Flower Units
Drape: excellent
Skill: experienced

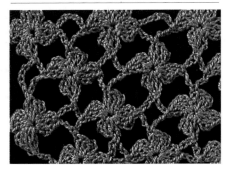

1ST ROW (RS): 7ch, ✳sl st into 4th ch from hook, 3ch, into ring just formed work a Base Flower Unit of [2dc, 3ch, sl st, 3ch, 2dc]✳✳, 10ch; rep from ✳ ending last rep at ✳✳ when fabric is required width, then keep same side facing and turn so as to be able to work along underside of Base Flower Units.

2ND ROW (RS): ✳3ch, sl st into ch ring at center of Flower, 3ch, [2dc, 3ch, sl st – center petal completed, 3ch, 2dc] all into same ring, skip 2ch of base chain which connects Units, sl st into next ch, 7ch, skip 2ch, sl st into next ch; rep from ✳ into next and each Base Flower Unit to end, turn.

NOTE: Check that each Base Flower Unit is not twisted before you work into it.

3RD ROW: 11 ch, sl st into 4th ch from hook, 3ch, 2dc into ring just formed, 3ch, sl st into top of 3ch of center petal of last flower made in previous row (see diagram), ✳10ch, sl st into 4th ch from hook, 3ch, 2dc into ring just formed, sl st into 4th of next 7ch arch of previous row, 3ch, [sl st, 3ch, 2dc] into same ch ring as last 2dc, 3ch, sl st into top of 3ch of center petal of next Flower in previous row; rep from ✳ to end, turn.

4TH ROW: 9ch, skip 2ch, sl st into next ch, ✳3ch, sl st into ch ring at center of Flower, 3ch, work [2dc, 3ch, sl st, 3ch, 2dc] into same ring, skip 2ch, sl st into next ch, 7ch, skip [3ch, sl st and next 2ch], sl st into next ch; rep from ✳ ending 3ch, sl st into ch ring at center of last Flower, 3ch, 2dc into same ring, turn.

5TH ROW: ✳10ch, sl st into 4th ch from hook, 3ch, 2dc into ring just formed, sl st into 4th ch of next arch of previous row, 3ch, [sl st, 3ch, 2dc] into same ch ring as last 2tr✳✳, 3ch, sl st into top of 3ch of center petal of next Flower in previous row; rep from ✳ ending last rep at ✳✳, turn.

Rep 2nd, 3rd, 4th and 5th rows.

When fabric is required length, finishing after a 4th (right-side) row, continue down left side to complete edge Flowers as follows: ✳3ch, [sl st, 3ch, 2dc, 3ch, sl st, 3ch, 2dc] all into ch ring at center of edge Flower, skip 3ch, sl st into next ch✳✳, 6ch, sl st into last ch before center petal of next edge Flower; rep from ✳ ending last rep at ✳✳ after last edge Flower. Fasten off.

4ch, tr2tog inserting hook into next ch for 1st leg and into last ch for 2nd leg, (missing 2ch between), turn.

2ND ROW: 6ch (count as 1tr and 2ch), 1tr into 1st st, ✳tr2tog inserting hook into next tr for 1st leg and then into next Cluster for 2nd leg✳✳, 4ch, 1tr into same place as 2nd leg of Cluster just made; rep from ✳ ending last rep at ✳✳ when 2nd leg is in Edge Cluster, 2ch, 1tr into same place, turn.

3RD ROW: 4ch, skip 2ch, 1 tr into next Cluster (counts as edge cluster), ✳4ch, 1tr into same place as tr just made✳✳, tr2tog inserting hook into next tr for 1st leg and then into next Cluster for 2nd leg; rep from ✳ ending last rep at ✳✳, tr2tog inserting hook into next tr for 1st leg and then into following 3rd ch for 2nd leg, turn.

Rep 2nd and 3rd rows.

Doubled Lattice Stitch

Starting chain: multiple of 6 sts + 5
Drape: excellent
Skill: intermediate
Note: For description of tr2tog see pages 187–188.

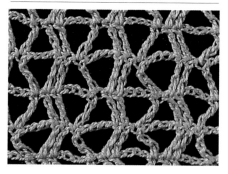

1ST ROW (RS): Skip 6ch, 1tr into next ch (counts as Edge Cluster), 4ch, 1tr into same ch as tr just made, ✳tr2tog inserting hook into next ch for 1st leg and then into following 5th ch for 2nd leg (missing 4ch between), 4ch, 1tr into same ch as 2nd leg of Cluster just made; rep from ✳ to last

dense lace patterns

This section contains a vast variety of patterns, ranging from the very simplest, as in Sieve Stitch (*page 269*) to quite bold patterns, such as 3-Strand Zigzags (*page 268*). In between are classic shell- and fan-type stitches, including the soft and graceful Fantail Stitch (*page 271*) and the more elaborate Open Crescent (*page 277*). The three shown below have a refreshingly crisp character. Alternating Clusters, for example, would lend itself to a summer jacket or a beach cover-up.

Alternating Clusters
Starting chain: multiple of 4 sts + 4
Drape: excellent
Skill: easy

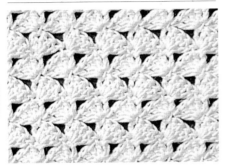

1ST ROW (RS): Work 4dc into 4th ch from hook, skip 3ch, 1sc into next ch, ✳2ch, 4dc into same ch as last sc, skip 3ch, 1sc into next ch; rep from ✳ to end, turn.
2ND ROW: 5ch, work 4dc into 4th ch from hook, ✳skip 4dc, 1sc between last dc skipped and next 2ch, 2ch, 4dc into side of last sc worked; rep from ✳ to last 4dc, skip 4dc, 1sc into next ch, turn.
Rep 2nd row.

Palm Pattern
Starting chain: multiple of 8 sts + 12
Drape: excellent
Skill: easy

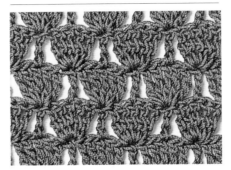

1ST ROW (RS): Work 5tr into 8th ch from hook, skip 3ch, 1tr into next ch, ✳skip 3ch, 5tr into next ch, skip 3ch, 1tr into next ch; rep from ✳ to end, turn.
2ND ROW: 4ch (count as 1tr), 2tr into 1st tr, skip 2tr, 1tr into next tr, ✳skip 2tr, 5tr into next tr, skip 2tr, 1tr into next tr; rep from ✳ to last 3 sts, skip 2tr, 3tr into next ch, turn.
3RD ROW: 4ch, ✳skip 2tr, 5tr into next tr, skip 2tr, 1tr into next tr; rep from ✳ to end placing last tr into 4th of 4ch at beg of previous row, turn.
Rep 2nd and 3rd rows.

Bauble Pattern
Starting chain: multiple of 5 sts + 6
Drape: excellent
Skill: easy

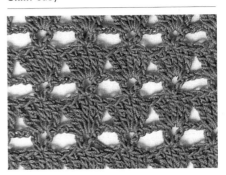

1ST ROW (WS): Work [1dc, 2ch, 1dc] into 8th ch from hook, ✳3ch, skip 4ch, work [1dc, 2ch, 1dc] into next ch; rep from ✳ to last 3ch, 2ch, 1dc into last ch, turn.
2ND ROW: 4ch (count as 1tr), skip 1st 2ch sp, work 5tr into next 2ch sp, ✳skip 3ch sp, work 5tr into next 2ch sp; rep from ✳ to last sp, skip 2ch, 1tr into next ch, turn.
3RD ROW: 5ch (count as 1dc, 2ch), skip 1st 3tr, into next tr work [1dc, 2ch, 1dc], ✳3ch, skip 4tr, into next tr work [1dc, 2ch, 1dc]; rep from ✳ to last 3tr, 2ch, 1dc into 4th of 4ch at beg of previous row, turn.
Rep 2nd and 3rd rows.

Stem and Petal Pattern

Starting chain: multiple of 13 sts + 9
Drape: excellent
Skill: intermediate

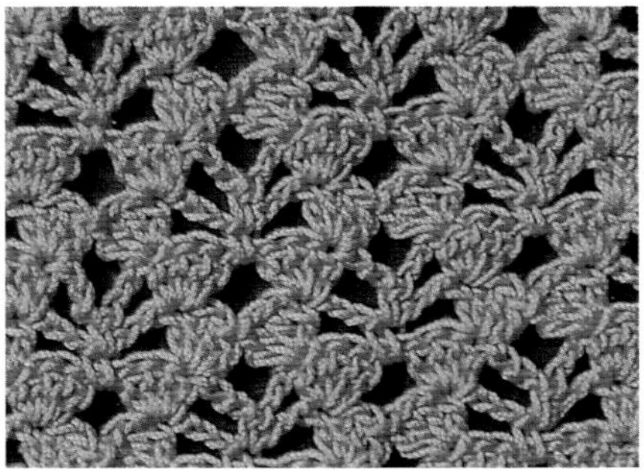

1ST ROW (RS): Work 3dc into 4th ch from hook, skip 4ch, 4dc into next ch, ✳3ch, skip 3ch, 1sc into next ch, 3ch, skip 3ch, 4dc into next ch, skip 4ch, 4dc into next ch; rep from ✳ to end, turn.
2ND ROW: 3ch (count as 1dc), 3dc into 1st dc, skip 6dc, work 4dc into next dc, ✳3ch, 1sc into next sc, 3ch, 4dc into next dc, skip 6dc, 4dc into next dc; rep from ✳ to end placing last group of 4dc into top of 3ch, turn.
3RD ROW: 6ch (count as 1dc, 3ch), work 1sc between next 2 groups of 4dc, ✳3ch, skip 3dc, 4dc into each of next 2dc, 3ch, 1sc between next 2 groups of 4dc; rep from ✳ to last group, 3ch, 1dc into 3rd of 3ch at beg of previous row, turn.
4TH ROW: 6ch, work 1sc into 1st sc, 3ch, ✳4dc into next dc, skip 6dc, 4dc into next dc, 3ch, 1sc into next sc, 3ch; rep from ✳ to last arch, 1dc into 3rd of 6ch at beg of previous row, turn.
5TH ROW: 3ch, 3dc into 1st dc, work 4dc into next dc, ✳3ch, 1sc between next 2 groups of 4dc, 3ch, skip 3dc, 4dc into each of next 2dc; rep from ✳ to end placing last group of 4dc into 3rd of 6ch at beg of previous row, turn.
Rep 2nd to 5th rows.

Seashell Pattern

Starting chain: multiple of 7 sts + 4
Drape: excellent
Skill: intermediate

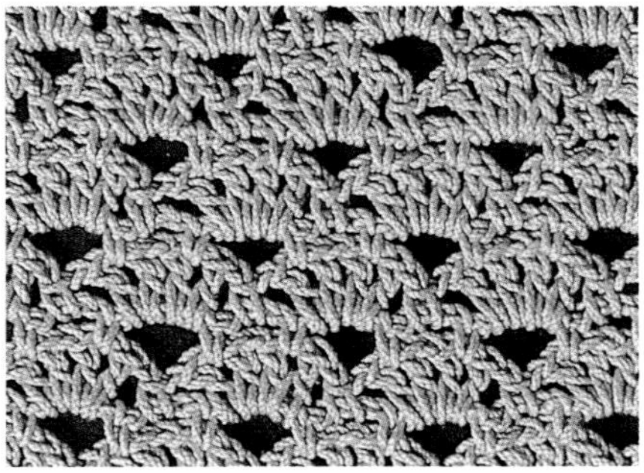

1ST ROW (WS): Work 1sc into 5th ch from hook, 3ch, skip 3ch, 1sc into next ch, ✳3ch, skip 2ch, 1sc into next ch, 3ch, skip 3ch, 1sc into next ch; rep from ✳ to last 2ch, 1ch, 1dtr into last ch, turn.
2ND ROW: 1ch, 1sc into 1st dtr, ✳1ch, into next 3ch arch work [1dc, 1ch] 4 times, 1sc into next 3ch arch; rep from ✳ to end placing last sc into 2nd ch, turn.
3RD ROW: 4ch (count as 1dc, 1ch), skip 1st ch sp, 1sc into next ch sp, 3ch, skip 1ch sp, 1sc into next ch sp, ✳3ch, skip 2ch sps, 1sc into next ch sp, 3ch, skip 1ch sp, 1sc into next ch sp; rep from ✳ to last ch sp, 1ch, 1dc into last sc, turn.
4TH ROW: 3ch (count as 1dc), work [1dc, 1ch] twice into 1st ch sp, 1sc into next 3ch arch, ✳1ch, work [1dc, 1ch] 4 times into next 3ch arch, 1sc into next 3ch arch; rep from ✳ to last sp, 1ch, work [1dc, 1ch, 1dc] into last ch sp, 1dc into 3rd of 4ch at beg of previous row, turn.
5TH ROW: 3ch (count as 1dtr, 1ch), 1sc into 1st ch sp, 3ch, skip 2ch sps, 1sc into next ch sp, ✳3ch, skip 1ch sp, 1sc into next ch sp, 3ch, skip 2ch sps, 1sc into next ch sp; rep from ✳ to last 2dc, 1ch, 1dtr into 3rd of 3ch at beg of previous row, turn.
Rep 2nd to 5th rows.

Block and Lattice Stitch

Starting chain: multiple of 6 sts + 6
Drape: excellent
Skill: intermediate

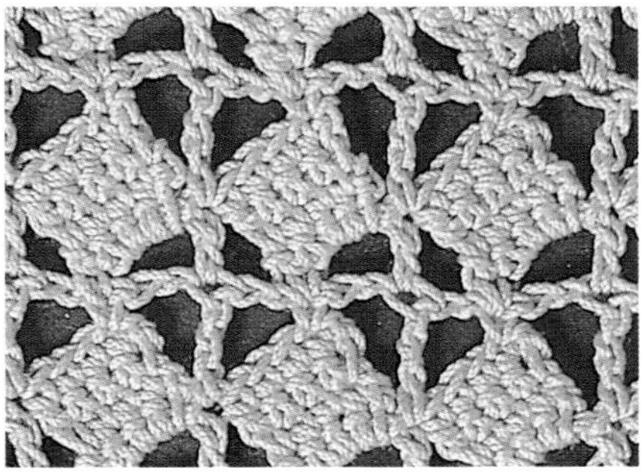

1ST ROW (RS): Work 1sc into 9th ch from hook (1dc and 3ch sp formed at beg of row), turn, 1ch, 1sc into sc, 3sc into 3ch sp, [turn, 1ch, 1sc into each of the 4sc] 3 times, skip next 2ch on starting chain, 1dc into next ch, ✳3ch, skip next 2ch on starting ch, 1sc into next ch, turn, 1ch, 1sc into sc, 3sc into 3ch sp, [turn, 1ch, 1sc into each of the 4sc] 3 times, skip next 2ch on starting ch, 1dc into next ch; rep from ✳ to end, turn.
2ND ROW: 6ch (count as 1tr, 2ch), skip 1dc and 3sc, 1sc into next sc, 2ch, 1tr into next dc, ✳2ch, skip 3sc, 1sc into next sc, 2ch, 1tr into next dc; rep from ✳ to end placing last tr into top of ch at beg of previous row, turn.
3RD ROW: 6ch (count as 1dc, 3ch), 1sc into 1st sc, turn, 1ch, 1sc into sc, 3sc into 3ch sp, [turn, 1ch, 1sc into each of the 4sc] 3 times, 1dc into next tr, ✳3ch, 1sc turn, 1 ch, 1sc into sc, 3sc into 3ch sp, [turn, 1ch, 1sc into each of the 4 sc] 3 times, 1dc into next tr; rep from✳ to end placing last dc into 4th of 6ch at beg of previous row, turn.
Rep 2nd and 3rd rows ending with a 2nd row.

Line shows direction of work for 1st part of 1st row.

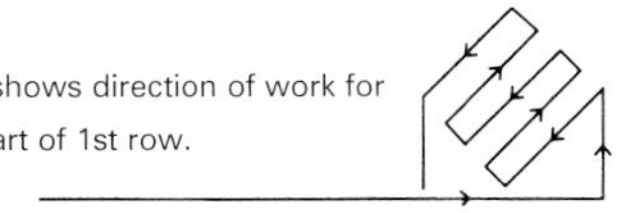

3-Strand Zigzags

Starting chain: multiple of 6 sts + 2
Drape: excellent
Skill: intermediate

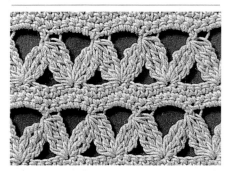

Special Abbreviations

Dtr Group = work 3dtr into next sc until 1 loop of each remains on hook, yo and through all 4 loops on hook.

Double Dtr Group = work 3dtr into same sc as last group until 1 loop of each remains on hook (4 loops on hook), skip 5 sc, into next sc work 3dtr until 1 loop of each remains on hook, yo and through all 7 loops on hook.

1ST ROW (RS): Work 1sc into 2nd ch from hook, 1sc into each ch to end, turn.

2ND ROW: 1ch, work 1sc into each sc to end, turn.

3RD ROW: 5ch (count as 1dtr), skip 1st 3sc, work 1Dtr Group (see Special Abbreviations) into next sc, 5ch, ✳1 Double Dtr Group, (see Special Abbreviations) 5ch; rep from ✳ to last 3sc, into same sc as last Group work 3tr until 1 loop of each remains on hook (4 loops on hook), 1dtr into last sc until 5 loops remain on hook, yo and through all 5 loops, turn.

4TH ROW: 1ch, 1sc into top of first group, 5sc into 5ch arch, ✳1sc into top of next group, 5sc into next 5ch arch; rep from ✳ to last group, 1sc into 5th of 5ch at beg of previous row, turn.

5TH ROW: 1ch, work 1sc into each sc to end, turn.
Rep 2nd to 5th rows.

Little Shells

Starting chain: multiple of 8 sts + 3
Drape: excellent
Skill: intermediate

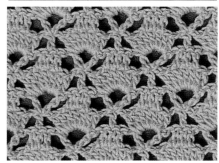

1ST ROW (WS): Work 1dc into 4th ch from hook, ✳1ch, skip 2ch, into next ch work [1dc, 3ch, 1dc], 1ch, skip 2ch, 1dc into each of next 3ch; rep from ✳ to end omitting 1dc at end of last rep, turn.

2ND ROW: 4ch (count as 1dc, 1ch), work 7dc into next 3ch arch, ✳1ch, skip 2dc, 1dc into next dc, 1ch, 7dc into next 3ch arch; rep from ✳ to last 3dc, 1ch, skip 2dc, 1dc into top of 3ch, turn.

3RD ROW: 4ch, 1dc into 1st dc, 1ch, skip 2dc, 1dc into each of next 3dc, ✳1ch, skip 2dc, into next dc work [1dc, 3ch, 1dc], 1ch, skip 2dc, 1dc into each of next 3dc; rep from ✳ to last 3dc, skip 2dc, into 3rd of 4ch at beg of previous row work [1dc, 1ch, 1dc], turn.

4TH ROW: 3ch (count as 1dc), 3dc into 1st ch sp, 1ch, skip 2dc, 1dc into next dc, ✳1ch, 7dc into next 3ch arch, 1ch, skip 2dc, 1dc into next dc; rep from ✳ to last 3dc, 1ch, skip 2dc, 3dc into last ch sp, 1dc into 3rd of 4ch at beg of previous row, turn.

5TH ROW: 3ch, skip 1st dc, 1dc into next dc, ✳1ch, skip 2dc, into next dc work [1dc, 3ch, 1dc], 1ch, skip 2dc, 1dc into each of next 3dc; rep from ✳ to end omitting 1dc at end of last rep and placing last dc into 3rd of 3ch at beg of previous row, turn.
Rep 2nd to 5th rows.

Easter Eggs

Starting chain: multiple of 9 sts + 2
Drape: excellent
Skill: intermediate

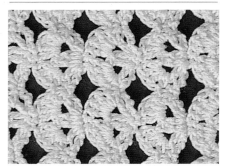

1ST ROW (RS): Work 1sc into 2nd ch from hook, ✳skip 3ch, into each of next 2ch work [1dc, 2ch, 1dc], skip 3ch, 1sc into next ch; rep from ✳ to end, turn.

2ND ROW: 1ch, 1sc into 1st sc, ✳into next 2ch sp work [1dtr, 3dc], into next 2ch sp work [3dc, 1dtr], 1sc into next sc; rep from ✳ to end, turn.

3RD ROW: 7ch (count as 1tr, 3ch), skip 1st 4 sts, 1sc into each of next 2dc, ✳7ch, skip 7 sts, 1sc into each of next 2dc; rep from ✳ to last 4 sts, 3ch, 1tr into last sc, turn.

4TH ROW: 1ch, 1sc into 1st tr, ✳into each of next 2sc work [1dc, 2ch, 1dc], 1sc into 7ch arch; rep from ✳ to end placing last sc into 4th of 7ch at beg of previous row, turn.

Rep 2nd to 4th rows.

Squares and Ladders

Starting chain: multiple of 16 sts + 8
Drape: excellent
Skill: intermediate
Note: For description of dc3tog see page 187.

BASE ROW (RS): 1dc into 6th ch from hook, ✳1ch, skip 1ch, 1dc into next ch; rep from ✳ to end, turn.

Commence Pattern

1ST ROW: 4ch (count as 1dc and 1ch), skip 1st st and next ch, 1dc into next dc, 1ch,

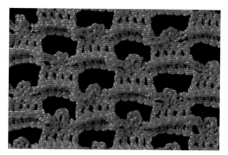

skip 1ch, 1dc into next dc, ✻5ch, skip 5 sts, dc3tog into next dc, 5ch, skip 5 sts, 1dc into next dc, [1ch, skip 1ch, 1dc into next st] twice; rep from ✻ ending last rep in tch, turn.

2ND ROW: 4ch (count as 1dc and 1ch), skip 1st st and next ch, 1dc into next dc, 1ch, skip 1ch, 1dc into next dc, ✻4ch, 1sc into 5ch arch, skip Cluster 1sc into next 5ch arch, 4ch, 1dc into next dc, [1ch, skip 1ch, 1dc into next st] twice; rep from ✻ ending last rep in tch, turn.

3RD ROW: 4ch (count as 1dc and 1ch), skip 1st st and next ch, 1dc into next dc, 1ch, skip 1ch, 1dc into next dc, ✻4ch, 1sc into 4ch arch, 1sc between 2sc, 1sc into next 4ch arch, 4ch, 1dc into next dc, [1ch, skip 1ch, 1dc into next st] twice; rep from ✻ ending last rep in tch, turn.

4TH ROW: 4ch (counts as 1dc and 1ch), skip 1st st and next ch, 1dc into next dc, 1ch, skip 1ch, 1dc into next dc, ✻5ch, dc3tog into 2nd of 3sc, 5ch, 1dc into next dc, [1ch, skip 1ch, 1dc into next st] twice; rep from ✻ ending last rep in tch, turn.

5TH ROW: 4ch (count as 1dc and 1ch), skip 1st st and next ch, 1dc into next dc, ✻1ch, skip 1ch, 1dc into next st; rep from ✻ ending last rep in tch, turn.

6TH ROW: As 5th row.
Rep these 6 rows.

Sieve Stitch

Starting chain: multiple of 2 sts + 2
Drape: good
Skill: easy

BASE ROW (WS): 1sc into 2nd ch from hook, ✻1ch, skip 1ch, 1sc into next ch; rep from ✻ to end, turn.

Commence Pattern

1ST ROW: 1ch, skip 1 st, ✻2sc into next ch sp, skip next sc; rep from ✻ until 1 ch sp remains, 1sc into last ch sp, 1sc into next sc, skip tch, turn.

2ND ROW: 1ch, skip 1 st, 1sc into next st, ✻1ch, skip 1 st, 1sc into next sc; rep from ✻ until only tch remains, 1sc into tch, turn.

3RD ROW: 1ch, skip 1st 2 sts, ✻2sc into next ch sp, skip next sc; rep from ✻ until only tch remains, 2sc into tch, turn.

4TH ROW: As 2nd row.

5TH ROW: 1ch, 1sc into 1st st, ✻skip next sc, 2sc into next ch sp; rep from ✻ ending last rep in tch, turn.

6TH ROW: 1ch, skip 1 st, ✻1sc into next sc, 1ch, skip 1sc; rep from ✻ ending 1sc into tch, turn.

7TH ROW: 1ch, skip 1 st, 1sc into next ch sp, ✻skip 1sc, 2sc into next sp; rep from ✻ ending skip last sc, 1sc into tch, turn.

8TH ROW: 1ch, 1sc into 1st st, ✻1ch, skip 1sc, 1sc into next st; rep from ✻ to end working last st into top of tch, turn.
Rep these 8 rows.

Picot Ridge Stitch

Starting chain: multiple of 10 sts + 9
Drape: excellent
Skill: intermediate
Note: For description of dc/rf see page 188 (Raised Stitches).

1ST ROW (RS): Skip 3ch (count as 1dc), ✻1dc into each of next 5ch, 3ch, skip 2ch,

[1sc, 4ch, 1sc] into next ch, 3ch, skip 2ch; rep from ✻ ending 1dc into last ch, turn.

2ND ROW: 8ch (count as 1dc and 5ch), skip 1st st and next 3ch arch, ✻1dc/rf round each of next 5 sts, 5ch, skip next 3 arches; rep from ✻ ending 1dc/rf round each of last 5dcs, 1dc into top of tch, turn.

3RD ROW: 6ch, skip 1st 3 sts, ✻[1sc, 4ch, 1sc] into next st, 3ch, skip 2 sts, 1dc into each of next 5ch✻✻, 3ch, skip 2 sts; rep from ✻ ending last rep at ✻✻, 1dc into next ch of tch, turn.

4TH ROW: 3ch (count as 1dc), skip 1st st, ✻1dc/rf round each of next 5 sts, 5ch✻✻, skip next 3 arches; rep from ✻ ending last rep at ✻✻, skip next 2 arches, 1dc into tch arch, turn.

5TH ROW: 3ch (count as 1dc), skip 1st st, ✻1dc into each of next 5ch, 3ch, skip 2 sts, [1sc, 4ch, 1sc] into next st, 3ch, skip 2 sts; rep from ✻ ending 1dc into top of tch, turn.
Rep 2nd, 3rd, 4th and 5th rows.

Half Double V Stitch

Starting chain: multiple of 2 sts + 2
Drape: good
Skill: easy

1ST ROW (RS): [1dtr, 1ch, 1dtr] into 4th ch from hook, ✻skip 1ch, [1dtr, 1ch, 1dtr] into next ch; rep from ✻ until 2ch remain, skip 1ch, 1dtr into last ch, turn.

2ND ROW: 2ch, ✻skip 2 sts, [1dtr, 1ch, 1dtr] into next ch sp; rep from ✻ to last ch sp, skip 1 st, 1dtr into tch, turn.
Rep 2nd row.

Double V Stitch

Starting chain: multiple of 2 sts + 2
Drape: good
Skill: easy

1ST ROW (RS): 2dc into 4th ch from hook, ✳skip 1ch, 2dc into next ch; rep from ✳ to last 2ch, skip 1ch, 1dc into last ch, turn.
2ND ROW: 3ch, ✳skip 2 sts, 2dc between 2nd skipped st and next st; rep from ✳ to last 2 sts, skip 1 st, 1dc into top of tch, turn.
Rep 2nd row.

Three-and-Two Stitch

Starting chain: multiple of 6 sts + 4
Drape: excellent
Skill: easy

1ST ROW (RS): Work a V St of [1dc, 1ch, 1dc] into 5th ch from hook, ✳skip 2ch, 3dc into next ch, skip 2ch, work a V St into next ch; rep from ✳ to

last 5ch, skip 2ch, 3dc into next ch, skip 1ch, 1dc into last ch, turn.
2ND ROW: 3ch, ✳skip 2 sts, work 3dc into center dc of next 3dc, work a V St into ch sp at center of next V St; rep from ✳ ending 1dc into top of tch, turn.
3RD ROW: 3ch, ✳V St into sp of next V St, 3dc into center dc of next 3dc; rep from ✳ ending 1dc into top of tch, turn.
Rep 2nd and 3rd rows.

Basket Stitch

Starting chain: multiple of 3 sts + 4
Drape: good
Skill: intermediate
Note: For description of working double stitches together see page 187.

1ST ROW (WS): Work a V St of [1dc, 1ch, 1dc] into 5th ch from hook, ✳skip 2ch, work V St into next ch; rep from ✳ to last 2ch, skip 1ch, 1dc into last ch, turn.
2ND ROW: 3ch, skip 2 sts, work a Double V St of [2dc, 1ch, 2dc] into ch sp at center of V St, ✳1ch, skip next V St, work a Double

V St into sp at center of next V St; rep from ✳ leaving last loop of last dc of last Double V St on hook and working it together with 1dc into top of tch, turn.
3RD ROW: 3ch, work a V St into each sp to end finishing with 1dc into top of tch, turn.
4TH ROW: 3ch, 1dc into first st, ✳1ch, skip next V St, work a Double V st into sp at center of next V St; rep from ✳ until 1 V St remains, 1ch, skip V St, 2dc into top of tch, turn.
5TH ROW: As 3rd row.
Rep 2nd, 3rd, 4th and 5th rows.

Empress Stitch

Starting chain: multiple of 18 sts + 4
Drape: excellent
Skill: intermediate
Note For description of Popcorn see page 190. Popcorns occur on both right-side and wrong-side rows alternately. Be sure to push them all out on the right side of the fabric as you complete them.

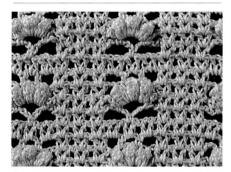

1ST ROW (WS): 1dc into 4th ch from hook, ✳skip 2ch, work a V St of [1dc, 1ch, 1dc] into next ch; rep from ✳ to last 3ch, skip 2ch, 2dc into last ch, turn.
2ND ROW: 3ch, 1dc into 1st st, V St into sp at center of next V St, ✳5ch, skip next V St, 1sc into sp at center of next V St, 5ch, skip next V st✳✳, [V St into sp at center of next V St] 3 times; rep from ✳ ending last rep at ✳✳, V St into sp at center of last V St, 2dc into top of tch, turn.
3RD ROW: 3ch, 1dc into 1st st, V St into sp at center of next V St, ✳[3ch, 1sc into next 5ch arch] twice, 3ch ✳✳, [V St into sp at

openwork patterns

center of next V St] 3 times; rep from ✳ ending last rep at ✳✳, V St into sp at center of last V St, 2dc into top of tch, turn.

4TH ROW: 3ch, 1dc into 1st st, V St into sp at center of next V St, ✳skip next 3ch arch, [5dc Popcorn, 2ch, 5dc Popcorn, 2ch, 5dc Popcorn] into next 3ch arch, skip next 3ch arch✳✳, [V St into sp at center of next V St] 3 times; rep from ✳ ending last rep at✳✳, V St into sp at center of last V St, 2dc into top of tch, turn.

5TH ROW: 3ch, 1dc into 1st st, V St into sp at center of next V St, ✳[3ch, 1sc into next 2ch sp] twice, 3ch✳✳, [V St into sp at center of next V St] 3 times; rep from ✳ ending last rep at ✳✳, V St into sp at center of last V St, 2dc into top of tch, turn.

6TH ROW: 3ch, 1dc into 1st st, V St into sp at center of next V St, ✳[V st into 2nd ch of next 3ch arch] 3 times✳✳, [V St into sp at center of next V St] 3 times; rep from ✳ ending last rep at ✳✳, V St into sp at center of last V St, 2dc into top of tch, turn.
Rep 2nd, 3rd, 4th, 5th and 6th rows.

Fantail Stitch
Starting chain: multiple of 10 sts + 2
Drape: excellent
Skill: intermediate

1ST ROW (RS): 1sc into 2nd ch from hook,1sc into next ch, ✳skip 3ch, work a Fan of [3dc, 1ch, 3dc] into next ch, skip 3ch, 1sc into next ch✳✳, 1ch, skip 1ch, 1sc into next ch; rep from ✳ ending last rep at ✳✳, 1sc into last ch, turn.
2ND ROW: 2ch (count as 1dtr), 1dtr into 1st

st ✳3ch, 1sc into ch sp at center of next Fan, 3ch✳✳, work a V St of [1dtr, 1ch, 1dtr] into next sp; rep from ✳ ending last rep at✳✳, 2dtr into last sc, turn.
3RD ROW: 3ch, 3dc into 1st st, ✳1sc into next 3ch arch, 1ch, 1sc into next arch✳✳, work a Fan into sp at center of next V St; rep from ✳ ending last rep at ✳✳, 4dc into top of tch, turn.
4TH ROW: 1ch, 1sc into 1st st, ✳3ch, V St into next sp, 3ch, 1sc into sp at center of next Fan; rep from ✳ ending last rep into top of tch, turn.
5TH ROW: 1ch, 1sc into 1st st, ✳1sc into next arch, Fan into sp at center of next V St, 1sc into next arch✳✳, 1ch; rep from ✳ ending last rep at ✳✳, 1sc into last sc, skip tch, turn.
Rep 2nd, 3rd, 4th and 5th rows.

Diamond Shell Trellis Stitch
Starting chain: multiple of 16 sts + 6
Drape: excellent
Skill: experienced

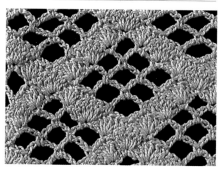

BASE ROW (RS): 1sc into 2nd ch from hook, [5ch, skip 3ch, 1sc into next ch] twice, ✳skip 1ch, 5dc into next ch, skip 1ch, 1sc into next ch✳✳, [5ch, skip 3ch, 1sc into next ch] 3 times; rep from ✳ ending last rep at ✳✳ when 8 ch remain, [5ch, skip 3ch, 1sc into next ch] twice, turn.

Commence Pattern
1ST ROW: ✳[5ch, 1sc into next 5ch arch] twice, 5dc into next sc, 1sc into 3rd of next 5dc, 5dc into next sc, 1sc into next arch; rep from ✳ ending 5ch, 1 sc into next arch,

2ch, 1dc into last sc, skip tch, turn.
2ND ROW: 1ch, 1sc into 1st st, skip 2ch, ✳5ch, 1sc into next 5ch arch, 5dc into next sc, 1sc into 3rd of next 5dc, 5ch, 1sc into 3rd of next 5dc, 5dc into next sc, 1sc into next arch; rep from ✳ ending 5ch, 1sc into tch arch, turn.
3RD ROW: 3ch (count as 1dc), 2dc into 1st st, ✳1sc into next 5ch arch, 5dc into next sc, 1sc into 3rd of next 5dc, 5ch, 1sc into next arch, 5ch, 1sc into 3rd of next 5dc, 5dc into next sc; rep from ✳ ending 1sc into next arch, 3dc into last sc, skip tch, turn.
4TH ROW: 1ch, 1sc into 1st st, ✳5dc into next sc, 1sc into 3rd of next 5dc, [5ch, 1sc into next arch] twice, 5ch, 1sc into 3rd of next 5dc; rep from ✳ ending 5dc into next sc, 1sc into top of tch, turn.
5TH ROW: 3ch (count as 1dc), 2dc into 1st st, ✳1sc into 3rd of next 5dc, 5dc into next sc, 1sc into next arch, [5ch, 1sc into next arch] twice, 5dc into next sc; rep from ✳ ending 1sc into 3rd of next 5dc, 3dc into last sc, skip tch, turn.
6TH ROW: 1ch, 1sc into 1st st, ✳5ch, 1sc into 3rd of next 5dc, 5dc into next sc, 1sc into next arch, 5ch, 1sc into next arch, 5dc into next sc, 1sc into 3rd of next 5dc; rep from ✳ ending 5ch, 1sc into top of tch, turn.
7TH ROW: ✳5ch, 1sc into next 5ch arch, 5ch, 1sc into 3rd of next 5dc, 5dc into next sc, 1sc into next arch, 5dc into next sc, 1sc into 3rd of next 5dc; rep from ✳ ending 5ch, 1sc into next arch, 2ch, 1dc into last sc, skip tch, turn.
8TH ROW: 1ch, 1sc into 1st st, skip 2ch, 5ch, 1sc into next 5ch arch, 5ch, 1sc into 3rd of next 5dc, ✳5dc into next sc, 1sc into 3rd of next 5dc, [5ch, 1sc into next arch] twice✳✳, 5ch, 1sc into 3rd of next 5dc; rep from ✳ ending last rep at ✳✳ in tch arch, turn.
Rep these 8 rows.

Fan Trellis Stitch

Starting chain: multiple of 12 sts + 12
Drape: excellent
Skill: easy

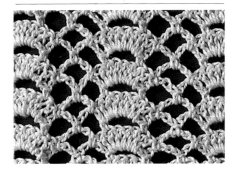

1ST ROW (WS): 1sc into 2nd ch from hook, ✳5ch, skip 3ch, 1sc into next ch; rep from ✳ to last 2ch, 2ch, skip 1ch, 1dc into last ch, turn.
2ND ROW: 1ch, 1sc into 1st st, skip 2ch sp, ✳7dc into next 5ch arch, 1sc into next arch✳✳, 5ch, 1sc into next arch; rep from ✳ ending last rep at ✳✳, 2ch, 1tr into last sc, skip tch, turn.
3RD ROW: 1ch, 1sc into 1st st, ✳5ch, 1sc into 2nd of next 7dc, 5ch, 1sc into 6th dc of same group✳✳, 5ch, 1sc into next 5ch arch; rep from ✳ ending last rep at ✳✳, 2ch, 1tr into last sc, skip tch, turn.
Rep 2nd and 3rd rows.

Single Trellis Stitch

Starting chain: multiple of 4 sts + 2
Drape: excellent
Skill: intermediate
Note: For description of dc2tog see page 187.

1ST ROW (RS): 1sc into 2nd ch from hook, ✳3ch, dc2tog inserting hook into same place as sc just made for 1st leg and then into following 4th ch for 2nd leg (skipping 3ch between), 3ch, 1sc into same place as 2nd leg of Cluster just made; rep from ✳ to end, turn.
2ND ROW: 4ch, 1dc into top of next Cluster (counts as Edge Cluster), 3ch, 1sc into

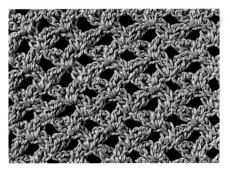

same place as dc just made, ✳3ch, dc2tog inserting hook into same place as sc just made for 1st leg and then into next Cluster for 2nd leg, 3ch, 1sc into same place as 2nd leg of Cluster just made; rep from ✳ ending 3ch, yo, insert hook into same place as sc just made, yo, draw loop through, yo, draw through 2 loops, [yo] twice, insert hook into last sc, yo, draw loop through, [yo, draw through 2 loops] twice, yo, draw through all 3 loops on hook, skip tch, turn.
3RD ROW: 1ch, 1sc into 1st st, ✳3ch, dc2tog inserting hook into same place as sc just made for 1st leg and then into next Cluster for 2nd leg, 3ch, 1sc into same place as 2nd leg of Cluster just made; rep from ✳ to end, turn.
Rep 2nd and 3rd rows.

Open Fan Stitch

Starting chain: multiple of 10 sts + 7
Drape: excellent
Skill: intermediate

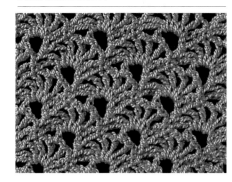

1ST ROW (RS): 1sc into 2nd ch from hook, ✳1ch, skip 4ch, into next ch work a Fan of 1tr, [2ch, 1tr] 4 times, then 1ch, skip 4ch, 1sc into next ch; rep from ✳ to last 5ch, 1ch, skip 4ch, into last ch work [1tr, 2ch] twice and 1tr, turn.
2ND ROW: 1ch, 1sc into 1st st, ✳3ch, skip next 2ch sp, 1dc into next sp✳✳, 2ch, skip next tr, sc and tr and work 1dc into 1st 2ch sp of next Fan, 3ch, work 1sc into center tr of Fan; rep from ✳ ending last rep at ✳✳, 1ch, 1tr into last sc, skip tch, turn.
3RD ROW: 7ch (count as 1tr and 2ch), skip 1st tr, work [1tr, 2ch, 1tr] into next 1ch sp, 1ch, skip 3ch sp, 1sc into next sc, ✳1ch, skip next 3ch sp, work a Fan into next 2ch sp, 1ch, skip next 3ch sp, 1sc into next sc; rep from ✳ to end, skip tch, turn.
4TH ROW: 6ch (count as 1tr and 1ch), skip 1st tr, work 1dc into next 2ch sp, 3ch, 1sc into center tr of Fan, ✳3ch, skip next 2ch sp, 1dc into next 2ch sp, 2ch, skip next tr, sc and tr, work 1dc into next 2ch sp, 3ch, 1sc into center tr of Fan; rep from ✳ ending last rep in 3rd ch of tch, turn.
5TH ROW: 1ch, ✳1sc into sc, 1ch, skip next 3ch sp, Fan into next 2ch sp, 1ch, skip next 3ch sp; rep from ✳ to last sc, 1sc into sc, 1ch, skip next 3ch sp, work [1tr, 2ch] twice and ltr all into top of tch, turn. Rep 2nd, 3rd, 4th and 5th rows.

Boxed Shell Stitch

Starting chain: multiple of 5 sts + 4
Drape: excellent
Skill: easy

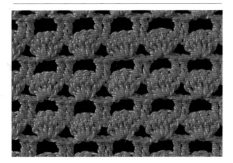

1ST ROW (RS): Skip 3ch (count as 1dc), 1dc into next ch, ✳3ch, skip 3ch, 1dc into each of next 2ch; rep from ✳ to end, turn.
2ND ROW: 3ch (count as 1dc), skip first st, ✳5dc into 2nd ch of next 3ch arch; rep from ✳ ending 1dc into top of tch, turn.
3RD ROW: 3ch (count as 1dc), skip first st, 1dc into next dc, ✳3ch, skip 3dc, 1dc into each of next 2dc; rep from ✳ to end, turn.
Rep 2nd and 3rd rows.

Boxed Block Stitch
Starting chain: multiple of 5 sts + 4
Drape: excellent
Skill: easy

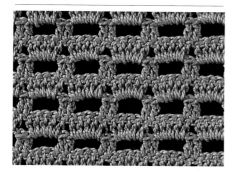

Worked as Boxed Shell Stitch, except that on 2nd and every alternate row 5dc are worked under 3ch arch instead of into actual st, thus making a block rather than a shell.

Norman Arch Stitch
Starting chain: multiple of 9 sts + 2
Drape: excellent
Skill: intermediate

1ST ROW (WS): 1sc into 2nd ch from hook, ✳3ch, skip 3ch, 1sc into next ch, 7ch, 1sc into next ch, 3ch, skip 3ch, 1sc into next ch; rep from ✳ to end, turn.
2ND ROW: 1ch, 1sc into 1st sc, ✳skip 3ch, work 13dc into next 7ch arch, skip 3ch, 1sc into next sc; rep from ✳ to end, skip tch, turn.

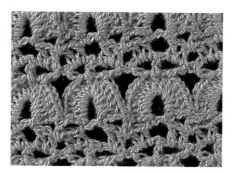

3RD ROW: 5ch (count as 1dtr), skip 1st sc and next 5dc, ✳[1dc into next dc, 3ch] twice, 1dc into next dc✳✳, skip [next 5dc, 1sc and 5dc]; rep from ✳ ending last rep at ✳✳, skip next 5dc, 1dtr into last sc, skip tch, turn.
4TH ROW: 3ch (count as 1dc), skip 1st st and next dc, ✳1dc into next ch, 1ch, skip 1ch, 1dc into next ch, 3ch, skip 1dc, 1dc into next ch, 1ch, skip 1ch, 1dc into next ch✳✳, skip next 2dc; rep from ✳ ending last rep at ✳✳, skip next dc, 1dc into top of tch, turn.
5TH ROW: 6ch (count as 1dc and 3ch), ✳skip next 1ch sp, work [1sc, 7ch, 1 sc] into next 3ch sp, 3ch, skip next 1ch sp✳✳, 1dc between next 2dc; rep from ✳ ending last rep at ✳✳, 1dc into top of tch, turn.
Rep 2nd, 3rd, 4th and 5th rows.

Fan and V Stitch
Starting chain: multiple of 8 sts + 2
Drape: good
Skill: intermediate

1ST ROW (RS): 1sc into 2nd ch from hook, ✳skip 3ch, 9dc into next ch, skip 3ch, 1sc into next ch; rep from ✳ to end, turn.
2ND ROW: 3ch (count as 1dc), 1dc into 1st st, ✳5ch, skip 9dc group, work a V St of [1dc, 1ch, 1dc] into next sc; rep from ✳ ending 5ch, skip last 9dc group, 2dc into last sc, skip tch, turn.
3RD ROW: 3ch (count as 1dc), 4dc into 1st st, ✳ working over next 5ch so as to enclose it, work 1sc into 5th dc of group in row below✳✳, 9dc into sp at center of next V St; rep from ✳ ending last rep at ✳✳ 5dc into top of tch, turn.
4TH ROW: 3ch, skip 5dc, V St into next sc, ✳5ch, skip 9dc group, V St into next sc; rep from ✳ ending 2ch, sl st to top of tch, turn.
5TH ROW: 1ch, 1sc over sl st into 1st st of row below, ✳9dc into sp at center of next V st, working over next 5ch so as to enclose it. Work 1sc into 5th dc of group in row below; rep from ✳ to end, turn.
Rep 2nd, 3rd, 4th and 5th rows.
End with a wrong-side row working [2ch, sl st to 5th dc of group, 2ch] in place of 5ch between the V Sts.

Peacock Fan Stitch
Starting chain: multiple of 12 sts + 2
Drape: excellent
Skill: intermediate

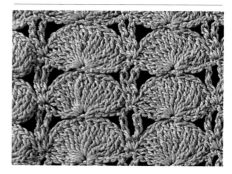

1ST ROW (RS): 1sc into 2nd ch from hook, ✳skip 5ch, 13dtr into next ch, skip 5ch, 1sc into next ch; rep from ✳ to end, turn.
2ND ROW: 5ch (count as 1dtr), 1dtr into 1st

st, ✳4ch, skip 6dtr, 1sc into next dtr, 4ch, skip 6dtr✳✳, work [1dtr, 1ch, 1dtr] into next sc; rep from ✳ ending last rep at ✳✳, 2dtr into last sc, skip tch, turn.

3RD ROW: 1ch, 1sc into first st, ✳skip [1dtr and 4ch], 13dtr into next sc, skip [4ch and 1dtr], 1sc into next ch; rep from ✳ to end, turn.

Rep 2nd and 3rd rows.

Soft Fan Stitch

Starting chain: multiple of 10 sts + 2
Drape: excellent
Skill: experienced
Note: For description of dtr3tog see page 191 (Puff Stitch).

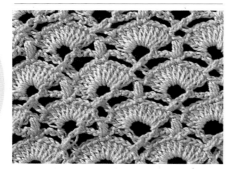

1ST ROW (WS): 1sc into 2nd ch from hook, ✳3ch, work 2 crossed dcs as follows: skip 5ch, 1dc into next ch, 5ch, inserting hook behind dc just made work 1dc into 4th of 5ch just skipped, then 3ch, skip 3ch, 1sc into next ch; rep from ✳ to end, turn.

2ND ROW: 3ch (count as 1dc), skip 1st st, ✳skip next 3ch sp, work a group of 11dc into next 5ch arch, skip next 3ch sp, work dtr3tog into next sc, 1ch; rep from ✳ omitting dtr3tog and 1ch at end of last rep and working 1dc into last sc, skip tch, turn.

3RD ROW: 2ch, skip 1st 2 dc, 1dtr into next dc, 4ch, 1dtr into top of dtr just made, ✳3ch, skip 3dc, 1sc into next dc, 3ch✳✳, work 2 crossed dcs as follows: 1dc into 2nd dc of next 11dc group, 5ch, going behind dc just made work 1dc into 10th dc of previous 11dc group; rep from ✳ ending last rep at ✳✳, 1dc into top of tch, 2ch,

going behind dc just made work 1dc into 10th dc of previous 11dc group, turn.

4TH ROW: 3ch (count as 1dc), skip 1st st, 5dc into next 2ch sp, ✳skip next 3ch sp, work dtr3tog into next sc, 1ch, skip next 3ch sp✳✳, 11dc into next 5ch arch; rep from ✳ ending last rep at ✳✳, 6dc into top of tch, turn.

5TH ROW: 1ch, 1sc into 1st st, 3ch, 1dc into 2nd dc of next 11dc group, 5ch, going behind dc just made work 1dc into 5th dc of previous 6dc group, ✳3ch, skip 3dc, 1sc into next dc✳✳, 3ch, 1dc into 2nd dc of next dc group, 5ch, going behind dc just made work 1dc into 10th dc of previous dc group; rep from ✳ ending last rep at ✳✳ in top of tch, turn.

Rep 2nd, 3rd, 4th and 5th rows.

Hearts and Diamonds Stitch

Starting chain: multiple of 10 sts + 12
Drape: excellent
Skill: intermediate

Special Abbreviation

Diamond = 4 rows inside a main row worked as follows: turn, 1st row: 1ch, 1sc. into 1st sc, 1sc into each of next 3ch, turn. Next row: 1ch, 1sc into each of next 4sc, skip tch, turn. Rep the last row twice more.

1ST ROW (WS): 1sc into 9th ch from hook, ✳2ch, skip 4ch, work a Heart of [3dc, 1ch, 3dc] into next ch, 2ch, skip 4ch, 1sc into next ch; rep from ✳ to last 3ch, 2ch, skip 2ch, 1dc into last ch, turn.

2ND ROW: 6ch, skip 1st st and next 2ch, 1sc into next sc, work a Diamond (see

Special Abbreviation), ✳skip 2ch, 1 Heart into ch sp at center of next Heart, 3ch, skip 2ch, 1sc into next sc, work Diamond; rep from ✳ ending skip 2ch, 1dc into next ch of tch, turn.

3RD ROW: 5ch (count as 1dc and 2ch), ✳1sc into top corner of next Diamond, 2ch✳✳, 1 Heart into sp at center of next Heart, 2ch; rep from ✳ ending last rep at ✳✳, 1dc into 3rd ch of tch, turn.

Rep 2nd and 3rd rows.

Butterfly Lace

Starting chain: multiple of 12 sts + 4
Drape: good
Skill: intermediate
Note: For description of dc2tog see page 187 (Clusters).

1ST ROW (RS): 1sc into 2nd ch from hook, 2ch, skip 1ch, 1sc into next ch, ✳skip 3ch, work [3tr, 4ch, 1sc] into next ch, 2ch, skip 1ch, work [1 sc, 4ch, 3tr] into next ch, skip 3ch, 1sc into next ch, 2ch, skip 1ch, 1sc into next ch; rep from ✳ to end, turn.

2ND ROW: 4ch (count as 1dc and 1ch), skip 1st sc, 1dc into next 2ch sp, ✳1ch, skip 3tr, 1sc into top of 4ch, 2ch, work dc2tog into next 2ch sp, 2ch, skip 3ch, 1sc into next ch, 1ch✳✳, work [1dc, 1ch, 1dc] into next sp; rep from ✳ ending last rep at ✳✳, 1dc into last sp, 1ch, 1dc into last sc, skip tch, turn.

3RD ROW: 1ch, 1sc into 1st st, 2ch, skip [1ch and 1dc], 1sc into next ch, ✳work [3tr, 4ch, 1sc] into next 2ch sp, 2ch, skip next Cluster, work [1sc, 4ch, 3tr] into next

2ch sp, 1sc into next 1ch sp, 2ch, skip 1ch, 1sc into next 1ch sp; rep from ✳ ending last rep in 3rd ch of tch, turn. Rep 2nd and 3rd rows.

Lacy Wave Stitch
Starting chain: multiple of 11 sts + 2
Drape: excellent
Skill: intermediate

1ST ROW (RS): 1sc into 2nd ch from hook, ✳2ch, skip 2ch, 1dc into each of next 2ch, 2ch, skip 2ch, 1sc into each of next 5ch; rep from ✳ to end, turn.
2ND ROW: 5ch (count as 1dc and 2ch), 1dc into 1st st, ✳[1ch, skip 1 st, 1dc into next st] twice, 1ch, 1dc into next 2ch sp, skip 2dc✳✳, 5dc into next 2ch sp, 2ch, 1dc into next st; rep from ✳ ending last rep at ✳✳, 4dc into last 2ch sp, 1dc into last sc, skip tch, turn.
3RD ROW: 5ch (count as 1dc and 2ch), 1dc into 1st st, ✳[1ch, skip 1st, 1dc into next st] twice, 1ch, skip 1 st, 1dc into next ch, skip [1dc, 1ch, 1dc, 1ch and 1dc], 5dc into next 2ch sp✳✳, 2ch, 1dc into next st; rep from ✳ ending last rep at ✳✳ in tch, turn.
Rep 3rd row.

Arched Lace Stitch
Starting chain: multiple of 8 sts + 2
Drape: excellent
Skill: intermediate

1ST ROW (RS): 1sc into 2nd ch from hook, 1sc into next ch, ✳5ch, skip 5ch, 1sc into each of next 3ch; rep from ✳ omitting 1sc at end of last rep, turn.
2ND ROW: 1ch, 1sc into 1st st, ✳3ch, skip next sc, 3dc into next 5ch arch, 3ch, skip 1sc, 1sc into next sc; rep from ✳ to end, skip tch, turn.
3RD ROW: 6ch (count as 1tr and 2ch), skip 3ch, ✳1sc into each of next 3dc✳✳, 5ch, skip [3ch, 1sc and 3ch]; rep from ✳ ending last rep at ✳✳, 2ch, skip 3ch, 1tr into last sc, skip tch, turn.
4TH ROW: 3ch (count as 1dc), skip 1st st, 1dc into 2ch sp, ✳3ch, skip next sc, 1sc into next sc, 3ch, skip 1sc✳✳, 3dc into next 5ch arch; rep from ✳ ending last rep at ✳✳, skip 1ch, 1dc into each of next 2ch of tch, turn.
5TH ROW: 1ch, 1sc into 1st st, 1sc into next st, ✳5ch, skip [3ch, 1sc and 3ch], 1sc into each of next 3dc; rep from ✳ to end, omitting 1sc at end of last rep, turn.
Rep 2nd, 3rd, 4th and 5th rows.

Petal Stitch
Starting chain: multiple of 8 sts + 2
Drape: excellent
Skill: intermediate

1ST ROW (WS): 1sc into 2nd ch from hook, ✳2ch, skip 3ch, 4tr into next ch, 2ch, skip 3ch, 1sc into next ch; rep from ✳ to end, turn.
2ND ROW: 1ch, 1sc into 1st st, ✳3ch, skip 2ch and 1tr, 1sc into next tr, 3ch, skip 2tr and 2ch, 1sc into next sc; rep

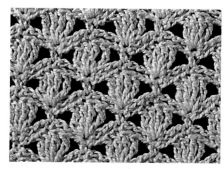

from ✳ to end, skip tch, turn.
3RD ROW: 4ch (count as 1tr), 1tr into 1st st, ✳2ch, skip 3ch, 1sc into next sc, 2ch, skip 3ch, 4tr into next sc; rep from ✳ to end omitting 1tr at end of last rep, skip tch, turn.
4TH ROW: 1ch, 1sc into 1st st, ✳3ch, skip 2tr and 2ch, 1sc into next sc, 3ch, skip 2ch and 1tr, 1sc into next tr; rep from ✳ ending last rep in top of tch, turn.
5TH ROW: 1ch, 1sc into 1st st, ✳2ch, skip 3ch, 4tr into next sc, 2ch, skip 3ch, 1sc into next sc; rep from ✳ to end, skip tch, turn. Rep 2nd, 3rd, 4th and 5th rows.

Webbed Lace Stitch
Starting chain: multiple of 7 sts + 4
Drape: excellent
Skill: easy

1ST ROW: 1dc into 5th ch from hook, ✳2ch, skip 5ch, 4dc into next ch✳✳, 2ch, 1dc into next ch; rep from ✳ ending last rep at ✳✳ in last ch, turn.
2ND ROW: 4ch, 1dc into 1st st, ✳2ch, skip

[3dc, 2ch and 1dc]✳✳, work [4dc, 2ch, 1dc] into next 2ch sp; rep from ✳ ending last rep at ✳✳, 4dc into tch, turn. Rep 2nd row.

Picot Fan Stitch

Starting chain: multiple of 12 sts + 2
Drape: excellent
Skill: intermediate

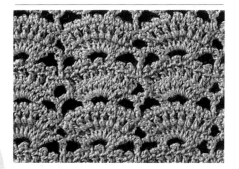

1ST ROW (RS): 1sc into 2nd ch from hook, ✳5ch, skip 3ch, 1sc into next ch; rep from ✳ to end, turn.
2ND ROW: 5ch (count as 1dc and 2ch), ✳1sc into next 5ch arch, 8dc into next arch, 1sc into next arch✳✳, 5ch; rep from ✳ ending last rep at ✳✳ in last arch, 2ch, 1dc into last sc, skip tch, turn.
3RD ROW: 1ch, 1sc into 1st st, skip 2ch and 1sc, ✳work a Picot of [1dc into next dc, 3ch, insert hook down through top of dc just made and sl st to close] 7 times, 1dc into next dc, 1sc into next arch; rep from ✳ to end, turn.
4TH ROW: 8ch, skip 2 Picots, ✳1sc into next picot, 5ch, skip 1 Picot, 1sc into next Picot, 5ch, skip 2 Picots, 1dc into next sc✳✳, 5ch, skip 2 Picots; rep from ✳ ending last rep at ✳✳, skip tch, turn. Rep 2nd, 3rd and 4th rows.

Open Pineapple Stitch

Starting chain: multiple of 15 sts + 3
Drape: excellent
Skill: experienced

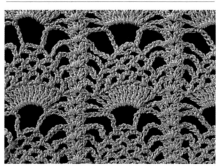

Special Abbreviation
DV St = Double V Stitch.
BASE ROW (RS): Skip 2ch (count as 1dc), 2dc into next ch, ✳7ch, skip 5ch, 1sc into next ch, 3ch, skip 2ch, 1sc into next ch, 7ch, skip 5ch✳✳, work a DV St (see Special Abbreviation) of [2dc, 1ch, 2dc] into next ch; rep from ✳ ending last rep at ✳✳, 3dc into last ch, turn.

Commence Pattern
1ST ROW (RS): 3ch (count as 1dc), 2dc into 1st st, ✳3ch, 1sc into 7ch arch, 5ch, skip 3ch, 1sc into next 7ch arch, 3ch✳✳, DV St into sp at center of DV St; rep from ✳ ending last rep at ✳✳, 3dc into top of tch, turn.
2ND ROW: 3ch (count as 1dc), 2dc into 1st st, ✳skip 3ch, 11tr into next 5ch arch, skip 3ch✳✳, DV St into next sp; rep from ✳ ending last rep at ✳✳, 3dc into top of tch, turn.
3RD ROW: 3ch (count as 1dc), 2dc into 1st st, ✳2ch, skip 2dc, 1sc into next tr, [3ch, skip 1tr, 1sc into next dir] 5 times, 2ch, skip 2dc✳✳, DV St into next sp; rep from ✳ ending last rep at ✳✳, 3dc into top of tch, turn.
4TH ROW: 3ch (count as 1dc), 2dc into first st, ✳3ch, skip 2ch, 1sc into next 3ch arch, [3ch, 1sc into next 3ch arch] 4 times, 3ch, skip 2ch✳✳, DV St into next sp; rep from ✳ ending last rep at ✳✳, 3dc into top of tch, turn.
5TH ROW: 3ch (count as 1dc), 2dc into 1st st, ✳4ch, skip 3ch, 1sc into next 3ch arch,

[3ch, 1sc into next 3ch arch] 3 times, 4ch, skip 3ch✳✳, DV St into next sp; rep from ✳ ending last rep at ✳✳, 3dc into top of tch, turn.
6TH ROW: 3ch (count as 1dc), 2dc into 1st st, ✳5ch, skip 4ch, 1sc into next 3ch arch, [3ch, 1sc into next 3ch arch] twice, 5ch, skip 4ch✳✳, DV St into next sp; rep from ✳ ending last rep at ✳✳, 3dc into top of tch, turn.
7TH ROW: 3ch (count as 1dc), 2dc into 1st st, ✳7ch, skip 5ch, 1sc into next 3ch arch, 3ch, 1sc into next 3ch arch, 7ch, skip 5ch✳✳, DV St into next sp; rep from ✳ ending last rep at ✳✳, 3dc into top of tch, turn. Rep these 7 rows.

Strawberry Lace Stitch

Starting chain: multiple of 12 sts + 8
Drape: excellent
Skill: experienced

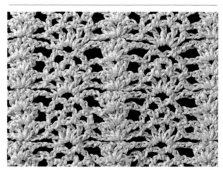

1ST ROW (RS): 1sc into 2nd ch from hook, ✳3ch, skip 5ch, into next ch work a 5 group of 1dc, [1ch, 1dc] 4 times, 3ch, skip 5ch, 1sc into next ch; rep from ✳ ending 3ch, skip 5ch, into last ch work 1dc, [1ch, 1dc] twice, turn.
2ND ROW: [3ch, 1sc into next ch sp] twice, ✳1ch, skip 3ch, work a DV St of [2dc, 1ch, 2dc] into next sc, 1ch, skip 3ch, 1sc into next ch sp, [3ch, 1sc into next sp] 3 times; rep from ✳ ending 1ch, skip 3ch, 3dc into last sc, skip tch, turn.
3RD ROW: 3ch (count as 1dc), 2dc into 1st st, ✳2ch, skip 1ch, 1sc into next 3ch arch✳✳, [3ch, 1sc into next 3ch arch]

twice, 2ch: skip 1ch, DV St into next ch sp; rep from ✳ ending last rep at ✳✳, 3ch, 1sc into tch, turn.

4TH ROW: 4ch, 1sc into next 3ch arch, ✳3ch, skip 2ch, DV St into next ch sp, 3ch, skip 2ch, 1sc into next 3ch arch, 3ch, 1sc into next 3ch arch; rep from ✳ ending 3ch, skip 2ch, 3dc into top of tch, turn.

5TH ROW: 1ch, 1sc into 1st st, ✳3ch, skip 3ch, 5 group into next 3ch arch, 3ch, skip 3ch, 1sc into next ch sp; rep from ✳ ending 3ch, skip 3ch, into tch work 1dc, [1ch, 1dc] twice, turn.

Rep 2nd, 3rd, 4th and 5th rows.

Open Crescent
Starting chain: multiple of 18 sts + 2
Drape: excellent
Skill: experienced

1ST ROW (WS): 1sc into 2nd ch from hook, ✳3ch, skip 2ch, 1sc into next ch, [5ch, skip 3ch, 1sc into next ch] 3 times, 3ch, skip 2ch, 1sc into next ch; rep from ✳ to end, turn.

2ND ROW: 3ch (count as 1dc), 1dc into 1st st, ✳3ch, skip 3ch, 1sc into next arch, 9dc into next arch, 1sc into next arch, 3ch, skip 3ch, 3dc into next sc; rep from ✳ working only 2dc at end of last rep, skip tch, turn.

3RD ROW: 1ch, 1sc into each of 1st 2 sts, ✳1ch, skip 3ch and 1sc, 1dc into next dc, [1ch, 1dc into next dc] 8 times, 1ch, skip 1sc and 3ch, 1sc into each of next 3 sts; rep from ✳ omitting 1sc at end of last rep, turn.

4TH ROW: 1ch, 1sc into 1st st, ✳skip 1sc

and 1ch, 1dc into next dc, [1ch, skip 1ch, 1dc into next dc] 3 times, 1ch, skip 1ch, work [1dc, 1ch, 1dc] into next dc, [1ch, skip 1ch, 1dc into next dc] 4 times (Crescent completed), skip 1ch and 1sc, 1sc into next sc; rep from ✳ to end, skip tch, turn.

5TH ROW: 6ch (count as 1dc and 3ch), ✳1sc into 3rd dc of next Crescent, 5ch, skip 1ch and 1dc, 1sc into next ch, 5ch, skip 1dc, 1ch and 1dc, 1sc into next ch, 5ch, skip 1dc and 1ch, 1sc into next dc, 3ch, skip remaining sts of same Crescent, 1dc into next sc, 3ch; rep from ✳ omitting 3ch at end of last rep, skip tch, turn.

Rep 2nd, 3rd, 4th and 5th rows.

Little Pyramid Stitch
Starting chain: multiple of 4 sts + 2
Drape: excellent
Skill: intermediate

1ST ROW (RS): 1sc into 2nd ch from hook, ✳work a Pyramid of [6ch, 1sc into 3rd ch from hook, 1dc into each of next 3ch], skip 3ch, 1sc into next ch; rep from ✳ to end, turn.

2ND ROW: 6ch (count as 1dtr and 1ch), ✳1sc into ch at tip of next Pyramid, 3ch; rep from ✳ ending 1sc into ch at tip of last Pyramid, 1ch, 1dtr into last sc, skip tch, turn.

3RD ROW: 10ch, skip 1ch, 1sc into next sc, ✳work Pyramid, skip 3ch, 1sc into next sc; rep from ✳ ending 5ch, skip 1ch, 1dtr into next ch of tch, turn.

4TH ROW: 1ch, 1sc into 1st st, ✳3ch, 1sc

into ch at tip of next Pyramid; rep from ✳ ending last rep in center of 10tch, turn.

5TH ROW: 1ch, 1sc into 1st st, ✳work Pyramid, skip 3ch, 1sc into next sc; rep from ✳ to end, skip tch, turn.

Rep 2nd, 3rd, 4th and 5th rows.

Chevron Lattice
Starting chain: multiple of 20 sts + 11
Drape: excellent
Skill: intermediate

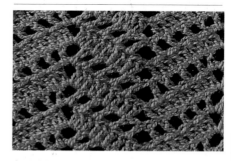

Special Abbreviation
Dc Cluster: leaving last loop of each dc on hook work 1dc into next ch, skip 3ch, and work 1dc into next ch, then yo and draw through all 3 loops on hook.

1ST ROW (WS): 1dc into 6th ch from hook, ✳[1ch, skip 1ch, 1dc into next ch] 3 times, 1ch, skip 1ch✳✳, work [1dc, 3ch, 1dc] into next ch, [1ch, skip 1ch, 1dc into next ch] 3 times, 1ch, skip 1ch, work a dc Cluster (see Special Abbreviation) over next 1dc, 3ch and 1dc; rep from ✳ ending last rep at ✳✳, work [1dc, 1ch, 1dc] into last ch, turn.

2ND ROW: 3ch (count as 1dc), 2dc into 1st st, ✳1dc into next ch sp, [1dc into next dc, 1dc into next ch sp] 3 times✳✳, leaving last loop of each dc on hook work 1dc into next dc, skip dc Cluster, work 1dc into next dc and complete as dc Cluster, [1dc into next ch sp, 1dc into next dc] 3 times, 1dc into next ch, work [1dc, 3ch, 1dc] into next ch; rep from ✳ ending last rep at ✳✳, work dc Cluster over next 2dcs, skip tch, turn.

3RD ROW: 3ch, skip 1st 2 sts, 1dc into next st, ✳[1ch, skip 1dc, 1dc into next dc]

277

3 times✳✳, 1ch, skip 1ch, work [1dc, 3ch, 1dc] into next ch, 1ch, skip 1ch, [1dc into next dc, 1ch, skip 1dc] 3 times, leaving last loop of each dc on hook work 1dc into next dc, skip 1dc, dc Cluster and 1dc, work 1dc into next dc and complete as dc Cluster; rep from ✳ ending last rep at ✳✳, 1ch, skip 1dc, work [1dc, 1ch, 1dc] into top of tch, turn. Rep 2nd and 3rd rows.

Fan Pattern

Starting chain: multiple of 5 sts + 2
Drape: good
Skill: intermediate

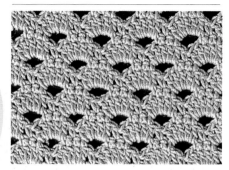

1ST ROW (WS): Work 1sc into 2nd ch from hook, 1sc into next ch, ✳3ch, skip 2ch, 1sc into each of next 3ch; rep from ✳ to end omitting 1sc at end of last rep, turn.
2ND ROW: 1ch, 1sc into 1st sc, ✳5dc into next 3ch arch, skip 1sc, 1sc into next sc; rep from ✳ to end, turn.
3RD ROW: 3ch (count as 1dtr, 1ch), skip 1st 2 sts, 1sc into each of next 3dc, ✳3ch, skip next 3 sts, 1sc into each of next 3dc; rep from ✳ to last 2 sts, 1ch, 1dtr into last sc, turn.
4TH ROW: 3ch (count as 1dc), 2dc into 1st ch sp, skip 1sc, 1sc into next sc, ✳5dc into next 3ch arch, skip 1sc, 1sc into next sc; rep from ✳ to last sp, 2dc into last sp, 1dc into 2nd of 3ch at beg of previous row, turn.
5TH ROW: 1ch, 1sc into each of 1st 2dc, ✳3ch, skip 3 sts, 1sc into each of next 3dc; rep from ✳ to end omitting 1sc at end of last rep and placing last sc into 3rd

of 3ch at beg of previous row, turn.
Rep 2nd to 5th rows.

Daisy Pattern

Starting chain: multiple of 11 sts + 3
Drape: good
Skill: experienced

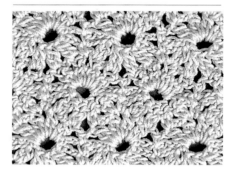

Special Abbreviation

Dc2tog = work 2dc into next st until 1 loop of each remains on hook, yo and through all 3 loops on hook.

1ST ROW (RS): Work 1sc into 2nd ch from hook, 1ch, skip 1ch, 1sc into next ch, [3ch, skip 3ch, 1sc into next ch] twice, ✳2ch, skip 2ch, 1sc into next ch, [3ch, skip 3ch, 1sc into next ch] twice; rep from ✳ to last 2ch, 1ch, skip 1ch, 1sc into last ch, turn.
2ND ROW: 3ch (count as 1dc), into 1st ch sp work [dc2tog—see Special Abbreviation, 2ch, dc2tog], 1ch, skip 1ch, 1sc into next sc, ✳1ch, skip 3ch sp, dc2tog into next 2ch sp, into same sp as last dc2tog work [2ch, dc2tog] 3 times, 1ch, skip 3ch sp, 1sc into next sc; rep from ✳ to last 2 sps, 1ch, skip 3ch sp, into last ch sp work [dc2tog, 2ch, dc2tog], 1dc into last sc, turn.
3RD ROW: 1ch, 1sc into 1st dc, ✳3ch, work 1dc2tog into top of each of next 4dc2tog, 3ch, 1sc into next 2ch sp; rep from ✳ to end placing last sc into 3rd of 3ch at beg of previous row, turn.
4TH ROW: 1ch, 1sc into 1st sc, ✳3ch, 1sc into top of next dc2tog, 2ch, skip 2dc2tog, 1sc into top of next dc2tog, 3ch, 1sc into next sc; rep from ✳ to end, turn.
5TH ROW: 1ch, work 1sc into 1st sc, ✳1ch,

skip 3ch sp, dc2tog into next 2ch sp, into same sp as last dc2tog work [2ch, dc2tog] 3 times, 1ch, skip 3ch sp, 1sc into next sc; rep from ✳ to end, turn.
6TH ROW: 3ch, work 1dc2tog into top of each of next 2dc2tog, 3ch, 1sc into next 2ch sp, 3ch, ✳dc2tog into top of each 4dc2tog, 3ch, 1sc into next 2ch sp, 3ch; rep from ✳ to last 2dc2tog, work 1dc2tog into each of last 2dc2tog, 1dc into last sc, turn.
7TH ROW: 1ch, 1sc into 1st dc, 1ch, skip 1dc2tog, 1sc into next dc2tog, 3ch, 1sc into next sc, 3ch, ✳1sc into top of next dc2tog, 2ch, skip 2dc2tog, 1sc into top of next dc2tog, 3ch, 1sc into next sc, 3ch; rep from ✳ to last 2dc2tog, 1sc into next dc2tog, 1ch, skip 1dc2tog, 1sc into 3rd of 3ch at beg of previous row, turn.
Rep 2nd to 7th rows.

Pansy Pattern

Starting chain: multiple of 10 sts + 2
Drape: excellent
Skill: experienced

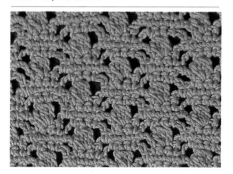

Special Abbreviations

Bobble = work 4dc into next st until 1 loop of each remains on hook, yo and through all 5 loops on hook.

Dc2tog = work 2dc into next st until 1 loop of each remains on hook, yo and through all 3 loops on hook.

1ST ROW (RS): Work 1sc into 2nd ch from hook, 1sc into each of next 2ch, ✳3ch, skip 2ch, 1 Bobble (see Special Abbreviations) into next ch, 3ch, skip 2ch,

1sc into each of next 5ch; rep from ❋ to end omitting 2sc at end of last rep, turn.

2ND ROW: 1ch, 1sc into each of 1st 2sc, ❋3ch, 1sc into next 3ch sp, 1sc into top of next Bobble, 1sc into next 3ch sp, 3ch, skip 1sc, 1sc into each of next 3sc; rep from ❋ to end omitting 1sc at end of last rep, turn.

3RD ROW: 3ch (count as 1dc), 1dc into 1st sc (half Bobble made at beg of row), ❋3ch, 1sc into next 3ch sp, 1sc into each of next 3sc, 1sc into next 3ch sp, 3ch, skip 1sc, 1 Bobble into next sc; rep from ❋ to end but working half Bobble of dc2tog (see Special Abbreviations), at end of last rep, turn.

4TH ROW: 1ch, 1sc into top of half Bobble, 1sc into 1st 3ch sp, 3ch, skip 1sc, 1sc into each of next 3sc, ❋3ch, 1sc into next 3ch sp, 1sc into top of next Bobble, 1sc into next 3ch sp, 3ch, skip 1sc, 1sc into each of next 3sc; rep from ❋ to last 3ch sp, 3ch, 1sc into last 3ch sp, 1sc into 3rd of 3ch at beg of previous row, turn.

5TH ROW: 1ch, 1sc into each of 1st 2sc, ❋1sc into next 3ch sp, 3ch, skip 1sc, 1 Bobble into next sc, 3ch, 1sc into next 3ch sp, 1sc into each of next 3sc; rep from ❋ to end omitting 1sc at end of last rep, turn. Rep 2nd to 5th rows.

Ostrich Plumes

Starting chain: multiple of 16 sts + 3
Drape: excellent
Skill: experienced

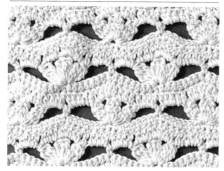

Special Abbreviations

Cluster = work 1dc into same arch as last

3dc until 2 loops remain on hook, skip 1sc, work 1dc into next arch until 3 loops remain on hook, yo and through all 3 loops on hook.

Bobble = work 3tr into next sc until 1 loop of each remains on hook, yo and through all 4 loops on hook.

1ST ROW (RS): Work 1dc into 4th ch from hook, 1dc into each of 6ch, work 3dc into next ch, 1dc into each of next 6ch, ❋work 1dc into next ch until 2 loops remain on hook, skip 1ch, 1dc into next ch until 3 loops remain on hook, yo and through all 3 loops on hook, work 1dc into each of next 6ch, 3dc into next ch, 1dc into each of next 6ch; rep from ❋ to last 2ch, work 1dc into next ch until 2 loops remain on hook, 1dc into last ch until 3 loops remain on hook, yo and through all 3 loops (Cluster made at end of row—see Special Abbreviations), turn.

2ND ROW: 1ch, work 1sc into each st to last dc, skip last dc, 1sc into top of 3ch, turn.

3RD ROW: 4ch, work 1tr into 1st sc (half Bobble made at beg of row—see Special Abbreviations), 2ch, 1 Bobble into same sc as half Bobble, 4ch, skip 7sc, 1sc into next sc, ❋4ch, skip 7sc, work 1 Bobble into next sc, into same sc as last Bobble work [2ch, 1 Bobble] twice, 4ch, skip 7sc, 1sc into next sc; rep from ❋ to last 8sc, 4ch, work 1 Bobble into last sc, 2ch, work 2tr into same sc as last Bobble until 1 loop of each remains on hook, yo and through all 3 loops on hook (half Bobble made at end of row), turn.

4TH ROW: 3ch (count as 1dc), 1dc into top of first half Bobble, work 2dc into 2ch sp, 1dc into next Bobble, 3dc into next 4ch arch, 1 Cluster, 3dc into same arch as 2nd leg of last Cluster, ❋1dc into top of next Bobble, 2dc into 2ch sp, 3dc into top of next Bobble, 2dc into next 2ch sp, 1dc into top of next Bobble, 3dc into next 4ch arch, 1 Cluster, 3dc into same arch as 2nd leg of last Cluster; rep from ❋ to last Bobble, 1dc into last Bobble, 2dc into next 2ch sp, 2dc into top of half Bobble, turn.

5TH ROW: 1ch, 1sc into each st to end, placing last sc into 3rd of 3ch at beg of previous row, turn.

6TH ROW: 1ch, 1sc into 1st sc, ❋4ch, skip 7sc, 1 Bobble into next sc, into same sc as last Bobble work [2ch, 1 Bobble] twice, 4ch, skip 7sc, 1sc into next sc; rep from ❋ to end, turn.

7TH ROW: 3ch, 4dc into 1st 4ch arch, 1dc into next Bobble, 2dc into next 2ch sp, 3dc into next Bobble, 2dc into next 2ch sp, 1dc into next Bobble, ❋3tr into next 4ch arch, 1 Cluster, 3dc into same arch as 2nd leg of last Cluster, 1dc into next Bobble, 2dc into next 2ch sp, 3dc into next Bobble, 2dc into next 2ch sp, 1dc into next Bobble; rep from ❋ to last 4ch arch, 3dc into last arch, 1 Cluster working into last arch and last sc; turn. Rep 2nd to 7th rows.

Crab Pattern

Starting chain: multiple of 8 sts + 2
Drape: excellent
Skill: experienced

Special Abbreviation

Bobble = work 4dc into next st until 1 loop of each remains on hook, yo and through all 5 loops on hook.

1ST ROW (WS): Work 1sc into 2nd ch from hook, 1sc into each ch to end, turn.

2ND ROW: 4ch (count as 1dc, 1ch), skip 1st 2sc, 1 Bobble (see Special Abbreviation) into next sc, 1ch, skip 1sc, 1dc into next sc, ❋1ch, skip 1sc, 1 Bobble into next sc, 1ch, skip 1sc, 1dc into next sc; rep from ❋ to end, turn.

3RD ROW: 1ch, work 1sc into each dc, ch sp and Bobble to end, working last 2sc into 4th and 3rd of 4ch at beg of previous row, turn.

4TH ROW: 1ch, 1sc into each of 1st 3sc, ✳5ch, skip 3sc, 1sc into each of next 5sc; rep from ✳ to end omitting 2sc at end of last rep, turn.

5TH ROW: 1ch, 1sc into each of 1st 2sc, ✳3ch, 1sc into 5ch arch, 3ch, skip 1sc, 1sc into each of next 3sc; rep from ✳ to end omitting 1sc at end of last rep, turn.

6TH ROW: 1ch, 1sc into 1st sc, ✳3ch, 1sc into next 3ch arch, 1sc into next sc, 1sc into next 3ch arch, 3ch, skip 1sc, 1sc into next sc; rep from ✳ to end, turn.

7TH ROW: 5ch (count as 1dc, 2ch), 1sc into next 3ch arch, 1sc into each of next 3sc, 1sc into next 3ch arch, ✳5ch, 1sc into next 3ch arch, 1sc into each of next 3sc, 1sc into next 3ch arch; rep from ✳ to last sc, 2ch, 1dc into last sc, turn.

8TH ROW: 1ch, 1sc into 1st dc, ✳3ch, skip 1sc, 1sc into each of next 3sc, 3ch, 1sc into next 5ch arch; rep from ✳ to end placing last sc into 3rd of 5ch at beg of previous row, turn.

9TH ROW: 1ch, 1sc into 1st sc, ✳1sc into next 3ch arch, 3ch, skip 1sc, 1sc into next sc, 3ch, 1sc into next 3ch arch, 1sc into next sc; rep from ✳ to end, turn.

10TH ROW: 1ch, 1sc into each of 1st 2sc, ✳1sc into next 3ch arch, 3ch, 1sc into next 3ch arch, 1sc into each of next 3sc; rep from ✳ to end omitting 1sc at end of last rep, turn.

11TH ROW: 1ch, 1sc into each of 1st 3sc, ✳3sc into next 3ch arch, 1sc into each of next 5sc; rep from ✳ to end omitting 2sc at end of last rep, turn. Rep 2nd to 11th rows.

Fan and Lattice Pattern

Starting chain: multiple of 10 sts + 2
Drape: excellent
Skill: intermediate

Special Abbreviation

Dc2tog = work 2dc into next 3ch arch until 1 loop of each remains on hook, yo and through all 3 loops on hook.

1ST ROW (WS): Work 1sc into 2nd ch from hook, ✳3ch, skip 3ch, 1sc into next ch, 3ch,

skip 1ch, 1sc into next ch, 3ch, skip 3ch, 1sc into next ch; rep from ✳ to end, turn.

2ND ROW: 1ch, 1sc into 1st sc, ✳1ch, skip next 3ch sp, dc2tog (see Special Abbreviation) into next 3ch arch, into same arch as last dc2tog work [3ch, dc2tog] 4 times, 1ch, skip next 3ch sp, 1sc into next sc; rep from ✳ to end, turn.

3RD ROW: 7ch (count as 1tr, 3ch), skip next 3ch arch, 1sc into next 3ch arch, 3ch, 1sc into next 3ch arch, 3ch, 1tr into next sc, ✳3ch, skip next 3ch arch, 1sc into next 3ch arch, 3ch, 1sc into next 3ch arch, 3ch, 1tr into next sc; rep from ✳ to end, turn.

4TH ROW: 1ch, 1sc into 1st tr, ✳1ch, skip next 3ch sp, dc2tog into next 3ch arch, into same arch as last dc2tog work [3ch, dc2tog] 4 times, 1ch, 1sc into next tr; rep from ✳ to end, working last sc into 4th of 7ch at beg of previous row, turn.
Rep 3rd and 4th rows.

Cloud Wisps

Starting chain: multiple of 6 sts + 2
Drape: excellent
Skill: experienced

Special Abbreviations

Dtr2tog = ✳yo, insert hook into st, yo and draw a loop through (3 loops on hook); rep from ✳ once more into same st, yo and through all 5 loops on hook.

Dc2tog = work 1dc into next ch sp until 2 loops remain on hook, work a 2nd dc into next ch sp until 3 loops remain on hook, yo and through all 3 loops on hook.

1ST ROW (RS): Work 1sc into 2nd ch from

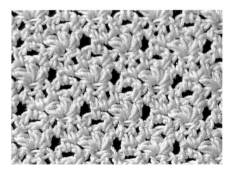

hook, ✳1ch, skip 2ch, into next ch work [dtr2tog—see Special Abbreviations, 1ch] 3 times, skip 2ch, 1sc into next ch; rep from ✳ to end, turn.

2ND ROW: 4ch (count as 1dc, 1ch), skip 1st ch sp, 1sc into next ch sp, 3ch, 1sc into next ch sp, ✳1ch, dc2tog over next 2ch sps, 1ch, 1sc into next ch sp, 3ch, 1sc into next ch sp; rep from ✳ to last sc, 1ch, 1dc into last sc, turn.

3RD ROW: 3ch (count as 1dtr, 1ch), dc2tog into 1st dc, 1ch, 1sc into next 3ch sp, 1ch, ✳into top of next dc2tog (see Special Abbreviations) work [dtr2tog, 1ch] 3 times, 1sc into next 3ch sp, 1ch; rep from ✳ to last ch sp, into 3rd of 4ch at beg of previous row work [dtr2tog, 1ch, 1dtr], turn.

4TH ROW: 1ch, 1sc into 1st dtr, 1sc into 1st ch sp, 1ch, dc2tog over next 2 ch sps, 1ch, ✳1sc into next ch sp, 3ch, 1sc into next ch sp, 1ch, dc2tog over next 2ch sps, 1ch; rep from ✳ to last ch sp, 1sc into last ch sp, 1sc into 2nd of 3ch at beg of previous row, turn.

5TH ROW: 1ch, 1sc into 1st sc, ✳1ch, into top of next dc2tog work [dtr2tog, 1ch] 3 times, 1sc into next 3ch sp; rep from ✳ to end placing last sc into last sc, turn.
Rep 2nd to 5th rows.

Feathers

Starting chain: multiple of 24 sts + 5
Drape: excellent
Skill: experienced

Special Abbreviations

Dc2tog = work 2dc into next st until 1 loop

openwork patterns

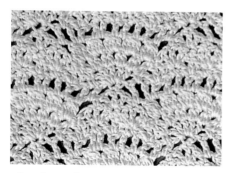

of each remains on hook, yo and through all 3 loops on hook.

Bobble = work 4dc into next st until 1 loop of each remains on hook, yo and through all 5 loops on hook.

Group = work 1dc into next st, into same st as last dc work [1ch, 1dc] twice.

1ST ROW (RS): Work 1dc into 5th ch from hook, skip 2ch, 1sc into next ch, skip 2ch, 1 Group (see Special Abbreviations) into next ch, skip 2ch, 1sc into next ch, skip 2ch, 5dc into next ch, ✳skip 2ch, 1sc into next ch, [skip 2ch, 1 Group into next ch, skip 2ch, 1sc into next ch] 3 times, skip 2ch, 5dc into next ch; rep from ✳ to last 12ch, skip 2ch, 1sc into next ch, skip 2ch, 1 Group into next ch, skip 2ch, 1sc into next ch, skip 2ch, into last ch work [1dc, 1ch, 1dc], turn.

2ND ROW: 1ch, 1sc into 1st dc, 1 Group into next sc, 1sc into center dc of next Group, skip 1dc, 2dc into each of next 5dc, ✳1sc into center dc of next Group, [1 Group into next sc, 1sc into center dc of next Group] twice, skip 1dc, 2dc into each of next 5dc; rep from ✳ to last Group, 1sc into center dc of next Group, 1 Group into next sc, skip [1dc, 1ch], 1 sc into next ch, turn.

3RD ROW: 4ch (count as 1dc, 1ch), 1dc into 1st sc, 1sc into center dc of first Group, 2ch, [1 Bobble (see Special Abbreviations) between next pair of dc, 2ch] 5 times, ✳1sc into center dc of next Group, 1 Group into next sc, 1sc into center dc of next Group, 2ch, [1 Bobble between next pair of dc, 2ch] 5 times; rep from ✳ to last Group, 1sc into center dc of last Group, into last sc work [1dc, 1ch, 1dc], turn.

4TH ROW: 1ch, 1sc into 1st dc, ✳1ch, 1dc into next 2ch sp, [1ch, 1dc into top of next Bobble, 1ch, 1dc into next 2ch sp] 5 times, 1ch, 1sc into center dc of next Group; rep from ✳ to end placing last sc into 3rd of 4ch at beg of previous row, turn.

5TH ROW: 3ch (count as 1dc), 2dc into 1st sc, ✳skip 1ch sp, 1sc into next ch sp, [skip 1ch sp, 1 Group into next dc, skip 1ch sp, 1sc into next ch sp] 3 times, 5dc into next sc; rep from ✳ to end omitting 2dc at end of last rep, turn.

6TH ROW: 3ch (count as 1dc), 1dc into 1st dc, 2dc into each of next 2dc, 1sc into center dc of next Group, [1 Group into next sc, 1sc into center dc of next Group] twice, ✳skip 1dc, 2dc into each of next 5dc, 1sc into center dc of next Group, [1 Group into next sc, 1sc into center dc of next Group] twice; rep from ✳ to last 5 sts, skip next dc and sc, 2dc into each of next 2dc, 2dc into 3rd of 3ch at beg of previous row, turn.

7TH ROW: 3ch (count as 1dc), dc2tog (see Special Abbreviations) between 1st pair of dc, 2ch, [1 Bobble between next pair of dc, 2ch] twice, 1sc into center dc of next Group, 1 Group into next sc, 1sc into center dc of next Group, ✳2ch, skip [1dc, 1sc], [1 Bobble between next pair of dc, 2ch] 5 times, 1sc into center dc of next Group, 1 Group into next sc, 1sc into center dc of next Group; rep from ✳ to last 3 pairs of dc, [2ch, 1 Bobble between next pair of dc] twice, 2ch, dc2tog between last pair of dc, 1dc into 3rd of 3ch at beg of previous row, turn.

8TH ROW: 4ch (count as 1dc, 1ch), 1dc into 1st 2ch sp, 1ch, [1dc into top of next Bobble, 1ch, 1dc into next 2ch sp, 1ch] twice, 1sc into center dc of next Group, ✳1ch, 1dc into next 2ch sp, 1ch, [1dc into top of next Bobble, 1ch, 1dc into next 2ch sp, 1ch] 5 times, 1sc into center dc of next Group; rep from ✳ to last 3 2ch sps, 1ch, 1dc into next 2ch sp, [1ch, 1dc into top of next Bobble, 1ch, 1dc into next 2ch sp] twice, 1ch, 1dc into 3rd of 3ch at beg of previous row, turn.

9TH ROW: 4ch (count as 1dc, 1ch), 1dc into 1st dc, skip 1ch sp, 1sc into next ch sp, skip 1ch sp, 1 Group into next dc, skip 1ch sp, 1sc into next ch sp, 5dc into next sc, ✳skip 1ch sp, 1sc into next ch sp, [skip 1ch sp, 1 Group into next dc, skip 1ch sp, 1sc into next ch sp] 3 times, 5dc into next sc; rep from ✳ to last 6 ch sps, skip 1ch sp, 1sc into next ch sp, skip 1ch sp, 1 Group into next dc, skip 1ch sp, 1sc into next ch sp, into 3rd of 4ch at beg of previous row work [1dc, 1ch, 1dc], turn. Rep 2nd to 9th rows.

Speckled Stitch

Starting chain: multiple of 7 sts + 4
Drape: excellent
Skill: intermediate

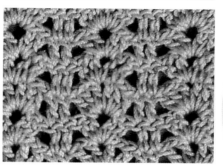

1ST ROW (RS): Work 1dc into 4th ch from hook, ✳skip 2ch, into next ch work [3dc, 1ch, 3dc], skip 2ch, 1dc into each of next 2ch; rep from ✳ to end, turn.

2ND ROW: 3ch (count as 1dc), skip 1st dc, 1dc into next dc, ✳skip 2dc, 1dc into next dc, 1ch, into next ch sp work [1dc, 1ch, 1dc], 1ch, 1dc into next dc, skip 2dc, 1dc into each of next 2dc; rep from ✳ to end placing last dc into 3rd of 3ch at beg of previous row, turn.

3RD ROW: 3ch, skip 1st dc, 1dc into next dc, ✳skip next ch sp, into next ch sp work [2dc, 3ch, 2dc], skip 2dc, 1dc into each of next 2dc; rep from ✳ to end placing last dc into 3rd of 3ch at beg of previous row, turn.

4TH ROW: 3ch, skip 1st dc, 1dc into next dc, ✳into next 3ch sp work [3dc, 1ch, 3dc], skip 2dc, 1dc into each of next 2dc; rep from ✳ to end placing last dc into 3rd of 3ch at beg of previous row, turn.
Rep 2nd to 4th rows.

Dock Leaf Pattern

Starting chain: multiple of 8 sts + 4
Drape: excellent
Skill: intermediate

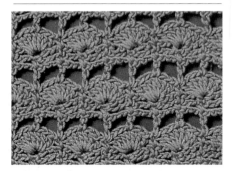

1ST ROW (RS): Work 3dc into 4th ch from hook, skip 3ch, 1sc into next ch, ✳skip 3ch, 7dc into next ch, skip 3ch, 1sc into next ch; rep from ✳ to last 4ch, skip 3ch, 4dc into last ch, turn.

2ND ROW: 6ch (count as 1dc, 3ch), 1dc into next sc, ✳3ch, skip 3dc, 1dc into next dc, 3ch, 1dc into next sc; rep from ✳ to last 4 sts, 3ch, 1dc into top of 3ch at beg of previous row, turn.

3RD ROW: 1ch, ✳1sc into next dc, 3ch; rep from ✳ to last st, 1sc into 3rd of 6ch at beg of previous row, turn.

4TH ROW: 1ch, 1sc into 1st sc, ✳3ch, 1sc into next sc; rep from ✳ to end, turn.

5TH ROW: 1ch, 1sc into 1st sc, ✳7dc into next sc, 1sc into next sc; rep from ✳ to end, turn.

6TH ROW: 6ch, skip 3dc, 1dc into next dc, 3ch, 1dc into next sc, ✳3ch, skip 3dc, 1dc into next dc, 3ch, 1dc into next sc; rep from ✳ to end, turn.

7TH AND 8TH ROWS: As 3rd and 4th rows.

9TH ROW: 3ch (count as 1dc), 3dc into 1st sc, 1sc into next sc, ✳7dc into next sc, 1sc into next sc; rep from ✳ to last sc, 4dc into last sc, turn. Rep 2nd to 9th rows.

Arch and Picot Pattern

Starting chain: multiple of 3 sts + 2
Drape: excellent
Skill: easy

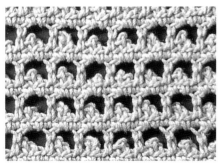

1ST ROW (RS): Work 1sc into 2nd ch from hook, 1sc into next ch, ✳4ch, sl st into 4th ch from hook (1 Picot made), 1sc into each of next 3sc; rep from ✳ to end omitting 1sc at end of last rep, turn.

2ND ROW: 5ch (count as 1dc, 2ch), skip 2sc, 1dc into next sc, ✳2ch, skip 2sc, 1dc into next sc; rep from ✳ to end, turn.

3RD ROW: 1ch, 1sc into 1st dc, ✳into next 2ch sp work [1sc, 1 Picot, 1sc], 1sc into next dc; rep from ✳ to end placing last sc into 3rd of 5ch at beg of previous row, turn. Rep 2nd and 3rd rows.

Fountain Stitch

Starting chain: multiple of 9 sts + 4
Drape: good
Skill: experienced

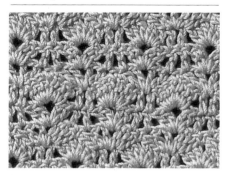

Special Abbreviations

Shell = work 1dc into next dc, 1ch, between last dc and next dc work [1dc, 1ch, 1dc], 1ch, 1dc into next dc.

Half Shell (at beg of row) = 4ch (count as 1dc, 1ch), 1dc between 1st 2dc, 1ch, 1dc into next dc.

Half Shell (at end of row) = 1dc into next dc, 1ch, 1dc between last dc worked into and last dc (the 3ch at beg of previous row), 1ch, 1dc into 3rd of 3ch at beg of previous row.

1ST ROW (RS): Work 1dc into 4th ch from hook, ✳skip 3ch, into next ch work [3dc, 1ch, 3dc], skip 3ch, 1dc into each of next 2ch; rep from ✳ to end, turn.

2ND ROW: Work Half Shell (see Special Abbreviations) over 1st 2dc, 1sc into next ch sp, ✳skip 3dc, 1 Shell (see Special Abbreviations) over next 2dc, 1sc into next ch sp; rep from ✳ to last 5 sts, skip 3dc, Half Shell (see Special Abbreviations) over last 2dc, turn.

3RD ROW: 4ch (count as 1dc, 1ch), 2dc into 1st ch sp, skip 1dc, 1dc into each of next 2dc, ✳skip 1ch sp, into next ch sp work [2dc, 3ch, 2dc], skip 1dc, 1dc into each of next 2dc; rep from ✳ to last 2dc, 2dc into last ch sp, 1ch, 1dc into 3rd of 4ch at beg of previous row, turn.

4TH ROW: 4ch (count as 1dc, 1ch), 3dc into 1st ch sp, skip 2dc, 1dc into each of next 2dc, ✳into next 3ch sp work [3dc, 1ch, 3dc], skip 2dc, 1dc into each of next 2dc; rep from ✳ to last 3dc, work 3dc into last ch sp, 1ch, 1dc into 3rd of 4ch at beg of previous row, turn.

5TH ROW: 1ch, 1sc into 1st dc, 1sc into 1st ch sp, ✳skip 3dc, 1 Shell over next 2dc, 1sc into next ch sp; rep from ✳ to end, 1sc into 3rd of 4ch at beg of previous row, turn.

6TH ROW: 3ch (count as 1dc), skip 1st sc, 1dc into next sc, skip 1ch sp, into next ch sp work [2dc, 3ch, 2dc], ✳skip 1dc, work 1dc into each of next 2dc, skip 1ch sp, into next ch sp work [2dc, 3ch, 2dc]; rep from ✳ to last 2dc, 1dc into each of last 2sc, turn.

7TH ROW: 3ch (count as 1dc), skip 1st dc, 1dc into next dc, ✳into next 3ch sp work [3dc, 1ch, 3dc], skip 2dc, 1dc into each of next 2dc; rep from ✳ to end placing last dc into 3rd of 3ch at beg of previous row, turn. Rep 2nd to 7th rows.

Bay Tree Stitch
Starting chain: multiple of 12 sts + 6
Drape: excellent
Skill: intermediate

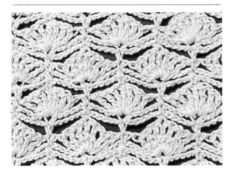

1ST ROW (RS): Work [1tr, 1ch] 3 times into 6th ch from hook, skip 5ch, 1sc into next ch, ✳1ch, skip 5ch, into next ch work [1tr, 1ch] 7 times, skip 5ch, 1sc into next ch; rep from ✳ to last 6ch, 1ch, into last ch work [1tr, 1ch] 3 times, 1tr into same ch as last 3tr, turn.
2ND ROW: 1ch, 1sc into 1st tr, ✳6ch, 1sc into next sc, 6ch, skip 3tr, 1sc into next tr; rep from ✳ to end placing last tr into 4th of 5ch at beg of previous row, turn.
3RD ROW: 1ch, 1sc into 1st sc, ✳6ch, 1sc into next sc; rep from ✳ to end, turn.
4TH ROW: 1ch, 1sc into 1st sc, ✳1ch, into next sc work [1tr, 1ch] 7 times, 1sc into next sc; rep from ✳ to end, turn.
5TH ROW: 1ch, 1sc into 1st sc, ✳6ch, skip 3tr, 1sc into next tr, 6ch, 1sc into next sc; rep from ✳ to end, turn.
6TH ROW: 1ch, 1sc into 1st sc, ✳6ch, 1sc into next sc; rep from ✳ to end, turn.
7TH ROW: 5ch (count as 1 tr, 1ch), into 1st sc work [1tr, 1ch] 3 times, 1sc into next sc, ✳1ch, into next sc work [1tr, 1ch] 7 times, 1sc into next sc; rep from ✳ to last sc, into last sc work [1ch, 1tr] 4 times, turn.
Rep 2nd to 7th rows.

Sea Anemone
Starting chain: multiple of 10 sts + 14
Drape: excellent
Skill: experienced

Special Abbreviation
Puff St = [yo, insert hook into sp, yo and draw a loop through] 3 times into same space, yo and through all 7 loops on hook, work 1 firm ch to close Puff St.

1ST ROW (WS): Work 1sc into 9th ch from hook, (1st 3ch sp made), 1ch, skip 1ch, 1sc into next ch, ✳3ch, skip 2ch, 1dc into next ch, 1ch, skip 1ch, 1dc into next ch, 3ch, skip 2ch, 1sc into next ch, 1ch, skip 1ch, 1sc into next ch; rep from ✳ to last 3ch, 3ch, skip 2ch, 1dc into last ch, turn.
2ND ROW: 1ch, 1sc into 1st dc, ✳3ch, skip 3ch sp, 1 Puff St (see Special Abbreviation) into next ch sp, 2ch, into same ch sp as last Puff St work [1 Puff St, 2ch, 1 Puff St], 3ch, skip 3ch sp, 1sc into next ch sp; rep from ✳ to end working last sc into 4th ch, turn.
3RD ROW: 1ch, 1sc into 1st sc, 3ch, skip 1st 3ch arch, 1dc into next 2ch arch, 1ch, 1dc into next 2ch arch, 3ch, 1sc into next 3ch arch, ✳1ch, 1sc into next 3ch arch, 3ch, 1dc into next 2ch arch, 1ch, 1dc into next 2ch arch, 3ch, 1sc into next 3ch arch; rep from ✳ to end placing last sc into last sc, turn.
4TH ROW: 6ch (count as 1dc, 3ch), skip 3ch arch, 1sc into next ch sp, ✳3ch, skip 3ch arch, 1 Puff St into next ch sp, 2ch, into same ch sp as last Puff St work [1 Puff St, 2ch, 1 Puff St], 3ch, skip 3ch arch, 1sc into next ch sp; rep from ✳ to last 3ch arch, 3ch, 1dc into last sc, turn.
5TH ROW: 6ch (count as 1dc, 3ch), 1sc into 1st 3ch arch, 1ch, 1sc into next 3ch arch, ✳3ch, 1dc into next 2ch arch, 1ch, 1dc into next 2ch arch, 3ch, 1sc into next 3ch arch, 1ch, 1sc into next 3ch arch; rep from ✳ to end, 3ch, 1dc into 3rd of 6ch at beg of previous row, turn. Rep 2nd to 5th rows.

Paired Cluster Pattern
Starting chain: multiple of 9 sts + 14
Drape: excellent
Skill: intermediate

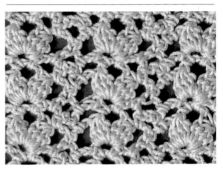

Special Abbreviations
Cluster = work 4dc into next 3ch arch until 1 loop of each remains on hook, yo and through all 5 loops on hook.
Dc2tog over next 3 3ch arches = work 1dc into next 3ch arch until 2 loops remain on hook, skip next 3ch arch, 1dc into next 3ch arch until 3 loops remain on hook, yo and through all 3 loops on hook.

1ST ROW (WS): Work 1sc into 6th ch from hook, 3ch, skip 2ch, into next ch work [1sc, 3ch, 1sc], ✳[3ch, skip 2ch, 1sc into next ch] twice, 3ch, skip 2ch, into next ch work [1sc, 3ch, 1sc]; rep from ✳ to last 5ch, 3ch, skip 2ch, 1sc into next sc, 1ch, skip 1ch, 1dc into last ch, turn.
2ND ROW: 2ch (count as 1dtr), 1dc into 1st 3ch arch, 3ch, into next 3ch arch work [1 Cluster (see Special Abbreviations), 4ch, 1 Cluster], 3ch, ✳dc2tog (see Special Abbreviations) over next 3 3ch arches, 3ch, into next 3ch arch work [1 Cluster, 4ch, 1 Cluster], 3ch; rep from ✳ to last 2 arches, work 1dc into next 3ch arch, skip 1ch, 1dtr into next ch, turn.
3RD ROW: 4ch (count as 1dc, 1ch), 1sc into next 3ch arch, 3ch, into next 4ch arch work [1sc, 3ch, 1sc], ✳3ch, [1sc into next 3ch arch, 3ch] twice, into next 4ch arch work

openwork patterns

[1 sc, 3ch, 1sc]; rep from ✳ to last 3ch arch, 3ch, 1 sc into last 3ch arch, 1ch, 1dc into 2nd of 2ch at beg of previous row, turn. Rep 2nd and 3rd rows.

Petal and Leaf Pattern

Starting chain: multiple of 10 sts + 5
Drape: excellent
Skill: intermediate

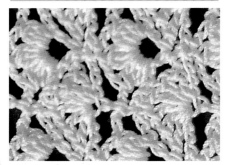

Special Abbreviation

Cluster = work 3dc into next space until 1 loop of each remains on hook, yo and through all 4 loops on hook.

1ST ROW (RS): Work [1dc, 1ch, 1dc] into 5th ch from hook (1dc and 1ch sp formed at beg of row), 1ch, skip 4ch, 1sc into next ch, ✳1ch, skip 4ch, into next ch work [1dc, 1ch] 6 times, skip 4ch, 1sc into next ch; rep from ✳ to last 5ch, 1ch, 1dc into last ch, [1ch, 1dc] twice into same ch as last dc, turn.

2ND ROW: 1ch, 1sc into 1st dc, 3ch, into next sc work [1dc, 3ch, 1dc], ✳3ch, skip 3dc, 1sc into next ch sp, 3ch, into next sc work [1dc, 3ch, 1dc]; rep from ✳ to last 3dc, 3ch, 1sc into 3rd of 4ch at beg of previous row, turn.

3RD ROW: 1ch, 1sc into 1st sc, ✳2ch, skip 3ch sp, 1 Cluster (see Special Abbreviation) into next 3ch sp, 2ch, into same sp as last Cluster work [1 Cluster, 2ch] twice, 1sc into next sc; rep from ✳ to end, turn.

4TH ROW: 7ch (count as 1dc, 4ch), ✳skip 1 Cluster, 1sc into next Cluster, 4ch, 1dc into next sc, 4ch; rep from ✳ to end omitting 4ch at end of last rep, turn.

5TH ROW: 4ch (count as 1dc, 1ch), into 1st dc work [1dc, 1ch] twice, 1sc into next sc, ✳1ch, into next dc work [1dc, 1ch] 6 times, 1sc into next sc; rep from ✳ to last dc, 1ch, work 1dc into 3rd of 7ch at beg of previous row, [1ch, 1dc] twice into same ch as last dc, turn. Rep 2nd to 5th rows.

Hands Pattern

Starting chain: multiple of 7 sts + 3
Drape: excellent
Skill: intermediate

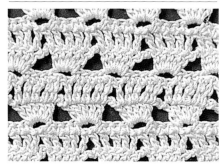

1ST ROW (RS): Work 1sc into 2nd ch from hook, 1sc into each of next 2ch, ✳3ch, skip 3ch, 1sc into each of next 4ch; rep from ✳ to end omitting 1sc at end of last rep, turn.

2ND ROW: 4ch (count as 1dc, 1ch), work 5dc into 1st 3ch sp, ✳3ch, 5dc into next 3ch sp; rep from ✳ to last 3sc, 1ch, 1dc into last sc, turn.

3RD ROW: 3ch (count as 1dc), skip 1st dc, ✳1dc into next dc, [1ch, 1dc into next dc] 4 times; rep from ✳ to last dc, 1dc into 3rd of 4ch at beg of previous row, turn.

4TH ROW: 1ch, 1sc into 1st dc, 1ch, [1sc into next ch sp, skip 1dc] 4 times, ✳3ch, [1sc into next ch sp, skip 1dc] 4 times; rep from ✳ to last 2dc, 1ch, 1sc into 3rd of 3ch at beg of previous row, turn.

5TH ROW: 3ch, 2dc into 1st sc, 3ch, ✳5dc into next 3ch sp, 3ch; rep from ✳ to last sc, 3dc into last sc, turn.

6TH ROW: 4ch, skip 1st dc, 1dc into next dc, 1ch, 1dc into next dc, ✳1dc into next dc, [1ch, 1dc into next dc] 4 times; rep from ✳ to last 3dc, [1dc into next dc, 1ch] twice, 1dc into 3rd of 3ch at beg of previous row, turn.

7TH ROW: 1ch, 1sc into 1st dc, [1sc into next ch sp, skip 1dc] twice, 3ch, ✳[1sc into next ch sp, skip 1dc] 4 times, 3ch; rep from ✳ to last 3dc, 1sc into next ch sp, skip 1dc, 1sc into next ch sp, 1sc into 3rd of 4ch at beg of previous row, turn. Rep 2nd to 7th rows.

Thistle Pattern

Starting chain: multiple of 4 sts + 3
Drape: excellent
Skill: intermediate

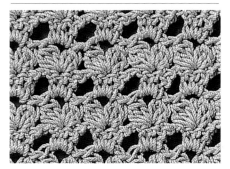

Special Abbreviation

Bobble = work 3dc into next st until 1 loop of each remains on hook, yo and through all 4 loops on hook.

1ST ROW (WS): Work 1dc into 4th ch from hook, 1dc into each of next 2ch, ✳2ch, skip 1ch, 1dc into each of next 3ch; rep from ✳ to last ch, 1dc into last ch, turn.

2ND ROW: 3ch (count as 1dc), skip 1st 2dc, into next dc work [1 Bobble (see Special Abbreviation), 3ch, 1 Bobble], ✳skip 2dc, into next dc work [1 Bobble, 3ch, 1 Bobble]; rep from ✳ to last 2dc, 1dc into 3rd of 3ch at beg of previous row, turn.

3RD ROW: 3ch, work 3dc into 1st 3ch arch, ✳2ch, 3dc into next 3ch arch: rep from ✳ to last 2 sts, 1dc into 3rd of 3ch at beg of previous row, turn.

Rep 2nd and 3rd rows.

Palm Tree Pattern

Starting chain: multiple of 10 sts + 2
Drape: excellent
Skill: experienced

Special Abbreviation

Dc2tog = work 2dc into next st until 1 loop of each remains on hook, yo and through all 3 loops on hook.

1ST ROW (RS): Work 1sc into 2nd ch from hook, 1sc into next ch, 3ch, skip 2ch, dc2tog (see Special Abbreviation) into next ch, 1ch, skip 1ch, dc2tog into next ch, ✳3ch, skip 2ch, 1sc into next ch, 1ch, skip 1ch, 1sc into next ch, 3ch, skip 2ch, dc2tog into next ch, 1ch, skip 1ch, dc2tog into next ch; rep from ✳ to last 4ch, 3ch, skip 2ch, 1sc into each of last 2ch, turn.

2ND ROW: 4ch (count as 1dc, 1ch), 1dc into 1st sc, 3ch, skip next 3ch sp, 1sc into next ch sp, ✳3ch, skip next 3ch sp, 1dc into next ch sp, 1ch, into same ch sp as last dc work [1dc, 1ch, 1dc], 3ch, skip next 3ch sp, 1sc into next ch sp; rep from ✳ to last 3ch sp, 3ch, into last sc work [1dc, 1ch, 1dc], turn.

3RD ROW: 3ch (count as 1dc), dc2tog into 1st ch sp, 3ch, 1sc into next 3ch sp, 1ch, 1sc into next 3ch sp, ✳3ch, dc2tog into next ch sp, 1ch, dc2tog into next ch sp, 3ch, 1sc into next 3ch sp, 1ch, 1sc into next 3ch sp; rep from ✳ to last ch sp, 3ch, dc2tog into last ch sp, 1dc into 3rd of 4ch at beg of previous row, turn.

4TH ROW: 1ch, 1sc into 1st dc, ✳skip next 3ch sp, 3ch, 1dc into next ch sp, 1ch, into same ch sp as last dc work [1dc, 1ch, 1dc], 3ch, skip next 3ch sp, 1sc into next ch sp; rep from ✳ to end placing last sc into 3rd of 3ch at beg of previous row, turn.

5TH ROW: 1ch, 1sc into 1st sc, 1sc into 1st 3ch sp, 3ch, dc2tog into next ch sp, 1ch, dc2tog into next ch sp, ✳3ch, 1sc into next 3ch sp, 1ch, 1sc into next 3ch sp, 3ch, dc2tog into next ch sp, 1ch, dc2tog into next ch sp; rep from ✳ to last 3ch sp, 3ch, 1sc into last 3ch sp, 1sc into last sc, turn. Rep 2nd to 5th rows.

Lattice Flakes

Starting chain: multiple of 6 sts + 3
Drape: excellent
Skill: intermediate

1ST ROW (RS): Work 1sc into 2nd ch from hook, 1sc into next ch, ✳6ch, skip 4ch, 1sc into each of next 2ch; rep from ✳ to end, turn.

2ND ROW: 3ch (count as 1dc), skip 1st sc, 1dc into next sc, ✳2ch, 1sc into 6ch arch, 2ch, 1dc into each of next 2sc; rep from ✳ to end, turn.

3RD ROW: 3ch, skip 1st dc, 1dc into next dc, ✳3ch, 1 sl st into next sc, 3ch, 1dc into each of next 2dc; rep from ✳ to end placing last dc into 3rd of 3ch at beg of previous row, turn.

4TH ROW: 1ch, 1sc into each of 1st 2dc, ✳4ch, 1sc into each of next 2dc; rep from ✳ to end placing last sc into 3rd of 3ch at beg of previous row, turn.

5TH ROW: 1ch, 1sc into each of 1st 2sc, ✳6ch, 1sc into each of next 2sc; rep from ✳ to end, turn.
Rep 2nd to 5th rows.

Turning Triangles

Starting chain: multiple of 6 sts + 2
Drape: excellent
Skill: easy

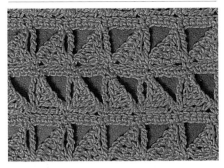

1ST ROW (RS): Work 1sc into 2nd ch from hook, 1sc into each ch to end, turn.

2ND ROW: 1ch, 1sc into 1st sc, ✳6ch, work 1sc into 2nd ch from hook, then working 1 st into each of next 4ch work 1dtr, 1dc, 1tr and 1dtr, skip 5sc on previous row, 1sc into next sc; rep from ✳ to end, turn.

3RD ROW: 5ch (count as 1dtr), ✳1sc into ch at top of next triangle, 4ch, 1dtr into next sc; rep from ✳ to end, turn.

4TH ROW: 1ch, work 1sc into each [dtr, ch and sc] to end, placing last sc into top of 5ch at beg of previous row, turn.
Rep 2nd to 4th rows.

Rows of Flowers

Starting chain: multiple of 12 sts + 11
Drape: excellent
Skill: intermediate

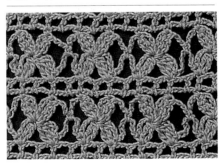

Special Abbreviation

Dc2tog = work 2tr into next st until 1 loop of each remains on hook, yo and through all 3 loops on hook.

1ST ROW (RS): Work 1dc into 8th ch from hook, ✳2ch, skip 2ch, 1dc into next ch; rep from ✳ to end, turn.

2ND ROW: 1ch, 1sc into 1st dc, ✳9ch, skip 1dc, into next dc work [1sc, 4ch, dc2tog (see Special Abbreviation)], skip 1dc, into next dc work [dc2tog, 4ch, 1sc]; rep from ✳ to last 2 sps, 9ch, skip 1dc, 1sc into 3rd ch, turn.

3RD ROW: 10ch (count as tr tr, 4ch), 1sc into 1st 9ch arch, ✳4ch, into top of next dc2tog work [dc2tog, 4ch, 1 sl st, 4ch, dc2tog], 4ch, 1sc into next 9ch arch; rep from ✳ to end, 4ch, 1 tr tr into last sc, turn.

4TH ROW: 1ch, 1sc into 1st tr tr, ✳5ch, 1sc into top of next dc2tog; rep from ✳ to end placing last sc into 6th of 10ch at beg of previous row, turn.

5TH ROW: 5ch (count as 1dc, 2ch), 1dc into next 5ch arch, 2ch, 1dc into next sc, ✳2ch, 1dc into next 5ch arch, 2ch, 1dc into next sc; rep from ✳ to end, turn. Rep 2nd to 5th rows.

Shell and Stripe Pattern

Starting chain: multiple of 16 sts + 7
Drape: excellent
Skill: intermediate

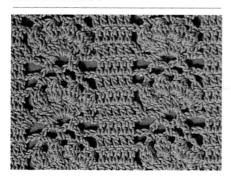

Special Abbreviation

Bobble = work 4dc into next st until 1 loop of each remains on hook, yo and through all 5 loops on hook.

1ST ROW (RS): Work 1dc into 4th ch from hook, 1dc into each of next 3ch, ✳4ch, skip 4ch, 1sc into next ch, 3ch, skip 1ch, 1sc into next ch, 4ch, skip 4ch, 1dc into each of next 5ch; rep from ✳ to end, turn.

2ND ROW: 3ch (count as 1dc), skip 1st dc, 1dc into each of next 4dc, ✳2ch, 1sc into next 4ch arch, 1ch, work 7dc into next 3ch arch, 1ch, 1sc into next 4ch arch, 2ch, 1dc into each of next 5dc; rep from ✳ to end placing last dc into top of 3ch at beg of previous row, turn.

3RD ROW: 3ch, skip 1st dc, 1dc into each of next 4dc, ✳1ch, 1 Bobble (see Special Abbreviation) into next dc, [3ch, skip 1dc, 1 Bobble into next dc] 3 times, 1ch, 1dc into each of next 5dc; rep from ✳ to end placing last dc into 3rd of 3ch at beg of previous row, turn.

4TH ROW: 3ch, skip 1st dc, 1dc into each of next 4dc, ✳2ch, 1sc into next 3ch arch, [3ch, 1sc into next 3ch arch] twice, 2ch, 1dc into each of next 5dc; rep from ✳ to end placing last dc into 3rd of 3ch at beg of previous row, turn.

5TH ROW: 3ch, skip 1st dc, 1dc into each of next 4dc, ✳4ch, skip 2ch sp, 1sc into next 3ch arch, 3ch, 1sc into next 3ch arch, 4ch, 1dc into each of next 5dc; rep from ✳ to end placing last dc into 3rd of 3ch at beg of previous row. Rep 2nd to 5th rows.

Cluster and Bobble Pattern

Starting chain: multiple of 12 sts + 8
Drape: excellent
Skill: experienced

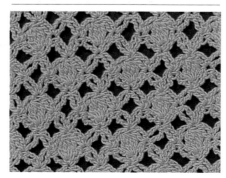

Special Abbreviations

Cluster = 3ch, 1tr worked until 2 loops remain on hook (1st leg), 1tr worked until 3 loops remain, yo and through all 3 loops, 3ch, 1sc into same stas last tr (2nd leg).

Bobble (on Cluster) = work 1st leg of Cluster then work 4tr into next sc until 1 loop of each remains on hook (6 loops on hook), work 2nd leg of Cluster but bringing yarn through all 7 loops on hook to finish tr, complete 2nd leg as for Cluster.

1ST ROW (RS): Work 1sc into 2nd ch from hook, ✳work 1st leg of Cluster (see Special Abbreviations) into same ch as last sc, skip 5ch, work 2nd leg of Cluster into next ch; rep from ✳ to end, turn.

2ND ROW: 4ch (count as 1tr), into top of 1st Cluster work [1tr, 3ch, 1sc], ✳work next Cluster placing 2nd leg into top of next Cluster; rep from ✳ finishing with 2nd leg worked into top of last Cluster, work 1st leg of Cluster, 1 tr into last sc until 3 loops remain, yo and through all 3 loops, turn.

3RD ROW: 1ch, 1sc into 1st st, ✳work Cluster placing 2nd leg into top of next Cluster; rep from ✳ to end but working Bobble (see Special Abbreviations) on next and every alt Cluster, turn.

4TH ROW: As 2nd row.

5TH ROW: As 3rd row but working Bobble on 1st then every alt Cluster, turn.
Rep 2nd to 5th rows.

mesh-type patterns

The patterns given here can be used either on their own or, in some cases, as a background for Irish crochet motifs (*pages 196 and 292*). The two Plain Trellis stitches (*below*) are especially well-suited to this purpose. The ever-popular Solomon's Knot (*below*) makes a gossamer-light curtain, if worked in fine crochet cotton, but it could equally well be worked in twine for a string bag. (*See page 190 for the technique.*)

(*See page 190 for the technique.*)

Solomon's Knot

Starting chain: multiple of 2 Solomon's Knots + 1
Drape: excellent
Skill: intermediate

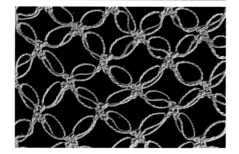

Special Abbreviations

ESK (Edge Solomon's Knot) = these form the base "chain" and edges of the fabric and are two-thirds the length of MSKs.
MSK (Main Solomon's Knot) = these form the main fabric and are half as long again as ESKs.
BASE "CHAIN" = 2ch, 1sc into 2nd ch from hook, now make a multiple of 2ESKs (say, 2 cm [¾ in]), ending with 1MSK (say, 3 cm [1⅛ in]).
1ST ROW: 1sc into sc between 3rd and 4th loops from hook, ✳2MSK (see Special Abbreviations), skip 2 loops, 1sc into next sc; rep from ✳ to end, turn.
2ND ROW: 2ESK (see Special Abbreviations) and 1MSK, 1sc into sc between 4th and 5th loops from hook, ✳2MSK, skip 2 loops, 1sc into next sc; rep from ✳ ending in top of ESK, turn.
Rep 2nd row.

Plain Trellis Stitch I

Starting chain: multiple of 4 sts + 6
Drape: excellent
Skill: easy

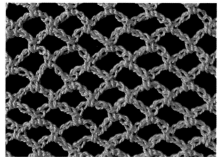

1ST ROW: 1sc into 6th ch from hook, ✳5ch, skip 3ch, 1sc into next ch; rep from ✳ to end, turn.
2ND ROW: ✳5ch, 1sc into next 5ch arch; rep from ✳ to end, turn.
Rep 2nd row.

Plain Trellis Stitch II

Starting chain: multiple of 4 sts + 2
Drape: excellent
Skill: easy

1ST ROW (RS): Work 1sc into 2nd ch from hook, ✳6ch, skip 3ch, 1sc into next ch; rep from ✳ to end, turn.
2ND ROW: 8ch (count as 1dtr, 3ch), 1sc into first 6ch arch, ✳6ch, 1sc into next 6ch arch; rep from ✳ to end, 3ch, 1dtr into last sc, turn.
3RD ROW: 1ch, 1sc into 1st dtr, ✳6ch, 1sc into next 6ch arch; rep from ✳ to end placing last sc into 5th of 8ch at beg of previous row, turn.
Rep 2nd and 3rd rows.

Lacewing Network

Starting chain: multiple of 16 sts + 2
Drape: excellent
Skill: intermediate

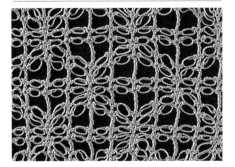

Special Abbreviation

SK (Solomon's Knot) = loop approx 1.5 cm.
Note: You may need to experiment with the number of ch in the base chain and length of loop, or even make the base "chain" itself out of Knots.
BASE ROW (RS) = 1sc into 2nd ch from hook, ✳1SK (see Special Abbreviation), skip 3ch, 1tr into next ch, 1SK, skip 3ch, 1 quad dc into next ch, 1SK, skip 3ch, 1tr into next ch, 1SK, skip 3ch, 1sc into next ch; rep from ✳ to end, turn.

Commence Pattern

1ST ROW: 3ch, 1sc into 2nd ch from hook, ✳1SK, skip SK, 1dc into next st; rep from ✳ to end, turn.
2ND ROW: 6ch, 1sc into 2nd ch from hook, ✳1SK, skip SK, 1tr into next st, 1SK, skip SK, 1sc into next st, 1SK, skip SK, 1tr into next st, 1SK, skip SK, 1 quad dc into next st; rep from ✳ to end, turn.
Rep the last 2 rows once then work 1st row again.
6TH ROW: 1ch, 1sc into 1st st, ✳1SK, skip SK, 1tr into next st, 1SK, skip SK, 1 quad dc into next st, 1SK, skip SK, 1tr into next st, 1SK, skip SK, 1sc into next st; rep from ✳ to end, turn.
7TH ROW: As 1st row.
8TH ROW: As 6th row.
Rep these 8 rows.

Horizontal Trellis

Starting chain: multiple of 5 sts + 7
Drape: excellent
Skill: easy

1ST ROW (RS): Work 1dc into 12th ch from hook, ✳4ch, skip 4ch, 1dc into next ch; rep from ✳ to end, turn.
2ND ROW: 6ch (count as 1tr, 2ch), 1dc into next 4ch sp, ✳4ch, 1dc into next 4ch sp; rep from ✳ to end, 2ch, 1tr into 5th ch, turn.
3RD ROW: 7ch (count as 1dc, 4ch), ✳1dc into next 4ch sp, 4ch; rep from ✳ to last sp, 1dc into 4th of 6ch at beg of previous row, turn. Rep 2nd and 3rd rows.

Small Picot Trellis

Starting chain: multiple of 5 sts + 2
Drape: excellent
Skill: intermediate

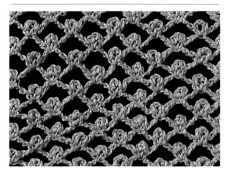

1ST ROW: 1sc into 2nd ch from hook, ✳5ch, skip 4ch, 1sc into next ch; rep from ✳ to end, turn.

2ND ROW: ✳5ch, work a Picot of [1sc, 3ch, 1sc] into 3rd ch of next 5ch arch; rep from ✳ ending 2ch, 1dc into last sc, skip tch, turn.
3RD ROW: 1ch, 1sc into 1st st, ✳5ch, skip Picot, Picot into 3rd ch of next 5ch arch; rep from ✳ ending 5ch, skip Picot, 1sc into tch arch, turn.
Rep 2nd and 3rd rows.

Clones Knot Trellis

Starting chain: multiple of 8 sts + 2
Drape: excellent
Skill: experienced

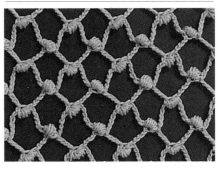

Special Abbreviation

Clones Knot = draw up a chain to required length and hold it in place, ✳yo, twist hook over, then under the loop, then pull the yarn back under the loop with the hook; rep from ✳ until the loop is completely covered. Yo, draw hook through all loops on hook. To secure knot work 1sc into last ch before Clones Knot.
1ST ROW (RS): Work 1sc into 2nd ch from hook, ✳4ch, 1 Clones Knot (see Special Abbreviation), 4ch, skip 7ch, 1sc into next ch; rep from ✳ to end, turn.
2ND ROW: 10ch (count as 1quad dc, 4ch), working behind 1st Clones Knot work 1sc into sc securing knot, ✳4ch, 1 Clones Knot, 4ch, 1sc into sc securing next Clones Knot as before; rep from ✳ ending with 4ch, 1 quad dc into last sc, turn.
3RD ROW: 1ch, 1sc into quad dc, ✳4ch, 1 Clones Knot, 4ch, working behind next Clones Knot work 1sc into sc securing

knot; rep from ✳ to end placing last sc into 6th of 10ch at beg of previous row, turn. Rep 2nd and 3rd rows.

Single Crochet Mesh
Starting chain: multiple of 5 sts + 2
Drape: excellent
Skill: intermediate

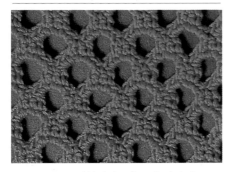

1ST ROW (RS): Work 1sc into 2nd ch from hook, 1sc into each ch to end, turn.
2ND ROW: 1ch, 1sc into each of 1st 2sc, ✳5ch, skip 2sc, 1sc into each of next 3sc; rep from ✳ to end omitting 1sc at end of last rep, turn.
3RD ROW: 1ch, 1sc into 1st sc, ✳5ch into next 5ch arch, skip 1sc, 1sc into next sc; rep from ✳ to end, turn.
4TH ROW: 6ch (count as 1tr, 2ch), skip first 2sc, 1sc into each of next 3sc, ✳5ch, skip 3sc, 1sc into each of next 3sc; rep from ✳ to last 2sc, 2ch, 1tr into last sc, turn.
5TH ROW: 1ch, 1sc into 1st tr, 2sc into 2ch sp, skip 1sc, 1sc into next sc, ✳5sc into next 5ch arch, skip 1sc, 1sc into next sc; rep from ✳ to last 2ch sp, 2sc into last sp, 1sc into 4th of 4ch at beg of previous row, turn.
6TH ROW: 1ch, 1sc into each of 1st 2sc, ✳5ch, skip 3sc, 1sc into each of next 3sc; rep from ✳ to end omitting 1sc at end of last rep, turn.
Rep 3rd to 6th rows.

Crested Mesh
Starting chain: multiple of 5 sts + 2
Drape: excellent
Skill: intermediate

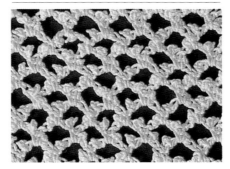

1ST ROW (RS): Work 1sc into 2nd ch from hook, ✳[4ch, 1sc into 3rd ch from hook] twice, 1ch, skip 4ch, 1sc into next ch; rep from ✳ to end, turn.
2ND ROW: 9ch (count as 1dtr, 4ch), 1sc into 3rd ch from hook, 1ch, 1sc into center of 1st arch, ✳[4ch, 1sc into 3rd ch from hook] twice, 1ch, 1sc into center of next arch; rep from ✳ to end, 4ch, 1sc into 3rd ch from hook, 1ch, 1dtr into last sc, turn.
3RD ROW: 1ch, 1sc into 1st dtr, ✳[4ch, 1sc into 3rd ch from hook] twice, 1ch, 1sc into center of next arch; rep from ✳ to end placing last sc into 5th of 9ch at beg of previous row, turn.
Rep 2nd and 3rd rows.

Coronet Ground
Starting chain: multiple of 8 sts + 1
Drape: excellent
Skill: intermediate

1ST ROW (RS): Skip 1ch, ✳1sc into each of next 4ch, work a picot of [3ch, insert hook down through top of last sc made and work sl st to close], 1sc into each of next 4ch, work 9ch then without turning skip 7 previous sc, work a sl st back into previous sc, then working in the normal direction work 7sc into 9ch arch, work a Coronet of [5ch, sl st into 5th ch from hook, 7ch, sl st into 7th ch from hook, 5ch,

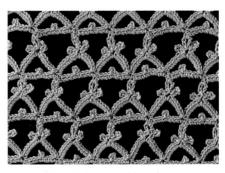

sl st into 5th ch from hook], work 7sc into arch; rep from ✳ ending sl st into last sc, turn.
2ND ROW: 11ch (count as 1quad dc and 4ch), ✳1sc into 7ch arch at center of next Coronet, 7ch; rep from ✳ ending 1sc into 7ch arch at center of last Coronet, 2ch, 1 quad dc into last sc, skip tch, turn.
3RD ROW: 1ch, 1sc into 1st st, 1sc into each of next 2ch and next sc, turn, 4ch, skip 3sc, 1tr in last sc, turn, 8ch, sl st into 7th ch from hook, 5ch, sl st into 5th ch from hook (half Coronet worked), 7sc into next 4ch arch, ✳1sc into each of next 4ch, 3ch Picot, 1sc into each of next 3ch, 1sc into next sc, work 9ch, skip 7 previous sc, sl st back into previous sc, work 7sc into 9ch arch, work a Coronet as before, then 7sc into 9ch loop; rep from ✳ ending 1sc into each of next 4ch of tch arch, 9ch, skip previous 3sc, sl st into previous sc, work 7sc into 9ch arch, work a half Coronet of [5ch, sl st into 5th ch from hook], 1sc into 9ch arch, 3ch, 1tr into last sc, turn.
4TH ROW: 1 ch, 1sc into top of 3ch, ✳7ch, 1sc into 7ch arch at center of next Coronet; rep from ✳ ending last rep in 8ch arch of half Coronet, turn.
5TH ROW: 1ch, 1sc into 1st st, 1sc into each of next 3ch, ✳3ch Picot, 1sc into each of next 3ch, 1sc into next sc, 9ch, skip 7 previous sc, sl st back into previous sc, work 7sc, Coronet and 7sc into arch✳✳, 1sc into each of next 4ch; rep from ✳ ending last rep at ✳✳, sl st into last sc, turn.
Rep 2nd, 3rd, 4th and 5th rows.

String Network

Starting chain: multiple of 4 sts + 6
Drape: excellent
Skill: easy

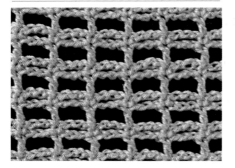

1ST ROW (RS): 1dc into 10th ch from hook, ✳3ch, skip 3ch, 1dc into next ch; rep from ✳ to end, turn.
2ND ROW: 1ch, 1sc into 1st st, ✳3ch, skip 3ch, 1sc into next dc; rep from ✳ ending 3ch, 1sc into 4th ch of tch, turn.
3RD ROW: 6ch (count as 1dc and 3ch), skip 1st st and 3ch, 1dc into next sc, ✳3ch, skip 3ch, 1dc into next sc; rep from ✳ to end, turn.
Rep 2nd and 3rd rows.

Offset Filet Network

Starting chain: multiple of 2 sts + 3
Drape: excellent
Skill: easy

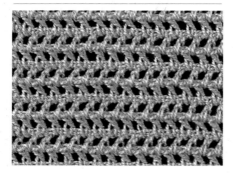

1ST ROW (RS): 1dc into 6th ch from hook, ✳1ch, skip 1ch, 1dc into next ch; rep from ✳ ending 1dc into last ch, turn.

2ND ROW: 4ch (count as 1dc and 1ch), skip 1st 2 sts, 1dc into next ch sp, ✳1ch, skip 1dc, 1dc into next sp; rep from ✳ to tch, 1dc into next ch, turn.
Rep 2nd row.

Embossed Flower Network

Starting chain: multiple of 24 sts + 8
Drape: excellent
Skill: experienced
Note: When working Embossed Flower always treat the various stitches and threads which form the four sides of the space as if they were the base ring of a motif, i.e. always insert hook through center of this "ring" to make stitches.

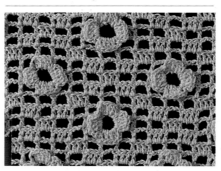

BASE ROW (RS): 1dc into 8th ch from hook, ✳2ch, skip 2ch, 1dc into each of next 4ch, [2ch, skip 2ch, 1dc into next ch] 3 times, 1dc into each of next 3ch, [2ch, skip 2ch, 1dc into next ch] twice; rep from ✳ to end, turn.

Commence Pattern
1ST ROW: 5ch (count as 1dc and 2ch), skip 2ch, 1dc into next st, ✳2dc into next 2ch sp, 1dc into next st, [2ch, skip 2 sts, 1dc into next st] twice, 2dc into next sp, 1dc into next st, [2ch, skip 2 sts, 1dc into next st] twice, 2dc into next sp, 1dc into next st, 2ch, skip 2ch, 1dc into next st; rep from ✳ to end, turn.
2ND ROW: 3ch (count as 1dc), skip 1st st, 2dc into next 2ch sp, 1dc into next st, ✳[2ch, skip 2 sts, 1dc into next st] twice, 2dc into next sp, 1dc into next st, 2ch, skip 2dc, 1dc into next st. Now work Embossed

Flower round space just completed, (see note above); with right side facing and working around counterclockwise, work 1sc into corner (top left), down left side work ✳✳3ch, 3dc, 3ch, 1sc into next corner✳✳ (bottom left), rep from ✳✳ to ✳✳ 3 more times, omitting sc at end of last rep and ending sl st to 1st sc, sl st to last dc made of main fabric. Continue working main fabric as follows: 2dc into next 2ch sp, 1dc into next st, [2ch, skip 2 sts, 1dc into next st] twice, 2dc into next 2ch sp, 1dc into next st; rep from ✳ ending last rep in 3rd ch of tch, turn.
3RD ROW: As 1st row.
4TH ROW: 5ch (count as 1dc and 2ch), skip 2ch, 1dc into next st, ✳2ch, skip 2 sts, 1dc into next st, 2dc into next 2ch sp, 1dc into next st, [2ch, skip 2 sts, 1dc into next st] 3 times, 2dc into next sp, 1dc into next st, [2ch, skip 2 sts, 1dc into next st] twice; rep from ✳ ending last rep in 3rd ch of tch, turn.
5TH ROW: 3ch (count as 1dc), skip 1st st, 2dc into next 2ch sp, 1dc into next st, ✳[2ch, skip 2 sts, 1dc into next st] twice, [2dc into next sp, 1dc into next st, 2ch, skip 2 sts, 1dc into next st] twice, 2ch, skip 2ch, 1dc into next st, 2dc into next sp, 1dc into next st; rep from ✳ ending last rep in 3rd ch of tch, turn.
6TH ROW: 5ch (count as 1dc and 2ch), skip first 3 sts, 1dc into next st. Now work Embossed Flower round space just completed as in 3rd row. Continue working main fabric as follows: ✳2dc into next 2ch sp, 1dc into next st, [2ch, skip 2 sts, 1dc into next st] twice, 2dc into next sp, 1dc into next st, [2ch, skip 2 sts, 1dc into next st] twice, 2dc into next sp, 1dc into next st, 2ch, skip 2 sts, 1dc into next st. Now work Embossed Flower round space just completed as before; rep from ✳ ending last rep of main fabric in top of tch, turn.
7TH ROW: As 5th row.
8TH ROW: As 4th row.
Rep these 8 rows.

openwork patterns

crochet motifs

These versatile motifs can be used in all sorts of ways: some of them can be joined up to form placemats, tablecloths, or bedspreads, whereas the Irish motifs are crocheted to a mesh background fabric. Motifs also have the advantage of being an easily portable kind of needlework—perfect for the airport departure lounge.

Irish motifs

For old-fashioned charm, these motifs are unsurpassed. They range from the sweet flowers given below to spectacular three-dimensional designs, such as Climbing Rose (*page 295*). Techniques for working Irish motifs and joining them to a mesh background are given on page 196. To make a pretty decoration for a window, crochet one of the large motifs in a fine cotton, immerse it in starch and pin it to a flat, protected surface to dry. Enliven a cushion by sewing on small motifs.

crochet motifs

Little Flower
Skill: intermediate

Special Abbreviation

Dc2tog = work 1dc into each of next 2sc until 1 loop of each remains on hook, yo and through all 3 loops on hook.

Make 6ch, sl st into 1st ch to form a ring.

1ST ROUND: 1ch, work 15sc into ring, sl st into 1st sc.

2ND ROUND: [3ch, dc2tog (see Special Abbreviation) over next 2sc, 3ch, sl st into next sc] 5 times placing last sl st into last sc of previous round. Fasten off.

Four-leaf Clover
Skill: intermediate

Special Abbreviation

Bobble = work 3tr into next sc until 1 loop of each remains on hook, yo and through all 4 loops on hook.

Make 5ch, sl st into 1st ch to form a ring.

1ST ROUND: 1ch, work 12sc into ring, sl st into 1st sc.

2ND ROUND: ✳4ch, work 1 Bobble (see Special Abbreviation) into next sc, 4ch, sl st into each of next 2sc; rep from ✳ 3 times more omitting 1 sl st at end of last rep, 7ch, work 1sc into 2nd ch from hook, 1sc into each of next 5ch, sl st into 1st sc on 1st round. Fasten off.

Daisy
Skill: easy

Make 6ch, sl st into 1st ch to form a ring and continue as follows: 1ch, work [1sc, 12ch] 12 times into ring, sl st into 1st sc. Fasten off.

Rose and Star
Skill: experienced

Special Abbreviation
3-Loop Cluster = 7ch, sl st into 1st of these ch, [6ch, sl st into same ch as last sl st] twice.

Make 8ch, sl st into 1st ch to form a ring.

1ST ROUND: 1ch, working into ring and over padding threads, work 18sc, sl st into 1st sc.

2ND ROUND: 6ch (count as 1hdc, 4ch), skip 1st 3sc, 1hdc into next sc, [4ch, skip 2sc, 1hdc into next sc] 4 times, 4ch, sl st into 2nd of 6ch at beg of round.

3RD ROUND: 1ch, work [1sc, 1hdc, 3dc, 1hdc, 1sc] into each of the 6 4ch arches, sl st into 1st sc. (6 petals.)

4TH ROUND: Working behind each petal, sl st into base of each of 1st 4 sts, [5ch, skip next 6 sts, sl st into base of next dc] 6 times, working last sl st into base of same dc as sl st at beg of round.

5TH ROUND: 1ch, work [1sc, 1hdc, 1dc, 5tr, 1dc, 1hdc, 1sc] into each of the 6 5ch arches, sl st into 1st sc.

6TH ROUND: Working behind each petal, sl st into base of each of 1st 6 sts, [6ch, skip next 10 sts, sl st into base of next tr] 5 times, 3ch, skip next 10 sts, 1tr into base of next tr.

7TH ROUND: Sl st into arch just formed, into same arch work [1sc, 6ch, 1sc], 6ch, ✳into next arch work [1sc, 6ch, 1sc], 6ch; rep from ✳ 4 times more, sl st into 1st sc.

8TH ROUND: Sl st into each of 1st 3ch of 6ch loop, into same loop work [1sc, 6ch, 1sc], 6ch, 1sc into next 6ch arch, 6ch, ✳into next 6ch loop work [1sc, 6ch, 1sc], 6ch, 1sc into next 6ch arch, 6ch; rep from ✳ 4 times more, sl st into 1st sc.

9TH ROUND: Sl st into each of 1st 3ch of 6ch loop, into same loop work [1sc, 6ch, 1sc], 6ch, [1sc into next 6ch arch, 6ch] twice, ✳into next 6ch loop work [1sc, 6ch, 1sc], 6ch, [1sc into next 6ch arch, 6ch] twice; rep from ✳ 4 times more, sl st into 1st sc.

10TH ROUND: Sl st into each of 1st 3ch of 1st 6ch loop, into same loop work [1sc, 3 Loop Cluster (see Special Abbreviation), 1sc], 6ch, [1sc into next 6ch arch, 6ch] 3 times, ✳into next 6ch loop work [1sc, 3 Loop Cluster, 1sc], 6ch, [1sc into next 6ch arch, 6ch] 3 times; rep from ✳ 4 times more, sl st into 1st sc. Fasten off.

Sun Star
Skill: intermediate

Make 16ch, sl st into 1st ch to form a ring.

1ST ROUND: 2ch (count as 1hdc), work 35hdc into ring and over padding threads, sl st into 2nd of 2ch at beg of round.

2ND ROUND: 1ch, work 1sc into same st as last sl st, [5ch, skip 2hdc, 1sc into next hdc] 11 times, 5ch, sl st into 1st sc. Fasten off.

Picot-edge Leaf
Skill: intermediate

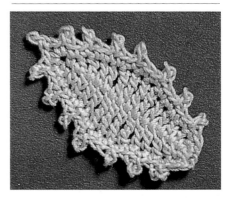

Special Abbreviation
Picot = make 3ch, sl st into 1st of these ch.

Make 15ch and work in a spiral as follows: 1sc into 2nd ch from hook, working 1 st into each ch work 1hdc, 3dc, 4tr, 3dc, 1hdc and 1sc, 3ch, then working 1 st into each ch on other side of starting chain work 1sc, 1hdc, 3dc, 4tr, 3dc, 1hdc, 1sc, 3ch, 1sc into 1st sc at beg of spiral, 1sc into next hdc, 1 picot, [1sc into each of next 2 sts, 1 Picot (see Special Abbreviation)] 6 times, into 3ch sp at point of leaf work [1sc, 4ch, sl st into 3rd ch from hook, 1ch, 1sc], [1 Picot, 1sc into each of next 2 sts] 7 times, sl st into 3ch sp. Fasten off.

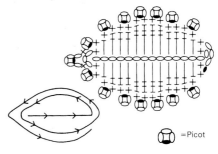

⬚ = Picot

Line shows direction
Line shows direction of work.

Trefoil Tracery

Skill: experienced

Special Abbreviation

Picot = make 3ch, sl st into 1st of these ch.

1ST ROUND: Make 10ch, sl st into 1st ch, [9ch, sl st into same ch as last sl st] twice (3 loops formed).

2ND ROUND: ✳1ch, working into next 9ch loop and over padding threads work [2sc, 1hdc, 11dc, 1hdc, 2sc], 1ch, sl st into same ch as sl sts of 1st round; rep from ✳ twice more.

3RD ROUND: Sl st into each of 1st 9 sts of 1st loop, [16ch, skip 1st 8 sts on next loop, sl st into next dc] twice, 16ch, sl st into same dc as last sl st at beg of round.

4TH ROUND: 1ch, working over padding threads, work 1sc into same dc as last sl st of previous round, 19sc into 1st 16ch arch, [1sc into same dc as next sl st of previous round, 19sc into next 16ch arch] twice, sl st into 1st sc. (60sc.)

5TH ROUND: 8ch (count as 1dc, 5ch), skip next 3sc, [1dc into next sc, 5ch, skip 3sc] 14 times, sl st into 3rd of 8ch at beg of round.

6TH ROUND: Sl st into 1st 3ch of 1st arch, 1ch, working over padding threads work 4sc into 1st arch, 7sc into each of next 14 arches, 3sc into same arch as 1st 4sc, sl st into 1st sc.

7TH ROUND: 6ch, [skip next 6sc, sl st into next sc] 14 times, 6ch, sl st into same sc as last sl st of previous round.

8TH ROUND: 1ch, into each 6ch arch and over padding threads work 2sc, [1 Picot (see Special Abbreviation), 2sc] 3 times. Sl st into 1st sc and fasten off.

Little Rose

Skill: intermediate

Make 5ch, sl st into 1st ch to form a ring.

1ST ROUND: 1ch, work 10sc into ring, sl st into 1st sc.

2ND ROUND: 1ch, work 1sc into each sc, sl st into 1st sc.

3RD ROUND: 2ch (count as 1hdc), skip 1st sc, work 2hdc into each of next 9sc, 1hdc into 1st sc, sl st into 2nd of 2ch.

4TH ROUND: ✳2ch, working into front loop only of each hdc work 2dc into each of next 3hdc, 2ch, sl st into next hdc; rep from ✳ 4 times more placing last sl st into 2nd of 2ch at beg of previous round. (5 petals made.)

5TH ROUND: Working behind each petal of previous round and into back loop of each hdc on 3rd round, sl st into 1st 2hdc, ✳4ch, work 2dtr into each of next 3hdc, 4ch, sl st into next hdc; rep from ✳ 3 times more, 4ch, 2dtr into next hdc, 2dtr into 2nd of 2ch at beg of 3rd round, 2dtr into next hdc, 4ch, sl st into next hdc. Fasten off.

Climbing Rose
Skill: experienced

Make 7ch, sl st into 1st ch to form a ring.
1ST ROUND: 1ch, work 16sc into ring, sl st into 1st sc.
2ND ROUND: 1ch, 1sc into 1st sc, [5ch, skip 1sc, 1sc into next sc] 7 times, 5ch, sl st into 1st sc.
3RD ROUND: Sl st into 1st 5ch arch, 1ch, work [1sc, 5hdc, 1sc] into each 5ch arch to end, sl st into 1st sc. (8 petals.)
4TH ROUND: 1ch, working behind each petal work 1sc into 1st sc on 2nd round, [6ch, 1sc into next sc on 2nd round] 7 times, 6ch, sl st into 1st sc.

5TH ROUND: Sl st into 1st 6ch arch, 1ch, work [1sc, 6hdc, 1sc] into each 6ch arch to end, sl st into 1st sc.
6TH ROUND: 1ch, working behind each petal work 1sc into 1st sc on 4th round, [7ch, 1sc into next sc on 4th round] 7 times, 7ch, sl st into 1st sc.
7TH ROUND: Sl st into 1st 7ch arch, 1ch, work [1sc, 7hdc, 1sc] into each 7ch arch to end, sl st into 1st sc.
8TH ROUND: 1ch, working behind each petal work 1sc into 1st sc on 6th round, ✻[9ch, sl st into 6th ch from hook (1 Picot made)] twice, 4ch, 1sc into next sc on 6th round, [13ch, sl st into 6th ch from hook (1 Picot made)] twice, 8ch, 1sc into same

sc as last sc, [9ch, sl st into 6th ch from hook] twice, 4ch, 1sc into next sc on 6th round; rep from ✻ 3 times more omitting 1sc at end of last rep, sl st into 1st sc.
9TH ROUND: Sl st into each of 1st 3ch, behind 1st picot and into next ch of arch between Picots, 1ch, 1sc into same arch as sl st, ✻✻[10ch, sl st into 6th ch from hook] twice, 5ch, 1sc into corner loop between 2 Picots, ✻[10ch, sl st into 6th ch from hook] twice, 5ch, 1sc into arch between 2 Picots; rep from ✻ once more; rep from ✻✻ 3 times more omitting 1sc at end of last rep, sl st into 1st sc.
10TH ROUND: Sl st into each of 1st 4ch, behind 1st Picot and into next 2ch of arch between 2 Picots, 1ch, 1sc into same arch between 2 Picots, ✻✻[10ch, sl st into 6th ch from hook] twice, 5ch, 1sc into next sc at top of loop, ✻[10ch, sl st into 6th ch from hook] twice, 5ch, 1sc into next arch between 2 Picots; rep from ✻ twice more; rep from ✻✻ 3 times more omitting 1sc at end of last rep, sl st into 1st sc. Fasten off.

5-Ring Rose
Skill: experienced

Make 8ch, sl st into 1st ch to form a ring.
1ST ROUND: 1ch, work 16sc into ring, sl st into 1st sc.
2ND ROUND: 5ch (count as 1dc, 2ch), skip next sc, [1dc into next sc, 2ch, skip 1sc]

7 times, sl st into 3rd of 5ch at beg of round.

3RD ROUND: Sl st into 2ch sp, 1ch, work [1sc, 1hdc, 1dc, 1hdc, 1sc] into each of the 8 2ch sps, sl st into 1st sc. (8 petals.)

4TH ROUND: Working behind each petal, sl st into base of each of next 2 sts, 1ch, 1sc into base of same dc as last sl st, [3ch, skip 4 sts, 1sc into base of next dc] 7 times, 3ch, sl st into 1st sc.

5TH ROUND: Sl st into 3ch arch, 1ch, work [1sc, 1hdc, 3dc, 1hdc, 1sc] into each of the 8 3ch arches, sl st into 1st sc.

6TH ROUND: Working behind each petal, sl st into base of each of next 3 sts, 1ch, 1sc into base of same dc as last sl st, [5ch, skip 6 sts, 1sc into base of next dc] 7 times, 5ch, sl st into 1st sc.

7TH ROUND: Sl st into 5ch arch, 1ch, work [1sc, 1hdc, 5dc, 1hdc, 1sc] into each of the 8 5ch arches, sl st into 1st sc.

8TH ROUND: Working behind each petal, sl st into base of each of next 4 sts, 1ch, 1sc into base of same dc as last sl st, [7ch, skip 8 sts, 1sc into base of next dc] 7 times, 7ch, sl st into 1st sc.

9TH ROUND: Sl st into 7ch arch, 1ch, work [1sc, 1hdc, 7dc, 1hdc, 1sc] into each of the 8 7ch arches, sl st into 1st sc.

10TH ROUND: Working behind each petal, sl st into base of each of next 5 sts, 1ch, 1sc into base of same dc as last sl st, [9ch, skip 10 sts, 1sc into base of next dc] 7 times, 9ch, sl st into 1st sc.

11TH ROUND: Sl st into 9ch arch, 1ch, work [1sc, 1hdc, 9dc, 1hdc, 1sc] into each of the 8 9ch arches, sl st into 1st sc. Fasten off.

Rose Window
Skill: experienced

Make 6ch, sl st into 1st ch to form a ring.
1ST ROUND: 3ch (count as 1dc), work 17dc into ring and over padding threads, sl st into 3rd of 3ch at beg of round.
2ND ROUND: 8ch (count as 1dc, 5ch), [1dc into next dc, 5ch] 17 times, sl st into 3rd of 8ch at beg of round.
3RD ROUND: Sl st into each of next 3ch of 1st arch, 1ch, into same ch as last sl st

work [1sc, 1ch, 1sc], ✳2sc into 2nd part of arch and 2sc into 1st part of next arch, into center ch of arch work [1sc, 1ch, 1sc]; rep from ✳ 16 times more, 2sc into 2nd part of last arch, 2sc into 1st part of 1st arch, sl st into 1st sc.

4TH ROUND: Sl st into 1st ch sp, 1ch, into same sp as last sl st work [1sc, 1ch, 1sc], 1sc into each of next 6sc, ✳into next ch sp work [1sc, 1ch, 1sc], 1sc into each of next 6sc; rep from ✳ 16 times more, sl st into 1st sc.

5TH ROUND: Sl st into 1st ch sp, 1ch, into same sp as last sl st work [1sc, 1ch, 1sc], 1sc into each of next 8sc, ✳into next ch

sp work [1sc, 1ch, 1sc], 1sc into each of next 8sc; rep from ✳ 16 times more, sl st into 1st sc.

6TH ROUND: Sl st into 1st ch sp, 1ch, into same sp as last sl st work [1sc, 1ch, 1sc], 1sc into each of next 10sc, ✳into next ch sp work [1sc, 1ch, 1sc], 1sc into each of next 10sc; rep from ✳ 16 times more, sl st into 1st sc.

7TH ROUND: Sl st into 1st ch sp, 1ch, work 1sc into same sp as last sl st, 5ch, [1sc into next ch sp, 5ch] 17 times, sl st into 1st sc.

8TH ROUND: 1ch, 1sc into 1st sc of previous round, 3ch, 1sc into next 5ch

arch, [3ch, 1sc into next sc, 3ch, 1sc into next 5ch arch] 17 times, 3ch, sl st into 1st sc.

9TH ROUND: Sl st into 1st ch of 1st 3ch arch, 1ch, 1sc into same arch as last sl st, ✳4ch, 1sc into next 3ch arch; rep from ✳ to end, 4ch, sl st into 1st sc.

10TH ROUND: Sl st into each of 1st 2ch of 1st 4ch arch, 1ch, 1sc into same arch as last sl sts, ✳5ch, 1sc into next 4ch arch; rep from ✳ to end, 5ch, sl st into 1st sc. Fasten off.

Pansy
Skill: experienced

Special Abbreviation
Picot = make 3ch, sl st into 1st of these ch.
Make 10ch, sl st into 1st ch to form a ring.

1ST ROUND: 1ch, into ring work 5sc, 1 Picot (see Special Abbreviation), [8sc, 1 Picot] twice, 3ch, sl st into 1st sc.

2ND ROUND: 1ch, 1sc into same st as last sl st, ✳12ch, skip [4sc, 1 Picot, 3sc], 1sc into next sc; rep from ✳ once more, 12ch, sl st into 1st sc.

3RD ROUND: Sl st into 1st 12ch arch, 1ch, into each of the 3 arches work [1sc, 1hdc, 2dc, 9tr, 2dc, 1hdc, 1sc], sl st into 1st sc.

4TH ROUND: ✳1ch, 1sc into next hdc, 1ch, [1dc into next st, 1ch] 13 times, 1sc into next hdc, 1ch, sl st into each of next 2sc; rep from ✳ twice more omitting 1 sl st at end of last rep.

5TH ROUND: Sl st into each of 1st [sl st, ch sp, sc and ch sp], 1ch,

into same ch sp as last sl st work [1sc, 4ch, 1sc], into each of next 13 ch sps work [1sc, 4ch, 1sc], ✳1ch, sl st into each of next [sc, ch sp, 2 sl sts, ch sp, sc and ch sp], 1ch, into same sp as last sl st work [1sc, 4ch, 1sc], into each of next 13 ch sps work [1sc, 4ch, 1sc]; rep from ✳ once more, 1ch, sl st into each of last [sc, ch sp and sl st]. Fasten off.

Picot-petal Rose
Skill: experienced

Special Abbreviation
Picot = make 3ch, sl st into 1st of these ch.
Make 8ch, sl st into 1st ch to form a ring.

1ST ROUND: 3ch (count as 1dc), work 15dc into ring, sl st into 3rd of 3ch at beg of round.

2ND ROUND: 5ch (count as 1dc, 2ch), [1dc into next dc, 2ch] 15 times, sl st into 3rd of 5ch at beg of round.

3RD ROUND: 1ch, work 3sc into each of the 16 2ch sps, sl st into 1st sc.

4TH ROUND: 1ch, work 1sc into same sc as last sl st, ✳6ch, skip 5sc, 1sc into next sc; rep from ✳ 6 times more, 6ch, sl st into 1st sc.

5TH ROUND: Sl st into 1st 6ch arch, 1ch, work [1sc, 1hdc, 6dc, 1hdc, 1sc] into each of the 8 6ch arches, sl st into 1st sc. (8 petals worked.)

6TH ROUND: 1ch, working behind each petal of previous round, work 1sc into 1st sc on 4th round, ✳7ch, 1sc into next sc on 4th round; rep from ✳ 6 times more, 7ch, sl st into 1st sc.

7TH ROUND: Sl st into 1st 7ch arch, 1ch, work [1sc, 1hdc, 7dc, 1hdc, 1sc] into each of the 8 7ch arches, sl st into 1st sc.

8TH ROUND: 1ch, working behind each petal of previous round, work 1sc into 1st sc on 6th round, ✳8ch, 1sc into next sc on 6th round; rep from ✳ 6 times more, 8ch, sl st into 1st sc.

9TH ROUND: Sl st into 1st 8ch arch, 1ch, work [1sc, 1hdc, 3dc, 1 Picot (see Special Abbreviation), 3dc, 1 Picot, 3dc, 1hdc, 1sc] into each of the 8 8ch arches, sl st into 1st sc. Fasten off.

Shamrock
Skill: intermediate

1ST ROUND: Make 16ch, sl st into 1st ch (1st loop formed), [15ch, sl st into same ch as last sl st] twice.

2ND ROUND: 1ch, working over padding threads work [28sc into next loop, 1 sl st into same ch as sl sts of 1st round] 3 times.

3RD ROUND: Sl st into each of 1st 3sc, 1ch, 1sc into same st as last sl st, 1sc into each of next 23sc, [skip 4sc, 1sc into each of next 24sc] twice, 17ch, working over padding threads work 1sc into 2nd ch from hook, 1sc into each of next 15ch, sl st into 1st sc. Fasten off.

5-Petal Flower
Skill: experienced

Make 8ch, sl st into first chain to form a ring.

1ST ROUND: 1ch, work 15sc into ring, sl st into first sc.

2ND ROUND: 5ch, skip first 3sc, [sl st into next sc, 5ch, skip 2sc] 4 times, sl st into sl st at end of previous round.

3RD ROUND: Sl st into first 5ch arch, 1ch, into same arch and each of next 4 arches work [1sc, 1hsc, 5dc, 1sc], sl st into first sc. (5 petals).

4TH ROUND: 1ch, working behin each petal of previous round, work 1 sl st into last sl st on 2nd round, 8ch, [1 sl st into next sl st on 2nd round, 8ch] 4 times, sl st into the same st as first sl st at beg of round.

5TH ROUND: Sl st into first 8ch arch, 1ch, into same arch and each of next 4 arches work [1sc, 1hsc, 8sc, 1hsc, 1sc], sl st into first sc.

6TH ROUND: 2ch, working behind each petal of previous round work 1 sl st into last sl st on 2nd round, 10ch, [1 sl st into next sl st on 2nd round, 10ch] 4 times, sl st into same st as first sl st at beg of round.

7TH ROUND: Sl st into first 10ch arch, 1ch, work 15sc into same arch and into each of next 4 arches, sl st into first sc.

8TH ROUND: Sl st into next sc, [4ch, skip 1sc, sl st into next sc] 6 times, turn, work 2 sl sts into first 4ch arch, [4ch, sl st into next 4ch arch] 5 times, turn, work 2 sl sts into first 4ch arch, [4ch, sl st into next 4ch arh] 4 times, turn, work 2 sl sts into first 4ch arch, [4ch sl st into next 4ch arch] 3 times, turn, work, work 2 sl sts into first 4ch arch, [4ch, sl st into next 4ch arch] twice, turn, work 2 st sts into first 4ch arch, 4ch, sl st into next arch and fasten off. [Turn, skip next 2sc on 7th round, rejoin yarn to next sc and rep from to] 4 times.

assorted motifs

There's a motif for every purpose in this section—square, round, hexagonal, solid, lacy, flat, and textured. Many of those shown in a single color could be worked in several colors, and vice versa. For example, the Traditional Square (*page 300*), also known as a Granny Square, is often worked in four colors, with black or another dark color used for the last round. Using four colors for Sunflower I (*below*) would accentuate its resemblance to a Gothic rose window.

page 300

Sunflower I
Skill: intermediate

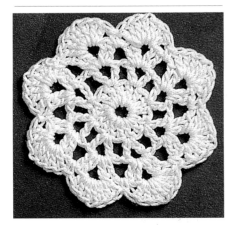

Make 6ch, sl st into 1st ch to form a ring.
1ST ROUND: 3ch (count as 1dc), work 15dc into ring, sl st into 3rd of 3ch at beg of round.
2ND ROUND: 5ch (count as 1dc, 2ch), 1dc into same st as last sl st, ✳1ch, skip 1dc, into next dc work [1dc, 2ch, 1dc]; rep from ✳ 6 times more, 1ch, sl st into 3rd of 5ch at beg of round.
3RD ROUND: Sl st into 1st 2ch sp, 3ch (count as 1dc), into same sp work [1dc, 2ch, 2dc], ✳1ch, into next 2ch sp work [2dc, 2ch, 2dc]; rep from ✳ 6 times more, 1ch, sl st into 3rd of 3ch at beg of round.
4TH ROUND: Sl st into next dc and 1st 2ch sp, 3ch, work 6dc into same sp as last sl st, 1sc into next ch sp, [7dc into next 2ch sp, 1sc into next ch sp] 7 times, sl st into 3rd of 3ch at beg of round. Fasten off.

Popcorn Wheel Square
Skill: intermediate
Note: For description of Popcorn see page 190.

Make 6ch, sl st into 1st ch to form a ring.
1ST ROUND: 3ch (count as 1dc), 4dc into ring and complete as for 5dc Popcorn, [3ch, 5dc Popcorn into ring] 7 times, 3ch, sl st to 1st Popcorn.
2ND ROUND: 3ch (count as 1dc), 1dc into next 3ch arch, [9dc into next arch, 2dc into next arch] 3 times, 9dc into last arch, sl st to top of 3ch.
3RD ROUND: 1ch, 1sc into same place as 1ch, 1sc into next st, ✳into next 9dc group work 1sc into each of 1st 3dc, skip 1dc, [1hdc, 4dc, 1hdc] into next dc, skip 1dc, 1sc into each of last 3dc✳✳, 1sc into each of next 2 sts; rep from ✳ twice and from ✳ to ✳✳ again, sl st to 1st sc. Fasten off.

Spider Square
Skill: intermediate
Note: For description of dc2tog and dc3tog see page 187.

Make 6ch, sl st into 1st ch to form a ring.
1ST ROUND: 1ch, [1sc into ring, 15ch] 12 times, sl st to 1st sc.
2ND ROUND: Sl st along to center of next 15ch arch, 3ch, dc2tog into same arch (counts as dc3tog), ✳4ch, dc3tog into same arch, [4ch, 1sc into next arch] twice, 4ch, dc3tog into next arch; rep from ✳ 3 times, omitting dc3tog at end of last rep, sl st to 1st Cluster.
3RD ROUND: Sl st into next arch, 3ch, dc2tog into same arch (counts as dc3tog), ✳4ch, dc3tog into same arch, [4ch, 1sc into next 4ch arch, 4ch, dc3tog into next 4ch arch] twice; rep from ✳ 3 times, omitting dc3tog at end of last rep, sl st to 1st Cluster. Fasten off.

Floral Triangle
Skill: experienced

Special Abbreviations

Popcorn = work 5tr into next ch, drop loop from hook, insert hook from the front into 1st of these tr, pick up dropped loop and draw through, 1ch to secure.

Picot = make 5ch, sl st into top of dc just worked.

Make 6ch, sl st into 1st ch to form a ring.

1ST ROUND: 6ch (count as 1dc, 3ch), into ring work [1dc, 3ch] 11 times, sl st into 3rd of 6ch at beg of round.

2ND ROUND: 1 sl st into each of 1st 2ch of 1st arch, 4ch (count as 1tr), work 4tr into same ch as last sl st, drop loop from hook, insert hook from the front into 4th of 4ch, pick up dropped loop and draw through, 1ch to secure (Popcorn—see Special Abbreviations—made at beg of round), 5ch, 1sc into next 3ch arch, [5ch, skip 1ch of next 3ch arch, 1 Popcorn into next ch, 5ch, 1sc into next 3ch arch] 5 times, 5ch, sl st into top of 1st Popcorn.

3RD ROUND: 4ch, into top of 1st Popcorn work [3tr, 5ch, 4tr], 3ch, 1dc into next sc, 1 Picot (see Special Abbreviations), 3ch, 1sc into top of next Popcorn, 3ch, 1dc into next sc, 1 Picot, 3ch, ✳into top of next Popcorn work [4tr, 5ch, 4tr], 3ch, 1dc into next sc, 1 Picot, 3ch, 1sc into top of next Popcorn, 3ch, 1dc into next sc, 1 Picot, 3ch; rep from ✳ once more, sl st into 4th of 4ch at beg of round. Fasten off.

Traditional Square
Skill: intermediate

Make 4ch, sl st into 1st ch to form a ring.

1ST ROUND: 5ch (count as 1dc and 2ch), [3dc into ring, 2ch] 3 times, 2dc into ring, sl st to 3rd of 5ch.

2ND ROUND: Sl st into next ch, 5ch (count as 1dc and 2ch), 3dc into same sp, ✳1ch, skip 3dc, [3dc, 1ch, 3dc] into next sp; rep from ✳ twice, 1ch, skip 3 sts, 2dc into same sp as 5ch at beg of round, sl st to 3rd of 5ch.

3RD ROUND: Sl st into next ch, 5ch (count as 1dc and 2ch), 3dc into same sp, ✳1ch, skip 3dc, 3dc into next sp, 1ch, skip 3dc✳✳, [3dc, 2ch, 3dc] into next sp; rep from ✳ twice and from ✳ to ✳✳ again, 2dc into same sp as 5ch, sl st to 3rd of 5ch.

4TH ROUND: Sl st into next ch, 5ch (count as 1dc and 2ch), 3dc into same sp, ✳[1ch, skip 3dc, 3dc into next sp] twice, 1ch, skip 3dc ✳✳, [3dc, 2ch, 3dc] into next sp; rep from ✳ twice and from ✳ to ✳✳ again, 2dc into same sp as 5ch, sl st to 3rd of 5ch. Fasten off.

Greek Cross Square
Skill: intermediate

Make 6ch, sl st into 1st ch to form a ring.

1ST ROUND: 3ch (count as 1dc), work 15dc into ring, sl st into 3rd of 3ch at beg of round.

2ND ROUND: 3ch (count as 1dc), 2dc into

same st as last sl st, 2ch, skip 1dc, 1dc into next dc, 2ch, skip 1dc, ✳3dc into next dc, 2ch, skip 1dc, 1dc into next dc, 2ch, skip 1dc; rep from ✳ twice more, sl st into 3rd of 3ch at beg of round.

3RD ROUND: 3ch, 5dc into next dc, ✳1dc into next dc, [2ch, 1dc into next dc] twice, 5dc into next dc; rep from ✳ twice more, [1dc into next dc, 2ch] twice, sl st into 3rd of 3ch at beg of round.

4TH ROUND: 3ch, 1dc into each of next 2dc, 5dc into next dc, ✳1dc into each of next 3dc, 2ch, 1dc into next dc, 2ch, 1dc into each of next 3dc, 5dc into next dc; rep from ✳ twice more, 1dc into each of next 3dc, 2ch, 1dc into next dc, 2ch, sl st into 3rd of 3ch at beg of round.

5TH ROUND: 3ch, 1dc into each of next 4dc, 5dc into next dc, ✳1dc into each of next 5dc, 2dc into next 2ch sp, 1dc into next dc, 2dc into next 2ch sp, 1dc into each of next 5dc, 5dc into next dc; rep from ✳ twice more, 1dc into each of next 5dc, 2dc into next 2ch sp, 1dc into next dc, 2dc into last 2ch sp, sl st into 3rd of 3ch at beg of round. Fasten off.

Picot Square
Skill: experienced

Special Abbreviation

Picot = 3ch, sl st into side of last sc worked.

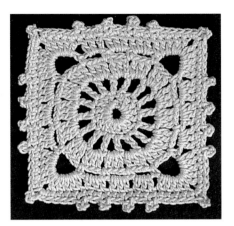

Make 6ch, sl st into 1st ch to form a ring.

1ST ROUND: 3ch (count as 1dc), work 15dc into ring, sl st into 3rd of 3ch at beg of round.

2ND ROUND: 5ch (count as 1dc, 2ch), [1dc into next dc, 2ch] 15 times, sl st into 3rd of 5ch at beg of round.

3RD ROUND: Sl st into 1st 2ch sp, 3ch (count as 1dc), work 2dc into 1st 2ch sp, 1ch, [3dc into next 2ch sp, 1ch] 15 times, sl st into 3rd of 3ch at beg of round.

4TH ROUND: Sl st into each of next 2dc, 1ch, 1sc into 1st ch sp, 3ch, 1sc into next ch sp, 6ch, ✳1sc into next ch sp, [3ch, 1sc into next ch sp] 3 times, 6ch; rep from ✳ twice more, [1sc into next ch sp, 3ch] twice, sl st into 1st sc.

5TH ROUND: Sl st into 1st 3ch sp, 3ch, work 2dc into 1st 3ch sp, into next 6ch arch work [5dc, 2ch, 5dc], ✳3dc into each of next 3 3ch sps, into next 6ch arch work [5dc, 2ch, 5dc]; rep from ✳ twice more, 3dc into each of last 2 3ch sps, sl st into 3rd of 3ch at beg of round.

6TH ROUND: 1ch, 1sc into same st as last sl st, 1sc into each of next 2dc, 1 Picot (see Special Abbreviation), 1sc into each of next 5dc, into next 2ch sp work [1sc, 1 Picot, 1sc], 1sc into each of next 5dc, ✳1 Picot, [1sc into each of next 3dc, 1 Picot] 3 times, 1sc into each of next 5dc, into next 2ch sp work [1sc, 1 Picot, 1sc], 1sc into each of next 5dc; rep from ✳ twice more, 1 Picot, [1sc into each of next 3dc, 1 Picot] twice, sl st into 1st sc. Fasten off.

French Square

Skill: intermediate

Note: For description of hdc3tog and hdc4tog see page 191 (Puff Stitch).

Make 6ch, sl st into 1st ch to form a ring.

1ST ROUND: 4ch (count as 1dc and 1ch), [1dc into ring, 1ch] 11 times, sl st to 3rd of 4ch. (12 spaces.)

2ND ROUND: Sl st into next ch, 3ch, work hdc3tog into same sp (counts as hdc4tog), ✳2ch, work hdc4tog into next sp, 3ch, 1tr into next dc, 3ch, work hdc4tog into next sp, 2ch✳✳, hdc4tog into next sp; rep from ✳ twice more and from ✳ to ✳✳ again, sl st to top of 1st Cluster.

3RD ROUND: 1ch, 1sc into same place, ✳2ch, skip next 2ch sp, 4dc into next 3ch sp, 2ch, 1tr into next tr, 3ch, insert hook down through top of last tr and work sl st, 2ch, 4dc into next 3ch sp, 2ch, skip next 2ch sp, 1sc into next Cluster; rep from ✳ 3 more times, omitting sc at end, sl st to 1st sc. Fasten off.

Italian Square

Skill: intermediate

Note: For description of hdc3tog and hdc4tog see page 191 (Puff Stitch).

Make 4ch, sl st into 1st ch to form a ring.

1ST ROUND: 3ch (count as 1dc), 11dc into ring, sl st to top of 3ch. (12 sts.)

2ND ROUND: 3ch, work hdc3tog into same place as 3ch (counts as hdc4tog),

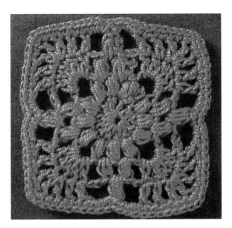

[1ch, work hdc4tog into next st] twice, 5ch✳✳, hdc4tog into next st; rep from ✳ twice more and from ✳ to ✳✳ again, sl st to top of 1st Cluster.

3RD ROUND: Sl st into next sp, 3ch, work hdc3tog into same sp (counts as hdc4tog), ✳1ch, hdc4tog into next sp, 2ch, 5dc into next 5ch arch, 2ch✳✳, hdc4tog into next sp; rep from ✳ twice more and from ✳ to ✳✳ again, sl st to top of 1st Cluster.

4TH ROUND: Sl st into next sp, 3ch, work hdc3tog into same sp (counts as hdc4tog), ✳3ch skip 2ch, [1dc into next dc, 1ch] twice, work [1dc, 1ch, 1dc, 1ch, 1dc] into next dc, [ch, 1dc into next dc] twice, 3ch, skip 2ch✳✳, work hdc4tog into next sp; rep from ✳ twice more and again from ✳ to ✳ ✳ sl st to top of 1st Cluster.

5TH ROUND: 1ch, 1sc into each ch and each st all round, but working 3sc into 3rd of 5 dc at each corner, ending sl st to 1st sc. Fasten off.

Square Flower

Skill: intermediate

Special Abbreviations

4dc Cluster = work 1dc into each of next 4dc until 1 loop of each remains on hook, yo and through all 5 loops on hook.

4dc Bobble or 5dc Bobble = work 4dc (or 5dc) into next ch until 1 loop of each remains on hook, yo and through all 5 (or

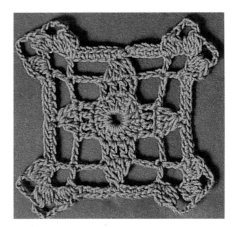

6) loops on hook.

Make 6ch, sl st into 1st ch to form a ring.

1ST ROUND: 3ch (count as 1dc), work 15dc into ring, sl st into 3rd of 3ch at beg of round.

2ND ROUND: 3ch, 1dc into each of next 3dc, [7ch, 1dc into each of next 4dc] 3 times, 7ch, sl st into 3rd of 3ch at beg of round.

3RD ROUND: 3ch, work 1dc into each of next 3dc until 1 loop of each remains on hook, yo and through all 4 loops on hook (1 Cluster made at beg of round), 5ch, skip 3ch, into next ch work [1dc, 5ch, 1dc], 5ch, ✳4dc Cluster (see Special Abbreviations) over next 4dc, 5ch, skip 3ch, into next ch work [1dc, 5ch, 1dc], 5ch; rep from ✳ twice more, sl st into top of 1st Cluster.

4TH ROUND: 1ch, ✳1sc into top of Cluster, 1sc into each of next 5ch, 1sc into next dc, 2ch, 4dc Bobble (see Special Abbreviations) into next ch, 5ch, skip 1ch, 5dc Bobble (see Special Abbreviations) into next ch, 5ch, skip 1ch, 4dc Bobble into next ch, 2ch, 1sc into next dc, 1sc into each of next 5ch; rep from ✳ 3 times more, sl st into 1st sc. Fasten off.

Daisy Cluster Square

Skill: intermediate

Note: For description of dc2tog and dc3tog see page 187.

Wrap yarn around finger to form a ring.

1ST ROUND: 1ch, 8sc into ring, sl st to 1st

sc. (8 sts.)

2ND ROUND: 3ch, dc2tog into 1st st (counts as dc3tog), [3ch, dc3tog into next st] 7 times, 3ch, sl st to top of 1st Cluster.

3RD ROUND: 3ch, 1dc into 1st st (counts as dc2tog), ✳skip 3ch, [dc2tog, 5ch, dc2tog] all into next Cluster; rep from ✳ 6 times, dc2tog into next Cluster, 5ch, sl st to top of 3ch.

4TH ROUND: Sl st into next Cluster, 7ch (counts as 1dc and 4ch), [1sc into next 5ch arch, 4ch, skip 1 Cluster, 1dc into next Cluster, 4ch] 7 times, 1sc into next arch, 4ch, sl st to 3rd of 7ch.

5TH ROUND: 1ch, 1sc into same place as 1ch, ✳4ch, skip 4ch, [1tr, 4ch, 1tr] into next sc, 4ch, skip 4ch, 1sc into next dc, 4ch, skip 4ch, 1hdc into next sc, 4ch, skip 4ch, 1sc into next dc; rep from ✳ 3 times, omitting sc at end of last rep, sl st to 1st sc. Fasten off.

Floribunda

Skill: intermediate

Using A, make 6ch, sl st into 1st ch.

1ST ROUND: 1ch, 16sc into ring, sl st to 1st sc. (16 sts.)

2ND ROUND: 6ch (count as 1dc and 3ch arch), skip 2 sts, [1dc into next st, 3ch, skip 1 st] 7 times, sl st to 3rd of 6ch.

3RD ROUND: 1ch, work a petal of [1sc, 1hdc, 5dc, 1hdc, 1sc] into each of

next 8 3ch arches, sl st to 1st sc. Fasten off.

4TH ROUND: Using B join between 2sc, 1ch [1sc between 2sc, 6ch behind petal of 3rd round] 8 times, sl st to 1st sc.

5TH ROUND: 1ch, work a petal of [1sc, 1hdc, 6dc, 1hdc, 1sc] into each of next 8 arches, sl st to 1st sc. Fasten off.

6TH ROUND: Using C join into 2nd dc of petal of 5th round, 1ch, 1sc into same place as 1ch, 6ch, skip 2dc, 1sc into next dc, [6ch, 1sc into 2nd dc of next petal, 6ch, skip 2dc, 1sc into next dc] 7 times, 3ch, 1dc into 1st sc.

7TH ROUND: 3ch (count as 1dc), 3dc into arch formed by dc which closed 6th round, ✳4ch, 1sc into next arch, [6ch, 1sc into next arch] twice, 4ch✳✳, [4dc, 4ch, 4dc] into next arch; rep from ✳ twice and from ✳ to ✳✳ again, ending [4dc, 4ch] into last ch arch, sl st to top of 3ch. Fasten off.

Sow Thistle Square

Skill: intermediate

Note: For description of dc2tog and dc3tog see page 187.

Using A, make 4ch, sl st into 1st ch.

1ST ROUND: 4ch (count as 1dc and 1ch), [1dc, 1ch] 11 times into ring, sl st to 3rd of 4ch. Fasten off. (12 spaces.)

2ND ROUND: Using B join into sp, 3ch, dc2tog into same sp (counts as dc3tog), [3ch, dc3tog into next sp] 11 times, 3ch, sl

st to top of 1st Cluster. Fasten off.

3RD ROUND: Using A join into 3ch arch, 1ch, 1sc into same arch, [5ch, 1sc into next arch] 11 times, 2ch, 1dc into 1st sc. Fasten off.

4TH ROUND: Using B join into same place, 1ch, 1sc into same place, ✳5ch, 1sc into next arch, 1ch, [5dc, 3ch, 5dc] into next arch, 1ch, 1sc into next arch; rep from ✳ 3 times, omitting 1sc at end of last rep, sl st to 1st sc. Fasten off.

Christmas Rose Square

Skill: intermediate
Note: For description of dc3tog, and dc4tog see page 187.

Using A, make 6ch, sl st into 1st ch.

1ST ROUND: 5ch (count as 1dc and 2ch), [1dc into ring, 2ch] 7 times, sl st to 3rd of 5ch. (8 spaces.)

2ND ROUND: 3ch, work dc3tog into next sp (counts as dc4tog), [5ch, work dc4tog into next sp] 7 times, 5ch, sl st to top of 1st Cluster. Fasten off.

3RD ROUND: Using B join into same place, 1ch, 1sc into same place, ✳2ch, working over the 5ch arch so as to enclose it work 1dc into next dc of 1st round, 2ch, 1sc into top of next Cluster; rep from ✳ all round omitting sc at end, sl st to 1st sc.

4TH ROUND: Sl st into next ch, 1ch, 1sc into same place, ✳3ch, 1sc into next sp;

rep from ✳ all round omitting sc at end, sl st to 1st sc.

5TH ROUND: Sl st into next ch, 3ch (count as 1dc), [1dc, 2ch, 2dc] into same arch, ✳2ch, 1sc into next arch, [3ch, 1sc into next arch] twice, 2ch✳✳, [2dc, 2ch, 2dc] into next arch; rep from ✳ twice more and from ✳ to ✳✳ again, sl st to top of 3ch. Fasten off.

Daisy Square

Skill: intermediate

Special Abbreviations

Tr2tog = work 2tr into ring until 1 loop of each remains on hook, yo and through all 3 loops on hook.

Cluster = work 3dc into sp until 1 loop of each remains on hook, yo and through all 4 loops on hook.

Make 10ch, sl st into 1st ch to form a ring.

1ST ROUND: 4ch, 1tr into ring, 2ch, into ring work [tr2tog (see Special Abbreviations,) 2ch] 11 times, sl st into 1st tr.

2ND ROUND: Sl st into 2ch sp, 3ch, into same 2ch sp as sl st, work 2dc until 1 loop of each remains on hook, yo and through all 3 loops on hook (1st Cluster made—see Special Abbreviations), 3ch, [1 Cluster into next 2ch sp, 3ch] 11 times, sl st into top of 1st Cluster.

3RD ROUND: 5ch (count as 1hdc, 3ch), skip 1st 3ch arch, into next 3ch arch work [1 Cluster, 2ch, 1 Cluster, 4ch, 1 Cluster, 2ch, 1 Cluster], 3ch, ✳skip next 3ch arch, 1hdc into top of next Cluster, 3ch, skip next 3ch arch, into next 3ch arch work [1 Cluster, 2ch, 1 Cluster, 4ch, 1 Cluster, 2ch, 1 Cluster], 3ch; rep from ✳ twice more, sl st into 2nd of 5ch at beg of round.

4TH ROUND: 1ch, work 1sc into same st as last sl st, ✳3sc into next 3ch sp, 1sc into top of next Cluster, 2sc into next 2ch sp, 1sc into next Cluster, 5sc into next 4ch arch, 1sc into next Cluster, 2sc into next 2ch sp, 1sc into next Cluster, 3sc into next 3ch sp, 1sc into next hdc; rep from ✳ 3 times more omitting 1sc at end of last rep, sl st into 1st sc. Fasten off.

Cranesbill Lace Square

Skill: intermediate
Note: For description of dc2tog and dc3tog see page 187.

Base ring: 6ch, join with sl st.

1ST ROUND: 3ch, dc2tog into ring (counts as dc3tog), [3ch, dc3tog into ring] 7 times, 3ch, sl st to top of 1st Cluster.

2ND ROUND: Sl st to center of next 3ch arch, 1ch, 1sc into same place, [5ch, 1sc into next arch] 7 times, 2ch, 1dc into 1st sc.

3RD ROUND: ✳5ch, [dc3tog, 3ch, dc3tog] into next arch✳✳, 5ch, 1sc into next arch; rep from ✳ twice and from ✳ to ✳✳ again, 2ch, 1dc into dc which closed 2nd round.

4TH ROUND: ✳5ch, 1sc into next arch, 5ch, [1sc, 5ch, 1sc] into corner 3ch arch, 5ch, 1sc into next 5ch arch; rep from ✳ 3 times, ending last rep into dc which closed 3rd round, sl st to 1st ch. Fasten off.

Rose Chain
Skill: experienced

Special Abbreviation

Dc2tog = work 1dc into next dc until 2 loops remain on hook, skip 2dc, work 1dc into next dc until 3 loops remain on hook, yo and through all 3 loops on hook.

Make 10ch, sl st into 1st ch to form a ring.

1ST ROUND: 3ch (count as 1dc), work 31dc into ring, sl st into 3rd of 3ch at beg of round.

2ND ROUND: [7ch, skip 3dc, sl st into next dc] 7 times, 3ch, 1tr into same st as last sl st of previous round.

3RD ROUND: 3ch, work 6dc into top of tr, [7dc into 4th ch of next 7ch arch] 7 times, sl st into 3rd of 3ch at beg of round.

4TH ROUND: Sl st into next dc, 6ch (count as 1dc, 3ch), ✳skip 1dc, into next dc work [1tr, 5ch, 1tr], 3ch, skip 1dc, dc2tog (see Special Abbreviation), 3ch, skip 1dc, 1sc into next dc, 3ch, skip 1dc, dc2tog, 3ch; rep from ✳ 3 times more omitting 1dc2tog and 3ch at end of last rep, skip 1dc, 1dc into next dc, sl st into 3rd of 6ch at beg of round.

5TH ROUND: 1ch, 1sc into same st as last sl st, ✳3sc into next 3ch sp, 1sc into next tr, 6sc into 5ch arch, 1sc into next tr, 3sc into next 3ch sp, 1sc into top of next dc2tog, 3sc into next 3ch sp, 1sc into next sc, 3sc into next 3ch sp, 1sc into top of next dc2tog; rep from ✳ 3 times more omitting 1sc at end of last rep, sl st into 1st sc. Fasten off.

Carnation
Skill: intermediate

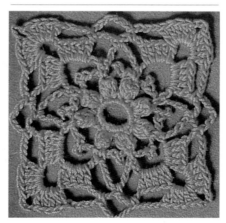

Special Abbreviations

Popcorn = work 5hdc into next sc, drop loop from hook, insert hook from the front into top of 1st of these hdc, pick up dropped loop and draw through, 1ch to secure Popcorn.

Picot = make 3ch, work 1sc into 1st of these ch.

Make 10ch, sl st into 1st ch to form a ring.

1ST ROUND: 1ch, work 16sc into ring, sl st into 1st sc.

2ND ROUND: 2ch, work 4hdc into 1st sc, drop loop from hook, insert hook from the front into 2nd of 2ch, pick up dropped loop and draw through, 1ch to secure (1 Popcorn—see Special Abbreviations—made at beg of round), 2ch, 1 Picot (see Special Abbreviations), 2ch, [skip 1sc, 1 Popcorn into next sc, 2ch, 1 Picot, 2ch] 7 times, sl st into top of 1st Popcorn.

3RD ROUND: 1ch, 1sc into same st as last sl st, [9ch, 1sc into top of next Popcorn] 7 times, 4ch, 1dtr into 1st sc.

4TH ROUND: Sl st into arch just formed, 3ch (count as 1dc), work 4dc into same arch as last sl st, 4ch, 1sc into next 9ch arch, 4ch, ✳work [5dc, 5ch, 5dc] into next 9ch arch, 4ch, 1sc into next 9ch arch, 4ch; rep from ✳ twice more, 5dc into same arch as 1st 5dc, 5ch, sl st into 3rd of 3ch at beg of round.

5TH ROUND: 7ch (count as 1dc, 4ch), ✳1sc into next 4ch arch, 4ch, 1sc into next 4ch arch, 4ch, work [5dc, 3ch, 5dc] into next 5ch arch, 4ch; rep from ✳ 3 times more omitting 1dc and 4ch at end of last rep, sl st into 3rd of 7ch at beg of round. Fasten off.

Sunflower II
Skill: intermediate

Special Abbreviation

Popcorn = work 5dc into next st, drop loop off hook, insert hook into 1st of these dc, pick up dropped loop and draw through. Make 5ch, Sl st into 1st ch to form a ring.
1ST ROUND: 4ch (count as 1dc, 1ch), work [1dc, 1ch] 11 times into ring, sl st into 3rd of 4ch at beg of round.
2ND ROUND: 6ch (count as 1dc, 3ch), 1 Popcorn (see Special Abbreviation) into next dc, 3ch, [1dc into next dc, 3ch, 1 Popcorn into next dc, 3ch] 5 times, sl st into 3rd of 6ch at beg of round.
3RD ROUND: 1ch, 1sc into same st as last sl st, 4ch, 1sc into top of next Popcorn, 4ch, [1sc into next dc, 4ch, 1sc into top of next Popcorn, 4ch] 5 times, sl st into 1st sc.
4TH ROUND: Sl st into 1st 4ch arch, 2ch (count as 1hdc), into same arch work [1dc, 1tr, 1dtr, 1tr, 1dc, 1hdc], into each of next 11 4ch arches work [1hdc, 1dc, 1tr, 1dtr, 1tr, 1dc, 1hdc], sl st into 2nd of 2ch at beg of round. Fasten off.

Star Flower
Skill: intermediate

Work as given for Sunflower II, but working 1st and 2nd rounds in A and 3rd and 4th rounds in B.

6-petal Flower
Skill: easy

Special Abbreviation

Bobble = work 5dc into next sc until 1 loop of each remains on hook, yo and through all 6 loops on hook.
Make 6ch, sl st into 1st ch to form a ring.
1ST ROUND: 1ch, work 12sc into ring, sl st into 1st sc.
2ND ROUND: 3ch, work 4dc into same st as last sl st until 1 loop of each dc remains on hook, yo and through all 5 loops on hook (1 Bobble—see Special Abbreviation—made at beg of round), ✳5ch, skip 1sc, 1 Bobble into next sc; rep from ✳ 4 times more, 5ch, sl st into top of 1st Bobble. Fasten off.

Eastern Star
Skill: intermediate

Make 6ch, sl st into 1st ch to form a ring.
1ST ROUND: 1ch, [1sc into ring, 3ch] 12 times, sl st to 1st sc
2ND ROUND: Sl st into each of next 2ch, 1ch, 1sc into same 3ch arch, [3ch, 1sc into next 3ch arch] 11 times, 1ch, 1hdc into top of 1st sc.
3RD ROUND: ✳6ch, 1sc into next 3ch arch✳✳, 3ch, 1sc into next 3ch arch; rep from ✳ 4 more times and from ✳ to ✳✳ again, 1ch, 1dc into hdc which closed previous round.
4TH ROUND: ✳[5dc, 2ch, 5dc] into next 6ch arch, 1sc into next 3ch arch; rep from ✳ 5 more times ending last rep in dc which closed previous round, sl st into next st.
Fasten off.

Little Gem
Skill: experienced
Note: For description of dc2tog and dc3tog see page 187.

Make 5ch, sl st into 1st ch to form a ring.
1ST ROUND: 4ch (count as 1tr), 2dc into 4th ch from hook, ✳3ch, 1tr into ring, 2dc into base of stem of tr just made; rep from ✳ 4 more times, 3ch, sl st to top of 4ch.
2ND ROUND: 3ch, dc2tog over next 2dc (counts as dc3tog), ✳6ch, skip 3ch, dc3tog over next 3 sts; rep from ✳ 5 more times omitting last dc3tog and ending sl st to top of 1st Cluster. Fasten off.

3RD ROUND: Using B join into center of 3ch arch of 1st round, then so as to enclose 6ch arch of 2nd round work 1ch, 1sc into same place as 1ch, ✳5ch, 1dc into top of next Cluster, 5ch, 1sc into 3ch arch of 1st round at same time enclosing 6ch arch of 2nd round; rep from ✳ 5 more times omitting last sc and ending sl st into 1st sc. Fasten off.

4TH ROUND: Using C join into same place, 1ch, 1sc into same place as 1ch, ✳5ch, skip 5ch, 3sc into next dc, 5ch, skip 5ch, 1sc into next sc; rep from ✳ 5 more times omitting last sc and ending sl st into 1st sc. Fasten off.

Scallop Flower
Skill: intermediate

Using A, make 6ch, sl st into 1st ch.

1ST ROUND: 3ch (count as 1dc), 17dc into ring, sl st to top of 3ch. (18 sts.)

2ND ROUND: 1ch, 1sc into same place as 1ch, ✳3ch, skip 2 sts, 1sc into next st; rep from ✳ 5 more times omitting last sc and ending sl st to 1st sc. Fasten off.

3RD ROUND: Using B join into next ch, 1ch, ✳work a petal of [1sc, 1hdc, 3dc, 1hdc, 1sc] into 3ch arch, sl st into next sc; rep from ✳ 5 more times.

4TH ROUND: Sl st into each of next 4 sts to center dc of next petal, 1ch, 1sc into same place as 1ch, ✳8ch, 1sc into center dc of next petal; rep from ✳ 5 more times omitting last sc and ending sl st to 1st sc.

Fasten off.

5TH ROUND: Using A join into next ch, 1ch, ✳work [1sc, 3hdc, 5dc, 3hdc, 1sc] into next arch; rep from ✳ 5 more times, ending sl st into 1st sc.
Fasten off.

Briar Rose
Skill: intermediate

Using A, make 3ch, sl st into 1st ch.

1ST ROUND: 5ch (count as 1dc and 2ch), [1dc into ring, 2ch] 7 times, sl st to 3rd of 5ch. Fasten off. (8 spaces.)

2ND ROUND: Join B into a sp, 9ch, sl st into 4th ch from hook, 5ch, sl st into 4th ch from hook, 1ch, ✳1dc into next sp, work a Picot of [5ch, sl st into 4th ch from hook] twice, 1ch; rep from ✳ 6 more times, sl st to 3rd ch of starting ch. Fasten off.

3RD ROUND: Join C into 1ch between 2 Picots, 1ch, 1sc into same place as 1ch, ✳7ch, skip [1 Picot, 1dc and 1 Picot], 1sc into next ch between Picots; rep from ✳ 7 more times omitting sc at end of last rep, sl st to 1st sc.

4TH ROUND: Sl st into next ch, 1ch, ✳work [1sc, 1hdc, 9dc, 1hdc, 1sc] into next arch; rep from ✳ 7 more times, sl st to 1st sc.
Fasten off.

Halley's Comet Motif
Skill: intermediate

Special Abbreviation
Ssc (Spike Single Crochet) = insert hook below st indicated 1 row down, i.e. into top of 1st round, yo, draw loop through and up to height of current round, yo, draw through both loops on hook (see also page 188).

BASE RING: using A, 4ch, sl st to join.

1ST ROUND: 5ch (count as 1dc and 2ch), [1dc into ring, 2ch] 7 times, sl st to 3rd of 5ch. (8 spaces.)

2ND ROUND: 3ch (count as 1dc), 3dc into next sp, [1dc into next dc, 3dc into next sp] 7 times, sl st to top of 3ch. (32 sts.) Fasten off.

3RD ROUND: Join B into same place, 1ch, 1Ssc (see Special Abbreviation) over 1st st, work a Picot of [3ch, insert hook down through top of sc just made and work sl st to close], ✳1sc into next st, 2sc into next st, 1sc into next st✳✳, 1Ssc over next st, Picot; rep from ✳ 6 more times and from ✳ to ✳✳ again, sl st to 1st Ssc.
Fasten off.

edgings

An edging isn't always needed on a crocheted fabric, as the fabric edges are usually firm or decorative. But crocheted edgings are wonderfully useful for other items—on woven-fabric items such as table linens, and often on knitted garments. The following pages hold an assortment to add to your crochet repertoire.

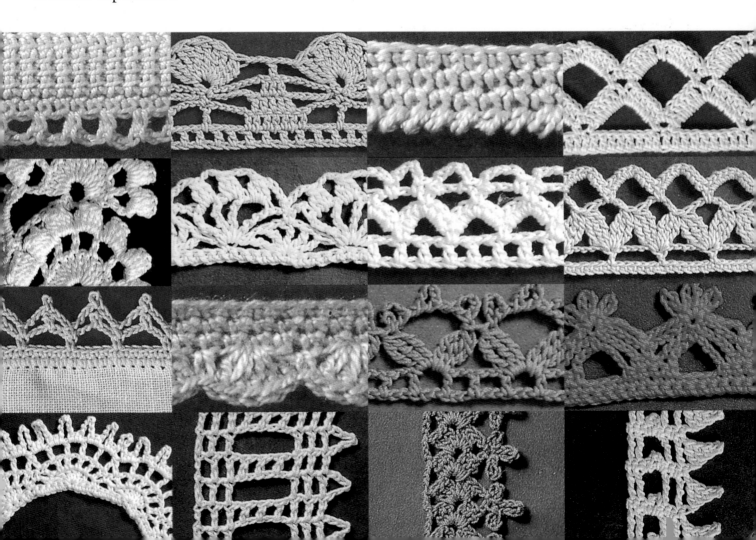

edgings worked on fabric

Some crochet edgings can be worked directly on a fabric edge—either crocheted (as shown in the samples below), knitted, or woven (*see page 309*). In the case of woven fabric, the relative closeness of the weave will govern the scale of the edging and the size of thread and hook used: the closer the weave, the finer the edging. Run a line of machine stitching just in from the finished edge, then trim close to it and work the first row of crochet over the stitching line.

Shell Edging
Multiple of 4 sts + 1
Skill: easy

1ST ROW (RS): 1sc, ✳skip 1 st or equivalent interval, 5dc into next st, skip 1 st, 1sc into next st; rep from ✳.

Chain Arch Edging
Multiple of 2 sts + 1
Skill: easy

1ST ROW (RS): 1sc into each st or at equivalent intervals, turn.
2ND ROW: 1ch, 1sc into 1st st, ✳3ch, skip 1 st, 1sc into next st; rep from ✳.

Corded Edging
Any number of sts
Skill: easy
Note: For description of Corded (or Reversed) sc see page 191.

1ST ROW (RS): 1sc into each st or at equivalent intervals. Do not turn or fasten off.
2ND ROW: ✳1sc back into last st just worked, ✳1sc into next st to right; rep from ✳.

Picot Edging
Multiple of 2 sts + 1
Skill: easy

1ST ROW (RS): 1sc, ✳3ch, sl st into 3rd ch from hook, skip 1 st or equivalent interval, 1sc into next st; rep from ✳.

edgings

edgings worked separately

The instructions in this section include a starting chain. In the case of edgings worked across, this chain is sewn to the fabric edge. (A few are worked lengthways, so that one side edge is joined to the fabric.) To work one of these edgings directly onto a fabric edge (see *page 308*), substitute the same number of single crochet for the number of chain given; or, if the first row is single crochet, omit the chain and begin with this, as shown in Arch and Picot in Rounds (*below*).

Simple Scallop Edging
Starting chain: multiple of 4 sts + 2
Skill: easy

1ST ROW (RS): Work 1sc into 2nd ch from hook, 1sc into each ch to end, turn.
2ND ROW: 1ch, 1sc into 1st sc, ✳5ch, skip 3sc, 1sc into next sc; rep from ✳ to end, turn.
3RD ROW: 1ch, 1sc into 1st sc, ✳7ch, 1sc into next sc; rep from ✳ to end. Fasten off.

Arch and Picot Edging
Starting chain: multiple of 5 sts + 2
Skill: intermediate

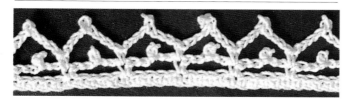

1ST ROW (RS): Work 1sc into 2nd ch from hook, 1sc into each ch to end, turn.
2ND ROW: 1ch, 1sc into 1st sc, ✳5ch, sl st into 3rd ch from hook, 3ch, skip next 4sc, 1sc into next sc; rep from ✳ to end, turn.
3RD ROW: 1ch, 1sc into 1st sc, ✳6ch, sl st into 3rd ch from hook, 4ch, 1sc into next sc; rep from ✳ to end. Fasten off.

Arch and Picot in Rounds
Starting chain: multiple of 5 sts + 1 for each side, plus 1 for each corner
Skill: intermediate

To make edging in rounds, make a starting chain of a multiple of 5 sts + 1 for each side + 1 for each of the 4 corners. Place a marker in last ch (4th corner ch) and in each of the other 3 corner ch. Sl st into 1st ch to form a ring.
1ST ROUND (RS): 1ch, work 1sc into same ch as last sl st, 1sc into each ch to 1st corner ch, [3sc into corner ch, 1sc into each ch to next corner ch] 3 times, 3sc into last corner ch, sl st into 1st sc.
2ND ROUND: 1ch, work 1sc into same st as last sl st, ✳5ch, sl st into 3rd ch from hook, 3ch, skip 4sc, 1sc into next sc; rep from ✳ to next corner, 6ch, sl st into 3rd ch from hook, 4ch, skip 3sc (corner scs), 1sc into next sc✳✳; rep from ✳ to ✳✳ 3 times more omitting 1sc at end of last rep, sl st into 1st sc.
3RD ROUND: 1ch, work 1sc into same st as last sl st, ✳6ch, sl st into 3rd ch from hook, 4ch, 1sc into next sc; rep from ✳ to next corner, 8ch, sl st into 3rd ch from hook, 6ch, 1sc into next sc✳✳; rep from ✳ to ✳✳ 3 times more omitting 1sc at end of last rep, sl st into 1st sc. Fasten off.

edgings

Lacy Fan Edging

Starting chain: multiple of 9 sts + 5
Skill: intermediate

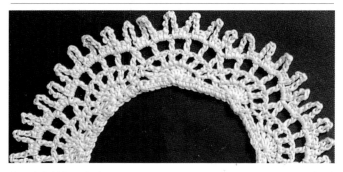

Special Abbreviation

Dc2tog = work 1dc into each of next 2dc until 1 loop of each remains on hook, yo and through all 3 loops on hook.

1ST ROW (RS): Work 1sc into 2nd ch from hook, 1sc into each ch to end, turn.

2ND ROW: 1ch, 1sc into 1st sc, 2ch, skip 2sc, 1sc into next sc, ✳skip 2sc, 6dc into next sc, skip 2sc, 1sc into next sc, 2ch, skip 2sc, 1sc into next sc; rep from ✳ to end, turn.

3RD ROW: 1ch, 1sc into 1st sc, 2ch, ✳1dc into next dc, [1ch, 1dc into next dc] 5 times, 1sc into next 2ch sp; rep from ✳ to last 2sc, omitting 1sc at end of last rep, 2ch, 1sc into last sc, turn.

4TH ROW: 3ch (count as 1dc), [1dc into next dc, 2ch] 5 times, ✳dc2tog (see Special Abbreviation), 2ch, [1dc into next dc, 2ch] 4 times; rep from ✳ to last dc, work 1dc into next dc until 2 loops remain on hook, 1dc into last sc until 3 loops remain on hook, yo and through all 3 loops, turn.

5TH ROW: 1ch, 1sc into 1st st, 3sc into 1st 2ch sp, ✳7ch, 3sc into next 2ch sp; rep from ✳ to last 2dc, 1sc into 3rd of 3ch at beg of previous row. Fasten off.

Crested Wave Edging

Starting chain: multiple of 17 sts + 3
Skill: experienced

Special Abbreviation

Bobble = work 3dc into next space until 1 loop of each remains on hook, yo and through all 4 loops on hook.

1ST ROW (RS): Work 1sc into 2nd ch from hook, 1sc into each ch to end, turn.

2ND ROW: 1ch, work 1sc into each sc to end, turn.

3RD ROW: 1ch, work 1sc into each of 1st 8sc, ✳4ch, skip 3sc, 1sc into each of next 14sc; rep from ✳ to last 11sc, 4ch, skip 3sc, 1sc into each of last 8sc, turn.

4TH ROW: 3ch (count as 1hdc, 1ch), skip 1st 2sc, 1sc into each of next 3sc, 1ch, into next 4ch sp work [1dc, 1ch] 6 times, skip 3sc, 1sc into each of next 3sc, ✳3ch, skip 2sc, 1sc into each of next 3sc, 1ch, into next 4ch sp work [1dc, 1ch] 6 times, skip 3sc, 1sc into each of next 3sc; rep from ✳ to last 2sc, 1ch, 1hdc into last sc, turn.

5TH ROW: 1ch, 1sc into 1st hdc, 2ch, [1 Bobble (see Special Abbreviation) into next ch sp, 2ch] 7 times, ✳1sc into next 3ch arch, 2ch, [1 Bobble into next ch sp, 2ch] 7 times; rep from ✳ to last 3ch, skip 1ch, 1sc into next ch, turn.

6TH ROW: 1ch, 1sc into 1st sc, 2sc into 1st 2ch sp, 1sc into top of 1st Bobble, 2sc into next 2ch sp, [3ch, 2sc into next sp] twice, 5ch, [2sc into next sp, 3ch] twice, 2sc into next sp, 1sc into top of next Bobble, 2sc into next sp, ✳skip 1sc, 2sc into next sp, 1sc into top of next Bobble, 2sc into next sp, [3ch, 2sc into next sp] twice, 5ch, [2sc into next sp, 3ch] twice, 2sc into next sp, 1sc into top of next Bobble, 2sc into next sp; rep from ✳ to last sc, 1sc into last sc. Fasten off.

Big and Little Scallops

Starting chain: multiple of 10 sts + 2
Skill: intermediate

Special Abbreviation

Bobble = work 3dc into next space until 1 loop of each remains on hook, yo through all 4 loops on hook.

1ST ROW (WS): Work 1sc into 2nd ch from hook, 1sc into each ch to end, turn.

2ND ROW: 5ch (count as 1tr, 1ch), work [1tr, 1ch] twice into 1st sc, skip 4sc, 1sc into next sc, ✳1ch, skip 4sc, into next sc work [1tr, 1ch] 5 times, skip 4sc, 1sc into next sc; rep from ✳ to last 5sc,

1ch, work 1tr into last sc, 1ch, into same st as last tr work [1tr, 1ch, 1tr], turn.

3RD ROW: 1ch, 1sc into 1st tr, ✳2ch, into next sc work [1dtr, 2ch] 4 times, skip 2tr, 1sc into next tr; rep from ✳ to end placing last sc into 4th of 5ch at beg of previous row, turn.

4TH ROW: 1ch, 1sc into 1st sc, ✳4ch, skip next sp, 1 Bobble (see Special Abbreviation) into next 2ch sp, [3ch, 1 Bobble into next 2ch sp] twice, 4ch, 1sc into next sc; rep from ✳ to end. Fasten off.

Shallow Scallop Edging
Starting chain: multiple of 6 sts + 3
Skill: intermediate

1ST ROW (WS): Work 1sc into 2nd ch from hook, 1sc into each ch to end, turn.

2ND ROW: 3ch (count as 1dc), skip 1st sc, 1dc into next sc, ✳1ch, skip 1sc, 1dc into each of next 2sc; rep from ✳ to end, turn.

3RD ROW: 5ch (count as 1dc, 2ch), 1sc into next ch sp, ✳4ch, 1sc into next ch sp; rep from ✳ to last 2 sts, 2ch, 1dc into 3rd of 3ch at beg of previous row, turn.

4TH ROW: 1ch, 1sc into 1st dc, ✳work 5dc into next 4ch sp, 1sc into next 4ch sp; rep from ✳ to end placing last sc into 3rd of 5ch at beg of previous row. Fasten off.

Soft Slope Edging
Starting chain: multiple of 6 sts + 3
Skill: intermediate

Special Abbreviation
Picot = make 3ch, sl st into 3rd ch from hook.

1ST ROW (WS): Work 1sc into 2nd ch from hook, 1sc into each ch to end, turn.

2ND ROW: 5ch (count as 1dc, 2ch), skip 1st 3sc, 1sc into next sc,

work 3 Picots (see Special Abbreviation), 1sc into next sc, ✳5ch, skip 4sc, 1sc into next sc, work 3 Picots, 1sc into next sc; rep from ✳ to last 3sc, 2ch, 1dc into last sc, turn.

3RD ROW: 1ch, 1sc into 1st dc, ✳8ch, 1sc into next 5ch arch; rep from ✳ to end placing last sc into 3rd of 5ch at beg of previous row, turn.

4TH ROW: 1ch, 1sc into 1st sc, ✳11sc into next 3ch arch, 1sc into next sc; rep from ✳ to end. Fasten off.

Aqueduct Edging
Starting chain: multiple of 4 sts + 4
Skill: intermediate

1ST ROW (RS): Work 1dc into 6th ch from hook, ✳1ch, skip 1ch, 1dc into next ch; rep from ✳ to end, turn.

2ND ROW: 1ch, 1sc into 1st dc, ✳5ch, skip 1dc, 1sc into next dc; rep from ✳ to last dc, 5ch, skip 1dc and 1ch, 1sc into next ch, turn.

3RD ROW: 1ch, 1sc into 1st sc, work 7sc into each 5ch arch to end, 1sc into last sc, turn.

4TH ROW: 5ch (count as 1dc, 2ch), skip 1st 4sc, 1sc into next sc, ✳3ch, skip 6sc, 1sc into next sc; rep from ✳ to last 4sc, 2ch, 1dc into last sc, turn.

5TH ROW: 1ch, 1sc into 1st dc, 5ch, 1sc into 2ch sp, into each sp work [1sc, 5ch, 1sc] to end placing last sc into 3rd of 5ch at beg of previous row. Fasten off.

Square Edging
Starting chain: multiple of 9 sts + 4
Skill: intermediate

1ST ROW (RS): Work 1dc into 4th ch from hook, 1dc into each ch to end, turn.

2ND ROW: 1ch, 1sc into 1st dc, 1ch, 1sc into next dc, 9ch, skip 7dc, 1sc into next dc, ✳3ch, 1sc into next dc, 9ch, skip 7dc, 1sc into next dc; rep from ✳ to end, 1ch, 1sc into top of 3ch, turn.

3RD ROW: 1ch, 1sc into 1st sc, 1sc into 1st ch sp, ✳5dc into next 9ch arch, 2ch, into same arch as last 5dc work [1sc, 2ch, 5dc], 1sc

into next 3ch arch; rep from ✳ to end placing last sc into last ch sp, 1sc into last sc, turn.

4TH ROW: 9ch (count as 1dtr, 4ch), 1sc into next 2ch sp, 3ch, 1sc into next 2ch sp, ✳9ch, 1sc into next 2ch sp, 3ch, 1sc into next 2ch sp; rep from ✳ to last 5dc, 4ch, 1dtr into last sc, turn.

5TH ROW: 3ch (count as 1dc), 5dc into 4ch arch, 1sc into next 3ch arch, ✳5dc into next 9ch arch, 2ch, into same arch as last 5dc work [1sc, 2ch, 5dc], 1sc into next 3ch arch; rep from ✳ to last arch, 5dc into last arch, 1dc into 5th of 9ch at beg of previous row. Fasten off.

Open Scallop Edging
Starting chain: multiple of 10 sts + 2
Skill: intermediate

1ST ROW (RS): Work 1sc into 2nd ch from hook, 1sc into each ch to end, turn.

2ND ROW: 3ch (count as 1dc), skip 1st sc, 1dc into each of next 3sc, ✳3ch, skip 3sc, 1dc into each of next 7sc; rep from ✳ to end omitting 3dc at end of last rep, turn.

3RD ROW: 1ch, 1sc into each of 1st 4dc, 3sc into next 3ch sp, ✳1sc into each of next 7dc, 3sc into next 3ch sp; rep from ✳ to last 4dc, 1sc into each of next 3dc, 1sc into 3rd of 3ch at beg of previous row, turn.

4TH ROW: 1ch, 1sc into 1st sc, 2ch, skip 2sc, 1sc into next sc, 8ch, skip 3sc, 1sc into next sc, ✳5ch, skip 5sc, 1sc into next sc, 8ch, skip 3sc, 1sc into next sc; rep from ✳ to last 3sc, 2ch, 1sc into last sc, turn.

5TH ROW: 1ch, 1sc into 1st sc, 19dc into 8ch arch, ✳1sc into next 5ch sp, 19dc into next 8ch arch; rep from ✳ to last 2ch sp, 1sc into last sc. Fasten off.

Egyptian Edging
Starting chain: multiple of 16 sts + 3
Skill: experienced

Special Abbreviation
Cluster = work 2dtr into next st until 1 loop of each remains on hook, yo and through all 3 loops on hook.

1ST ROW (RS): Work 1dc into 4th ch from hook, ✳1ch, skip 1ch, 1dc into next ch; rep from ✳ to last ch, 1dc into last ch, turn.

2ND ROW: 3ch (count as 1dc), skip 1st dc, 1dc into each of next dc, ch sp and dc, 5ch, skip 2 sps, 1tr into next sp, 5ch, skip 2dc, 1dc into next dc, ✳[1dc in next sp, 1dc in next dc] 3 times, 5ch, skip 2 sps, 1tr into next sp, 5ch, skip 2dc, 1dc into next dc; rep from ✳ to last 3 sts, 1dc into next sp, 1dc into next dc, 1dc into top of 3ch, turn.

3RD ROW: 3ch, skip 1st dc, 1dc into each of next 2dc, 7ch, 1sc into next tr, 7ch, ✳skip 1dc, 1dc into each of next 5dc, 7ch, 1sc into next tr, 7ch; rep from ✳ to last 4 sts, skip 1dc, 1dc into each of next 2dc, 1dc into 3rd of 3ch at beg of previous row, turn.

4TH ROW: 3ch, skip 1st dc, 1dc into next dc, 7ch, into next sc work [1sc, 5ch, 1sc], 7ch, ✳skip 1dc, 1dc into each of next 3dc, 7ch, into next sc work [1sc, 5ch, 1sc], 7ch; rep from ✳ to last 3 sts, skip 1dc, 1dc into next dc, 1dc into 3rd of 3ch at beg of previous row, turn.

5TH ROW: 6ch (count as 1dc, 3ch), ✳skip 7ch arch, work 1 Cluster (see Special Abbreviation) into 5ch arch then [1ch, 1 Cluster] 4 times into same arch, 3ch, skip 1dc, 1dc into next dc, 3ch; rep from ✳ to end omitting 3ch at end of last rep and placing last dc into 3rd of 3ch. Fasten off.

Diamond and Heart Edging
Starting chain: multiple of 6 sts + 2
Skill: intermediate

Special Abbreviation

Bobble = work 3dtr into next st until 1 loop of each remains on hook, yo and through all 4 loops on hook.

1ST ROW (RS): Work 1sc into 2nd ch from hook, 1sc into each ch to end, turn.

2ND ROW: 8ch (count as 1dc, 5ch), skip 1st 6sc, 1dc into next sc, ✳5ch, skip 5sc, 1dc into next sc; rep from ✳ to end, turn.

3RD ROW: 6ch (count as 1tr, 2ch), work 1 Bobble (see Special Abbreviation) into 1st dc, ✳into next dc work [1 Bobble, 5ch, 1 Bobble]; rep from ✳ to last dc, into 3rd of 3ch at beg of previous row work [1 Bobble, 2ch, 1tr], turn.

4TH ROW: 1ch, 1sc into 1st tr, ✳7ch, 1sc into next 5ch arch; rep from ✳ to end placing last sc into 4th of 6ch at beg of previous row, turn.

5TH ROW: 1ch, 1sc into 1st sc, ✳9sc into next 7ch arch, 1sc into next sc; rep from ✳ to end. Fasten off.

Thorny Crown Edging
Starting chain: multiple of 9 sts + 5
Skill: intermediate

Special Abbreviation

Bobble = work 3dtr into sp until one loop of each remains on hook, yo and through all 4 loops on hook.

1ST ROW (WS): Work 1dc into 8th ch from hook, ✳2ch, skip 2ch, 1dc into next ch; rep from ✳ to end, turn.

2ND ROW: 3ch (count as 1dc), skip next sp, work 1 Bobble (see

Special Abbreviation) into next sp, [6ch, 1dc into 1st of these ch] 3 times, 1 Bobble into same sp as last Bobble, ✳skip 2 sps, work 1 Bobble into next sp, [6ch, 1dc into 1st of these ch] 3 times, 1 Bobble into same sp as last Bobble; rep from ✳ to last sp, skip 2ch, 1dc in next ch. Fasten off.

Clover Leaf Edging
Starting chain: multiple of 11 sts + 3
Skill: intermediate

Special Abbreviation

Bobble = Work 3dtr into 3ch loop until 1 loop of each remains on hook, yo and through all 4 loops on hook.

1ST ROW (RS): Work 1dc into 4th ch from hook, 1dc into each ch to end, turn.

2ND ROW: 1ch, 1sc into 1st dc, ✳9ch, sl st into 3rd ch from hook, 7ch, skip 10dc, 1sc into next dc; rep from ✳ to end placing last sc into top of 3ch, turn.

3RD ROW: 5ch, ✳work 1 Bobble (see Special Abbreviation) into next 3ch loop, 5ch, into same loop as last Bobble work [1 Bobble, 5ch, 1 Bobble], 1dtr into next sc; rep from ✳ to end. Fasten off.

Haystacks Edging I
Starting chain: multiple of 8 sts + 2
Skill: intermediate

Special Abbreviation

Triple Loop = sl st into next sc, [7ch, 1 sl st] 3 times into same sc.

1ST ROW (WS): Work 1sc into 2nd ch from hook, 1sc into each ch to end, turn.

2ND ROW: 1ch, work 1sc into each sc to end, turn.

3RD ROW: 1ch, 1sc into each of 1st 3sc, ✳9ch, skip 3sc, 1sc into each of next 5sc; rep from ✳ to end omitting 2sc at end of last rep, turn.

4TH ROW: 1ch, 1sc into each of 1st 2sc, ✳5ch, 1sc into next 9ch arch, 5ch, skip 1sc, 1sc into each of next 3sc; rep from ✳ to end omitting 1sc at end of last rep, turn.

5TH ROW: 1ch, 1sc into 1st sc, ✳5ch, skip 1sc, 1sc into next sc; rep from ✳ to end, turn.

6TH ROW: 1ch, 1sc into 1st sc, ✳5ch, work 1 Triple Loop (see Special Abbreviation) into next sc, 5ch, 1sc into next sc; rep from ✳ to end. Fasten off.

Flamenco Edging
Worked lengthways
Skill: experienced

1ST ROW (RS): Make 31ch, work 1dc into 7th ch from hook, [2ch, skip 2ch, 1dc into next ch] 8 times, turn. (9 sps.)

2ND ROW: 5ch (count as 1dc, 2ch), skip 1st dc, 1dc into next dc, [2ch, 1dc into next dc] 3 times, 5ch, skip next 4 sps, 1dc into next sp, work [3ch, 1dc] 3 times into same sp as last dc, turn.

3RD ROW: 1ch, 1sc into 1st dc, into 1st 3ch sp work [1hdc, 1dc, 1tr, 1dc, 1hdc, 1sc], into next 3ch sp work [1sc, 1hdc, 1dc, 1tr, 1dc, 1hdc, 1sc], into next 3ch sp work [1sc, 1hdc, 1dc, 1tr, 1dc, 1hdc], 1sc into next dc, 5ch, 1dc into next dc, [2ch, 1dc into next dc] 4 times placing last dc into

3rd of 5ch at beg of previous row, turn.

4TH ROW: 5ch (count as 1dc, 2ch), skip 1st dc, [1dc into next dc, 2ch] 4 times, 1dc into 5ch sp, 7ch, skip 1st group of 7 sts, work 1dc into tr at center of next group of 7 sts, [3ch, 1dc] 3 times into same st as last dc, turn.

5TH ROW: 1ch, 1sc into 1st dc, into 1st 3ch sp work [1hdc, 1dc, 1tr, 1dc, 1hdc, 1sc], into next 3ch sp work [1sc, 1hdc, 1dc, 1tr, 1dc, 1hdc, 1sc], into next 3ch sp work [1sc, 1hdc, 1dc, 1tr, 1dc, 1hdc], 1sc into next dc, 5ch, 1dc into 7ch sp, [2ch, 1dc into next dc] 6 times placing last dc into 3rd of 5ch at beg of previous row, turn.

6TH ROW: 5ch (count as 1dc, 2ch), skip 1st dc, [1dc into next dc, 2ch] 6 times, 1dc into 5ch sp, 7ch, skip 1st group of 7 sts, work 1dc into tr at center of next group of 7 sts, [3ch, 1dc] 3 times into same st as last dc, turn.

7TH ROW: 1ch, 1sc into 1st dc, into 1st 3ch sp work [1hdc, 1dc, 1tr, 1dc, 1hdc, 1sc], into next 3ch sp work [1sc, 1hdc, 1dc, 1tr, 1dc, 1hdc, 1sc], into next 3ch sp work [1sc, 1hdc, 1dc, 1tr, 1dc, 1hdc], 1sc into next dc, 5ch, 1dc into 7ch sp, [2ch, 1dc into next dc] 8 times placing last dc into 3rd of 5ch at beg of previous row, turn. Rep 2nd to 7th rows, end with a 7th row.

Citrus Slice Edging
Worked lengthways
Skill: experienced

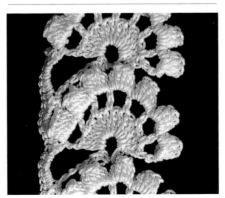

Special Abbreviations
Popcorn (at beg of row) = 3ch, work 6dc into 1st sp, drop loop from hook, insert hook from the front into top of 3ch, pick up dropped loop and draw through, 1ch to secure.

7dc Popcorn = work 7dc into next sp, then complete as for Popcorn at beg of row inserting hook into top of 1st of these dc. Make 10ch and join into a ring with a sl st.

1ST ROW (RS): 3ch (count as 1dc), work 14dc into ring, turn.

2ND ROW: 5ch (count as 1dc, 2ch), skip 2dc, 1dc into next dc, [2ch, skip 1dc, 1dc into next dc] 6 times placing last dc into 3rd of 3ch at beg of previous row, turn.

3RD ROW: Work 1 Popcorn (see Special Abbreviations) at beg of row, [3ch, 1 7dc Popcorn (see Special Abbreviations) into next 2ch sp] 6 times.

4TH ROW: 10ch, skip 1st 2 sps, work [1sc, 5ch, 1sc] into next 3ch sp, turn.

5TH ROW: 3ch (count as 1dc), work 14dc into 5ch sp, turn. Rep 2nd to 5th rows until edging is required length, ending with a 3rd row. Do not turn work but continue along side edge as follows:

1ST FINAL ROW: 3ch, 1sc into sp formed at beg of 2nd row of pattern, ✳5ch, 1sc into sp formed at beg of 4th row of pattern, 5ch, 1sc into sp formed at beg of 2nd row of pattern; rep from ✳ to end, turn.

2ND FINAL ROW: 1ch, 1sc into 1st sc, ✳5sc into 5ch sp, 1sc into next sc; rep from ✳ to end. Fasten off.

Portcullis Edging
Worked lengthways
Skill: intermediate

1ST ROW (WS): Make 20ch, work 1dc into 6th ch from hook, ✳1ch, skip 1ch, 1dc into next ch; rep from ✳ to end, turn.

2ND ROW: 7ch, 1dc into 1st dc, [1ch, 1dc into next dc] twice, 7ch, skip 3dc, [1dc into next dc, 1ch] twice, skip 1ch, 1dc into next ch, turn.

3RD ROW: 4ch (count as 1dc, 1ch), skip 1st dc, 1dc into next dc, 1ch, 1dc into next dc,

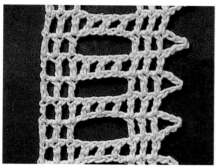

[1ch, skip 1ch, 1dc into next ch] 3 times, [1ch, 1dc into next dc] 3 times. Rep 2nd and 3rd rows.

Little Fans Edging
Worked lengthways
Skill: intermediate

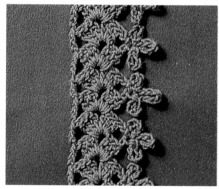

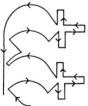

1ST ROW (WS): Make 4ch (count as 1dc, 1ch), work 2dc into 1st of these ch, 2ch, 3dc into same ch as last 2dc, turn.
2ND ROW: 8ch, sl st into 6th ch from hook, 7ch, sl st into same ch as last sl st, 5ch, sl st into same ch as last 2 sl sts, 2ch, 3dc

into 2ch sp, 2ch, 3dc into same sp as last 3dc, turn.
3RD ROW: Sl st into each of 1st 3dc, 3ch (count as 1dc), 2dc into 2ch sp, 2ch, 3dc into same sp as last 2dc, turn.
Rep 2nd and 3rd rows until edging is required length, ending with a 2nd row. Do not turn work but continue along side edge as follows:
FINAL ROW: ❋3ch, 1sc into top of 3ch at beg of next Fan, 3ch, 1sc into 1st sl st at beg of next Fan; rep from ❋ to last Fan, 1sc into top of 4ch at beg of 1st row. Fasten off.

Spiked Edging
Worked lengthways
Skill: intermediate

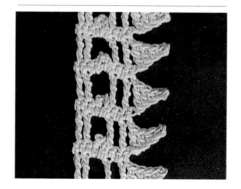

1ST ROW (RS): Make 14ch, work 1sc into 3rd ch from hook, 1hdc into next ch, 1dc into next ch, 1tr into next ch, [1ch, skip 1ch, 1tr into next ch] twice, 2ch, skip 2ch, 1tr into each of last 2ch, turn.
2ND ROW: 1ch, 1sc into each of 1st 2tr, 1sc into 2ch sp, 4ch, 1sc into same sp as last sc, 1sc into next tr, 1sc into ch sp, 1sc into next tr, turn.
3RD ROW: 7ch, work 1sc into 3rd ch from hook, 1hdc into next ch, 1dc into next ch, 1tr into next ch, 1ch, 1tr into next sc, 1ch, skip 1sc, 1tr into next sc, 2ch, skip 2sc, 1tr into each of last 2sc, turn.
Rep 2nd and 3rd rows.

edgings

Index